KING ARTHUR Pendragon

EPIC ROLEPLAYING IN LEGENDARY BRITAIN

by Greg Stafford

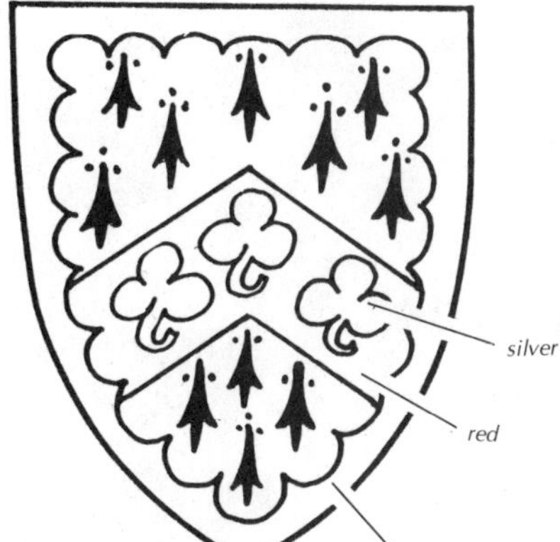

EDITOR, GRAPHIC DESIGNER: William Dunn

ASSISTANT EDITORS: Sam Shirley, Charlie Krank, Anne Merritt

PRODUCTION: John B. Monroe, Mike MacDonald

COVER ARTIST: Mike Weaver

COVER DESIGN: Charlie Krank

CARTOGRAPHY: Carolyn Savoy

ARTISTS: Lisa Free, Gus diZerega, Carolyn Savoy, Arnie Swekel, Teanna Byerts, Michael Blum

CELTIC DECORATIONS: Gus diZerega

CHAOSIUM INC.
1990

Credits

SPECIAL THANKS GO to these people, who contributed greatly or a little, but whose impact has affected the game: Stephen Abbot, Don Alaman, Marcie Alaman, Matt Bailey, Mike Beavers, Christopher Beiting, Michael Blinde, Derek Boain, Martin J. Bourne, Heather Bryden, John Carnahan, Yurek Chodak, Morgan Conrad, Suzanne Courteau, Bogdan Dabrowski, Gigi D'Arn, Philippe Dohr, Bruce Dresselhaus, Christer Edling, Steve Englehart, Jason Fink, Scott Fitz, Sean Fitzpatrick, Lisa A. Free, Don Frew, Rick Geimer, Sharon M. Grant, Marc Grossberg, Steve Hartman, Keith Herber, Ed Holtz, Jim Hooker, Tony Hughes, Bill Johnson, Sherman Kahn, Ken Kaufer, Katharine Kerr, Bill Keyes, Eric Krupa, Mike Koop, Freya Reeves Lambides, Peter Larsen, Gary May, Treesa McLean, Hal Moe, Ed Mooring, Ellen Munro, Henri Naccah, Helmut Nikel, Daniel Nolte, Michael North, Carol Parker-Pollock, Gleb Perfiloff, Sandy Petersen, Jon Quaife, Richard A. Rian, Rory Root, Wolfe Schaaf, Studette Scoflaw, Frank Shewmake, Leigh Skilling, Benjy Sikora, Noah Stafford, Bob Starfire, Andy Tauber, Marcus Thomas, Anne Vetillard, David W. Wilkins, Lynn Willis, Marc Willner, Elizabeth Wolcott, Bill Zurn... and my apologies to any others who were unrecorded.

This work was prepared using the Penguin Classics edition of *Le Morte D'Arthur,* edited by Janet Cowen.

The arms of King Arthur's knights are based on the 15th-century document known as *La forme quon tenoit des tournoys* in the collection of Harvard University, attributed to Jacques d'Armagnac, Duc de Nemours.

KING ARTHUR PENDRAGON is published by Chaosium Inc.

Address questions concerning this book as well as requests for free catalogs of Chaosium products to Chaosium Inc., 950-A 56th St., Oakland CA, 94608.

Chaosium Publication 2709. Published in June 1990. ISBN 0-933635-59-1. Printed in the United States of America.

Table of Contents

Welcome to Pendragon 4
Article: Which Arthur Is This? 5
The Quotations 6
Quote: Introduction to King Arthur 7
Article: What Does "Pendragon" Mean? 7
Table: A Pendragon Chronology 9
Quote: Three Damosels Incite Adventure 10

What Your Character Knows . 11
The Feudal World 11
The Realm of Chivalry 12
Quote: Sir Ywaine is Described 16
Britain and Europe 16
Article: Armies of Logres 18
Camelot 22
The High Order of Knighthood 25
Magic 30

Character Generation 32
Your First Character 32
Blank Character Sheet 35, 36
Default Characters 37, 38
Coats of Arms 43, 44
Article: Introducing Your Knight 46

Your Family 48
Table: Family History 48

Glory and Ambitions 56
Table: Glory Ranking 57
Table: Basic Glory Awards 58
Article: Extra Glory 58
Quote: Comparing Glory 59
Table: Sample Glory 60-62
Ambitions 64
Quote: Class Distinction, Arthurian Style 64
Quote: Sir Balin Defends Poor Knights 65
Quote: Sir Palomides Fights for the Right of a Quest . . .66
Quote: Who Are Noblemen? 67
Quotes: Names Written in Gold 70

Game Mechanics 71
Basic Concepts 71
Resolution 72
Time Scales 74
Table: Calendar 75
Experience 76
Movement 77
Quote: King Arthur Encounters Travel Difficulties 80
Combat 81
Quote: Sir Lancelot Adventures 83
Questions and Answers: Game Mechanics 84
Skills 90
Injury and Health 102
Terminology: Injury and Health 104
Quote: Two Knights Fight to the Death 107
The Winter Phase 109

Ideals and Passions 115
Personality Traits 116
Quote: Lancelot Fumbles His Energetic 117
Quote: King Arthur's Justice 118
Quote: King Mark Gets a Cowardly Check 119
Passions 122
Table: Dishonor 123
Quote: Sir Berluse Gets a Hospitality Check ... 123
Quote: Sir Lamorak's Loyalty (Pendragon) Overcomes His Hate (Orkney Clan) 124
Quote: Sir Palomides Is Inspired by His Love (Isoud) Passion 126
Quote: Sir Alisander Is Besotted by Love 128
Quote: Sir Lancelot Goes Mad 129

Your Home 130
The County of Salisbury 130
Your Manor 137
Castles 140
Travel In Britain 141

Wealth 143
Quote: Sir Galeron Eats A Fine Feast 144
Table: Standard Price List 146, 147
Table: Major Investment List 148

Chivalric Duties 150
Courtesy
The Hunt 151
Quote: The Boar is Found 152
Tournament 152
Quote: Sir Marhaus Takes the Prize 153
Romance 155
Religion 157
Article: Swearing 157
Adventuring 159
Battle 159
Quote: Battle, A Poem 160
Quote: The Army Marches 162
Article: The Battle System 163-166

Scenarios 167
Introductory Scenario 167
Article: The Knighting Ceremony 173
Solos 174
Adventures 179
Short Adventures 183
Stories 191

Characters and Creatures ... 192
Ordinary Characters 192
Famous People 195
The Stable 200
Hunted Beasts 202
Monsters 203

Appendix 206
Designer's Notes 206
Bibliography 206
Measurements 207
Watch Your C's and K's 207
Glossary and Abbreviations 207
Index 208

Index of Maps, Shields, and Illustrations

THE MAPS
Color Map of Logres .... between 16-17
Color Map of Salisbury .... between 144-145
Map of Britain 21
Travel Times in Salisbury 135
Map of Salisbury Manors 138

THE SHIELDS
Color page of Shields .... between 80-81
Sample Coats of Arms 43-44
Arthur 1
Bors de Ganis 97
Brus sans Pitie 85
Dinadan 153
Gawaine 41
Kay the Seneschal 74
Lancelot 9
Lamorak 27
Sir Thomas Malory 1
Marhaus 10
King Mark 156
Mordred 121
Palomides 69
Sagramore 101
Tristram 51
Turquine 142
Ywaine 17

THE ILLUSTRATIONS
The Avanc 185
A Battle Scene 161
Camelot 23
Castles 140-141
Earl Robert Creates a Knight 172
Faerie Horses 151
A Forest Scene 78
Sir Gawaine 40
The Great Hall of Salisbury Castle 132
Griffin 29
Horses 201
A Joust 63
Sir Lancelot 8
Merlin 91
Sir Mordred 120
Morgan le Fay 15
A Quintain 169
Queen Guenever 127
The Questing Beast 188
Raven Witch Transforming 73
The Redcap 205
A Roe Deer 112
Sarum and Salisbury Castle 131
A Spriggan 159
A Typical Manor 139
The White Horse 182

Welcome to Pendragon

Join the Story of King Arthur!

PENDRAGON IS UNLIKE any game you have played. It has many revolutionary features which are novel to roleplaying games. It provides an imaginary method for you to participate in the wondrous world of King Arthur.

This game portrays the legendary era of King Arthur Pendragon, the mythical ruler who unified Britain, repelled the Roman Empire, vanquished the Saxons, and led the invincible brotherhood of heroes called the Round Table. The myth of Arthur's world has grown over the fourteen centuries of its literary existence, added to by many authors, whose ranks you are about to join.

The game world of *King Arthur Pendragon* (hereafter known as *Pendragon*) is a place of high chivalry and glittering armor. In it meet the many interpretations of King Arthur, from the barbaric tribal realm of the ancient Welsh texts to the modern Hollywood glamor. *Pendragon* is a literary game, based on the pioneering works of Chretien de Troyes, the later French *Vulgate* texts, and the culminating work of Sir Thomas Malory, *Le Morte D'Arthur*.

It is a land where jousting and romance are the common sports, and where killing enemies is daily work. In this arena Christian virtues struggle to vanquish savage passions and worldly motives. Characters are clothed in noble court fashions, and equipped with medieval customs and morals.

It is a time of glorious and deliberate anachronisms, brought together because they are of King Arthur, a timeless hero. To start with, we have two chronologies crunched together. The dates and politics are those of the sixth century, the so-called Dark Ages or Early Middle Ages, when King Arthur really lived. But the customs and fashions are those of the High Middle Ages, when the literature about him was first written. As a result, in this chronology feudalism was instituted by Uther Pendragon circa 480-495, in the style of his contemporary, Clovis of the Franks. Chivalry, which refines the brute ways of knighthood, is introduced by young King Arthur after he ascends to the high kingship in 510. Romance, the art of *fine amor*, is popularized by Queen Guenever after her marriage to Arthur in 514.

This setting is not fair to people outside Britain, and does not strive for game balance for everyone. The untamed Celts, Saxons, and Picts who defy Arthur's rule must rely upon their own barbaric cultures, devoid of the anachronistic gifts which feudalism, chivalry, and romance deliver. Their warriors might be addressed as knights, and their chieftains might be called kings, but these enemies of the Pendragon are deluded and are destined to be conquered by him.

Between the kingdoms of men lie the mythical domains of Faerie — great dark woods and bright shining fields unexplored by human foot or thought. Entire kingdoms of immortals lie beyond and within Arthur's realm. Their cities and castles appear and vanish like mist. Their magical residents, such as the Green Knight, often visit the world of men. In turn, bold human questers enter the Faerie realm to seek the greatest adventures.

From the domains of the faerie comes the magic which enchants Britain in Arthur's time. Merlin, Morgan le Fay, and the Lady of the Lake are the foremost practitioners of the occult arts, twisting enchantments to their own hidden goals. Ancient rites echo in the challenges of the magical foes found in lonely places, and old folk songs remember other stories with similar prizes. The world of Arthur is sometimes not at all what it seems, and much is yet to be discovered.

Play

MOST OF US, AS CHILDREN, engaged in some sort of "make believe." "Cops and Robbers" is common, or some variant of "guns." (Or the ever-present "knights," if swords and shields are in fashion this year).

A roleplaying game is a lot like that kid play, except in instead of running around the back yard you use your collective imaginations. And instead of the incessant "Got you!" and "No you didn't!" arguments, we use dice to settle disputes. Game play is mostly talk about and for your character, who is your "pretend guy" in the imaginary world.

It seems strange at first, but give it a try. It is something you have done in the past. And it's entertaining fun. If it seems embarassing, relax: fun is its own reward and needs no justification.

What Is Roleplaying?

Roleplaying games give the players a way to rationally interact with a fantasy world. In a roleplaying game the players make up an imaginary person called a *character*. Then they direct the actions of this character as he interacts with other imaginary characters. Through the actions of their imaginary characters the players are like actors in the legendary world. The players, through the actions of

their character-knights, visit and explore the enchanted medieval world of *Pendragon.*

Most of the game is verbal interchange. Most actions are automatically successful: everyone can walk, talk, ride a horse under calm conditions, and so on. Dice rolls are used to determine whether or not a character succeeded at performing an act which is not automatically successful, such as fighting, leaping his horse over a ditch, or arguing with another person.

The players control characters who are household knights, bachelor knights, or banneret knights. If someone already knows how to play this game they can probably explain most of the necessary rules in half an hour.

Typical adventures of player characters are to combat robber barons, rescue damsels in distress, hobnob with famous knights at court, hunt fabulous monsters, and cross lances with the likes of Lancelot, Tristram, Gawaine, and Palomides. Knights will travel throughout an enchanted land to see many marvels and curiosities.

To play the game a second task must be undertaken by one player: that of the gamemaster. The gamemaster describes the world and events within it to the players. He controls the non-player characters.

The gamemaster in a roleplaying game directs the flow of the game while the players control the actions of the characters. As the gamemaster describes what is

❊ WHICH ARTHUR IS THIS? ❊

MANY VERSIONS OF KING ARTHUR exist. Stories have been told and retold about him for 1400 years, changing a little or a lot to suit the audience. The *Pendragon* game uses parts from all literary versions. However, in this introductory book some version are emphasized over the others. Supplements to *Pendragon* will reveal other aspects of the legends. The first planned supplement is *Knights Adventurous.*

English

Personal heroism, chivalrous honor, and a refreshing simplicity mark the English tales. King Arthur is a vigorous, wise and benevolent monarch. Sir Gawaine is by far the favorite English knight.

Best known stories include *Sir Gawaine and the Green Knight* and *Sir Gawaine and Dame Ragnell.*

Malory's *Le Morte D'Arthur,* the first modern English interpretation of French and English sources, serves as the basis for this game.

French

Most medieval Arthurian legends are in French, the tongue of aristocrats in the era they were written. The stories range from brilliant to insipid, but are characterized by a colorful, romantic, and artistic treatment. King Arthur is often portrayed as inefficient and uninspiring. Sir Lancelot is the favored knight among the French.

Chretien de Troyes is the Father of Arthurian Literature. The sprawling *Vulgate* and *Prose Tristram* were among the most copied manuscripts of their day. These latter two are the "French books" which Malory used in his version, and have inevitably influenced the game.

Chronicle

Characterized by relatively sober reporting, chronicles reported purportedly historical events.

The best known of these is the first, Geoffrey of Monmouth's *History of the Kings of Britain.* Modern fiction which follows this tradition portray the Dark Ages, devoid of medieval flourishes. Mary Stewart's series on Merlin is the best-known of these modern novels.

Facts drawn from this type of history are used to supply background political detail for *Pendragon.*

Modern

King Arthur is wise beyond his era, forshadowing democratic and other common institutions; he is vaguely aware of being a tool of some greater Fate; he courageously but vainly struggles against a certain doom.

T.H.White's *Once and Future King* is closest to the spirit of the basic *Pendragon* game. Howard Pyle's compilation exhibit a sanitized idealism. Hal Foster's *Prince Valiant* comic strip provides a background similar to the chornicles, and to *Pendragon.*

The idealism and enlightment of King Arthur in *Pendragon* comes from White's stories.

Welsh

Primitive and wild, the Welsh tales go hand-in-hand with the supernatural and fantastic. Arthur is a vigorous warrior, more a chieftan than king or emperor.

The best known Welsh Arthurian story is *Culhwch and Olwen,* found in *The Mabinogion.*

The wonder and fantasy of this Arthurian tradition are reserved for exposure in *Knights Adventurous.*

Radical

Some stories, mostly modern, provide novel interpretations of people and events. They tend to psychologize the heroes. Favorite characters are often the "bad guys" from medieval story. These include a confused, but not evil, Mordred in Stewart's *That Wicked Day;* a justifiably short-tempered Sir Kay in *Idylls of the Queen;* and a good-bad pagan Morgan le Fay in *The Mists of Avalon.*

The complexity of the corpus of legend leaves room for these kinds of interpretations. They can be explored more thoroughly in *Knights Adventurous.*

⁂ THE QUOTATIONS ⁂

Scattered throughout this book are many quotations from Arthurian literature. These are of three types. The most common are those which illustrate some rule or part of the game with an example taken from the literature. Thus you will find "King Mark Gets a Cowardly Check" or "King Arthur Encounters Travel Difficulties." Others are included to give a feel for some of the high adventure typical of the Arthurian era. These include such entries as "The Army Marches." Finally, some have incidental notes relevant to the text.

How to Read the Quotations

Most of the quotations in this book are taken from the works of Sir Thomas Malory, a gifted writer of the fifteenth century. The 500 years of literary development from then until now can be seen, even in this translated text, and needs some comment for the newcomer.

The text for the quotations has been translated and transliterated to modern English, but not entirely updated.

Some of the archaic vocabulary is probably unfamiliar to the casual reader. Clarifyications have been inserted into the text in [brackets] to make understanding easier.

Run-on sentences are the rule, rather than the exception.

Bad pronoun usage is common, and it is hard to sometimes understand who the "him" and "he" refers to. I can only urge patience.

The major changes which I have made to the published texts are to spell the names consistently, using the forms I prefer.Thus we use Lancelot du Lac rather than Launcelot du Lake, or Isoud, not Isolt.

See the Bibliography at the end of the book for further literary notes. Attribution is not given for sections quoted from, except for Malory.

going on, where they are, and other details of the plot, the players choose actions for their characters, thus cooperating with him in creating the adventure.

The gamemaster oversees the imaginary world, describing it in detail and directing its course. He is not an adversary, but rather the key to the world of Arthurian Britain. He brings both friends and enemies to life for the players. When they have questions or need help, players turn to the gamemaster for answers. Likewise, the gamemaster must ask for opinions from the players to make it an acceptable game.

One-on-one gaming is possible, with one gamemaster and one player. This type of adventure where a single knight travels alone against all odds is *very* Arthurian and should not be avoided.

Also, solitaire gaming is possible with a single person taking the both roles of gamemaster and player. The rules will help to guide you through adventures. Remember, however, that it is much more fun with another player, and that the worst problem of solitaire play is when someone cheats.

Pendragon presents an on-going story. It is a campaign roleplaying game in which time progresses, unique events occur, and characters age. If the players play through the whole Arthurian campaign the players' characters at the end will be the grandchildren of the original characters. Player-characters normally have one big adventure per game year, each of which will last one or more sessions.

The player characters' knowledge of their world is different from the players'. Players should remember to differentiate between their knowledge and that of their characters. A good gamemaster will accept the players' assistance and ask for their help when needed. Success in *Pendragon* comes through cooperation between player characters with each other, and also between players and gamemaster.

Some familiarity with medieval history and customs is useful before play, but not much is needed. Seeing almost any film about knights, or reading almost any book about King Arthur will supply the minimal information needed.

The Unique Features of *Pendragon*

Some players may be new to this type of game, while many may already be familiar with other roleplaying games. Both should read this section, because *Pendragon* presents a novel approach to roleplaying, combat, and magic. To enjoy the game at its fullest you must use all the game elements summarized below. The game works best as a totality, and you will fail to give *Pendragon* a fair try if you start playing the game without understanding the intentions and overall concept of the game. Once you have experienced the game, you can go ahead and change parts you are unhappy with; but try the total package at least once before you judge it.

Knighthood

Pendragon is a game about knighthood. It compares and contrasts the beauty and high chivalry of the literary romances with the brutal reality of the Middle Ages. The game tries less to adapt the milieu to the modern mind than to instruct the modern mind to the milieu. It is a realm of paradoxes: inspirational love and festering wounds; communication with elf-kind and brutal plunder; ecstatic spiritual visions and stillborn children. The beauty and inspiration of the legendary world take on depth and meaning within this contrast.

Knights are an elite and privileged part of a working society. This game provides the structure around which to build your personal knight in Arthur's glorious and squalid age.

An Arthurian knight is part of a larger world, and cannot function for long without it. Without a larger

world he has no place to exercise his privileges or uphold his responsibilities. A knight's world is primarily the realm of his family and his lord, both of which support him and may call upon his strength and even his life in time of need. However, during the great events of Arthurian legend, broad political and cultural themes will present themselves to the players and require decisions from their characters that go beyond the daily considerations of family and lord.

What does an Arthurian knight seek? Fame is important, but so is power: a knight yearns for lands and a castle of his own, so that he can become a lord in his own right, and carry on his family to greatness. A great knight in Arthur's Britain will rarely be a lone warrior. To be truly great he must be a leader of men, a subtle intriguer, a great lover, or an expert in battle strategy as well as a superlative killer of men and monsters.

The rules of *Pendragon*, summarized here, reflect these concepts of Arthurian knighthood. They are the heart of the game and need to be understood and used in unison. Please refer to the specific details of the rules only after you have read these introductory passages.

Mortality

All *Pendragon* characters will eventually die. This is a basic fact of the design. This must be so if the game is to reflect the important issues of legends and of life.

The world of *Pendragon* is more immediately violent than ours, and so combat is a regular part of the game — but combat in *Pendragon* is a more serious matter than in most other adventure games. The chance of death or permanent injury is great. Worse, healing from damage is slow and uncertain, and magical healing is rare. Thus actions must be planned carefully, and violence cannot be used to solve all problems.

Aging is a part of the game, and includes the effects of old injuries, the ravages of disease, and other cruel realities ignored by most roleplaying games.

Psychological effects also exist in the game, as they do in the literature. Madness or other emotional trauma can permanently affect a character, perhaps fatally in rare instances.

All of these factors impose an awareness on the players which provides motivation to play. After all, everyone is a knight, and everyone is going to die, so the only variable to address is: what kind of knight are you going to be?

Ideals and Motivations

In *Pendragon* roleplaying and behavior is much more significant to a character's success or failure than in other adventure games. *Pendragon* challenges roleplaying skills. Rather than simply letting players state that their characters always act the right way, *Pendragon* uses a system of Ideals and Passions to quantify your character's patterns of behavior. This insures reasonable consistency and gives player knights an accurate record of their reputation as regards chivalrous, cultural, and romantic ideals.

This does not have to result in your character being forced in a mold, nor is the intention of the system to take away the player's ability to make decisions for his character. The system simply makes sure that the Gamemaster has some control over this vital aspect of the game.

Personality quantification also permits the gamemaster to be impartial and consistent when gamemaster characters such as Sir Lancelot must make personal decisions or consult their code of ethics during a game.

There is no single "right" way for a knight to act. The behavior patterns of different characters vary tremendously. Some knights are chivalrous and just, while others are treacherous and cruel. The numbers that quantify these traits are more secret than Glory. A character may adventure for years with a group without revealing his darker side to anyone other than the Gamemaster. The range of ideals and passions includes many individual variations on the themes of piety, vengeance, or true

Introduction to King Arthur

LISTEN AND HEAR the life of a great lord who, while he lived, had no equal in cottage or castle. This event took place in the time of Arthur, that King, courtly and royal, and is about one of his great adventures. Wherever he went, of all kings, Arthur bears the flower; of all knights, he bears the honor. The whole country was chivalrous in those days. All knights were valiant, and cowards were forever disgraced.

— from *The Wedding of Sir Gawaine and Dame Ragnell*

What Does "Pendragon" Mean?

Pendragon is a title which roughly corresponds to "High King." Arthur's uncle, Aurelius Ambrosius, first held it when he regained his patrimony from the usurper Vortigern, a hated tyrant who invited the Saxons to Britain. After Aurelius his brother, Uther, held it. He was Arthur's father, and Arthur holds the title now, and no one will hold it after him. Thus it became, in effect, a family name.

The word comes from the ancient British (Cymric) tongue. It means *ben*, or chief, and *dragon*, or warlord. Dragons have been associated with warlords ever since the coming of the Romans, who carried draconic banners as legionary standards. Aurelius Ambrosius is called by Nennius "the last Roman," and probably bore such a banner before his army. The modern descendants of Arthur's people, the Welsh, still revere the symbol in their national arms: a red dragon.

Young Sir Lancelot du Lac

love, any of which are possible for your character. The choice is up to you.

Pendragon characters are not supposed to be without common sense or logic, but they possess strong feelings and act with consistency to those feelings, even when there is a cost. Illogical (but meaningful) actions may be limited or even exaggerated in particular situations. For example, even a notably honest character might behave dishonestly if the situation forced him into it, while a situation that made honesty the logical choice might *guarantee* that he would be honest. A situation that affect behavior is handled by imposing strong modifiers to a character's normal behavior, within limits and as the players and gamemaster feel are appropriate. Characters should never act randomly.

Passions are the strongest behavior factors. An Arthurian knight is not usually a cold-blooded warrior for hire. He is an emotional being with strong feelings about his world. These feelings, known as passions, may inspire him to superhuman feats, and may cause him to age prematurely when his hopes are blasted. A character without passions will always be weak (but will be more under the control of the player). Great glory can also be gained by strong passions.

Ideals, treated as groups of Personality Traits, are less powerful factors, and can neither inspire or harm as easily. They are based initially on the character's cultural and religious background. Great glory can be gained from certain dramatic patterns of personality traits.

The Passage of Time

Time in *Pendragon* passes at a faster and more clearly defined rate than in other adventure games. The general rule is that one year passes each time a knight has an adventure or fights a battle. Thus in a month of weekly playing four game-years will have passed. After a real year and a half your initial character will be slowly aging, and his eldest sons will be preparing to enter play.

Like the tale of Arthur, the game spans several generations. Important Arthurian events, such as the Grail Quest, begin in a specific year, and may take years to

unfold. Families grow and gain interest as game-years pass and dynastic influences take effect. The passage of time in the game also serves to compensate for the escalation of power which inevitably occurs as a roleplaying game progresses. Finally, Arthur's reign has a start and a finish, and time must progress to witness both events.

Events relating to characters should take more than an evening's game play to resolve. Feuds may fester and love affairs may linger for many sessions of *Pendragon*.

Glory

Glory measures character success. It includes many concepts of success. A knight's personal confidence, notoriety, heroic qualities, and social recognition are all quantified in *Pendragon* as Glory. Glory gives the players something else to work for besides character experience, and makes sure that any successes within the world of the game are recognized and dealt with in the rules, not just relegated to roleplaying considerations.

Glory has the power to raise a knight beyond the lot of normal persons. A knight that gains significant glory may take on heroic traits.

Glory can be increased in many ways, not just by success in war or personal combat. Among these alternate sources of glory are offices and high rank; chivalrous, religious, or romantic personal behavior, the ownership of land and castles; and many others.

Glory is not experience, though it may reflect experience.

Glory is not reputation: this is handled by the Ideals and Passions system.

Glory is an innate thing, unmeasured in the world, but always recognized. Everyone knows how much Glory a knight has, and great Glory augments the chance of recognition.

Families

A knight without a family is a lonely and isolated person in the violent world of *Pendragon*. A family includes the following, in order of importance: eldest son; parents; siblings; other children; one's wife; and distant relatives.

A knight's family supports him against his enemies, ransoms him when captured, and sustains him emotionally. All these functions are important during the play of the game, and are not just considerations for roleplaying.

For example, a threat to knights who routinely injure other player knights is the possibility of a blood feud, carried on against him by the relatives of their victims. This threat is strongly present in the literature and takes its place in the game as well. For example, a knight out to revenge his brother's death could be played by the same player whose previous character was murdered.

Just as importantly, families are the biological solution to mortality. The most important member of the knight's family is his heir, hopefully a son. Having a son means that a knight has a heir to inherit his weapons, his castle, a portion of his Glory, and a good degree of his personality, if desired by the player. Once a knight has a son, his death does not mean the loss of the character. The knight lives on in his son, and will be in many ways a more interesting and powerful character than his father; a son of a

Lancelot du Lac

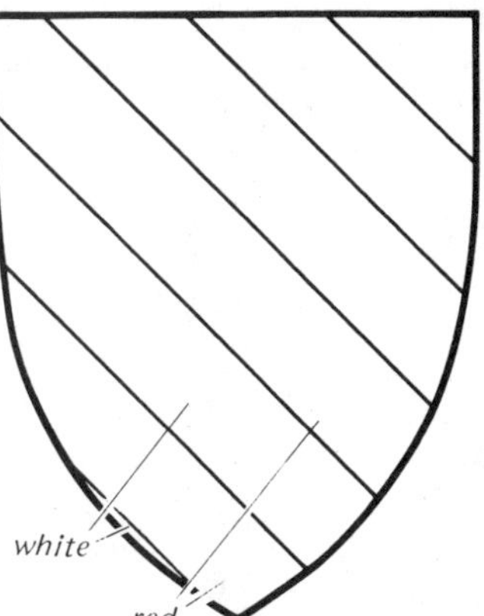

A *Pendragon* Chronology

This chronology lists the crucial phases and events in King Arthur's long reign. It can only hint at the richness of detail and variety to be found in the various Arthurian sources. Subsequent *Pendragon* supplements will present these events in detail.

495: Battle of St. Albans — King Uther Pendragon dies without a known heir. Anarchy reigns.
510: Arthur draws the Sword from the Stone, and is declared High King.
510-525: Period of Unification. King Arthur fights many fierce wars to unify Britain.
514: King Arthur marries Guenever and institutes the Brotherhood of the Round Table.
515: The Dolorous Stroke begins the Enchantment of Britain.
525: Sir Lancelot arrives at court.
525-540: Period of Consolidation. Romance and knight errantry are popular. Hints of what is to come, both good and bad, begin to appear, but are ignored or unrecognized by participants.
531: This is the suggested starting year for campaigns using this book. In only a decade Arthur's reign will reach its glittering height. The year 531 is notable for several reasons. The sinister Sir Mordred arrived at court earlier this year. Lancelot will be made a member of the Round Table this year. Finally, during the Irish Tournament that crowns the year, an unknown knight, Sir Tramtrist (Tristram), will defeat all participating Round Table knights, and begin a legendary love affair with Queen Isoud of Cornwall.
540-555: Period of Apogee. A period of magical quest and adventure as the enchantment of Britain is at its peak.
549: Miraculous healings by the Grail begin.
553: The Lonazep Tournament is held, the last and greatest. Dark forces appear and tragedy looms.
554: The Quest for the Holy Grail begins.
555 and later: Period of Decline. Intrigue, murder, and rebellion disrupt the realm.
563: Lancelot and Guenever are caught in adultery, shattering the unity of the Round Table and Britain.
565: At the disastrous battle of Camlann Mordred wounds King Arthur, who is removed to the Isle of Avalon. The magic fades and history intervenes.

player-character knight will always start play with more Glory and lands than a newly-created knight, and the scions of several generations will be awesome characters indeed if they survive to full maturity.

Epic Scale

Unlike characters in most adventure games, *Pendragon* characters are part of a larger world. The game is epic in its scope and scale. Characters are members of the elite ruling class and wield awesome power and privilege. They are movers and shapers of society, not unknown outsiders struggling to be recognized. Player characters must fulfil the obligations of their office and take part in the larger events of their time to maintain their proper status as knights.

Players will also benefit from the rich ongoing myth of King Arthur by having their characters fulfill their responsibilities.

The most significant events are those that affect the fate of Britain, such as the great battles, or the crucial magical events, such as the Grail Quest. See the nearby chronology for more information.

Marhaus

Three Damosels Incite Adventure

AT THE LAST they came into a great forest, that was named the country and forest of Arroy, and the country of strange adventures.

"In this country," said Sir Marhaus, "came never a knight since it was christened, but he found strange adventures."

And so they rode, and came into a deep valley full of stones, and thereby they saw a fair stream of water; and above thereby was the head of the stream a fair fountain, and three damosels sitting thereby. And they rode to them, and either saluted the other, and the eldest had a garland of gold about her head, and she was three score winter of age or more, and her hair was white under the garland. The second damosel was of thirty winter of age, with a circlet of gold about her head. The third damosel was but fifteen year of age, and a garland of flowers about her head. When these knights had so beheld them, they asked them the cause why they sat at that fountain.

"We be here," said the damosel, "for this cause: if we may see any errant knights, to teach them unto strange adventures; and ye be three knights that seeken adventures, and we be three damosels and therefore each one of you must choose one of us; and when ye have done so we will lead you unto three highways, and there each of you shall choose a way and his damosel with him. And this day twelvemonth ye must meet here again, and God send you your lives, and thereto ye must plight your troth."

"This is well said," said Sir Marhaus.

— Malory IV, 18

The Hidden World of Magic

Magic is a vital part of the Arthurian knight's world, but it is a total mystery. Magic takes different forms, and includes holy Christian miracles, Pagan sorcery and nature reverence, dark Wotanic dooms, and wicked necromancy. Magical swords and deadly enchantments abound, and more than one miraculous potion has come from the magician's hoard. An invisible land with supernatural inhabitants hides within the woods, and eerie creatures sometimes wander out.

A knight can never practice magic. To become a practitioner of the occult a person would have to have spent his lifetime training to become something other than a knight. Thus magic is always uncertain and fearful, even to the most powerful of members of chivalry. Even Sir Lancelot survived many contests only because of a very potent magic ring given to him by his step-mother, and without it was helpless before the power of a single young sorceress.

To simulate the terror and uncertainty of Arthurian magic, the *Pendragon* gamemaster has total control over all magic in the campaign, and is encouraged to create his own conception of how magic works as well as using the forms suggested in this book (see the "What Your Character Knows" chapter below).

Many sources of ideas are available in Arthurian literature. Later *Pendragon* supplements will go into detail about magic and its possible forms.

What Your Character Knows

Roleplaying requires a consensual setting which everyone agrees upon. This chapter gives the basis for that agreement.

THE SETTING for *Pendragon* is that of an idealized Middle Ages. It is a world very different from our 20th century life, with some very different basic assumptions. If we lack understanding of the basic facts then we can not understand the fabric of the fantasy. Some parts of the best-known Arthurian stories do not make sense if viewed only from a modern perspective.

This chapter gives you information which is known to everyone. Your character knows everything in this section. The information provides the unspoken background for everything which goes on. It includes political, geographic, social, and economic information, and a bit of very important folklore as well.

It is very important to understand these things if you wish your character to succeed. Your character may choose not to act within these parameters during the game, but it is still important to know these things because this is how almost everyone else is going to act.

Two types of information are given on the pages of this chapter. The main text provides an ideal and romanticized history of Britain, taken primarily from the literature. Players unfamiliar with the literature should read this to get an idea of what has been going on lately in their world. Players familiar with the literature should read it to see what has *not* yet occurred.

The lower panels of boxed text give basic historical facts essential to understanding the middle ages, feudal society, and the attitudes of the privileged society of knights.

The contrast of the two points of view is emphasized here, at the start of the game, because much of the play of *Pendragon* will find itself in such a contrasting position. Much of the intense drama in Arthurian literature is gained through a conflict between the ideal and the human.

⁜ THE FEUDAL WORLD ⁜

THIS BOXED PORTION of the chapter deals with facts which were prevalent in the middle ages, but unknown to most people today. They are the historical facts — the reality of a brutal and violent world. Players must be at least vaguely familiar with these factors in order to understand their characters fully.

Feudalism

In this section the medieval concept of feudalism is presented as your character knows it. Many complicated rules derive from the basic idea.

Feudalism is the belief that everything belongs to the king, as highest lord of the land. All rights derive from the king, who has distributed some of his rights and responsibilities among his lords who, in turn, distribute some of them to their knights. All obligations are personal, dependant upon the relationship between a lord and his followers. The followers swear to follow the lord, and afterwards are known as vassals of that lord.

The lord ensures the loyalty of his followers by giving them land, the single most valuable, and permanent, commodity in the realm. To receive gold is a slightly dubious honor, since even a peasant can be bribed with gold. But a transfer of land is sacred.

Two types of land transfer are common. A *gift* is given for the duration of the recipient's life but upon death reverts to the lord. A *grant* is given for the life of the recipient and the life of his heirs.

A vassal does not own the land, but he does own all the granted benefits collected from that land. The vassal receives his grant in return for loyalty and services.

As long as the obligations are satisfied, then the benefits are legally his and cannot be justly taken away. Typically, a knight's obligations are to serve in his lord's military campaigns and to advise his lord on important matters.

The lord owes his vassal protection, sustenance, and livelihood. The vassal owes loyalty, advice, and military service.

Thus there is a non-equal, but reciprocal agreement between lord and vassal.

Obligations may be changed only if both parties agree. Usually they are only changed when one person has done something significant for the other. If the vassal rescued the king on the battlefield he might receive his former gift as a permanent grant. Typical reasons for land to revert to the lord are: treason, failure to support the lord, or the lack of an heir when the grant holder dies. Daughters may inherit their father's grants only if there are no male heirs.

Ranks of feudal vassalage begin with those closest to the king, both in friendship and in wealth. In *Pendragon* they are the British kings, lords, and office holders. In turn those men appoint their own vassals. Knights (and squires, as knights-in-training) are the lowest class of noble vassals. They may hold their land from the king, a count, a lower lord, or even from another knight.

The Realm of Chivalry

Recent History

This is a good time to be alive. King Arthur's realm is well-established and approaching its glittering height. Although the realm may never be entirely peaceful, the only menaces extant now are those which can be handled by the vigorous activity of the Round Table and other chivalrous knights.

No recent wars have plagued the land. The greatest adventures lie within the forests and off the beaten tracks. At the center of the land lies Camelot, the enchanted city and center of all civilization.

King Arthur ascended to the throne of Britain 21 years ago after the wondrous deed of pulling a sword from an anvil and stone to prove his right to kingship. He acquired the magical sword, Excalibur, from Dame Viviane, the Lady of the Lake, who preceded Nimue in that position. Arthur fought several great wars against rebellious kings who denied his right to rule, and then went on to conquer foreign nations who sought to destroy him.

King Arthur instituted the Order of the Round Table to honor the greatest knights of the realm and unify them under his leadership. He now reigns over a magnificent realm, sending loyal knights out to conquer the robber barons and evil knights who have taken refuge in the wild lands farther from his central Kingdom of Logres. Since his accession to the throne many magical events have occurred, and to the discerning eye of those who care to study such things, it seems that the enchantments have grown ever more numerous and wondrous of late.

Famous People

In this section is what your character knows of the most notable persons of Britain. It is important to understand that the information given here is simply common knowledge, not necessarily the most accurate data possible. A Saxon raider or a Pict might have a totally different perspective on these people. The descriptions below are by no means impartial, nor even necessarily true. They do represent what most people of your society and culture have accepted as fact.

These extraordinary individuals are known throughout Britain and beyond. Your character has not personally met any of these people yet.

Reduced character sheets for most of these important figures are available for the gamemaster's use in the "Characters and Creatures" chapter of this book. Players are advised to review these characters to get an idea of the highest level of success and power which can be reached by characters in the game.

KING ARTHUR

King Arthur is the greatest king who has ever lived. He is the High King of Britain, Chief Knight of the Round Table, and conqueror of Europe. For two decades Arthur has fought great wars to unify Britain and maintain his claim against foreign kings. Now his court, at Camelot, is the center of civilization, and from there spring the greatest adventures of the island.

Church officials and monasteries also rely upon land grants to knightly vassals in return for loyal service. Monasteries often became powerful landowners with their own knights to protect them.

Homage and Fealty

Everyone but the king is someone's vassal. Everyone who has a lord has taken an oath of loyalty, a ritual composed of *homage* and *fealty* pledging two people to an unbreakable, permanent bond of loyalty.

Homage is an act of submission. The first part of the ceremony, homage, is ancient and originated among the Franks and Saxons. It is the personal oath of an underling to his lord. The vassal kneels before his lord and raises his clasped hands to his lord, who encloses them in his own. The vassal gives a brief oath promising aid and counsel. *Aid* means military assistance, while *counsel* means support of the lord in his business and the granting of advice. Then the lord gives a similar promise of leadership, and of support expressed as a *beneficium*, or a gift. The beneficium is usually a land grant, or *fief*. After swearing, the vassal rises, and both men kiss once to seal the oath. This finishes the act of homage.

Fealty is an oath of faithfulness. It is a solemn oath, often sworn upon saints' relics. Fealty's most common clause includes a promise never to attack the lord. Unlike homage, which can be sworn only once, a fealty oath is sometimes resworn to remind someone of his place, or whenever otherwise felt by the lord to be necessary.

After both of these oaths the vassal is the "man of another man." He is also sometimes called "a man of hands and mouth."

Multiple loyalties are possible. The issue is confused at court, but currently the most popular solution offered to the problem of multiple lords is the practice of having a *liege lord*. That is, among all of one's lords one is selected to be liege, and he has priority to the vassal's loyalty in case of conflict.

Your character has only one lord to begin, which creates no problem. However, if he acquires lands elsewhere the character will eventually have to choose one as liege.

King Arthur is great as well as mighty. All the virtues of a king spring from him. He is generous to everyone, he upholds the rights of his vassals, he delivers justice both high and low without favoritism if at all possible. He is brave and does not shun personal combat, and he is a great military leader, being unbeaten in battle.

King Arthur is yet more. He seeks to ensure his royal justice and protection for ever person in his realm, rich or poor, man or woman, noble or commoner. This is a novel idea, embraced by commoners and those who love or admire Arthur. It is manifest in the extraordinary ideals of chivalry and of "noblesse oblige," exemplified in the cry of "Might for Justice" as well as the normal standards expected of a king.

QUEEN GUENEVER

The wife of King Arthur is the most beautiful woman of the realm. She has introduced many civilizing influences to the realm, most notably that of courtly romance. She is the object of many man's Amor, but correctly refuses all serious advances, maintaining the lofty ideals of this delicate concept. In addition, she is a skilled politician and ably assists King Arthur in maintaining the glory of the realm.

SIR GAWAINE

The most renowned knight of the realm, Gawaine is Arthur's eldest nephew, and thus according to the Celtic reckoning special to the king, being Champion or, sometimes, even heir-apparent. Sir Gawaine has shown no political ambition, being content to serve the greatest king in Christendom.

Sir Gawaine is noted for his extraordinary courtliness and manners, his extravagant courtesy and flirting with women, his great prowess at battle, and his unrelenting vengeance when motivated by his love of family.

Sir Gawaine is the head of the Orkney clan, the most powerful family of northern Britain.

SIR LAMORAK DE GALES

This knight is the greatest fighter in the realm, though the newcomer from France shows great promise.

Many years ago Lamorak's father, King Pellinore, was treacherously murdered in secret, and since then Sir Lamorak has rarely appeared at court. Instead he prefers to wander the countryside seeking adventure, even appearing at tournaments in disguise.

Sir Lamorak is head of the de Gales family which was once powerful in Cambria. Since the death of King Pellinore the influence of the de Gales clan has diminished considerably. Thus, even though Lamorak and two of his brothers are members of the Round Table, their patrimony of the Kingdom of Gomeret and The Isles has been seized by King Maelgwyn.

SIR LANCELOT DU LAC

This knight is a newcomer to court, having arrived only a few years ago. He is the youngest member of the famous de Ganis clan which has taken refuge with King Arthur. Originally from Ganis, on the continent, they were driven out many years ago by the French king. They impatiently await their opportunity to regain their lands.

Although present at court for only six winters, this Lancelot has already impressed everyone with his courtly manners, prowess at battle, and success at adventure. Recently he killed Sir Carados of the Dolorous Tower, an evil knight of awesome prowess who had troubled the realm for many years.

Social Classes

SOCIETY CONSISTS OF three strictly separate social classes: nobles, clergy, and commoners. Everyone believes in this system. People are born into a specific class and enter the same occupation as their parents. People do not usually expect to change their status.

This seems shocking to us today, when individual freedom is the highest ideal. Members of our modern, democratic society have difficulty understanding the class system which dominates medieval society, but an understanding of it is necessary to capture the feel and meaning of the literature and events of the Middle Ages.

Strict social classes are not inherently bad. Many people find comfort in avoiding responsibilities and knowing that their daily routine will be predictable and unchanging. It is not being in a caste which is bad, but rather being in an exploited and abused caste. Thus, although many miserable serfs would like to have their condition improved, they figure that they would still, always, be serfs, and have all the advantages of being a man or woman of the soil.

The ruling class of nobles jealously holds its prerogatives. So insistent are noblemen on maintaining class differences that a knight will lose his status for engaging in non-knightly behavior, such as physical labor or money-lending. The unarguable belief in "might makes right" allows noblemen to maintain their prerogative at everyone else's expense.

It is important, however, to remember that these are social classes, not strictly hard castes. For instance, any knight might attain to the status of lord by being richly rewarded by his own lord. Furthermore, a commoner might attain knighthood through prowess or arms displayed on the battlefield. Finally, the clergy fill their ranks from people of all classes.

Admittedly, every age has people who do not fit into their class. Such people are exceptional, and like exceptional people anytime, will find a way through or around the system to their advantage. In the Middle Ages exceptional commoners

When Is This?
King Arthur's reign lasts for 55 years, from the time that he draws the sword from the stone (510 A.D.) until he boats to Avalon (565). The *Pendragon* rules depict the central period of Arthur's reign, starting around 531. Your game could be set earlier or later, in which case some information here is not yet relevant. Be sure to check with your gamemaster on the precise date of your campaign.

Sir Lancelot is often absent from court, searching out glory in adventure. He is King Arthur's shining example of a dutiful knight, traveling into unsettled realms to bring the High King's justice and custom to the realm.

Everyone is certain that he will soon be admitted to the high honor of the Round Table.

MERLIN

The most skilled and revered of all magicians, Merlin disappeared some fifteen years ago. He was instrumental in helping Arthur establish his throne, and his mysterious absence is a sore grievance to the king, who has ordered a search that continues to this day. Throughout his life Merlin has been known to disappear on previous occasions, not returning to court for years at a time, and so many believe he may yet reappear, or at least is still alive. Thus the search goes on.

Even without his actual presence the magician's influence is everywhere. He set many great events into motion, and the greatest of these are not yet finished, especially including the events of the Grail Quest.

NIMUE

Nimue is the Lady of the Lake, a powerful enchantress and head of a sisterhood of powerful pagan priestesses. She is not only a priestess, but also studied under the great Merlin. Nimue is among the most firm supporters of the king. She has taken over the magical protection once provided by Merlin, who has mysteriously disappeared.

Her home is beneath a magical lake which comes and goes at her call, and which may appear in almost any land. Beneath it is a great palace where her lover, Sir Pelleas, lives, and where Lancelot, Bors, and Lionel were raised.

The Isle of Avalon, the home of her pagan sisterhood, is a magical place like Nimue's lake. It exists at the edges of normal reality, sometimes not in this world at all. It, however, does not move about, and if found is found in the marshes of Somerset.

SIR YWAINE

Sir Ywaine is the son of King Uriens of Gorre and Morgan le Fay, the wicked sister of King Arthur. Sir Ywaine is one of the great knights of the Round Table even though he was once banished by Arthur. Ywaine has since continually proved his unswerving loyalty to the High King. Ywaine has participated in many great adventures, and in them has acquired the friendship of a mighty lion which is as peaceful as a lap dog when Ywaine is present.

THE FISHER KING

King Pellam, better known by his title of Fisher King, is the Keeper of the Holy Grail. His realm is normally hidden from mortal eyes, known only through legend. But rumor insists that his land had been growing outward, filling the deep woods and hidden realms with its pres-

usually joined the church, or became personal employees of a nobleman. Exceptional members of the ruling class became saints, like St. Francis, or heroes, like King Arthur.

The Noble Class
The nobility is the upper class. Noblemen are the leaders and warriors of society. They do not work for their own maintenance, but acquire the food and goods of their life from others.

However, within this class not all persons are equal. Two distinct divisions exist, commonly called the higher and lower nobility. The lower nobility are the knights. The higher nobility are called lords. Lords include all knights who have vassals who are knights or lords, and includes all the hereditary landholders. Lords are also knights, of course, but are usually referred to by their higher rank.

This division is common among most feudal cultures. In English the terms for higher and lower nobility are Lords (higher) and Gentry (lower); in French barons and *chevaliers*; in German *Herren* and *Ritter*; and in Spanish *grandes* and *hildagos*.

Within the category of lord are several ranks of noblemen, ranged from lowest to highest: banneret, baron, earl, duke.

Knights' primary responsibility is to serve as the military force for their lord. They have many privileges and freedoms which are not available to the lower classes, gained in exchange for the pledge that they will die if necessary for their lord.

Knights fill the most advantaged class, and thus have the greatest freedom and most privileges of anyone else in the game. *Pendragon* concerns itself primarily with this class of men.

The Clerical Class
The clergy includes all members of the church, a powerful institution which owns considerable lands and has many rights of its own. Churchmen are exempt from most ordinary laws, and claim loyalty to God, a higher authority than the king — a claim which is a source of great conflict between clergy and royalty.

The clergy, supposed to be chaste, can hardly be expected to reproduce itself and so draws members from both the nobility and the commoners. It is not unusual for younger sons of the nobility to join the

ence, threatening to engulf even the lands of men with its enchantment. But though the realm grows, the secret Castle of the Holy Grail remains undiscovered.

MORGAN LE FAY

This wicked witch is the youngest sister of King Arthur. Morgan was once friendly, but has proved herself treacherous and been driven into hidden exile. She has maneuvered many plots against the king and his knights, and her secret strongholds throughout the land provide refuge for bandits, and meeting places for conspirators.

Morgan is a powerful sorceress, known to commune with faeries and other pagan powers. Her powers of seduction and lust are rumored to be as great as her magic.

SIR MORDRED

Sir Mordred has recently come to Camelot. He is the youngest son of King Lot, who was once an enemy of King Arthur. Thus he is Sir Gawaine's brother, and a member of the Orkney clan. His mother is Queen Margawse, Arthur's sister, who is explained below.

Sir Mordred has a strong personality, and is both cynical and sly. More, he seems sinister, as if possessing some dark secret, and his mere presence often makes men uncomfortable, as if his shadow is too large and cold. Everyone believes that the Pendragon tolerates the young man because of his natural love for the Orkney kinsmen of his family.

QUEEN MARGAWSE

The Wicked Queen of the North is the oldest sister of King Arthur. She holds a deep and relentless grudge against her younger brother, seeking vengeance for the wrongs done to her father and mother by Arthur's father. Her husband, King Lot, was killed in the wars of unification, and she took refuge with her youngest son, Mordred, in the far northern realm of the Orkney Islands.

Ironically, her eldest son, Sir Gawaine, is Arthur's most sincere follower, having made his choice of loyalties many years ago. Young Mordred has also deserted his mother's cause, having arrived this very year at court to be knighted.

KING MARK

The King of Cornwall is the most powerful British king who has not yet paid homage to King Arthur. He rules over Cornwall, a rich and powerful kingdom, and much of Brittany. His rule is maintained by political diplomacy, good trade agreements, a strong army, and the powerful sword arm of Sir Tristram, a promising young knight who is the king's nephew.

Morgan le Fay

Sir Ywaine is Described

Sir Ywaine, hard on an adventure, has discovered the woman of his dreams. After a remarkable wooing, he gets his wish, and a marriage is planned. The Duchess introduces Ywaine to her court.

"You should know that he is no lesser man that King Urien's son. Apart from his being of high birth, he is of such great valor and is so courtly and intelligent that nobody should advise me against accepting him. I suppose you've all heard of my lord Ywaine; it is he who is seeking my hand."

—from *Yvaine, or The Knight with the Lion*, by Chretien de Troyes (D.D.R Owen Trans.)

King Mark's wife Isoud is famous for her wit and beauty, which some compare even to Queen Guenever.

SIR TURQUINE OF THE DOLOROUS TOWER

This unrepentant Saxon rebel hates King Arthur and all good knights, especially those of the Round Table. His brother Carados was recently slain by Sir Lancelot and so Turquine has sworn unrelenting vengeance on Arthur and his realm, sallying forth from his hidden stronghold to raid and plunder. Anyone who brings Turquine's head to Arthur would probably warrant membership in the Round Table, and even information leading to his demise would be greatly appreciated.

SIR BRUS SANS PITIE

A treacherous, back-stabbing knight and slayer of women, Sir Brus has been sighted in many places across the island wreaking terrible havoc against all that is good. He owns an incredibly swift horse of magical origin which has saved him many times from the king's justice.

Britain and Europe

IN THIS SHORT SECTION the basic geographical and political organization of your character's world is revealed. Because your character is a knight he probably has memorized this material a long time ago.

Players should note that the information here represents commonly accepted estimates, not the work of trained geographers, demographers, or other technical specialists, who will not exist for perhaps a thousand years. Thus it is always up for reappraisal.

As you will see, your character knows little about the world outside his own homeland of Logres, less of Europe, and nothing about lands and peoples outside of Europe.

clergy rather than be landless knights, seeking whatever opportunity the church can give them. For bright and ambitious commoners the church provides the best opportunity for advancement.

Churchmen may be secular clergy or monastics. Secular clergy includes bishops and the village priests who administer the sacraments to commoners, and who oversee the spiritual development of their parish. Monastics are men or women who have taken the religious path of isolation and joined special communities which practice devotion apart from the ways of ordinary mankind.

The Common Class

Everyone who is not noble or clergy is a commoner. They are the basis for society. They are the ordinary people who provide the food and goods which allow noblemen and clergy to pursue their specialized functions. Commoners are mostly farmers, whether poor serfs without any freedom or rich landholders who maintain the right to change lords at will. The artisans who populate cities and make their wares are commoners. The merchants who act as middlemen for trade and cross Britain with their goods are also commoners.

Members of the nobility can become commoners. A squire's sons are considered commoners, though of good status within the broad spectrum of commoners.

Commoners can enter the ranks of knight as well. Anyone who can acquire weapons and employment in the ranks of mercenaries might rise further through recognition by his leader. Commoners who perform outstandingly, even off the battlefield, can be raised to the status of squires or even knights by their grateful lords. Sometimes lords desperate for money sell knighthood to rich men.

KEY
City
Large City
Old fortification
Small Castle
Large Castle
Medium Castle
Seaport
Baron
Count
Duke
King
High King
Road
Trail
River
Trees
To Bedegraine
To Cameliard
Leicester
Wuerensis
Arden Forest
Warwick
Avon River
To Estregales
Clarence
To Glastonbury
Bourton
Wanborough
Thames River
Cirencester
Wells
Bath
Compacorent Forest
Jagent
Morgaine's Forest
Somerset
Ilchester
Dorset
Dorchester
To Cornwall

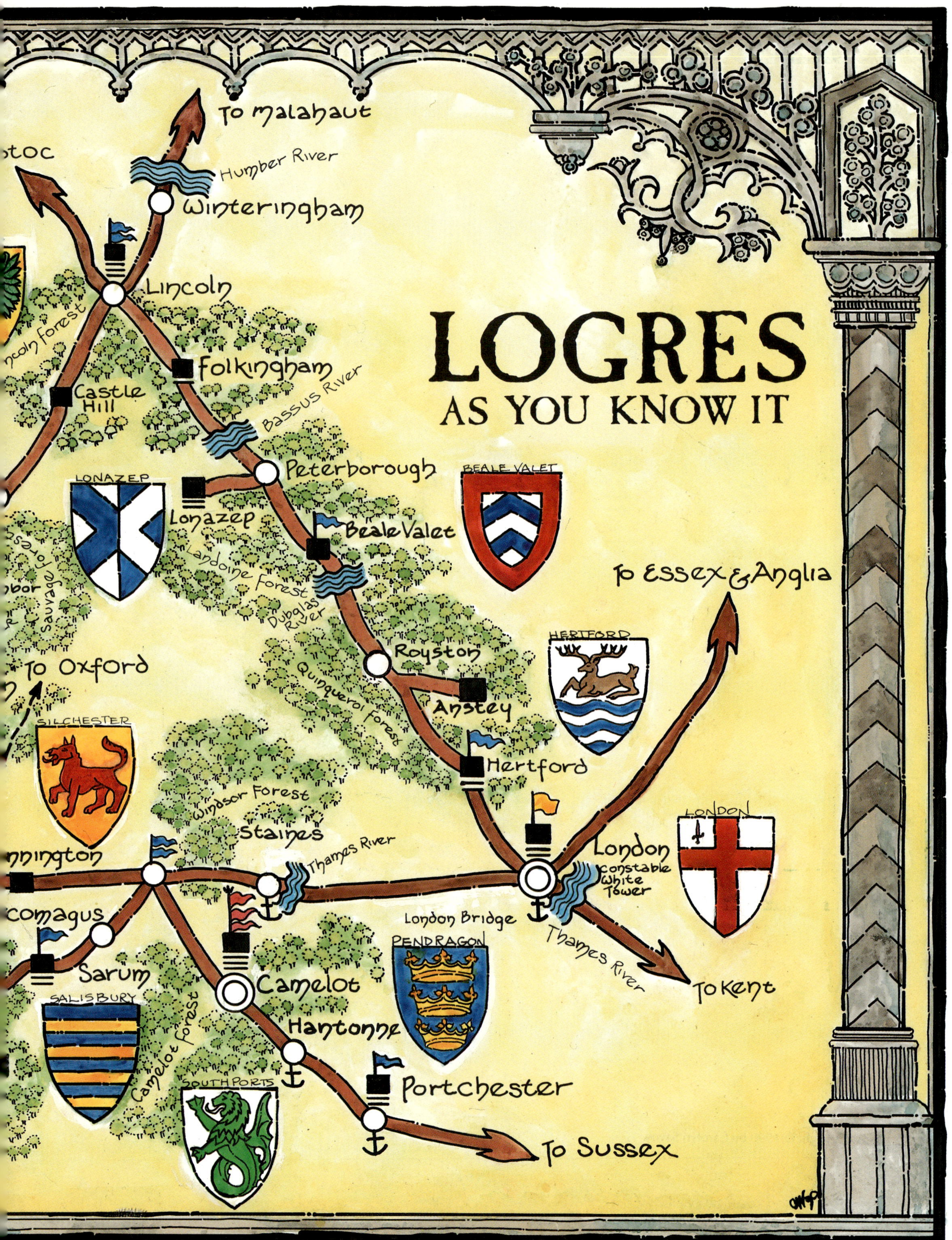

LOGRES
AS YOU KNOW IT
To Malahaut
Humber River
Winteringham
Lincoln
Folkingham
Castle Hill
Bassus River
Peterborough
LONAZEP
Lonazep
Landoine Forest
BEALE VALET
Beale Valet
Dubglas River
Sauvage Forest
To Essex & Anglia
Royston
Anstey
HERTFORD
Hertford
To Oxford
Quinqueroi Forest
SILCHESTER
Windsor Forest
Staines
Thames River
London
Constable White Tower
LONDON
London Bridge
Thames River
To Kent
Sarum
PENDRAGON
Camelot
SALISBURY
Hantonne
Camelot Forest
Portchester
SOUTH PORTS
To Sussex

Political Divisions of Britain

Britain is divided into five areas. They are Logres, Cambria, Cumbria, Pictland, and Cornwall. Logres is by far the most important.

Logres, Arthur's Kingdom

This is information which your character knows about his homeland, the Kingdom of Logres. This information is generally known by all informed knights.

Logres is King Arthur's kingdom. Your character's home county, the County of Salisbury, is located in Logres. Logres is the largest and most powerful kingdom of Britain, and includes most of the lowland areas of the southeast. It is the home of British civilization and culture, and includes about one half of the island's population. Most of the large cities of Britain are in Logres, including Camelot, the cultural center, and London, the economic center.

Many great lords rule portions of Logres, and populate Arthur's court as courtiers and fill his army with knights. Four nobles are the *really great* landholders: the Dukes of Clarence, Lindsey, Anglia, and the Archbishop of Carlion.

The many lesser ones include the war-worn Duke of Silchester, several Earls (including the Earl of Salisbury) and other barons.

The Christian Church in Logres has one supreme churchman, the Archbishop of Carlion, a Cymru, Dubricus by name, twelve Bishops, and a dozen or so Abbots of great houses. Churchmen are not considered noble unless they are also landlords, which is not uncommon.

Merlin the Enchanter was the only Archdruid, but the position has not been filled since his disappearance. Many lesser druids and enchantresses also exist, but generally as local covens without much central organization. Thus druids are not normally considered noblemen, but sometimes continue to have a noble status in lands where the ancient pagan ways are upheld.

Ywaine le Chevalier au Lion

silver

blue

The Map of Logres

Elsewhere is a color map of Logres as you know it. This map is strange to the modern eye. We are accustomed to reading a map and seeing objective data. This map is more medieval in its flavor, showing subjective knowledge rather than accurately measured distances. Many maps of this medieval type will probably be encountered by your character during a *Pendragon* campaign, so I provide this as an example. You are encouraged to keep similar maps of your character's travels.

This map may be understood to be what most knights of Logres know of their land. If your character spent a year with Arthur's peacetime army riding its usual

Customs of Society

The Universal Laws

Certain customary laws are universal among all the peoples of Britain. They are the unwritten laws of loyalty, family, hospitality, and honor. Your character knows these laws well. From childhood on they have been a part of life for every knight.

Players must understand that these laws precede and underlie the bold new concepts of chivalry that King Arthur is promoting. Even the most barbaric or vicious groups in Britain accept these ancient traditions as necessary and essential for survival in a hostile world.

These laws are respected even between enemies. For instance, when an enemy Pictish king accepts the hospitality of King Arthur, he is confident that he can eat and relax in the Pendragon's halls without fear of murder, even if he is dead drunk. Only the Saxons and other dastards perfidiously break this rule, and then only occasionally. Similarly, if the enemy Pict king was conquered by Arthur and swore loyalty, then Arthur can be confident that he will be obeyed by his new vassal. Finally, if someone marries into a family, even that of his enemy, he becomes a kinsman and can therefore be trusted.

Every player must remember that these rules are the keystones of his character's society and of the world. They are what make people into people, and set them apart from beasts.

This is not to say that your character must *always* abide by the four laws, or that he must assume that others will. You control your own character, and tricky issues, such as consistency of behavior or your character's reputation, are handled by the game rules, not just left to the gamemaster to enforce or ignore. In game terms, these laws are the four basic Passions. See the "Ideals and Passions" chapter for further information.

Hospitality

Among the divergent cultures of Britain there is one matter upon which all agree: the rules of hospitality.

Armies of Logres

The only detailed information known by your character about Logres is military, as would be expected from a warrior. Below is a list of the various subdivisions of the kingdom and their armies. The term "Soldiers" indicates foot-soldiers.

Anglia
Army: 75 knights, 250 soldiers

Bedegraine
Army: 75 knights, 75 soldiers

Brun
Army: 50 knights, 250 soldiers

Clarence
Army: 100 knights, 300 soldiers

Dorset
Army: 50 equites (a Roman term for knights), 2000 soldiers

Essex
Army: 60 knights, 200 soldiers

Hampshire
Army: 100 knights, 300 soldiers

Hertford
Army: 80 knights, 100 soldiers

Huntington
Army: 90 knights, 200 soldiers

Jagent
Army: 75 knights, 150 soldiers

Kent
Army: 80 knights, 250 soldiers

Lambor
Army: 75 knights, 150 soldiers

Lindsey
Army: 300 knights, 1000 soldiers

Lonazep
Army: 75 knights, 75 soldiers

London
Army: 70 knights, 1000 soldiers

Rydychan
Army: 60 knights, 150 soldiers

Salisbury
Army: 75 knights, 165 soldiers

Silchester
Army: 150 knights, 1000 soldiers

Somerset
Army: 100 knights, 500 soldiers

Southports (including Wight)
Army: 35 knights, 125 soldiers
Navy: 25 war ships with 500 sailors

Sussex
Army: 60 knights, 250 soldiers

Tribruit
Army: 50 knights, 500 soldiers

Wuerensis
Army: 70 knights, 125 soldiers

rounds, this is the route which they took. If your character has asked other, more experienced knights about Logres, the information which they gave is on this map. Note that most of the information is military in nature, as befitting a simple knight's area of interest.

Your character also knows things about his own homeland, Salisbury, which do not appear on this map. You can assume that everyone from Logres knows this map's information, plus something more about their own homeland.

Exploration and questing are themes of the *Pendragon* game, and adventures will often consist of investigating other areas, sometimes to just sight-see the marvels of enchanted Britain, at others to fulfill some heroic task.

The roads shown are all Royal Roads. They are considered to be the property of King Arthur himself, and anyone who commits violence incurs the penalty as if violating the sanctity of Arthur's feast hall. Other Royal Roads also exist in Logres.

A man's house is considered to be sacrosanct, protected by whatever powers watch over mankind. This is true whether he lives in a hovel or a mighty castle. This sanctity does not mean the powers intervene to protect a house if it is attacked. It does mean that the offender is never trusted in anyone's house again if he breaks the rules, and that an ill fate will dog the offender's footsteps from then on.

The rules insist that a person need not invite anyone into the safety of his hearth, but if he does, then *both* people must obey certain rules of respect and safety. Once inside, peace must reign between them, even if they discover they are deadly enemies. They can go outside and fight, or one of them can leave and then return with hostile intentions, if he is permitted back in. But while inside both men must be peaceful and the visitor must even aid the owner of the hearth to defend it if they are attacked.

The host may never act against his visitor, but must treat him as an honored guest. The visitor must in turn be civil and not insult his host.

Any breach in this unwritten contract is seen and corrected by the powers that oversee the laws of hospitality. They will see that justice is eventually delivered. Superstition assures your character that if a person abuses this rule, something terrible will occur to him at the most inconvenient time, whether delivered by God, Llew, or Wotan, all of whom protect the hearth. The famous events in the Grail Castle, precipitated by the unlucky Sir Balin, illustrate the workings of fate as regards hospitality. First Sir Garlon, a vile knight, insulted and struck his brother's guest, Sir Balin. Then Sir Balin committed another crime when he killed Sir Garlon. Thus King Pellam, the host, was caught in a trap of honoring either his own hospitality and maintaining peace, or his own family loyalty and avenging his brother. He chose the latter, and in the fight against Sir Balin Pellam suffered the Dolorous Stroke. For these wrongs the hapless Sir Balin was condemned to a useless and tragic death, and King Pellam suffered terribly until finally healed by the celebration of the Mass of the Holy Grail many years later.

Trust Your Kin

The world is a dangerous place. There is plenty to mistrust in others, even if they are not strangers who speak a different

Foreign Britain

To the knights of Logres, all the rest of Britain is full of foreign lands. These lands are commonly grouped into several large regions, each of which has several kingdoms within it.

Cambria

Cambria is the western region of Britain. It is sometimes called Wales, or in the French fashion as Gales. Cambria, however,includes modern Wales and a much larger region in the east. Two strong kings contend for power in Cambria.

The King of Estregales rules the southern regions, even over some lowland areas taken from Logres in earlier days. Its king has always been friendly to Arthur and, since he is heirless, has willed his lands to the Pendragon.

The lands of Gomeret and Isles are ruled by King Maelgwyn, an ambitious and difficult king. After King Pellinore was killed many lords vied for the kingship, and Maelgwyn was victorious. He has since sworn fealty, but his kingdom has never been conquered by Arthur, and Maelgwyn uses Arthur's sense of justice to protect his own prerogatives. Maelgwyn is always late on paying his tribute, never catches robbers who ambush Arthur's men, and cannot find the knights who steal cattle from neighboring Cameliard. Christian churchmen all hate Maelgwyn. Yet his people love him, and his son Rhun is one of the most respected princes in Cambria.

Cumbria

The people of Cumbria are often called the "northern British." Cumbria includes all the lands north of the Humber River and south of the Pictish mountains. The kings from this region initially resisted Arthur's kingship, but were conquered and are now his vassals. Much of the region is rugged mountains and dense, unexplored forest.

The Kingdom of Malahaut is one major power in Cumbria. Sir Barant de Apres has almost as many titles as King Arthur does: the Centurion King, King of the Brigantes, heir of King Coel the Old, and King of One Hundred Knights. He rules a mixed population of British, Saxons, and Romans from the city of Eburacum (York). He pays his tribute and houses the Pendragon's men, but he is formal and reluctant rather than enthusiastic.

King Uriens is the other powerful king, ruling from the mountainous land of Gorre and receiving vassalage from most surrounding lands. He is heir to the unity established by King Lot many years ago. His widespread lands are thinly populated and full of wild forests, mountains, and unexplained landmarks. His wife, Morgan le Fay, fled from Uriens' house many years ago, but the king still loves Arthur as a brother-in-law and kinsman.

Pictland

Pictland includes everything north of Cumbria. Most of it is mountain, unexplored and unknown to anyone except the wild, tattooed natives. Much of it is rugged coastline, occupied in part by Irish from the powerful kingdom of Dal Riada. The region is called the Long Isles. Other island kingdoms, like the Out Isles and Orkneys, once submitted to Arthur but have since reverted to a piratical independence. Since they primarily prey upon each other, King Arthur generally leaves them alone.

tongue and worship alien gods. Foreigners are, *a priori,* hostile and threatening.

However, one's kin group should always be trusted. Even if a kinsman acts despicably he is still to be trusted. Only the family can be counted upon in an emergency — any emergency. Thus an individual is not helpless against the world, but can always count on his kin for aid.

The loyalty and affection of a person for his family is considered to be inherent to nature. It is unthinkable that someone would turn against his family. A kinslayer is unheard of — inhuman, almost demonic.

Sometimes a knight has to choose between loyalty to his kin and loyalty to his lord. There may be no way to resolve problems without offending someone important. Such dilemmas are what the greatest stories are made of, and offer the best chances to roleplay.

Some of the commonly-used family terms are:

clan: all people who claim descent from a common ancestor.

lineage: all people who can actually trace their ancestry to a common ancestor. This is the *Pendragon* family.

kindred: all people who are relatives of an individual, including those which are outside his lineage (i.e. his wife's family).

Loyalty

Loyalty is acknowledged as the basis for all of society beyond the family. All members of society except the mad hold loyalty to someone. For warriors and soldiers (like your character), loyalty is particulary important because it is the foundation of military organization and the basis of survival in battle.

Logic and self-interest both provide a basis for loyalty. No one would consider it fair or just to perform hostile acts against the person who supports them with food, protection, and comfort. Moreover, loyalty to a leader extends a person's influence outside of his own family, giving him a place in the larger world.

Loyalty is assured by ritualized pledges and oaths which establish the relationship between two people. As noted above, feudal loyalty is an agreement between two parties: a leader and a follower.

Those who break their oath of loyalty are outcasts from society and will never

Cornwall

Cornwall is the last area of Britain. It includes the entire southwestern peninsula, an area much larger than the Cornwall of today. Cornwall is famous for its rich tin mines, and its close political connections with Brittany. The Kingdom of Cornwall has never submitted to Arthur, but is neutral at worst. Its king is named Mark. King Mark is known to be ruthless and, as convenient, perfidious even to his kinsmen. Such traits in a king are reflected in his knights, and Cornishmen are generally considered to be inferior to other knights and are the butt of numerous jokes.

Brittany: Brittany is a peninsula on the continent which has recently been settled by emigrants from Britain. Its lands are rich and growing, although the interior is a wild and enchanted forest. The most powerful king here is Mark of Cornwall, thanks to the additional strength provided by his estates in Britain. King Conon of Vannetais is the other major ruler, ambitious and troubled by a hatred for the King of France.

Areas Outside Britain

Ireland

Ireland is a wild and barbarous island populated by five great kingdoms which are filled with unruly Irish clansmen. Ireland is beset by all the difficulties inherent in decentralized tribal government. Its High King rules more in name than in fact.

Europe

Little is known of Europe in King Arthur's time, except for Rome, Brittany, Ganis, and Gaul.

The great Roman Empire of the Caesars has fallen, replaced by warring barbarian kingdoms ruled by grandsons of the ancient German war gods. A few years ago Theoderic (a Goth) conquered his neighbors and named himself Emperor. Theoderic made a fatal mistake in offending the High King several years ago, provoking the Roman War. Arthur and his greatest warriors marched to Rome, crushed Theoderic's armies, and slew the Gothic overlord. The Pope then anointed Arthur as Emperor, and Arthus is still emperor today.

Gaul is occupied by Franks. Once great under King Clovis, the French kings continually bicker among themselves. Thus the fate of Brittany and Ganis, occupied by French troops, wavers continually in the unruly continental politics.

Sailors of Ganis and Brittany control the Atlantic trade routes between Britain and the Mediterranean. From that distant market come exotic commodities such as destriers, two-handed greatswords, horse barding, and sumptuous goods.

Every other land in Europe may be treated as a feudal kingdom, except the Byzantine Empire which is so far away it is out of play. The farther north the kingdom lies the more barbaric it is likely to be, making the Picts and the Scandinavians among the most barbaric.

lationship between two people. As noted above, feudal loyalty is an agreement between two parties: a leader and a follower.

Those who break their oath of loyalty are outcasts from society and will never be trusted by right-thinking people. As with the laws of hospitality and kinship, the supernatural powers that watch over man may intervene to bring oathbreakers to a terrible end.

Loyalty and the further implications of this concept on your character's life are discussed in detail below.

Honor

Honor is the last of the universal laws of society. Honor is required of knights, but not of everyone else. Having honor is one of the things which sets a knight apart from all others. Churchmen do not need honor, for they are supposed to put the interests of God and Church before their own. Commoners do not need honor, for they have enough difficulty just staying alive. Women do not need honor, because they are just women, although women who have honor are esteemed above others. Knights, however, must have honor because they have agreed to take the oath of knighthood. Without honor no oath is worth anything, for without it the sworn word will soon be broken. It is conceivable that a knight could cheat and connive, but still maintain his own sense of honor as long as the oath of knighthood was never violated.

Honor includes your character's personal code of integrity, pride, and dignity, which is important enough to be backed up by force of arms. Beyond these words, however, definition gets more difficult. Difficulty stems from using the critical adjective "personal." Every knight has agreed that it includes some things. For instance, the Dishonorable Acts Table in the "Ideals and Passions" chapter lists the things which everyone agrees are dishonorable actions for a knight. Performing these deeds (killing a woman, for example) always diminishes honor. Knights have agreed not to do these things.

However, the concept of a personal definition of honor is important. It means two things. First, some aspects of honor are determined by the individual, not by common social consent. Secondly, "personal" is used to separate honor from the other sworn or innate social obligations, including the other unwritten laws of society or any others, which are determined socially.

REGIONS of BRITAIN

•Key•
•also showing the major political powers•
Kingdom's:
•centre of power
•influence only
•ocean •land
REGION (name)
•Kingdom name

PICTLAND
Long Isles
EIRE
CUMBRIA
Malahaut
Gore
Gomeret
Leinster
CAMBRIA
LOGRES
Saxon Logres
Escavalon
Cornwall

Camelot

CAMELOT IS THE CENTER of Arthur's magnificent realm. It is a place of man-made magic conjured into being by Arthur's dreams and hard work.

In ancient times Camelot was the capital of a pagan kingdom which was converted to Christianity by Joseph of Arimathea. However, the place lost its importance between then and Arthur's time, for it is not mentioned again except as Arthur's city.

Arthur chose the site to be his capital and began construction in 522 after his political and military situation was secure. The central palace was finished in less than a year as the laborers worked as if by magic, inspired by Arthur's dream and hard cash. The rest of the city was added over the years, always growing in splendor. The immense castle-palace is so extensive that it will never be finished.

The courts and customs of the High Court originate at Camelot. King Arthur and Queen Guenever set the fashions of the kingdom here, imitated closely by the courtiers and visiting kings. Those powerful personages each have their own private quarters in the city, varying in size and splendor according to the status of the individual. These private courts imitate the styles of the High Court as best possible. The biggest courts, banquet halls, and gardens which are most like the Pendragon's court are the sections belonging to the Kings of Malahaut, the Dukes of Britain, and so on.

Other significant parts of Camelot include its cathedral, gardens which house parts of the famous Camelot menagerie, stables which hold thousands of steeds, lofty mews with magical birds, and the stadium-sized tournament field.

Arthur has three main courts in Camelot: the Outer Court, King's Throne Room, and Round Table Hall. The Queen's Court is indoors, while her Court of Love usually meets in a magical garden outdoors. A Visitor's High Court is available for important occasions. The Great Banquet Hall is where the knights closest to Arthur normally eat, with several other banquet halls for lesser knights and servants.

The Outer Court is a parade ground and courtyard capable of holding both a teeming mass of commoners and a proud display of chivalry at once. Public assembly occurs here.

The King's Court holds the thrones of the High King, his Queen, and the heir-presumptive. The last-titled is hoped to be the son of the king and queen. Most of the time, however, it is Sir Gawaine's seat.

The Round Table Hall is used only when the Round Table meets, either annually at the Pentecost (the seventh Sunday after Easter), or at Arthur's command (such as the Christmas when Gawaine meets the Green Knight). The magnificent Round Table measures one hundred and fifty feet in diameter, and is housed beneath a lofty dome. Singing birds fly overhead. The table has an open center

Customs of the Family

Patriarchy

The rules and laws of *Pendragon* are based on those of Europe in the 12th and 13th centuries, not the sixth century of the historical Arthur. Feudalism and vassalage, already discussed, are the most obvious examples of these customs. The laws of family, property, and marriage are others.

The laws are based on Roman models and are reinforced by the beliefs of both the Judeo-Christian and the Germanic warrior traditions. These three systems uniformly place men and male things to be more important than women and female things. Property belongs to the father, or *patriarch*. Thus the system is called patriarchal.

The position of women in this system is sad. They are degraded by the church and the legal system. Women are promised as pledges of friendship between would-be allies, and allowed to oversee the household. Everything of importance revolves around the family head.

Marriage and Inheritance

Marriage is a sacred and legal institution which is supposed to secure certain inheritance rights for all members involved. It is sanctioned and blessed by pagan and Christian churches, and is recognized by all government authorities.

Divorce is not allowed. Occasional annulments are made by the Pope on grounds of consanguinity (i.e., that the person whom you married is more closely related to you than you originally believed). In general, marriages between any person more closely related than third cousins is prohibited.

Note that there are absolutely no emotional requirements for marriage. It is a political act, with little care for individual feelings. Thus it is not surprising that both men and women sought love, emotional expression, and satisfaction in extramarital affairs. These affairs eventually acquired unofficial sanction in the Courts of Love, wherein the art of Fine Amor was developed and exercised.

Rules of Marriage

In marriage a woman leaves her blood family and takes up residence with her husband, thereby joining herself and her children to his family. Marriage is a legal institution upheld by society, and a religious sacrament upheld by religion.

accessible to dancers, musicians, jugglers, and other performers, and the floor there is slightly lower than the knights' level. Thus the servants, entertainment, and miraculous events of the Pentecost assemblies occur in the middle, where all the Round Table knights can see. Banners and tapestries line the walls, commemorating the grand deeds of the noble knights. The seats of the knights are each ornate and beautiful, with their names gleaming in gold.

The Queen's Court is decorated with pale glowing marble imported from the Antipodes Islands, beyond the edge of the world. Despite any severe weather outside, sunshine always beams through the open skylight sections of the roof in daytime, and clear starlight at night. Guenever's throne alone sits atop the dais, and from here the Queen rules her private domains and affairs.

The Court of Love is a garden paradise of flowers, where each blossom symbolizes some portion of love's splendor and agony. Within its pathways are places for lovers to discover the symbolic truths of love, and to find inspiration for immortal private poetry. It mirrors the truth of the world and changes with each season, to test the passions of lovers. Although glorious under sunlight, this garden is most beautiful under the moon.

The Great Banquet Hall serves most of Arthur's knights for daily eating. Only other honored guest eat here; most knights eat at their own lord's hall, or at one of the dozen auxiliary feast halls used to feed lesser knights, unknown visiting knights, and the hordes of squires left to fend for themselves. Other halls with simpler fare feed the city-sized population of servants and workers.

The cathedral of Camelot is a lofty buttressed structure with fifty stained-glass windows fifty feet high, each showing a portion of Christ's life and the Holy Grail. Masses are sung every day at Prime (about 6:00 AM), Sext (12:00 noon), and Vespers (about 6:00 PM). A dozen confessionals are always open. The areas around the cathedral house the priests, visiting clergy, and their knights and staffs. Several independent monasteries have separate quarters in other parts of the palace.

Camelot's gardens are cared for by expert gardeners, with each trying to outdo the other with imported plants from far lands of the known and invisible worlds. None outdoes Guenever's Garden of Love, although some have special effects which temporarily eclipse the queen's in novelty. All the gardens contain decorated pens for display and control of wild beasts according to their needs. For instance, the Deer Garden has several herds of roving animals which do not molest the vegetation or landscaping, but carefully prune and clip it according to the gardener's command; but the lions are kept caged, and the fierce wyrm is held behind a magical barrier.

The stables are immense, and the magic of Camelot overcomes the Augean task of cleaning them each night. Thus, of all the stables in the world, these do not offend the civilized noses of the daintiest maiden or city-dweller. In Arthur's central stable, oats are always the fare, and sometimes destriers or magical steeds ridden by heroes can be seen.

The mews of Camelot house a miraculous variety of sporting birds. Every known species is present, including species of eagles which only the king and queen, and their hawkers, may command. Only the healthiest birds are kept here, shining and keen-witted enough to help even the most amateur hunter.

The vast tournament field of Camelot is generous enough for two teams of a thousand knights each to charge each other comfortably in front of immense stands for the two thousand viewers, a small town of

A critical function of marriage is to produce an heir who will obtain control of the properties of both father and mother, as ordained by law. Thus marriage is a legal institution, and children born to a legally married couple are *legitimate,* or within the law, and can inherit things without problem or question. Children born outside of wedlock are illegitimate, commonly called bastards, and discussed below.

Marriage also serves to increase property holdings, may be performed for political ends, and (on rare occasions) serves emotional needs as well.

Marriage and love are entirely separate matters for most medieval couples. Many marriages are arranged, and some couples see each other for the first time on their wedding day. The occasional happy marriage inspires bards to write poetry, spiteful overlords to become jealous and cruel, and lovers to take heart.

Marital fidelity was a constant issue in the Middle Ages. The desire for the lord to maintain his blood line demanded fidelity from his wife, and fearful punishments could be invoked upon her for having a lover. Churchmen, themselves servants of a jealous Father God, constantly thundered about chastity from their pulpits. Undoubtedly, most women followed the social norm and remained faithful to their loveless marriage, just to keep things simple and safe.

Such fidelity was not expected, or at least not *as* expected, from men. The now-infamous "double standard" was in its heyday. Women could be murdered for having a lover, but men were admired for their capacity to engender children upon numerous women.

Illegitimacy

Many children were born out of wedlock. Noblemen seemed especially subject to propagating this vice. Their partners were sometimes called lovers, concubines, courtesans, or paramours, and were frequently of a social class significantly lower than the nobleman.

Children of such issue were illegitimate, or basely said, bastards. The issue is not one of knowing one's father or not. Often the children knew quite well who their father was, but because they were born outside of marriage they had fewer rights than legitimate children. Most importantly, illegitimate children had no

shelters and storage sheds for lances, saddles, and spare weapons, with a nearby 250-bed hospital.

Camelot seems even bigger on the inside than on the outside. The spaces between important places are crammed with roomy quarters for the thousand of anonymous servants and workers necessary to maintain the splendor. It works in magical ways beyond the understanding of the participants.

The High Order of Knighthood

IN THIS PART of the chapter, the concept of knighthood as your character knows it is introduced. As a knight, your character knows all this information intimately. Further important information about knighthood is found in the "Glory and Ambitions" and "Chivalric Duties" chapters.

The Origins of Knighthood

In the beginning all men were equal, but the original sins of Adam and Eve condemned all humanity to live in the world. Envy and covetousness came into being, and might triumphed over right. Knighthood was instituted to restrain the unjust and to defend the weak. One man in every thousand (*ex mille electus*), the most strong, courageous, and loyal, was chosen to be a knight (*miles.*) He was given a horse, the most noble of beasts, weapons, and armor. He was given a squire to serve him, and placed over the common people who were to till the earth and support the knight. Since then it has been the duty of each knight to train his son to follow in his noble steps, and so the institution has continued. Biblical heroes were knights: Judas Maccabeus and King David, for instance. Ancient pagans were knights as well: Alexander and Julius Caesar are among their number.

Becoming a Knight

A formalized sequence for learning the skills of knighthood is an established part of the feudal tradition. Except under very special conditions, every aspirant to knighthood must follow these steps.

Page

Pages are young boys and girls between the ages of 10 and 15 who are learning the ways of courtly life by observing their elders and doing those tasks assigned to them. After serving as pages most girls become maids-in-waiting and wives. Boys become squires.

Squire

Boys may become squires at age 15. Squires are servants of their knights. They study the ways of knighthood while they serve. Those who are confident in themselves, who show promise, and have the right connections may become knights. Most will remain squires.

Knight

Most aspirants must wait until age 21 to be knighted after serving six years as squires. Men knighted younger are

rights to inherit any property from their father.

Illegitimate children could be legally adopted and, therefore, allowed to inherit, but only if no legitimate children lived. Even then their rights could be challenged by other kinsmen close to the deceased father.

Noblemen often provided for their concubines after they were dismissed. Sometimes the women were married to one of the noble's retainers as a reward. Often the women received valuable properties which would be passed on to the bastard afterwards. The fathers often kept half an eye on their illegitimate sons, too, and used their influence to help them advance in station beyond their mother's class. This influence might be quite overt. The illegitimate sons often helped their more legitimate brothers as loyal, reliable retainers.

Divorce

Divorce is the dissolution of the sacred bond of matrimony. It is not a legal matter, but a religious one. But the parts are so bound together that no one in the Middle Ages ever got a legal divorce without church approval (at least not until Henry VIII, at the end of the late era).

Divorce is allowed only for adultery and *consanguinity*. Adultery meant the woman had a lover, and was never applied to men. Consanguinity meant that the couple were too closely related to each other, as defined by the rules of the Church. Proving consanguinity was an expensive and laborious matter, usually left only to kings or others who could afford the immense cost of pontifical procedure.

Inheritance

Strict laws govern inheritance. They may be bent, but they cannot be broken without someone intervening. Parties who defend the laws are usually the next of kin who stand to inherit the property, and the lord, who has much to say in its governing.

The British cultures of *Pendragon* follow the custom of *primogeniture*. The eldest son of the father is held to be the heir. As a rule, the eldest son gets everything. If the father is rich, then the younger sons might get something, though if they are knighted and receive sets of armor, they should be grateful. If a lord is very rich he is more likely to give small parts of his

exceptional but not unknown. Lancelot was knighted at age 18. Sometimes a young heir must be hastily knighted and ennobled upon reaching his majority at age 18 or, even rarer, 15.

Grades of Knighthood

All knights share certain duties and traits. However, all knights are not equal, and there exists several grades of knighthood. The difference between these is primarily the source of income for the knight.

Note that the descriptive term to describe a knight may either precede or follow the word "knight." Thus it is equally correct to say knight bachelor or bachelor knight. This is a vestigial remnant of the French influence on old English.

Here I deal with only what your character actually knows. The grade or rank that your character attains affects the course of the game in many ways. The rules for the effects of varying incomes are given in the "Game Mechanics" chapter. The rules for how increased prestige affects the game, as derived by increasingly powerful and respected grades of knight, are found in the "Glory and Ambitions" chapter.

Knight Mercenary

Knights without a lord are the lowest class of knights. They are called *mercenary* because they must seek to sustain themselves through work for money. Since knights are fighting men, they generally make their living by seeking mercenary soldier employment, and differ from ordinary mercenary cavalry (serjeants) only in that they have taken the oath of knighthood to a lord.

Knight Bachelor

Knights whose income is derived directly from their lord, either through direct maintenance or by cash payments, are called knights bachelor. The word comes from *bas chevalier*, or "low knight." The word "bachelor" has come to be associated with unmarried men because bachelor knights were generally not rich enough to support a wife.

Knights bachelor are also called household knights because they live in their lord's household, not on their own land. They are his bodyguard and standing army, and travel wherever their lord takes them. Their loyalty is crucial to the lord's success, perhaps even to his survival, so they are treated well and receive great honor.

A knight bachelor may bear a *pennocelle* (a small pennant) upon his lance to distinguish his rank from the commoners, who wear no decoration.

Knight Vassal

Knights who own their own land are knight vassals. They are substantial landlords and capable of equipping themselves for war. Knight vassals generally live at their own home, but are obliged to serve for 40 days per year at war, plus a customary extension of 20 more if the lord demands it. They must also serve three months of castle garrison duty, and at court to offer advice whenever the lord demands it.

A knight vassal may bear a pennant on his lance.

Knight Lord

Knights are sometimes lords over other knights, and are thus called knight lords. Knight lords are the upper rank noblemen, the lords of the land. In this book, when I

wife's property to his younger sons, but keep his patrimony intact.

The Merovingian French divide their estates among all their sons, but the result of the practice is seen in the impoverished and anarchic state of that kingdom. The lesson is not lost to the British.

The eldest son also inherits his father's coat of arms. Thus his arms are exactly the same as his father's, but with a small mark called a *difference* to set them apart as long as both father and son live. This *difference* has been established by tradition to be a horizontal stripe with downward tabs, and is used for eldest sons in *Pendragon.* Although a tradition of other differences is present, younger sons can also choose their own coats of arms.

If there are no sons, the eldest daughter often inherits the land, or the widow might keep it. There is, however, a good chance that some other male of close kinship receives it instead. Likely candidates are the brother to the dead lord, or his bastard son, or the father if he lives. In all cases the lord of the lands has some say about who gets disputed property. If a woman, whether daughter, widow, or mother retains property rights, a lord always has final say on who she marries.

Wills may specify the inheritance preference of a deceased property holder. Your character sheet has a place for Heir to be written in. Use it. The gamemaster need not accept any unrecorded will.

Second only to war, litigation is a lord's favorite activity. Few of us want to game out constant legal wranglings. If legal disputes do arise, they should be settled through trial by combat, or be referred to the judgment of the next highest common lord, or perhaps High King Arthur Pendragon himself.

refer to a "lord" I mean any knight who has taken on other knights as followers.

The lowest grade of lord is a banneret knight. The highest is the high king.

Customs of Knighthood

King Arthur: the Fount of Chivalry

King Arthur has revitalized the order of knighthood by reminding everyone of its ancient origins and sacred social duty. He has reminded everyone that the King is the origin of all knighthood, and has taken it upon himself to provide the most shining example of what a knight can, and ought, to be.

King Arthur has also provided a means whereby any knight may accept the challenge of his new type of knighthood by instituting the Companions of King Arthur. Membership in The Companions is voluntary. A knight must travel to wherever King Arthur holds his Pentecost feast for the year, and join in a mass swearing to uphold the Companions by swearing knight-allegiance to King Arthur. Since loyalty is the primary virtue of knighthood, this allegiance is stronger that knights' loyalty to their lords.

Anyone who has taken the oath of Companionship can state, without reserve, that he is a "knight of King Arthur."

The Coat of Arms

Each knight has his individual coat of arms. This is a design commonly carried on a shield or surcoat, but which can be used to mark anything of the owner's as a personal possession. Only the man, his wife, and his hired herald (who must wear a special coat called a tabard) can wear a knight's arms. His eldest son wears the arms, but with a difference which is taken off after he inherits the title and other rights of his dead father.

Heraldry, the art and science of understanding coats of arms, is discussed in many books, and only touched upon in *Pendragon.*

Lamorak de Gales

silver

purple

The Shield of Peace

Knights all have a regular shield with their coat of arms painted prominently upon it. Lately many knights have taken to the latest custom out of Camelot which is to also have a shield of peace.

The shield of peace does not carry the coat of arms of the knight, but instead some other personal device by which he wishes to recognized. This custom is becoming popular at tournaments, where the shield is often a square shape, called *targe*, with the device painted on.

According to the latest fashion, the shield of peace is to be used at tournaments where rebated weapons are used. It is also being carried by young Sir Lancelot, the trend-setter, as he goes on his many quests these days.

Badges

A coat of arms is individual. Members of a family share similar coats of arms which designate their relationship. But sometimes another sign is needed to show individuals' relationships which are not based upon family. Badges are used.

Customs of Knighthood

You Are the Law

Knights are sheriff, judge, and jury for all matters of Low Justice on their own domains (see below for the three types of justice). If a character has land, then it is his responsibility to maintain justice within it. Likewise, on their lord's land, knights must act in their lord's behalf, either delivering justice then and there or else taking the wrongdoer to the lord's court.

Knights who break the law are subject to justice in the courts of whoever was offended. If in their own domain, then their own lord makes judgement. The only exception to this is when a knight breaks a rule of his lord's, in which case the other knights of the court stand to deliver a judgement.

Appeal to a higher court can be made, but it is at the mercy of the higher lord's court whether to even hear the petition.

Knights accused of wrongdoing at any time may claim trial by combat instead of normal court justice.

Trial by Combat

In any case of justice, any knight may choose trial by combat instead of the normal court justice. In this trial everyone knows that God will favor the right party, and that might will aid right.

A lord can and a woman must choose a knight to fight in their stead. The fight may be for love of fighting (the first combatant to be knocked down or wounded loses the fight), for conquest (the knight who yields loses), or to the death. The ruling made by the god of battles cannot be reversed or appealed.

Justice

Three types of justice exist.

Low Justice is available to any noble of a land, including knights. They can

Badges are used by knights to designate members of their household. Thus everyone, commoners included, who live in the lord's household may wear a badge upon their clothing. A lord with multiple manors may have different badges for each household.

Badges may be used by knights to show their membership in a group. The green sash worn by Round Table knights is a badge. So was the *planta genet*, or broom plant, which was worn by soldiers of Anjou and gave its name to a dynasty of English kings; or the red and white roses worn by opposing households in the English War of the Roses.

Oaths

An oath is a promise made under the witness of God. An oath is the most sacred form of promise, and cannot be broken except with the most serious consequences. To Christians, lying to God provides one of the consequences, with its subsequent threat of eternal damnation in Hell. Perhaps just as important are the more immediate social consequences.

Oath-breakers are shunned by all normal people. A man's sworn word is one of the few possession that he has after all material goods are taken away. It measures his soul and personality. A breaker of oaths has a shrivelled and tiny soul, is not to be trusted, and forfeits the rights which he had as a member of society. Since all of society is based upon oaths and keeping one's word, anyone who fails in this duty fails to uphold society and, therefore, cannot be part of it.

Oaths can be taken literally or figuratively. However, most common people look to the spirit to be fulfilled, but intellectuals sometimes allow only the letter to be fulfilled. Such misunderstandings are the cause of much friction between classes.

In game terms, oaths are handled using the Honor passion. See the "Ideals and Passions" chapter for more information.

Combat for Love or Conquest

Knights may decide to do combat for love or for conquest. Both knights must agree to the terms, or else the combat is for conquest.

"For Love" means that the knights will fight for the love of fighting, not for personal gain. Thus when there is a friendly joust the winner will receive the Glory for winning,but nothing else. Fellows of the Round Table are always expected to joust and fight one another for love. See the "Glory and Ambitions" chapter for more information on Glory.

"For Conquest" is more serious. This combat is hostile, roughly equivalent to an act of war. This does not always mean that it will end in death, but it might. The loser in the struggle is not always held for ransom, but may be. Alternatively, and more popularly, the winner will seize the loser's horse, weapons, and armor as his reward, and let the man go.

Some vile knights fight for conquest, but accept no ransoms, preferring to keep the prisoners in shameful imprisonment. Such villains include the late Sir Carados of the Dolorous Tower, his brother Sir Turquine, and others.

Adventuring

A primary activity of all the famous knights is to adventure. Adventuring, in fact, is the activity which sets fa-

judge any case which is less critical than murder, rape, or other capital crime. Knights can deliver justice to commoners, including imprisonment and the cutting off of hands, ears, and other body parts of commoners. They cannot judge on capital crimes or deliver a sentence of death, or judge other nobles or members of the clergy (who have their own separate system of justice).

High Justice is reserved for higher nobles, usually only kings. They make rulings on anything that may be rewarded with the death penalty. This includes treason, rape, murder, and theft of the lord's goods.

Arthur's Justice, or the King's Justice, is a humanitarian system of rules inaugurated by King Arthur to pacify his lands and to keep the peasants happy and whole. The ideals of the Round Table are extended not just to the noble class, but to all of humanity. Thus a peasant may not be murdered for cursing at a knight who has trampled his crops and carried off his daughter, if the place is protected by the King's Justice. Thus, as Arthur's bold fellowship conquers the island the reign of peace grows, and fair (if not exactly equal) justice is available to all.

Noble Prisoners

Knights are often captured and held in various states of arrest. Often they are held shamefully in dark dungeons, dirty and unfed. Sometimes they are maintained according to their station, sharing in their captor's table and making no attempt to escape since they have given their word of surrender.

Surprisingly, even enemies of the worst kind do not kill their enemies. Hated murderers languish away in prison rather than being hung or killed. Player character knights may occasionally spend years in prison this way, and the gamemaster should know why.

The answer lies in the fact that most knights and lords do not have the right of life and death over their prisoners. This is determined by the division of Justice into High and Low, as mentioned above. Most lords have the rights only to Low Justice, which allows them to enforce most laws *except* those of capital crimes. Any crime which warrants death of the culprit are High Justice, enforceable only by the king. To execute a criminal would be unusual, illegal, and draw the lord's attention and wrath significantly enough that the knight

mous knights apart from the ordinary knights who stay at home and acquire Glory passively (out of play).

Adventuring is an activity which is recognized as a legitimate knightly duty by the Arthurian court. Under the reign of King Arthur, knights have a duty to seek adventure which is as important as their duty to stand garrison and serve an active 40 days in the field.

Most knights do not take the job. For them the everyday activities of guard duty, tournaments, and battles, are enough to satisfy their sense of adventure. Other knights, like the player knights, seek more, and undertake quests.

Most of the lords of Logres are in favor of the new sport of adventuring, and are happy to oblige their knights who wish to engage in it. The recent lull in peace has left the castles full of boisterous fighters with nothing to fight. Adventuring sends the knights to work off their energy elsewhere, perhaps even far away from Logres. Undoubtedly the lord hopes that the questing knights will arouse something from the other, less enthusiastic knights as well.

Adventures abound. Even the normal, stay-at-home knights have adventures as part of their routine, without having to seek them out. Adventures include going to tournaments, participating in battles, engaging in romance, visiting unusual sights, and encountering unusual beings.

Questing

Quests are adventures, but not all adventures are quests. A quest is a protracted adventure and must also include several elements to qualify as such: going to an unknown place, encountering something mysterious or unusual, facing unusual dangers, and (always) facing death.

A griffin

Quests must, by definition, occur in the strange lands, where High Adventure and opportunity wait to test the neat ideals of the heartland of civilization.

Thus knights must request a leave from their lord and normal duties to quest and adventure. A knight always represents not only himself, but also his lord, and so the lord will try to send only individuals who he will not have to get out of trouble, or who will not bring shame or dishonor to them.

A time limit is often imposed on absentee time for questing. The proverbial "year and a day" is a good starting time period. At the end of the time the knight must return to court and report the results of his activities. Later on the time limit may be longer, indefinite, or geared to the specific task. Not that this cycle is the same as that

might lose his station for disobedience to his office. Remember, most knights are still law-abiding in their own realm and sworn to uphold their king's justice. Thus, instead of killing their foes, the knight simply throws the offender into jail, a thing which is within the rights of his office.

Punishments

Knights can be punished for disobeying their lord's laws or the custom of the land. Usually the punishment is a fine. A more severe penalty is banishment, during which the knight must depart all of his lord's holdings for the term of the banishment, which is typically a year and a day for the first such offense. The banished knight is considered an enemy of the lord, even unto being able to be killed without his kin justly claiming revenge. During his absence the lord controls all the lands and obtains all income and benefits therefrom. More serious offenses can be punished by outlawry, which is permanent banishment, and is usually accompanied by forfeiture of all lands and titles out of the knight's family to the lord. Finally, degradation is the ultimate punishment, for the knight is stripped of his title and right to his rank. The ceremony is a public humiliation, and is permanent, so that another lord cannot re-bestow knighthood.

The Church

Christianity came to Britain with Joseph of Arimathea, the friend of Jesus' who lent his tomb to the Savior. Joseph reached western Britain a few years before the first Romans invaded the eastern island. Many druids converted to the new faith, and started the Culdee sect. Much later King Lucius asked Rome to send some missionaries to enlighten his folk. When they arrived they discovered a thriving Celtic Christian community already in place. Centuries later Christianity became the

which occurs with the Round Table knights at Arthur's court.

Questing is the excuse for player knights to wander the roads and trails of Britain. Questing is the activity which sets an Arthurian knight apart from the ordinary knight.

Thus, whereas knighthood is the heart of *Pendragon*, Questing is its soul.

Magic

Magic in *Pendragon* exists. It is a factor of great mystery, uncertainty and danger. It is unknown in every way and facts about magic are unknown to both characters and players in the game.

Pendragon has no magic system. All magic is within the hands of the gamemaster, and is used to imitate traditional magical effects seen in Arthurian literature, rather than to make comic-book flash-bang nonsense spells. It is impossible for characters to be magicians of significance. This is not to say that the magic of Britain is not powerful. It is extremely potent, partially because of its very mystery. *Pendragon* magic is also dangerous, because it is hidden and subtle. But your character knows that magic is more likely to drive him mad or age him a century in a day than to toast him with a fireball. Magic in this game is for purposes of roleplaying, not for cartoon violence.

Everyone in the world of *Pendragon* knows that magic exists. Magic includes everything which is unknown, which is plenty. Fate and luck are important components of magic, not just spells and spellcasters. The fundamental laws of society, such loyalty or hospitality, are enforced by the decrees of fate, and thus enter the realm of magic.

People accept the world of magic as a normal part of the great unknowable reality, even though they do not understand it. Men cannot explain how Merlin marched King Ban's army over 165 miles in a few days, even if they remember doing it. Men know that druid shapeshifters change their appearance, that magical ladies live beneath enchanted lakes, and that another invisible world exists with a populace of frightful beings. They have heard about, and perhaps seen, magical objects like the sword Excalibur and the Holy Grail. But men do not hope to understand it, and in fact mistrust it immensely.

Magicians are not to be trusted. Everyone knows some reasons for this, though the reasons vary depending on the point of view of the observer. Some mistrust them because they can alter reality, or because they talk to the dead, or because they can tell what the weather is going to be and change it if they don't like it. Other people dislike magicians because they believe that all occult powers come from the Devil. Some don't like anyone who is strange, and magicians have access to the unknowable, and what is not known cannot be trusted.

Different types of magic are recognized: druid magic, Christian miracles, native Old Heathen magic, Saxon battle magic, necromancy. The primary types are the druidic and Christian. The main difference between Christianity and the others is that druidic magic is immediate and demonstrative, while Christian magic is subtle and assertive.

Roman state religion, and it is still the main religion throughout the former Roman colony. A couple of centuries ago the local British belief, called Pelagianism, was condemned as heresy by the Roman Pope, the leader of the Church. Despite that, the beliefs expressed are still current as Semi-Pelagianism, although condemned from Rome.

Christianity, despite these minor differences, unifies all of western mankind. It is, in fact, one of the two factors which unify all European peoples (the other being the feudal system). A person can travel from Ireland in the west to Italy in the east, and from Germany in the north to Spain in the south, and in every place he stops he will find the same ceremonies, the same holy days, and the same morality administered and overseen by clergy.

Christianity believes in a single God who created the world and everything in it. Adam and Eve were the first human beings, and because they sinned all of the world became corrupted, Death was loosed upon humanity, and evil became stronger than good.

During the Roman times God incarnated Himself as a human being, and after a short life on earth allowed Himself to be killed by being tortured and nailed to a cross. He was buried, but three days later rose from the dead and ascended into Heaven.

He did this to fix the wrongs done by Adam and Eve and to return sanctity to the world. This sacrifice by God allowed humans to obtain eternal salvation and, after death, to join God in Heaven.

Saints are also important in the religion. They are exceptionally holy persons who are rewarded after death for a lifetime of dedication to the church. They have the power to intercede between God and his worshipers. Many saints are important in the Arthurian era, but one of the foremost in Britain is Saint Mary, the Mother of God.

Philosophically speaking, Christianity is focused on the transcendent aspect of God, to the exclusion of the immanent. Its promise of eternal salvation for each individual is intimately associated with that person's understanding and contact with

Druidic magic stems from mastery of the power of *glamour*, which is the ability to create a temporary reality. Its effects are obvious, material, personal, and generally flashy. These include pyrotechnics, castles in the air, great clouds of dense mist, kingdoms hidden under lakes, silent warriors raised from the dead, and healing with the use of potions, unguents, and charms.

Christian magic, on the other hand, is subtle, long-term, and miraculous. Often the effects are permanent, rather than temporary. A fountain once blessed may last for generations. Knowledge and wisdom are two of the best-known applications of Christian magic. Magical healing is done by laying on of hands rather than using physical components.

Curses, blessings, and healing are common to both types of magic. Spirits are acknowledged, and can be summoned, banished, or exorcised.

Old Heathen magic is the integral magic of the land which predates all humanity. It can be sensed in the rocks, in the earth and tides, and in the glimpses of gods' minds caught on holy, moon-bright nights. It is the power of the Forest, of Moor or of the ever-changing river which exists with or without mankind.

Necromancy is speaking with the dead, and gaining magical powers from them. Everyone knows that people have spirits which survive their corporal death, but varying theories exist about where the spirits go, and so people view this practice differently.

Saxon magic makes users mad in battle. It is gained from a blessing from Wotan, their war god. But few Saxons in Britain worship Wotan any more.

Demonic magic, the least important type, gives magic which is gained from making deals with the truly evil forces of Satan, the Christian god of evil.

Not everyone believes in these forces (for instance, among 6th century Christians belief in Satan was not universal.) Some or all of these forces may be totally false. Part of the adventure is to figure out what scheme the gamemaster has adopted to use for his magic.

Magic should never dominate the game. Gamemasters should feel free to make magic take whatever form they wish, as long as it is subtle. Establish a mood with magic: let palaces glow from a warm internal light, serve exotic and intoxicating wines from Cathay, mark trails through the forest with glowing stones.

Magic is an essential plot device for gamemasters. A magical event or curse can form the basis for an adventure. Magic can be used to save villains or player knights. But never should the plot rely upon a magician to do something or not do something magical — this is an example of the gamemaster working against himself, which only occurs at the players' expense.

The Enchantment of Britain

The magic of Arthur's reign comes from the Enchantment of Britain. The causes of this enchantment are not clear: they began when Balin, the Knight of Two Swords, struck down good King Pellam; or as divine retribution to punish King Arthur for the sins which he committed; or simply because Arthur is the King of Adventure.

The era in which this book's *Pendragon* campaign is set is the time when the Enchantments begin to flow out of the magical lands into the world of Logres. Encounters with human beings continue to be the most common event, but magic seems to be more common than in the past.

the transcendent reality which can be reached only through imitation of Christ's virtues.

The holy days of the Christian religion mark the significant parts of the life of Jesus. Christmas, which occurs at midwinter, celebrates His birth day and is a day of joyful celebration marked by exchanges of gifts. The spring season has the most holidays, starting with Good Friday, which marks the day that He died, sacrificed upon the cross for the redemption of Mankind. Easter is next, three days after Good Friday, and is the most important holy day because it is the anniversary of the day which He proved His divinity by rising from the dead. Pentecost, celebrated on the 7th Sunday after Easter, commemorates the moment when the followers of Jesus were gifted with knowledge of foreign tongues to facilitate their mission to spread the Good Word of God's miraculous life, death, and rebirth. Saints have their own holy days, too, and are so numerous that every day is dedicated to one or another of them.

Mass is the name of the most common type of formal worship service. Sacraments of the church are the most holy rituals which the Christian religion has. They include: baptism, which is given upon entering the religion; communion, the basic act of participation with God, around which the Mass is centered; confirmation, which initiates members of the church as Soldiers of Christ; matrimony, which blesses marriage; Holy Orders, by which a man is made a priest; and Extreme Unction, given at death to ease a person's journey to Heaven.

Character Generation

You must have a character to play. In this chapter you create your first character, an experienced squire from Salisbury who is ready to be knighted.

THE IMAGINARY *PERSONAE* used for play in *Pendragon* sessions are called characters. Characters controlled by players are called player characters. Characters used by the gamemaster are called gamemaster characters or non-player characters. Not including player characters, the gamemaster controls everyone from High King Arthur Pendragon to the half-wit gooseboy.

The Character Sheet

Players use the two-sided character sheets to record all information pertinent to the play of their imaginary *Pendragon* personae. This information includes such things as the characters' physical qualities, appearance, family data, personality, equipment, and personal history. Each character requires a separate character sheet. Once the generation of a player character is completed, the character sheet is the only piece of paper that is necessary for play.

If your character dies during the game, give his character sheet to the gamemaster. Gamemasters should keep these together in a "cemetery" for later reference, and to use as instant gamemaster characters by changing their name and origin. The character sheet should be filled out using a pencil. The information contained on it will change during play.

Creating a Character

You can create your first *Pendragon* character while you learn the contents of the character sheet. When you are finished, and have read the "What Your Character Knows" chapter, your character will be on the verge of knighthood. All you need then is to play the game.

Two methods exist to create a player character: the default character and the designed character. I recommend that you actually create a designed character, if at all possible. This chapter is your guide.

The Default Characters

The Default Characters found below have all values given in full already. To create a character, simply copy the information from your favorite default knight's sheet onto a blank character sheet and determine a name.

All the default knights are complete, except for names, and have been constructed to represent standard types. They are all from the county of Salisbury, and have spent all their life there. Although these characters are quite ordinary and rather bland, several sessions will reveal individual personality (see the "Ideals and Passions" chapter below for more information on personality).

Note that the default knights do not have character sheet backs provided.

The Designed Character

With this method you create your character the way you wish him to be. Players choose the qualities and attributes for their desired characters. This assures you that you will not have to play a character you despise.

Limits are given within which to create your character. Also, some guidelines are given to steer beginners towards important points.

Other Methods

Other more complex and variable methods of character creation are given in the second *Pendragon* book, *Knights Adventurous*.

Rounding Off Fractions

When performing calculations in *Pendragon,* round .5 up and lower fractions down. For example, a character with a Damage value of 4.43 would have a 4 and a character with a Damage value of 4.5 would have a 5.

Your First Character

FOLLOW THESE STEPS to create your first character. This procedure creates characters which fits into the mainstream of central Arthurian society. All the characters generated through this procedure will come from Salisbury, an important land loyal to King Arthur. They will speak the same native language, live by the same culture, and will have been raised as Christians. They will be experienced squires, ready to become knights.

Many characters who you will meet during play are not from this mainstream. They may be of different gender, nationality, social class, or religion, and may belong to some esoteric organization such as the Templars.

Once you have gained experience with your first character, feel free to create your own type of character, with gamemaster approval. *Knights Adventurous* will offer advanced character generation, even including female knights!

Procedure

Several steps must be considered when creating a character. The first seven steps are essential for the play of *Pendragon.* Step Eight, the Character Sheet Back, is not as important but is highly recommended. The steps are:

1. Determine Personal Data
2. Allocate Personality Traits and Passions

3. Allocate Prime and Derived Statistics
4. Determine Starting Skills and Combat Skills
5. Determine Previous Experience
6. Knighthood
7. Determine Other Data
8. The Character Sheet Back

Note: located just below the *Pendragon* name, above "Personal Data," is a space labeled "Player". The name of the player needs to be written here before start of play. This will help the character sheet find its way back to the player if misplaced.

1. Personal Data

This information includes such items as the character's name, homeland, culture, character age, date of birth, and so forth.

Name

Write in your character's name. Here are some sample names, taken from obscure characters in *Le Morte D'Arthur*, to use:

Adtherp, Alein, Aliduke, Annecians, Archade, Arnold, Arrouse, Bandelaine, Bellangere, Bellias, Berel, Bersules, Bliant, Breunis, Briant, Caulas, Chestelaine, Clegis, Cleremond, Dalan, Dinaunt, Driant, Ebel, Edward, Elias, Eliot, Emerause, Flannedrius, Florence, Floridas, Galardoun, Garnish, Gerin, Gauter, Gherard, Gilbert, Gilmere, Goneries, Gracian, Gumret, Guy, Gwinas, Harsouse, Harvis, Hebes, Hemison, Herawd, Heringdale, Herlews, Hermel, Hermind, Hervis, Hewgon, Idres, Jordans, Lardans, Leomie, Manasan, Maurel, Melion, Miles, Morganor, Morians, Moris, Nanowne, Nerovens, Pedivere, Pellandres, Pellogres, Perin, Phelot, Pillounes, Plaine, Plenorias, Sauseise, Selises, Selivant, Semond.

Homeland, Culture, Religion

All initial characters are from Salisbury, were raised in a Cymric culture, and are Christian.

Father's Name

Choose another name from the above list to be your character's father's name.

A campaign takes on appropriate tone when the characters have appropriate names. It is impossible to stop some people from using ridiculous names like Exxon, Frodo, or Conan in a campaign, but it is possible to forestall most of this foolishness by using only names found in popular or historical literature.

Characters should have one name only. Last names or family names are not used. Instead the name is modified by the addition of a title: a physical distinction, a description of origin such as "of such-a-place," or a family link such as "son of so and-so." Titles such as "the Bold" are also important and may be self-given or earned in play. Many Malorian names are given in French, and if you use a French title it rings with authenticity. See below for more information on titles.

Examine the name list or select a name that sounds right to you. If you have trouble pronouncing it write it down the way you think it sounds. It is important that you be comfortable with the name.

Sounds can be arranged and re-arranged to make new names. Feel free to make a name which you can live with without ridiculing the campaign (i.e. no Xerox or Groucho).

Don't choose names which you already know from the King Arthur stories since those are most likely the most famous characters in the story. It gets confusing during play to have to keep saying that you are not *that* Tristram or Lancelot.

Titles

Characters often have descriptive titles as well as a name. These are taken only after the character is knighted and experience has been gained, but you may wish to plan for one now.

Titles are often in French, even though the characters is from another country. You decide if it sounds better in English or French. Some are descriptive: *le blank* (the white), *le noir* (the black), *le petit* (the little). Some simply tell where they are from: de Ganis, of the Orkneys, and so on. Some are more descriptive of actions: *le Desirious* (the Desirer [of battle]), *le Chevalier au Leon* (the knight of the lion), of the Seven Adventures, of the Golden Ring, of the Hat.

It is often best to wait until your character *earns* a title for his actions.

Father's Class

Vassal knight. All characters created using this book are sons of a vassal knight.

Son Number

You are the eldest son of your family. Write a "1" here. Eldest sons have a big advantage in *Pendragon*. Primogeniture is the law of the land, meaning that the eldest son will inherit everything (or almost everything) from his father. The younger sons are left out, to make their own way as knights in whatever service they can find.

Liege Lord

Your character's only lord is Sir Robert, Earl of Salisbury. Listing a lord's title in this space is sufficient. If a knight has multiple lords one will be selected as liege, and should be specially marked here.

Current Class

Your first character is a squire on the verge of knighthood. He will become a vassal knight during the course of play. Leave this space blank for now.

Current Home

Your home is the manor which is your inheritance, as the eldest son of your father. This manor often provides the knight's title, as discussed above, being from (*de*) the manor. Roll 1d20 to get the name of a Salisbury manor from this list:

Salisbury Manor Table

d20	*manor*
01	Baverstock
02	Berwick St. James
03	Broughton
04	Burcombe
05	Cholderton
06	Dinton
07	Durnford
08	Idmiston
09	Laverstock
10	Newton
11	Newton Tony
12	Pitton
13	Shrewton
14	Stapleford
15	Steeple Langford
16	Tisbury
17	Winterbourne Gunnet
18	Winterbourne Stoke
19	Woodford
20	Wylye

Only one person may inherit each manor, so gamemasters should modify

this list by eliminating manors already taken.

These places can all be found on the map of Salisbury manors, in the chapter titled "Your Home."

Age, and Year Born

This entry should remain blank until character generation is completed. At the end of character generation your character will be 21 or more years old, based on your preferences for the character's amount of previous experience. Once character generation is complete, go back to this entry and ask your gamemaster the year that his campaign is currently in (campaigns usually begin in 531 A.D.). Subtract your age from the current game year to find the year your character was born. Write it down.

2. Personality Traits and Passions

Every reference to King Arthur and his knights is full of personality and passion, whether taken from the romances, legends, or Hollywood movies. The game emphasizes those points. The personality traits and passions are methods of quantifying your character's inner self. They record both reputation and propensity. They help you to run your character in a consistent manner and according to his actual play activity.

A value of 16 or more indicates great interest and activity in that Trait or Passion, perhaps bordering on the fanatical. The behavior is very obvious to everyone, and thus significant in game terms.

New characters start play with only one value of 16, in the trait of your choice. No passions begin at 16.

Personality Traits

The personality traits used in *Pendragon* consist of thirteen opposed pairs of virtues and vices. But what is a virtue in one culture is sometimes a vice in another. Thus the Christian and Saxon cultures view Modesty and Pride differently. However, all initial characters begin from the same Christian moral base. And all characters, regardless of culture, determine Chivalry from the same five traits. Use these three steps:

Check Religious Background: Initial traits are modified by the religious background. Here are the traits which Christianity deems the most important. They are already underlined on your character sheet.

Christian Virtues Table

Traits: Chaste, Forgiving, Merciful, Modest, Temperate

Assign Traits: The Valorous trait always begins at a value of 15, reflecting your character's martial training. The Christian traits listed above begin at a value of 13. The remaining traits to the left of the slash (/) begin at 10, Pious for example.

You may assign any one trait a value of 16 if you so desire. This includes traits on the right side of the slash, such as Worldly or Reckless.

The total on the two sides of the slash *must equal 20.* Complete the traits by subtracting the values you have assigned from 20, and filling in the resulting number opposite the chosen trait.

As your character develops, these initial values will change, and various rewards may become available.

Your Famous Trait: Assigning a 16 is optional. If you do assign a 16, put it in a trait which denotes the behavior you wish your character to be famous for.

For your first character, be sure to choose a value 16 trait which you can live with. Since this will show how your character *has acted,* try to make the trait in line with your intended actions and attitudes for the character.

This will affect the player's actual control over his character; the character's actions may be determined by the trait and contrary to the wishes of the player. For example, a character with an Honest trait of 16 will tell the truth in most situations, even those where honesty might be inadvisable! See the "Ideals and Passions" chapter for more information.

Directed Traits

Leave these blank for now. They will be used during game play.

Passions

Passions are strong emotions within a single individual. They include love, hate, amor, loyalty, envy, and honor, among others. Beginning characters all begin with five passions: Loyalty to their lord, Love of family, Hospitality, Honor, and Hate (Saxons).

Loyalty is the prime virtue of the medieval world — without it the feudal system could not exist. Most knights believe in "King before God." Showing obedience to one's immediate overlord is correct behavior, and disobedience to a lord is shocking to all true knights.

Love of family is a natural emotion common to mankind in any age. To most people, Family = society = their world. The travel restrictions of the era emphasize family closeness.

Everyone learns Hospitality at their mother's knee, and it is so ingrained that it is almost subconscious.

Honor is the knight's special passion. All knights must have honor (in other words, a value greater than 0) in order to be knighted.

Other passions may be allowed at the beginning by the gamemaster, and characters will acquire passions as the result of game play. Note that Hate (Saxons) is an inherited passion of all Salisbury residents, whose lands suffered heavily under their invasion and raiding some years ago.

Enter the values below onto the character sheet (these values are also listed on the character sheet).

Passions Value Table

passion	*starting value*
Loyalty (lord)	15
Love (family)	15
Hospitality	15
Honor	15
Hate (Saxons)	Roll 3d6 to find this value.

3. Statistics

The physical traits of any *Pendragon* character are quantified by five statistics. Various other statistics are derived from this group. These crucial five prime statistics and their common abbreviations used in *Pendragon* are Size (SIZ), Dexterity (DEX), Strength (STR), Constitution

KING ARTHUR

Pendragon

Player . . . .

Personal Data

Name . . . .
Homeland . . . .
Culture . . . . Religion . . . .
Father's Name . . . .
Father's Class . . . . Son Number . . . . .
Liege Lord . . . .
Current Class . . . .
Current Home . . . . Age . . . Year Born . . . .

Personality Traits

Chivalry Bonus [•] *(total = 80+)* . . . .
Religious Bonus *(underlined traits all 16+)* . . . .

- ☐ Chaste . . . . . . / . . . . Lustful ☐
- • ☐ Energetic . . . . . / . . . . Lazy ☐
- ☐ Forgiving . . . . . / . . . . . . Vengeful ☐
- • ☐ Generous . . . . . . / . . . . Selfish ☐
- ☐ Honest . . . . / . . . . . . Deceitful ☐
- • ☐ Just . . . . / . . . . . . Arbitrary ☐
- • ☐ Merciful . . . . . / . . . . Cruel ☐
- • ☐ Modest . . . . / . . . . Proud ☐
- ☐ Pious . . . . / . . . . Worldly ☐
- ☐ Prudent . . . . / . . . . . . Reckless ☐
- ☐ Temperate . . . . . / . . . . . . Indulgent ☐
- ☐ Trusting . . . . / . . . . . Suspicious ☐
- • ☐ Valorous . . . . . . / . . . . . . Cowardly ☐

Directed Trait . . . .
Directed Trait . . . .

Passions

Loyalty (lord) *(15)* . . . . ☐
Love (family) *(15)* . . . . ☐
Hospitality *(15)* . . . . ☐
Honor *(15)* . . . . ☐
Hate (Saxons) *(3d6)* . . . . ☐
. . . . ☐
. . . . ☐
. . . . ☐

Equipment Carried

Armor Type [......... points] . . . .
Clothing [......... Librum value] . . . .
☐ Personal Gear [on horse #.........] . . . .
☐ Travel Gear [on horse #.........] . . . .
☐ War Gear [on horse #.........] . . . .
. . . .
. . . .

Statistics

SIZ . . . . (Knockdown)
DEX . . . .
STR . . . .
CON *(+3)* . . . . . (Major Wound)
APP . . . .
Damage *((STR+SIZ)/6)* d6
Healing Rate *((STR+CON)/10)* . . . .
Movement Rate *((STR+DEX)/10)* . . .
Total Hit Points *(SIZ+CON)* . . . . . .
Unconscious *(HP/4)* . . . .

Distinctive Features

. . . .
. . . .
. . . .

Skills

Awareness *(5)* . . . . ☐
Boating *(1)* . . . . ☐
Chirurgery *(0)* . . . . ☐
Compose *(0)* . . . . ☐
Courtesy *(3)* . . . . ☐
Dancing *(2)* . . . . ☐
Faerie Lore *(1)* . . . . ☐
†First Aid *(10)* . . . . ☐
Flirting *(3)* . . . . ☐
Folk Lore *(2)* . . . . ☐
Gaming *(3)* . . . . ☐
Hawking *(3)* . . . . ☐
Heraldry *(3)* . . . . ☐
Hunting *(2)* . . . . ☐
Industry *(0)* . . . . ☐
Intrigue *(3)* . . . . ☐
Orate *(3)* . . . . ☐
Play (....................) *(3)* . . . . ☐
Read (....................) *(0)* . . . ☐
Recognize *(3)* . . . . ☐
Religion (................) *(2)* . . . ☐
Romance *(2)* . . . . ☐
Singing *(2)* . . . . ☐
Stewardship *(2)* . . . . ☐
Swimming *(2)* . . . . ☐
Tourney *(5)* . . . . ☐
. . . . ☐
. . . . ☐
. . . . ☐
. . . . ☐

Squire

Name . . . .
Age . . . .
First Aid *(6)* . . . . ☐
Battle *(1)* . . . . ☐
Horsemanship *(6)* . . . . ☐
. . . . ☐

Glory

Glory This Game

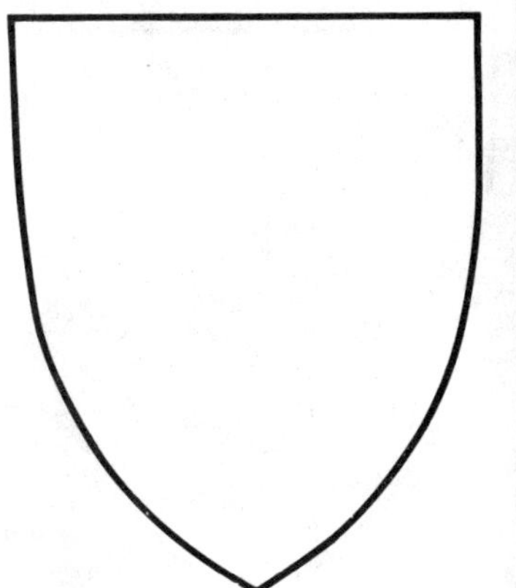

Current Hit Points

Wounds . . . .
. . . .
☐ Chirurgery Needed

Combat Skills

†Battle *(10)* . . . . ☐
†Horsemanship *(10)* . . . . . . ☐

Weapon Skills

†Sword *(10)* . . . . ☐
†Lance *(10)* . . . . ☐
Spear *(6)* . . . . ☐
Dagger *(5)* . . . . ☐
. . . . ☐
. . . . ☐
. . . . ☐
. . . . ☐
. . . . ☐
. . . . ☐
. . . . ☐

Joust Score

Wins . . . . Losses . . . . . .

Horses

Best Warhorse (#1)

Type . . . .
Damage . . . . Move . . . .
Armor . . . . HP . . . .
SIZ . . . . CON . . . DEX . . . .

Other Horses

Own Riding (#2) . . . . . CON . . . .
Squire's (#3) . . . . CON . . . .
(#4) . . . . CON . . . .
(#5) . . . . CON . . . .

Family

Year Wed ..... Spouse Name .... Family Characteristic ....

Will

Children To Reach Majority

History

Date	Important Event	Glory New	Glory Total

Selected Events

Born ...... Ennobled ......

Squired ..... Landed ......

Knighted

Member of Round Table

Died

Holdings

Equipment at Home

Denarii

Libra

Army

Old Knights

Middle-Aged Knights

Young Knights

Total Family Knights

Vassal Knights

Other Lineage Men

Levy

The Default Characters

For an instant character, copy the information on the small character sheet of your choice (using a pencil) onto a photocopy of the character sheet.

KING ARTHUR Pendragon

Player ....
Personal Data de Falt
Name ....
Homeland Salisbury
Culture Cymric Religion Christian
Father's Name ....
Father's Class Vassal Son Number 1
Liege Lord Earl Robert
Current Class ....
Current Home Dinton Age 21 Year Born 510

Personality Traits
Chivalry Bonus [•] (total + 80+) No
Religious Bonus (underlined traits all 16+) NO

	Trait			Trait
□	Chaste	13 / 7	Lustful	□
• □	Energetic	10 / 10	Lazy	□
□	Forgiving	13 / 7	Vengeful	□
• □	Generous	10 / 10	Selfish	□
□	Honest	10 / 10	Deceitful	□
• □	Just	10 / 10	Arbitrary	□
• □	Merciful	13 / 7	Cruel	□
• □	Modest	13 / 7	Proud	□
□	Pious	10 / 10	Worldly	□
□	Prudent	10 / 10	Reckless	□
□	Temperate	13 / 7	Indulgent	□
□	Trusting	10 / 10	Suspicious	□
• □	Valorous	15 / 5	Cowardly	□

Directed Trait ....
Directed Trait ....

Passions
Loyalty (lord) (15) .... 15 □
Love (family) (15) .... 15 □
Hospitality (15) .... 15 □
Honor (15) .... 15 □
Hate (Saxons) (3d6) .... 11 □

Equipment Carried
Armor Type (12 points) Reinforced Chain
Clothing (1 Librum value)
☑ Personal Gear (on horse # 2)
□ Travel Gear (on horse #)
☑ War Gear (on horse # 1) 2 Spears. 5 Jousting lances. 1 Librum

Statistics
SIZ 13 (Knockdown)
DEX 12
STR 12
CON (+3) 14 (Major Wound)
APP 12
Damage ((STR+SIZ)/6) 4 d6
Healing Rate ((STR+CON)/10) 3
Movement Rate ((STR+DEX)/10) 2
Total Hit Points (SIZ+CON) 27
Unconscious (HP/4) 7

Distinctive Features Curly Hair

Skills
Awareness (5) 10 □
Boating (1) 1 □
Chirurgery (0) □
Compose (0) □
Courtesy (3) 10 □
Dancing (2) 2 □
Faerie Lore (1) 1 □
†First Aid (10) 10 □
Flirting (3) 3 □
Folk Lore (2) 2 □
Gaming (3) 3 □
Hawking (3) 3 □
Heraldry (3) 3 □
Hunting (2) 3 □
Industry (0) □
Intrigue (3) 3 □
Orate (3) 3 □
Play (Harp) (3) 3 □
Read (....) (0) □
Recognize (3) 3 □
Religion (Christ) (2) 2 □
Romance (2) 2 □
Singing (2) 2 □
Stewardship (2) 2 □
Swimming (2) 2 □
Tourney (5) 5 □

Squire
Name Oswald
Age 15
First Aid (6) 6 □
Battle (1) 1 □
Horsemanship (6) 6 □
Sword 5 □

Glory 175
Glory This Game

Current Hit Points
Wounds ....
□ Chirurgery Needed

Combat Skills
†Battle (10) 13 □
†Horsemanship (10) 10 □

Weapon Skills
†Sword (10) 15 □
†Lance (10) 13 □
Spear (6) 9 □
Dagger (5) 5 □

Joust Score
Wins .... Losses ....

Horses
Best Warhorse (#1)
Type Charger
Damage 6d6 Move 8
Armor 5 HP 46
SIZ 34 CON 12 DEX 17

Other Horses
Own Riding (#2) Rouncy CON 14
Squire's (#3) Sumpter CON 16
(#4) .... CON ....
(#5) .... CON ....

A Man of the de Falt Clan

This young man, like most of his family, is average in all ways for his homeland, culture, and religion. As the eldest son of the family (like all player characters), he will hold the very ordinary Falt manor to the southeast of Sarum as soon as he is knighted. De Falt is unremarkable in reputation and behavior, with no famous personality trait, and only an average dislike of Saxons.

Choose this character if you wish to start the game simply, and learn the rules without receiving any surprises from your character. De Falt is not exceptional, but neither does he have any major flaws or weaknesses.

Like many experienced squires, de Falt has chosen to concentrate on his Sword skill.

Note that "Current Class" is left blank because de Falt will soon become a knight.

KING ARTHUR Pendragon

Player ....
Personal Data Courtier
Name ....
Homeland Salisbury
Culture Cymric Religion Christian
Father's Name ....
Father's Class Vassal Son Number 1
Liege Lord Earl Robert
Current Class ....
Current Home Pitton Age 21 Year Born 510

Personality Traits
Chivalry Bonus [•] (total + 80+) NO
Religious Bonus (underlined traits all 16+) NO

	Trait			Trait
□	Chaste	13 / 7	Lustful	□
• □	Energetic	10 / 10	Lazy	□
□	Forgiving	13 / 7	Vengeful	□
• □	Generous	10 / 10	Selfish	□
□	Honest	10 / 10	Deceitful	□
• □	Just	16 / 4	Arbitrary	□
• □	Merciful	13 / 7	Cruel	□
• □	Modest	13 / 7	Proud	□
□	Pious	10 / 10	Worldly	□
□	Prudent	10 / 10	Reckless	□
□	Temperate	13 / 7	Indulgent	□
□	Trusting	10 / 10	Suspicious	□
• □	Valorous	15 / 5	Cowardly	□

Directed Trait ....
Directed Trait ....

Passions
Loyalty (lord) (15) .... 15 □
Love (family) (15) .... 15 □
Hospitality (15) .... 15 □
Honor (15) .... 15 □
Hate (Saxons) (3d6) .... 11 □
Amor (Guenever) .... 15 □

Equipment Carried
Armor Type (12 points) Reinforced Chain
Clothing (1 Librum value)
☑ Personal Gear (on horse # 2)
□ Travel Gear (on horse #)
☑ War Gear (on horse # 1)
Sacred Christian Relic (blood)

Statistics
SIZ 14 (Knockdown)
DEX 11
STR 11
CON (+3) 11 (Major Wound)
APP 16
Damage ((STR+SIZ)/6) 4 d6
Healing Rate ((STR+CON)/10) 2
Movement Rate ((STR+DEX)/10) 2
Total Hit Points (SIZ+CON) 25
Unconscious (HP/4) 6

Distinctive Features Tall and Thin

Skills
Awareness (5) 5 □
Boating (1) 1 □
Chirurgery (0) 0 □
Compose (0) 0 □
Courtesy (3) 15 □
Dancing (2) 5 □
Faerie Lore (1) 1 □
†First Aid (10) 10 □
Flirting (3) 5 □
Folk Lore (2) 2 □
Gaming (3) 3 □
Hawking (3) 3 □
Heraldry (3) 5 □
Hunting (2) 2 □
Industry (0) 0 □
Intrigue (3) 10 □
Orate (3) 5 □
Play (Lute) (3) 3 □
Read (Latin) (0) 1 □
Recognize (3) 3 □
Religion (Christn) (2) 2 □
Romance (2) 10 □
Singing (2) 2 □
Stewardship (2) 2 □
Swimming (2) 2 □
Tourney (5) 5 □

Squire
Name ....
Age 15
First Aid (6) 6 □
Battle (1) 1 □
Horsemanship (6) 6 □
Play (Harp) 5 □

Glory 175
Glory This Game

Current Hit Points
Wounds ....
□ Chirurgery Needed

Combat Skills
†Battle (10) 10 □
†Horsemanship (10) 10 □

Weapon Skills
†Sword (10) 10 □
†Lance (10) 10 □
Spear (6) 6 □
Dagger (5) 5 □

Joust Score
Wins .... Losses ....

Horses
Best Warhorse (#1)
Type Charger
Damage 6d6 Move 8
Armor 5 HP 46
SIZ 34 CON 12 DEX 17

Other Horses
Own Riding (#2) Rouncy CON 14
Squire's (#3) Sumpter CON 16
(#4) .... CON ....
(#5) .... CON ....

The Courtier

This young man pursues Glory at court, through romance, chivalrous actions, and courtesy. Though average on the field of combat, he shines in court situations.

Select this character if you are interested in Glory derived from roleplaying as well as combat. He can be a spokesman for the rest of the party, and will do very well with the ladies (note his Appearance).

Avoid this character if you are primarily interested in killing enemies and monsters.

Master of the Tourney

This young man wishes to be the jousting champion of all Britain. He has studied all the skills important to the tourney, including the use of the lance and the lore of Heraldry.

Select this character if you wish to gain Glory from chivalrous as well as lethal combat. The Master of the Tourney is somewhat less biased towards roleplaying than ~~the Courtier~~, and represents a good compromise.

KING ARTHUR **Pendragon**

Player
Personal Data Master of the Tourney
Name
Homeland Salisbury
Culture Cymric Religion Christian
Father's Name
Father's Class Vassal Son Number 1
Liege Lord Earl Robert
Current Class
Current Home Tisbury Age 21 Year Born 510

Personality Traits
Chivalry Bonus [•] (total = 80+) NO
Religious Bonus (underlined traits all 16+) NO
- □ Chaste 13 / 7 Lustful □
- • □ Energetic 10 / 10 Lazy □
- □ Forgiving 13 / 7 Vengeful □
- • □ Generous 10 / 10 Selfish □
- □ Honest 10 / 10 Deceitful □
- • □ Just 10 / 10 Arbitrary □
- • □ Merciful 13 / 7 Cruel □
- • □ Modest 13 / 7 Proud □
- □ Pious 10 / 10 Worldly □
- □ Prudent 10 / 10 Reckless □
- □ Temperate 13 / 7 Indulgent □
- □ Trusting 10 / 10 Suspicious □
- • □ Valorous 16 / 4 Cowardly □

Directed Trait
Directed Trait

Passions
Loyalty (lord) (15) 15 □
Love (family) (15) 15 □
Hospitality (15) 15 □
Honor (15) 15 □
Hate (Saxons) (3d6) 8 □

Equipment Carried
Armor Type (12 points) Reinforced Chain
Clothing (1 Librum value)
☑ Personal Gear (on horse # 2)
□ Travel Gear (on horse #)
☑ War Gear (on horse # 1) 2 Spears
5 jousting lances
Decorated Saddle (1 librum)

Statistics
SIZ 14 (Knockdown)
DEX 13
STR 12
CON (-3) 14 (Major Wound)
APP 10
Damage ((STR+SIZ)/6) 4 d6
Healing Rate ((STR+CON)/10) 3
Movement Rate ((STR+DEX)/10) 3
Total Hit Points (SIZ+CON) 28
Unconscious (HP/4) 7

Distinctive Features
Burly

Skills
Awareness (5) 7 □
Boating (1) 1 □
Chirurgery (0) □
Compose (0) □
Courtesy (3) 5 □
Dancing (2) 2 □
Faerie Lore (1) 1 □
†First Aid (10) 10 □
Flirting (3) 3 □
Folk Lore (2) 2 □
Gaming (3) 3 □
Hawking (3) 3 □
Heraldry (3) 10 □
Hunting (2) 2 □
Industry (0) □
Intrigue (3) 3 □
Orate (3) 3 □
Play (Harp) (3) 3 □
Read ( ) (0) □
Recognize (3) 4 □
Religion (Christ.) (2) 2 □
Romance (2) 2 □
Singing (2) 2 □
Stewardship (2) 2 □
Swimming (2) 2 □
Tourney (5) 10 □

Squire
Name Will
Age 15
First Aid (6) 6 □
Battle (1) 1 □
Horsemanship (6) 6 □
Hunting 5 □

Glory 175
Glory This Game

Current Hit Points
Wounds
□ Chirurgery Needed

Combat Skills
†Battle (10) 10 □
†Horsemanship (10) 13 □
Weapon Skills
†Sword (10) 12 □
†Lance (10) 15 □
Spear (6) 6 □
Dagger (5) 5 □

Joust Score
Wins Losses

Horses
Best Warhorse (#1)
Type Charger
Damage 6D6 Move 8
Armor 5 HP 46
SIZ 34 CON 12 DEX 17
Other Horses
Own Riding (#2) Rouncy CON 14
Squire's (#3) Sumpter CON 16
(#4) CON
(#5) CON

The Berserker

This fierce young warrior is big, strong, and ugly. He bears the scars of many fights, although only 21 years old. Reckless by nature, and famous for his wild acts, he has the constitution to survive most injuries with little permanent effect.

Choose this character if your primary interest lies in combat. He will not do very well in formal situations, however.

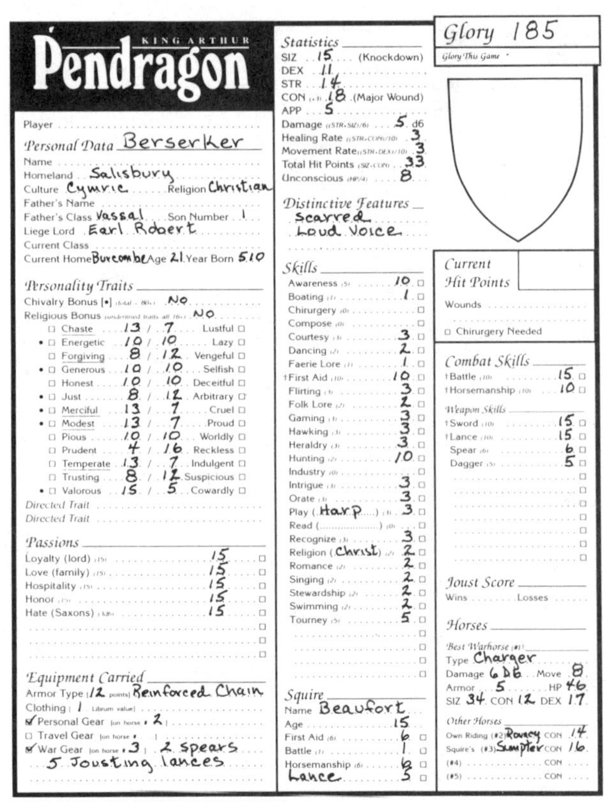

KING ARTHUR **Pendragon**

Player
Personal Data Berserker
Name
Homeland Salisbury
Culture Cymric Religion Christian
Father's Name
Father's Class Vassal Son Number 1
Liege Lord Earl Robert
Current Class
Current Home Burcombe Age 21 Year Born 510

Personality Traits
Chivalry Bonus [•] (total = 80+) NO
Religious Bonus (underlined traits all 16+) NO
- □ Chaste 13 / 7 Lustful □
- • □ Energetic 10 / 10 Lazy □
- □ Forgiving 8 / 12 Vengeful □
- • □ Generous 10 / 10 Selfish □
- □ Honest 10 / 10 Deceitful □
- • □ Just 8 / 12 Arbitrary □
- • □ Merciful 13 / 7 Cruel □
- • □ Modest 13 / 7 Proud □
- □ Pious 10 / 10 Worldly □
- □ Prudent 4 / 16 Reckless □
- □ Temperate 13 / 7 Indulgent □
- □ Trusting 8 / 12 Suspicious □
- • □ Valorous 15 / 5 Cowardly □

Directed Trait
Directed Trait

Passions
Loyalty (lord) (15) 15 □
Love (family) (15) 15 □
Hospitality (15) 15 □
Honor (15) 15 □
Hate (Saxons) (3d6) 15 □

Equipment Carried
Armor Type (12 points) Reinforced Chain
Clothing (1 Librum value)
☑ Personal Gear (on horse # 2)
□ Travel Gear (on horse #)
☑ War Gear (on horse # 3) 2 Spears
5 Jousting lances

Statistics
SIZ 15 (Knockdown)
DEX 11
STR 14
CON (-3) 18 (Major Wound)
APP 5
Damage ((STR+SIZ)/6) 5 d6
Healing Rate ((STR+CON)/10) 3
Movement Rate ((STR+DEX)/10) 3
Total Hit Points (SIZ+CON) 33
Unconscious (HP/4) 8

Distinctive Features
Scarred
Loud Voice

Skills
Awareness (5) 10 □
Boating (1) 1 □
Chirurgery (0) □
Compose (0) □
Courtesy (3) 3 □
Dancing (2) 2 □
Faerie Lore (1) 1 □
†First Aid (10) 10 □
Flirting (3) 3 □
Folk Lore (2) 2 □
Gaming (3) 3 □
Hawking (3) 3 □
Heraldry (3) 3 □
Hunting (2) 10 □
Industry (0) □
Intrigue (3) 3 □
Orate (3) 3 □
Play (Harp) (3) 3 □
Read ( ) (0) □
Recognize (3) 3 □
Religion (Christ) (2) 2 □
Romance (2) 2 □
Singing (2) 2 □
Stewardship (2) 2 □
Swimming (2) 2 □
Tourney (5) 5 □

Squire
Name Beaufort
Age 15
First Aid (6) 6 □
Battle (1) 1 □
Horsemanship (6) 6 □
Lance 5 □

Glory 185
Glory This Game

Current Hit Points
Wounds
□ Chirurgery Needed

Combat Skills
†Battle (10) 15 □
†Horsemanship (10) 10 □
Weapon Skills
†Sword (10) 15 □
†Lance (10) 15 □
Spear (6) 6 □
Dagger (5) 5 □

Joust Score
Wins Losses

Horses
Best Warhorse (#1)
Type Charger
Damage 6D6 Move 8
Armor 5 HP 46
SIZ 34 CON 12 DEX 17
Other Horses
Own Riding (#2) Rouncy CON 14
Squire's (#3) Sumpter CON 16
(#4) CON
(#5) CON

(CON), and Appearance (APP). Statistics are determined by allocation from a pool of 60 points.

Definitions

Size (SIZ) reflects the bulk and height of your character. The smallest that a normal human can be is SIZ 8. Bigger characters are superior in combat because bigger men do more damage, can absorb more damage, and because SIZ is also used to calculate Knockdown, as explained in the Combat section of the "Game Mechanics" chapter.

Dexterity (DEX) reflects your character's quickness, agility and manual dexterity. In game terms, the higher the DEX value the better your character's sense of balance.

Strength (STR) reflects your character's ability to lift and carry weight. High STR indicates a strong character. STR influences combat and movement rate.

Constitution (CON) reflects the health of your character. A CON value less than 5 indicates a sickly character, while a value greater than 15 indicates robust health. For combat, CON determines how severe a wound a character can take and still be unaffected, called the Major Wound.

Appearance (APP) reflects the physical beauty of a character. APP over 15 indicates a handsome or beautiful person, while APP below 5 is extremely ugly and repulsive. Do not neglect this stat! It is tempting to reduce this in favor of combat-oriented stats, but handsome knights have a distinct advantage in some situations.

Distinctive Features, below, help define the exact appearance of your character more fully than a simple number can.

Allocate Statistics

Distribute a total of 60 points among the five statistics, keeping in mind the restrictions below.

CON will automatically increase by +3 during the next step, "Cultural Modifiers," regardless of allocation, and the maximum for CON is 21, so if you allocate more than 18 to CON, the extra points will be wasted.

Restrictions: No statistic can have an initial value greater than the maximum possible for a character of that culture (15-21, depending on culture and statistic). Minimum value for a statistic is always 5 or higher, again depending on culture. In this book, all knights come from the Cymric culture.

Cymric Statistics Table

statistic	*minimum*	*maximum*
SIZ	8	18
DEX	5	18
STR	5	18
CON	5	21
APP	5	18

Suggestions: Your first character should be designed so that STR and SIZ have a total of at least 21. This gives him a respectable Damage statistic of 4d6 (see below for more information on the Damage statistic). His CON also ought to be at least 11 (you need allocate only 8 points to CON, given the cultural modifier below). Characters with less than these values will be handicapped in combat.

You have plenty of points to work with. For example, assigning values of SIZ 11, STR 10, and CON 8 (recommended minimums) yields 31 more points to be allocated to DEX and APP (for example, DEX 13 and APP 18).

Effects of Low Statistics: As you can see, no statistic can have an initial value of less than 5, and SIZ must be at least 8. Don't be tempted to assign more than one of these minimums to statistics. Statistics will be reduced during the game, and when any statistic is at 3 the character is bedridden and cannot leave his room. Worse, any statistic value at 0 indicates death. Thus even a low APP can be hazardous, due to aging and wounds (see the "Game Mechanics" chapter for more information).

Cultural Modifiers

Your character's original culture modifies his statistics. This modification is done after the above step is completed. The modifiers are based on culture, and all initial characters in this book are Cymric.

Cymric Modifiers Table

Modifier:	+3 CON

Yearly Statistic Increases

Characters can slowly increase their statistics up to the maximum values given above through a yearly procedure known as the *Winter Phase*. You may perform several simplified Winter Phases as a part of character generation (see "Previous Experience" below).

This process is considered to be physical growth or training, or some combination of the two. Two limitations apply: SIZ can be increased only up to age 21 (few persons grow significantly after that age); and all other statistics can be increased only up to age 35.

After age 35, only magic or Glory can increase statistics: see the "Glory and Ambitions" chapter and the "Magic" section in the "What Your Character Knows" chapter.

Derived Statistics

Some of the statistics are derived from those already determined above.

Damage: A character's Damage value reveals his potential to do harm to his foe. The value acquired from the equation below indicates the number of six-sided dice which the player rolls when his character successfully hits something or someone with a sword or other heavy weapon.

Damage = SIZ + STR divided by 6

Healing Rate: The healing rate of a character indicates the number of hit points which can be regained during a week of game time by the character, as long as that character is quietly resting. Refer to the "Damage and Health" section of the "Game Mechanics" chapter for additional details.

Healing Rate = CON + STR divided by 10

Movement Rate: This value indicates the number of yards per melee round that your character can walk while in armor. The Movement Rate number also affects daily overland rates for forced march. See the "Game Mechanics" chapter for more information on movement.

Move = STR + DEX divided by 10

Total Hit Points: Total Hit Points are used in combat to determine how much damage a character may sustain before going unconscious or being killed.

Total Hit Points = CON + SIZ

Unconscious: This value acts as a threshold below which a character falls unconscious. If any character's current hit points fall below this value then that character falls unconscious.

Unconscious = Total Hit Points divided by 4

Distinctive Features

APP measures relative appearance, determining whether a character is handsome or beautiful, or ugly. The higher APP statistics indicate a more handsome character, while numbers below 5 indicate real ugliness.

Distinctive features allow for objective differences between characters with the same subjective value.

A distinctive feature is not always a negative quality, though you may wish to make it so. The following list of suggestions includes ideas for both positive and negative features.

The number of features your character receives is determined by the character's APP, cross-indexed on the table below.

Sir Gawaine

Distinctive Features Table

APP value	number of features
1-4	3
5-8	2
9-12	1
13-15	2
16 or more	3

Players are free to choose the specific details which best fit their characters, rather than making a roll.

Distinctive Features Detail Table

d6 roll	distinctive feature
1	Hair (very long, curly, red, crewcut, blond, excessively hairy, huge beard, prematurely gray, glossy, bald, a particular cut, etc.)
2	Body (slouched, barrel-chested, hunchback, tall, thin, broad-shouldered, high-shouldered, very muscular, burly, squat, smooth skin, etc.)
3	Expression (bright-eyed, proud, sneering, haughty, nice smile, hidden behind beard, straight teeth, dour, cheerful, squint, piercing glance, etc.)
4	Speech (lisp, stutter, accent, basso, sharp, nasal, shrill, squeaky, musical, loud, soft, strong, national accent, etc.)
5	Facial Feature (noble nose, scarred, darkly tanned, black eyes, bushy eyebrows, deep-set eyes, high cheekbones, red and weatherbeaten skin, braided beard, big ears, long moustache, small nose, facial blemishes, birthmark, etc.)
6	Limbs (short legs, bulging biceps, one arm longer than the other, rough hands, long nails, hairy arms and hands, bow legs, limp, big feet, long fingers, etc.)

4. Skills

Skills in *Pendragon* define those activities which characters commonly perform during game play. The numerical value of these skills reflects the chance of successfully completing that action during the game. As a result of different personal experience, not all characters have equal ability in these skills. Characters who matured within the same culture show certain similarities in their abilities.

The values for each character's skills are derived from three sources: the character's culture, his social class, and from the individual choices of the player. Once skill determination is complete, your character will have the skills of a 21 or more-year old squire who is ready to be knighted.

Beginning Cultural Values and Beginning Class Values

A character's beginning skills values are shaped by his environment, especially his culture and his father's social class. In this book, all characters are of the Cymric culture, and are sons of a knight. The character sheet has the beginning skill values written in (parentheses). These serve as the basis for most skill values. However, you may pick the skills that your character will specialize in.

Individual Skill Choices

During youth each person discovers those things which interest him most, and he spends as much time as possible in doing those things. The following process lets the player pick the things that interested his character most.

No skill may ever be raised above 15 by these extra points. Also, no skill with a beginning value of 0 may be augmented, except for weapons skills. Hence, no Cymric character can have a Chirurgery skill before starting play.

- Choose any 2 non-combat skills other than First Aid which will be used to qualify your character for knighthood (any will do; Dancing, for example). Make each of them 10.
- Choose any one combat or non-combat skill at which you excel. Make it 15. The Sword skill is a popular choice.
- Add 10 more points to any number of combat or non-combat skills of your choice, within the limits given above.
- Give the other skills listed on the sheet the value given in parentheses. For example, if you did *not* pick Hunting in any above step, write in a value of 2 (the same number in parentheses) into that space now.

5. Previous Experience

As figured thus far, your character is 21 years old and has already gained the reputation, connections, and minimum skills needed for knighthood. You may wish to add some years to your character's age before play, allowing him to gain some further pre-play experience. Each additional year of age provides a character with one (not two or all) of the following benefits, which are based on the Winter Phase system of the game (see the "Game Mechanics" chapter below). You should normally not age your character more than 5 additional years using this table.

Gawaine

Yearly Previous Experience Table

Pick one action from below per year

1. Distribute 1d6 points among the character's skills as desired, except that no non-weapon skills with a beginning value of 0 may be augmented, and no skill may be raised above value 15. Make a note that your character is a year older. Or...

2. Add one point to any personality trait or passion, up to a maximum of 19 for traits and 20 for passions. Make a note that your character is a year older. Or...

3. Add one point to a statistic. No statistic can be raised to a value greater than the maximum possible for a character of that culture. Make a note that your character is a year older.

Notes: If you simply wish to play an older character, the easiest way of aging him is to determine what age you wish him to be, then roll 1d6 worth of skill points per year beyond age 21 (a 24-year old character would roll 3d6 for his points).

6. Knighthood

New characters created using this book always qualify for knighthood, and the gamemaster should make sure that they become knights as soon as the ceremony can be integrated into play.

The Importance of Knighthood

Knighthood is an extraordinary and rare honor, too important to be conferred automatically on characters. Instead, the ceremony is part of the game. Players must speak the part of their character in taking the oath of knighthood. If this is their first knight, the oath will be the first words they speak "in character." The oath appears in a boxed article discussing the knighthood ceremony, found in the "Scenarios" chapter.

Beginning knights receive a full 1000 Glory points upon being knighted, are entitled to use the title Sir before their name, and also qualify for a heraldic coat of arms.

Note that new characters are assumed to have contacts at court who will sponsor them properly, and it is further assumed that their lord needs another knight. In the companion to this book, *Knights Adventurous,* characters are created who will have to strive for knighthood, rather than gain it so easily.

New Campaigns

If the gamemaster is just beginning a campaign, then he should refer to the "Scenarios" chapter once characters are complete, and conduct the beginning scenario. At the appropriate point he will perform the knighthood ceremony for all the characters in the campaign, who will then have the same lord and homeland, an important bond between them.

Ongoing Campaigns

If your new character is entering an ongoing campaign in which the other characters are already knights, then as soon as you've finished your character, the gamemaster should announce a court session, and conduct the ceremony of knighthood, with the other player knights as witnesses.

If the other player knights are all in the middle of an adventure elsewhere, and cannot come to court, the gamemaster should still interupt the action long enough to conduct the knighthood ceremony, with non-player characters as witnesses.

7. Other Information

Glory

This space is provided to display the accumulated Glory acquired by your character every winter.

Characters gain Glory through family ties. Every son receives Glory equal to 1/10 of his father's Glory, determined either when the character begins play or when the father dies, whichever comes first. Determine it now for your starting character, using the simple table below.

When your character is knighted, he will gain a massive 1000 Glory points. If your gamemaster practices the custom of "The Leap", then your character may have jumped onto his horse after he was knighted, and his Glory would then be increased by 10.

Inherited Glory Table

father's social class	*inherited Glory*
Knight	6d6 + 150

Glory This Game: The "Glory This Game" box is provided to keep track of new Glory gained during game play, but not actually displayed because winter has not yet arrived in game time. See the "Glory and Ambitions" chapter for more information.

Coat of Arms

When your character is knighted, you may color in the shield here in a design of your own making. Every knight deserves his own coat of arms. Confer with the gamemaster about your chosen coat of arms. Nearby pages include coats of arms that you can trace.

A coat of arms is the design worn by a knight on the outside surface of his shield. This design serves to identify the knight and his family when he wears full armor and is not otherwise identifiable. The skill that allows the identification of a coat of arms is called Heraldry. A group of people, called heralds, spend all their lives mastering this skill.

A knight is entitled to bear his own, unique, coat of arms. If your character does not have a ready-made coat of arms and you cannot make one up on the spot, your character may apply for provisional arms and ride for a year with a blank shield. Additionally, a squire may reserve his design ahead of time by checking with the Royal Herald (the gamemaster).

Draw the coat of arms you want or trace a design from the nearby pages.One page of Charges (pictorial elements) and one page of Ordinaries (geometrical background designs) are given.

Label each section with the desired color, or color it in with pencils. Normally a coat of arms includes a color and a metal. Colors available are red, green, blue, purple, and black. Metals include silver (white) and gold (yellow). "Furs" are also possible. For the sake of readability, do not use a metal adjacent to another metal, or a color adjacent to another color. For example, if you chose a Lorraine cross as your charge and Barry as your ordinary, the stripes could be silver and blue, with a black cross, but *not* black and blue with a silver cross, or silver and gold, with a blue cross.

Be sure you do not use the same color scheme and arms as recorded for someone else who is listed in this book. Each coat of arms must be unique, otherwise it is not fulfilling its purpose of identifying an individual.

Feel free to invent, alter, and otherwise be creative in your heraldic devices. Remember that the gamemaster has final say about the design which you choose. Simplicity is the key of heraldic design. The symbol should be easily recognizable from a distance or it will not achieve its purpose.

Joust Score

This space is provided to record the results of every joust resolved during game play. You will start with zero in each category.

Add one to the Wins column every time that your character wins a joust, and add one to the Losses column every time that your character loses a joust. These tallies are mainly for the amusement of the players, and do not directly affect the game unless the gamemaster wishes them to.

Charges

Trace the Charge of your choice onto your character's coat of arms and use an Ordinary to vary the background colors.

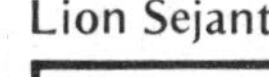

Lion Sejant

Crescent

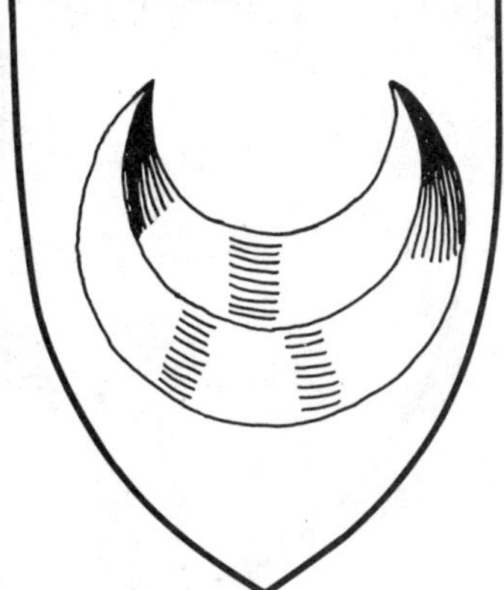

Lion Rampant Reguardant

Quatrefoil

Lorraine Cross

Lion Couchant

Maltese Cross

Latin Cross

Dolphin Naiant

Boar's Head Couped

Martlet

Rose

Stag Trippant

Eagle Rising, Wings Elevated and Addorsed

Tau Cross

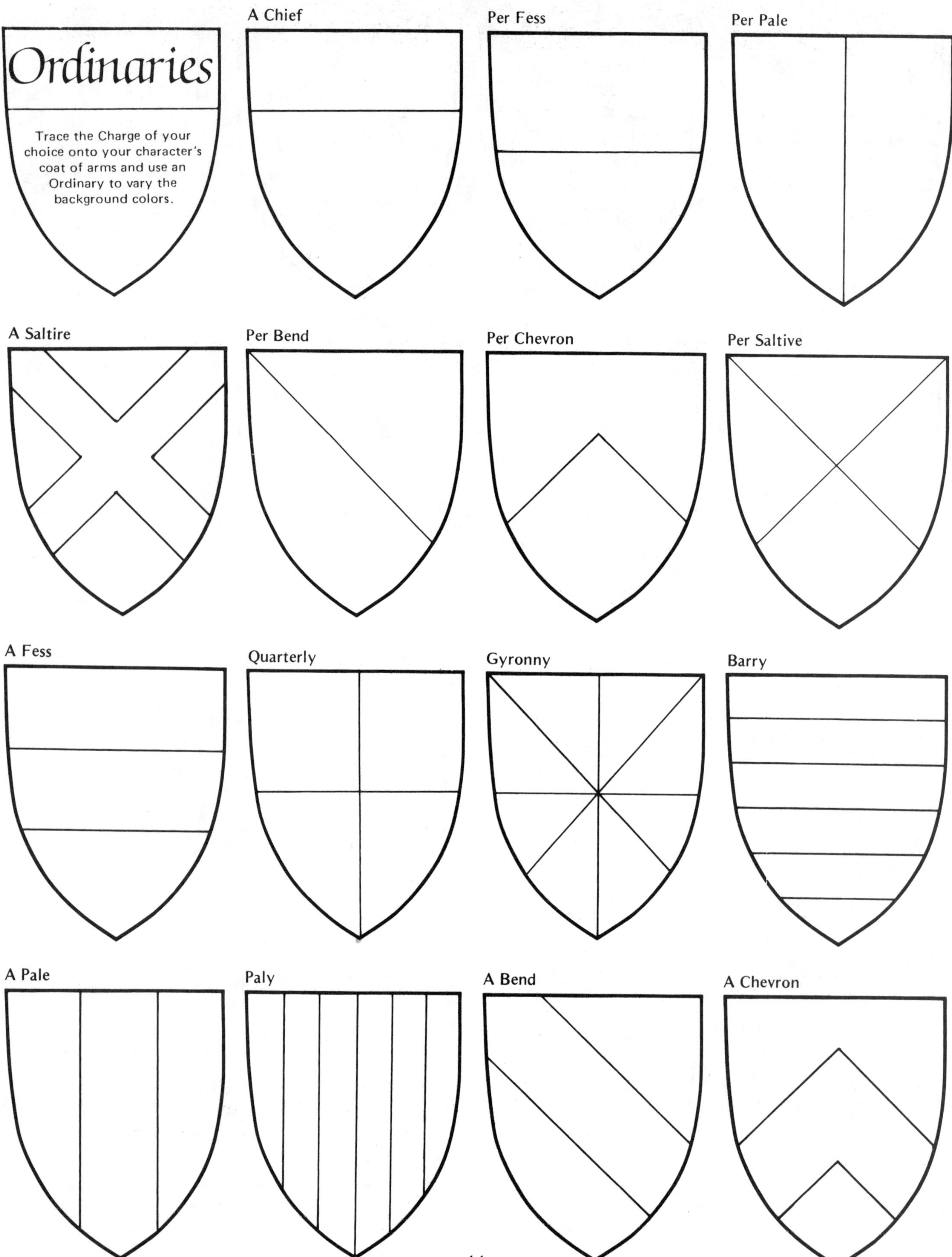
A Chief
Per Fess
Per Pale
Ordinaries
Trace the Charge of your choice onto your character's coat of arms and use an Ordinary to vary the background colors.
A Saltire
Per Bend
Per Chevron
Per Saltive
A Fess
Quarterly
Gyronny
Barry
A Pale
Paly
A Bend
A Chevron

Horses

In this space you keep track of your five most important horses. Most characters begin play with only three horses, but eventually your character may accumulate an entire stable. Your character starts with one of each of the following horses, and luck may give you another.

- Charger (your warhorse).
- Rouncy (a small horse for riding; also carries equipment).
- Sumpter (for carrying equipment).

List the horse's type and selected statistics under each number. Characters usually ride a rouncy, listed under Own Riding horse (#2) and keep their warhorse (#1) to use in a fight.

Sample stats for each type of horse are:

***Horse Table** (by type)*

	charger	*rouncy*	*sumpter*
Damage	6d6	4d6	3d6
Movement	8	6	5
Armor	5	4	3
SIZ	34	26	22
CON	12	14	16
DEX	17	10	12
HP (hit points)	46	40	38

Checklist of Equipment Carried

This entry is further explained below, under Equipment Carried.

Squire

After knighthood, characters are assigned a squire by their lord or a subordinate. Starting squires are always age 15. Usually a squire's success at performing his duty is determined by attempting a Squire Roll (see the "Game Mechanics" chapter. Sometimes a simple Squire Roll does not seem appropriate, or the squire requires more definition. Thus skills are given; the skills we use here are taken from the son of a Cymric squire, and are given on the character sheet in parentheses.

First Aid 6; Battle 1; Horsemanship 6; and [Your choice of skill in blank] 5.

Equipment Carried

Beginning characters start with standardized equipment. Write the values listed here in the spaces provided (in parentheses).

***Starting Equipment** (as the son of a knight)*

Your starting character gets:

Reinforced chain mail (12 points).

2 spears, shield, sword, dagger, 5 jousting lances.

Fine clothing worth 1 £.

Charger, rouncy, sumpter (listed above).

Personal gear, travel gear, war gear.

Locating Equipment

The simplest way to divide a knight's cargo among several steeds is to classify it into one of these types, and write in the number for the appropriate steed to locate it (the character does not normally carry these items himself).

Personal Gear: includes money, documents, best set of clothing, favorite secondary weapons, and so on. Generally a small bundle, very portable. It is generally carried on the knight's riding horse (rouncy). Note any unusual item in the small space provided to the right.

Travel Gear: This includes a tent, blankets, tent stakes, cooking and eating materials, horse-tending equipment, cold weather and rain cloaks, and so on. This can be carried on a horse which is also being ridden, and is about a quarter horse load per person (you and your squire, once you are a knight), without much food or water. If your character has something special in his travel gear, such as a mirror or a wig, write this in the small space provided.

War Gear: This includes things for extended military camping, such as more warm socks, rope, paint to fix up shields, whetstones, pieces of armor, mail-polishing keg of sand, spare weapons, a couple bottles of wine, and anything which might not be replaced while on campaign. This is about one horse-load per knight and squire team, and includes the Travel Gear for each person. These possessions are usually kept in a trunk in the lord's hall. When a knight goes on campaign with his lord, the lord lends the knight a horse to carry this gear. If adventuring on his own, a knight must find, borrow, buy, or otherwise obtain a horse if he wishes to both carry this gear and allow his squire to ride.

Luck Benefits

This table gives various colorful items to beginning characters. Make up the where and why of this, if necessary. Most of the entries are simple references to money. This extra money can be used to purchase something from the Price List, found in the "Wealth" chapter. Money in *Pendragon* is measured in Libra (singular Librum), abbreviated £. A Librum can be divided into 240 denarii, also called pennies, and abbreviated d.

Roll 1d20 to find your Luck.

Luck Benefits Table

d20	*Result*
01	Money. 3d20 denarii.
02-03	Money. 3d20+100 denarii.
04-06	Money. 1 £. (240 d.)
07	Money. 1d6 £.
08	Family Heirloom: sacred Christian relic. Roll 1d6 (1=finger, 2=tears, 3-4=hair, 5=bone fragment, 6=blood)
09	Family Heirloom: ancient bronze sword. +1 modifier to Sword skill value when used. Weak blade; it will break in combat as if it was not a sword (see the "Game Mechanics" chapter below). Value = 2 £.
10	Family Heirloom: blessed lance. Add +1 modifier to Lance skill value when using this lance until it breaks. Value = 25 d.
11	Family Heirloom: decorated saddle. Value = 1 £.
12	Family Heirloom: engraved finger ring. 1d6 roll for value: 1-4 = silver, worth 0.5 £.; 5-6 = gold, worth 2 £.
13	Family Heirloom: arm ring. (roll 1d6: 1-5 = silver, worth 1£., 6 = gold, worth 8 £.)
14	Family Heirloom: valuable cloak worth 1£. from (roll 1d6: 1-2 = Byzantium, 3 = Germany, 4-5 = Spain, 6 = Rome.)
15	A magic healing potion, heals 1d6 damage once. Priceless.
16-17	A rouncy
18	A charger
19	A destrier (a huge warhorse: see the "Characters and Creatures" chapter for statistics).
20	Roll twice more, re-rolling further rolls of 20.

Heirlooms

For heirlooms, you can make up a story of how it came into the family's possession. It might be from the mother's side of the family, a gift from a lord, a war trophy, and so on.

Introducing Your Knight

Before a game everyone usually introduces their character. Here are two such descriptions, for two sample knights that will appear again in examples of play. They are young Sir Ambrut (a new player character) and his lord, Sir Yvane (an experienced player character).

"This is Sir Ambrut, a household knight of Sir Yvane le Cour, baron of the King of Listeneise. He is 22 years old, dresses very well, and has pale skin and a deep voice. He is not notably Pious or attendant at church, but holds to the Christian virtues. He has the Glory of an Ordinary Knight. He is proud of the fact that he is the oldest of the four brothers who make up the leaders of his family clan. His father, the famous knight known as Ambrut of the White Hawk, died heroically some years ago at the battle of the River Tribuit."

"I am playing Sir Yvane le Cour, a Baron of Listeneise, age 29. He has blond hair, a shining smile, and a braided beard. He is a pious pagan, but keeps it to himself. He is noted for his great courage. He has the Glory of a Praiseworthy knight."

8. The Character Sheet Back

Use the back of your character sheet to record the game history and significant facts of your character. You do not have to write things down, but you should. You lose much of the long-term impact of playing this game if you don't. *Pendragon* is a campaign, with knights staking their lives for glory. Their play-lives are worth the minor effort of a one-line synopsis for each of their adventures.

Selected Events

Use this box to record the dates upon which these seven critical events of a character's life occur:

Born - Your character's birth date.

Squired - Birth date plus 15 years, and to whom squired, if part of the campaign.

Knighted - the year in which your character is knighted, and by whom.

Titled - the year in which the character receives a lord's title, if ever.

Landed - The year in which a household knight becomes a vassal knight. Your character, being the eldest son of a vassal knight, will be landed when knighted.

Member of the Round Table - the year in which your knight is accepted at the Round Table — a rare honor!

Died - the year in which your character died. Useful if you created a family for your character.

Family

Use this space to record family information.

Year Wed - The year in which your character marries, if at all.

Spouse Name - The name of your character's wife. No knights start the game already married. However, marriage is an important part of the *Pendragon* fantasy, and most player knights should wish to be married. See the chapters entitled "Your Family" and "Glory and Ambitions" for more information.

Will - Write here the name or relationship of the person whom your character has designated as heir to his property. "Family" is usually sufficient. Only personal property is transferred — gifts from a lord return to him. If nothing is written here then everything goes to the lord.

Children to reach majority - the date of birth and name of any children your character may have.

Family Characteristic - A family characteristic is some unusual feature which everyone in the family has. Figure it now, from the table below, and add the value to the appropriate skill. Please roll this randomly, even though the other components of your character were yours to chose. This addition can violate the rules previously established for limitations. Thus it might raise a skill above 15, or perhaps even above 20.

This feature is transferred through the male line, and is given to all children of all men of this line. Thus your brothers and sons will also have this characteristic.

Note the feature carefully: some have advantages which will not become apparent until you play the game.

Family Characteristic Table

d20	characteristic
1-2	Good with horses (+5 Horsemanship)
3	Excellent voice (+10 Singing)
4-7	Keen sighted (+5 Awareness)
8	At home in nature (+5 Hunting)
9	Light-footed (+10 Dancing)
10	Natural healer (+5 First Aid)
11	Naturally lovable (+10 Flirting)
12	Never forgets a face (+10 Recognize)
13	Surprisingly deductive (+5 Intrigue)
14	Like otters in the water (+10 Swimming)
15	Natural speaker and storyteller (+10 Orate)
16	Natural musician (+15 Play (all instruments))
17	Good with words (+15 Compose)
18	Natural affection for armory (+10 Heraldry)
19	Good with birds (+15 Hawking)
20	Clever at games (+10 Gaming)

Holdings

Your character begins as the eldest son of a vassal knight. List the name of his future holding here — it is the same as his Current Home. If he acquires more land, list each manor or larger holding by name. List the number of manors in any larger holding.

Equipment at Home

Knights often accumulate Denarii, Libra, extra weapons, addition mounts, sumptuous goods, and so forth. If your character does not carry these things everywhere he goes, list them here.

Army

Family Knights: These are your relatives who are knights, whether uncles, brothers, or other relations.

One of the most important factors in the game is how many knights you can

potentially call to your side in a crisis. Family knights are either Old (over 55), Middle-aged (35-55), or Young (20-35 or so.) Only the numbers are needed now, not the names or other information. The "Characters and Creatures" chapter gives sample data for each of the three categories of knight.

Determine them by rolling as follows, and then enter the numbers on the character sheet back.

Add all three numbers together, plus one more young knight (your character), to find the number for Family Knights, Total.

Old Knights: 1d6-5
Middle-Aged Knights: 1d6-2
Young Knights: 1d6+1

Vassals: Starting characters are never lords holding other knights as vassals; leave this blank for now. If your character acquires vassals during the campaign, list the number of vassals here. These knights are obliged to come to battle if summoned, and are probably close associates of the lord as well.

Other Lineage Men: Other adult men from the family can be useful in a fight. They are never well armed, and are generally unskilled at fighting, but at least they won't run away immediately upon being attacked by the enemy. They, as blood members, have much to gain in any family victory.

Total Number = 3d6+5

Levy: The levy calls forth every able-bodied man of the holding. Though the total population of your manor is around 420 people, this includes only 100 or fewer able-bodied men other than knights and squires. Not all of these peasants will come to fight.

For the sake of information, this number is the number anticipated *per manor*. So if your character gains more manors, roll again for each new manor and write the combined total down here. A knight with many manors can call upon a large levy!

Your gamemaster will decide how effective the men of your levy are in combat. The "Characters and Creatures" chapter gives sample data for an adult peasant.

Total Number = 5d20

History

Use this area to record various events of your character's life. Begin each entry with the date. The year designation is usually enough since most characters engage in only one adventure per year. At the end of each line is a column for listing any new glory gained in the adventure, plus a column to list the total glory gained by your character. Also list this total glory on the front of the character sheet.

After experiencing several adventures with a number of characters, you will begin to sense the history and movement which pervades Arthurian Lore, and your characters will grow into the story.

Conclusion

If you have followed instructions this far you now have a character ready to play. The character is a squire, 21 or more years old, possessing the connections, skills, and reputation necessary to become a knight immediately. As noted above, knighthood is a great honor. The Glory received from knighthood reflects this. The actual events leading to knighthood, and especially the ceremony, should best be played out during the game.

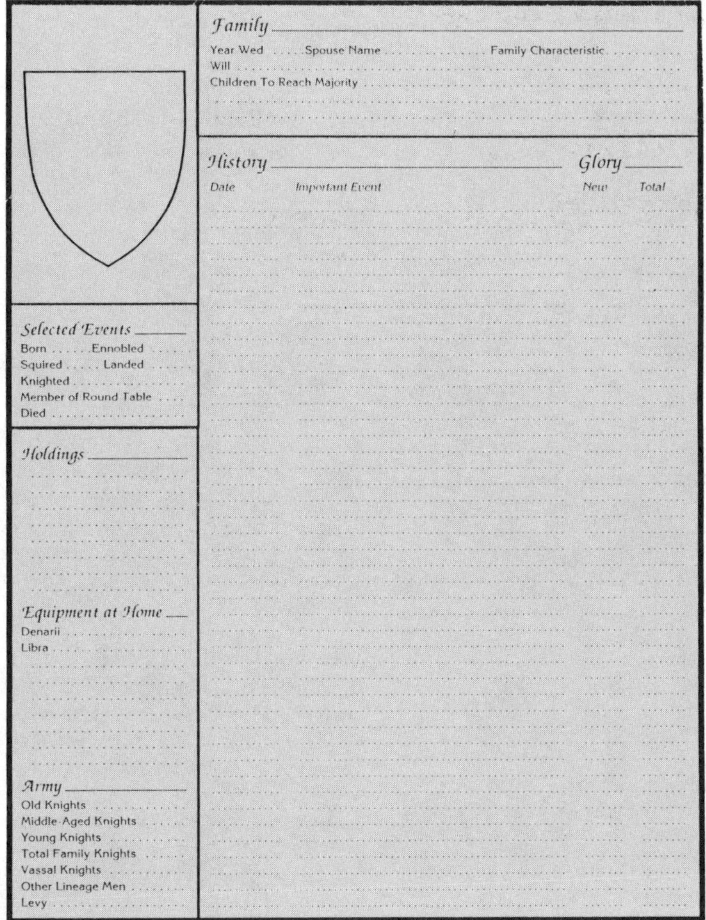

Family
Year Wed ..... Spouse Name .... Family Characteristic ....
Will ....
Children To Reach Majority ....

History
Date Important Event
Glory
New Total

Selected Events
Born ...... Ennobled ......
Squired ...... Landed ......
Knighted ....
Member of Round Table ......
Died ....

Holdings

Equipment at Home
Denarii ....
Libra ....

Army
Old Knights ....
Middle-Aged Knights ....
Young Knights ....
Total Family Knights ....
Vassal Knights ....
Other Lineage Men ....
Levy ....

Your Family

Your family is one thing you can ***always*** *count on.*

A KNIGHT'S FAMILY is his most precious and reliable resource. The family I am discussing here consists of your closest relatives — those who can be relied upon to help each other out in any circumstances, against any odds. These are the ones who, if they heard you were in mortal danger, would get up from whatever they were doing to come help immediately. You, of course, would do the same for them.

Why A Family?

Several reasons exist to have some further knowledge of your family than you have already gained from character generation.

Historical Perspective

Even if you have no desire to maintain your own dynasty, your roleplaying will be enhanced if you know about your family's past.

The extensive Family History table below helps you figure out what your character's grandfather and father did. Naturally both did much more than this, but here are the salient facts to incorporate the family into Arthurian history.

Your character will gain not only a family history but a portion of his grandfather's and father's Glory, and one or more inherited traits or passions derived from your ancestors' experiences over the last generation.

Character Protection

A family provides many kinds of protection from enemies. The ultimate expression of this protection is whether they are willing to enter mortal combat for your welfare.

In game play one of the most useful functions of the abstracted family is to give player knights a small back-up army of their own. In this way everyone has an emergency force at their beck and call.

You have already calculated the basic numbers for your private army during Character Generation. In this chapter you will learn a little more. Actual statistics for most of your family are available in the "Characters and Creatures" chapter.

The Dynastic Segment

Pendragon is designed to include long-term events which may take longer than a single character's lifetime to be finished. *Pendragon* time advances regularly. Some stories take the whole of King Arthur's 55 year-reign to complete — enough time for grandchildren of the original character to become knights.

✪ FAMILY HISTORY TABLE ✪

Introduction

This long table provides several things:

1. Some past history important to the game campaign, and,

2. Your grandfather's and father's actual part in these great historical events.

3. At least one family passion or directed trait that is handed down from father to son. These may be gained from some of the more dramatic and sanguinary historical events, mostly battles. Hate (Saxons) is mandatory, with others possible (see the "Ideals and Passions" chapter for more information on passions and traits).

4. Realistic and individual Inherited Glory from your ancestors, based on their actual achievements. This augments the Glory already gained from the Inherited Glory table (in Step 7 of character generation).

This table is based on your entering the game as a knight at age 21, in the year 531 A.D. Your father died one or more years ago, and you have been made a vassal knight, taking over from your father as head of the family.

If you took some previous experience during character generation, assume that it took place during your career as a squire, so that it is still 531. You will be older than the text assumes, but this presents no problem.

How to Use This Table

Your family history is determined year-by-year. The first year, 490 A.D., includes a detailed explanation of the method to be used for both grandfather's and father's histories.

Read the opening entry to get information, and then go to the year's Event Table. Roll the 20-sided die to determine your ancestor's part in the year's events, if any. For example, in 490 your grandfather may have fought in the great battle of Windsor. On the other hand, he may have died without achieving anything notable that year.

Check for a passion or trait at the end of the year's entries before you go on. If the ancestor is dead, the son gains the passion after hearing his father's last words. The son will either be you, or your father.

A pencil and paper to keep track of details will be needed (unless you wish to write in the book). Write down each year's event, if any, any Glory gained, and any passions or directed traits gained (by either grandfather, father, or your character).

When your grandfather dies, determine 1/10th of his final Glory and add this to your father's initial 1000 points. Note grandfather's passions and traits, if any, and assign one or more to your father (your choice), using the same numerical value that your grandfather had (for example, Hate (Saxons) at 15).

When your father finally dies the sequence is over. Take 1/10th of his final Glory as extra Inherited Glory beyond that already gained during character generation (which was based on a character having ordinary knights for ancestors).

If the text called for your character to take a passion or trait, write it down, including the value you rolled. You also may pick any one other passion or trait from

To participate fully in a long-term *Pendragon* campaign every knight should raise a family that can bring a player through the entire saga. The best *Pendragon* history is established if your campaign begins early and continues through to the end: guidelines for this are contained later, in *Knights Adventurous*. But in this basic *Pendragon* book, the campaign begins a generation or so later, so to help work your character into history the Family History table is provided.

Going Beyond the Single-Character Game

The emotional content of the game is changed by having a family. With a family a knight has someone other than himself for whom to live and to die. The motivation of individual characters changes when they have someone whom they love and for whom they will fight. The gamemaster should urge development of character families to provide that critical motivation.

Your character's sons can be given the same family characteristic, traits, passions, equipment, and starting statistics that your previous character had. Thus a character with a family doesn't really die.

Families allow players to interact in a natural way. When character knights marry into the same family, perhaps each others' sisters, they become enmeshed. This provides an excuse for the various knights to mingle so trustingly on adventures.

An established family provides a source of rank, power, traditions, knowledge, and even heirlooms. Thus the magic sword which your knight cherished does not disappear from the game at his death. Instead it, with his coat of arms, title, possessions, and other neat stuff, goes to his son.

When the new character enters the game the old ones might say "I was with your father at Badon," or "I remember when he messed up at the Adventure of the Knight of the Parrot." And your new character, of course, knows the details of the Adventure of the Knight of the Parrot. Thus death does not diminish the family, which is heir to the accumulated property and Glory of the deceased.

Connections

Relatives may provide opportunities: if someone becomes well-placed then his relatives will benefit as well.

However, in *Pendragon* the player knight is the leader of the family. He is an unusual and adventurous, and successful, individual, from the moment he first becomes a squire. It is to your character that others turn for leadership. You won't find a rich uncle in *Pendragon* — your character is that rich uncle for the other nonplayed family members.

More important are the connections which a family provides between the successive knights of a single player. Your experience of the game will take on depth and elegance if most of your own player characters come from a single family.

your father. Write down the same value that he had.

Hate (Saxons) is mandatory; it is already on your character sheet from the character generation procedure. If you inherit a higher Hate (Saxons) value than the one rolled during character generation (for example, a 15 rather than a 10), then erase the old number and write in the new one.

Note that passions of 16 or more gain their value in Glory during the winter. See the "Game Mechanics" and "Ideals and Passions" chapters for more information.

Your Grandfather's History

GRANDPA WAS BORN when Ambrosius Pendragon ruled Britain. Everyone knows that Ambrosius was "the last Roman," and that he ended the rule of the evil overlord Vortigern. Merlin the Magician was a young boy when Ambrosius destroyed Vortigern and reclaimed Logres. Ambrosius' reign was troubled by wars with the Saxons and northern British.

After Ambrosius died his brother, Uther Pendragon, inherited the kingdom. When your grandfather reached military age he followed his lord, the earl of Salisbury, in the many wars waged by King Uther against the Saxons. Your grandfather was successful. He had a good horse, armor, and the weapons of a heavy cavalry soldier. He was also lucky enough to survive the dangers of battle, at least until 490, the first year in this history. Sometime or other, he met your grandmother.

Start your grandfather's Glory at 2500 (he was a notable but not famous knight). He begins with no passions or directed traits. He may gain more Glory or a passion if you are lucky with your rolls on the tables below.

YEAR 490 (Sample Year)

This was almost an ordinary year. The Saxons raided heavily and were driven off. Of special note: a son was born — your father. *For this first year, italicized notes like this are included to explain the text above each note.*

A sentence always introduces events for the year. Usually, either nothing happens, or a famous battle occurs. For each event, you need a d20. Roll it, and refer to the subsequent table for the event that occurs that year:

Year 490 Events Table

d20	event
01-05	Nothing significant happened.

An easy entry, self-explanatory. Go to the next year when you roll this result.

d20	event
06	Died of Other Causes. See Miscellaneous Cause Table, Male.

This means grandfather died of something other than the main battle fought that year. The Miscellaneous Cause Table determines the exact cause.

d20	event
07-20	He fought at the Battle of Windsor.

Whenever you have this entry, it means you have to make another d20 roll on a

Your Past Family

Causes of Death

Two tables are used to determine a random cause of death for past family members.

Miscellaneous Cause Table, male

d20	death
1-3	in battle with personal feud
4-6	in battle with neighboring land
7-8	in battle with foreign invaders
9	entered monastery
10-11	hunting accident
12-13	other accident
14-16	old age, illness
17-20	Unknown cause, just never came home

Miscellaneous Cause Table, female

d20	death
01-07	sickness
08-09	old age
10-12	accident
13	killed by raiders
14-15	captured by raiders
16-18	died of pregnancy difficulties
19	entered convent
20	unknown cause, just disappeared

When a Character Dies

When a favorite character dies you should be ready for a moment of emotion. You decide what it is and how to handle it. It may be one of elation at some heroic deed, or it may be dejection over bad dice rolls. Among everything else a touch of sadness is likely.

The other players must decide what to do with the body. The now lordless squire might voice his dead lord's concerns and former desires. See what was written on the character sheet back as "Will." Check whether he died among people who will know where to return the body or news of the character's death.

Bookkeeping follows. Add up the final Glory which the character had. If he has a son, you cannot help but calculate the 10% which is going to be passed on. Make a list of all equipment to be passed on. Make a list of fiefs.

List the Traits, Directed Traits, and Passions of 16 or more and list them for later reference.

Take a deep breath and reflect for a moment on his life. Then write a one-line epitaph which will be on the headstone of his grave.

Store the character sheet in the "graveyard." Players usually want to keep treasured characters in their own graveyard, or might not care, and so should give the sheet to the gamemaster to keep.

separate table about the battle which follows. The results change on each table.

BATTLE OF WINDSOR (80)

This is the name of the battle. The number in parentheses shows the amount of Glory gained by participants in the battle. Write this number down immediately under your ancestor's running Glory total.

d20	*event*
01	He died with Great Glory (add 1000 Glory).

He was killed in the battle, but acted with great heroism — record an extra 1000 Glory and conclude the history for this ancestor. Check to see if the son gained a passion or directed trait. Whenever any character dies refer to the section on "Character Death," in the rules in the main text above.

02	Died in Battle. End history.

As above, this entry finishes your ancestor's life history. Check for a passion or trait below.

03-20	He survived, continue history.

Your ancestor fought in the battle and survived: check to see if he gained a passion or directed trait from the battle before you go on to his next year.

d20 Passion Roll, 01-05 = success.

This section doesn't always appear. If it does, it means you make another d20 roll. If you achieve a success by rolling equal to or less than the number shown, then your ancestor (if he lived) or his son (if the father died) got a passion or directed trait as a result of this experience, possibly one that is handed down to your character.

3d6 Hate (Saxons)

("Those shifty ambushers! There's neither courage or honor among them.")

The result of the second die roll shows how strong your or your ancestor's passion was, and what the type of passion is. The quotation is more or less what everyone remembers your ancestor used to say about this particular battle (or his last words, if he died).

Your ancestors may later get duplicate passions. Use whichever is higher than the other for the final number.

This ends the explanatory year. The remaining years follow the same pattern.

YEAR 492

In this year King Uther went to war against the rebellious Duke of Cornwall.

Year 492 Events Table

d20	event
01-03	Served Garrison duty, and survived Saxon raiding. Get 25 Glory.
04-05	Served Garrison duty, and killed by Saxon raiders. Get 25 Glory. End history.
06-09	Grandpa fought at the Siege of Tintagel, an indecisive siege even though Merlin was there to help the king. Get 10 Glory.
10-20	Grandpa fought at the Battle of Castle Terrabil.

BATTLE OF CASTLE TERRABIL (100)

01	He died with Great Glory (add 1000).
02-03	Died in battle. End history.
04-20	He survived, continue history.

INTERRUM YEARS 493-494

During these years wars with the Saxons continued. The king wed the Lady Igraine, widow of the Duke of Cornwall, but

Your Current Family

Players usually want to know a little bit more about the rest of their family. These tables provide the naked facts for individualized information.

Knights in Your Family

You have already determined the number of knights in your family and their relative ages during Character Generation. The information is on the back of your character sheet.

Given here are tables to construct the rest of your family based on the number of knights.

Old Knights

Old knights are age 55 or more. Whatever their precise relationship, they are likely to be addressed by the honorific "grandfather" during family discussions. They are counted among the elders of the community, for they have survived both years of warfare and the Aging Table.

Old Knights Table

d20	result
01-15	Your grandfather's younger brother
16-20	Your grandfather's illegitimate brother

Middle-Aged Knights

Middle-aged knights are between 36-54 years old. They are usually addressed as uncle by younger knights, whatever their status. They have begun using the Aging Table.

Middle-Aged Knights Table

d20	result
01-13	Your father's younger brother
14-17	Your mother's brother
18-20	Your father's illegitimate brother

Young Knights

Younger knights are between 20-35. They do not use the Aging Table yet.

Tristram de Lyonesse

Younger Knights Table

d20	result
01-08	Your younger brother
09-14	A first cousin, on your father's side
15	Your brother-in-law
16-17	A first cousin, on your mother's side
18	An illegitimate brother, older
19-20	An illegitimate brother, younger

shortly afterwards Uther was struck low by illness.

Years 493-494 Events Table

d20	event
01-02	Died. Roll on Miscellaneous Cause Table, Male.
04-20	Alive, continue history.

YEAR 495

The Saxons exploited the weak kingdom led by a sick king, but Uther mustered all his forces and surprised the invaders with a pitched battle.

Year 495 Events Table

d20	event
01-05	Nothing significant happened.
16-20	He fought at the Battle of St. Albans.
BATTLE OF ST. ALBANS (150)	
d20	*event*
01	He died with Great Glory (add 1000).
02-04	Died in battle. End history.
05-20	He survived, continue history.

King Uther slaughtered the Saxons. As the victorious Britons were celebrating a treacherous Saxon, masquerading as a doctor, poisoned the water. The king, and most of the reigning nobility, died.

YEARS 496-507

Anarchy reigned as noblemen killed each other to seize positions of power vacated by the mass death of the lords. Your grandfather supported the rightful earl of Salisbury. Saxons use the opportunity to seize many lands, including founding Wessex, a land south of Salisbury.

Year 496-507 Events Table

d20	event
01-02	Died. Roll on Miscellaneous Cause Table, Male.
04-20	Alive, continue history.

YEAR 508

The son of Vortigern the Tyrant, King Cerdic of Wessex, gained reinforcements and attacked Salisbury.

Year 508 Events Table

d20	event
01-05	Grandpa served garrison duty in Sarum. Take 10 Glory.
06-20	He fought at the Battle of Winchester.
BATTLE OF WINCHESTER (175)	
d20	*event*
01-04	He died with Great Glory (add 1000).
04-20	Died in battle. End history.
d20 Passion Roll, 01-20 = success	
2d6+6 Hate (Saxons) gained by your father.	
(Grandfather's last words: "Watch out for those guys that wear bear skins and roar.")	

At the end of this section your grandfather will be dead, having acquired during his career the fief of his manor in Salisbury. Your father, meantime, has begun his own career, and has started his own family, beginning with you, his eldest son.

Other Family Members

Constructing a family proceeds from the eldest relevant generation to the youngest. The oldest generation is that of your character's father and mother.

These calculations determine, in every case, legitimate kin only. Illegitimate sons, determined on the tables above, do not enter into these calculations, but are added on to the family tree at the end, separately.

These also cover only adults. Children under the age of 15 are ignored.

Father's Siblings

To start, we know that your father is deceased. Roll 1d6 to find the total number of siblings.

Roll 1d6 for each sibling, where an even number = male, and an odd number = female. These are your paternal uncles and aunts.

Now match the number of your uncles with the number of father's brothers who are knights. If the number of knights is smaller than the number of brothers, add brothers to reach the right number of knights.

Mother's Siblings

Follow the same process as used for Father's Siblings.

Your Character's Siblings

Once again, follow the same process as for Father's Siblings.

Living or Dead?

All of the knights shown on the list so far are known to be alive, as determined during Character Generation. Your father is known to be dead, as is your grandfather. The status of the rest of the family (women and unknighted men) is determined now.

Kinfolk Status Table

1d20 roll	*results*
01-07	alive, married
08-14	alive, unmarried
15-17	dead, was married
18-20	dead, never married

Once again, check to make sure this does not conflict with the information on knights. If it does, change the fact to suit the needs of the knights.

For the relatives who are deceased, use the Misc. Cause of Death Tables to find out how they died.

Your Father's History

YOUR FATHER WAS beginning his career as a knight when you were born, 21 years ago. Start your new tally with your father's initial Glory = 1000 + (grandfather's Glory/10). Your father has the Hate (Saxons) passion rolled above, at a minimum, and will pass this on to you.

Remember to note any Glory, passions, or directed traits gained by your father in the process below.

YEAR 510

This is Arthur's first year as king.

Your father saw young Arthur pull the magical sword from the stone and anvil, thereby declaring his kingship and inaugurating his reign. He was also present at Arthur's coronation, and fought in the wars against the rebels who did not accept the young king's right to rule.

Year 510 Events Table

d20	*events*
1-10	He was present at the first public drawing (Glory = 25).
11-20	He was present at one of the subsequent drawings (Glory = 10).

The earl of Salisbury was among the first lords of Logres who declared their support of King Arthur. As a knight of Salisbury, your father was present at the declaration of Arthur as warlord (or *dux bellorum*) in London, and shortly afterwards at his coronation at Carlion (Glory = 10).

Right after the coronation, your father fought at the subsequent Battle of Carlion. The northern kings, though outnumbering Arthur's forces, were driven off in their first attempt to defy the "Boy King."

BATTLE OF CARLION (250)

d20	*event*
01	He died with Great Glory (add 1000 Glory). End history. Take a +5 to the Passion Roll below, for your character (not father), with a maximum of 20 as the result.
02	Died in battle. End history. +10 to the Passion Roll below, for your character (not father), maximum 20.
03-20	Survived, continue history.

d20 Passion Roll, 01-10 = success.

Value = 3d6 Hate (Cumbrians) ("Their northern hearts are cold, like the snow there.")

Later that same year the northern lords, under King Lot, invaded again. Your father fought against them at the Battle of Bedegraine. Arthur won, but it was a very bloody battle, even for the victors.

BATTLE OF BEDEGRAINE (700)

d20	*event*
01	He died with Great Glory (add 1000 Glory).
02-04	Died in battle. End history.
05-20	Survived, continue history.

d20 Directed Trait Roll, 01-03 = success.

Value = 2d6 Mistrust Magicians (add to Suspicious) ("We won because of Merlin's tricks, and it should have been our chivalrous valor that took the day.")

YEARS 511-512

Two years of peace followed, broken only by minor skirmishing with the Saxons.

Years 511-512 Events Table

d20	*events*
01	Go to Miscellaneous Cause Table.
06-20	Served Garrison Duty.

YEAR 513

The northerners invaded again in even greater strength. King Arthur was surprised, and hard-pressed, but ultimately victorious. This victory secured the loyalty of the northern Britons.

Your Future Family

Your Wife

The selection of a wife is one of the most important points in a knight's life. As you will see from the "Glory and Ambitions" chapter, this importance is born out in the amount of Glory that can potentially be gained by marriage to the right woman.

Your gamemaster may introduce your character to several non-player character women of appropriate status for marriage in the course of the campaign. Many will be related to other player characters. This is the best way to find a wife. However, the "Winter Phase" section of the "Game Mechanics" chapter includes a family creation segment. In this segment you will find a random marriage table that can be used to generate random wives immediately. Of course, you take your chances this way.

Many game possibilities will be opened up for you and the gamemaster once your character is married.

I stress that a legitimate wife is necessary. Read the information in the "What Your Character Knows" chapter to understand the fine points of inheritance and legitimacy.

Your Son

Once you have a wife, the Winter Phase system will give you a chance every year of producing offspring. Usually a few years of game time have to pass before you achieve the success of having a male heir. There is no rule for reduction of fertility due to old age or wounds in *Pendragon*, so your character and his wife may become quite old and still produce a son.

The child will need to survive until the son reaches age 21, whereupon he qualifies to become a new player character knight. He can then carry on your aged or dead character's dynastic goals, interests, and even his rivalries, while letting you participate in the latest phase of the campaign with a strong, vital young knight as your primary character.

Your new character will not enter into a history constructed from rolling d20s on too many tables. He enters into a history constructed by you, the player, and his father, your former character.

You, the player, make most of the decisions in his makeup, a few of which are dependant on gamemaster approval.

What If the Heir Is Underage?

Your main character may die before any son reaches age 21. Your gamemaster will help you through here. First, gener-

Year 513 Events Table

d20	event
01-05	Go to Miscellaneous Cause Table.
06-10	Served Garrison Duty.
11-20	Your father fought at the Battle of Terrabil.

BATTLE OF TERRABIL (600)

d20	event
01	He died with Great Glory (add 1000 Glory).
02-04	Died in battle. End history.
05-20	Survived, continue history.

d20 Passion Roll, 01-09 = success.

Value = 1d6 Fear (Norgales knights). ("Seems like they all have giants for fathers, or witches for mothers, or magical Pict blood.")

YEAR 514

This year King Arthur married the most beautiful woman in the land. Your father attended the wedding, and participated in the great tournament afterwards.

Year 514 Events Table

d20	event
01-07	Was on losing team in the tournament's Melee (Glory = 15).
08-14	Was on winning team in the tournament's Melee (Glory = 50).
15-20	Received additional honors during the tournament: add 5d6 Glory, and then roll again, taking rolls of 15-20 as no further result.

INTERRUM YEARS 515-517

War against the Saxons continued. Every time they were defeated another migration from the continent arrived to renew conflict. Raids and skirmishes were continual, and battles common.

515-517 Years Events Table

d20	event
01-03	Go to Miscellaneous Cause Table.
04-17	Raided, skirmished, served Garrison Duty. Take 50 Glory.
18-20	Died in a skirmish or minor battle. Take 100 Glory. End history.

YEAR 518

The Saxon menace reached its height this year, and the largest army ever mustered marched up the Thames Valley to destroy the Pendragon once and for all. King Arthur stripped his land of garrisons to meet this threat. This was the largest battle ever fought in Britain. King Arthur won, exterminating the hostile Saxons and decimating his own army.

Year 518 Event Table

d20	event
01-20	Your father fought at the great Battle of Badon.

BATTLE OF BADON (1150)

d20	event
01-04	He died with Great Glory (add 1000 Glory).
05-10	Died in battle. End history.
11-20	Survived, continue history.

d20 Passion Roll, 01-10 = Success.

Value = 2d6+6 Hate (Saxons) ("I've seen too many of my good friends die to forgive them now.")

d20 Directed Trait Roll, 01-05 = Success.

Value = +5 Reckless against Saxons. ("Everyone of us was wounded, and them too, like berserkers. We had to meet them fanatic to fanatic.")

YEARS 519-525

A long period of relative peace followed the Battle of Badon, during which many of the outlying kingdoms and hidden robber barons were defeated by small armies and the knights of the Round Table. By 525 most of Britain had been unified under the rule of Arthur.

ate a ward for the child. This should be a relative, one of the other knights generated during character generation. He then becomes the head of the family, your character to play until the young heir reaches majority. By that time you may not care about the heir, or you might choose to have two characters from the same family to play.

The gamemaster will have to determine whether the youth may be knighted upon reaching majority (he may have lost his lands, his family connections, or even worse).

Bad Family Luck

Sometimes it seems impossible to generate an heir. The frustration of this fact illustrates one of the unwritten sorrows of the Arthurian legend. Will consolation be found comparing the plight to King Arthur's?

Frustration is not necessarily the desired end of this process, however. If your children continue to die as the years pass, talk to the gamemaster about the situation. Your gamemaster may wish to give you some help if you've been plagued with bad luck; perhaps a cousin can be discovered who can be adopted and played.

Creating a Player Character Son

Once a son survives to 21, you have an eldest son, a squire, who is ready to play. As with all player characters generated using this book, it is assumed that the father has trained the boy to be ready for knighthood, and prepared the way with his lord.

Knights Adventurous provides a random method to generate new characters. Even the random method should be modified using this important process for inheriting personality traits, passions, and attributes.

Create the character using the normal character generation procedure, but with some differences, as follows (remember that the standard character creation system assumes that new characters do not have families in the campaign).

Personal Data

Most of this is determined by the father's ancestry. Year born is written on the father's character sheet back. Calculate the age to the campaign date. Check these carefully.

Check the list of fiefs which will be gained upon knighthood.

Traits, Directed Traits, and Passions

Players choose whether they wish to keep the same Traits, Directed Traits, and/or Passions for which their father was famous. If they want to keep them they can get them at the same value as their father had, although the gamemaster must approve of any value of 20 or more.

Years 519-525 Event Table

d20	event
01-05	Died: go to Miscellaneous Cause Table.
06-10	Served Garrison Duty. Add 10 Glory
11-20	Went Adventuring.

During this period your father went on one of the new-fangled adventures that had become popular recently, to see what knight errantry was like. Roll on the next table for results. Though he may have survived, he did not resolve any of these challenging adventures, which can still be found for your character to complete in the "Short Adventures" section of the "Scenarios" Chapter.

Father's Adventure Results Table (75)

d20	result
01-03	The Redcap
04-06	The Adventurous Shield
07-09	The Tomb of Lions
10-12	The Basilisk
13-15	The Perilous Cemetery
16-18	The Raven Tower
19-20	Roll twice more, treating a second roll of 19-20 as indicating that your father died on the adventure. Make a note of the adventure, and remember that your father died trying to complete it. If you managed to roll 19-20 three times, your father died in the adventure of the Perilous Cemetery.

YEAR 526

During the High King's Pentecostal feast a Roman embassy entered the hall and demanded tribute from Britain. King Arthur refused, and after conferring with his vassals, summoned his army to fight. The army shipped to France, where it met the Roman army in battle. After a victory over natural and magical opponents, the army marched on and took Rome.

Year 526 Events Table

d20	event
01-20	Your father fought at the Battle of Flanders in France in which the main elements of the Roman army were defeated. Giants were encountered by some of Arthur's troops during this remarkable battle.

BATTLE OF FLANDERS (150)

d20	event
01	He died with Great Glory (add 1000 Glory).
02-03	Died in battle. End history.
04-18	Survived, continue to Battle in Italy.
19-20	Fought against giants. Roll again, -7 on d20 roll for results of the battle (i.e. a 19 becomes a 12). A result of 0 or a negative number = a roll of 1. It is likely that your father died fighting the giants, in which case you inherit the passion below.

Passion *only* if your father fought against giants, no roll necessary.

Value = 3d6 Fear (Giants). ("I don't care what anyone thinks, they are more than any man can handle.")

If he survived the earlier fighting in France, your father continued the invasion with King Arthur. Your father fought during the invasion of Italy, and helped to conquer the Roman Empire, which had hired mercenaries after the defeat of its main army in Flanders.

Equipment

Eldest sons inherit everything which their father owned. Check the list of items which was taken from his body.

Statistics

Statistics are done as usual, with 60 points distributed. If you wish, these may be identical to the original statistics of the father.

Skills

Skills and combat skills are done the usual way.

Coat of Arms

The coat of arms is that of the father, with the heraldic mark (the "difference") for the son if the father yet lives. This may not be changed, although a son can choose an entirely new device for his Shield of Peace if he wishes.

Glory

Initial Glory is 1/10th of the father's Glory when the knight is made, or when the father died. The character will also get 1000 points for being knighted, and perhaps some more if other inheritances are involved.

Equipment

Equipment may be whatever the father provides.

Luck

There will be no luck benefits except those provided by the father and other family members to the young man.

Back of Sheet

Data on the character sheet back should be derived from the father and the family. For example, the family characteristic is the same as the father's.

Other

Family data as provided by this chapter is obviously replaced by the history of the father as gained in play.

Year 526: Events In Italy Table

BATTLE IN ITALY (150)

d20	*event*
01	Died in Battle. End history.
02-20	Survived, continue to a Visit to Rome.

d20 Directed Trait Roll, 01-15 = Success

Value = 1d6+5 Mistrust Mercenaries (add to Suspicious). ("They were dangerous to everyone except us, their enemy.")

After the battle Rome surrendered, and the Pope appealed to Arthur to spare the sacred city, which was granted. The triumphant army entered the city in procession, and was given great treasures as gifts. Like most of the soldiers, your father took the opportunity to tour Rome.

Year 526: Events in Rome Table

d20 Directed Trait Roll, 01-10 = Success

Value = 1d6+5 Mistrust Romans (add to Suspicious). ("I was impressed by the ancient magnificence, the decay, and the dishonest and corrupt people of the city.")

YEARS 527-529

A period of relative peace followed, during which more of the outlying kingdoms and hidden robber barons were defeated by the knights of the Round Table.

Years 527-529 Events Table

d20	*events*
01-15	Go to Miscellaneous Cause Table.
16-10	Served Garrison Duty.

YEAR 530

Britain's western coast had long been subject to raids from the Irish, and last year the Pendragon set sail with a great army to punish the Irish once and for all. Arthur was victorious, but after the campaign, a magical quest was taken that few knights survived.

Year 530 Events Table

d20	*events*
01-05	Go to Miscellaneous Cause Table.
06-20	Your father was among the expeditionary army to invade Ireland. He fought at the Battle of Tara against the Irish.

BATTLE OF TARA (100)

d20	*event*
01	He died with Great Glory (add 1000 Glory). End history.
02	Died in battle. End history.
03-20	Survived unwounded, go to Battle of Castle of Bones.

d20 Directed Trait Roll, 01-07 = Success

Value = 3d6 Contempt for the Irish (add to Proud).

FURTHER 530 EVENTS

While in Ireland, your father was among those chosen to accompany King Arthur in his midnight ride to attack the Castle of Bones, reportedly to recover marvelous artifacts. Everyone now believes this was an attack against the faerie forces of the Other World. Only seven men survived this, and your father was not among them.

BATTLE OF THE CASTLE OF BONES (100)

d20	*event*
01-20	He died with Great Glory (add 1000 Glory). End history.

d20 Passion Roll, 01-02 = Success

Value = 2d6+3 Fear (Faerie Things) gained by your character. ("I have come to you, Son, from beyond the wall of Death to warn you of the horrors awaiting you if you fall to their black spears...")

Glory and Ambitions

A knight's primary goal is to gain Glory through the pursuit of adventure, love, and power.

THE OBJECT OF THE GAME for players in *Pendragon* is to experience the magical world of King Arthur through the actions of their character knights. The object of the game for *characters* is to get Glory. Players control the actions of their characters, who receive Glory for notable actions and behavior, and for attaining ambitions.

The pursuit of Glory and knightly ambitions need not force your character into a chivalrous mold. You will find that success in *Pendragon* is based upon the ancient warrior virtues as well as the chivalrous ideals of King Arthur.

What is Glory?

Glory is the chief mode of reward in the game. The gamemaster always awards Glory. Players are free to ask for Glory at anytime during the game, but the gamemaster is in charge of who gets Glory, when they get it, and how much they receive. This chapter contains guidelines for the gamemaster, not exact rules that must be followed slavishly.

The concept of Glory is new in the mainstream of roleplaying games. It has proven to be fairly intuitive in play, but, it is important to read the information below, especially if you intend to be the gamemaster.

What Does Glory Measure?

Glory measures a character's fame, success, confidence, importance, influence, and status. A person's Glory is expressed in minstrel's songs, court gossip, peasant chatter, the prayers of holy men, enemies' curses, traders' tales, and nobles' praises. People are aware of each others' Glory rating because they all participate in the same society and hear the same things about each other. Characters do not really know their exact number. But everyone is extremely conscious of their status relative to others. Thus the Glory number is a quantification of your character's position in comparison to others.

Glory does not measure the quality of a character's reputation. Reputation is the purpose of the traits and passions system. A glorious knight may walk about proudly, lording it over other knights, yet be despised for his cowardly or treacherous deeds. King Mark of Cornwall is an excellent example of such a character. It is important for players to understand that, since Glory measures status but not reputation, evil knights who are extremely successful will attain the same Glory as some chivalrous knights. Evil knights lose reputation, not Glory, for their vile deeds. See the "Ideals and Passions" chapter for more information on honor and reputation.

How Is Glory Gained?

Characters get Glory by many different means in *Pendragon*. Players may choose entirely different paths to Glory for their characters. This promotes roleplaying and ensures that characters will not all be the same, or competing for the same rewards.

Any dramatic event during the game offers a potential Glory award. But routine events rarely gain much Glory. Sometimes simple participation in a significant event is enough, but often successful action will be required for Glory to be received.

Glory once gained cannot be lost.

Almost any action that an ambitious knight performs can gain Glory. Examples of events that normally gain Glory include defeating an enemy in personal combat, getting married, being made a lord, successfully exhibiting a skill at court, spending a great deal of money, and finding the solution to an eerie magical riddle.

Glory can even be gained outside the game itself. Ownership of land and castles gains Glory every year. Notoriety and reputation also gain yearly Glory.

Because society is concerned with personal behavior as well as combat and adventure, high passions and faithful service to chivalrous, romantic, or religious ideals can gain much Glory. In *Pendragon,* behavior and reputation are quantified using various character attributes and codes of behavior. See the "Ideals and Passions" chapter for more information on these patterns.

Specific ways to get Glory are discussed in detail, under the heading "Areas of Glory Gain," below.

Who Can Gain Glory?

Any character, whether peasant or king, may gain Glory. For the same action, both characters will gain the same amount of Glory. However, knights and higher-ranking members of the noble class are very jealous of their prerogatives. Squires, sergeants, and other characters below the status of knight may frequently be denied the opportunity to gain Glory. This must be the case in order to keep the game authentic to its sources.

Most courtly situations in which Glory can be gained will be off-limits to characters of less than knightly status. For example, feasts and tournaments will be held for knights and their ladies only. Squires will be expected to serve, not dance with the ladies or show off their skills before the court.

On adventures, all sergeants (mercenary cavalry) or squires must be under the orders of a knight; either a player knight or a gamemaster knight. As the premier warriors, knights are expected to do most of the fighting, while their squires render assistance by fetching new lances and horses, providing first aid, and fighting off foot soldiers and other rabble. Squires and sergeants will be expected to fight when the combat is either unchivalrous or when the knights

ask for help. But in many cases only the knights will fight, and thus they will get all the Glory from such events. During combat, any sergeant or squire who rudely shoulders aside knights in order to grab Glory may be declared outlaw, or simply killed immediately. In non-combat situations, a presumptuous sergeant or squire will simply be removed from the room, or placed in a dungeon if he resists. Gamemasters must enforce these points consistently to maintain the authenticity of the game.

Ranges of Glory

Once your character begins to accumulate Glory, the question becomes "how much is a lot?" The nearby Glory Ranking Table answers this question, and defines the range of Glory for all player and gamemaster characters.

The high end is left open; awesome heroes such as Sir Lancelot are far superior in Glory to almost all other knights in Britain, with good reason. The rules of the game do not permit player characters to attain Glory similar to that of King Arthur or Sir Lancelot; there can be only one High King and one perfect knight in Britain.

Players should set themselves realistic goals, and not expect the gamemaster to let their characters become famous after only a few adventures. Only characters who have been played through scores of adventures can hope to attain the status of Extraordinary Knight. Even a very active and very successful knight errant should collect around 100-200 Glory per adventure, and perhaps another 100 at the end of the year for maintaining ideals and passions.

✤ GLORY RANKING TABLE ✤

Glory	*Class of Knight*
1 - 999	Non-Knight (squire, damsel)
1,000 - 1,999	Ordinary Knight
2,000 - 3,999	Notable Knight
4,000 - 7,999	Famous Knight
8,000 or more	Extraordinary Knight

Glory Awards

Exactly how much Glory should a character be awarded for performing significant actions and participation in great events? In the section below I offer guidelines, but not absolute rules. *Pendragon* is a social game, not a wargame, and Glory represents good opinions, not something palpable like gold. So to a great extent Glory is dependent on the reaction of the gamemaster and the other players to your roleplaying.

If you impress everyone with your character's actions, chances are that you will receive more Glory. If your character's actions and speeches during the game are dull, or if you rely on a powerful character to gain attention and success, you should expect to receive less than normal Glory.

Glory has nothing to do with experience. Cowardly or foolish characters may gain little Glory, but they will receive experience checks on occasion, and may certainly practice and train during the Winter Phase of the game. See the "Game Mechanics" chapter for more information on experience and training.

Group Glory Awards

Glory is often attained by a lone individual, but not always. Sometimes the player characters will cooperate to achieve some task or goal. The gamemaster divides his Glory award among several characters whenever it is unclear that one individual was solely responsible for a success. For example, if five characters cooperate to defeat a group of bandits, each of the five would receive some of the credit.

The gamemaster always determines the division of Glory. Usually Glory is divided equally among all the participants, with an extra portion awarded to any deserving individual for heroic behavior. But the gamemaster may choose to award most of the Glory to one of the participants, rather than giving anything extra, with the rest receiving very small awards. The gamemaster's decision is final.

If desired, a generous character may assign his portion of the Glory to someone else. Sir Lancelot does this occasionally. The gamemaster may choose to award a Generous check to the character for such an action (see the "Ideals and Passions" chapter for more information on trait checks).

How Much Glory Is Enough?

In this section I state the magnitude of Glory awards that should be given to characters. There are four basic categories: minimum, ordinary, heroic, and extraordinary. Situations will also occur in which important events take place, but zero Glory is gained. This will be because the action taken, though successful, was dishonorable.

The Basic Glory Awards table shows the four basic, non-zero categories, while the Sample Glory table shows many examples (many of which do not fit the four categories exactly).

The gamemaster must use the examples given in this chapter as guidelines for awarding Glory in the special situations that will arise.

Most successes in the game are not worth Glory, and those that are will usually gain a character only ordinary Glory: 10 points. But the high points in a character's career, like the ceremony of knighthood, will be accompanied by the maximum Glory award of 1000 points. An occasion from which more than 1000 points can be gained will be unique and

✤ BASIC GLORY AWARDS ✤

Glory Gained	Category
1	Minimum
10	Ordinary
100	Heroic
1000	Extraordinary

deadly (the Battle of Badon Hill, for instance).

Gamemasters will be tempted to award excessive Glory during moments of excitement and drama. Keep to the guidelines printed here: once a bad precedent is set, every player will expect that much Glory in subsequent games, and Glory inflation can ruin a campaign very quickly.

Zero Glory

Some activities gain no Glory. Any activity which diminishes Honor gets zero Glory.

Extra Glory

Sometimes the nature of a deed, or its circumstances, warrants a bonus to the Glory given. Gamemasters and players both should be alert for unusual situations, desperate successes, exciting solutions, and dramatic incidents which might warrant a bonus.

Some reasons to award extra Glory might include:

- Success against bad odds (worse then 3:1): add 100 per knight.
- Extraordinary witness to the event: add 25 for a greater noble (earl, duke), 50 for a king or Round Table knight, 100 for your lord, 150 for the Pendragon or High Queen.
- Helped a famous hero (for instance, a Round Table knight), add 100 Glory.
- Extraordinary flourish and show, add 10.
- Made the gamemaster laugh with pleasure, add 10.

Occasionally an act will gain zero Glory, but side effects of the action will gain great Glory. For example, when Sir Balin decapitated the Lady of the Lake in King Arthur's Court he got no Glory for the killing, for he had committed a dishonorable act of treason by so offending the king's hospitality. However, he did get Glory for achieving such a dramatic and violent success with his Sword skill (instantly killing his foe), for a critical success roll on his Love (family) passion, and for another critical success on his Hate (Lady of the Lake) roll.

Minimum Glory

The minimum Glory that a character can gain from a significant event is 1 point. Killing a huge snake might be worth 1 Glory point if circumstances were appropriate. In most cases, if an event is worth Glory at all, the character should gain more than 1 point.

If the gamemaster is dividing Glory among a group, and each individual would receive less than 1 point by a strict division of the Glory, then each individual gains 1.

Ordinary Glory

The ordinary, common amount of Glory that the gamemaster should award for an action or event is 10 points. Most normal actions during the game that are worth praise should receive 10 Glory. These might include victory over a bandit, a successful speech, or an act of courage.

Use 10 points as the default Glory award. The gamemaster should hand out 10 Glory whenever he is in doubt over how much to award, or whenever an argument over Glory seems likely.

Gamemasters may reward players who are excellent roleplayers with 10 Glory (per action) as a reward for their fine play-acting and authentic decisions.

Heroic Glory

100 points of Glory is the proper award for most heroic acts or important events. A heroic event is an order of magnitude more significant than an ordinary event. Some heroic events and actions are worth as much as 250 or more points (see the nearby Sample Glory table for several examples). But even 100 points is a lot for a single action or event, and 100 should be the highest amount awarded in most cases where no sample is given.

Extraordinary Glory

An action or event can be truly extraordinary; a once-in-a-lifetime opportunity. 100 Glory is clearly not enough for such a situation. Extraordinary actions or events gain 1000 points, an order of magnitude over heroic actions.

Adventures yielding opportunities for extraordinary Glory are extremely rare. Only something incredible, an awesomely heroic and successful action, or a unique magical or sacred ritual, qualifies as extraordinary. Perhaps one adventure in twenty might offer this opportunity. Such opportunities must involve great risk or demand great roleplaying from characters. For example, defeating an extraordinary monster like a huge fire-breathing wyrm (with attributes tougher than those in this book) might gain 1000 points, should the gamemaster feel it appropriate. But such creatures should be rare indeed, and should easily kill most knights foolish enough to go against one single-handed.

Adventures involving tasks crucial to the realm, such as rescuing Queen Guenever, might yield extraordinary Glory if completed successfully. However, only Extraordinary knights (those of 8,000 or more Glory) who are known to King Arthur personally will even be *considered* for participation in such important events — these sort of adventures are the domain of the Round Table. Until they attain great fame and excellent reputation, player knights will have to accustom themselves to tasks of lesser significance.

The fact that it usually takes a group of knights to achieve such great things (unless the knight is Sir Lancelot) means that few knights will gain a full 1000

Glory for successfully completing any adventure.

Only a few extraordinary non-adventuring acts gain extraordinary Glory, and each of them can occur only once in a knight's life. They include: being knighted; dying heroically in battle; being made a king; joining the Round Table; and participating in the High Mass of the Holy Grail.

One single act might be repeated to gain extraordinary Glory: marriage.

Comparing Glory

Sir Tristram is traveling incognito and staying at a friendly castle. He and his host discuss who are the best (i.e. Glorious) knights of the realm. Tristram defends his opinions vigorously except when one knight is concerned.

NOW TURN WE unto Sir Tristram, that asked the knight his host if he saw late any knights adventurous.

"Sir," he said, "the last night here lodged with me Ector de Maris and a damosel with him, and that damosel told me that he was one of the best knights of the world."

"That is not so," said Sir Tristram, "for I know four better knights of his own blood, and the first is Sir Lancelot du Lak, call him the best knight, and Sir Bors de Ganis, Sir Bleoberis, Sir Blamore de Ganis, and Sir Gaheris."

"Nay," said his host, "Sir Gawaine is a better knight than he."

"That is not so," said Tristram, "for I have met with them both, and I felt Sir Gaheris for the better knight, and Sir Lamorak, I call him as good as any of them except Sir Lancelot."

"Why name ye not Sir Tristram?" said his host, "for I account him as good as any of them."

"I know not Sir Tristram," said Tristram.

— Malory IX, 43

Note on personality traits (see the "Ideals and Passions" chapter): for this behavior, Sir Tristram would receive a Modest check for his self-effacing modesty, despite the fact that Tristram is hiding his identity.

Areas of Glory Gain

The following section lists the primary areas of the game from which Glory may be gained. The Sample Glory table shows specific Glory awards in these categories. The gamemaster should be wary of adding other things to the list, especially if they do not fit into one of the following categories: not everything a character does is worth Glory.

Glory from Individual Combat

Knights are warriors first and foremost, and their fame is most greatly increased by combat. Combat may be against bandits, monsters, soldiers, or occasionally, other worthy knights. The basic rationale for combat Glory is simple: the more fearsome or important the foe, the greater the Glory.

If the loser had an unusual advantage in the combat, such as a large damage value, or a magic shield, or inspiration from a passion, then more Glory for the winner is appropriate, since the risk was greater. Creatures follow the same rationale as human opponents: a creature with an unusual power or attribute yields the victor extra Glory.

If the enemy defeated has Glory, or is significant in some way beyond its simple combat ability, then Glory should be increased. Thus an old but famous knight would be worth somewhat more Glory to defeat than a bandit with the same skills and equipment.

Sample enemies, both humans and creatures of all kinds, and the Glory gained for defeating them, are listed in the "Characters and Creatures" chapter. The gamemaster must determine the amount of extra Glory if the creature has different attributes or capabilities from those given in the "Character and Creatures" chapter.

Situations of extreme danger or importance, or those combats that take place in a famous noble's court or tournament field, may gain more Glory, with the extra amount determined by the gamemaster.

Mortal combat with another knight is the supreme challenge, and great Glory may thereby accrue. However, combat between knights in *Pendragon* is often initiated "for love" (of fighting). Such combat is normally performed with one or more customary restrictions that reduce the chance of maiming or fatal injury. Combat is resolved by some minor event, such as knockdown, rather than by the surrender or death of the loser. Glory for such safe, formalized combat is calculated normally, but the victor receives only 1/10th the normal award.

Example of Combat Glory: *Young Sir Ambrut, a household knight introduced at the end of the "Character Generation" chapter, jousts "for love" with a knight met at a river ford.*

Ambrut is a new knight on his first year's adventuring, and his father was only an Ordinary knight, so he has only 1100 Glory.

The joust ends with Ambrut losing, so the other knight gains the usual amount of Glory for defeating an Ordinary knight, 50 points (derived from the Sample Glory table nearby). Because the joust was "for love" the knight receives only 1/10th of 50, 5 Glory.

Marriage Glory

Marriage gains both participants Glory, and usually gets the woman more than the man.

Each partner acquires Glory equal to their partner's Glory, up to a maximum of 1,000. Thereafter each continues to collect Glory individually, not mutually.

Death of a partner allows remarriage, and the subsequent Glory gains for the marriage are as for previous marriages.

Glory From Non-Combat Actions

Although combat is the premier area of Glory gain, the gamemaster should award Glory for *any* chivalrous, dra-

✻ SAMPLE GLORY TABLE ✻

USE THESE GUIDELINES as the starting point for Glory awarded.

In a few cases there is a limit on the maximum Glory to be obtained from a source.

Defeating Enemies

Consider "defeat" to mean that the enemy surrendered, or was captured, incapacitated, or killed. If the enemy's plans were defeated but he escaped, no Glory is gained for the defeat (but see "Successful Tasks" later in this table).

If several knights cooperate to defeat an enemy, the Glory given below is divided among them.

Knights

If the combat was "for love" (to knockdown, first blood) then the number should be reduced to a tenth of the number given.

Ordinary Knight (1000-1999 Glory) = 50
Notable Knight (2000-3999 Glory) = 100
Famous Knight (4000-7999 Glory) = 250
Extraordinary Knight (8000+ Glory) = 500

Other Human Foes

unruly peasant = 1
thief = 5
ordinary bandit = 10
notable bandit = 25
armored and mounted non-knight = 35
Saxon raider = 35
Pict raider = 20

Animals, Monsters, and Magical Beings

vicious rat = 0
huge snake = 1
large wolf = 5
bear = 10
huge white bear = 100
witch = 25
ogre = 25
small giant = 100
unicorn = 100
lion = 250
griffin = 250
giant = 250
fire-breathing wyrm = 400
huge giant = 500
basilisk = 500

Skill Success

Any successful use of a skill in an important or critical situation may warrant a Glory award for the action.
10 points is the ordinary award.
20 is appropriate for a critical success.
20 is awarded for performing before royalty, 40 for a critical success.

One-time Honors, Titles, and Ceremonies

Glory is gained for receiving the honors which are significant to a knight and his society. This one-time Glory is received at the end of the year.

If a character regains a title a second time after losing it for some reason, no Glory is gained. See the "Ambitions" section of the chapter for more information on titles and their ramifications.

A heroic death, the last great honor a knight can achieve, is listed here.

Knighted = 1000
Vassal Knight = 50
Banneret Knight = 100
Earl = 350
Duke = 750
King = 1000
Officer to an Earl = 35
Officer to a Duke = 75
Officer to a King = 100
Officer to the Pendragon = 250
Companion of Arthur = 100
Joined Round Table = 1000

matic, or prestigious actions of note during the game, such as an act of great generosity or courage, or a remarkable performance with a harp or lute during a feast. Usually the action must entail a successful die roll, but not always.

If the gamemaster feels it is appropriate, a character who succeeds in a statistic, skill, personality trait, or passion roll during courtly or other public circumstances may gain Glory equal to the adjusted number rolled (1-20). Remember that any critical success is considered to be a roll of 20. See the "Game Mechanics" chapter for information on die rolls and successes.

A non-combat action of great significance to an adventure may gain Glory equal to double or more the success rolled, at the gamemaster's option. In the court of King Arthur, a success can gain five times the number rolled in Glory. Five is the maximum multiplier, and should rarely be used except in extremely dramatic or complicated situations. Simply awarding 100 points for a heroic action will do as well or better.

Glory may be gained from chivalrous actions even without a roll. For example, a player may simply state that his character will perform a remarkably generous act. As long as this is consistent with the character's normal behavior and reputation, no roll is really needed. Of course, in such cases the gamemaster has no starting number of points to award. Usually he should award 10 points of Glory, the normal amount, or if the action was heroic, 100 points.

Example of Non-Combat Action Glory: *Sir Ambrut goes on a hazardous magical adventure later in his first year, in which someone must suffer being bitten by a panther before the group can pass through the gate that the sinister beast guards.*

Every knight on the adventure attempts to make a Valorous roll, but either the players are unlucky, or their characters are daunted by the panther's cruel appearance, and only Sir Ambrut succeeds. He steps forward, presenting his naked arm to the slavering jaws, and receives 100 Glory for his heroic and selfless action.

Glory From Participation in Important Events

Great events such as tournaments, battles, and religious or feudal ceremonies are at the heart of the game. Simply participating in such exciting events gains characters a Glory award, of a magnitude based on the importance of the event.

Receiving a high rank or honor such as the Round Table is classified as participation Glory because the event does not require any successful die rolls or actions other than acceptance (note that qualification to *receive* such honors may require many successful actions, however).

Example of Participation Glory: *Sir Ambrut and his lord Sir Yvane (knights introduced at the end of the "Character Generation" chapter) enter a chapel, where Ambrut is magically healed of a terrible wound (inflicted by a panther) by a priest garbed all in white.*

Celebrated High Mass of the Holy Grail = 1000
Heroic Death = 1000

Getting Married

When officially wed, the husband and wife each collect Glory equal to the Glory of their spouse, up to a maximum of 1000 points. If a spouse has in excess of 1000, the extra points are not gained.

If a spouse dies and a character remarries, he or she collects the new Glory for the new spouse normally.

Subsequent Glory gains during the campaign (from defeating enemies, etc.) are personal to the husband and wife, not shared, unlike the mutual Glory collection upon marriage.

Conspicuous Consumption

Generally, each 1 £. spent gets 1 Glory. However, money spent over 100 £. gains only 1 Glory per 10 £. spent. So a gift of 120 £. would gain the giver 102 Glory.

Sponsoring a Tournament

This Glory is per tournament, and is received at the end of year in which the tournament took place.
Neighborhood = 50
Local = 100
Regional = 200
Regal = 300

Quality of Maintenance

This Glory is received annually. It equals the amount of extra money spent on the knight's maintenance. See the "Ambitions" section for more information. Numbers shown are typical, not fixed.
Ordinary = none
Rich = 10/year
Superlative = 15/year

Holding Land

This Glory is received annually. See the "Ambitions" section of the chapter for more information. Annual Glory = the year's income in £., up to a maximum Glory of 100 for one year. Even King Arthur receives only 100 Glory per year for his vast holdings of land because of this important maximum.
A Manor, typical of a vassal knight = 6/year
Several Manors, typical of a banneret knight = 30/year
Many Manors, typical of an earl or duke = 100/year

Holding Castles

Annually, up to 100 maximum per year, as with land.
Motte and bailey = 8/year
Small castle = 26/year
Medium castle = 36/year
Large castle = 51/year
Very strong castle = 66/year
Tintagel Castle = 55/year
Camelot, Pembroke Castle, Beaumaris Castle (the ultimate castles) = 100/year

All Traits and Passions

Any trait or passion of 16+ gains Glory equal to the value each winter.

Ideals

Meeting the requirements for a Chivalrous or Religious Knight gains the character 100 Glory each winter, in addition to points gained from the required traits.

Romantic knights gain 50 Glory for their first successful year of romance, and the annual number increases by 50 for each subsequent successful year.

Battle Participation

Awards for battle depend on how well the character and the army fought. Glory is gained on a per-round basis, and is derived from the size of the battle, with adjustments for various factors. See the "Chivalric Duties" chapter for more information on battles.

Both knights gain 10 Glory simply for being involved in a miraculous event.

Passive Glory

Glory can be gained without any action during the game taking place. The Glory award is collected during the Winter Phase of the game. See the "Game Mechanics" chapter for more information on the Winter Phase.

Inherited Glory: Every son receives Glory equal to 1/10 of his father's Glory, determined either when the character is knighted or when the father dies, whichever comes first. In the case of player characters created using this book, knighthood will be one of the first events they experience during play, so each character receives 1/10th their father's Glory immediately after the ceremony.

Note that if a character is created using the optional data generated in the "Your Family" chapter, then the character's father is already dead (and thus 1/10th his Glory has been received even before knighthood).

Glory from Reputation and Ownership: Characters can earn passive Glory by maintaining a reputation or holding possessions during the game. Reputation includes any traits or passions of 16 or more, maintaining a wealthy lifestyle, exhibiting patterns of behavior such as chivalrous, romantic, and so on.

Just being rich or powerful can gain Glory. Ownership of lands or castles gains a Glory award during the Winter Phase. If a character loses ownership he gets no Glory for it that winter.

Example of Passive Glory: *Sir Eoric the Golden is famed for his lack of caution. In game terms this translates into a value of 16 in Eoric's Reckless trait. He will gain 16 Glory for his notorious recklessness every year during the winter, as long as he maintains the trait. Eoric is also wealthy, holding 3 manors, for which he gains 18 Glory, also collected each winter.*

Rewards of Glory

A character of 1000 or more Glory has attained heroic stature, and gains special benefits and advantages thereby. The obvious benefit is enhanced status, which can aid the character in many ways. The second, more exciting advantage is the enhancement to personal confidence that great Glory fosters. In game terms this gain in confidence is simulated by magical increases in the character's attributes.

The rewards of Glory accrue at the end of the year, after any adventures are over or on hold, and after all Glory gained during the year has been calculated, in the latter part of the Winter

Glory per Battle Round
Small Battle = 15
Medium Battle = 30
Large Battle = 45

Result Multipliers: How well your character did with his weapon skill roll during the round makes a big difference. And being on the field, but disengaged, is worth far less in Glory.
Critical Success = x2
Success = x1
Failure = x.5
Fumble = x.01
Disengaged = x0.1

Victory Multipliers: Participation in a victory is far more glorious than surviving a humiliating defeat.
Clear Victory = x2
Indecisive = x1
Clear Loss = x0.5

Odds Multipliers: If the odds in battle were against your side, more Glory is gained.
Outnumbered more than 2:1 = x1.5
Outnumbered more than 5:1 = x2

Tournaments

Glory in tournaments may be gained two ways. First, through combat, with the usual "for love" rules (a tenth of normal Glory). Secondly, by winning in either of the two main events, the Joust or the Melee, which gives the Glory below. See the "Chivalric Duties" chapter for more information on tournaments.

Neighborhood Tournament (about 100 knights participating, in total)
50 Glory to the Melee Champion, to the Winner of the Joust, and to the Sponsor (as noted above under "Sponsoring a Tournament"); about 5 Glory for average participants.

Local Tournament (500-1000 knights participating)
These are the most common tournaments.
100 to the Melee Champion, the Winner of the Joust, and the Sponsor; and about 10 for average participants.

Regional Tournament (1000-2500 participants)
200 to the Melee Champion, Winner of the Joust, and the Sponsor; and 20 for average participants.

Regal Tournament (2500-5000 participants)
300 to the Melee Champion, the Winner of the Joust, and Sponsor; and 30 for average participants.

Successful Tasks

This Glory is gained when a task is successfully completed. A scenario or adventure may require several tasks to be completed as part of the process.

Award task Glory whenever a task is important to a scenario, and offers some challenge. Rolls are not mandatory, and no enemies need be killed. The Glory awarded may supplement incidental Glory gained for defeating enemies, participation in important events, etc. If a knight is specifically ordered by his lord to slay a famous ogre, he gains both defeating enemy Glory and task Glory.

Assuming cooperation and similar contributions, each participant receives an equal share of the Glory. The gamemaster should reduce or eliminate the share of any character who held the others back or was uninvolved.

Trivial Task (save a maid from a wolf) = 1
Ordinary Task (carry a message through unknown territory) = 10
Heroic Task (free prisoners from a tribe of giants, or carry a message safely into a very dangerous place) = 100
Very Heroic Task (lead a tiny army to repel a huge group of Irish invaders) = 250
Extraordinary Task (rescue Queen Guenever from death) = 1000

Phase (see the "Game Mechanics" chapter).

Bonus Points from Glory

Characters that gain 1,000 or more Glory derive heroic benefit from their status. Each 1,000 Glory points gained allows the character to freely add one point to any one trait, passion, statistic, or skill. These extra points are called *Bonus Points*, and are added during the Winter Phase of the game.

Bonus points allow characters to bend or break certain game rules, and can confer heroic attributes on characters with already high abilities. This bending of the rules occurs in two ways. First, statistics can be increased using bonus points, even when at the cultural maximum, and even after age 35! Second, bonus points allow any attribute (statistics, traits, passions, skills) to increase freely, without the character having to allocate training points or make a successful experience check roll (see the "Winter Phase" section of the "Game Mechanics" chapter).

Thus you will occasionally hear of extraordinary knights with attribute values of 25 or even greater.

Once bonus points are added, they are not kept track of. They cannot be taken away directly, but their results can be lost. For example, a statistic to which a bonus point was once added could still decrease due to aging, all the way down to 0.

Using Bonus Points

Although Glory may be recorded immediately during a scenario, the effects do not accrue until winter. Any resultant bonus points are gained and *must* be used during the Winter Phase. Glory takes effect on a year-by-year basis. Thus a bonus point cannot be saved over to next year's Winter Phase, but must be spent during the winter immediately following the adventure that it was gained.

Players are advised to spend development points on one skill or attribute that is earmarked for a heroic value. Once the skill or attribute is brought up to its normal maximum, a bonus point from Glory will increase it to the heroic level.

Example of Bonus Point Use: *Sir Ambrut has been developing his Constitution every year while a squire. It reaches a value of 21 on the year he is knighted. 21 is the maximum normally possible for Ambrut's culture. Next winter, Ambrut gains a bonus point from his Glory, which has increased to 1210 points from adventures described in examples above. Ambrut uses the bonus point to increase the value of his CON to a heroic 22.*

Game System Consequences of Heroic Attributes

Characters with significant Glory are likely to have values over 20 in one or more attributes. As noted in the "Game Mechanics" chapter, whenever any skill,

A joust before King Arthur and Guenever

passion, trait, or statistic has a value greater than 20, the die rolls for that attribute are increased, making critical or opposed successes more likely.

Status From Glory

The following rules give the basic ways in which increased status and prestige from Glory translates into game terms. However, both players and gamemaster should be alert for other ways to bring Glory into the story. Glory should be a source of pride, and can be an excellent basis for roleplaying.

Increased Recognition

Glorious individuals are well-known in the lands of Britain. Each 1,000 Glory adds 1 point to a knight's chance of being identified using Recognize or Heraldry skills (see the "Game Mechanics" chapter for more information on skills).

Example of Increased Recognition from Glory: *Baron Yvane is taking part in a tournament, at which evil Lady Sangive le Noir, wife of an enemy, has secretly arrived. Sangive has a respectable Recognize skill of 15. Yvane has 4,500 Glory, so Sangive gains a +5 modifier, and is guaranteed to recognize her husband's enemy if she spots him in the crowd or at tourney.*

Character Precedence

When characters are in a social or chivalrous situation, the character with the highest Glory takes precedence over others of equal title (a king is unlikely to defer to an ordinary knight, no matter what the knight's Glory).

Example of Precedence: *Four knights are preparing to enter a mysterious ruined castle. By the laws of courtesy and chivalry, the knight of highest Glory is accorded the right to enter first. If there is only one enemy to defeat inside the castle, he will get the chance to fight it first, and gain all the Glory thereby.*

Skill Modifiers

Glory indicates status and importance, not just notoriety. In formal situations where characters interact, such as the courts of nobles, this status may enhance the character's capabilities to influence or impress others. Normally the character must have a respectable reputation to do so. Evil knights with no honor, even if very powerful and influential, won't usually be invited to court.

Only non-combat skills such as Flirting, Singing, or Oratory can be enhanced by Glory. The rationale is that characters of great Glory are much more likely to receive attention and praise, and less likely to be judged harshly if their performance is mediocre.

If the gamemaster approves, the character gains a modifier of up to +1 per 1,000 points of Glory, added to the skill being used (see the "Game Mechanics" chapter for information on modifiers). Thus a character of 8,200 Glory could gain a maximum modifier of +8 to a courtly skill from his prestige. Players may always request a Glory bonus to skills when in court, but the gamemaster is always the arbiter of how much, or how little, a bonus the character actually gains. The gamemaster may choose to permit *no* modifier, or he may permit only a portion of the total possible modifier.

Class Distinction, Arthurian Style

Sir Tristram and Sir Palomides find the corpse of a nobleman, the king of the Red City, floating down a stream. In his hand is a letter explaining the conditions of his murder. Rather than trusting his kinsmen the dead king trusted two commoners who he raised to be knights. They feloniously murdered him. The dead man's letter admits the error of his democratic point of view with these bitter words:

"Give a churl rule and thereby he will not be sufficed; for whatsomever he be that is ruled by a villain born, and the lord of the soil to be a gentleman born, that same villain shall destroy all the gentlemen about him: therefore all estates and lords, beware whom ye take about you. And if ye be a knight of King Arthur's court remember this tale, for this is the end and conclusion."

— Malory X, 61

Example of Skill Modifiers from Glory: *Sir Yvane (Glory 4500) wishes to impress a lady with his charm and wit. Yvane will use his Flirting skill, and his player requests a positive modifier to take into account his character's impressive Glory. The gamemaster agrees, but feels that the lady is not particularly influenced by Yvane's Glory (she is far more concerned with his appearance and his money). The gamemaster decides that Sir Yvane will gain only a +1 modifier to Flirting in this situation, even though his Glory would permit a far greater modifier of +5 (rounding .5 up as always).*

Keeping Track of Glory

A character's Glory may increase many times during his career. The player should keep careful track of each major award. Part of the fun in the game is looking back with pride on the adventures, tournaments, and battles your character was involved in.

Glory is gained as soon as it is written down on the character sheet, under the heading of "Glory This Game." Do this whenever the gamemaster gives you Glory points.

At the end of the session or adventure the back of the character sheet is used. Usually a year of game time will have passed, or more. You will see a large space labeled "History" in which you should record all significant events in the adventure that gained Glory, with the year clearly noted in the space provided.

What constitutes a major event? Each adventure qualifies, even if little Glory was gained, and certain events within an adventure, such as a battle or tournament, should also be recorded separately. Special ceremonies, such as marriage, or the gaining of Round Table status, should definitely be recorded separately. These events are also provided with a space for the date achieved.

Example — Recording Glory: *In game year 532, his second year in play, Sir Ambrut participates in an adventure in which he and his comrades successfully vanquish a powerful group of faerie knights in a castle. The gamemaster's title for the adventure is "The Dark Tower." During the adventure Sir Ambrut also slays a lion in an incident unconnected with the main story.*

At the end of the adventure, during which Ambrut earned 45 miscellaneous points, the gamemaster announces that all participants gain 100 adventure Glory for their clever and successful solution to the adventure, which he feels was heroic in overall significance and drama (see the Sample Glory table). The gamemaster also awards Ambrut 250 Glory for singlehandedly defeating the lion (a remarkable feat). Sir Ambrut's player adds two entries on the back of the character sheet:

Year	*Important Event*	*New*	*Total*
532	"The Dark Tower"	45+100	1355
532	Slew a lion singlehanded	250	1605

In later years, Sir Ambrut will be able to look back with pleasure at this record of his success and courage. When someone asks, "What deeds of fame have you performed?" Ambrut's player can check the back of the character sheet and answer accurately.

Ambitions

YOUR CHARACTER will gains experience and Glory during the game, and you may aspire to achieve some of the higher ambitions of knighthood. These include rank and wealth as well as chivalrous virtue and other ideals of behavior.

This game gives several roles which may be fulfilled. Knights may attempt to fulfill several of these at once in their never-ending quest for Glory. Some are, of course, incompatible. I encourage the player to focus on those ambitions that are most interesting and ignore the others; knights are not identical to one another.

If the reader has created a character using this book, the character has already achieved one of the great ambitions of the gentry; becoming a landowner, a vassal knight. Being a vassal knight makes your character one of an elite group that makes up less than 5% of Britain's population.

As the campaign progresses, your new character may attain even more.

Differences Between Knights

Knighthood is the unifying factor among members of the noble class in the Middle Ages. Knighthood sets a man apart from the common folk and defines the aristocracy of society. All knights, despite any differences between them, have more in common with each other than they have with the peasant class. The richest knights hobnob with the poorest and acknowledge each other as brothers of the military class.

Differences between knights do exist. Primarily this is measured by Glory, but behavior, rank, and wealth also can have a strong effect. Who would say that a humble household knight is equal in importance to Sir Gawaine, the preeminent baron of the land with hundreds of

knights at his beck and call? As brothers in arms they may stand together on the battlefield, or cross lances in a tournament, but if they both reached a doorway together, is there argument about who has the right to choose whether he goes first or second? (Gawaine, of course, as a man known for his chivalrous behavior, would probably go second, and receive a Modest check).

Non-Glory differences between *Pendragon* knights are measured by several factors. First, the quality of a knight is determined by the amount of money spent in his yearly maintenance. Secondly, a knight may be titled and gain the honor and Glory of his rank, as explained later. Finally, a knight may live in accordance with a chivalrous or religious idea.

Qualities of Knights

In *Pendragon* the economic difference between knights is quantified by the annual income allotted to them each Winter Phase. Five categories of knights exist: impoverished, poor, ordinary, rich, and superlative. The game effects of the categories are listed in the "Game Mechanics" chapter, except for Glory, which is listed here.

Impoverished Knights

Knights with an income of less than 3 £. per year are described as impoverished. Theirs is a miserable lot. He appears ragged, his armor dented and rusty, and is lean and sickly. He has no squire and usually lacks a horse of any kind. As a result, an impoverished knight counts only as a sergeant in battle, even though he may be far more skilled or valorous.

Legally, impoverishment means trouble. A impoverished bachelor knight, who normally lives at the hall of his lord, is not required to remain loyal to his lord since the feudal oath promises him sustenance. He may leave, or may be sent away on a quest by the helpless lord.

On the reverse, if a vassal knight neglects his land to the point of impoverishment, the lord has the right to cancel their agreement and take the land back. The knight has clearly failed to maintain the land and uphold his end of the feudal bargain.

Glory: no Glory is gained for suffering the life of an impoverished knight.

Poor Knights

Poor knights receive too little economic support to maintain themselves in the manner in which they ought. A knight who receives between 3-5 £. per year is considered poor. A nearby essay expounds at length upon this state of relative poverty. In general a poor knight has no squire; rides a mangy, sway-backed horse; is hungry, lean and ragged; and wears dented armor.

Glory: no effect. There is no shame, but no special fame, in being a poor knight.

Ordinary Knights

Regular, or ordinary knights are the knights most often discussed in *Pendragon*, and details about what they receive each year are given in the "Wealth" chapter. Whenever the word knight is used, unmodified by adjective, it refers to this type of person. Ordinary knights comprise the majority of chivalry. Player character knights always begin the game as ordinary knights in terms of economic quality.

An ordinary knight receives 6 £. per year in money and food which keeps himself, his family, a single squire, and his horses in a healthy and robust manner of living, and keeps his equipment in good repair.

Glory: no effect.

Sir Balin Defends Poor Knights

A MYSTERIOUS WOMAN has come to Arthur's court with a challenge: she seeks an excellent knight who has the virtue and courage to draw forth the sword from the scabbard which is strapped about her waist. All the knights of Arthur's court try, and fail, and with discouraging words the maiden prepares to depart when she is confronted by Sir Balin, a knight of notable Glory but poor.

"DAMOSEL, I PRAY you of your courtesy, suffer me as well to assay as these lords; though that I be so poorly clothed, in my heart meseemeth I am fully assured as some of these other, and meseemeth in my heart to speed right well."

The damosel beheld the poor knight, and saw he was a likely man, but for his poor arrayment she thought he should be of no worship without villainy or treachery. And then she said unto the knight, "Sir, it needeth not to put me to more pain or labour, for it seemeth not you to speed thereas other have failed."

"Ah! fair damosel," said Balin, "worthiness, and good tatches [qualities], and good deeds, are not only in arrayment, but manhood and worship is hid within man's person, and many a worshipful knight is not known unto all people, and therefore worship and hardiness in not in arrayment."

"By God," said the damosel, "ye say sooth [truth]; therefore ye shall assay to do what ye may."

Then Balin took the sword by the girdle and sheath, and drew it out easily; and when he looked on the sword it pleased him much. Then had the king and all the barons great marvel that Balin had done that adventure; many knight had great despite at Balin.

— Malory, II, 2

Thus did Sir Balin prove that clothes do not make the man, and became known as the Knight of Two Swords, and began his great adventure.

Rich Knights

Rich knights receive between 9 and 12 £. per year to spend on their maintenance, significantly above normal standards.

Rich knights wear clothing of rich fabrics and furs in the latest style, use silver-decorated tack for their glossy-coated horses, and enjoy rich feasts. They have two squires in attendance, both well-mounted and attentive to their lord's needs. Their families live well, off the fat of the land.

Glory: Knights who live above their expected means (6 £. per year) gain yearly Glory equal to the number of maintenance Libra spent (typically 10 Glory/year for Rich knights). If a lord supplies their maintenance, rather than their providing the money themselves, the lord also gains this Glory.

Superlative Knights

Superlative knights are the most extravagant and impressive of all, requiring more than 12 £. per year for upkeep. Their armor shines brightly, their clothing is sumptuous with intricate stitching, extensive use of gold thread, jewels, imported feathers, and furs from fantastic beasts. Three squires, each proud in matching livery, attend their lord's needs. Superlative knights also benefit from their superior health and the aid given in battle by well-equipped, loyal squires (important benefits in battle for being well-maintained are described in the "Chivalric Duties" chapter of this book).

Glory: As above, knights who live above their expected means (6 £. per year) gain additional yearly Glory equal to the number of maintenance Libra spent (typically 15 Glory/year for Superlative knights). A lord who supplies their maintenance also gains this Glory.

Rank

High rank is a source of both power and Glory. The allure of high rank is well documented historically. In this book I deal only briefly with rank: further supplements to *Pendragon* will approach the subject in all its splendor.

The "Wealth" chapter in this book discusses the benefits of rank in terms of ransoms, spending money, etc.

Vassal Knights

Knights may obtain special honors from their lord. Simple gifts are common, usually as horses, better armor, and so on. The most prestigious honor is to receive a *fief*. This is a manor to be held by the vassal, which raises a bachelor knight to the status of vassal knight.

Player knights, as characters outside the ordinary, begin the game by receiving this great honor. The gamemaster may wish to have player knights created subsequently in his campaign begin as ordinary knights, not vassal knights, in which case this becomes an ambition of great importance.

The land received by a vassal knight may be a gift or a grant. A gift belongs to the recipient for his life, but may not be passed on to his heirs. Thus, upon the holder's death the gifted land returns to the lord. A grant is permanent, assignable to the holder's heirs. Thus a granted fief is inherited after death by the legitimate heir. The property usually goes to the oldest surviving son, to a daughter if no sons live, otherwise to the nearest other kin, as long as it is kept in the hands of the knightly and noble class. Player knights created using this book hold their land as a grant unless the gamemaster chooses to say otherwise.

A vassal knight holds at least a manor and its land. This gives him enough income to provide his own food and equipment, and supports him at an ordinary level of economic quality. He may also get married at this time, with his lord's permission. He usually lives on his land, which has a nice hall, when he is not serving his share of castle garrison duty, serving summer active duty time, or visiting court to offer his advice.

Requirements to be a Vassal Knight

To be a vassal knight the character must either inherit the land, or be granted or gifted the land by a lord, or conquer it.

Duties of a Vassal knight

The duties of a vassal knight are the same as those of any knight: to serve and protect his lord. As a knight given a special

Sir Palomides Fights for the Right of a Quest

SIR PALOMIDES HAS taken upon himself the quest to avenge the murdered king of the Red City.

AND AS HE came nigh the city, there came out of a ship a goodly knight armed against him, with his shield on his shoulder, and his hand upon his sword. And anon as he came nigh Sir Palomides he said, "Sir knight, what seek ye here? Leave this quest for it is mine, and mine it was or [before] ever it was yours, and therefore I will have it."

"Sir knight," said Palomides, "it may well be that this quest was yours or it was mine, but when the letter was take out of the dead king's hand, at that time by likelihood there was no knight had undertake to revenge the death of the king. And so at that time I promised to revenge his death, and so I shall or else I am ashamed."

"Ye say well," said the knight, "but wit ye well then will I fight with you, and who be the better knight of us both, let him take the battle upon hand."

"I assent me," said Sir Palomides.

— Malory X, 63

So, with typical chivalrous logic, they fight for the right of the quest, and Sir Palomides wins.

honor by his lord, it is expected that a vassal knight will perform his duties with consummate skill and energy.

Benefits

A vassal knight is increased in influence. His land gives him rank and prestige, and raises him in the hierarchy of knighthood over all landless knights.

A vassal knight receives a regular income to maintain his appropriate life style.

A vassal knight has a higher ransom than bachelor knights, and is more likely to be spared in a fight. See the "Wealth" chapter for more information on ransoms.

A vassal knight's future is secure beyond his life. A knight with a land grant receives the knowledge that his sons, should he have any, can inherit his property and status after he dies.

A vassal knight usually receives a wife if he does not have one, completely at the will of his lord. The woman may be the heiress of the land, or simply be provided to maintain stewardship. Whatever the case, the wife remains nameless and faceless, unless otherwise desired by the player.

Glory: A vassal knight receives 50 Glory upon receiving the title, once only. He receives annual Glory for his land equal to the income generated by the fief, usually 6 points, but perhaps more. If he maintains himself at a higher than ordinary quality of life (rich or superlative), an ambition which is often easier for vassal knights to achieve than for ordinary knights, then the knight receives annual Glory based on the quality sustained that year.

Who Are Noblemen?

AND SO, my lord, it is needful both in this regard and others that you should know who they are who you should hold for gentlemen, who for nobles, and who for non-nobles.

The Gentleman is he who from old springs from gentlemen and gentlewomen, and such men and their posterity by marriage are gentle.

And with regard to nobility, which is the beginning of gentility, it is acquired firstly by those who hold great office under the prince, and by this means they are ennobled and their posterity after them. And the heirs of such, who come after, may, by maintaining the free condition and leading the honorable life of the nobleman, call themselves gentlemen.

Thirdly, when the servant of the prince of any other has led an honorable existence, and the prince has made him a knight, he thus ennobles him and his posterity.

Fourthly, to follow the profession of arms in the rank of man-at-arms and to serve the prince valorously and long at war, this ennobles a man.

And fifthly, when a prince wishes to ennoble a man, he may do so and may give him letters to make him noble, for his good or his virtuous living, or for his riches. And although it is true that to be ennobled by letters patent is the least well authorized manner of ennoblement, yet it is apparent enough that ancient nobility comes from ancient riches. And he is the happier, and is to be the more esteemed, who commences his nobility in virtue, than he who brings his to an end in vice.

— Oliver de la Marche

Knight Lord

The lowest rank of knight lord, and that rank most accessible to the player knights, is that of banneret. A banneret knight holds several manors and estates. He must have at least three other knights holding land from him as well, but typically about seven or eight. He also has a hall nicer than a vassal knight's, but usually not fortified.

Requirements to be a Banneret Knight

To be a banneret knight the character must either inherit the land, or be granted or gifted the land by a lord.

Duties of a Banneret Knight

The duties of a banneret knight are the same as those of any knight: to serve and protect his liege. But because he has enfeoffed other knights his responsibility as a leader is greater.

When summoned to battle, the banneret must bring his knights as well.

Benefits

A lord knight is increased rank and prestige, and raises him in the hierarchy of knighthood over all landless and vassal knights. He will always be seated higher at table, enter the room later, and be served before lower knights.

A banneret knight receives a generous income to maintain his appropriate life style as a rich knight. He eats well, maintains good health, and wears rich clothing. When he travels, he can go with a full retinue. He usually has money to spend.

A banneret knights has a private army which is pledged to obey him. These are his enfeoffed knights, and their followers.

A banneret knight has a higher ransom than bachelor or vassal knights, and is thus more likely to be spared in a fight.

A banneret knight's future is secure beyond his life. A knight with a land grant receives the knowledge that his sons, should he have any, can inherit his property and status after he dies.

A banneret knight is a prime candidate for a wife, if he does not have one already. The decision may be completely at the will of his lord. Whatever the case, the wife remains nameless and faceless, unless otherwise desired by the player. The gamemaster must ensure that, as the wife of a lord knight, she is more individualized and more wealthy than the wives of mere vassal knights (those wives provided by the Random Marriage Table in the "Game Mechanics" chapter).

Glory: A banneret receives 100 Glory when first titled. This Glory is added during the Winter Phase that concludes that year.

The banneret gets annual Glory points thereafter equal to the income value of his estate, as long as he holds it.

This is at least 30 points, often much more.

A banneret is wealthy enough to maintain himself at the quality of a Rich knight as long as famine or raids do not interfere. This yields around 10 Glory annually (see above for more information on qualities of maintenance).

Ideals

A knight may take up the ambition of living in accordance with an ideal of behavior. Some famous knights maintain two ideals at once, though this is a great challenge.

Chivalrous Knight

Chivalry is a method of behavior introduced by Arthur early in his reign and popularized by his Round Table knights. Chivalrous behavior is in vogue during the middle part of the *Pendragon* campaign in which this book is set, and it is one of the major civilizing influences which makes Arthur's reign so outstanding. To be chivalrous is to be civilized. Much of the early campaign consists of spreading this belief by beating down everyone who disagrees (chivalry does not preclude violence).

Chivalry supports the protection of the weak by the strong. Before chivalry's acceptance most knights live by the attitude that "might makes right." Chivalry seeks to turn that attitude into one of *noblesse oblige* — nobility obligates responsible persons of high birth or rank to benevolent and honorable behavior.

This definition of chivalry places its emphasis upon refining the knights' duty.

Requirements to be a Chivalrous Knight

Chretien de Troyes wrote the first stories of high chivalry and adventure in Arthurian romance. He wrote the earliest known stories of Lancelot and the Holy Grail, and his definition of chivalry was imitated by less skillful writers and poets for centuries afterwards.

To Chretien, chivalry embodied the loftiest values of "chevalerie et clergie." "Chevalerie" is "bravoire et justice," or true courage and a passion for justice. "Clergie" is "elegance et culture," or right conduct, sensibility, and proper handling of personal relationships.

Chivalrous knights are recognized solely by their ideals, behavior, and reputation. Although six different traits are admired, chivalry does not hold a person to be perfect in all traits. Instead, chivalry strives for an average high quality from among them. Thus you must add together a character's personality traits to find the total. A total of 80 or more in the Generous, Energetic, Modest, Just, Merciful, and Valorous personality traits yields recognition that a knight is chivalrous. These virtues are already marked on the character sheet with a "bullet" (•). See the "Ideals and Passions" chapter for more information on traits.

Oath: as part of being a chivalrous knight, one swears to uphold the following:

"To protect the widow, the orphan, the poor; not to slay a vanquished and defenseless adversary; not to take part in a false judgment or treason, or to withdraw if it cannot be prevented; to never give evil counsel to a lady; to help, if possible, a fellow being in distress."

Duties of a Chivalrous Knight

A chivalrous knight must use his skills to protect the weak, spread culture and civilization, and uphold the law of the land. He must strive to bring the King's justice to all.

Benefits of Being a Chivalrous Knight

Chivalrous knights gain the Armor of Honor: 3 points of magical protection against all physical damage. Whether naked or fully armored, the Armor of Honor protects the Chivalrous knight against attack. The gamemaster will have to decide if the Armor of Honor protects against drowning or other such unpleasant effects.

Glory: Chivalrous knights get a reward if they maintain their status for a year: 100 Glory points. This is in addition to any Glory acquired for chivalrous traits at 16 or higher. The Glory is gained during the Winter Phase of the game.

Chivalrous knights also gain the prestige and enhanced reputation which their behavior deserves, and are considered greater than other knights of equal Glory who are not chivalrous.

Romantic Knight

Queen Guenever introduced the first Court of Romance to Arthurian Britain. It has been followed by formalized social events called the Courts of Love. This event marks the start of the popular activity of *fine amor,* and allows a character to gain Glory for romantic affairs.

Requirements for Being a Romantic Knight

Characters must have a lover to qualify for Glory through romance. The precise nature of the amorous affair is shaped by the individuals involved. Given here are some typical examples, which are by no means exclusive to your imaginations.

He must have five of the following skills at 10 or more: Compose, Dance, Flirting, Game, Hawking, Intrigue, Orate, Play (Harp), Read (Latin), Sing, and Tourney. The lady, of course, decides which five.

Further requirements are that a knight must prove his passion for his lady at least once per year by doing her bidding, occasionally even under duress. This activity must be played out, or done solitaire using the Lover's Solo (see the "Scenarios" chapter).

A knight must also entertain his amor with presents equalling at least one full Librum per year.

Duties of a Romantic Knight

A knight of romance honors all women and must do everything in his nature and ability to protect women, to deliver them justice, to respect them, and to do their bidding. He must honor every lady as if she were his own lover.

A lover must also be true to his love. Infidelity is the worst offense committed against a lover.

If the deed to prove love is not played out as an adventure created by the gamemaster, then the knight must play through the Lover's Solo during the Winter Phase to see if he succeeds in gaining the Glory.

Benefits of Being a Romantic Knight

Successful lovers gain Glory, even during the time their love is secret. Their behav-

ior betrays their activities, if not the objects of their affections.

Success at Romance gets 50 Glory the first year, and the magnitude of Glory gained increases by 50 each successful year thereafter (thus 100 is gained the 2nd year, 150 the third, and so on).

Companions of Arthur

Many people voluntarily espouse the ways and beliefs of King Arthur, even though they may never meet the High King individually, or hope to join the honored Table Round. It is simply that many knights take pride in their support of the High King and his ideals, and are willing to work for the cause even without being Arthur's direct vassals.

This support for the Pendragon is given by taking the Companion's Oath of Allegiance. If this oath has been performed a knight may call himself "King Arthur's man." Thus when stopped on a road a knight may be asked, "Are you Arthur's man?" and reply, "Yes, I am a Companion," even if he has another liege lord, is a member of another organization, or whatever.

Requirements to Become a Companion

Every year a special ceremony is held during the Pentecost feast at Camelot, or wherever King Arthur may be found. At it knights may take an oath of allegiance to the High King.

Knights must first present themselves to any Round Table knight, who will speak with him and test the knight's knowledge of Arthur's ideals. This is handled by the gamemaster, who checks the character's traits and passions. Desirable areas include the traits of Energetic, Generous, Honest, Just, Merciful, Modest, and Valorous, and the passions of Loyalty, Honor, and Amor (Lady). If five or more of these have a value of 16 or better, the test is passed. If less than five have a value of 16 or better, and any have a value of 4 or less, the test is failed. Otherwise the gamemaster must make a decision in character, as the Round Table knight (probably Sir Gawaine) administering the test. Requesting a speech about Arthur's ideals from the player is a fair and entertaining solution to the problem, with a good speech permitting the test to be passed.

If the test is passed the Round Table knight acts as sponsor to the would-be Companion. On the day before the Great Feast, when new Round Table knights are ordained, the oath is administered in the presence of the High King. New candidates are brought forward and take the oath, *en masse*. Then all knights who wish to may renew their oaths in another public ceremony which is, of course, much larger since it is customary for all Companions to participate.

Duties of a Companion

Membership is voluntary and unofficial, and so are the duties. But knight should always seek to maintain honor, keep their word, and support the ideals of the High King whenever possible.

Benefits

The benefit is to become part of a widespread network of people working to further the cause of the High King. Companions also gain 100 Glory for receiving the honor, once only.

Gamemasters should permit player characters who are Companions to more easily gain assistance and make important contacts during adventures, at least in Logres. Most knights of Logres are Companions, as are many in Cambria (including the Irish there) and Cumbria. However, it is as yet accepted among Saxons only by a few individuals, and the Picts do not like it at all.

Christian Knight

Christianity is the dominant religion of Britain, slowly ousting the native religions despite their recent resurgence. Most people in Logres believe that Christianity is the True Religion, but these knights go one step further and work hard to promote the religion through their exemplary lifestyle.

Requirements to be a Christian Knight

Knights must have a passion of Love (Christ). Christian knights embrace the Christian ideal. This consists of fame (a value of 16 or more) in each of the traits of Chaste, Forgiving, Merciful, Modest, and Temperate. These traits are underlined on the character sheet. This requirement is extremely difficult to maintain.

Palomides the Saracen

Duties of a Christian Knight

Christian knights must strive to exercise their virtues during their daily lives. They must attend Mass as much as possible, and at least once per year (at Easter).

Benefits of being a Christian Knight

If a Christian knight has 16 or more in all his Christian virtues he gains Spiritual Vigor: +6 hit points. These hit points are added onto the Total Hit Points value on the character sheet. If the knight ever fails to maintain his required passion or trait values, even by a single point, during the Winter Phase, he begins the next adventure without the extra hit points. However, any healing from wounds is performed first, so the loss of virtue will never instantly kill a character.

Glory: A Christian knight also gets 100 Glory points over the Winter Phase. This is in addition to the 80+ Glory which a Christian knight acquires for traits equal or greater than 16.

Round Table Knight

The ultimate ambition is to become a knight of the Round Table. The Round Table refers to a body of hand-picked knights who serve at Arthur's personal command. They are chosen because they personify the virtues which Arthur wishes to bring to his land: knighthood, chivalry, and romance.

150 knights have seats. The Round Table is a marvelous piece of furniture

Names Written In Gold

EARLY IN ARTHUR'S reign, when he chose the first members of his Round Table, the last available seat was given to Sir Tor, a new knight, instead of Sir Bagdemagus, an experienced and loyal knight.

SO WHEN THEY were so chosen by the assent of all the barons, so were there founden in their sieges [seats] every knight's names that here are rehearsed; and so they were set in their sieges, whereof Sir Bagdemagus was wonderly wroth, that Sir Tor was advanced afore him...

— Malory IV, 5

Forty years later, at the annual Pentecost feast, after other miracles, the knights of the Round Table sit to eat. Suddenly the doors and windows all slam shut. The court falls dark. An elderly monk in shining robes reveals a young man, clothed all in red armor, and introduces the youth as the person who shall fulfill many marvels, beginning with the Siege Perilous [Seat of Danger.]

AND THE OLD KNIGHT said unto the young knight, "Sir, followeth me."

And anon he led him unto the Siege Perilous, where beside sat Sir Lancelot; and the good man lift up the cloth, and found there letters that said thus:

This is the Siege of Galahad, the Haut Prince.

"Sir," said the old knight, "wit ye well that place is yours."

And then he set him down surely in that siege. And then he said to the old man, "Sir, you may now go your way, for well have ye done that ye were commanded to do; and recommend me unto my grandsire, King Pelleas, and unto my lord Petchere, and say them on my behalf, I shall come and see them as soon as ever I may."

So the good man departed...

— Malory XIII, 4

given to Arthur by his father-in-law at his wedding. Each knight has a seat with his name engraved on a gold plaque. The name magically appears on the plaque sometimes even before the king knows that the knight will be chosen.

Requirements to become a Round Table Knight

A candidate for the Round Table must be a Chivalrous knight sponsored by another member of the Round Table (see above for the requirements for a Chivalrous knight).

There must also be a vacancy, which only occurs when a member dies or retires from active campaigning. The gamemaster will determine this.

A member must strive to attend Arthur's great Pentecostal feasts, there to relate the deeds of the year gone by and to renew his Round Table oath which goes as follows:

"I swear, by the honor done me by my lord Arthur and the Table Round, to never commit violence without good purpose, to shun all murder and treason, and to give mercy where it is asked. I swear, upon pain of death, to always protect ladies, gentlewomen, damsels, and widows. I promise to never fight for an unjust cause, and to never fight for personal gain."

Duties of a Round Table Knight

A Round Table knight must attend Arthur's court at least once a year, unless he is upon some quest or important business. He must acknowledge Arthur as his lord. He must perform every deed with a mind towards the betterment of Arthur's name and the glory of Britain.

Knights of the Round Table act as leaders in war, especially as officers over other knights, war councilors, bodyguards to the Pendragon, and as an elite battle unit.

Knights of the Round Table act as leaders in peace. Their duty is to deliver the High King's justice across the land, and to act as models of behavior for all to emulate. They carry the king's messages, conduct his business, and protect his roads, people, and property.

Benefits of being a Round Table Knight

Upon selection to the Round Table a knight receives 1000 Glory points for the honor, and a place at the magical table.

A knight of the Round Table possesses the greatest honor in the land, and is always respected by those who revere peace, wisdom, and the King's justice. Knights of the Round Table are respected by men, admired by women, and always welcome in any house in Britain, once their origins are made known.

Since the adventure of Gawaine and the Green Knight the knights of the Round Table have worn ceremonial green belts ("girdles") as marks of their office.

Game Mechanics

How does a character use his skills? How are random factors determined? Game mechanics determine these answers.

IN THIS CHAPTER I deal with the fundamental mechanics of the game. It is important that the gamemaster be expert in these rules; players need not memorize them.

A brief, informal "Questions and Answers" section has been provided midway through the chapter to answer some of the most frequently-asked questions about game mechanics.

Gamemasters can use the Introductory Scenario at the beginning of the "Scenarios" chapter to introduce the players to the mechanics of the game while playing. Various brief adventures take the player characters through the essential rules, ending with knighthood as the culmination of the scenario.

Basic Concepts

Character Attributes and Values

As you learned in the "Character Generation" chapter, the numbers on the character sheet are used to rate your character's various attributes. Your character has five sets of attributes listed on the sheet; traits, passions, statistics, skills, and combat skills. Spaces are also given for squire and horse attributes.

Attributes have numerical values ranging from 5 to 25 for most characters in the game. What is a good value to have? In general, values around 10 are ordinary and mediocre. Values over 15 are considered superior. Values over 20 are heroic. Values lower than 5 are inferior. This is the range for humans; some monsters or magical characters have values of 30 or more in certain attributes.

A normal character's Chaste trait might have a value of 10. A Round Table knight's Sword skill might have a value of 25. An aged knight's Strength might have dwindled to 5.

Roll, Check

During the game, your character will be tested in certain ways; in personal combat, for example. Rather than your just saying "I win" or "I succeed," the gamemaster will sometimes require you to make a *roll* on d20 versus an appropriate attribute. For example, in combat, you will roll versus a combat skill. The random result is compared with the value of your attribute to determine whether you succeed or fail.

Next to some of the attributes on your character sheet (skills, traits, and passions) you will note small, hollow boxes. "Check" means put a check mark in one of these boxes. It means your character did something significant enough to deserve a learning experience. Normally a successful roll will be necessary for a check.

Sometimes no roll is needed. If you describe your character's actions in a very convincing or creative fashion, you may not need to roll: your ideas or tactics were good enough to ensure success. The character may also receive a check. The gamemaster always decides if a roll is necessary or a check is warranted.

Dice

Two types of dice are used to aid the play of *Pendragon:* 20-sided and 6-sided. To use them, the die is rolled on a table or other smooth surface. When the die comes to rest, the number that can be read on the top provides the rolled result. For a 20-sided die, the number will be between 1 and 20. For the 6-sided die, the number will be between 1 and 6.

d20: the abbreviation for using the 20-sided die. If the rules ask, "Roll d20" it means that the player rolls the die, and the number which is left face-up is the result.

d6: means roll one 6-sided die. However, usually more than one of these are used at once. The abbreviation for multiples of the d6 are made by putting a number before the "d," such as in 4d6. Thus, if the rules say 5d6, it means that the player rolls five 6-sided dice and adds their results together.

d3: means the player should roll one 6-sided die, then divide the result by two, with the results that 1 or 2 = 1, 3 or 4 = 2, and 5 or 6 = 3.

x1/2: this means the player rolls all the die normally rolled in that situation, then divides the result by 2.

x2: means the player rolls the number of dice two times and adds all the results. Also referred to as "double," as in double damage.

Rounding Off

Whenever a number must be rounded off in *Pendragon* and there is a remainder that is equal to or greater than .5, then round up to the next whole number. If the remainder is less than .5, then round down. For example, 4.4 would be considered 4, but 4.5 would be considered 5.

Resolution

DURING CRITICAL TIMES of play the gamemaster asks his players to make die rolls for their characters to see whether they are successful in what they are trying to do. Such rolls are required whenever a character is in a situation of stress or otherwise acts without deliberate forethought.

To determine success or failure, roll d20 and compare the result with the character's attribute value. If the die roll is *equal to or less* than the number indicated then the character succeeded at what he was trying to do.

Unopposed Resolution

Unopposed resolution rolls are made directly against the character's attribute value.

Modifiers to the value may apply, raising or lowering the number on the character sheet temporarily. The value may be lowered to zero, in which case failure is certain, or above 19, in which case success is certain. The die should still be rolled to see whether a fumble or critical success occurs (see below for more information on modifiers, fumbles, and critical successes).

Example of Unopposed Resolution: *In a forest quest that begins the year's scenario, Sir Ambrut (a sample knight first introduced at the end of the "Character Generation" chapter) tries hard to recognize the noise he just thought he heard. His player tries to make an Awareness roll on d20, gets a 7, which is higher than Ambrut's Awareness value of 5, and so fails. Without warning (since Ambrut failed to hear him), a robber on a vine swings down from a tree and attacks.*

Opposed Resolution

Opposed resolution rolls are made versus the opponent's rolled number. Simple success may not be enough to defeat the opponent. To win the player must succeed with his own roll, and also roll a number on d20 that is *higher* than the number that the opponent's player (usually the gamemaster) rolls.

A failure is considered a rolled number of 0, regardless of the actual number rolled on the die.

Winners and Losers: An opposed resolution may result in either a winner and loser, a tie, or two losers. A winner must roll equal to or under his own skill value, and also achieve a success that is higher than his opponent. Both opponents may be losers if both fail their roll. A loser may also have a partial success (see below).

Modifiers: Modifiers may adjust values up or down. Values over 20 increase the rolled number, but the maximum success roll is always 20.

Tie: A tie in *Pendragon* means that the situation is unresolved, although time has passed. Continue with resolution. Ties may have results in certain special instances; for example, in personal combat, a tie means that certain weapons are broken by a character using a sword.

Partial Success: A loser in an opposed resolution may have a partial success. A partial success is a successful roll which loses. Some minor benefit is usually gained from a partial success. In combat, a character achieving a partial success may parry with a shield, if using one.

Example of Opposed Resolution: *To continue the robber's attack from above — Ambrut sees the robber charging and draws his sword. A fight ensues, wherein the robber has a skill of 12 and Ambrut 15. In the first round (combat is resolved in "melee rounds") the robber rolls a 13 and fails, but Ambrut rolls a 1, a success and higher than the robber's roll, since a failure is considered to be a roll of 0. Ambrut is the winner of the resolution. He inflicts minor damage on the robber.*

In the next round, Ambrut rolls a 12, the robber an 11. Both succeed this time, but Ambrut wins, since his d20 roll is higher. The robber, although the loser in the round, also succeeded this time, so he achieves a partial success and parries Ambrut's blow with his shield. However, Ambrut strikes a mighty blow that goes through the robber's shield and armor to wound him severely, and the scoundrel surrenders. Ambrut receives a check to his Sword skill.

Critical Success

Whenever a character attempts a resolution roll of any type he has a chance for a critical success. A critical success is achieved whenever a character rolls a number exactly equal to his modified attribute value (see below for modifier rules). The character has achieved the ultimate success: regardless of the number rolled on the die, a critical success is considered a successful roll of 20. This is true even if a character with an attribute of 1 rolls a 1. A roll of 20 beats any lesser roll in opposed resolution, so a critical success guarantees a win or a tie.

Special Results of a Critical Success: In most cases unusually favorable results will obtain from a critical success.

In some situations there will be no special benefit, and no difference between a critical and a normal success: in particular, a critical success with a statistic (Dexterity, Strength, etc.) often gives no special result.

A critical success with a skill has two potential benefits. First, the results were extraordinarily successful, and the gamemaster relates the specific game effects. In combat, a critical success with a weapon skill indicates that the character inflicts double damage (his player rolls the normal number of dice twice.) Second, the skill may be checked with gamemaster approval, indicating a chance to learn from experience during the winter (see the "Experience" and "Winter Phase" sections of the chapter below).

A critical success with a trait or passion works in a similar way to skills, giving increased benefits and an experience check. A critical trait or passion roll also indicates extreme, perhaps even fanatical behavior in accordance with the trait or passion that was rolled.

Fumble

A fumble occurs whenever a character receives a roll of 20, unless his modified attribute value is 20 or more, in which case he has no chance to fumble (and in such cases, a critical success is achieved by a die roll of 20).

A fumble is a disastrous stroke of bad luck resulting in such things as dropping or breaking your weapon during combat, or coughing or cursing in the midst of a romantic ballad. Gamemasters relate the specifics of a fumbled roll, based on the guidelines given in the sections below.

Most situations not covered by the rules will present a possible fumble result.

Note that in many cases statistic rolls are either a success or a failure, with neither fumbles or critical successes having any special effect.

Fumbles occur frequently in *Pendragon*. This is done in order to provide many opportunities for storytelling to the gamemaster. In many cases a fumble will let the gamemaster balance out a situation that has gotten out of hand, feed the players false information, or simply interject some humor and excitement into the story. But as a result of the frequency of fumbles, the way is opened for bad gamemasters to inflict incessant grief on their players. Ideally the effects suffered by the fumbling character should be interpreted in the character's favor. Gamemasters who insist that every fumble means a disaster will soon spoil the game for everyone.

A raven witch transforming

Modifiers

Modifiers to all attributes may be applied by the gamemaster whenever useful or realistic. The gamemaster should be consistent in applying these to both gamemaster and player characters. Modifiers are always added or subtracted from the character's attribute values. However, modified values over 20 increase the die roll (see below under "Values Greater Than 20"). Critical success is based on rolling equal to the character's modified value, not his unmodified value.

Modifiers represent temporary advantages or difficulties in a situation. Thus a mounted man fighting against an unmounted one gets +5 to his attack skill. A special hawk might add +5 to a character's Hawking skill. A wounded knight asked to surrender by a troop of enemy knights might suffer a -5 modifier to his Valorous trait.

Range of Modifiers Table
+/- 5 = ordinary modifier (used for most situations)
+/- 10 = strong modifier (for dramatic situations)
+/- 15 = extreme modifier

Normally +/-15 should be the maximum modifier used. But modifiers of +/-20 or even more may occur on rare occasions. These will guarantee success or failure, but the die should be rolled anyway to see if a critical success or fumble occurs.

Types of Modifiers

Modifiers can be used with any attribute. The following are the standard types.

Reflexive Modifiers: In many cases of opposed resolution, modifiers will be reflexive. This means that both participants are affected, but in opposite ways. For example, in the case of the mounted man attacking a man on foot with a +5 modifier, the man on foot also suffers a -5 modifier to his weapon skill when attacking the mounted man.

Since reflexive modifiers widen the gap between character capabilities, a -5/+5 modifier is equivalent to an ordinary +/- 10 point modifier in strength.

Reflexive modifiers may be mixed with regular modifiers in a few cases.

Combat Modifiers: These are based on weapon types, position of combatants, etc. The standard combat modifier is a reflexive -5/+5 as listed above. Combat modifiers are discussed in the "Combat" and "Skills" sections of the chapter.

Skill Modifiers: These are used to adjust a character's skill to a particular situation. Modifiers make skill use harder, or less commonly, easier. They should be used whenever the situation calls for it. Most combat modifiers are skill modifiers.

Example of Skill Modifier: *In the same forest quest described above, Sir Ambrut again attempts to spot an ambush using his Awareness skill of 5. This time the player states that Ambrut is carefully scanning each tree near the trail for robbers before passing under-*

Kay the Seneschal

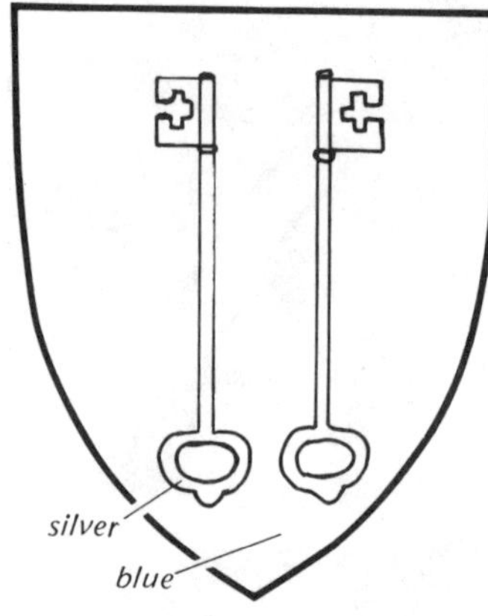

neath. The gamemaster permits Ambrut a +5 modifier to his normal skill value because treetops are indeed the favorite ambush spot for the local group of bandits.

A few moments later, Ambrut rolls a 10, a critical success (given the +5 modifier). He spots two robbers lurking in a tree about 200 yards ahead, and quietly leaves the trail, bypassing them before they see him. The gamemaster decides that Ambrut receives a check for his Awareness skill.

Note that if the bandits had been hiding on the ground instead of up in a tree, Ambrut would still receive a modifier for his tactic (or else the player would be tipped off that the treetops were not the place to look), but the gamemaster would not have to reveal the bandits' presence, even with a critical success. He might say "You spot a very rare bird in the next tree with that crit, but no robbers."

Personality Trait and Passion Modifiers: These are used to modify traits or passions when the current situation is likely to influence a character's normal behavior. For example, a character whose family had betrayed him to an enemy might receive a -10 modifier to his Love (family) passion.

Trait and passion modifiers may also be used when a player feels that his character would act differently than would be determined by a simple die roll. The objective is to make everyone comfortable with the personality trait or passion roll that is about to be made. The gamemaster must permit realistic modifiers whenever the players ask for them: characters should *not* behave randomly. +/- 5 is the recommended modifier when a player feels his character deserves a modifier to his behavior. See the "Ideals and Passions" chapter for more information.

Example of Trait Modifier: *Sir Moris of the Tower, a notoriously lazy knight, is asked to perform a difficult task by a beautiful damsel. Although the lazy knight is normally unlikely to undertake such a task, the presence of the damsel might make a difference. The player asks for a modifier before he makes his character's Energetic roll. The gamemaster agrees and gives Sir Moris a +5 modifier for this special situation.*

Statistic Modifiers: Sometimes a statistic roll may be modified. The most common use of this is the negative modifier which armor gives to DEX rolls in some situations. In such cases leather armor gives a -5 modifier, and metal armor gives a -10 modifier. See the "Movement" and "Combat" sections below for more information on DEX rolls, armor, etc.

Values Greater Than 20

If a character has a attribute value greater than 20, or temporarily modified to be greater than 20, then every die roll which he makes versus that value is *increased.* The increase is equal to the amount of the value over 20. Thus a knight with a Dexterity of 25 would increase the number rolled by 5 every time (unless a modifier to DEX reduced its value).

Note that the die roll can never be reduced, only increased, in *Pendragon*.

The increased die roll is considered to be the number "rolled." The maximum possible roll is still a 20, not a 21, 22, etc.

A value greater than 20 increases the chance of a critical success and eliminates the chance of fumble. For the purpose of determining critical success, a value greater than 20 is considered to be 20. Since the maximum possible roll is 20, this means that a roll of 20, or a roll increased to 20, is equal to the skill value, and is thus a critical success.

Example of Values Greater Than 20: *Sir Yvane (a sample character introduced in the "Character Generation" chapter) fights from horseback against a footsoldier. Yvane's sword skill is normally 19, but the combat modifier for attacking unmounted foes gives him an increase of +5, so Yvane's Sword skill value is temporarily 24. His die roll is increased by +4. Thus if he and the footsoldier both rolled 13 on their dice, Yvane would win because his increased roll equals 17. For Yvane against the footsoldier, a roll of 16, 17, 18, 19, or 20 counts as a roll of 20, a critical success. A fumble cannot occur.*

Values of Zero

Due to negative modifiers it is possible that an attribute value will be temporarily reduced to zero or worse. The rule is that in such circumstances, the character attempting to roll against the modified value receives an automatic failure. Players should still roll to see if they also fumble, as normally, on a roll of 20.

Negative values are not used in *Pendragon,* even if a modifier would reduce the value to a negative number. Instead the value is considered to be zero.

Time Scales

TIME IN *PENDRAGON* passes at a faster and more clearly defined rate than in other adventure games.

The general rule is one scenario per game year, a scenario being defined as a linked series of adventures, feasts, combats, battles, quests, tournaments, or other knightly activities selected by the gamemaster for the player knights to participate in.

Usually a scenario will last no more than one or two seasons of game time. There are a number of reasons why the one scenario per year rule is useful.

1. Much of a knight's time is not his own. Training, duties to one's lord, and the needs of one's family take precedence over the pursuit of personal fame. Travel times are very slow as well. The period of good weather and free time available in a typical year in Arthurian Britain only suffices for a single scenario, and some years may pass without any scenarios at all occurring.

2. Part of the fun of the game is the dynastic segment. Also, death is more likely than in games with more magical healing. Children are a solution to both these points. If player knights are to have children who grow to adulthood during a

campaign, game-years must pass quickly.

3. Glory is the goal of the game. Since Glory only accrues after time has passed and one's exploits become part of heroic legend, time needs to pass briskly. Glory, coming as it does from public recognition, gives its benefits only during the Winter Phase of the game, not at the immediate conclusion of glorious events.

Characters receive Glory for the passage of a year's normal activities, not just for combat and adventuring. Some characters may achieve more Glory from annual sources than they can easily achieve in scenarios, and may choose to stay home certain years, maintaining their lands and raising a fine family.

4. *Pendragon* characters improve quickly and age slowly as the years pass. As each year passes, it is possible to augment characters significantly due to Glory, experience, and training. This character improvement is based on yearly updating, and aging doesn't necessarily spoil characters. In fact, the Aging Table is designed so that player knights can live to about 70 years of age or even older.

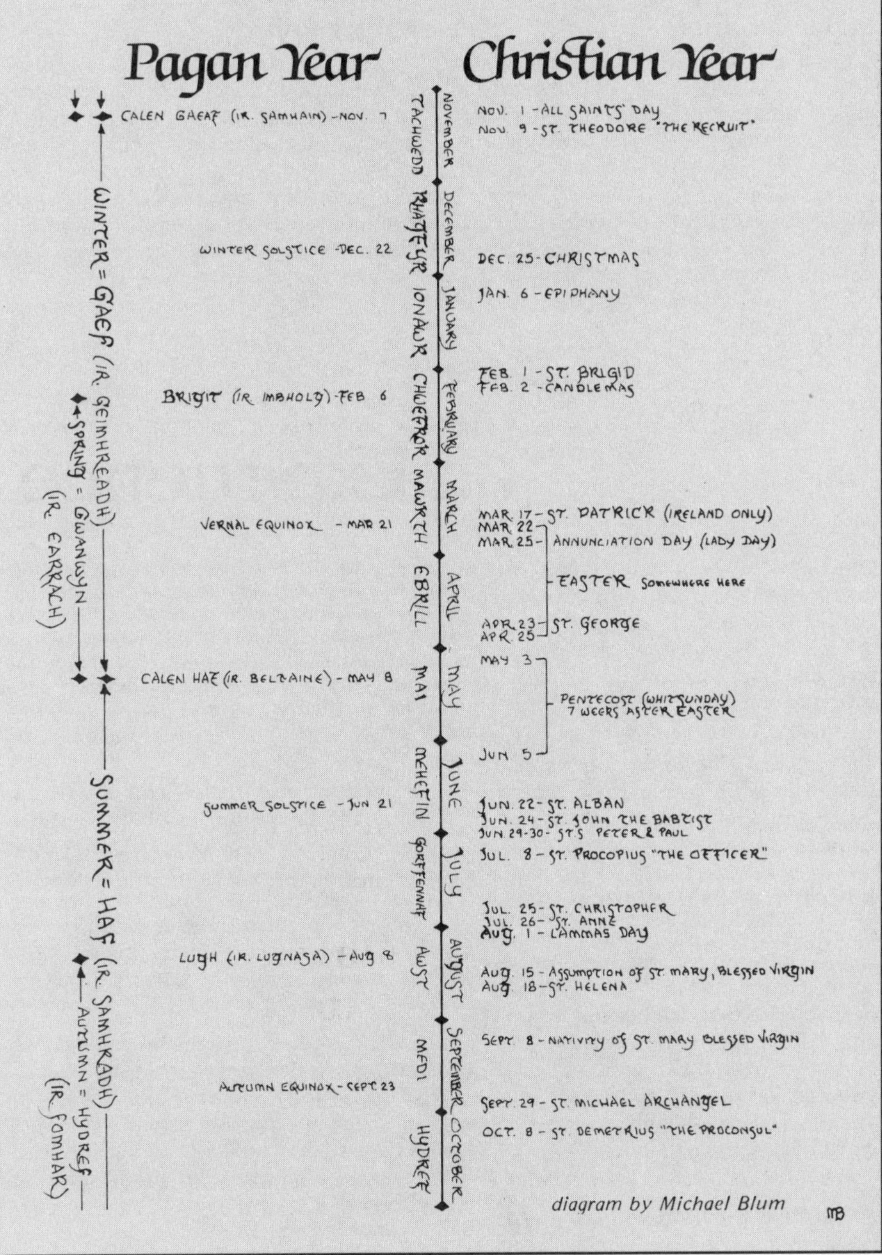

diagram by Michael Blum

Narrative Time

Narrative time is the quick passage of time which moves the game along. For example, most travel time is narrative in nature. The gamemaster says, "It takes you twelve days to get there," or "You search the woods for a week and nothing happens." Other examples are easy to imagine. "It is 20 days until you are fully healed again." "The storm lasts for two days." "You wait two weeks for the enemy fleet to show up." "Nothing happens for the whole summer."

Scenario Time

Scenario time is divided into two types. First are hours and minutes, called time passage, and then there is real time.

The gamemaster controls time by stating how it passes, in terms of hours and minutes. He tells what is going on by saying, "It takes five minutes for you to reach them," or "You have to wait here for an hour, will you do anything?" or "The giant will reach you in one minute, so get prepared fast."

Real time occurs in scenarios when players speak in character, or otherwise play the 'here and now' of the game action. You say, "My knight is walking to stand beside the courtier who is speaking," or, "I want to ask the king something before I depart," or, "I will speak to the herald to try to gain access to the duke."

Battle Rounds

When a battle takes place during a scenario, time passes in battle rounds. Battle rounds are approximately 30 minutes in duration. A battle lasts from two to twelve rounds. Pursuit rounds are also possible, with basically the same duration as a battle round.

Because of the confused state of affairs in battles (the "fog of war" and so forth), only one combat skill use is performed during a battle round, though many other mass events may occur.

Skirmishes are lesser events than battles, and time is measured in melee rounds rather than battle rounds.

See the Battle skill description, under the "Skills" section below, and the "Chivalric Duties" chapter, for more information on skirmishes and battles.

Melee Rounds

When the game turns into split-second action, especially during fighting, it uses melee rounds. The melee round is a brief period of time. The exact duration is abstract. It is not measured in seconds, but in terms of activities performed. Specifically, one action can be performed in a melee round. This important time scale is treated in more detail in the "Movement," "Skills," and "Combat" sections of the chapter below.

Winter Phase

The annual Winter Phase is a non-playing measure of time used by characters for training and many other important pursuits. The character sheet is updated by the player during each Winter Phase, and various bookkeeping tasks are performed. Details are covered later in the "Winter Phase" rules below.

Annual Time

This is one year of game time. Each year begins with the Winter Phase. Changes are figured at the beginning of the year, during winter, when most people retire from the foul weather. As noted above, scenarios occur, on the average, once per year, usually during the fine weather of summer.

Experience

One of the most exciting things to occur in roleplaying games is the growth and change of characters as game time progresses. In *Pendragon* these changes are brought about by Glory, by training, and by experience in the field.

Experience is handled using experience checks. The results of experience, as well as Glory and training, are noted during the Winter Phase.

Obtaining Experience

Every skill, trait, or passion which can change as a result of learning is marked on the character sheet by having a box (□) near it. The box is checked when the character gains significant experience during an adventure with a skill, trait, or passion (statistics do not change as a result of learning, though annual training may increase them).

Procedure for Skills: There are times during play when the gamemaster tells the player to check one of his character's skills (under "Skills" or "Combat Skills" on the sheet). This means that the character has successfully used the skill in a time of crisis and may learn from the experience. This box is checked only when the skill is used successfully, and only when the gamemaster say the player may do so. The mark reminds the player to check the skill later, over the Winter Phase, to see if any learning occurred.

Note that a character's squire's skills may increase in the same manner as normal skills.

Example of Skill Check: *Sir Ambrut, in love with a lady, announces that he will write a love poem to her. Ambrut's player actually writes the poem and reads it to the group. The poem is reasonably good, and the gamemaster decides that Ambrut has succeeded with his Compose skill, and states that it may be checked. Note that no roll was necessary here, only success and the gamemaster's approval.*

Procedure for Traits and Passions: there are times during play when the gamemaster will tell the player to check one of his character's traits or passions. This means that the character has displayed significant behavior in accordance with the trait. The action does not necessarily have to be observed by others.

If the rules for traits or passions request a roll this means that your character *might* learn something, if he acts or feels the right way. But his actions are not yet clear, or significant enough. A successful roll means he might get the check, too.

Example: *Fickle Sir Ambrut, now in love with a new lady, is asked if he has ever loved any woman as deeply as he loves her. Ambrut answers "Never has my love been so deep," choosing not to tell the woman of his recent obsession with her predecessor. The gamemaster feels that Ambrut is being dishonest, given the depth of feeling he claimed in the poem he wrote a few weeks earlier, and states that Ambrut gets a Deceitful check.*

Skills and Experience: Experience checks for skills are intended to be very difficult to get, and are *not* automatic whenever a success is achieved. Gamemasters must explain this point to the players. The ability to award or deny an experience check is one of the key powers of the gamemaster.

A check for a skill is possible only if at least one or more of the following statements obtain:

1) A critical success is achieved. If a character does his best possible, learning is likely.

2) A success in a significant situation was achieved. Even a dozen successful attacks on a gang of helpless peasants would not be justification for a check to a weapon skill, since no risk or challenge was incurred by the attacker, and nothing important was achieved.

And I repeat: no check can be gained unless the gamemaster assigns it. Players can ask if they deserve one, of course, but the gamemaster is not obliged to grant it.

Example: *From the examples above, Sir Ambrut ends up with the following: a check for Sword, for striking the robber several times and defeating him; a check for Awareness, since Ambrut spotted the bandits with a critical success; a check for Compose, from the poem written by Ambrut's player; and a check for Deceitful, derived from his dishonest behavior with a lover.*

Results of Experience Checks

When a character has a check next to a skill, trait, or passion, the player must make an experience check roll during the Winter Phase. If the roll is successful, the checked value increases by one point. Experience check rolls may bring skills over 20 with luck. See the "Winter Phase" section below for more information.

Movement

DIFFERENT RATES OF MOVEMENT are figured according to different time scales. Of significance are Melee Movement and Scenario Movement. The DEX roll is also an important part of movement.

Movement during the game is one of the most complicated subjects that the gamemaster has to handle. In *Pendragon*, movement and actions are highly abstracted for the purposes of quick resolution and simplicity. The gamemaster must be ready to adjudicate specific situations using the following rules as guidelines.

Melee Movement

A melee round is used for game situations that must be handled second-by-second. Duration is defined as the time needed to plan and perform one action.

Melee combat is the chief situation that calls for melee round resolution, but the gamemaster may use the melee round for non-combat events if necessary. For example, if two knights are racing their horses through a crowded village, melee movement may be needed to determine who won.

Man-to-man combat and movement are the two basic actions performed by characters in melee. Here I analyze movement, including several maneuvers performed during a melee round. See the "Skills" and "Combat" sections below for more information on fighting, tactics, and weapons.

Basic Rules

Movement in melee rounds is done by moving characters one yard at a time until all character have moved their permissable distance in yards (their Movement Rate statistic). Miniature figures may help determine yard-by-yard movement distances, but are not essential. In many cases it will not be important to determine exactly how many yards a character moved, only that they entered a door, or approached another character close enough to engage in combat.

Characters fighting one another are considered to be engaged in combat and may not move or do anything else other than fight without suffering a penalty assigned by the gamemaster.

Remember that a character may normally perform only one action in a round.

The Movement Rate

This statistic determines how many yards per melee round a character or creature can move. It also affects forced march movement rates (see "Scenario Movement" below).

Normal Melee Movement: Movement on foot uses the character's Movement Rate. If the character is mounted than the mount's Movement Rate is used. Each melee round the character may move a number of yards equal to his Movement Rate or a multiplier thereof as his sole action.

- Movement Rate = the number of yards which an encumbered character or creature (an armored warrior, or a horse carrying a rider, for example) can walk per round of melee combat.
- For humans, Movement Rate = (STR+DEX) divided by 10. For animals, Movement Rate formulas vary. Four-legged animals' movement equals (STR+DEX) divided by 5, with adjustments for some creatures.

Rapid Melee Movement: Characters will often prefer to run or sprint during melee movement. In crowded combat situations, this may be inappropriate. The gamemaster always determines whether movement over the base rate is permitted.

- Running (cantering for horses) doubles the basic Movement Rate. There is no express penalty for running or pressing a mount to a canter, but gamemasters should be wary of players who wish to run through a crowd of combatants or a battle. If sustained for a long period of time, running or cantering will tire the character or creature (see "Sprinting" for suggested effects).
- Sprinting (galloping for horses) triples the basic rate, but if sustained for more than a few melee rounds, may require a DEX roll or CON roll every subsequent round, at the gamemaster's option. Failure indicates that the character slows down, while a fumble indicates exhaustion and collapse. Modifiers may be applied if the sprint is continued.

Special Situations

The rules below attempt to deal with some of the questions that can arise when characters interact during movement. Gamemasters are advised to keep the game simple.

Initiative: If it is important to decide who moves first, the character with the highest Movement Rate moves first. If two characters have the same Movement Rate, the person with the highest DEX has the option to decide whether he will take the initiative or let another character move first.

Moving In Conjunction With Other Actions: If a character or creature moves only a portion of their Movement Rate in a round then the gamemaster decides if other actions are also allowed. Normally the "one action in a round" rule should be enforced, but note that a lance attack is always done in combination with movement on horseback. See the "Skills" and "Combat" sections below for more information.

Movement and Evasion: If a character moves within one yard of an enemy with the intention of moving on past, or if a character in combat wishes to disengage from an opponent, evasion must be attempted as part of movement. See the "DEX rolls" section below.

Friendly characters or creatures may move past each other freely without becoming entangled unless their paths converge.

A surprised enemy, or one engaged in combat with other opponents, or with his back turned, may be moved past freely with gamemaster approval.

Encumbrance: A character or creature may be "encumbered" in *Pendragon*. Knights and horses are usually encumbered during the game as their normal state of affairs, and no special rules apply. However, characters and horses that are *unencumbered* gain an increase of +2 to their basic Movement Rate. Thus a man with a Movement Rate of 3 would walk 5 yards when unencumbered.

A typical forest in Britain. Note the various hazards for mounted movement.

Encumbrance is defined as a heavy load. Clothing, or even a sword and shield, aren't enough to constitute a heavy load for a character, but full armor, weapons, and combat gear do qualify as a heavy load. An armored knight and heavy saddle are clearly a heavy load for a horse to carry, while a small girl riding bareback is not much of a burden for most steeds.

As always, the gamemaster is in charge of judging specific cases. In borderline situations, add 1 point, rather than 2, to the Movement Rate of the character or creature in question.

If a character or creature is bearing an extremely heavy load, perhaps carrying another armored knight on his back, the gamemaster may wish to reduce the Movement Rate by 1 point.

Note that a +1 or +2 bonus is already figured into the Movement Rates for characters and creatures that do not normally bear heavy burdens (i.e. giants, bandits, hawks, bears, wyrms, peasants, and so forth).

Horses are assumed to be encumbered by the weight of an armored rider or a heavy pack. So a sumpter horse bearing an empty pack would have a Movement Rate of 7 (5+2).

Encumbrance affects skill as well as movement: whenever a knight fights without any leather or metal armor, he gets a +5 modifier to his weapon skill. See the "Combat" section of the chapter for more details.

Chases: Sometimes two characters will chase each other on foot or on horse, or a creature will be chased by several characters, and so forth. If the Movement Rates are different, the character or creature with the higher rate catches the lower. If the rates are the same, but one is more encumbered than the other, the gamemaster must make a ruling based on common sense. For example, two characters racing on identical horses might find that the horse carrying the lighter load (the rider with the lower SIZ) gradually outdistanced the other. Alternatively, opposed rolls on appropriate character attributes can resolve these situations. For instance, when a knight chases another, opposed Horsemanship, Energetic, or DEX rolls might be appropriate, with the winner catching or escaping the other. As always, modifiers can be applied if necessary.

Scenario Movement

Scenario movement covers vast distances in a few words. The Travel Distances Table below offers detailed guidelines for scenario movement. The gamemaster can use the table to determine travel times for specific situations.

The distances for normal travel, as shown on the table, do not vary for individuals but are based on average travel times. On the other hand, forced marching puts character or horse movement ability to the test, and movement is affected by individual Movement Rates. See the "Forced March" rules below.

Given below are travel distances along different types of roads and paths. The pace of travel is also important.

Travel Pace: Normally, player knights move at the "Normal" pace. If something important is occurring, they may move at

the "Hurried" pace without penalty, unless they are unmounted.

Certain persons or groups may only travel at the slowest, "Leisurely" travel pace; ladies, siege trains, merchants, monks on donkeys, and especially injured characters needing Chirurgery. In other cases the gamemaster must decide which pace is appropriate.

Note that people on horse and on foot move at the same general pace for a day's travel. However, parties on foot can not move at the "Hurried" pace. "Normal" is the best they can do, unless they wish to Forced March.

Travel Distances Table (in miles per day)

Type	*Leisurely*	*Normal*	*Hurried*
Royal or Trade Road	15	20	30
Road, Local	10	15	25
Path	5	8	12
Track	2	3	4

Traveling Unknown Routes

Often characters will enter unfamiliar areas of Britain. A successful Hunting skill roll is needed to make progress while traveling in such areas.

Success = move at a Leisurely pace.
Critical Success = move at Normal pace.
Failure = character is confused, and must stop the trip to get his bearings, delaying the journey for at least an hour or more, depending on gamemaster preference.
Fumble = character takes the wrong direction, and is thoroughly lost.

Road Terminology

Royal Road: A road protected by the laws of the High King. Crimes committed against anyone on the Royal Road are treated as an offense against the king; High Treason. Otherwise this is like a Trade Road.

Trade Road: A raised dirt or stone road, repaired occasionally.
Local Road: An undrained, ill-repaired dirt road.
Path: This is a well-marked path through woods or fields.
Track: A barely-discernable series of marks.

Forced March

Forced march is a deliberate effort to go farther and faster than normal. Add the character or mount's Movement Rate x3 as a bonus in miles to the distances given in the Travel Distances Table above, with adjustments if the gamemaster deems it necessary.

Forced marches require a CON roll. A normal or critical success indicate successful completion of the trip. Failure indicates exhaustion: the character or mount stops after moving half the attempted distance and must rest for several hours, perhaps for the rest of the day (the gamemaster must determine the exact time spent resting). A fumbled CON roll in a forced march indicates that a serious injury was taken during the trip. Distance traveled and rest needed are the same as for failure, but if a horse fumbles the roll, it is ruined (crippled, wind lost). A character fumbling the roll takes 2d6 damage from heat stroke, a sprained leg, or some other travel mishap. See the "Injury and Health" section below for more information on damage and recovery.

Example: *Sir Ambrut must ride hard to rescue his brother. He decides to make a forced march. His best riding horse, a charger given the name "Flame," is available. He takes another horse, an unusually hardy rouncy, as a backup. The trip will be entirely on a trade road well-known to Ambrut, so he will make good time.*

Ambrut and his squire (leading his master's special rouncy and mounted on his own rouncy) leave at dawn. Ambrut's brother is imprisoned in a castle about 50 miles away, so a single day's forced march should easily do it.

Ambrut's charger Flame has a Movement Rate of 9 and a CON of 13. Ambrut's player successfully makes a CON roll for Flame, so the trip is made successfully. The bonus for forced marching gained by this particular horse is (9x3) = 27 miles. The Travel Distances Table shows that a day's movement on a trade road, at a hurried pace, is 30 miles. 30+27 = 57 miles, so Ambrut covers the 50 miles easily and arrives at the castle before sunset. He defeats the ogre that lives there and rescues his brother before the ogre's evening meal takes place, gaining a check on Love (family) from the gamemaster for his timely and single-handed rescue.

The squire's horse also sustains the pace, but being a much slower horse, gains less of a forced march bonus and is gradually left behind as the day progresses. The squire will not arrive until the next day, even if he tries to ride all night: the forced march rule puts an absolute limit on what can be achieved in a day.

The DEX Roll

Game play presents hazards and difficulties which challenge characters' manual dexterity, agility, reactions, or other movement-related abilities, such as climbing, sneaking, and balancing. All these situations use a DEX (dexterity) roll to determine success, usually unopposed. Brawling also uses DEX rather than a skill, and characters may oppose their DEX in such fights. The gamemaster may find other occasions to use the DEX roll as well.

Critical Successes and Fumbles

As with most statistic rolls, success and failure are usually the only possible results of a DEX roll — neither a critical success or a fumble gives any special result. However, several special uses of the DEX roll are an exception to this pattern, brawling and sneaking for example. Furthermore, the gamemaster may see something appropriate in a particular situation; if storytelling is enhanced, by all means let a critical DEX success gain some extra benefit or a fumble extract a special penalty.

DEX Roll Modifiers

Many situations in which the DEX roll is used require negative modifiers. A few usages gain positive modifiers. Each specific use of the DEX roll below lists specific suggestions for modifiers in addition to the general points given here. Modifiers from sources such as passions apply to DEX rolls as they do to all rolls. In borderline situations the gamemaster decides whether a modifier to DEX is appropriate.

Encumbrance: For actions involving a lot of movement, such as climbing or dodging, DEX is reduced by armor worn or heavy items carried. A modifier of -5 to DEX is used for leather armor or a light load. A modifier of -10 is used for metal armor (of all grades) or for persons carrying heavy objects. Actions such as balancing, in which little actual movement is intended, do not require a modifier for encumbrance.

Footing: Most DEX rolls should also receive a negative modifier for difficult or slippery surfaces, when appropriate. For example, a character attempts to balance on a narrow wooden beam across a chasm, or attempts to climb a wet and slippery wall of polished rock. Usually the negative modifier should be no more than -10.

Cumulative modifiers may be applied to DEX rolls. For example, a climber carrying a wounded knight on his back, and attempting to climb up a

King Arthur Encounters Travel Difficulties

The king has been marching with his men, but experiences some of the difficulties of medieval travel.

But many days passed before the king found food or fire, only deep valleys, one after the other, hills and dales, mountains and morasses and many rank quagmires, groves of birches, swamps and springs, without decent shelter, no barns or sheds. The rocks and narrow paths were harrowing even in the telling. So terribly damp was the way that they became worn and fatigued, for even the best men can tire, as you may well know. All their food was gone that once they had in great plenty, nor could they find shelter, which might have given them relief.

– from *Golagros and Gawaine*

difficult surface might suffer a -15 or even worse to DEX. Certain feats are impossible and a negative modifier should stress this.

DEX Roll Uses

Balance: The balance roll is the most common DEX roll. Whenever a character or creature receives their Knockdown statistic or more in damage they must make a balance roll to recover and remain on their feet. Whether the recipient is on horseback or on foot, a DEX roll determines success. Balance might also be tested when a character crosses a narrow bridge, stays afoot on the heaving deck of a ship, or staggers about when the earth shakes from magic.

Encumbrance, whether from armor or other heavy items, is *not* used to modify a DEX roll for balance unless the gamemaster insists. Difficult footing may require a negative modifier, however.

If the roll is successful, the character remains upright; if not, he falls down. He falls off his horse if mounted, taking 1d6 damage from the fall. This roll is often needed during combat. A critical balance success gains no special advantage unless the situation presents an obvious extra benefit. A fumble does no further harm.

Once knocked down, a character needs no roll to get up again, even if in heavy armor. However, in combat he must fight from a disadvantage while clambering back to his feet, and suffers a -5 modifier to his weapon skill while any opponents gain a +5 modifier. See the "Combat" section below for more information on the complicated issues of combat modifiers and actions during a melee round.

Brawling: If a character wishes to strike another with his fist or otherwise engage in casual, unmilitary violence like any peasant, DEX/2 is used as the skill value, and opposed rolls may be made. See the "Skills" and "Combat" sections of the chapter for the rules of brawling.

Climb: A character may attempt to clamber up a surface using a DEX roll. If it is an easy slope, perhaps a sand dune, the DEX roll might be without modification, if a roll is needed at all. A -5 modifier might be needed for the character to climb a smooth stone wall. Encumbered characters who are climbing suffer normal modifiers to DEX. Bad footing may also dictate a modifier.

Normally one DEX roll is made per 30 feet of height or fraction thereof. So a 65-foot-tall tower would require three successful DEX rolls to climb.

Ropes or convenient vines may add to the chance of success. A rope gives a +5 modifier to DEX. A proper ladder gives a +10 modifier. Siege ladders, which may have suffered hasty construction or damage from usage or defenders, have a modifier of +1d6+4.

Dodge: A character may choose to avoid an incoming blow by throwing himself out of the way. He can do this by opting to dodge instead of using his combat skills. Treat a dodge as a simple unopposed resolution roll, performed simultaneously to the enemy's unopposed weapon skill roll.

A critical or successful dodge means the character avoided the blow and remained on his feet, regardless of the roll of the enemy. A failed or fumbled dodge means that the character fell onto the ground as a result of his violent movement, being hit by the enemy if the latter was successful in his unopposed roll. Damage is inflicted normally (although balance is not tested).

As always, if in combat the fallen character will have to take the next round getting to his feet, fighting at a disadvantage (modifiers of -5 to character, +5 to enemy).

Modifiers for encumbrance and footing apply normally to dodging.

The Double Feint Tactic: In the "Combat" section of the chapter is a list of combat tactics usable with gamemaster approval. This includes the Double Feint tactic, which requires a DEX roll. Normal modifiers for encumbrance and footing apply. See that chapter for more information.

Evasion: This is similar to a dodge, but less likely to succeed since an opposed roll is required. To evade another character, the moving character must make an opposed DEX roll (if on foot), or Horsemanship skill roll (if mounted), against the opponent's modified weapon skill.

If the moving character wins the opposed roll, he evades the attack and may move normally. If the enemy beats the evading roll he does damage normally, and the moving character stops where he is. The moving character may not fight or use his shield, since his intended action for the round was movement, not combat.

If both characters fail, or a tie results, both are losers in the round. In this case the evading character fails to move but is not hit.

If the evading character fumbles, he falls down. If on horseback, he falls off and take 1d6 damage from the fall.

Evasion is handled slightly differently depending on whether a character is attempting to move past an enemy, or is already engaged and is attempting to escape melee before he moves. Both follow the same rules given above, but escape requires an additional prerequisite: the evading character must have a *higher Movement Rate* than the opponent he is disengaging from, or escape is impossible.

FAMOUS KNIGHTS
Gawaine
Lamorak de Galis
Arthur Pendragon
Lancelot du Lac
Ywaine
le Chevalier au Lion
Brus Sans Pitie
Turquine
Mordred
CMGP

Also, moving out of engagement in melee is considered a tactical option, and the gamemaster may wish to circumscribe or forbid usage of tactics in combat in order to keep the game simple. See the notes in the "Combat" section of the chapter, below, under "Special Combat Tactics," particularly the "Escape Melee" tactic.

Encumbered characters who are evading suffer normal encumbrance and footing modifiers. Note that since this particular movement option involves Horsemanship as well as DEX, "footing" must include things like a broken saddle girth.

Jumping: A character may jump horizontally to cross a wide chasm or hole, or vertically up or down. Both types of jumps require DEX rolls.

A jump may have a modifier for difficulty assigned to it, based on the distance in yards and the encumbrance carried. This will make certain jumps impossible.

For simplicity, distance modifiers are based on a basic -3 modifier per yard of height or width. For example, a one yard high wall gives a -3 modifier to DEX for jumping, while a five yard wide ditch gives a -15 to characters trying to jump across. A professional moat has no modifier — it is too wide to ever jump, even for naked screaming Picts.

Encumbered characters who are jumping suffer normal modifiers to DEX.

Sneaking: Stealth and detection are complicated subjects, and the gamemaster should be ready to adjust or amplify the basic rules given here as needed.

If a character wishes to sneak up on someone, he makes a DEX roll. This is opposed by the Awareness of the victim, or by a guard, if any guards stand between the sneaker and his goal. Success in the opposed DEX roll indicates that the sneaker remained in cover, unless the Awareness roll of the victim or guard overcame the roll. Failure means that the hider revealed himself somehow. Of course, if the guard also failed his Awareness, he might still miss the noisy sneaker.

Unlike most DEX rolls, a critical success has an effect: a critical success while sneaking always succeeds unless the opponent also achieves a critical, in which case a tie results, meaning that the sneaker moves forward, but the victim is alerted that something suspicious is going on. A fumble while sneaking ensures detection.

Characters who are sneaking suffer a -5 modifier for metal armor. A +5 or better modifier should be gained if there is a lot of cover or noise, or the victim is engaged in an activity rather than devoting his attention to watching and listening for intruders.

Throwing Objects: To have your character throw a rope to a drowning person, or throw an unconscious enemy over the parapet, use a DEX roll. Success indicates that the objective was achieved, failure that it was not.

The gamemaster rules on the modifier, if any, which should be applied to the task. Throwing a heavy object at a tiny target far away might suffer a -10 modifier, while a throw from the top of a wall at a huge target below might gain a +10 modifier.

Encumbrance or footing do not hinder a throw unless the gamemaster feels the circumstances warrant a negative modifier.

If damage is intended to a target, a weapon skill such as Javelin should normally be used. However, if the gamemaster permits an attack throw using DEX, a critical success indicates that double damage is done, and a fumble might hit a nearby friend instead of the target.

Combat

Combat is perhaps the most important part of *Pendragon*. But even combat can involve roleplaying in this game. The usual enemies are other knights, honorable opponents and fellow nobles.

Combat and Roleplaying

The best combats in *Pendragon* are those with purpose, particularly in battle or adventure. Knights fight for reasons that go far beyond the crude concerns of unscrupulous mercenaries and plundering Saxons. Knights may even refuse combat on rare occasions, should loyalty dictate it.

In combat situations where love, honor, or another powerful passion is invoked, knights may be inspired to greatness and fight with superhuman strength and skill. See the "Ideals and Passions" chapter for more information.

Pomp and circumstance are also a part of combat, although blood may be drawn without ritual or preamble when characters are angry or impassioned. Miniature figures painted using heraldic coats of arms can add to the pageantry of the game during combat.

Much Glory can be gained from combat. Glory is included to ensure that combat is directed more towards roleplaying than towards basic concerns like experience and treasure. For example, the monsters and magical beings that your character will encounter are worth only moderate Glory by themselves (unless they are exceedingly rare and fearsome, like the dreaded basilisk). More important is the purpose behind their appearance in the scenario: the secret they hide, or the sorceress they guard, or the magical riddle that they will reveal to you if they are vanquished and spared. If such underlying mysteries are handled well by characters, in addition to simply defeating the creature, the gamemaster should award additional Glory.

For an example of how combat could be directly affected by roleplaying concerns, imagine meeting a young knight whose father is the hated enemy of your father. Do you challenge the knight or leave him be, knowing that his only crime is to be the son of *his* father? If you do fight, do you plan on a combat to the death or a fight "for love" of fighting? Once combat is joined and you are victorious, do you accept the lad's surrender chivalrously, or mock his humiliation before slaying him?

The best games of *Pendragon* include these emotional and intellectual decisions in much of the combat that occurs. This is why the combat rules below are relatively simple and flexible in com-

parison to many games. Gamemasters are free to add more detail to suit their personal preference.

Primary Combat Rules

These include the way damage is determined, the difference between damage that knocks someone down and that which causes actual injury, the concept of the melee round, and so forth.

Note that the rules for weapon skills and for handling injury are found in their own sections, under "Skills" and "Injury and Health."

Your Character's Damage Statistic

The Damage statistic on the character sheet tells you how much harm your character can do when he strikes with a normal knight's weapon, such as a heavy sword or a battleaxe. Damage = (SIZ + STR) divided by 6 = number of d6s rolled.

Weapons such as daggers or greatswords do 1d6 less or more damage than the Damage statistic (see the "Combat Skills" section for more information on weapons). Brawling weapons (fists, kicks, chairs) or shields do 2d6 less damage than the statistic, down to a minimum of 1d6.

Naturally other characters use the same rating to determine damage. Creatures using natural weapons use a slightly different formula that varies depending on size, magic, and other factors.

Knockdown

Knockdown is equal to a character's SIZ. Whenever a character receives a hit, through combat or some other means (such as riding into a tree limb), the damage must be compared to his SIZ. If the points of damage received are equal to or greater than SIZ, then the character has received a blow which sends him reeling for balance.

When unbalanced, the knight must receive a successful DEX roll, whether on foot or mounted. If the roll is successful then he does not fall down, but can continue fighting. If he falls and was mounted or on a wall or other high position, he takes damage from the fall.

When knocked down, the knight may struggle back to his feet without a DEX roll, taking a round to do so. But if attacked while getting up, he receives a -5 modifier to his weapon skill that round, while each opponent receives a +5. Unless knocked down again, he regains his normal footing at the beginning of the next round.

Whenever a character receives damage equal to twice or more than his knockdown, he does not even have a chance to make a DEX roll, but always is bashed down. No extra damage is taken.

Gamemaster creatures and even monsters must roll DEX just as knights do when their Knockdown statistic is equaled or exceeded.

Armor

Armor protects characters from weapon damage (but not from other damage, such as falling.) When a character is hit by a weapon but is wearing armor, check for knockdown, after which the value of the armor is subtracted from the total damage to yield a wound. See the "Injury and Health" section for more information on wounds.

As described above in the "Movement" section of the chapter, armor gives a negative modifier to DEX in many situations, climbing for example. In most cases this is simplified as -5 for all leather and -10 for all metal armor, as given in the table below. However, balance rolls suffer no modifier for armor, while armor worn while swimming gives a -1 modifier per point of armor protection. The gamemaster is free to adjust these modifiers to suit the logic of unusual situations, such as a fight in a muddy field during a rainstorm.

Magical armor, like the Armor of Honor described in the "Glory and Ambitions" chapter, is possible but should be very difficult to get. Magical armor may have certain limitations, which are up to the gamemaster to enforce.

Animals and monsters have "armor" equal to the thickness of their skin, subcutaneous muscle and fat, magical nature, and other factors. This armor gives no penalty to DEX (nor can it be removed and made into armor).

Chargers, the ordinary warhorses, may wear 1 point of armor in the form of a caparison. Destriers are strong enough to wear battle caparisons known as "trappers," worth 5 points of armor, without penalty to DEX or movement. Chainmail bardings are also possible, for destriers, but rare. See the "Warhorses" section below for more information.

In the table below partial plate armor is listed. This sophisticated form of armor is rare and extremely valuable, and is made only by a few extraordinary armorers in Britain.

Example: *Sir Ambrut has been struck for 17 points while wearing reinforced chainmail worth 12 points of protection. This is greater than his knockdown statistic, so he rolls unmodified DEX, successfully. Now armor is considered. After subtracting the value of the armor, only 5 points of damage actually penetrate the armor and injure the knight.*

The table below assumes complete suits of armor, including a helmet of the appropriate type. Padding is worn underneath armor, again varying with the type. The gamemaster will have to determine the protection and encumbrance of a partial suit of armor or the results of padding worn without armor.

Armor Table

armor	*protection*	*DEX modifier*
Clothing of all types	0-2*	none
Leather Armor	4	-5
Cuirboilli (hard, boiled leather)	6	-5
Norman Chainmail Armor	10	-10
Reinforced Chainmail Armor	12	-10
Partial Plate Armor	14	-10

* at gamemaster option

The Melee Round

The basic time measure for combat is the melee round. This is a short elastic unit of time — the time required to plan and perform one action in melee. Melee rounds continue in succession until everyone is done fighting, either through incapacitation, death, surrender, or flight.

In these rules, the limit of one "action" per round means one *category* of action, not one physical movement, per round. For example, combat is not a single blow — it is an exchange of attacks and parries, and of cautious waiting for an opening.

Sir Lancelot Adventures

Sir Lancelot continues a series of adventures. He has just finished speaking to a damosel.

And so Sir Lancelot and she departed, and then he rode in a deep forest two days and more, and had strait lodging. So on the third day he rode over a long bridge, and there start upon him suddenly a passing foul churl, and he smote his horse on the nose that he turned about, and asked him why he rode over that bridge without his license.

"Why should I not ride this way?" said Sir Lancelot, "I may not ride beside."

"Thou shalt not choose," said the churl, and lashed at him with a great club shod with iron.

Then Sir Lancelot drew his sword and put the stroke aback, and clave his head unto the paps.

At the end of the bridge was a fair village, and all the people, men and women, cried on Sir Lancelot, and said, "a worse deed didst thou never for thyself, for thou hast slain the chief porter of our castle."

Sir Lancelot let them say what they would, and straight he went into the castle; and when he came into the castle he alit, and tied his horse to a ring on the wall, and there he saw a fair green court, and thither he dressed him, for there him thought was a fair place to fight in. So he looked about, and saw much people in doors and windows that said, "Fair knight, thou art unhappy."

Anon withal came there upon him two great giants, well armed all save the heads, with two horrible clubs in their hands. Sir Lancelot put his shield afore him and put the stroke away of the one giant, and with his sword he clave his head asunder. When his fellow saw that, he ran away as he were wood, for fear of the horrible strokes, and Lancelot after him with all his might, and smote him on the shoulder, and clave him to the navel.

Then Sir Lancelot went into the hall, and there came after him three score ladies and damosels, and all kneeled unto him, and thanked God and him of their deliverance.

— Malory VI, 10, and VI, 11

In game terms, Sir Lancelot achieved several critical successes with his Sword skill here. The death of the second giant also shows an example of a fumbled Valorous roll, failed Escape Melee tactic, attack from behind, and the consequences.

The limit of one action per melee round is a loose one, with several apparent exceptions. For example, a character whose Knockdown statistic is exceeded must make a balance roll that round, which might be considered a second category of action. Defining balance as a part of routine combat maneuvering makes it clear that the limit is still valid.

The point of the one action limit is simply to keep the game moving. Players and gamemaster must cooperate or the game will be bogged down in pointless minutia.

Melee Round Procedure

Pendragon uses the following personal combat system to determine the winners and losers of a fight. Each time combat is joined the following procedure should be followed:

1. Determination Phase
2. Resolution Phase
3. Winner's Phase
4. Loser's Phase
5. Movement Phase

1. Determination Phase

All combatants state what they intend doing this round, including the weapon they will use. Targets and opponents are named. The gamemaster decides whether the players or their gamemaster-run opponents first make their statements of intent.

Characters can fight, or do something else, as listed below under "Actions Permitted in Melee." Generally, characters can fight or move, not both. Lance charges are exceptional: knights then may both move and fight.

- If the optional list of combat tactics is in use (see below), the choice of tactic, if any, must be stated out loud, or written down secretly if necessary.
- Enemies within a yard of each other are engaged, and need not move to fight. Otherwise movement must take place before combat can be resolved.
- If the gamemaster permits combat in combination with another action, characters attempting such combat suffer -5/+5 reflexive modifiers to weapon skills (modifiers where one combatant has a negative modifier and the opponent a positive modifier), or other penalties as appropriate.

2. Resolution Phase

Both combatants roll their respective modified weapon skills, using opposed resolution. The rolled number, considering any increases due to values over 20, should be announced out loud by gamemaster and player. The results leave a winner and a loser, or two losers. In

❊ Game Mechanics: Questions and Answers ❊

Question. *"The crit rules don't make sense. My character and another guy's were both using their Singing skills to charm a lady. My character is excellent at Singing, and I succeeded with a roll of 16, but the other character got lucky and rolled an 5, which is a crit, since his character's Singing is only 5. The gamemaster said he won the contest. Why does a lousy roll of 5 beat a 16, which is more than three times as good?"*

Answer. A critical success = a successful roll of 20. Even if a character has a miserable skill of 1, if he is lucky enough to roll a 1, he does as well as Sir Gawaine or Sir Lancelot can do. Remember that this will only happen 5% of the time. The idea is to give even weak characters a chance at greatness. It proved to be frustrating for players to never be able to do as well as more powerful characters, thus the rule.

Q. *"The players in my campaign keep asking for experience checks even when they hit the enemy just once or twice during a fight. I feel they should have to work for their checks a lot more, but the rules seem vague about how many successes they need for a check. Should I be more generous?"*

A. The decision is yours. In *Pendragon* the gamemaster is king. The rules deliberately leave interpretation in your hands. Go with your own feelings about experience, and remind your players that their characters can train a d6 worth every winter.

Q. *"My character was attacked by three bandits and two got +10 modifiers, even though I wasn't surprised or knocked down. This doesn't seem fair.*

A. The rules leave modifiers up to the gamemaster in specific situations. The bandits do seem to have gotten a good deal, but your gamemaster apparently felt that they had your character in a bind. If you don't like the interpretations you're getting, set a good example instead of complaining: offer to be the gamemaster yourself and show people how you think modifiers should be handled.

Q. *"The rules on healing make it impossible to have combat — when my character gets hit he always takes weeks and weeks to heal and misses the rest of the scenario. How can you design a game where the characters are knights and then make fighting no fun?"*

A. The combat and healing rules are certainly brutally realistic in terms of the lingering effects of injury. But the game has to be faithful to the literature, or why bother calling it *Pendragon?* Next time, ask your gamemaster if you can stay with the rest of the party even though you need Chirurgery. Your character may get worse, or even die, due to the aggravation rules, but at least you'll be involved in the scenario, and you can still fight if you have to.

Regarding healing times, I'll bet your character has a low CON and a low STR, so that his healing rate is poor. I'll also bet he has inferior armor. Spend a couple of years training up your character's CON instead of his skills, and buy, beg, borrow, or steal some better armor!

addition, ties, critical success, and fumbles have special meaning in combat.

If both fighters roll the same number, and both are successful, then both are losers. If one person's weapon is a sword and the other's is not, the sword breaks the other weapon.

If both fighters fail to make their success rolls, then both missed that round and both are losers. They can try again next round, or try something else.

A fumble means one of two things: either that the fighter dropped his weapon (if it was a sword) or that his weapon broke (if it was any other weapon). Either way the fighter must rearm himself to strike back. If fighting with a two-handed weapon, he is completely disarmed and must dodge, rearm, or run away. However, most weapons are used one-handed, with a shield. In that case, to block incoming blows with the shield, the character who fumbled may still make the roll of the weapon lost, though he cannot damage his opponent.

- A roll of 1 on d20, before any increase due to values over 20, is important if a character is using a flail or warflail. See the "Weapon Skills" section below.

3. Winner's Phase

The winner rolls his damage done. He may also receive a check for experience in the weapon used, with gamemaster approval (unless he already has such a check).

4. Loser's Phase

The loser first checks for knockdown, rolling DEX if unbalanced. If the total damage is equal to or greater than twice his knockdown, the loser cannot attempt the DEX roll. He is simply knocked down, or off his horse. See the DEX rolls section of the "Movement" section, above, for more information.

If the loser received a successful skill roll, and if he was using a one-handed weapon and shield, then he adds 6 points of shield protection to his armor that round. If he did not receive a successful skill roll, he does not gain the benefit of his shield.

Then he receives his damage, subtracting any protection gained from his armor, shield, and magical protection (such as the Armor of Honor) from the damage the opponent did. Any points greater than the armor are recorded under "Wounds" on the character sheet, and the number is then subtracted from current hit points to leave a revised number. The damage amount should be compared with CON for possible Major Wounds, and current hit points should be compared with the Unconscious statistic to see if the character has dropped below the threshold and collapsed. See the "Injury and Health" section below for more information.

- A character who falls unconscious during combat, due to a Major Wound or many small wounds, may still attempt a DEX roll if on horseback or balancing on a wall. Success indicates a gentle fall that does less or no damage, at the gamemaster's discretion. The DEX roll here is an involuntary reaction to years of training, and has nothing to do with consciousness or awareness.

5. Movement Phase

Characters who did not fight may move. Everyone moves their first yard of movement at once, then moves the second, third, and so on. Riders can move up to their horse's Movement Rate this way (a horse gives a great advantage in melee movement).

Characters do not have to move their whole rate but, if they stop, they cannot add the distance later in the phase.

Note that movement is basically for the purposes of determining whether one character has approached or catches another. Thus a character needing to walk 30 yards would take ten rounds to do so, given a Movement Rate of 3. Complicated issues such as facing and engaged initiative are not normally concerns during movement. Nor are miniature figures essential as long as issues like facing are left out.

- When characters move within one yard of enemies, evasion may be necessary for movement to continue. Once within this distance, combat becomes possible.

- A character cannot move full Movement Rate and initiate an attack unless the attack is a lance charge.

- Characters may wish to move a portion of their Movement Rate and then attack an enemy. This is a tricky issue, since in theory extra time is available in the round if partial movement occurs. The gamemaster will have to make a decision regarding his approach to partial movement and combat.

  The issue of partial movement and combat is handled here by making it one of many optional combined actions. These are possible options in a round only if the player is willing to take a penalty modifier. See the "Combined Actions" section below.

- Characters may wish to move at an increased speed. For simplicity's sake, it's best to restrict running or sprinting (cantering or galloping for horses) while characters are in close combat. If the gamemaster chooses to permit different rates during melee, characters moving at different rates (for example, one character is walking while another sprints) still move yard by yard. The gamemaster will have to determine whether interception or other important events occur between characters moving at different rates, using common sense.

Movement Example: *Sir Ambrut is riding his charger into a melee. He states in the Determination Phase that he will run down an enemy knight on foot some twenty yards away. Both characters move three yards (the enemy knight's Movement Rate), a yard at a time, after which the knight can move no further. Ambrut moves five more yards, using the horse's Movement Rate of 8, but still does not come within the one yard distance needed to attack, so no combat takes place.*

Actions Permitted In Melee

Action in melee includes the following standard actions. Other actions are certainly possible, and the gamemaster should not be too formal in defining what an action is.

Combined actions are not normally allowed, although a few borderline or arguable cases exist. For example, fighting several opponents might be considered multiple actions. Overtly combined actions should either not be permitted, or should entail a penalty. Gamemaster interpretation will, as always, be necessary.

A list of combined actions is provided below for those characters who wish to perform them while suffering a negative or reflexive modifer.

Standard Actions

- Exchange blows with one or more opponents using opposed resolution, dividing weapon skill among multiple opponents or ignoring them as desired.

- Attack a surprised or helpless enemy, or one ignoring your attack, with an unopposed weapon roll.

- Move full Movement Rate on foot or on horse. This may be at a run (canter for horses) or even a sprint (gallop), giving a x2 or x3 multiplier to Movement Rate, if the gamemaster permits.

- Move a portion of the Movement Rate and stop, possibly adjacent to an enemy. No further action.

- Move full Movement Rate on horse and make a lance charge during movement. Rapid movement may be permitted by the gamemaster during a a lance charge.

- Make a squire roll to get help or a new weapon. If more than one squire is available, multiple rolls may be made as one action. See below for the Squire Roll definition.

- Mount or dismount a horse.

- Perform a maneuver on horseback (turn around, leap a fence, etc.). A Horsemanship roll may be required.

- React to the appearance of a terrifying monster. A Valorous roll will be required, with a modifier if appropriate.

Brus Sans Pitie

- Give commands to followers.

- Engage in a brief conversation with a comrade.

- Rearm with a new weapon or a shield.

- Get up from the ground after a fall, even while wearing heavy armor.

- Get up from the ground while fighting, suffering a reflexive modifier of -5/+5 that round to character and opponent weapon skills.

- Fire an arrow from a bow or light crossbow and reload. A skill roll will be needed, with a modifier for range and target if necessary.

- Exchange blows with one or more opponents, from a height disadvantage, incurring a reflexive modifier for height of -5 to the lower combatant and +5 to the higher.

- Reload a medium crossbow.

- Scrutinize the surroundings, using Awareness or Hunting skill.

- Attempt a combat tactic such as Double Feint in melee (tactics are optional: see below).

- Attempt to dodge rather than fight. A DEX roll will be needed.

Combined Actions (Optional)

If the gamemaster approves, characters may combine actions, usually with a substantial penalty. Alternatively, gamemasters may simply refuse to permit multiple actions in order to keep the game simple.

Normally a negative modifier should be applied to any skills used in a multiple-action round. If combat is one of the

actions, a reflexive modifier should be applied. That is, a negative modifier to weapon skill must be imposed on the character attempting combined actions, while opponent(s) gain a positive modifier.

Here are some examples of combined or multiple actions (many others are possible).

- Move a portion of the Movement Rate and fight. A reflexive -5/+5 modifier should be applied to the moving and stationary combatants. If both moved, both suffer a -5 modifier.
- Mount or dismount a horse while giving commands. A DEX roll might be required, with failure indicated that the horse was not mounted, and a fumble indicating a fall with 1d6 damage.
- Scrutinize the surroundings with an Awareness roll while dodging: -5 modifiers to DEX and Awareness (in addition to the usual modifiers for dodging) should be applied.
- Arm or rearm while fighting, suffering a reflexive modifier of -5/+5 that round to character/opponent weapons skills.
- Climb over a wall while fighting, with a height disadvantage, suffering a reflexive modifier of -10/+10 that round to weapon skills (-5 for combining movement and combat, plus another -5 for the height difference).

Combat Modifiers

Some conditions may affect the skill of the fighters. These are, as always, applied to the weapon skill value, not the die roll.

Difficulty Seeing: In darkness, fog, smoke, or other similar conditions, characters' weapon skills are reduced by -10, unless they make their Awareness roll that round (an exception to the "one action per round" rule). Only the wildest Picts are exempt from this requirement, since they normally move about at night.

Fatigue and Minor Wounds: In general, combat in *Pendragon* is over fast enough that fatigue and minor wounds do not have a chance to overcome adrenalin and valor. However, in the literature knights are sometimes too exhausted and wounded to continue their fight, and agree to rest for an hour or so before continuing. The Major Wound and Unconscious rules insure that characters will collapse if they fight on after serious injury, rather than continuing until all hit points are lost. But minor injuries and fatigue are not covered, in order to keep the game simple and fast-moving.

The gamemaster must always determine if a combat modifier for fatigue and minor wounds is necessary and appropriate, and normally it should be kept to -5. For example, if a knight must fight three or more combats without rest, or must fight after a whole day's forced march, fatigue and minor injury should probably modify the exhausted knight's skill by -5.

If a single fight lasts for ten or more melee rounds, fatigue should reduce *both* combatants' skills, possibly leading to fumbles, mutual failed rolls, etc. Such extended combats will usually occur only between Extraordinary knights with very high weapon skills, or between two knights using the optional Defense tactic.

Height Advantage (horse vs. foot, man on wall vs. man climbing over, etc.): Height produces a reflexive combat modifier of -5/+5. If the foe is above you: -5, foe below: +5. When opponents are separated by less than six feet of height this modifier is used; otherwise the combatants are too far apart to engage in melee.

This includes situations where one character is mounted and the other afoot, or when one character is on a ladder and the other above him on a wall, or one has fallen on the ground and the other is standing, or when a character climbs a steep castle stairwell while fighting a defender above. The gamemaster may encounter other situations as well.

Immobilized: Characters in combat that are grappled, partially tied up, stuck in quicksand, or otherwise unable to move properly suffer a reflexive combat modifier of -10/+10.

Lance Charge Modifier: The lance charge gives a +5 combat modifier against all weapons except the great spear and another lance charge. Remember that a lance used without charging uses the Spear skill.

Multiple Actions: Characters attempting combat in combination with another action such as partial movement incur a reflexive combat modifier of -5/+5, assuming the gamemaster permits such action. The lance charge is the only exception.

Surprised: +5 combat modifier to attacker. A foe surprised includes those attacked from behind, or without warning. The attack is always unopposed, with this modifier. It is dishonorable to attack in this manner (see the "Ideals and Passions" chapter for more information on Honor).

Unencumbered: Knights not wearing armor, and carrying items no heavier than a weapon and a shield, gain a combat modifier of +5. Characters like bandits or Picts who are untrained in the wearing of armor do not gain this modifier.

Warhorses

Horses are essential vehicles for riders in *Pendragon*. They give many advantages in combat. A knight without a horse is just a man! Future supplements will contain additional rules for warhorses that will further enhance their interest.

Your Stable

The "Horses" area on the character sheet includes space for information about five horses from your character's stable, including the squire's horse. Your character's best warhorse gets space for most important information, including armor, a space for an attack skill using hooves or bites, and damage for such attacks (see below). Other horses have space only for their type and their CON.

Your character's best warhorse is by far the most important of your stable. This horse may be nothing but a standard charger, easily replaced, or he may be a mighty destrier, perhaps a gift from a grateful lord. Either way, statistics are as noted in the "Characters and Creatures" chapter. Prices are as noted in the "Wealth" chapter.

Lance Charge

A lance charge gains the initiative over lesser weapons. It also is the only attack that must always be made while moving in *Pendragon*. As already noted above, if

a lance charge is made against any other weapon except another lance charge or a great spear, the charging knight gets a +5 modifier to his Lance skill.

In a lance charge the horse's Damage statistic is used, not the rider's. The horse must move at least 10 yards in a straight line to build up enough speed for lance charge damage, although the gamemaster should not insist that each yard's movement be charted and plotted before combat takes place.

Average horse Damages are as follows: Rouncy = 4d6; Charger = 6d6; Destrier = 8d6. Note that these stastistics are different from most creatures in the game. They assume that the horse's weight is put behind the attack of a heavy steel-headed spear. So hoof or biting damage is reduced from these numbers.

Against Unmounted Foes

A mounted man fighting an unmounted one always gets a +5 to his weapon skill while the footman gets -5 unless the footman is armed with a great spear or halberd. In the latter case, there is no penalty for the footman, but still +5 for the mounted man.

Fast Melee Movement

A horse moves faster than any man in melee. A very fast horse (Movement Rate 10 or more) may gallop 30 yards in a round, normally in a straight line. The gamemaster should require a Horsemanship roll if any turns or tricky maneuvers are executed. Failure indicates that you stop moving where you are, while a fumble means that the rider falls off.

Two-handed Weapons on Horseback

No two-handed weapons may ever be used from horseback in this game. Grapple may be attempted, since it is used in the literature from horseback, but gamemasters should apply common sense to the results.

Destriers and Magical Horses

In general, only a banneret or higher-ranking noble can easily marshal the influence and funds necessary to obtain a destrier, the huge new breed of warhorse now coming into Britain. As sons of vassal knights, some lucky player characters will receive a destrier from their family as part of character generation (see the Luck Benefits Table). Most player knights can only hope to receive such priceless beasts as rewards for valor or loyalty from a grateful lord. Alternatively, they may fight and defeat the owner of a destrier, who should usually be a Famous or even Extraordinary knight.

Magical horses are even more rare than destriers, and may have unique features, even wings. Or they may be simply faster and more beautiful than ordinary steeds. The "Characters and Creatures" chapter lists several magical horses that serve as examples. As always, the gamemaster is in charge of all things involving magic.

Attack-Trained Horses

At some stage in the campaign the gamemaster may allow player knights to use horses trained to fight. Destriers and chargers are normally the only animals ever trained, and few attack-trained steeds are for sale with such training.

The rules for attack-trained horses are found in the "Characters and Creatures" chapter.

Horse Armor

The basic caparison worn by most warhorses, perhaps bearing the arms of the owner, is worth 1 point of armor. Actual armor worn by horses is usually called barding. Heavy caparisons known as trappers are also possible, and more commonly available than barding.

Only a destrier can bear armor beyond the basic caparison. Destriers are, by definition, the only horses which are big and strong enough to bear an armored rider and their own armor as well. Characters may be able to locate destriers and equip them with trappers, but barding is an extremely rare commodity in *Pendragon*, primarily because destriers are also rare and thus demand is negligible. Destriers have only begun to be seen in Britain, so only the gamemaster may release barding into the game. Chainmail barding should be particularly rare, made only in the private smithy of a duke or king, and not for sale.

Caparisons, trappers, and barding all work exactly as human armor does. Even barding rarely provides more than 10 points of protection. This includes chain mail, padding, and quilted caparison.

Characters may insist on equipping chargers or even lesser horses with armor, but gamemasters should severely reduce an overburdened mount's DEX and Movement Rate.

Horse Armor Table

type	*protection*	*horse*
Normal Caparison	1	any
Trapper	5	destrier
Light barding	8	destrier
Chainmail barding	10	destrier

Other Combat Notes

Blunt Weapons and Withheld Blows

During a tournament a knight may use blunt, or "rebated," weapons. Such weapons strike with force, but without the damage a sharp edge would wreak.

Roll damage and figure for knockdown as usual. However, blunt weapons do no damage at all unless a critical success is rolled. A critical success for a blunted weapon does normal damage, not the double damage of a real weapon. This damage is treated as normal in every way, may penetrate armor, and so on.

Combatants may voluntarily hold back the force of their hit through the use of a withheld blow. In such cases the attack is exactly the same as a blunt weapon, above. Blows are often withheld in tournaments instead of rebating a good weapon. A critical success does normal damage, regardless of the intent of the attacker.

Broken or Dropped Weapons

Weapons broken in combat cannot be fixed. New ones must be obtained at normal cost, or captured from an enemy. All weapons except swords and great swords break in combat when the fighter fumbles. Swords and great swords are dropped instead, and can be recovered in one melee round, even if the fighter is on horseback, for the weapon is normally tied to the knight's wrist or belt by a cord. Finally, remember that a sword always breaks a non-sword if both get the same roll in combat.

Combat Against Creatures

In general, combat against creatures follows normal rules. For example, a creature who achieves a critical success does double damage. However, creatures do

not suffer broken weapons upon fumbles or ties, a significant benefit. On the other hand, they may not use shields, so gain no benefit from partial success.

Many creatures in *Pendragon* have special abilities in combat to reflect their unique and magical characteristics. For example, the lion is permitted two attacks in a single round, and is given an armor value of 10 to reflect his legendary prowess. A boar fights for a round after death (zero or negative hit points). A griffin is so fearsome that opponents are required to make a Valorous roll before engaging it in combat, with a -5 modifier.

These rules are specific to the listed creatures, and may not be gained by player characters.

Creatures should normally not be able use the optional tactics listed in this section. They may dodge as needed.

Further rules for creatures and monsters are found in the "Characters and Creatures" chapter.

Fighting Without Armor

Knights are trained to fight wearing a full set of heavy armor covering all areas of the body. Their lifelong training allows them to fight at full capacity even though an ordinary man would be badly encumbered by the weight. The contrary is also true: whenever a knight fights without any leather or metal armor, he gets a +5 modifier to his weapon skill, simulating his ability to maneuver and attack better and faster without the weight and encumbrance of armor.

A sword and shield, or even a two-handed weapon like a halberd, may be used without armor, and the +5 modifier is still gained.

Characters that do not normally wear armor during training and warfare do not get the +5 modifier. Thus the skill of Picts, bandits, rebellious peasants, or other non-knights is unmodified.

The Movement Rate of unencumbered characters is increased by +2. See the "Movement" section of this chapter for more information.

Finally, gamemasters may wish to give a +5 modifier to Awareness when characters wear no armor, to simulate the increased sensitivity gained when the heavy, confining helmet of a knight is removed. Again, characters who normally do not wear heavy armor gain no modifier.

Jousting Lances

Jousting lances break very easily. They break any time that an odd number is rolled on d20, as well as on a fumble.

Damage is handled differently from other combat. In an opposed joust, the loser is simply knocked from his horse. No damage is rolled, and no chance for a DEX roll is allowed. The loser takes 1d6 from the fall, but no other damage. A critical success with a jousting lance, however, does normal horse damage as if it was a real strike with a real spear. Damage in this special case is resolved normally (check for knockdown, wounds, etc.) Such an accident is seen as unavoidable in the sport, and sometimes good knights are killed this way.

A fumbled roll indicates that the jouster did something terribly wrong, like striking his foe's horse, falling without being struck, or having the saddle girths break, as well as uselessly breaking his lance.

Multiple Opponents

Characters may be attacked by more than one opponent at a time. Up to three may do so on foot, or two if everyone is mounted. Defenders may fight against as many attackers as they wish, dividing their weapon skill among them. The skills must be rolled separately on the resolution rolls. Unopposed opponents make unopposed resolution rolls.

Multiple attacks may not be made by one character, although some unusual creatures are permitted multiple attacks.

Shield

The shield normally used in *Pendragon* is a small or medium-sized knight's shield, pointed at the bottom. Larger, heavier shields such as those born by the ancient Romans are not used.

The shield may be used in conjunction with any one-handed weapon skill, but not with two-handed weapons. It may also be used while re-arming, letting the user oppose an attack but not do damage. It gives 6 points of armor protection to the loser of an opposed resolution if his roll was a partial success (successful though outclassed by his opponent's roll).

If a knight has been disarmed of weapons, but still has his shield, he may use the special tactic of Defense, explained below, but no damage is done, unless the gamemaster wishes to permit shield attacks.

For shield attacks, reduce the character's damage by two dice and halve the character's best one-handed weapon skill for determining skill value. For example, a character with a Damage statistic of 5d6 and a Sword skill of 21 would do 3d6 with his shield, using a skill value of 11. 1d6 is the minimum amount of damage that a character's damage can be reduced to when using a shield.

Also note that a shield attacker cannot use other weapons simultaneously, or make two-handed attacks. He may not use tactical options without gamemaster approval.

Two-Handed Weapons

Two-handed weapons are longer than usual, but only the great spear and halberd are long enough to alter the disadvantage which footmen have fighting mounted men.

Two-handed weapons all do an additional +1d6 damage when they hit, except for the great spear, which does normal damage.

When the weapon is dropped or broken by a fumble, two-handed weapon users cannot try to parry with their shield, since they do not have it in use. They may instead dodge or run away, or receive an unopposed attack while they rearm (see the "Multiple Actions" section above, however).

Unopposed Two-Handed Strikes

It is possible to wield any one-handed weapon with two hands to cause extra damage, even though it is normally used one-handed with a shield. This can only be done when unopposed, and in that case the attack skill is still the same but gets an extra 1d6 damage added. Any shield or item held in the other hand must be dropped first.

Unopposed two-handed attacks may be done only against foes who do not know the attacker is there (perhaps a surprise attack from behind) or when the defender cannot protect himself (perhaps because he is unconscious, restrained, or asleep). In both these cases a modifier may be applied, but this is due to the circumstances, not because the weapon is used two-handed.

Special Combat Tactics

Tactics allow more direct player and gamemaster involvement in the fortunes of combat. These tactics are optional, not mandatory. The gamemaster is in charge of whether to permit special combat tactics in any specific situation.

If players have a problem deciding on a tactic to use, or two player knights fight one another, the tactic used should be written down beforehand.

Gamemasters may wish to insist that, once chosen, a tactic cannot be changed; the character must fight for as many rounds as necessary using whatever tactic was first selected.

Dodging is *not* considered a special combat tactic and may always be attempted. See the "Movement" section of the chapter.

Defense

Knights may choose to fight a defensive combat. This is especially useful when a knight is beset by multiple enemies and needs to divide his defense, but it can also be used against a single foe.

Many knights use this tactic to avoid injury, resulting in the prolonged combats described in Arthurian literature. No Honor is lost for this option, nor is Glory reduced for victory.

During the Declaration Phase the player declares that his knight is going to defend. He gains +10 to his weapon skill for purposes of combat that round, the skill may be divided, and the player rolls normally.

Although the character may be the winner in the opposed roll, no hit occurs unless the player rolls a critical success, in which case the damage is calculated as regular damage, not double damage.

Partial successes, failures, fumbles, and ties have normal results in the opposed resolution. Obviously the tactic is less useful without a shield.

If two characters both opt to Defend, both gain the +10 modifier and damage is done only if one character wins with a critical success. Such combats may last for hours of game time.

If a character using the Defend tactic is attacked by a character using the Berserker tactic (see below) the two tactics cancel each other out. A normal opposed resolution without modifiers due to tactics takes place.

Berserker Attack

Combatants may make an all-out, no-defense attack, known among the northerners as a *berserk* attack. Sir Turquine is feared for his use of the Berserker Attack.

The user of the tactic must state the intent to do so in the Declaration Phase of the combat round.

In a berserker attack, the enemy takes his attack first, unopposed. If he hits, he does damage normally. If the berserker is conscious and on his feet, he then gets an attack with a +10 to his weapon skill, unopposed. Carnage is guaranteed.

In a fight between two berserkers, the character with the highest Movement Rate attacks first. If Movement Rates are the same, the highest DEX goes first. Both attacks are unopposed.

Escape Melee

To escape melee once engaged in combat, a character must attempt an Evade roll, opposing modified DEX to the enemy's weapons skill, as described in the "Movement" chapter. However, this tactic can only be used successfully if a character's Movement Rate is *higher* than the opponent's. If his Movement Rate is equal to or lower than the opponent, he can not escape by running away and is automatically hit (a character that panics due to a fumbled Valor roll may attempt to flee anyway, as often happens in battle).

If multiple opponents are involved, this tactic cannot be used at all unless the gamemaster approves. Each opponent must be rolled against separately.

If both opponents opt to Escape Melee, they both flee without rolls.

Double Feint

This agile tactic confuses the opponent and permits a strike at an unarmored or vulnerable area of the body. Sir Lamorak is feared for his use of the Double Feint. The Picts are also effective with this tactic.

The Double Feint cannot be used with the spear or lance in a mounted charge, or with the great spear or halberd versus cavalry charges. The flail and warflail are also unsuitable weapons for a Double Feint.

During the Determination Phase the player declares that his knight is going to attempt a Double Feint. Before making the usual opposed roll, the character must attempt a DEX roll, as modified by armor, load carried, footing, etc. The user may be mounted, but still suffers the modifier to DEX. See the "Movement" section, above.

A successful DEX roll indicates that, should damage be done in the subsequent opposed roll by the user, the opponent's armor is halved. The user has managed to maneuver so that the opponent's armpit, groin, or other vulnerable area is hit. If the opponent is a creature, it is hit in its soft underbelly or other less armored zone.

If the DEX roll is a critical success, all armor is ignored. The victim is hit in the eyeslit of his helmet, or other unarmored location.

A failed DEX roll indicates that the tactic fails, and that the character does no damage that round (the weapon hits thin air). All other rules are still in effect, so the opponent may still lose; but the user still does no damage due to his failed tactic.

A fumbled DEX roll indicates that the character broke or dropped his weapon (and it fell too far away to just pick up the next round).

If the victim of a Double Feint is unarmored, the result of a DEX success is to give the user a +5 modifier to weapon skill for the subsequent opposed resolution. A critical success gives a +10 modifier.

The only protection against a successful Double Feint is a magical effect that covers the entire body, such as the Armor of Honor (gained by chivalrous knights) or magical Pictish tattoos. The gamemaster may determine other protective magical effects that work. The magical armor of a creature like a lion or griffin is not considered to cover the entire body.

If two characters attempt Double Feints, both roll DEX and both may receive the benefits of the tactic in the subsequent opposed roll.

Skills

CHARACTER ADVANCEMENT in *Pendragon* is partially measured by the increase of your character's skills. Skills express the social and physical activities popular in the Arthurian mythos. No knight is expected to master all or most of the possible skills.

Improving Skills

The character sheet lists the starting values for every ordinary skill and for the standard combat skills of the Cymric culture in parentheses to the right of the skill's name. Non-standard weapon skills like Great Axe are not printed, and start with a value of 0. Starting values may be increased during the Winter Phase of the game.

The blanks on the character sheet permit you to write in ordinary skills of your own devising, or special skills from *Pendragon* supplements like *Knights Adventurous*. The blanks under combat skills permit you to write in the non-standard weapon skills of your choice.

Skills in *Pendragon* can be increased in many ways. In the game a character may raise a skill value by training with a teacher, by diligent practice on his own, by first-hand experience in the field, by means of a major increase in self-confidence and reputation, or by magic.

All these improvements occur during the Winter Phase (see the "Winter Phase" section below). Experience is dealt with during the "Experience Check Rolls" step of the phase. The training of skills is handled in the "Training and Practice" step. The effects of self-confidence and heroic reputation are simulated using the Glory system, which involves two steps during the Winter Phase: "Compute Glory" and "Add Bonus Points."

The gamemaster must handle any magical skill increases that might occur during his scenarios (there should be a prerequisite action, a risk of unexpected side effects, or a corresponding penalty involved in any magical increases of a skill).

Note that Glory is not experience. Characters may be very skilled, due to the experience check system, while possessing only modest Glory. Of course, such characters will usually be bandits, squires, or sergeants, not knights.

Part of the fun in the game is seeing your character increase in skill. Most players focus on a half-dozen or less skills that they will increase through all the methods listed above, over several decades of game time. Using training and practice these skills are gradually raised to a value of 20. Then experience checks and Glory are used to raise each skill into the realm of heroic mastery.

Skill Categories and Special Types

Skills in *Pendragon* are divided into two broad categories: *ordinary* skills, which include a wide range of different skills useful in various circumstances, and *combat* skills, the crucial military skills that are the traditional area of expertise for knights. The two categories are listed in two separate areas on the character sheet, and described in separate parts of this section.

Skills also include several special types. Many skills are defined in *Pendragon*, but some are unusual in one way or another. These types are indicated in the individual skill descriptions that follow these general rules, and are defined here:

Optional Skills: Optional skills are any skills not essential to knighthood. Some players will wish to run characters with skills rarely mentioned in traditional Arthurian romances, such as Boating. For these players, optional skills are given.

Blank spaces have been provided on the character sheet, allowing more optional skills to be entered in by hand. The gamemaster is in charge of deciding which, if any, optional skills are in use in his adventure or campaign. He must also provide a written skill definition for any new skill to the players.

Non-knightly Skills are those which are often used in the game, but not by knights. The extreme example is Industry, the making of valuable items, which is normal for women or tradesmen, but which will cost a knight his title if he engages in it.

Knowledge Skills: Some skills are mentioned in the descriptions as Knowledge skills. These include knowledge normally associated with social classes, such as Courtesy (noble customs), Folk Lore (peasant customs), Religion (clerical or druidic customs); and with specialized practices, such as Romance or Tourney. These are bodies of information which require special knowledge to execute properly. The skill includes the what, when, where, why, and how of these activities. Success in a Knowledge skill does not always indicate that the knight *did* something, but that he knew or recognized something important or useful.

Sometimes a player will know something related to one of the Knowledge skills, but will be unable to make a successful die roll. In such cases the gamemaster should accept the fact that the player, and thus the character, knows the fact being requested: remember that there is no intelligence statistic in this game. He may reward the knowledge by awarding an experience check to the character.

Skills Needed for Knighthood: Certain skills are marked here and on the character sheet with a dagger (†). These are the skills considered to be essential to the duties of knighthood, mostly combat skills.

A note on non-standard characters: if the gamemaster is permitting non-knight player characters in his campaign, and your character is a squire or sergeant hoping to attain knighthood, it will be useful to practice and train in these skills. A minimum value of 10 will be needed in each daggered skill, plus a 10 in two ordinary (non-combat) skills of your own choice, such as Awareness. Before admitting a worthy sergeant or squire to knighthood, an experienced knight will administer tests to make sure minimum skill qualifications are met. Certain martial traits and passions such as Loyalty will also be tested: see the "Ideals and Passion" chapter for more information.

Aspects of Skill Use

Success or Failure

Success or failure with skills is resolved using normal resolution rolls. Most skills

may be used in unopposed resolution. Sometimes they are used in opposition against each other, in contests or challenges. Modifiers may be applied to any of these resolutions.

The results of a critical success or fumble with an ordinary skill are given in the individual skill descriptions below when significant. Otherwise the gamemaster describes the results, based on the situation. The "Combat Skills" section gives the results of criticals and fumbles for combat skills.

Glory from Skills

Situations where Glory could result from a successful use of the skill in question are mentioned briefly in most skill descriptions. Other situations worthy of Glory will doubtless occur to gamemaster and players.

Success with any skill may gain the character ordinary Glory, normally 10 points, at the gamemaster's option. The usual requirement is that the success must have contributed to the player characters' goals in the scenario. A critical success is worth double the ordinary award; 20 Glory. Successes in the court of a king double the basic skill awards. A heroic use of a skill, perhaps to save a character's life, might gain 100 Glory. This should be rare.

Combat skills are a special case, and may permit great Glory to be gained under appropriate circumstances. However, Glory for success in combat is based upon victory, not particular skill rolls. After all, killing a giant should gain Glory even if the character used cunning rather than any particular skill. The gamemaster will adjust the award to suit the circumstances as he sees fit.

Note that combats "for love" or victories gained by using missile weapons gain only 10% of normal Glory.

Skills and Honor

The Honor passion reflects your character's

Merlin the magician

code of behavior and reputation as a knight. Fumbled or failed skill rolls do not affect your character's Honor value: Honor cannot be lost simply because of a bad die roll. The penalty for a fumbled skill roll is the social embarrassment suffered, which the gamemaster must keep to an appropriate level. Honor is lost only due to character actions.

Certain situations might occur in which gamemasters could feel justified in subtracting Honor because a skill was used unwisely. For example, causing harm to another character through failure or fumble in a skill might lose the character a point of Honor if another character with a better skill value was available, and the failing character insisted taking responsibility for the task anyway. The gamemaster is always the final arbiter in such difficult situations. See the "Ideals and Passions" chapter for more on Honor.

Ordinary Skills

Awareness

This skill measures the knight's awareness of all activity in his surroundings, using both the five senses and the mysterious "sixth sense" to recognize that something dangerous or unusual is about to occur. Use it when a knight is listening for a sound, trying to spot a hidden Pict, or anything similar.

A critical success in Awareness might reveal extra information, while a fumbled Awareness should reveal incorrect information.

A success using Awareness that reveals an ambush or other crucial information may be worth Glory, at the gamemaster's option.

Boating *(optional)*

To boat is to handle a small water craft, whether a rowboat, skiff, coracle, or Saxon rowing ship. Successful rolls indicate the boat did what it was supposed to do. In calm waters Boating is unmodified, but during storms or floods varying modifiers may be assigned.

A success with the Boating skill can gain the character Glory if lives were saved thereby.

Chirurgery *(non-knightly)*

This ancient practice of healing and care includes much useful knowledge, such as herbal medicine and bone-setting. It also includes folk knowledge, simple prayers, and heaps of misinformation. Thus its use is fraught with uncertainty.

Chirurgery does little to heal the patient directly, but is a process which keeps the patient alive so that the natural healing processes of the body may take effect.

Chirurgery is a most important skill for women to have. Many holy people also know it. However, it is not the duty of a knight to learn the skill, and many knights feel uncomfortable performing a skill associated with women.

Chirurgery is pronounced "Ki-rir-ger-y," or "Kirgh-rir-gur-y." In modern times the word has evolved in spelling, pronunciation, and usage to be Sur-ger-y.

Badly wounded, ill, or debilitated characters often require chirurgery to heal. The gamemaster is the judge; if your character needs Chirurgery, for whatever reason, the gamemaster will tell you to check the box on the character sheet entitled "Chirurgery Needed." See the "Injury and Health" section below for more information on the complicated processes of chirurgery and healing.

Glory should always be gained for successful use of the Chirurgery skill. The amount gained can be increased in proportion to the Glory or rank of the character being treated if the gamemaster feels this is appropriate. More Glory should be gained if a life was saved thereby.

Compose

This skill permits the user a chance to create original musical works suitable for use by voice or by one or more medieval instruments. The quality of the piece composed is equal to the number rolled for the success. A critical success indicates that the piece created has beauty, quality of rhyme and emotion, originality, and that it sprang right to life, on the spot. A piece of this quality might bring a listener to tears, or even more.

A fumble indicates an embarrassingly bad piece.

The composer's ability to perform his work is limited by his Play (Instrument) and Singing skills.

The gamemaster may award Glory to a successful composer, particularly if the song is dedicated to a lady.

Courtesy

Courtesy is a knowledge skill defining a knight's knowledge of court manners. It could almost be called Court Lore. Court manners of all types are included, from etiquette to precedence to table manners. Issues of speech include modes of speech, protocol, vocabulary, style, and forms of address. Also included are all types of decorum and manners appropriate to a lord's court, around superiors, around women, and around disliked or disfavored people. The minimum Courtesy value of 3 indicates that the character understands precedence and knows the basic forms of address for court.

Courtesy does not include the art of the formal dance, heraldry, or the forms of the tournament. These areas of expertise are so complicated that they are treated as separate skills.

With the gamemaster's approval, characters of high Glory may receive a positive modifier to Courtesy, with a maximum modifier equal to Glory/1000.

Successful Courtesy means that the knight performed correctly in the formal manner appropriate to the relative stations of the witnessing court members. Courtesy is inappropriate to use with commoners.

A critical success indicates great elegance and style in the performance, while a success simply ensures that a good impression is made. A failure means incorrect behavior, while a fumble indicates that a silly or even offensive act was performed, with consequent humiliation. Haughty or cruel lords may become insulted and angry at characters who fumble their Courtesy roll in court, with dramatic consequences.

Glory may be gained by any significant use of Courtesy in a court or formal situation, particularly a critical success.

Dancing

This skill measures the character's ability to move gracefully to music, and his knowledge of the many styles of formal dancing done at court. This elegant style of dancing depends primarily on experience and knowledge of forms rather than agility.

With the gamemaster's approval, characters of high Glory may receive a positive modifier to Dance, with a maximum modifier equal to Glory/1000.

A critical success indicates superb grace and verve, while a success indicates accuracy to the forms of the dance being performed. Failure shows error,

while a fumble means that the character went the wrong way, probably bumping into other dancers. The gamemaster may even rule that the fumbler tripped and fell over his own feet. A fumble in Dance is a humiliating experience.

Glory can be gained from Dance if the dancer(s) are the center of attention.

Faerie Lore

Faerie lore is a knowledge skill which quantifies how much a knight knows about the mysterious ways of the faerie and the Invisible World. It is used to identify a type of faerie which was sighted, to recognize a faerie encounter as such, or to aid communication with them.

Modern opinion condemns faerie lore, but every person in King Arthur's Britain knows that this ancient wisdom is truth. Everyone knows that whenever something uncanny occurs it is due to some elf or faery, and anything which is not immediately recognizable is probably made by them as well.

Every character in *Pendragon* is superstitious to some extent and this is expressed by the initial skill value of 2. This minimum means that all characters know common legends. For example, everyone knows that a lone faery probably intends harm, while a band of faeries may not.

Although characters must be roleplayed as superstitious, the gamemaster decides to what extent the magic of Britain will be real within his campaign. This fact is up to the players to discover through play. Some gamemasters like to have magic as a common thread running throughout the game, while others prefer that actual magic appear only in the most unusual and terrifying circumstances.

A Faerie lore skill success reveals magical information, which the gamemaster must present in an entertaining way. However, this information may be sheer superstition, or incorrect in detail. A failure or fumble gives erroneous information. A critical success always reveals some important fact, as secretly communicated to the player of that character by the gamemaster (for example: "Sir Ambrut realizes that the three witches are actually the mad daughters of the king.").

Characters may gain Glory for a success with Faerie Lore if it reveals information crucial to a scenario. Usually, however, little Glory is to be gained from knowledge of the faerie realm — Glory is gained from *interactions* with that world, not talk.

† First Aid

First Aid provides immediate medical assistance to wounds. It is actually more reliable than the medieval treatments to be used later in treatment (chirurgery). Characters that gain successful First Aid for all their wounds usually do not require chirurgery, unless they have suffered a Major or Mortal wound. Successful First Aid reduces the chance of infection, and returns 1d3 hit points to the injured character. A critical success returns 1d3+3 hit points, while a fumble removes a further 1d3 hit points. Characters cannot First Aid themselves.

First Aid, like Chirurgery, is an important and complicated subject. See the "Injury and Health" section of this chapter, below, for more information.

Glory should usually be gained for successful use of the First Aid skill. The amount gained should be increased in proportion to the Glory and rank of the character being treated. If a life is saved, more Glory should be gained.

Flirting *(optional)*

In *Pendragon* terms, Flirting is a courtly skill that can be mastered to convey sensuality and sexuality. It includes use of specific words, tones of voice, expressions, movements, gestures, and attitudes. The primary purpose is to gain the attention of a member of the opposite sex.

Success simply indicates that a message of sensuality was conveyed, which the recipient may ignore or respond to. The higher the number rolled, the more potent the message conveyed. However, a critical success indicates that the listener was moved somehow, and was unable to hide his feelings whether he wanted to or not. Failure indicates that the message was not conveyed during the conversation. A fumble shows that the speaker mispoke something terribly, and caused embarrassment, perhaps even offense.

Although seduction certainly requires flirtation during its initial stages, flirtation does not mean seduction. It is not uncommon to flirt for amusement's sake, although this practice may be misinterpreted and incite passions among the unlettered and ignorant.

It is more exciting to flirt with a handsome or beautiful character than an ugly one. The gamemaster may wish to impose a modifier on the Flirting skill of any character with unusually high or low APP.

With the gamemaster's approval, characters of high Glory may receive a positive modifier to Flirting, with a maximum modifier equal to Glory/1000.

Success with the Flirting skill gains Glory only if the subject of the opposite sex becomes infatuated with the character.

Note that the Flirting skill is deliberately set apart from the far less vulgar activity of Romance.

Folk Lore *(optional, non-knightly)*

Folk Lore is a knowledge skill for the peasant way of life. It stems from familiarity with the land which has been gained over thousands of years of experience. Folk Lore includes information on many subjects, from such ordinary things as the lore of pigs or local landmarks, all the way to the household herbal cures of old women. Folk Lore includes thousands of tiny facts useful to daily living, such when to plant, how to tell if winter will be hard, and how to cheat the tax collector, as well as a certain amount of nonsense, such as how to rid oneself of warts, charms to kill rats, and songs to make the plants grow.

Folk Lore is used in play when a knight observes peasants at work to determine what they are doing, or when trying to evaluate how they feel.

Folk Lore may be used to gain a benefit in communicating with peasants. A successful Folk Lore roll shows that the knight communicated his friendliness and knowledge of the folk ways, presumably making the peasant more agreeable and less afraid. Failure reveals the knight to be a typical upper-class oppressor. Fumble indicates a major social *gaffe* which offends, and possibly enrages, the peasant.

Glory is not normally gained through Folk Lore. What Glory is there in dealing with commoners and peasant matters?

Gaming

The Gaming skill allows the user to perform certain types of medieval play effectively and with aplomb, whether in competition or for entertainment. This skill does not include ability in physical sports such as wrestling and jousting, and has nothing to do with them.

All types of common gaming, including simpler forms of gambling, are included. Common games include: Roman

Tabula (backgammon), Saxon *Hnaeftafl* (swords-and-shields), Cymric *Gwyddbwyll* (wooden wisdom), and the continental *Les Dames* (checkers).

Two characters playing a game together make opposed Gaming rolls, and the higher number rolled successfully wins. If a monetary stake is involved, the difference between the two numbers rolled can be used by the gamemaster to determine the amount of money won (i.e. a difference of 3 might indicate that 3 denarii were won).

Glory may be gained from success with the Gaming skill only if the situation is unusually chivalrous; ordinary gaming or gambling never gains Glory.

Hawking

Hawks can be trained to hunt birds and other small prey. Such sport is the pleasure of nobles, who sometimes spend considerable money to maintain a first-class mews (name for a building reserved for the maintenance of hunting hawks).

The Hawking skill is used whenever knights and ladies take the birds into the fields to hunt. The skill indicates how well the character knows the sport, such as when to let the bird go, how to call it back, and how to handle it.

Critical success means the bird caught its prey with a flourish and returned with it to the hawker's feet. Success indicates that the bird just got its prey. Failure shows it missed. A fumble means the hawk flew away.

Individual birds may be trained by their masters, and a well-trained bird can actually improve a knight's Hawking skill.

Tradition insists that certain birds be used only by certain ranks of nobility.

eagle: emperors
jerfalcon: kings, princes
peregrine falcon: earls
merlin: ladies
goshawk: knights
sparrow hawk: clergy

Note that the cover painting of this book shows King Arthur with his favorite jerfalcon.

Glory is gained for every success in hawking using a sparrow hawk or better. Most successes gain ordinary Glory (10 points), but a spectacular critical success before King Arthur and the assembled court might gain as much as 100 points.

Heraldry

A knight is known by his coat of arms. When in armor, everyone looks the same, except for the coat of arms blazoned on the shield and banner. Surcoats also carry this identification.

Members of families commonly display similar arms, such as the 2-headed eagle in the Orkney clan coats of arms. Sons often design their arms to resemble their fathers'. Quite by accident some coats of arms are similar to one another, making perfect identification difficult. Examples of large groups with similar coats of arms include the aforementioned Orkney clan, the de Ganis clan, Cornish knights, and the royal families of any kingdom. Other less coherent groups include groups of arms which all have horses, arms which have ships, or arms which have red on top.

Successful use of this skill indicates your character knows the members of the group or family for that coat of arms, or the several most likely holders of the arms. A critical success indicates the precise person is recognized, as well as the general group. Failure means the character has no idea who it is, and a fumble means he will not recognize it even if it is as obvious as King Arthur or Lancelot, or alternately it means that he identifies the coat of arms positively, but wrongly.

The gamemaster may require a Heraldry roll to see if the characters properly identify the coat of arms of someone they already know. Success means the gamemaster will state who the individual is (or at least whose shield the individual bears).

A knight's Glory modifies another character's Heraldry skill. One point is added to the skill value of the observer for every 1000 points of glory a knight has. Thus if a knight tries to recognize the arms of Sir Ambrut, with 1605 Glory by his second year, the skill value is raised by 2 points: trying to identify Sir Dodinas le Savage, with 4800 glory, adds 5 to the observer's Heraldry skill, and no one can miss King Arthur's arms.

A success with Heraldry gains Glory if vital information is gained thereby, normally 10 points.

Hunting

The Hunting skill includes the entire variety of tasks performed during the noble sport of the chase, except for weapon skills. Hunting includes knowing what the different blasts on the horn mean, knowing whether an animal is a "beast of chase, venery, or vermin." It includes care of hounds, understanding of their methods of hunting and what their cries mean; tracking the spoor and identifying beasts from it; knowing the best way to quickly kill each animal; and the skill of cutting it up properly afterwards so everyone, from hounds and dog boys to the sponsor, gets their correct share.

Hunting skills are also used to test general woodland and wild land knowledge. Hunting is used when trying to find your way through woods, wastes, or unfamiliar territory. A modifier may be added if following an established trail.

Successful hunts usually are worth modest Glory, but this is normally based on what animals are caught. See the "Characters and Creatures" chapter for more information on Glory for various game animals. Glory may be directly gained using the Hunting skill if scenario goals are met or lives are saved.

Industry *(optional, non-knightly)*

Knights never engage in Industry, and are in danger of losing their high rank if they do. Industry is the woman's work of creating things with her hands. This is most often expressed in the arts of spinning, weaves, and sewing. These are tasks for noblewomen, who create fashionable clothing for both men and women; large tapestries, to hang upon walls; ornate church vestments; and perhaps even simple table linen.

Industry can also be applied to churchmen who make fine books, and to witches or druids who create fetishes and charms. It is a very common peasant skill. Note, however, that this is not a knightly skill and is used by none.

The quality of work produced by Industry is based on the number rolled for success. A critical success creates a work of great craftsmanship or even art.

Glory can be gained by non-knights from the use of this skill, if a particularly beautiful item is made and presented to someone in public. Usually this should be only ordinary Glory (10 points).

Intrigue

Intrigue is the skill of knowing what is going on inside the court. Everyone has access to gossip, but hard work and clever conversations help to pry out the real facts. Skill is needed to know who to ask, when, what to say to learn half of a secret, and how to sift truth from lies. Personal contacts cultured through long,

often secret, relationships are another key and may provide modifiers. Thus young Sir Mordred, with his remarkable Intrigue skill, already has contacts among most of the noble families of Britain.

Intrigue is not used to poison people in secret, to foment rebellion, or to assassinate rivals. Such dark practices must be roleplayed, not left to random die rolls.

Many modifiers may be applied to an Intrigue roll. For instance, trying to find out secrets in a castle whose entire staff has been briefed on a plan, and who agree with its intent, will give a negative modifier. A sympathetic resident, perhaps because both he and the characters are from the same homeland, gives a positive modifier. A normal castle or court situation, with nothing unusual going on, gives no modifiers.

Success with Intrigue indicates you learn something true and probably useful. Critical success indicates you learn a special and important fact known only to you and the direct participants (perhaps a fact overheard at a critical juncture, or seen by accident, or discovered in a lost note). Failure indicates nothing new was learned, fumble means that a close contact lies, or is thought to have lied, to you. The gamemaster can exploit this uncertainty at his leisure.

An Intrigue success gains Glory if facts critical to the characters' success in a scenario are gained.

Orate

The art of speaking fluently, with poetic grace and with charismatic delivery, is useful in any situation which requires a character to speak, especially in public.

With the gamemaster's approval, characters of high Glory may receive a positive modifier to Orate, with a maximum modifier equal to Glory/1000.

A success at Orate indicates the speech was florid and well-delivered. A critical success indicates the listeners were genuinely moved by the speech. Failure shows that the speech was boring. A fumble indicates that the speaker made a fool of himself.

Ordinary Glory (10 points) is gained from a typical successful oration, while a speech that swayed a crowd at a crucial time, or impressed an angry king, might gain more.

Play (instrument) *(optional)*

Everyone appreciates a good tune to wile away the winter and after-dinner hours. Some women prefer men with this entertaining skill.

Characters should choose an instrument from the list below. If more than one instrument is played, write a new entry onto the character sheet.

Success indicates a good tune was played, while failure indicates the song was out of tune, off-beat, or in the wrong chord. Critical success indicates a rousing tune which evoked an emotional response from normal people, while fumble means the character played so badly that everyone laughed at him.

This skill is specific for each instrument. The name of the instrument should be inserted into the parentheses on the character sheet. Most characters will be familiar with only one instrument, but if more than one is known then the blank spaces on the sheet can be used.

Glory for playing music can only come from playing instruments appropriate to a courtly audience (see the list of instruments below). No Glory is gained for a Saxon warrior tootling his horn in court, or for someone entertaining peasants on a bagpipe. Normally ordinary Glory (10 points) should be gained.

Musical Instruments

Pendragon music is medieval. It uses a variety of instruments which are unfamiliar to us today, but which were popular in the Middle Ages. This list includes many instruments popular with the non-knightly classes.

Harp: The primary instrument played by the nobility. Most harps are small enough to be hand-held and are rested on the left shoulder (in contrast to modern harps). Most harps have five to ten strings. Harps are strummed and plucked for music.

Lute: The basic troubadour instrument. A lute has a round body and long neck with two to ten strings running along its length. It is played while the left hand presses the strings against frets in the neck and the right hand strums or picks the strings (like a modern guitar).

The rest are non-knightly instruments:

Flute: An ordinary instrument, used by entertainers but not encouraged because puffing distorts a nobleman's face to look silly. It is held horizontally and wind blows across the sound hole. Up to nine fingerholes make a wide variety of notes possible.

Recorder: Another ordinary instrument, used by entertainers and occasionally by women. It is played by blowing into one end, and covering or uncovering holes along its length.

Double Pipes: Another ordinary instrument not encouraged among noblemen because puffing distorts his face and looks silly. Two pipes, each with up to five holes, are bound side by side to be played at the same time by blowing into a single mouthpiece at one end. Sometimes one pipe is much longer than the other.

Horn: Only Saxons consider this instrument to be capable of music. Others may use it to color tales of the hunt or war. They are made of animal horns, and sometimes have holes to modulate the sound.

Bagpipes: A popular folk instrument. Used primarily among commoners to accompany dances and other festivities, the Irish also use it in battle to frighten their foes and to signal their friends. All other noblemen scorn its use.

Trumpet: The "Prince's Instrument." This is a metal horn, often up to three feet long or bent into an S-curve. It is incapable of music and is used only for battlefield signalling and courtly fanfares. Only royal houses may have trumpeters, hence its nickname.

Drums: A military instrument. Drums are used to signal forces on the battlefield, occasionally to send signals over a distance, and often among peasantry to accompany dances. No one in their right mind considers its use for music.

Read (symbols) *(optional)*

Several esoteric forms of writing exist in Britain, known to only the initiates of ancient lore. They are generally not used for messages or books, but instead document magical powers and serve as focus of spells and ritual. Latin is the closest equivalent to modern writing, and even Latin is rarely encountered in a written form. Characters might encounter symbols written on sticks, on stone menhirs, or inscribed over mysterious cave mouths.

Read (symbols) is a knowledge skill.

A successful roll at Read (symbols) indicates that the symbols were read and understood. A critical success means that only a short time was needed to read the

document. A failure indicates that the symbols remain incomprehensible, while a fumble means that misinterpretation occurs. Some pieces may have negative modifiers for reading, depending on the age, complexity, and subject of the manuscript. Ciphers and secret words are also possible, making the task of reading difficult or impossible to the uninitiated.

The gamemaster will have to determine how much time reading a document requires, based on its size and other factors.

Given society's belief in the power of symbols for spells and ritual, the gamemaster's interpretation of magic might include Read (symbols) as a component.

Glory could be gained for a use of Read (symbols) if important information for a scenario or hidden secrets were revealed thereby.

Four types of symbols are commonly known and read:

Ogham is from the old Cymri and Irish. It looks like bunches of lines, parallel within a group but not parallel with each other, scratched along a straight line. It is most often used on sticks. Sometimes the symbols are phonetic sounds, strung together like words. Sometimes they are not. Ogham is called the Language of Trees, and was discovered by the god Ogmios, who passed it on to his followers.

Runes are from the Saxons. They are a series of simple, angularly-cut symbols which each possess a specific type of power. Each is also a phonetic sound. They are cut into rocks or sticks in patterns to bless and empower magic spells, or to cast for divination. The first runes were discovered by Wotan, who sacrificed his own life to obtain the wisdom for himself and his followers.

Glyphs are Pictish signs, most often carved into rocks which serve as border markers and altars to local spirits. They tell the name of the local people responsible for the upkeep of the altar, and of the power which can be invoked. The first glyphs were placed there by Earth Mother to help her people, and the Picts can still work magic at those sites.

Latin: This language was originally from Rome. Reading Latin means literacy, or being able to read and write Latin, the old Roman tongue. Few people are well-versed in the skill of Read (Latin) other than churchmen, city merchants, and classical scholars.

Recognize

Not everyone can always put together a face and a name or, in *Pendragon*, a face and a coat of arms. When everyone mingles at court there are hundreds of nobles and knights, along with thousands of servants and commoners. In such a crowd you may see someone, perhaps even be introduced, and forget him as one among many. Likewise, after viewing several hundred jousters all but the best among them tend to blur into one indistinct figure. Disguised characters can also be encountered.

Recognize is the skill of putting together clues: a face, jousting style, distinctive feature, or other characteristic which identify a person. You must have previous reason to recall it at all. Thus if you never heard about or saw someone before, even a critical success would not help — it is impossible to use this skill to learn something about a complete stranger. On the other hand, the gamemaster may tell you to make a Recognize roll when you don't think of it, and may also assign a positive modifier to your skill if an acquaintance is nearby but unrecognized.

A successful Recognize roll indicates that you remember a character, and recall what you know about him. A critical success means that you recognize the person even if he is in disguise. A failed roll indicates that you don't remember this person. A fumble indicates that you think you recognize him, but the gamemaster can give you either false or true information. A character who fumbled his Recognize is thus always insecure about his identification.

A success with Recognize might gain Glory if recognition was crucial to a scenario.

Religion (..........)

This is a knowledge skill which quantifies how much is known concerning the beliefs, rites, sacred calender, and practices of the religion noted in parentheses. It also indicates a person's ability to follow a ceremony and do what is appropriate to his station within a sacred context. His station is that of the initiate — of an informed worshiper.

A high Religion skill does not necessarily indicate belief: this is measured by the Piety trait. Nor does it indicate sincerity: this is measured by passions. Believers know their own religion, acquired by attending normal worship. The common religion for player knights of Logres is Christianity. Less common are Paganism and Wotanism, and truly exotic are Islam and Judaism. Non-believers may have this skill for any religion.

Success or failure with the Religion skill should normally not affect magical events. Piety and passions are better sources of miracles and magic in the game than expertise in the forms and dogma of a religion.

Successful use of the Religion skill does not usually gain Glory unless a successful prayer or ritual was crucial to the scenario.

Romance

Romance is a knowledge skill concerning the practice of *fine amor*. This custom of the court adores women and holds that men are inspired and improved by their emotional commitment to women. The Romance skill includes the basic knowledge and procedures for this custom. It encompasses the rules of love, as detailed by Andreas Capellanus.

A Romance roll might be required to know how to approach a woman for the first time; how to properly avert one's eyes; how to kiss a hand, wrist, elbow, or other part of the body; and, especially, what is the best type of present to buy. For a woman it includes knowing when to refuse an audience, when to accept a tryst, how to say no, an understanding of constructive cruelty, how to tell whether entertainment is new or customary, and how a man lies.

Romance is an elegant and courtly skill, and success should gain ordinary Glory in most instances. See "The Lover's Solo" in the "Scenarios" chapter for further Glory from romance.

Singing

Music produced by voices pleases all listeners, whether sung in church, in court, or for a lover in a warm summer glade. Professional bards and minstrels wander from court to court with a repertoire of ballads and lays. Noblemen create love poems and romances, and find honor in their title of troubadour. The poorer troubadours perform their own songs, while the richer hire singers, called *jongleurs*, to perform. Women sing both to entertain the household on lonely winter nights and to please lovers.

I imagine that on some fine spring days Arthur's court is very much like the

musical *Camelot,* or like a very pleasant dream.

A critical success at Singing indicates a powerful and emotional performance, while a simple success indicates a pleasant experience. A failure indicates slurred or incorrect words, or worse, while a fumble indicates something causing social embarrassment.

Successful Singing always gains Glory, usually an ordinary award (10 points). More Glory might be gained if some scenario goal was achieved thereby (a savage guardian soothed, for example). Successful singing in a lord's court gains additional Glory.

Stewardship

This ability to plan, administer, and oversee the keeping of a farm or similar holding is not normally required for knights. It is an important women's skill. It is used to maintain and improve the income generated from land. On a knight's holding the bailiff usually knows the Stewardship skill.

Glory is not found by being a farmer, although Glory may be derived from Stewardship if a success contributes to a battle victory or saves a knight or greater noble from poverty or humiliation.

Swimming *(optional)*

Swimming is used to move successfully through water. The roll is normally unmodified, but in stormy or flooded conditions there may also be negative modifiers involved. Swimming is reduced by one point per point of armor worn, so a character with a Swimming value of 10 would have a modified skill of 6 while wearing 4-point leather armor.

A successful Swimming roll indicates that the character remained above water and moved in the desired direction. A critical success indicates that he did so at double speed. A failure or fumble indicates that he did not do so, and must attempt a CON roll. If both are failed the character begins drowning, taking 1d6 damage each melee round after the CON roll fails.

A Swimming roll also can be used to remove armor while underwater, if stated to the gamemaster at the beginning of the round. A successful roll removes 2 points of armor. But during this time, the character suffers drowning damage with no CON roll possible.

Glory is gained only if someone is saved by a Swimming roll.

Tourney

Tourney is a knowledge skill used for correct procedures, customs, and behavior at that spectacle of chivalrous entertainment, the tournament. Thus a Tourney skill roll is required to find out if the knights registered with the correct person at the right time, or whether they embarrassed themselves by arriving at the last minute. A roll could be used to see if the knights understand what certain trumpet blasts mean, where failure indicates that they did not place their helmets and surcoats out for the *helm show,* or that they missed a feast or a important speech. Alternately, a failed roll might mean that the knight did not know who to address, what do upon winning a joust, or how to properly ask for, receive, or handle a lady's favor. A fumble can be humiliating.

Glory can be gained with most successful uses of the Tourney skill. Usually this should be an ordinary award (10 points). A crucial use of the skill that gains an advantage in combat or foils a villain's plans should gain additional Glory.

Combat Skills

History, romance, and legend all agree that fighting is a knight's primary work. Thus these skills are considered separately from ordinary skills such as Singing. Following this section is the "Combat" section, in which you will learn more of how these skills are used.

Combat skills are organized into two parts: first, the two non-weapon combat skills of Battle and Horsemanship; second, the various weapons, arranged in alphabetical order (the sword, as the premier weapon of the knight, is listed first on the character sheet).

Notes on Combat Skills

Glory from Combat Skills

The successful use of combat skills does not necessarily gain Glory directly. Instead, various criteria are used, such as victory, opponents defeated, and other issues. See the "Glory and Ambitions" chapter.

Bors de Ganis

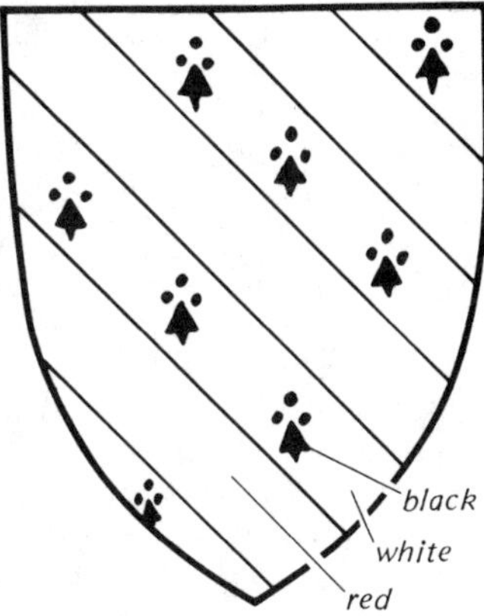

Base Combat Skill Values

Note that some combat skills are marked with a dagger (†). These are the crucial combat skills which every squire or sergeant must have with a value of 10 to qualify for knighthood.

On the character sheet only the traditional knightly weapons are listed: sword, lance, spear (also the favorite weapon of the Cymric culture), and the ubiquitous dagger. All squires and sergeants receive some degree of training in each of these weapons. Many other weapon skills exist. If a character wishes to learn one of these, write the name in one of the blanks provided on the sheet, starting the skill at 0.

Unknightly Combat Skills

Two common forms of combat can be considered unknightly: brawling and the use of missile weapons. Grapple is a skill that appears similar to brawling, but is used in serious combat while wearing armor.

Brawling: Occasionally during a session a character will hit another with his fist, a chair, or whatever is handy. There is no special skill defined for such attacks, nor are characters trained in such unmilitary forms of combat. This uncouth kind of violence is more appropriate to commoners than members of the nobility. Note that if a character pulls out his dagger, the situation is no longer a casual brawl but deadly serious combat.

DEX/2 is used as the skill value for brawling. This use of the DEX roll can be done using opposed resolution. A critical success with this DEX roll does double damage as always, while a fumble indicates that the brawler fell down clumsily.

Modifiers for drunkenness, bad footing, encumbrance, and so forth all apply to DEX rolls for brawling. The gamemaster should decide whether other modifiers are appropriate, depending on what the character is attempting; for example, hitting an enemy from behind would gain a +5 modifier to DEX/2, just as with a weapon skill.

If two characters wrestle or pull at each other, and neither has the Grapple skill, opposed STR rolls can be made instead of DEX/2 rolls, at the gamemaster's option. A STR roll is never used to see if a character hit another, however.

Damage for fists, kicks, etc. is equal to normal damage minus two dice, with 1d6 being the lowest possible brawling damage. For example, a character with a 3d6 Damage statistic would do 1d6 with his fist, as would a character with a 2d6 Damage statistic.

Brawling damage from casual weapons (chairs, candlesticks, rocks, beef bones, etc.) must be determined by the gamemaster, but should never be more than the character's damage with a dagger (normal Damage statistic minus 1d6).

Glory should rarely be gained from brawling, and only if no alternative form of combat was possible.

Should the gamemaster wish it, engaging in a serious brawl might lose a knight 1 Honor point, particularly if the results are disgraceful (a character killed or maimed in front of the court, for example). If the experience was unavoidable the shame may not be so great. See the "Ideals and Passions" chapter for more information on Honor.

Grapple: The Grapple skill defines a special form of unarmed combat that is not usually considered brawling, and occurs often in the literature. Grapple is very different from other weapon skills, and may almost be considered a tactical option rather than just another skill. See the "Grapple" entry below.

Missile Weapons: Three missile weapon skills are defined in *Pendragon:* Bow, Crossbow, and Javelin. Also, a DEX roll can be used to throw a stone or heave a boulder at an enemy, but there is no throw skill. Normal rules for weapons apply to missile weapons, and in addition range modifiers are needed.

Knights disdain to use missile weapons in combat, except for the short-ranged javelin once used by Rome. Only cowards fight from a distance, and personal honor requires men to confront each other body to body.

Hunting is different, and missile weapons are sometimes used, especially where food-gathering is more important than sport.

There is no penalty to Honor for using missile weapons, but the Glory gained from defeating an opponent or creature is 1/10th of normal, the same as in combats "for love." This is the penalty whether a thrown rock or a crossbow is used, and is extracted regardless of whether melee combat was also part of the victory or not.

Non-Weapon Combat Skills

† Battle

The Battle skill measures an individual's knowledge and use of individual tactics in skirmishes and battles. A high Battle skill means that a knight knows how to look around a battlefield to recognize what is dangerous or advantageous, and how to take advantage of what he sees.

Two general uses for the Battle skill exist: for leadership, and for tactical decisions when separated from your unit in battles. Leadership usage occurs in both battles and skirmishes (skirmishes are a separate form of mass combat from battles).

In both skirmish and battle, special rules are used to resolve what happens, but the procedure for a skirmish is much shorter and simpler, is likely to be used more often, and is given here.

Rules for large-scale battles are given later, in the "Chivalric Duties" chapter. Gamemasters in a hurry to finish a battle can use the skirmish rules given here instead, though this is not the best solution.

Following are some important general points on mass combat, and the rules for skirmishes.

Victory or Defeat: The actual resolution of a battle or a skirmish is normally up to the gamemaster. The decision should be based on commanders' Battle rolls, on the player knights' success or failure, and on storytelling factors.

In a skirmish, the player knights can make a big difference. If the player knights all do well in melee, then as the most important warriors in the group, their success should usually affect morale and drive their unit to victory.

In a battle, where the player knights may be minor or even insignificant participants, their success or failure should not usually affect the outcome.

Glory: Glory is gained in both skirmishes or battles.

Skirmish Glory is normally derived only from melee combat (i.e. Glory for defeating enemies, for heroic actions, etc.). However, if a player character is a commander or subordinate leader in a skirmish, Glory for successful Battle skill use may be gained if appropriate. There is no Glory just for participation in a skirmish unless the situation is something very special, in which case the gamemaster will determine the appropriate Glory awarded.

Battle Glory is a different story. This Glory is based on participation. Just being there can be worth Glory. Battle Glory is determined per battle round. The bigger the battle, the greater the Glory.

The Skirmish: A skirmish is a special form of melee combat which opens with a mass attack by one or both sides. One side or the other gains an initial advantage, and combat then dissolves into individual melee. Most mass combat during scenarios is of this type.

In a skirmish only the commander of the force and his subordinate leaders, if any, make Battle rolls. If the commander is not a player knight, the gamemaster determines the commander's skill and makes the roll. This roll is always unopposed. The roll is made on the Commander's Battle Roll Results Table, below.

The modifier from the table is applied to everyone's combat skills in the first melee round (usually Lance, Sword, and Horsemanship, but not DEX or Valorous rolls or any other non-skill rolls).

After the commander's roll, combat is joined and resolved character by character using normal melee combat rules. Each player knight should face an enemy knight unless the enemy unit is entirely composed of inferior troops. After the first round of the skirmish, combat modifiers are normal.

Commander's Battle Roll Results Table

result	modifier
Critical	+5
Success	+0
Failure	-5
Fumble	-10

Even in a skirmish, most of the combatants on each side will be non-player characters (nobody runs a game with 30 or 40 player knights). The skirmish does not end until the situation regarding the non-player characters is resolved. It may be that the player knights will be totally victorious, only to look up and see that the rest of their unit has been routed. Or they may be defeated by their opponents, only to be rescued by their non-player companions.

To determine what the rest of the unit has done, one or more Followers' Fate rolls must be performed, using the table below. Usually this should be delayed for one to five rounds of melee, while the gamemaster deals with individual combats. Eventually a player knight will look around and ask what is happening with the rest of the unit, or the gamemaster will feel it time to make the roll.

Every character who leads any troops other than squires requires a Followers' Fate roll, including the overall commander. In most cases the overall commander will have all non-player characters under his command, but player characters such as banneret knights are considered to be subordinate leaders, responsible for their own men.

A Fate roll is done using each leader's Battle skill, as modified by the commander's initial result on the Commander's Table above. The result of the Fate roll is checked on the table below.

Note that being a subordinate leader is the only way that a player can make a Battle roll in a skirmish if his character is not the overall commander of the unit.

Non-Player Followers' Fate Table

result	fate
Critical	A great victory! No losses, and 1 enemy of appropriate rank is captured per five non-player characters.
Success	10% losses (2% killed, 8% wounded). Survivors are victorious against their opponents.
Failure	50% losses (10% killed, 25% wounded, 15% captured) and surviving troops must retreat from the field.
Fumble	75% losses (50% killed, 25% captured), surviving troops routed from field.

Losses from groups that contain different classes of troops require a ruling from the gamemaster to ascertain who was captured, wounded, or killed. Wealthy knights with several squires are far less likely to be killed than sergeants or impoverished knights with no squires, but are prime targets for capture.

Each Fate roll determines what happened to that sub-section of the unit. The gamemaster must make sure that each non-player character in the skirmish is clearly assigned a leader for the purposes of Fate rolls, with no confusing overlaps.

Skirmish Example: *The famous warlord, Earl Crassus, with a band of 19 other knights and 30 sergeants, is riding northward. He personally leads 10 non-player knights, and the 30 sergeants are also under his direct command. Sir Yvane leads a subordinate troop of household knights (three other player character knights including Sir Ambrut, plus five non-player knights). The unit totals 50 men, including the earl.*

The group sights a party of 75 Saxon warriors who must, of course, be raiding. Crassus decides to smash the invaders, and the knights prepare to make a charge with lances.

Crassus, handled by the gamemaster, is responsible for the fate of his 10 non-player knights and 30 non-player sergeants, while Yvane, a player character, is responsible for five non-player knights. The three other player knights are responsible for their own fate. Crassus, as the commander of the unit, will also roll to determine the first round modifier for the skirmish.

Earl Crassus begins the skirmish by making his roll as commander, and receives a lucky Battle roll of 18, indicating a critical success. Since Crassus is a gamemaster character, no Glory is recorded for the success. Consulting the Commander's Battle Roll Results Table, the gamemaster announces that all members of the unit have +5 modifiers to their initial Lance attack in melee. The unit charges with a cheer, and the Saxons are caught in the flank. Yvane, as a subordinate leader, will have a +5 for his Followers' Fate roll, as will Crassus himself for his Followers' Fate roll, due to this roll.

The success or failure of individual characters in the skirmish will be determined by normal melee combat. On the first melee round of combat, Sir Ambrut's unmodified Lance skill of 10 is modified by Crassus' successful Battle roll to a value of 15. Ambrut rolls a 14 on the first round and hits a Saxon. Yvane skewers a Saxon with a critical Lance success on the first round, thanks to the +5 modifier from Crassus' Battle roll. The other player characters also do well in the first round, defeating several more Saxons. Glory is gained for each defeated enemy by the victors.

In subsequent rounds, the +5 modifier no longer applies, and combat is resolved normally. No one performs any unusual or heroic acts in the skirmish, so no other Glory is gained by the player characters.

Later in the fight, after resolving three rounds of melee for the players, the gamemaster decides to see what has happened to the non-player characters. He starts by rolling for the fate of Crassus' knights and sergeants.

Crassus has a +5 modifier to Battle from his initial roll as commander, and achieves success in his Fate roll. The results of a successful roll on the Followers' Fate Table are applied to all the men directly following the earl with these results: the men are victorious, and take 10% losses.

2% killed out of 40 = .8 = one non-player character killed. The gamemaster rules that it is one of the youngest non-player knights, who was reckless during the charge and attacked three Saxons at once.

8% wounded out of 40 = 3.4 = three non-player characters are wounded. The gamemaster rules that all three are sergeants.

Now Yvane rolls for his five non-player knights. He also has a +5 modifier from the commander's initial roll, but manages to fail his Battle roll. His surviving men must retreat. Results are as follows.

10% killed out of 5 = .5 = 1 household knight killed.

25% wounded out of 5 = 1.25 = 1 household knight wounded.

15% captured out of 5 = .75 = 1 knight captured.

The gamemaster rules that the skirmish ends with Crassus' troop of sergeants driving off the surviving Saxons. The player knights were all victorious in melee, so no special results obtain. Sir Yvane's non-played followers were driven back, but since his player knight followers did so well, the gamemaster rules that no loss or humiliation occurred as a result of Yvane's failed Battle roll.

Since Crassus' force won the fight, the knight of Yvane's that was captured is rescued, and no ransom need be paid.

† Horsemanship

Horsemanship is the ability to perform expected activities while mounted on a moving horse. Activities include fighting, jumping obstacles, and galloping.

In most normal uses success indicates that the horse did what it was expected to do. Failure indicates it did not. Critical success shows it went faster, jumped farther, or whatever is appropri-

ate for greater than normal effort. A fumble indicates that the horse tripped, the rider fell off, the saddle girths broke, or that the ride has otherwise ended.

Glory can be gained for a success in Horsemanship in various ways. Usually the Glory is gained not for the successful roll but for the results. Carrying a message swiftly might gain 10 Glory, for example. Winning a race would gain the same. A heroic use of Horsemanship, perhaps rescuing a child from a burning barn by riding in and out, might gain 100 Glory.

Weapon Skills

Axe

This one-handed weapon is favored by many Saxons and may be single or double-edged. The weapon easily shatters or splits open shields. It does normal rolled damage against all targets, and an additional 1d6 damage against any combatant using a shield. A fumble indicates the weapon broke.

Bow

This is a wooden missile weapon normally used by peasants for hunting and by footsoldiers in war. Knights normally do not use bows in combat.

A bow does 3d6 damage regardless of the user's Damage statistic. It is used two-handed and no shield can be used while shooting a bow. The maximum range is 150 yards. Modifiers must be applied for close or long-range shots, small or covered targets, etc. A fumble indicates that the weapon has a broken string or has cracked.

Crossbow

This is a mechanical missile weapon invented, some say, by the devil. The Pope has outlawed its use against Christians, but the damnable commoners seem not to have heard. Knights normally do not use crossbows in combat.

As with the bow or any missile weapon, negative modifiers must be used for longer ranges.

Different strengths of crossbows do different damage, and take different times to reload and shoot. A light crossbow fires at the same rate as a bow, but a heavy crossbow requires three full rounds of cocking before it can be fired.

Crossbow Table

type	*damage*	*rate of fire*	*maximum range*
Light	1d6+10	1/melee round	150 yards
Medium	1d6+13	1/2 melee rounds	200 yards
Heavy	1d6+16	1/4 melee rounds	250 yards

Dagger

This skill uses the knife as a weapon. The tool is usually metal but also possibly of stone. This includes all one-handed knives and even shortswords: everything from long dirks to table knives.

This small weapon is ineffective against heavily armored knights, but is carried by everyone, including women and priests. A knight usually has a dagger sheathed on his swordbelt, ready for use in close quarters.

Due to its small size, a dagger does one die less damage when it strikes. Thus a character who normally does 4d6 damage would do 3d6 with a dagger.

If a character with a tiny table knife is attacked by an enemy wielding a two-foot long dirk, the gamemaster may wish to adjust the damage done slightly to reflect the difference between the two similar but not identical weapons.

A fumble indicates the weapon was broken.

Flail

This wicked weapon has many spiked heads mounted on the ends of chains, which are in turn attached to a handle. It is a one-handed weapon and can be used with a shield. The flail is sometimes referred to as a "morning star" because of the spiked heads.

A flail ignores all protection given by shields, wrapping around any obstacle to damage its target. The flail also does an extra 1d6 damage to all opponents wearing chainmail armor. However, the weapon is extremely clumsy, and on a roll of 1 (the raw number on d20, before any increases due to values over 20) it always strikes the user, doing full damage. With a fumble, the weapon breaks.

Grapple

Characters in Arthurian literature often throw down their weapons and grapple an opponent in dramatic fashion. This skill simulates such tactics.

Fisticuffs are unknown in Arthur's Britain, but common brawling includes wrestling, bashing, gouging, biting, kicking, and so on. This is handled under the "Brawling" section, above, using DEX/2, and no skill is given.

Quarrelsome knights in their cups may often wrestle to prove their manhood, but this is considered brawling, not a use of the Grapple skill. Normal brawling rules apply, except that STR is used instead of DEX, to determine a winner. If a wrestling knight knows Grapple, he may use the skill, but get no Glory or experience checks.

Grapple is normally used in armed combat, either when every other weapon is broken, or when stalemate has set in between two knights with excellent weapon skills, and neither can easily hurt the other. Grappling is a risky but viable option in such instances.

Armor has no effect on the skill, nor does sitting on a horse affect it unless the gamemaster rules otherwise.

A grapple in combat must be done with the opposed resolution system. The character attempting a grapple must drop weapon and shield and tackle his enemy. This is extremely dangerous against an experienced knight with a good Damage statistic, but the reward for success may be a quick finish to a fight.

A winning Grapple roll indicates that the grappler has seized his opponent in a hold. This occurs whether the opponent is using a weapon skill or also using Grapple. A partial success does the loser no good in this instance. If the grappler loses the resolution against an opponent using a weapon, he is hit normally. Ties indicate stalemate, even if the opponent is using a sword; go on to the next round. This is an exception to the rule that a sword breaks any other weapon on a tied roll.

Once the opponent is in a hold, the grappler has a choice of two options for the following round: to attempt to immobilize the opponent with a second Grapple use, or to throw the grappled opponent down (no roll required).

The second Grapple roll is less risky. Once held, the grappled person is incapable of any action except trying to grapple the opponent back to break the grasp and allow escape (which may not be attempted if the victim's Grapple value is 0), or of trying to rearm himself with his dagger and attack the grappler. The dagger is the only weapon which can be used by a grappled person. Remember that fighting while rearming incurs the usual +5/-5 modifiers to the respective combatants.

If the hold is maintained successfully on the second round of opposed rolls,

the opponent is immobilized. In one famous instance, a knight is immobilized by Sir Turquine, who then tucks the hapless victim under his mighty arm and rides off.

If the immobilized victim attempts further combat, reflexive modifiers are +10/-10 for grappler and opponent. Assume that the loser is flat on his back, with the winner sitting on his chest, or has both arms twisted behind his back. The grappler may do normal brawling damage to the immobilized victim if no weapon is available to be picked up, and no friends are around to threaten the victim. In several cases in the literature, the winning grappler unlaces the downed character's helmet and pulls it off, creating a situation of great vulnerability for the victim, who usually surrenders at that point.

If thrown, the grappled person has no chance to resist, and takes 1d6 damage from the fall and is sprawled on the ground. +5/-5 modifiers apply on the following round. As usual, armor does not protect against this type of damage. If thrown from horseback, he also takes the normal 1d6 for the height of the fall for a total of 2d6. Further falls are obviously possible.

A fumbled Grapple indicates the would-be grappler falls down, and off his horse if mounted, taking falling damage.

Great Axe

Two-handed and double-headed, this weapon cannot be used with a shield. It does 1d6 extra damage against all targets, and an additional 1d6 against any combatant using a shield. A fumble indicates the weapon broke.

Great Spear

This is a two-handed heavy spear used to stab. It gains a +5 modifier for footsoldiers against horsemen, negating the footmen's normal disadvantage. The great spear is long enough that it also negates the +5 lance modifier versus non-lance weapons.

A fumble indicates that the spear has broken.

The Great Spear skill is used to wield a boar spear.

Great Sword

This two-handed sword cannot be used with a shield. It does 1d6 extra damage against all targets. On a fumble the great sword is dropped, but not broken, and can be recovered. On a tied resolution roll, the great sword breaks the opponent's weapon, unless it was a sword, too.

Halberd

This is a heavy, two-handed combined spear and axe which can be used to both cut and stab. It cannot be used from horseback or with a shield. Its length gains a +5 modifier for footsoldiers against horsemen, negating the footsoldier's normal disadvantage. It also does +1d6 extra damage. A fumble indicates that the halberd has broken.

Hammer

The military hammer is a blunt impact weapon which is particularly useful against plate armor. It is normally used one-handed with a shield. It gives an additional 1d6 damage against suits of partial plate, full plate, and gothic plate armor (the latter are not available until the last phases of the campaign).

A fumble indicates that the hammer broke.

Javelin

Spears that can be thrown at a nearby opponent or game animal are javelins. This is not the same weapon as a lance or spear, but is much shorter and lighter. Maximum range is 30 yards. It does two dice less than the character's Damage statistic, with a minimum of 1d6 being done. A fumble indicates the weapon broke.

Jousting Lance

The jousting lance is used just like a normal lance, as detailed below under "Lance." However, a jousting lance is a piece of sport equipment, not a weapon, and so is designed not to destroy the loser of a joust, just to knock him from his horse. This results in special rules for using jousting lances. There is no actual "Jousting Lance" skill. Instead, Lance is used. For more information on jousting lances, see the "Combat" section of the chapter.

† Lance

This is a spear used in a horse charge. It is held in the right hand and crossed over the horse's neck, allowing the knight to crouch behind his shield and impact directly with his target. Because of the type of attack, the damage done with a Lance charge uses the horse's Damage factor rather than the rider's.

Sagramore le Desirous

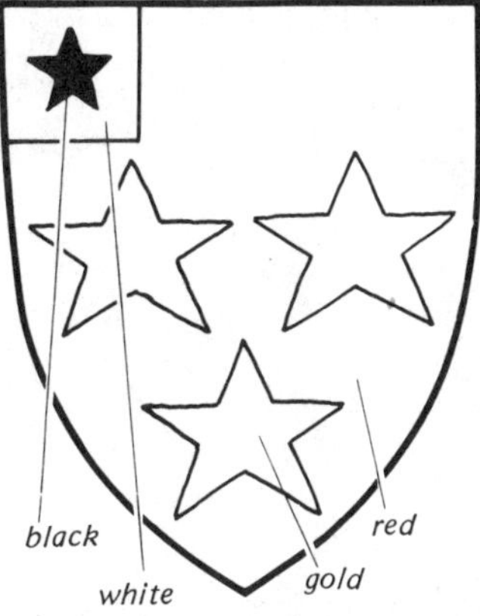

To use the horse's Damage factor in a lance charge, the character must commit to a charge during the Determination Phase explained in the "Combat" section. He must then move in a straight line for at least one melee round to get the lance charge modifier, and may move as many more as necessary to reach the target. This may be at whatever rate of movement desired (but most realistically, at a gallop).

Lance strikes are done while passing the target, who may strike back in opposed resolution if such was his intent in the Determination Phase. Unless unhorsed, the lancer must further continue in the straight line for at least one full melee round.

A lance attack uses the Damage factor of the horse rather than the rider, as written on the character sheet. Average horse Damage values of each size are:

Rouncy = 4d6
Charger = 6d6
Destrier = 8d6

The lance charge is devastating against opponents using ordinary melee weapons. When one combatant uses a lance and the other does not have a lance or great spear, the lancer receives a +5 modifier to his Lance skill.

Fighting with the lance from horseback without the charge is the same as using a spear. Use the character's Spear skill, not Lance, and remember that he does not get the additional +5 for using the charge against other weapons, and he inflicts his Damage value, not the horse's.

A lance may break more easily than some weapons: if the damage done is an odd number then the lance breaks. Also,

a fumble indicates the weapon broke before doing damage.

Lance skill is also used to joust, a friendlier and less lethal show of a martial skill. See the "Combat" section for more information.

Mace

This is a crafted weapon with flanged edges or spikes. It is one-handed. It does 1d6 additional damage against chainmail armor. A fumble indicates the mace has broken.

Morning Star

This long two-handed weapon ends in a clubbed head with spikes. It cannot be used with a shield, and does 1d6 extra damage against all targets, and an additional 1d6 damage against chainmail-armored foes. A fumble means the morning star breaks.

Spear

This is a long stick with a pointed head on the end. It is used one-handed, unlike the great spear, and it can also be used from horseback as a lance. It can not be thrown like a javelin, which is much smaller. It does normal damage. A fumble indicates the spear broke.

† Sword

This essential knightly weapon is one-handed and used with a shield. Favorite weapons have names and their own histories. A sword is of varying length but always of the best possible iron. It is called *spaetha* by the Romans, *seax* by the Saxons, and *cleddyf mawr* by the Cymri.

It does normal damage and has two advantages over all other weapons. Swords do not break when the user fumbles, but are dropped instead and can be recovered, and if a tie (identical successful skill rolls) occurs in any resolution, a sword always breaks a nonsword (excepting the Grapple skill, of course).

Warflail

This is a two-handed flail. It does +1d6 additional damage against all targets, and also wraps around all shields and ignores any protection provided by their use. An additional 1d6 damage is done to chainmail-armored foes.

Because it is a clumsy weapon, a user always strikes himself for normal damage on a straight roll of 1 (before any increases due to values over 20). On a fumble the warflail breaks.

Injury and Health

PENDRAGON IS A GAME about knighthood. The primary purpose of the knight is fighting, and much of the action in the game is personal or military combat that results in injury, whether minor or significant.

Knights expect to take injury, and wear their many scars proudly. In Arthurian literature knights often suffer great wounds, and thereafter go through long periods of healing and rest to recover. Such events are realistic as well as authentic to the stories. The following rules attempt to formalize this process, while leaving the gamemaster enough flexibility to deal with all possible situations. Violence in *Pendragon* should be realistic and terrifying, never casual or routine, and the best way to achieve this is to make injuries a serious matter.

Knights sometimes languish in foul dungeons or become feverish in the literature. Thus illness, physical deterioration, and other sources of damage beyond combat are included here, although such sordid forms of damage as disease should rarely kill a brave knight.

Keeping track of injuries and healing is a complicated process. Both the gamemaster and players are responsible for recording information accurately and honestly. You may wish to simplify portions of these rules while learning the game, but they should be used in full once familiarity is gained. The reward will be a more authentic and dramatic experience.

Hit Points

Health in *Pendragon* is measured primarily through the Total Hit Points statistic (SIZ+CON). This number represents the character's capacity to absorb injury. Death is imminent if a character has zero or negative hit points. A character with only half his hit points is half dead.

Losing Hit Points

As damage is taken during the game, hit points are lost. This loss is recorded by the player, in pencil, using the workspace on the character sheet labelled "Current Hit Points."

Damage can be partially or completely absorbed by armor, but not in all cases (see the "Sources of Damage" section below).

Characters may lose hit points from many different sources in *Pendragon*. Some forms of damage cause wounds, while some act directly on hit points. Fatigue alone never causes hit point loss.

Once injured, characters may lose further hit points through illness, excess activity, blood loss, or worse. These factors are summarized under the "Deterioration and Aggravation" rules below. Deterioration may be prevented by the unsophisticated medicine of the times, which I call Chirurgery (Chirurgery is a medieval word that is used here to mean medical care). Aggravation is caused by excess activity while a character is injured or ill, and may be averted only by avoiding activity.

Regaining Hit Points

A character's recovery from injury is a natural bodily process, which is quantified as a character's Healing Rate ((STR+CON)/10). Characters normally recover hit points equal to their Healing Rate every week (on Sunday at noon), although the gamemaster may adjust this schedule if necessary.

A critical success with Chirurgery augments the Healing Rate.

First Aid lets the injured character regain hit points immediately, and ensures that bleeding is stopped, infection prevented, and so forth, This process is independent of the character's Healing Rate, but only a few points are regained.

Magical healing spells or items, such as the potion some characters receive in character generation, may return hit

points, or otherwise magically improve a character's health, at the gamemaster's option. As always, the details of healing magic are secrets known only to the gamemaster and to a few rare gamemaster characters.

In all cases, any hit points regained over the value of the Total Hit Points statistic are not used.

Unconscious

As a character loses hit points he reaches a point at which he becomes unconscious. This important threshold is represented by the Unconscious statistic. Characters with current hit points *below* the Unconscious value are out of the action. At the moment they go below the threshold, they slump slowly to the ground, possibly staggering a few yards first, or sliding off a horse before collapsing. A DEX roll is allowed, with success indicating that any falling damage is averted. Once below the threshold, they are no longer capable of fighting, riding, or even standing.

The gamemaster may wish to let unconscious characters have brief periods of lucidity. With gamemaster approval, they may be allowed to speak quietly. For example, they might be capable of slowly dictating a will, praying for divine guidance, or describing an assailant in a weak whisper. See the nearby quotation, "Two Knights Fight to the Death."

Since they have been injured so heavily, they are unhealthy and need Chirurgery, and the "Chirurgery Needed" box is checked immediately. They continue to require chirurgery until the gamemaster says otherwise. See the "States of Health" and "Recovery from Injury and Illness" sections for more information.

Example of Injury and Unconsciousness: *A small battle with the Saxons ends the year's scenario for our sample knight, Sir Ambrut. After fighting one round of battle successfully, Sir Ambrut is caught alone (see the rules on battles in the "Chivalric Duties" chapter), and chased off the field by a band of lightly-armored but skillful mercenary sergeants. The gamemaster decides to run the combat using regular melee rounds.*

In a tremendous fight, Sir Ambrut is victorious over two assailants, also gaining a Horsemanship check for successfully outriding the remaining enemies. Ambrut takes no Major Wound in the fight, due to his heroic CON of 22 (see the "Wound Classification" section). However, the knight takes many minor injuries, including a fall from his horse, for a total of 26 points of damage, leaving him with 8 current hit points. 8 is under his Unconscious value of 9. He staggers into a wood near the battlefield, and falls unconscious. The "Chirurgery Needed" box is checked.

Zero or Negative Hit Points

As a character continues to suffer injury or deteriorate, current hit points may become a negative number. The player must continue to keep track of the number. A character at zero or negative hit points for any reason or combination of reasons (disease, drowning, wounds, deterioration, etc.) is on the verge of death. First Aid or magic may restore and preserve his feeble life enough for healing to be possible, but unless healed to positive points before midnight of that same day, the character dies. Even then Chirurgery is needed.

Example of Negative Hit Points: *After the fight mentioned above, Sir Ambrut lies unconscious on the field, with 8 hit points remaining. In his delirium he cries out. An enemy footsoldier wanders past, and seeing another victim, he brutally stabs Ambrut with his spear for 9 more points of damage: Ambrut writhes and goes limp. His current hit points are now -1. He will die later that evening, at midnight, if not given successful First Aid.*

Luckily, his squire, although separated from his knight, eventually manages to get help (a Squire roll is made successfully), and Ambrut receives First Aid for 2 points. Back to 1 point, he survives, with many new scars. The squire also takes charge of Ambrut's share of the plunder after the battle, which is won by Ambrut's side.

Recording Injuries

The workspace labelled "Current Hit Points" is used to record all important information on a character's physical state. The character's current hit points, recorded in the "Current Hit Points" box in the upper left-hand corner, measure how much damage the character is recovering from. The section also includes a space labelled "Wounds" to record the magnitude of new, untreated injuries. At the bottom can be seen the crucial "Chirurgery Needed" check-box. The state of this box indicates whether the character is healthy or unhealthy overall.

Procedure

Step 1. Write the magnitude of the injury on the lines labeled "Wounds" in the "Current Hit Points" box. Record the actual points of damage (i.e. -4, -17, etc.) that the character has just taken as a wound. Bigger wounds are much worse than small, so it is important to keep track of the magnitude of each wound taken.

Occasionally an insidious injury will be received that affects hit points without inflicting a visible wound. This is the case, for example, with disease, or if First Aid is fumbled, or if deterioration sets in after a previous injury. In these cases go directly to Step 3, without recording a wound number or checking the injury magnitude.

Step 2. Check to see if the magnitude of the injury qualifies for a Major or Mortal Wound. Check the "Wound Classification" section below.

Step 3. Subtract the magnitude of the injury from current hit points. Erase the current hit points number in the smaller, inner box in the upper left-hand corner, and put down the new total (21, 10, 3, -4, etc.).

Depending on wounds, the character's surroundings, his activity level, and other factors, the number recorded in this space may change many times during a play session.

Step 4. Check to see if current hit points have gone below the unconscious threshold. If so the character sways and passes out. A DEX roll is possible if the character is on horseback or balancing. See the "Movement" section of the chapter.

First Aid

First Aid can return lost hit points to wounded characters. It is applied on a per-wound basis.

As emergency battlefield treatment, it is only useful immediately or shortly after a wound is received. It cannot be applied to wounds more than a day old, and its benefits can only be received once per wound. If no wound is recorded, First Aid cannot be used.

Each use of First Aid takes several minutes, or 3d6 melee rounds. More serious wounds should take longer to deal with, but this is up to the gamemaster to decide. If a failed attempt is made, it is

too late for further tries. Any subsequent medical attention is subsumed under the heading of Chirurgery.

Note that many small wounds can be taken care of using First Aid and the knight returned to full hit points, but a severe wound leaves him still damaged.

Procedure

1. Determine who will make the First Aid attempt. Usually the most skilled person available should make the attempt, even if that person is a gamemaster character. Injuries are too serious in *Pendragon* to be handled by anyone but experts.

2. Determine *which* wound is being treated, and its magnitude (see the "Wounds" line: the number might be -3, -14, or whatever) before making an attempt.

3. Roll normally (modifiers may apply at gamemaster option) and see results below.

4. Adjust current hit points. Excess points gained beyond the magnitude of the wound are not used.

5. *Regardless of result,* erase the number on the "Wounds" line to show that the wound has been treated by First Aid. No further attempts can be made.

Results of First Aid

Critical Success: Patient gains 1d3+3 hit points.

Success: Patient gains 1d3 hit points.

Failure: No improvement.

Fumble: Patient loses 1d3 hit points directly from current hit points (but no new wound number is recorded). The patient's condition has been worsened, and the wound is now infected, bleeding further, or otherwise exacerbated. The character is unhealthy: check the "Chirurgery Needed" box.

Wound Classification

When a character is wounded, the magnitude of damage is crucial. Three classifications of wounds are recognised for game purposes, based on the wound magnitude in comparison to the character's CON (Major Wound) and Total Hit Points (Mortal Wound) statistics. Characters with high SIZ and CON values suffer less severely from injuries.

Remember that even at full hit points a knight is likely to have huge bruises, cuts, scrapes, and pulled muscles capable of disabling the normal 20th century male. These guys are tough!

Light Wounds

Damage less than CON (the Major Wound threshold) indicates bruises, cuts, or other minor injuries which are highly painful, but do not in themselves cause any serious effects. A light wound may later fester and worsen if not dealt with properly (see the "First Aid" and "Recovery From Injury and Illness" sections), but it has no immediate effect on combat or any other abilities. Aggravation damage may occur if a character fights or takes other violent activity after receiving several light wounds, at gamemaster option.

Cumulative light wounds may bring the character below his Unconscious threshold. Once the character has become unconscious, Chirurgery is needed, and deterioration may set in. See the section entitled "Recovery from Injury and Illness" below.

Bodily weakness from cumulative light wounds, unhealthy resting conditions, or fumbled First Aid rolls, may also result in the character becoming ill, again at the gamemaster's option.

Terminology: Injury and Health

Aggravation: The result when an injured or ill character is excessively active. Does 1 or more points of damage per incident of activity, based on the character's state of health, current hit points, activity level, duration of activity, and gamemaster interpretation.

Activity Level: A measure of how physically demanding various activities like eating or fighting are, particularly in terms of fatigue, the possibility of reopening old wounds, or other events capable of interfering with the healing process. *Moderate* activity causes aggravation for unhealthy characters. *Strenuous* activity causes aggravation of all injured characters. Subject to gamemaster interpretation.

Chirurgery: Medieval medical care. This skill prevents deterioration if applied successfully. Rolled once a week, normally at the beginning of the week. Modifiers may be applied to the skill.

A critical success at chirurgery doubles the character's Healing Rate for the week.

Conditions: A measure of how healthy the environment of a healing character is, in terms of dirt, flies, extremes of heat or cold, ventilation and other factors. Characters in the game will be only vaguely aware of these points, unless professional chirurgeons. Bad conditions may cause a -5 modifier to the Chirurgery skill, or cause an illness to be gained, both at the gamemaster's option.

Current Hit Points: Number expressing the current overall level of injury (not health) of a character. May be zero or negative, indicating imminent death.

Damage: Raw damage rolled and inflicted on a character; usually reduced by armor. Causes wounds and injuries.

Deterioration: The result when an unhealthy character fails to receive successful chirurgery. 1d6 damage is inflicted from deterioration every week, at the same time as natural healing, on Sunday at noon.

First Aid: Emergency medical treatment. 1d3 damage is healed with a success. Fumbled First Aid causes a character to become unhealthy.

Healing Rate: Derived statistic. Quantifies the rate at which a character's body heals its injuries naturally, with or without chirurgery (although a critical success with chirurgery doubles the rate). Equals (STR+CON)/10. Expressed in number of current hit points recovered

Major Wounds

Damage from a single injury that is equal to or greater than CON (the Major Wound threshold) represents serious damage that the character's constitution is too weak to shrug off. Examples might be a concussion, crushed or broken bones, heavy bleeding, or damaged internal organs. There are several negative consequences to Major Wounds in game terms.

1) The character immediately goes unconscious unless he makes a successful d20 roll against his current hit points (for example, a character with 10 hit points left would need to roll a 10 or less to stay conscious).

2) Should the character avoid unconsciousness he may wish to continue fighting or performing some similarly active task. The character must make a successful Valorous roll if in combat, possibly with a modifier. Failure indicates the knight cannot summon up the courage to continue fighting. He hesitates, and may not enter combat unless forced into it. A fumbled Valorous roll means the knight flees in fear, or surrenders. A critical success may gain some benefit. See the "Ideals and Passions" for the full rules on trait rolls.

If a character takes a Major Wound while out of combat (say from a fall), and makes a hit point roll, the gamemaster decides if a Valorous roll is needed to continue taking action.

3) The player must make a roll on the Statistics Lost Table (see the "Winter Phase" section below) immediately to discover the permanent effect of the Major Wound, if any. All derived statistics, such as Movement Rate or Unconscious, must be refigured immediately if a loss to a statistic occurs from this roll. If the Total Hit Points statistic drops, current hit points are not affected unless the character is at full hit points currently (in which case they drop to the new maximum).

4) The Chirurgery Needed box must be checked. The character requires the attention of an expert in order to avoid infection and other dangers resulting from his injury, described as deterioration in these rules.

5) If further action is taken once a Major Wound is suffered, both aggravation and deterioration may set in. See the section entitled "Recovery from Injury and Illness" below.

Major Wound Example: *Hunwulf the Red, a huge, fat old knight (SIZ 18, CON 9, Valorous 17, Hit Points 27, Unconscious 7) has become too old and unhealthy to fight safely. Even a 9-point wound is a Major Wound for him, given his mediocre constitution.*

Hunwulf rashly charges into one last fight, and takes 9 points of damage through armor, exactly the minimum for a Major Wound. His player checks the Chirurgery Needed box. He then rolls against Hunwulf's current hit points of 18 on d20 and easily succeeds, indicating that Hunwulf stays conscious. The player also easily succeeds with a Valorous roll — Hunwulf is well-known for his valor. So Hunwulf does not surrender or hesitate to attack. Now the player rolls on the Statistics Lost Table for the Major Wound's effects, and rolls a 2, so Hunwulf loses a point of DEX. Checking the character sheet, the player adjusts Hunwulf's statistics to take into account the DEX loss: sadly, Hunwulf's Movement Rate goes down a point. At this juncture in combat, Hunwulf may fight on, with no immediate penalty to skills or restrictions on actions (except the fear of death). Aggravation may occur over the longer term, however.

Mortal Wounds

Damage from a single blow that is equal to or greater than the Total Hit Points statistic is usually mortal, thus the term. The character has received a horrible injury; his skull is cracked, an artery severed, internal organs punctured, or even a limb amputated, if the gamemaster so rules. The character is incapacitated and totally helpless. However, he may still survive, if certain criteria are met. Follow the steps below.

per week of game time. Healing occurs on Sunday at noon. The effects of natural healing may be reduced or eliminated by the process of deterioration, which occurs simultaneously when chirurgery is not received successfully.

Healthy: The normal state of health. A character may be injured and missing hit points, but still healthy overall.

Injury: The results of damage, subtracted from current hit points.

Light Wound: A magnitude of injury that is not likely to cause problems unless a character is excessively active after injury. Equals a number less than CON.

Magnitude of Wound: A number equal to the injury received, checked against Major Wound and Mortal wound levels.

Major Wound: A serious magnitude of injury. Often has permanent effects. A number equal to or over CON, but less than Total Hit Points.

Mortal Wound: A lethal magnitude of injury. Usually leaves permanent effects if survived. A number equal or greater than Total Hit Points.

Natural Healing: The body's normal healing process, quantified as a character's Healing Rate statistic.

"Needs Chirurgery" Box: The box in the lower portion of the Current Hit Points area of the character sheet. Indicates an unhealthy character. Once checked, may be erased only with gamemaster approval after appropriate rest and healing.

Total Hit Points: a statistic, starting point and maximum for Current Hit Points. Equals Mortal Wound level.

Unconscious: Threshold number of current hit points, below which character becomes unconscious. Equals Total Hit Points/4. If a character is unconscious, no actions may be taken without gamemaster approval. When a character falls unconscious, either from normal damage, illness, or aggravation damage, the character relaxes and slumps to the ground. A DEX roll may be made to avoid a fall off a horse or precarious position.

Unhealthy: A sickly, vunerable state of health. Characters may become unhealthy through injury or through illness and disease. Unhealthy characters need chirurgery. Deterioration sets in if chirurgery is not received.

An unhealthy state is indicated by a character's "Chirurgery Needed" box being checked.

The gamemaster determines when a character becomes healthy again: normally this should be after several weeks of rest, with hit points regained to above the Unconscious statistic.

1) First Aid must be successfully applied within one hour or the character will die, and even then recovery is doubtful. First Aid must restore enough lost hit points to give the character at least 1 current point. Obviously, if the character is more than 5 points negative, the wound is always fatal. Chirurgery cannot help until the character is out of immediate danger. The only escape is magic healing, which is totally under the control of the gamemaster.

2) If the character is brought back to 1 or more hit points he lives, but immediately suffers 3 rolls on the Statistics Lost Table to determine permanent effects. Derived statistics must be refigured immediately if losses to statistics occur (current hit points are not reduced).

3) The "Chirurgery Needed" box must be checked if a character receives a Mortal Wound and receives successful First Aid, bringing him back to one hit point or better. He lies unconscious, and his future is still in grave doubt.

States of Health

As noted above, a character in *Pendragon* is either healthy or unhealthy. For the sake of simplicity, there is no middle ground. A character may have a reasonable number of hit points and still be unhealthy, or he may have only a few hit points above Unconscious and still be active. The "Chirurgery Needed" box at the bottom of the "Current Hit Points" section shows the current situation.

Healthy: Healthy individuals are all those who do not require Chirurgery: if the box is not checked, the character is fine and may function normally. The character is considered healthy even if not at full hit points: knights are trained to live with minor injuries. The injuries of healthy individuals heal weekly at the Healing Rate (see "Recovery from Injury and Illness" below).

Even if an injured character is healthy, excessive strenuous activity will cause aggravation, which is handled by incident, not by week. See below.

Unhealthy: If the "Chirurgery Needed" box is checked, the character is unhealthy and needs care. Rest is needed and action is liable to worsen his condition.

Normally the check is gained by:

1. Characters losing hit points to below the Unconscious level.

2. Characters who took a Major Wound.

3. Characters who took a Mortal Wound (and survived).

4. Characters who received a fumbled First Aid roll.

5. Characters contracting an illness due to unhealthy conditions or other sources. This might include poisoned characters.

Unhealthy characters are incapable of taking care of themselves properly and natural deterioration (see below) may set in unless someone else actively tends to their needs. This active attention is called Chirurgery. Success at Chirurgery prevents deterioration.

Once a character is unhealthy and the "Chirurgery Needed" box is checked, it remains checked until the gamemaster approves its removal, normally after several weeks of rest. At a minimum, the character must be conscious before the check is erased. After that the character's status is upgraded to healthy, and he does not need chirurgery any more.

Recovery from Injury or Illness

Recovery is unpredictable. Many situations will cause recovery to be delayed or even retarded, and weak characters may require months of convalescence before full recovery takes place. It is even possible for unhealthy characters to die during convalescence, should they be badly cared for. In the literature, even Sir Lancelot is often out of action due to injury.

Once a character is injured, recovery from injury or illness is determined for every week of game time.

If injured characters insist on activity instead of resting, aggravation damage must be applied on a per-action basis, although chirurgery, natural healing, and deterioration are always determined on a weekly basis.

Natural Healing

Natural healing occurs at noon on Sunday (game time) in the form of hit points gained equal to the Healing Rate statistic. Unhealthy characters who failed to receive successful chirurgery during the week also suffer 1d6 points of deterioration damage at this time.

Even if a character is injured on Saturday he normally heals (and may suffer deterioration) on the following day. Gamemasters will have to determine partial healing and deterioration rates when necessary.

In all cases, natural healing occurs weekly, regardless of what form a character's injuries or illness have taken, or whether he is resting or active during the week.

Due to damage caused by deterioration and aggravation, the final result of a week's cycle of rest and activity may be nil, or a loss of hit points. Chirurgery is used to stave off deterioration, but nothing can save an overly active character from aggravating his illness or injuries.

Deterioration and Aggravation

Injuries or illness may grow worse rather than better. If the character is active enough to interfere with healing, or if he is not tended properly, then he may take further hit point damage. This may be due to blood loss, dehydration, infection, further illness, and more. The damage from deterioration and aggravation indicates the effects of all these factors.

Deterioration

Deterioration only affects unhealthy characters who do *not* get a successful Chirurgery roll during that week. Only one Chirurgery roll is allowed per week, with deterioration occurring if failure or fumble occurs.

Deterioration causes the loss of 1d6 hit points per week directly to current hit points (no wound is recorded and First Aid cannot help). As with natural healing, this damage occurs on Sunday at noon. The net result of the two hit point

adjustments may be a gain in hit points, a loss, or nil.

Aggravation

Gamemasters must inevitably face situations where knights who should be resting insist on activity, perhaps "to travel just for a few hours" or "One good fight..." During a scenario an injured character may choose (or be forced) to leave his sickbed for several days, then rest, then ride many miles, then rest again. The rules for aggravation take care of this. For simplicity's sake, cumulative resting between actions is not tracked, only damage from specific activities.

Aggravation means making a condition worse by activity while ill or injured. *Each incident* of aggravation causes 1 or more points of damage directly to current hit points, and no wound is recorded. 1 point is the normal loss, but up to 3 points may be suffered from extremely violent or sustained activities, such as mortal combat with an ogre, at the gamemaster's option.

Aggravation damage is inflicted after the activity is complete unless the gamemaster decides otherwise. The extra damage caused by aggravation may cause a character to become unconscious immediately after his rash action.

Current health, extent of injuries, and duration and intensity of activity are all important in determining aggravation. See the table below. Aggravation is possible for all injured characters, healthy or unhealthy, when strenuous activity is undertaken. Aggravation also may occur for unhealthy characters when even moderate activity is undertaken. Note that characters below the Unconscious threshold cannot receive aggravation damage because they can, at best, perform only light activities. Normally they will be comatose.

A brief and trivial incident, such as a ten-minute dance during a feast, should rarely cause aggravation except to a severely wounded character, probably one with a major wound who happens to still be conscious. The gamemaster will have to judge each incident separately, based on the Activity Level definitions below, storytelling concerns, and common sense.

Aggravation can be heaped upon deterioration, but aggravation cannot be halted by Chirurgery, or any other die roll.

Two Knights Fight to the Death

Two knights, met as strangers in a forest, fight a duel and find they are well-matched, the older knight's skill being countered by the strength of the younger knight, Sir Percivale. Too stubborn to halt the combat, they fight until they are unable to continue, each taking many light wounds. Neither notices the other's serious condition until too late.

In game terms, the two knights fight until their hit points go below the Unconscious threshold. This example serves to illustrate a generous gamemaster interpretation of the Unconscious rules. Although scarcely able to stand, and certainly not capable of further fighting, Sir Percivale is able to speak to his opponent and to make a successful prayer.

...Thus they fought near half a day, and never rested but right little, and there was none of them both that had less wounds than fifteen, and they bled so much that it was marvel they stood on their feet. But this knight that fought with Sir Percivale was a proved knight and a wise fighting knight, and Sir Percivale was young and strong, not knowing in fighting as the other was.

Then Sir Percivale spoke first, and said, "Sir knight, hold thy hand a while still, for we have foughten for a simple matter, and quarrel overlong, and therefore I require thee tell me thy name, for I was never or this time matched."

"So God me help," said that knight, "and never or this time was there never knight that wounded me so sore as thou hast done, and yet have I foughten in many battles; and now shalt thou wit that I am a knight of the Table Round, and my name is Sir Ector de Maris, brother unto the good knight, Sir Lancelot du Lac."

"Alas," said Sir Percivale, "and my name is Sir Percivale de Gales that hath made my quest to seek Sir Lancelot, and now I am siker [certain] that I shall never finish my quest, for ye have slain me with your hands."

"It is not so," said Sir Ector, "for I am slain by your hands, and may not live. Therefore I require you," said Sir Ector unto Sir Percivale, "ride ye hereby to a priory and bring me a priest that I may receive my Saviour, for I may not live. And when ye come to the court of King Arthur tell not my brother, Sir Lancelot, how that ye slew me, for then he would be your mortal enemy, but ye may say that I was slain in my quest as I sought him."

"Alas," said Sir Percivale, "ye say that thing that never will be, for I am so faint for bleeding that I may unnethe [scarcely] stand, how should I then take my horse?"

— Malory XI, 13

Accidentally they have broken their Round Table vows to never fight against each other. Having rashly quested without squires, there is no one to help them or go for aid. Both would have died eventually from deterioration, except that Percivale prays with great faith and piety, and the Holy Grail, born by a maiden, miraculously appears and heals both of them.

Activity Levels Table

No Activity: Resting, eating, or sleeping. No aggravation. The best way to recover.

Light Activity: Walking short distances slowly, eating heavily, talking, writing short letters. No aggravation, even for unhealthy characters, unless the activity is performed to excess.

Moderate Activity: walking longer distances, riding a horse (even for a few minutes), celebrating, dancing, engaging in romance, engaging in an angry argument. Aggravation is possible for unhealthy characters, at gamemaster option.

Strenuous Activity: fighting, running, climbing, traveling a significant distance on horse or on foot (or even in a litter, if the gamemaster so rules). Aggravation is certain for unhealthy characters, and possible for healthy characters who are injured.

These rules are intended to permit freedom of action for players, as opposed to simply forbidding injured characters to be involved in the game. Players who wish to risk their character by taking actions while wounded or unhealthy are free to do so, with realistic consequences. Sometimes in *Pendragon* action may be more important than life: perhaps a character wishes to avenge a brother, or deliver a vital message, even if it means riding or fighting while injured.

Aggravation and Deterioration Example: *Sir Ambrut enters a rowdy tournament held on a Saturday to celebrate the victorious battle fought earlier that year by Baron Yvane's men.*

As the day progresses, Ambrut fights many times, and takes several light wounds, gaining successful First Aid for most, after which he fights again. After the third wound, the gamemaster rules that Ambrut is performing strenuous actitivity while injured, and tells the player to record 1 point of aggravation damage. First Aid may not be gained for this damage.

At the end of the day, still conscious, Ambrut staggers to his tent to rest. On the first evening of his convalescence he is down 13 points. He is healthy, so deterioration will not occur, nor is chirurgery needed. Conveniently, he will gain points the very next day, Sunday, when natural healing is normally applied.

Sir Ambrut rests Sunday morning. His comrades stop in to say hello, but do not insist that he join them that day. So his level of activity is light. At noon, Ambrut gains his Healing Rate of 3 hit points as his natural healing for the week. Further healing will occur normally on the following Sunday.

Ambrut decides to rest the requisite number of weeks to return to full hit points, avoiding any further strenuous activity in order to ensure quick recovery. Being healthy, he is able to engage in moderate activity freely, such as dancing and romance.

Chirurgery

Chirurgery is applied to unhealthy patients only. Chirurgery's purpose is to halt deterioration. Successful application means that deterioration does not occur. The successful chirurgeon has counteracted the forces which would have caused the additional damage from deterioration.

Only one Chirurgery roll per patient may be attempted per week. Normally the roll should be attempted during the beginning of the week, and the result noted by the gamemaster for future reference. If failure or even fumble is the result, the result is not obvious until the following Sunday. Note that if more than one chirurgeon try to use their arts on a single patient in a week, all automatically fail.

Results of Chirurgery

Critical Success: The patient's health improves rapidly. The patient gains double his normal Healing Rate that week, in addition to avoiding deterioration.

Success: Patient does not suffer deterioration.

Failure: Patient suffers deterioration (see "Recovery from Injury" below).

Fumble: Patient loses 1d3 hit points directly from current hit points immediately (but no new wound number is recorded), and suffers deterioration at the end of the week.

Modifiers to Chirurgery

If unclean or unhealthy conditions (disease, severe filth, freezing cold) predominate in the area that a patient is recuperating in, a -5 modifier to the Chirurgery skill is applied. Other modifiers must be determined by the gamemaster.

Sources of Damage

Many things cause physical damage. Weapons are foremost, but sometimes accidents are not far behind. Magic can also inflict damage, but this is unusual: the effects of magic are normally more subtle.

All damage is figured in the same way: by subtracting damage points from current hit points. Wounds and recovery may be handled differently, however, at the gamemaster's option. Suffocation and disease do not normally cause Major or Mortal wounds, but on the down side, cannot be dealt with using First Aid unless the gamemaster wishes it.

Aggravation: Caused by excess activity while already injured. See above. First Aid is not allowed.

Battle or Combat Wounds: The primary injury sustained during the game. If the character is wearing armor then it absorbs some or all of the damage. A wound number is recorded for wound damage, so Major and Mortal wounds must be checked for, and First Aid may be applied.

Deterioration: Suffered by unhealthy characters who do not receive proper care, in the form of chirurgery. See above. First Aid may not be used on damage from deterioration.

Disease: This should be a rare event in *Pendragon*. Usually disease results only from incarceration in a deep dungeon, rather than from a casual trip to a large city or similar action. The gamemaster will have to determine damage and whether the disease causes a wound that First Aid can help. Normally no wound is inflicted, only general loss of hit points. A diseased character is unhealthy, regardless of hit points. Check the "Needs Chirurgery" box and proceed normally.

Dropped Objects: Dropped objects do damage dependent upon their size and the height from which they are dropped. Size is determined in pounds, with each 10 lbs. = 1 point of damage. Height adds damage at the rate of 1 point of damage per 3 feet dropped. Thus a 35 lb. rock, dropped from 23 feet, causes (size = 3.5

pts. = 4 pts.) + (height = 8 pts.) = 12 points of damage. Armor protects against dropped objects, and a wound number is recorded, with normal results.

Falling: Falling from a distance of less than three feet results in no damage. Each six feet or fraction thereof adds 1d6 damage. For instance, falling off a horse, about a five-foot drop, causes 1d6 damage. A fall of twelve feet, from a house roof, causes 2d6. A fall of 50 feet, from a castle wall, causes 8d6. Armor does not absorb falling damage. A wound number is recorded for falling damage.

Fire or Heat: Fire in contact with skin does 1d6 damage per melee round, cumulatively. Thus after four rounds, a character would have taken a wound of 4d6 magnitude from a torch thrust against his body. Fires may also cause suffocation damage through smoke (see below).

Armor protects against fire damage for only one melee round, after which it becomes too hot to protect the body. Armor cools off in only one turn as well.

Huge fires, or sources of heat such as boiling lead, may well be hotter than normal fire, doing 2d6 damage per round or even more, and may do damage at a distance. The gamemaster must determine fire damage beyond the basic 1d6. However, no natural fire causes damage to something over twelve feet distant.

Fire wounds can be tricky to handle in game terms. A wound number should be recorded for fire damage if fire actually is brought in contact with the character, but it should be based on the total damage inflicted, not the damage per round. Heat simply causes general hit point damage.

First Aid is useful for dealing with most fire and heat damage. But when no wound numbers are recorded, only one or two First Aid rolls should be made.

Suffocation: Inhaling water, smoke, or poisonous vapors may be averted by attempting a CON roll. This simulates holding one's breath. Each melee round the roll must be made. If successful there is no damage. If sustained for many rounds, a negative modifier to CON may be imposed. Once the CON roll is failed, the character takes 1D6 damage to hit points per melee round thereafter while within the substance, even more if damage in addition to suffocation (like poison or heat) is being inflicted by the inhaled substance. No actual wound is inflicted.

Recovery from simple suffocation may be more rapid than from physical wounds at the gamemaster's option.

The Winter Phase

EACH SESSION OF *Pendragon* begins with the Winter Phase. The winter is a time to engage in training, in amorous pursuits, and in gossip. In game terms, the players perform character updating.

Although most military activity stops for the winter, people still are active. They gather for the feasts and holy days. These meetings are of major importance; a lord often calls his vassals to feast at his castle, or travels through the snow to visit each of them at their own holdings.

Thus most of the wintertime is spent in non-scenario action. Gamemasters may wish to run scenarios that take place during the winter, and if so, will have to rule as to whether the normal opportunities for training are available during that same year, or lost due to the characters being in action instead.

The Winter Phase is formalized into these steps:

1. Perform Solo (if applicable)
2. Experience Check Rolls
3. Aging (if applicable)
4. Check Economic Circumstances
5. Stable Rolls
6. Family Rolls
7. Training and Practice
8. Compute Glory
9. Add Glory Bonus Points (if applicable)

Step 1: Perform Solo

Your character may have opportunity to participate in one or more of the Solo Scenarios. This is particularly important if you have a romantic knight, or a knight that missed the last game year of play. Check with the gamemaster. If a solo is performed, it is always done first thing in the Winter Phase, to acquire checks, etc. Solo Scenarios are found in the "Scenarios" chapter.

Step 2: Experience Check Rolls

Characters spend some of the winter reflecting back over the year that has gone by. This process is simulated using an experience check roll. Improvements are recorded as an increase in the checked skill, passion, or trait value. The process is the same to increase any skill, passion, or trait. Statistics cannot be increased by experience.

Roll a d20 once for each experience check. If the number rolled is greater than the current value, then the character learned from experience and adds one point to that value. If the value is at 20 or greater, a roll of 20 still boosts it by another one point. So a character with a checked Proud trait of 24 who received a 20 on the experience check roll would increase his Proud to 25.

The process is repeated for every check. Each skill gets only one check per year, but any number of skills may be checked. The number of successes achieved during play is not relevant: only one check is needed, and more gain no bonus. The player determines the order in which he rolls for checks.

If your primary squire has any checks, roll for each skill normally.

Step 3: Aging

Increase the character's age by one year at this time. All aging is done during the Winter Phase, regardless of actual birthdate (it is as if all characters were born in January or February). Your primary squire also ages at this point, and is replaced with a new 15-year-old squire upon becoming age 21.

Every character of 35 years of age or more must roll on the Aging Table every new year. The result of aging is a random reduction in one or more of the character's statistics. For example, a character might lose a point of STR and a

point of CON, or two points of SIZ, in a given year.

The range is from zero to four. In most years of aging no statistics will be lost, and no more than four points can be lost in a single year's aging.

Aging will eventually take a character out of play, usually around age 50 or later. When any statistic reaches a value of 3 or less, even APP, the character is bedridden and may no longer participate in active play. A bedridden character no longer receives Glory unless circumstances are truly unusual, but continues to age. He may still give orders (which will probably be ignored), write a will, tell tales of his adventures, or take other actions that the gamemaster permits.

When any statistic reaches 0, the character dies.

Aging Procedure: Aging uses two tables in sequence. The Aging Table shows the number of dice rolled on the Statistics Lost Table, where stats are actually reduced.

To determine aging, roll 2d6 and consult the Aging Table to find the number of statistics affected by aging this year. This is given in terms of the number of dice rolled on the Statistics Lost Table. For example, if the first roll is a 4, this calls for two dice to be rolled on the second table. Often the number of dice called for by the Aging Table will be zero. But if not, continue.

After rolling the required number of d6s called for from the Aging Table, consult the Statistics Lost Table to determine which statistic values, if any, were reduced by one point. For example, if three dice are rolled, and all are 2s, the character loses three points of DEX. Note that a roll of 6 on the Statistics Lost table indicates that no statistic was lost from that die roll.

A character may die as a result of the second roll.

Galeholt the Haut Prince

Aging Table

2d6	*Statistics Affected*
2	4
3	3
4	2
5	1
6–8	0
9	1
10	2
11	3
12	4

Statistics Affected shows the number of d6s to roll on the Statistics Lost Table below.

Statistics Lost Table: Besides aging, this crucial table is also used when a character receives a Major or Mortal Wound, suffers a shock from a failed invocation of a passion, or perhaps suffers from some magical effect. See the "Injury and Health" section of this chapter and the "Ideals and Passions" chapter for more information.

When characters lose statistics from this table, various natural forces such as disease or inimical magic are blamed. For example, characters who suffer a loss of SIZ (muscle or bone mass reduced) are considered to have been afflicted with the "Evil Eye."

Statistics Lost Table

1d6	*result*	*blamed affliction*
1	SIZ	Evil Eye
2	DEX	Palsy
3	STR	Elf Stroke
4	CON	Consumption
5	APP	Pox
6	no loss	

Step 4: Check Economic Circumstances

4a. Determine Grade of Maintenance

Every character must determine his situation as regards food, money, clothing, and shelter in consultation with the gamemaster. An overall grade of maintenance will be established for your character (i.e. Impoverished Knight, Rich Knight).

Household knights usually have little control over their state of maintenance: their lord gives them the necessary things as the normal course of affairs. They will almost always be maintained as Ordinary Knights, unless greatly favored by their lord.

Vassal knights (player characters) usually are capable only of maintaining themselves at a Ordinary Knight's grade, unless they have gained wealth from plunder or ransoms.

Lord knights are usually expected to maintain themselves at a Rich Knight's grade. They have the resources to do this unless disaster or war strikes their lands.

Only the richest knights and greatest lords maintain themselves at the grade of Superlative Knight.

Perform this check by asking the gamemaster if anything important has happened to the character's lands and economic needs, keeping notes as needed. Raids, unscheduled visits by a lord, or even faerie curses might reduce a knight's economic circumstances, forcing a reduction in his grade of maintenance, while a very good harvest might let a knight increase his grade of maintenance.

Gifts given by the lord to the knight should be determined now, and any plunder or other valuable items gained during the last year evaluated for worth. This may be enough that the knight may increase his grade of maintenance, even though the lord has not provided for it. Buying and selling may have to be done in order to convert goods into cash: see the "Wealth" chapter.

4b. Reduce Clothing Value

For all grades of maintenance, reduce the character's best suit of clothing (listed under "Equipment Carried" on the character sheet) to 1/2 its previous value in Libra. This reflects the fact that even the most expensive formal clothes go quickly out of style, in addition to suffering normal wear and tear. New clothes can be purchased if desired.

4c. Apply Economic Effects

Knights incur various modifiers to rolls on subsequent tables in this segment of the Winter Phase. Keep track of these modifiers on a piece of scrap paper. Die rolls modified to less than 1 are considered rolls of 1, while rolls greater than 20 are considered rolls of 20.

Impoverished Knights: This is a disastrous economic state to be in. No knight should suffer such a state if any alterna-

tive is available and consistent with the dictates of loyalty and honor.

If the knight has a horse, it will die during the winter on any roll except a 19 or 20 during the Stable segment (found in Step 5, below). An impoverished knight's children suffer a -15 on the Child Survival Table found under Step 6, below. No further children are born to the starving and diseased household of an impoverished knight. The knight's armor suffers a permanent 1-point loss of protection value every winter due to severe rust and neglect of proper repair and care. All knights who are impoverished must make a CON roll or lose 1 CON point during the winter.

However, even with all this to suffer, the knight loses no Glory nor do his traits and passions change. The state of a knight's reputation is independent of such petty issues as money.

Poor Knights: This grade of maintenance is unfortunate but not disastrous. Many knights occasionally suffer this state for a year or two during their careers.

Horse Survival Table rolls suffer a cumulative -3 reduction for each consecutive poor year. Thus, during the first poor year, horses die on a roll of 1-5. In the second poor year, they die with a 1-8 result. After the sixth straight year that a knight is maintained at a Poor Knight's grade, the reduction is -18, so all remaining horses die. Child Survival Table rolls also suffer this -3 reduction for each successive poor year, so after the sixth such year, no children live. Childbirth Table rolls suffer a -5 modifier.

Ordinary Knights: No special effects apply. All tables are rolled on normally.

Rich Knights: Child Survival Table rolls receive a +1 modifier. All Childbirth Table rolls receive a +3 modifier. Horse Survival Table rolls are normal.

Superlative Knights: Horse Survival Table rolls receive a +2 modifier, thus no horses die. Furthermore, the horses are sleeker and trimmer, with silver tack and bells on the reins. Child Survival Table rolls receive a +3 modifier, so no children die in a superlative knight's family. Childbirth Table rolls receive a +5 modifier.

Step 5: Stable Rolls

Every horse in active play must be checked to see if it made it through the adventures of being a knight's steed. Horses may die, with bad luck or poor conditions of care.

The table below determines that, on average, horses will live to age 10. But some horses may get lucky and live to an absurd age. Characters riding the same favorite warhorse for year after year must have their situation reviewed by the gamemaster.

All knights with a lord get new animals as needed to maintain the minimum stable of one charger, one rouncy, and one sumpter, but any extra or unusual horses (superior chargers, destriers, unique gamemaster horses) are not replaced.

Roll d20 for each horse owned, applying modifiers as needed.

Horse Survival Table

d20	*result*
1-2	Horse dies, breaks a leg, loses its wind, etc.
3-20	Horse is healthy

Step 6: Family Rolls

Your family already exists, but children are desirable, especially for a vassal knight. The ideal way to gain children is through marriage. Once a marriage is achieved, legitimate children are possible. The wife's Glory and dowry are also useful: see below.

If your character is unmarried and wishes to remain so this winter, skip to step 6c, in which you determine events for your family overall.

6a. Marriage

When a character wishes to marry, the player should inform the gamemaster, who will rule whether this honor is possible for the character.

A marriage may require some game play to find the wife, or the Random Marriage Table can be used. Either way, no characters may start the game already married.

Most marriages are one of two types: below your class and within your class. To marry above your class, into a count's or a duke's holding, requires game play, not random die rolling.

Marriage Below Character's Class: Use this course of action whenever your character wants to have a wife, no matter what or who. She will probably be a handmaid of your lord's wife, a serving woman, an assistant seamstress to some rich merchant woman, or the younger sister of a knight. Household knights usually marry this way.

The gamemaster should almost always permit this form of marriage, unless the character has been absent from home for years, has been shamed, or unless the fact of marriage would not fit in well with the scenarios he intends to run.

The procedure is simple. Get permission from the character's lord with a roll of Loyalty (Lord). If successful, the lord grants the boon to wed. If your knight has not already chosen an available woman, the lord selects an appropriate match. Once successful, the character is married to an ordinary woman who has a dowry of 1d6 Libra and 10 Glory.

If the loyalty roll fails then the lord refuses permission to wed. The knight may ask again next winter. A fumble might indicate that the lord was offended somehow, or that something humorous happened, but a fumble should not indicate marriage to an unsuitable woman.

Marriage Within Character's Class: For a vassal knight or higher noble it may take time to find a likely candidate for marriage. The gamemaster should personalize potential wives who hold great dowries and have great Glory. See the "Glory and Ambitions" chapter for more information on Glory derived from marriage.

To find an ordinary wife within the character's class, roll his Courtesy once each winter. If successful, you may either roll on the Random Marriage Table below, or wait a year. If you choose to put it off, just note "met candidate for marriage, still waiting" in your character's history. You can wait for years if you want, if there is no pressure from your lord.

Each year you wait, add one to the d20 die roll on the Random Marriage Table when you do roll. A roll over 20 is considered a roll of 20.

If you fail your Courtesy roll, you do not add one to the Random Marriage Table for that year.

When time for marriage, roll on the table. Only one chance is allowed. If you

A roe deer.

get what seems to be a bad match, it is obviously at the political will of your lord.

On the table under dowry, "Goods" refers to valuable items like rugs or furs that are worth 1 Librum in value per point listed. See the "Wealth" chapter for more information.

Random Marriage Table

d20	dowry	Glory
1-4	no holding, 1d3+6 goods	10
5-7	1 manor, 1d6 goods	25
8-17	1 manor, 1d6+3 goods	50
18-19	2 manors, 1d6+6 goods	100
20	2 manors, 2d6+6 goods	250

6b. Children

Players make a d20 roll on the Childbirth Table once per year for player character wives, concubines, lovers, camp followers, and carnal paramours.

Nonwives may be kept by any knight, but they each require a fee of .5 £. per year, subtracted from records before the childbirth roll is made. If payment can't be made then the knight was unable to maintain the woman's interest or health and she has departed; childbirth is not performed for that character.

Wives do not require extra payment. Their costs are figured into the knight's stipend or holding. However, not having a wife does *not* mean that a surplus from the ordinary 6 £. is gained, since the wive's work is not gained either.

Childbirth: One annual childbirth roll may be attempted per wife, paramour, or concubine, if sufficient opportunity was fulfilled to possibly allow conception. Gamemasters must rule on the results of irregular liaisons.

Childbirth Table

d20	result
1-10	No birth
11	Mother and child die at childbirth
12	Mother dies in childbirth, child lives*
13-19	child born*
20	Twins born*

**Roll 1d6 for each child born, where an odd number = female, and even = male.*

Child Survival

Each year, roll d20 per child *under 15 years* and consult this table, applying modifiers to the die roll as needed. Children who survive to age 15 are expected to live to adulthood.

Child Survival Table

d20	result
1-2	Child dies
3-10	Child is sick, but lives
11-20	Child lives

6c. Family Events

This portion of the Winter Phase determines if any important or interesting events occur in your greater family. Note that the fathers of player knights created in this book are already dead, and all inherited Glory and items already gained. If the system in the chapter known as "Your Family" was used, the character's grandfather is also dead.

Family Events Table

1-2	death in family*
3-7	marriage in family*
8-12	birth in family
13-15	missing, may be lost
16-18	no event
19-20	scandal in family*†

* *Indicates roll on Family Member Table (below) to find person affected. If the result is ridiculous, like your mother remarrying when your father is still alive, just ignore it as a silly or nasty rumor and reroll.*

† *Indicates a roll on the scandal table, below.*

Family Member Table

d20	person
1-3	Father
4-6	Mother
7-11	Brother
12-15	Sister
16	Uncle
17	Aunt
18	Grandfather (even on d6) or Grandmother (odd on d6)
19-20	Cousin

Scandal Table

d20	result
1	insulted their lord
2-3	cheated at a tournament
4	badly in debt
5-7	adultery accusations
8	kidnap accusation
9-10	horse stealing accusation
11-16	messy love affair *almost* proved
17	murder rumored
18	heresy rumored
19	necromancy rumored
20	roll again, rerolling 20s, but this time the event is *proved true!*

Step 7: Training and Practice

Figure any training or practice done over the winter. This step also includes the natural growth of young player characters, and deliberate changes to reputation and behavior, affecting traits or passions.

If the gamemaster allows, your knight's squire can increase one or more of his three primary skills (listed on the character sheet) at this time, with the same choices as your knight.

You have a choice of three things to do:

1. Change a Personality Trait, Statistic, or Passion.

Only one trait, statistic, or passion value may be changed. It will change by one point, up or down, though in the case of personality traits this always alters the value of the opposite trait as well.

Several restrictions apply during this step. Traits cannot be increased over 19 by training and practice. Passions cannot be increased over 20. No statistic can be

raised higher than its maximum cultural value, which is usually 15, 18, or 21. See the "Character Generation" chapter for Cymric cultural maximums. Important age restrictions also apply on statistic increases: SIZ may not be increased after age 21 (so player knights who are already 21 or older cannot increase SIZ), and no statistics may be increased after age 35.

2. Train Skills Up To 15

Roll 1d6 for the number of points available if you wish to improve skills only to a value of 15. Any combination of one or more ordinary skills or combat skills may be improved, within the limit of the 1d6 roll. For example, if a 3 was rolled, Orate, Sword, and Lance could all be increased by one point, as long as none went over 15, or Sword could be increased by three points.

3. Train a Skill Up to 20

You may alternatively choose to increase one skill by one point, to a maximum value of 20. Skills can go beyond 20 only through experience or Glory.

Step 8: Compute Glory

During winter all Glory gained in the previous year's play is computed. Additional Glory may also be gained during the Winter Phase itself. A total is determined, and added to the current number in the main "Glory" box on the character sheet.

This sequence is one of the high points of the game for many players, as they see their character's fame and prestige increase through Glory.

Glory from Play: This is the primary source of Glory. If you participated in a scenario last game year, the Glory gained by your character should already be written in the "Glory This Game" box on the character sheet, and ideally recorded in detail on the back of the sheet with a date attached. For example, if you killed a bear while hunting, you should have recorded an award of 10 Glory. Participation in a neighborhood tournament should have gained about 5 Glory.

If you remember something the character did during the scenario that is not recorded, check with the other players and the gamemaster now. If they don't remember it, you're out of luck.

Glory from Solo Scenarios: Your character may have gone through a Solo Scenario. With gamemaster approval, Glory may have been gained thereby. For example, the solo scenario entitled "Your Own Land" may have gained you special Glory equal to your Just trait.

Glory from One-Time Honors: If any special honor or ambition was achieved last year, such as marriage to an heiress, this honor should have been recorded on the back of the character sheet. If not, check the "Glory and Ambitions" chapter now and review your character's achievements for the previous year.

Annual Glory: Many sources of Glory are annual. For example, holding a motte and bailey castle gains 8 Glory per year. Annual Glory accrues now, during the Winter Phase.

Check with the gamemaster to be sure you have recorded all the various Glory awards correctly. Refer to the "Glory and Ambitions" chapter if you have any questions.

"Compute Glory" Example: *After the first year of play, each new player knight gains a great deal of Glory, all of which comes into effect when the Winter Phase arrives after the first year of play.*

This example serves as a checklist for new characters as well as a sample of Glory gain. If your character just started play in the previous session, check this example carefully and talk to the gamemaster if you missed any of the listed Glory.

Glory was probably gained during the previous year for participation in a scenario, for defeating enemies, for courageous actions, and so forth. This should have been written in the "Glory This Game" box.

Honors are as follows. New characters receive 1000 Glory for the sacred ceremony of knighthood, as enacted during play. 10 more Glory from knighthood will have been gained if "The Leap" was performed successfully. An additional 50 one-time Glory for becoming vassal knights is also due for new player knights.

Annual Glory is received now; 6 Glory for holding land with an income of six Libra (one manor) for a year, and 16 Glory for exhibiting a famous personality trait, as selected during character generation (note that the value may now have increased to 17 or even 18 during previous steps in the Winter Phase, in which case 17 or 18 Glory points are gained).

If any passions have been increased to 16+, they gain Glory equal to the value.

Finally, one-time Glory should have been inherited from the character's father, both from the Inherited Glory Table in the "Character Generation" chapter, and additionally (if the chapter was used) 1/10th the father's actual Glory number, as determined in the chapter entitled "Your Family."

All this Glory should be added together now, and the total written in the main "Glory" box.

The 6 Glory for holding land and the Glory for any famous trait or passion will be gained every year that the land is held and the reputation maintained, while the Glory gained for knighthood, the leap, vassal knight status, and inherited Glory are all one-time only, and are gained after the first year of play.

Step 9: Add Glory Bonus Points

The last thing done in the Winter Phase is to add any Glory bonus points to the character's attributes. Bonus points are gained whenever a character's Glory total passes a 1000 point threshold (for example, a knight's Glory might increase from 1800 to 3010 in an extraordinary year, yielding two points). One or more bonus points become available and must be spent immediately to raise one attribute (a trait, passion, statistic, skill or combat skill) by one point. No restrictions apply to the increase. Refigure derived statistics now if you increase a statistic.

If a trait or passion has just been increased to 16 by means of a bonus point, Glory is *not* gained until next year's Winter Phase. The same is true for Glory if a character now qualifies for a Chivalrous or Religious bonus, but the bonus itself (the Armor of Honor, for example) is gained immediately and may be used during the year's scenario.

Winter Phase Example

Once again we encounter Sir Ambrut, the young household knight of Baron Yvane used in many previous examples. He has survived another year of play by the time of this example, including a skirmish and a battle. At the beginning of the new year, let's review his activities, and follow him through the Winter Phase.

Ambrut was knighted at age 21, in 531, though he was not made a vassal knight — the gamemaster wanted to run a campaign with less influential characters (remember that the gamemaster is king in *Pendragon*).

This Winter Phase takes place following Ambrut's third year of play, so the new year is 534. Glory accrued will be

from the events of 533, along with any annual Glory.

1. Perform Solo: *Ambrut took part in a scenario last year, and chose not to participate in the Lover's Solo over the winter. So nothing is noted in this step.*

2. Experience Check Rolls: *Reviewing the examples of play in this chapter, we see Ambrut received checks in the following skills, traits, and passions for the year: Awareness, Compose, Deceitful, Horsemanship, Lance, Love (family), and Sword. Ambrut's player attempts to roll over each checked value. For Awareness (value 5), a 5 is rolled; bad luck, no gain. For Compose a 3 is rolled, so the value increases from 2 to 3. Deceitful receives a roll of 16, so it increases from 11 to 12. Love (family) increases from a 15 to a 16. The other experience check rolls all yield numbers under the values, so fail.*

Ambrut's squire received no experience checks from play last year.

3. Aging: *A new year has come, so Ambrut's player changes his character sheet to show he is now age 24. Ambrut is still far too young to age. The player also raises the age of Ambrut's squire by one year, to 18.*

4. Check Economic Circumstances: *First Ambrut's grade of maintenance is established. Sir Ambrut is a household knight, not a vassal knight like normal player knights, so his circumstances are almost entirely the responsibility of his lord, Baron Yvane.*

Yvane's year was normal, so Ambrut is maintained at the grade of an Ordinary knight, with no special effects. Ambrut's plunder from the skirmish and battle he participated in gained him only 2 Libra over his normal stipend of 6 £. This is not quite enough to raise him up to a Rich knight's grade (minimum of 9 £.). He can save the plunder and spend it in play, during a scenario.

Second, Ambrut's court clothes, valued at 1 Librum, are reduced in value to .5 £.

Third, economic effects are applied. We saw from above that Ambrut's grade was that of an Ordinary knight, so no special effects accrue to any rolls below, and no notes need be made.

5. Stable Rolls: *Although only a household knight, Ambrut now has six horses in his stable, including his squire's rouncy. He has a very fast charger and a special rouncy, both described briefly in the example of Forced March given in the "Movement" section of this chapter, in addition to the normal charger, rouncy, and sumpter provided by his lord.*

Rolls are made for each of the six horses, and a roll of 2 occurs for Ambrut's special rouncy. Even though it has a better CON than normal, the animal becomes useless for some reason this winter, with no CON roll intervening. Since it is not a standard horse, it is not replaced by Ambrut's lord, and Ambrut must rely upon his normal rouncy for riding purposes in this year's scenario.

6. Family Rolls: *After his near escape in battle, Sir Ambrut realizes his mortality for the first time. He becomes interested in marriage and a family of his own. As a household knight, marriage within his class is only a remote possibility, as with most such knights. So he opts to marry below his class, and begins courting a young serving woman of Yvane's court. Unfortunately, when it comes time to ask permission to wed, Ambrut fails his Loyalty (Lord) roll and Yvane harshly forbids him to marry that winter. The value of the passion is reduced to 14 and Ambrut becomes disheartened and melancholic (see the "Ideals and Passions" chapter).*

Perhaps he will wait till he gains the high status of a vassal knight and use the Random Marriage Table to gain a wife. In the meantime, the unhappy Ambrut takes a woman as his concubine, expending .5 £. from his extra funds. A childbirth roll is made for the entire year to come at this time, and a 10 is rolled, indicating no children are born this year (remember that for convenience, all characters are considered to be born during the Winter Phase, in January or February, including any sons Ambrut might have this year).

Now Ambrut's family events are rolled for, on the Family Events Table. A 13 is rolled, indicating that a family member is missing, and may be lost. Now a roll on the Family Member Table is made. A 16 is the result, indicating that an uncle has disappeared. The gamemaster makes a note of this fact for possible tie-in to his planned scenario for the year.

7. Training and Practice: *Ambrut feels comfortable with his current traits and passions, so he does not practice or adjust them. He wants to improve his skills up to a value of 15. A roll of 1d6 = 4, a fair roll. Ambrut's player decides to add one point to his Awareness, one to his Lance, and two to a new skill of Flail, bringing it from the starting value of 0 up to 2.*

8. Compute Glory: *Glory from game play is determined first. In the previous year's scenario, Ambrut had quite a bit of combat: he defeated a robber in the woods; he killed a Saxon warrior in a skirmish; and finally, he fought one round in a small battle, after which he became separated from his unit and fought a group of mercenaries against terrible odds, defeating two before falling unconscious from his wounds. Ambrut later participated in a tournament to celebrate the battle, but failed in combat, was injured badly, and did not participate long enough to gain Glory. Ambrut also composed a love poem successfully, and rescued his brother from an ogre single-handed, after a forced march on his famous charger Flame.*

Glory for game play events has been already awarded by the gamemaster as follows: 10 for the robber, 35 for the Saxon raider, 30 for the battle round fought (15 Glory, x2 for a clear victory, otherwise normal), and 70 for the two mercenary sergeants (35 each, treated as armed and mounted bandits for Glory) that were killed before Ambrut was defeated. Glory for the poem was ordinary, 10 points. The rescue of Ambrut's brother gained Glory for successful completion of a task or adventure. Although the rescue was only a minor episode in a large scenario, it was significant to an ordinary degree, so 10 Glory was gained for the task, plus 25 for the defeat of an ogre. The total, which Ambrut's player has already listed in the section of the sheet entitled "Glory This Game," is 190 points.

Now annual Glory is determined. Ambrut has no manor, unlike normal player characters (vassal knights), so no annual Glory is gained for ownership. However, he does have several traits and passions at a value of 16 or more by this mid-point in his career: Love (family) at 16, Valorous at 17, and his originally selected famous trait of Modest, at 16. It will be years before Ambrut qualifies as a Chivalrous knight, but he is getting closer. The total is 49.

Ambrut's total Glory, listed in the main "Glory" box at the beginning of this step, was 1605, as accrued during last year's Winter Phase. 1605 + 190 + 49 = 1844, the new total that Ambrut will bear proudly for the coming year's scenario.

Add Glory Bonus Points: *Ambrut did not go over a 1000-point threshold this year, so no Bonus Points become available. He would have needed to gain a full 395 points to reach the minimum 2000-point threshold for a Bonus Point.*

Ideals and Passions

Idealism and passion make a man into a hero.

KING ARTHUR'S EPIC is a story of personality and action on a grand scale. Everyone whose name is remembered is known for both deeds and feelings. No great character is merely a two-dimensional cutout whose history consists solely of high scores and lists of events. Everyone feels strongly about something.

Personality in *Pendragon* is depicted through personality traits and passions. Together they provide guidelines for playing characters who may be quite different from the player.

Traits and passions are used to quantify character behavior. They are used to make the player's roleplaying task easier by providing guidelines for how the character acts, has acted, and is likely to continue to act. Numerical values are assigned to each trait and passion, and rolls are made using the values to determine behavior.

Of the two systems of character behavior, personality traits are more often used than passions.

Personality traits and passions should always be written in pencil, because they may change often.

Why Do We Need Traits and Passions?

Actually, not all players will wish to use traits and passions. The system offers tremendous scope and flexibility to those players who wish to use it, yet it can be ignored by players who prefer that their characters have no explicit personality.

For players who do happen to be interested in their character's personality, the system gives the following benefits.

Reputation

Keeping track of character reputation is an important function. Characters with similar Glory may have very different reputations, some good, some bad, some simply colorful.

Entertainment Value

The interplay of personalities provides much of the fun in *Pendragon* roleplaying. With the traits and passions system, each character's personality is different. A character may be pure of heart like Galahad, a courteous womanizer like Gawaine, or an ordinary knight with a streak of cruelty, like Agravaine. Each character has a well-defined and colorful basis for roleplaying and action within the game.

Traits and passions are also entertaining because they can provide increased character power, or lead to amusing results. Some successful trait or passion rolls result in the character becoming inspired, with temporary benefits to die rolls. Fumbled passion rolls may result in madness.

Glory

Any dramatic pattern of behavior gains Glory. Characters with interesting personalities will gain more Glory than those without. However, behavior in accord with society's ideals gains more Glory than idiosyncrasies. Thus Gawaine gains much more Glory for his chivalrous nature than Agravaine gains from his streak of cruelty.

Accuracy

The personality traits and passions define the way your character feels and acts. During play various emotions are revealed and traits and passions receive experience checks, like skills. Passions are also reduced at gamemaster option. Over time characters' traits and passions will reflect the story of their lives. The system allows characters to record the change in their attitudes and behavior with accuracy and consistency.

Authenticity

Pendragon is a roleplaying game dealing with the greatest of all medieval stories: the tragic tale of King Arthur and the Round Table. The game takes place in a world of knights and their ladies, in an age of feudalism and chivalry wherein democracy is seditious and unequal authoritarianism the norm. Players control the actions of characters sometimes quite unlike themselves, and are expected to act appropriately to their station. How can you know what is appropriate and correct? Traits and passions are the primary indicators that you will use to determine "correctness" in the Arthurian setting. If your character gains the proper traits and passions, then your character will be doing just exactly those things which constitute correct behavior in Arthurian society.

If you wish to run a character that defies the traditions of society you can and may, but your character will probably lose points in various passion values for acting outside the norms of society. The gamemaster must decide whether a loss is warranted and how much the loss should be, based on the specific circumstances. Acts such as accidental murder, stealing horses, participating in ambushes, or unmerciful behavior are not villainous: death, slaughter, and misery are a normal part of a knight's life. See the "Passions" section below for more information.

Using Traits and Passions

Traits and passions are important in that they are the primary component of the character's reputation, along with Glory, which is the general indicator of success in the game. Traits and passions measure such things as honor or trustworthiness, while Glory measures raw prestige and power. The two systems are linked, for traits and passions may gain Glory.

Famous Traits or Passions

The threshold value for gaining Glory and reputation from a trait or passion is 16. If your knight has a Valorous personality trait of 15 he is brave, but not particularly noteworthy for courage. Nor is a priest with a Piety of 6 particularly impious, nor is a passionate love of 11 worth great notice. But he whose Valorous is 16 is considered heroic, and he whose Piety is 18 is nearly a saint, while a lover of 20

is famous throughout the realm for his passion.

When Are Traits and Passions Rolled?

During play, character behavior is often challenged by the gamemaster. Temptations are paraded forth, moral crises leap up, and critical judgments and actions must be made.

Since traits and passions define character personality, they must be consulted whenever the gamemaster determines that a critical decision is at hand. In crises, individuals act according to character, not choice. At times, players will not want their characters to do something dictated by a die roll, but free choice is not always possible.

Famous Traits and Passions: Only famous traits and passions are noted by society, or gain Glory, and such traits or passions *must* be tested with a die roll when character behavior is challenged in a crisis. Basically, if you get Glory for a trait or passion, rolls based on the value must be made when required by the gamemaster.

This does *not* mean that trait rolls must be used whenever the character makes any decision in the game. And even characters with famous characteristics are allowed free choice of behavior except when the plot demands otherwise. The gamemaster should request trait rolls only when a trait is tested in an important situation. In general, trait rolls simulate situations in which a crisis forces the character to act unconsciously.

Ordinary Traits and Passions: Traits and passions which are between 5-15 do not have to be rolled against if the player wishes to use his personal will to determine an action, although rolling is obviously the most impartial way to determine action.

Characters who consistently act a certain way will eventually have traits or passions valued at 16 or higher, due to the rules below, at which time they will either have to make the required rolls or retire the character.

Modifiers: Trait or passion values may be modified based on situations, in order to keep the game realistic. Players are responsible for reminding the gamemaster when a situation might call for a trait or passion modifier. The gamemaster determines whether such modifiers are valid.

Increases and Reductions

Values for traits and passions will rise and fall repeatedly during the game. Experience checks for traits and passions are assigned by the gamemaster in a slightly different fashion from checks for skills. Players who are reluctant to roll should not be forced to, but the gamemaster must often insist that they check the trait or passion they exhibited, in order to simulate the possibility of a change in the character's psychology and reputation.

Passions are particularly vulnerable to reduction. When a character acts against a passion, no check is assigned: instead the gamemaster simply instructs the player to reduce the value of the passion by one point immediately. Also, any failed passion roll causes the character to lose a point.

Acting consistently, according to the role of your character, will prevent compulsory checks and reductions from being necessary.

The traits and passions system is not to be used to turn the player knights into puppets. Most of the time characters just do whatever the player wishes them to do, collecting checks along the way. However, if your character has a reputation, it's only fair that he maintain it, or lose it. The system ensures that this will occur.

Evil or Undesirable Behavior

It is not in the spirit of the game for player characters to become evil knights. However, players are encouraged to take minor character flaws such as cruelty or laziness for their characters; such traits can be very amusing in moderation, and the gamemaster also has more opportunities to create interesting situations.

With one or two undesirable traits or inferior passion values, characters can have weaknesses other than those revealed only in mortal combat, giving the gamemaster the possibility of creating non-lethal challenges for characters. Given the dangers involved in combat, this is a useful opportunity.

Personality Traits

TRAITS ARE DUALISTIC personality factors. A trait and its opposite both exist in every individual. They define a person's feelings and tendencies.

Pendragon has thirteen pairs of personality traits which are important. Characters certainly display other traits, but those listed are the ones critical to the Arthurian literature of the game.

The personality traits are presented in opposed pairs. The total value of the pair must always equal 20 at the time when the character is first created.

When one trait increases the opposite normally decreases by the same amount. No trait may ever be higher than 19, nor lower than 1, except by experience or by the use of increased Glory.

Any trait with a value between 5 and 15 is considered normal, while those less than 5 and greater than 15 are excessive and deserve to be noticeable, even famous. For instance, a man whose Modest trait is 15 and whose Proud trait is 5 does not have either trait in a notable proportion. Some extraordinary characters have a trait of 20, 25, or perhaps even more! They always have 0 for the opposite trait and are known through all the land for their unrelenting, fanatical behavior.

Personality traits should be listed in pencil on the character sheet as whole numbers, each to one side of the slash (/) mark.

Chaste/Lustful

To be chaste is to be monogamous, or faithful to one's sexual *mores*. It does not always require virginity — a man being faithful to his wife is being chaste. A chaste person is modest and decorous in behavior. A fanatically chaste person is celibate and probably virginal.

Lustful describes sexual desire, and implies activity, often without personal commitment between the persons involved. The pagan virtue of Lustful recognizes the value of this sensual art to

appreciate the immanence of the Goddess. Excessive promiscuity is called lechery, wantonness, and bawdiness.

Famous Characters: *Sir Bors de Ganis is respected for his chaste behavior.*

Lancelot Fumbles His Energetic

Lancelot and his cousin Lionel are adventuring on a very hot day. Riding in armor under the summer sun is hot enough to require an Energetic roll.

So they mounted on their horses, armed at all rights, and rode into a deep forest and so into a deep plain. And then the weather was hot about noon, and Sir Lancelot had great lust to sleep. Then Sir Lionel espied a great apple tree that stood by an hedge, and said, "Brother, yonder is a fair shadow, there may we rest us on our horses."

"It is well said, fair brother," said Sir Lancelot, "for this seven year I was not so sleepy as I am now."

And so they there alighted and tied their horses unto sundry trees, and Sir Lancelot laid him down under an apple tree, and his helm he laid under his head. And Sir Lionel waked while he slept. So Sir Lancelot was asleep passing fast.

— Malory VI, 1

Lionel receives a check for Energetic, Lancelot receives one for Lazy.

Energetic/Lazy

A vigorous person is Energetic. It includes the natural ability to get up and go to work, and to apply oneself to the tasks at hand. The comparable Christian virtue is Industry. Persons who are energetic are called vigorous, robust, and industrious.

Laziness includes all slothful activity, such as loafing and general sedentary behavior. At the end of the spectrum lies indolence.

Famous Characters: *Sir Lamorak de Gales is often admired for his energetic nature.*

Forgiving/Vengeful

To be forgiving means that a character can take insult without injury, and that he is unlikely to seek revenge for injuries intended or done to him. Extremely forgiving people are called meek, in the Biblical sense.

Vengeful indicates a character's propensity to seek revenge, perhaps petty, but possibly sweeping and grandiose, for wrongs done or imagined done to him. This trait also includes spitefulness.

Generous/Selfish

To be Generous includes the impulse, learning, or desire to share. It includes the *largesse* of the Saxon and Cymric chieftains, and also the Christian virtue of Charity. Extremely generous persons are called unselfish, magnanimous, and bighearted.

Selfish is the desire to possess, keep, and further accumulate things for yourself. Greed is usually a component of selfishness. Possession could be of material property, with the character being known as a miser or hoarder, or of credit, like hogging attention (Glory). Very selfish persons are labeled both stingy and self-seeking.

Famous Characters: *King Arthur and Queen Guenever are revered for their generosity.*

Honest/Deceitful

To be Honest is to deal truthfully in matters of importance or triviality, no matter what the consequences. Persons of extreme honesty are said to have integrity and to be trustworthy, scrupulous, and reliable.

Deceitful means that a person is likely to distort truth to his own or other end. Chronically deceitful people are called liars, frauds, and false-hearted.

Modest/Proud

To be Modest means that your character is quiet and does not seek excessive attention in the recitation of his deeds. He is glad to bask in the mere doing of his deeds, rather than in the repeated glory of hearing about them. Very modest people are called humble and reserved, perhaps even shy.

Proud means that a character gets pleasure from hearing and/or boasting of his deeds. Both Germanic and Pagan ways value Pride in a character. Excessive pride implies arrogance, and likely a boastful nature.

Famous Characters: *Sir Turquine, the feared Saxon knight, is notorious for his great pride.*

Just/Arbitrary

Just means that a character is capable of telling what is right and wrong, and is desirous of making a judgment on that information. A very just person is called fair and impartial.

Arbitrary means that the character has no concern for what is right or wrong, and uses other information in his decision making. Very arbitrary people are labeled unjust, unfair, wrongful, and probably biased and partial.

Famous Characters: *King Arthur is perhaps most famous for his extraordinary sense of justice.*

Trusting/Suspicious

To be Trusting is to believe information without any inclination to suspect its falsity. An excessively trusting person is gullible and credulous, perhaps even a dupe.

Suspicious indicates that a person is an unbeliever and unlikely to believe what he hears unless proof is offered. An extremely suspicious person is called a skeptic or a doubter.

Jealously is included under the trait of Suspicious. Jealousy cannot exist without suspiciousness. Thus when someone acts jealous, they get a check for their Suspicious.

Famous Characters: *Young Sir Mordred, recently arrived at court, has already caused a stir with his suspicious and skeptical behavior.*

Merciful/Cruel

Merciful means that a character is willing to extend unusual pity or aid to others. This includes sparing an enemy, giving money to the poor, helping the weak, and any other act which is not expected of one's rank and station. A very merciful person is called compassionate.

King Arthur's Justice

...such custom was used in those days, that neither for favor, neither for love nor affinity, there should be none other but righteous judgement, as well upon a king as upon a knight, and as well upon a queen as upon another poor lady.

— Malory, XVIII

Cruel indicates a disregard for the feelings and needs of others, or lack of sympathy. Extreme values indicate the character even enjoys others' discomforts and troubles.

Pious/Worldly

Pious shows that a character thinks often of the spiritual matters of the world and is aware of them and their implications. This should be contrasted with Worship, which is an action rather than a belief. A pious person is a spiritual person. An extremely pious person is devout, zealous, and saintly.

Worldly indicates a disregard or disbelief in the spiritual side of life. Extreme values might indicate blasphemy and sacrilege. Alternatively, it might just indicate great pleasure in mundane and profane delights such as fine clothes, comfortable furnishings, good music and poetry, and the best company.

Prudent/Reckless

Prudent means that a character gives thought to what he does before he acts. Such a character is called cautious, and excessively prudent people are slow to act or thoughtful.

Reckless means that the character acts before he thinks, without concern for anything but the immediate consequences. Almost any time someone gets a check for acting according to a passion they will act rashly. An extremely reckless character is called careless, or a hothead.

Famous Characters: *Sagramore le Desirious is decidedly rash, and Sir Dinadan is noted for being prudent.*

Temperate/Indulgent

Temperate means that a character takes only what he needs of food and drink. He is frugal and abstains from excess. Extreme temperance indicates asceticism, perhaps even self-mortification.

Indulgent means that a character takes pleasure in food and drink, both in quality and quantity. Extremes of this indicate gluttony and drunkenness.

Valorous/Cowardly

To be valorous means you are brave and courageous, willing to place yourself in danger for the sake of victory, your friends, or for the simple love of battle. Normal knights are doughty, stalwart, and valiant. Extremely heroic individuals are called fearless and intrepid.

Cowardly means to be fearful and afraid enough to affect actions. Someone who is extremely fainthearted is labeled as a poltroon, dastard, craven, caitiff, or recreant.

Valor may be exhibited not only in combat, but whenever risks are involved.

Famous Characters: *Sir Lancelot and Sir Lamorak are well-known as the most valorous knights in Britain.*

Using Traits

These traits define characteristic behavior. When the opportunity arises to behave one way or another, these can either be used as casual guidelines, or rolls may be imposed by the gamemaster.

Most of the time you simply state what you want your character to do and he does it, possibly receiving an experience check in the process. Sometimes, though, in a non-thinking situation, behavior takes over instead of conscious intent. Almost everyone of us has experienced doing something without thinking, and a trait roll duplicates that kind of situation. Modifiers may be used to underscore the dictates of a situation.

Trait Results Table

Critical Success: An experience check is normally gained, and the character acts strongly in accordance with the trait.

Success: The character feels the trait enough to act in accordance with it. The player may decide what action ensues. An experience check is gained on the rolled trait if an appropriate and significant action follows.

Failure: Roll the opposed trait. Success in this one means the character acts as rolled. Failure indicates the player gets his choice. No checks are given.

Fumble: The opposite trait is checked, and the character immediately acts in the opposite manner from what was attempted.

Interpreting Trait Results

Each result of a trait roll has special implications, and high or low trait values may influence interpretation.

Critical Success: A critical success in a trait roll indicates that the character *must* act in the manner described by the trait. The action needs not be totally outrageous and extreme, but is visible and overt enough to be noticed enough by others, and to make the character feel that he has revealed strong emotions or even compromised himself. Thus we can imagine that Sir Bors de Ganis gains a critical success on his Lustful trait of 1. Certainly he does not rape the girl. The gamemaster declares that he gently touches the maiden's fair cheek, causing her to blush. This is enough for Sir Bors to feel embarrassed and ashamed of perverting his ideals.

At gamemaster option, minor inspiration may be gained from a critical success with a trait, gaining the character a +5 modifier to one skill selected by the player, lasting for the duration of the situation that provoked a roll. Inspiration should only be gained in rare instances from a critical success: such inspiration is usually the domain of passions, not traits. But when a truly dramatic trait roll occurs, inspiration can make the process far more exciting. The possibility of inspiration also makes trait rolls more entertaining in general.

Success: Success in a trait roll indicates that the knight felt, and was moved by, the feelings expressed in the trait. Thus if he made a Merciful roll he feels that he should grant mercy in this instance. However, the player may choose to have

the character act in the opposite manner. The penalty for disobeying one's character's feelings is a check in the opposite trait.

Failure: Use of personality traits is not the same as striking with a weapon or using a skill. The traits quantify a character's likelihood to act in one of two opposed ways. Thus it is not enough to know that a character does not feel merciful. The player must know whether the character acts cruelly. The traits define the chances of either.

Failure at a single die roll is not enough to force a character to act the opposite way. The player must also check to see if chance and statistics force his character to act. Thus only a successful roll within the range of a trait will force an action. Failure to succeed at either option will allow free will. Success at either has determined that the character's innate behavior has overcome his free will.

Example of a Failed Trail Roll: *Sir Ambrut has accompanied a distressed damsel to her inheritance, which has been seized by a wicked uncle. The uncle refuses to return the land and gladly agrees to duel for it. The fight is fierce, but at last Ambrut's enemy collapses and begs for mercy. The damsel urges Ambrut to kill her foe despite Ambrut's desire to be merciful. The gamemaster asks for a roll of Ambrut's Merciful.*

Ambrut receives a failed Merciful of 18. Now his player must attempt a Cruel trait roll, and that result is also a failure at 12. The choice is up to Ambrut's player. Given the fact that Ambrut hopes to marry this harsh but beautiful woman, the player chooses death for the unhappy uncle. The damsel is given revenge, and a marriage is planned, but no experience checks are given since both rolls failed, even though a very significant event took place.

Opportunities to Avoid Trait Rolls

Players will often become aware of impending personality trait rolls, and should take action as needed to keep the game going without arguments. They can have their characters avoid conflict, but not after the gamemaster initiates the challenge process.

Example of Trait Roll Avoidance : *While lost in the woods some months after his marriage, Sir Ambrut finds a brightly-lit tower amid the trees. He asks for refuge and is granted it from the beautiful female host. The player is suspicious, and states that over dinner Ambrut tries to recognize his hostess. The Recognize skill roll is successful and Ambrut abruptly realizes he is supping with Morgan le Fay, the wicked sister of King Arthur. Fearful for Ambrut's life and virility, the player announces that Ambrut will attempt to avoid all lustful relations with the woman, and requests a modifier to Chaste. The gamemaster grumbles, but because Ambrut was forewarned he cannot be imposed upon by Morgan's lascivious beauty. The gamemaster rules that Ambrut's Chaste trait is modified by the addition of his new Love (wife) passion value, raising Chaste above 20 and making it possible to overcome Morgan's advances. If Ambrut had failed to recognize his hostess then he might not have tried to avoid the affair at all.*

Casual Use of Traits

A player often does not know what his character would do under specific circumstances. This might be because the player either never thought about it, does not care, or because the character has mid-range personality traits.

In such circumstances the player should roll d20 to determine behavior. If the number rolled is equal or less than the number in the left column then the character does that type of action. If the number rolled is greater than the left hand column then the character does what is shown on the right. A modifier may be applied if the situation warrants one.

Example of Casual Trait Use: *Sir Ambrut is one among seventeen knights riding to hunt the fabulous White Hart. A mysterious huntress comes from the woods and speaks privately with each man while he is resting. On Ambrut's turn she quietly asks him, "Are you seeking the White Hart?"*

A simple question, but coming from such a mysterious character it seems fraught with danger. Neither player nor gamemaster knows whether Ambrut's reply would be truthful or not.

His player rolls a d20 for his Honest trait and gets a 18, which is over the value. Therefore Ambrut replies, "No, not exactly..."

She replies, "Take the left fork on the road, then," and moves on.

Characters never receive experience checks for actions imposed on themselves this way. Sometimes the gamemaster might reward characters with a check for doing something, but it is still always the gamemaster's decision to give out checks.

Qualifying for a Moral Test

Arthurian adventure is full of magical and moral tests. A magical shield may be wielded only by a chaste knight, or an enchanted sword may be withdrawn only by a courageous knight, and so on.

King Mark Gets A Cowardly Check

Sir Dinadan plots to shame the dastardly King Mark. Dinadan has described Sir Mordred's arms to Mark, claiming that they are actually Sir Lancelot's. A short time later Sir Dinadan meets a party of Round Table knights and explains his plan to them. Sir Mordred complains that he cannot help because he is wounded, and comes up with an even better plan using Sir Dagonet, the king's fool, instead.

Then anon was Dagonet armed him in Mordred's harness and his shield, and he was set on a great horse, and a spear in his hand.

"Now," said Dagonet, "show me the knight, and I trow [believe] I shall bear him down."

So all these knights rode to a woodside, and abode till King Mark came by the way. Then they put forth Sir Dagonet, and he came on all the while his horse might run, straight upon King Mark.

And when he came nigh King Mark, he cried as he were wood [mad], and said, "Keep thee, knight of Cornwall, for I will slay thee!"

Anon, as King Mark beheld his shield, he said to himself, "Yonder is Sir Lancelot; alas, now I am destroyed;" and therewithal he made his horse to run as fast as it might through thick and thin. And ever Sir Dagonet followed after King Mark, crying and rating him as a wood man, through a great forest.

— Malory X, 12

Some of these tests use absolute trait values. For example, only those characters with Honest traits of 15 or more can go uninvited through the doorway into the Palace of the Lake, where lives the fay Nimue.

In other cases, the character must pass a less rigorous test and receive a successful unopposed d20 roll on a trait to determine success. Success gains the reward, while failure indicates that the consequences of failing the test ensue. Thus anyone who answers a Justice riddle (succeeds in a Just roll) can enter into the great feast hall of King Bagdemagus every St. John's Day, while failure to answer the riddle means a meal outside.

Sir Mordred

Conflicting Emotions

Players may wish to use trait tests privately to determine a character's actions. This method allows you to play your character's emotions against each other. It mimics the deep introspection of someone tortured by internal doubts. The gamemaster may also oppose tests of conflicting emotions. The exact rolls will be determined by the gamemaster. He may require you to make several coincidental personality trait rolls, with varying results depending on what was made and what was failed. Whatever traits are successful (if unopposed), or win (if opposed), receive experience checks if approved by the gamemaster.

Example of Conflicting Emotions: *Sir Ambrut, while wandering through the forest, has been ambushed and attacked by a ferocious knight with a black shield. By dint of much effort Ambrut has defeated his foe, who lies helpless on the ground before him and cries for mercy. Just as Ambrut is about to spare him a maiden rush from the woods and cries, "Good Sir Knight, I call on you to slay this villain. For he has slain his wife, my sister, and all of my other sisters as well. As you revere God, do not spare him!"*

Ambrut is caught between conflicting emotions. Justice demands that he kill this villainous knight, but Mercy calls on him to spare his defeated foe. Neither trait has an unusual value in Ambrut's case. So Ambrut gets an opposed resolution roll matching his Justice versus his Merciful. His Justice roll is a 4, his Merciful a 7, so his mercy wins and Ambrut spares the caitiff. He didn't have the stomach to cold-bloodedly slaughter a helpless man. The damsel curses Ambrut for a false knight and leaves. The defeated knight swears eternal gratitude to Ambrut for his wisdom and charity. Ambrut receives a check on Merciful.

Personality Disputes and Conflicting Emotions

Personality disputes between individuals are determined by opposed resolution rolls of traits. The challenger matches his personality against his rival's.

Example: *Sir Douglas the Red states that Sir Ambrut is too slothful to amount to much. Ambrut challenges Douglas to an endurance contest of wearing arms and armor day and night until one of them falls asleep. Players of both characters attempt Energetic rolls, and both succeed. However, Ambrut's roll of 9 is higher than Douglas' roll of 2. When Douglas falls asleep after two days and two nights Ambrut is declared winner. Thus Ambrut wins and gets the experience check. And promptly takes a nap.*

Because personality traits have opposites, results are more complex when someone fails during opposed trait resolution than is the case with simple opposed skill rolls.

Whenever a character receives a failed personality trait roll during a personality dispute, his player must then attempt to roll the opposite trait. If that roll succeeds then the character acts accordingly, even though this means that behavior is not as intended.

Challenged victims of a personality dispute who fail *both* trait rolls have free choice to do as they please. They have managed to control their inclinations.

Example of a Personality Dispute: *Sir Yvane and some of his men are visiting their newly-conquered lands. They are eating dinner with a petty Saxon lord who somehow survived the battle of Badon.*

With a loud voice Sir Aethelfrith engages the visitors with boasts of his courageous martial exploits. After a pause for breath the Saxon asks Sir Yvane what he has done to compare with such bravery. Sir Yvane hates such boors and so he tries to be Modest in response to his host's Pride. A personality dispute occurs, and an opposed resolution is performed. Because the Saxon is so overbearing, the player requests and receives a +5 modifier to Modest.

Sir Aethelfrith receives a successful roll of 6 for his Proud trait, while Yvane receives a roll of 18, failing to be modest. The Saxon chuckles over Yvane's hesitation.

Since Sir Yvane failed to be modest, he will attempt to outboast his opponent after all. Yvane's player rolls a second time, this time with no modifier. The player rolls a 9 for Yvane's Proud trait, a result greater than the Saxon's roll of 6. Yvane speaks harshly of his recent victory in battle over a Saxon army, and wins the personality dispute. Yvane gets an experience check for such proud behavior. Although he wanted to remain modest, his natural personality won out over both his initial desire and the influence of the situation.

If Yvane had received a successful Modest trait roll that was inferior to the Saxon's Proud trait he would not have had a chance to receive a Proud roll. His humility would not have been enough to put down the boastful Saxon, and silence would have fallen over Yvane's side of the dinner table.

Other Experience Checks for Traits

Remember, the task of the gamemaster is to decide when an action performed by the player deserves an experience check. The action need not have been preplanned as a test or challenge. For instance, if a player decided that his knight would kill a peasant who had insulted him, the gamemaster may give that knight an experience check for both his Proud and Cruel traits, though no resolution rolls took place.

Mordred

Ideals and Virtues

Chivalry

Perhaps the most potent ideal in *Pendragon* is that of chivalry. As noted in the "Glory and Ambitions" chapter, Chivalrous knights are recognized by their ideals, behavior, and reputation. A total of 80 or more in the Generous, Energetic, Modest, Just, Merciful, and Valorous personality traits yields recognition that a knight is chivalrous. These traits are marked on the character sheet with a "bullet" (•).

Chivalrous knights gain 100 Glory yearly, and receive the Armor of Honor: 3 points of magical protection against all physical damage.

Virtue

Virtue is the sum of the traits which a culture finds admirable, necessary, and important. Virtues are not fixed, but vary according to the beliefs of the people. Whatever behavior is the opposite of a virtue is perceived as a vice.

The virtues of the cultures in *Pendragon* are partially determined by the different religions. For comparison purposes, the virtues of the major British religions are given here:

Christian: Chaste, Modest, Forgiving, Merciful,Temperate.

Pagan: Generous, Energetic, Honest, Proud, Lustful.

Wotanic: Generous, Proud, Worldly, Indulgent, Reckless.

Bonuses are awarded to characters who fulfill specific virtuous roles. These peo-

ple are personifications of certain ways, and they receive benefits for their roles.

Benefits of Virtues

There are two benefits derived from great religious behavior: Glory, and a magical reward as well.

Every character who qualifies receives 100 Glory during winter, and gains the appropriate bonus below as long as he qualifies.

Religious Virtues Bonus Table
Christian bonus: +6 to Total Hit Points.
Pagan bonus: +2 to Healing Rate statistic.
Wotanic bonus: +1d6 to Damage statistic.

Qualification

All five virtues must be at 16 or more to gain the bonus. A character does not need to have a high Worship or Pious Trait skill rating to receive the virtue bonus.

Directed Traits

Some characters have strong feelings about someone or something which modify one or more of their traits. These are called Directed Traits. The most common are Distrust (Someone) and Pride (in something). Many others are possible and will be revealed during play.

Directed traits are strong emotions, but not strong enough to drive your character crazy, like a passion might.

Directed traits are entered in the blanks beneath the "Personality Traits" list on the character sheet. Write in the specific trait which is modified, its object, and the value of the modifier.

Example: *Sir Yvane has a directed trait of Mistrust (Romans) +3. While on an investigative mission for his lord he is invited to a hunt by the Roman lord he is visiting. The gamemaster asks everyone to make a Suspicious roll. Yvane must add his Mistrust (Romans) value of +3 as a modifier to his normal Suspicious roll.*

Acquiring a Directed Trait

Directed traits can be gained from parents, by assignment by the gamemaster, or voluntarily by the player. Randomly determined directed traits are equal to +2d6.

Advanced character generation, available in the supplement *Knights Adventurous,* sometimes imposes a directed trait upon the character. These reflect the common beliefs of an area and may be quite illogical and prejudicial.

Parents who have strong directed traits can pass them on to their children: see the chapter entitled "Your Family."

Gamemasters can assign a directed trait to a character who consistently displays specific prides or prejudices. The value is usually random, or not more than +5.

Players can choose to have a directed trait, with gamemaster approval. The value should be +2d6, or whatever value both player and gamemaster agree upon.

Passions

THE ARTHURIAN TALES are full of intense emotion, much of it uncontrolled. Beautiful women drive men to incredible and outrageous actions to prove their love. Family feuds turn otherwise sane men into wild avengers. An idealistic young king determines to bring everyone his extraordinary justice against all odds.

Every reference to King Arthur and his knights is full of personality and passion, whether taken from the romances, legends, or Hollywood movies.

Passions provide a method of measuring a character's inner self. They help the character follow the morals of his age, and let him benefit from being a notable example of proper behavior.

Passions are strong personal emotions. They include religion, love, hate, amor, loyalty, envy, and anything else which the gamemaster will admit into the game.

The most universal emotions of player characters have been isolated for game use. Expect to encounter these in your game. These typify the types of feeling felt most intensely by *Pendragon* characters. Some of these are so common they appear on the character sheet, while blanks are provided for further passions.

The Characteristics of Passion

Several characteristics mark a passionate person. Some are admirable, others less so. Players must make an effort to play their passions actively, and to act in accordance to them.

Passionate people may perform with superhuman effort and a greater likelihood of success. This is accomplished through the Inspiration rules. Passionate people are volatile. Their feelings may change instantly due to success or failure. Passionate people are extreme, and likely to be found in any of several states of mind which are not found among dispassionate folk. These states include: inspiration, introspection, melancholy, shock, and even madness. All have effects in game terms.

The Basic Passions

These passions are obligatory because everyone has them, or is expected to. They are the unwritten laws of your society. See the chapter entitled "What Your Character Knows" for more information. The experienced squire created in character generation has unusual values in all these passions to denote his special nature as a player character. If the gamemaster wishes, subsequent characters may roll for passions normally, as given below.

Loyalty (lord)

Loyalty is the prime virtue of the medieval world — without it the feudal system could not exist. Most knights believe in "King before God," no matter what the priests tell them. Showing obedience is

correct behavior, and disobedience to a lord is shocking to all true knights.

The character sheet shows a printed Loyalty (lord) passion. All knights must be knighted by someone, and this space is used for the character's loyalty to that initial lord.

The starting Loyalty (lord) value is 15 for vassal knights. If the gamemaster permits the play of an ordinary knight character, a household knight with an assured household but no land, like Sir Ambrut, you roll 2d6+6 for this passion. If you have a homeless knight, Loyalty (lord) is only 2d6 to whoever knighted him.

Love (family)

Love of family is a natural emotion common to mankind in any age. The travel restrictions of the medieval era were severe, and reinforced family closeness. Serfs almost never travelled more than a day's walk from their birthplace. Noblewomen were fortunate to travel across the country once a year. Turning to one's kin for help was the universal answer to any problem.

The less fortunate younger sons, sent from the hearth, found fault with their kin.

Starting Love (family) value is equal to 2d6+6 for first sons, and all daughters. Younger sons are less dutiful. The second son gets 2d6+5, the third 2d6+4, 4th 2d6+3, 5th 2d6+2, 6th 2d6+1, 7th and any others 2d6.

Other modifiers to the starting value may apply. In character generation, new characters, who are eldest sons and the heads of their immediate families, start with a powerful love for their family. A starting Love (family) value of 15 is given to these basic characters.

Hospitality

This measures how much your character respects this honored institution. In extreme cases, a person would feel bound to correct others' behavior, perhaps even to seek out and destroy those who break the rule of hospitality. On the other hand, anyone with disregard of hospitality (less than 5) is likely to steal without compunction.

Inversely as well, whenever someone's behavior warrants it, the statistic should be changed. If they go lurking around someone's castle, especially if they actually rob it of goods, they should lose a point immediately for breaking the rules of hospitality. If they rise to defend someone else's hospitality, they get a check (no check is given to someone defending their own home, which is expected of them, and is not extraordinary enough to warrant it).

Starting Hospitality value = 15.

Honor

Honor is the passion which sets knights apart from ordinary people. It is a combination of personal dignity, integrity, and pride.

Personal honor is not always a slippery issue. The nearby Dishonorable Acts Table lists things which everyone agrees are dishonorable actions for a knight. Performing these deeds diminishes honor. This is the code of knighthood which knights have agreed to. However, beyond that list disagreement arises about what is or is not honorable, because it is personal rather than social. "Personal" is also carefully used to separate honor from other sworn or innate social obligations, including the three other basic passions or any others. Thus it is not possible to have one's personal honor abused if someone insults your family — Love (Family) covers that. Likewise, someone insulting your lover

Dishonor Table

Honor lost	*Dishonorable Event*
-1	Attacking an unarmed knight.
-1	Cowardice.
-1	Desertion from battle or military service.
-1	Plundering a holy place of your religion.
-2	Killing an unarmed holy person of your religion.
-2	Killing, kidnapping, or raping a noblewoman.
-2	Performing physical labor.
-2	Lending money at a profit.
-3	Flagrant cowardice.
-3	Breaking an oath.
-5	Treason (against your lord).
-5	Treachery against a member of your family.
-6	Killing a kinsman.
-10	Degradation (character loses the status of a knight).

Sir Berluse Gets a Hospitality Check

Sir Dinadan, Sir Lamorak, and a disguised King Mark are travelling together and seek lodging at a castle. They are admitted. Sir Berluse makes a successful Recognize roll.

And then they came into a fair court well repaired, and they had passing good cheer, till the lieutenant of this castle, that hight Berluse, espied King Mark of Cornwall. Then said Berluse,

"Sir knight, I know you better than ye ween, for ye are King Mark that slew my father afore mine own eyen; and me had ye slain had I not escaped into a wood; but wit ye well, for the love of my lord of this castle I will neither hurt you ne harm you, nor none of your fellowship. But wit ye well, when ye are past this lodging I shall hurt you and I may, for ye slew my father traitorly. But first for the love of my lord, Sir Tor, and for the love of Sir Lamorak, the honourable knight that here is lodged, ye shall have none ill lodging; for it is a pity that ever ye should be in the company of good knights; for ye are the villainous knight or king that is now known alive, for ye are a destroyer of good knights, and all that ye do is but treason."

— Malory X, 9

Thus did Sir Berluse uphold the laws of hospitality despite his enmity for the murderer of his father.

should incite the Amor (Lady) passion, not honor.

But Honor can still cover many other things. In fact, it can include almost anything which a character chooses to include. Someone with an extremely high honor may be offended by anything which anyone says that he does not like. Rationality may not be relevant.

Honor is tied into the personality traits more deeply than other passions usually are. The "integrity" component of Honor, for instance, is closely linked to the trait of Honest, and "pride" is obviously linked with the Proud trait. Thus a knight with a high trait of Proud might be required to make a roll by the gamemaster, have his pride offended, and then invoke the Honor passion to help him through the event.

A dishonorable character will suffer considerably in his society. He loses the trust of those about him, and in committing dishonorable acts probably incurs various punishments ranging from money fines, banishment, and forfeiture to blood feud with those he has wronged. These social troubles are further reflected by rules concerning this passion.

Whenever a character's Honor is reduced to 4 or lower, he has proved himself unfit to bear the title of knight and serve a lord. His lord must either outlaw him or degrade him. To fail to do so places the lord's own status in jeopardy because he would be failing to uphold his own government. Honor may eventually be regained at this grim point in a character's career, through appropriate actions.

Finally, if a character's Honor reaches 0 he must be removed from active play by the player. Recovery from such a low state is not possible. If the player wishes to see him in the campaign he must turn the character sheet over to the gamemaster, who can play him as a gamemaster character if he wishes.

Starting Honor value = 15.

Other Common Passions

Loyalties

Loyalty is the basis for all society. Knights may be Loyal to more than one person.

Loyalty (lord)

A knight's initial lord is the one who knights him, and for whom he harbors a special passion, detailed above. A knight may later acquire other lands, and therefore other lords as well.

Starting Loyalty (lord) value = 3d6 for lords other than the one who knighted you.

Possible Modifiers:

Manors Granted: +1d3 per manor.

Rich Estates = +1 per 1£.

Loyalty (Pendragon).

Only a few characters will be direct vassals of the High King. Everyone else may get this passion if they take the Companion's Oath of Allegiance and become Companions of Arthur. See the "Glory and Ambitions" chapter.

Starting Loyalty (Pendragon) value = 2d6+6

Possible Modifiers:

Father killed fighting against Arthur = -1d6

You are socially conservative = -6

You already Hate (Arthur) = - value of the Hate (Arthur) passion.

Your lord Hates (Arthur) = - value of the lord's Hate (Arthur) passion.

You agree strongly with Arthur's aims = +6

Sir Lamorak's Loyalty (Pendragon) Overcomes His Hate (Orkney Clan)

At the great tournament at Surluse Sir Lamorak has been recognized, despite his disguise. The event begins when King Arthur succeeds at a Recognize roll, and they exchange regrets over recent events.

"Alas," said Arthur, "now wot I well it is Sir Lamorak de Gales. O Lamorak, abide with me, and by my crown I shall never fail thee; and not so hardy in Gawaine's head, nor none of his brethren, to do thee any wrong."

"Sir," said Sir Lamorak, "wrong they have done me, and to you both."

"That is truth," said the king, "for they slew their own mother and my sister, the which me sore grieveth: it had been much fairer and better that ye had wedded her, for ye are a king's son as well as they."

"O Jesu," said the noble knight Sir Lamorak unto King Arthur, "her death shall I never forget. I promise you, and make mine vow unto God, I shall revenge her death as soon as I see time convenable. And if it were not at the reverence of your highness I should not have been revenged upon Sir Gawaine and his brethren."

"Truly," said Arthur, "I will make you at accord."

"Sir," said Lamorak, "as at this time I may not abide with you, for I must to the jousts where is Sir Lancelot, and the Haut Prince Sir Galahaut."

— Malory X, 46

Because Sir Lamorak refused the king's offer to make peace between himself and Gawaine the awful feud between the houses of Orkney and de Gales continued.

Loyalty (vassals)

The feudal arrangement calls for mutual loyalty between vassals and lord. Most knights never have other knights as vassals and have no need for this passion. However, any knight who does have other knights under his command should have this trait. This trait might be used to determine whether a lord will ransom his vassals (never required by the lord). Other game uses will inevitably come up.

Starting Loyalty (vassals) value = 2d6+6

Loyalty (group)

Knights may join, or even form, temporary fellowships.

Starting Loyalty (group) value = 3d6

Possible Modifiers:

You are kinsmen, or from the same kingdom = +6

You are the same culture = +1d6

You know each other previously = +/- [a number] as appropriate.

Amor

The art of love for love's sake was inaugurated by Queen Guenever. The conventions of courtly romance, detailed elsewhere, insist upon the utter devotion of the knight to his lady. The amor relationship is totally chaste, as between Sir Galahad and Amide, Sir Percivale's sister — if it is not, then the relationship becomes one of Love (amor), as described below.

Unless the lady is Guenever (see below) the name of the individual for whom Amor is held is a secret. The gamemaster must be informed as to who the lady is, but the other players need not be told. The name of the Amor should be written into the parentheses when her name is no longer a secret.

Amor (individual)

This is the standard Amor passion.

Starting Amor (individual) value = 3d6

Possible Modifiers (maximum total modifier = +10):

She (or he) flirted successfully = +1d3

She is an heiress = +1 per 1£. annual income

She (or he) has significant Glory = +1 per 1000 Glory

Stunning Beauty = +1 per point over 20

She brought him back from the brink of death = +6

He saved her from a dire fate = +6

She/he is an enemy = -1 per Hate (enemy)

Commonly, knights will travel about seeking the one who will be their amor. In such a case the knights may make a roll for their starting passion, and discard any rolls which are below 16 if they wish. However, any roll of 16 or greater is a true passion, and cannot be discarded.

Amor (Guenever)

Sighting Queen Guenever for the first time requires a character to see if a passion is acquired. Roll the basic 3d6, ignoring the usual rules for modifiers to the starting Amor value. If the viewer already has a Love or Amor which is *greater* than the number just rolled for Guenever, then no passion for the queen is gained at this time. Otherwise the queen's regal beauty has instantly kindled a new Amor (Guenever) passion that, at gamemaster option, may replace the previous Love or Amor.

Characters may also deliberately take the Amor (Guenever) passion, in which case normal rules apply, and 3d6+10 is rolled. A safe alternative to secret amor exists in this option. A convention of the era admits that the high queen is a great and noble woman and that she is admired by many knights who work for her ideals. Thus a knight may make the queen his Amor openly, striving to impress her enough to be invited to join her Queen's Knights. He does not expect to become her lover, just her sincere admirer. Thus someone stricken with a passion for an unsuitable amor can journey to see Guenever, and with any luck, can find an outlet this way.

The effect of the queen's extraordinary charm and beauty is well-known. A character not wishing to put his Love or Amor passion at risk upon first sight needs only to state that when in the presence of the queen for the first time, he will think only of his love. The 3d6 roll is not made.

Love

Love is an emotional bonding or attraction felt by one individual for another individual, group, or deity. A character may have many loves, but it is best if only one counts for Glory points each year, normally the highest.

Love must always be for *someone*. It is not possible to love an abstraction. Thus there is no Love (country) passion or Love (fighting) passion possible.

Love (amor)

The Amor (individual) passion, as noted above, often becomes a Love (amor). The term (amor) replaces a name here, indicating it is a secret affair. Secret or not, a Love (amor) indicates that an affair has been culminated in physical and carnal commitment.

A character may have either Amor (individual) or Love (amor), but not both.

The value of the Love (amor) passion is derived from the number rolled previously, as it stands when amor changes to love. No new number is rolled.

As long as the name of the lover is secret, the gamemaster must be told who that person is, but other players need not be informed. If the name of the lover is revealed, write the name onto the character sheet.

Love (spouse)

Deep feeling and attraction for one's husband or wife was apparently quite uncommon in the feudal world of arranged marriages. Two significant exceptions in the romances are the loves of Duke Gorlois for his wife Ygraine, and of Arthur for his wife, Guenever.

Starting Passion = 3d6

Optionally, the modifiers listed above for Amor may be used for Love (spouse).

Love (God)

This passion is required of Christian clergy. The cynical nature of many clergymen proves that this passion does not have to be *high* to join the church, but it is a requirement. Religiously oriented knights may also have this passion.

Starting Passion value = Piety trait value of the beginning clergyman or religious knight

A critical success in this passion gives the character an ecstatic vision in which they receive a check to all their appropriate religious traits, and are otherwise incapacitated and cannot act at all in the mundane, physical world, for a period of time determined by the gamemaster (at least an hour).

Hate

Hatred motivates many people in *Pendragon*, especially poltroons who are driven to dastardly deeds. For instance,

King Mark assuredly hates Tristram, and Morgan le Fay hates Guenever. Even some of the good guys develop a hatred because of their Love (family). The best instance is Gawaine's unrelenting Hate (Lancelot) brought about by Lancelot's slaying of Gareth, the brother whom Gawaine most Loved (Family).

Hatred may be for an individual, a people, a kingdom, a religion, for magicians or monks, a station or class, or whatever the gamemaster agrees to.

Starting Hate values are up to the gamemaster, but should have a value of at least 10. A Hate value should be based on the event that provoked the passion.

Fear

Fear is a negative emotion which can possibly be inherited as a family curse, but is normally gained only through personal experience (that is, game play.) A Fear is an irrational and absolute, mindless state of panic. Only extraordinary adventures can instill such terror in knight characters (lesser characters may be more vulnerable). Such Fear usually stems from supernatural places or creatures. Fear is often wisdom in disguise, since many supernatural creatures are immensely powerful and mean only harm to humans. Some sample Fears might be for hags, sailing, sea monsters, crazed holy men, standing stones which move, or Picts in the wild.

Fears give no benefits. They are an exception to the normal rules. There is no Glory gained, and no inspiration possible. A Fear only places the character out of the player's control under specific situations.

The gamemaster may create an opportunity to overcome a Fear. Such a chance will probably only come once, and if the character succeeds in overcoming his Fear, he may gain Glory for it. This Glory gift should be about ten times the value of the character's former Fear.

Using Passions

Invoking a passion is a good way for the gamemaster to add excitement to a scenario. But passion rolls are a risky business for players. The results vary, but are likely to be dramatic. Normally a passion roll will result in a particular state of mind, such as inspiration or madness. See the "States of Passion" section below.

Gaining a Passion

Passions may be gained during play. Plenty of opportunities will be given to gain enemies, lovers, and loyalties.

Passions should be agreed upon by both players and gamemasters. When something significant occurs to a character the gamemaster or player may suggest that a passion has been generated. They will discuss it, then determine the starting value.

The starting value is an entirely subjective amount agreed upon by both player and gamemaster. Suggested guidelines for starting passions are given above.

Benefits and Disadvantages of a Passion

Passions define the character's life intentions. Characters who share similar passions have much in common. Passions such as Loyalty (lord) provide common ground between strangers and make introductions easier.

Of all that passions do, most notable is that they serve to inspire their possessors. Rules for the state of Inspiration follow.

Famous passions generate Glory. Each winter, a character receives Glory for most high-valued passions. Only passions with a value of 16 or more generate Glory, and several restrictions and exceptions apply, as detailed above.

The gamemaster may call for a passion roll, possibly with a modifier for the particular situation. At other times the player may request a roll, with the gamemaster's approval. Remember that the gamemaster has final word on the appropriateness of attempting to use a passion for Inspiration. Players are warned that passion rolls can be extremely risky as well as rewarding; passions may subject a knight to several unusual states of mind, including introspection, melancholy, and madness.

Sir Palomides is Inspired by his Love (Isoud) Passion

Palomides is at the Lonazep tournament, where his would-be amor, Queen Isoud, watched her own lover, Sir Tristram.

And as it happened, Sir Palomides looked up toward her where she lay in the window, and he espied her how she laughed; and therewith he took such a rejoicing that he smote down, what with his spear and with his sword, all that ever he met; for through the sight of her he was so enamoured in her love that he seemed at that time, that and both Sir Tristram and Sir Lancelot had been both against him they should have no worship of him; and in his heart, as the book sayeth, Sir Palomides wished that with his worship he might have ado with Sir Tristram before all men, because of La Beale Isoud.

Then Sir Palomides began to double his strength, and he did so marvelously that all men had wonder of him, and ever he cast his eye unto La Beale Isoud. And when he saw her make such cheer he fared like a lion, and there might no man withstand him.

— Malory X, 70

Queen Guenever and her favorite hawk

Passion Results Table

Critical Success: Character is Inspired, and acts strongly in accordance with the passion. One skill of player's choice is temporarily *doubled* in value, and remains so throughout the duration of the task or situation that evoked the passion roll (maximum duration of one day). Immediately go up one point in the Passion. An experience check is gained as well.

Success: Character is Inspired, and acts in accordance with the passion. Immediately, but temporarily, add +10 to one skill of the player's choice, with the same duration as above. Experience check gained.

Failure: Character is Disheartened. He may act as the player chooses, but a modifier of -5 is applied to *all* subsequent rolls for the duration of the situation that evoked the passion roll. After the action is over he will be Melancholic. Immediately lose one point of passion unless the gamemaster rules otherwise.

Fumble: Character is crushed by negative thoughts. He goes mad, either immediately or after the action is over, as determined by the gamemaster. Immediately lose one point of passion.

Frivolous Passion Rolls

Players will often request a passion roll in inappropriate or borderline circumstances, hoping for inspiration. If a player insists on rolling his passion, is inspired, but then fails to win his goal (defeat an enemy, win a lady's heart, capture the stag, etc.), then the character receives a Shock — a roll on the Aging Table caused by grief and frustration.

Mandatory Passion Rolls

Glorious passions place your character at the mercy of the gamemaster and the scenario. As noted in the introduction to traits and passions, values of 16 or higher require mandatory rolls whenever the gamemaster chooses.

Lowering a Passion

Once gained, a passion can only be lowered or replaced (see Amor, above).

It is possible to *reduce* an unwanted passion by loudly declaiming so in public, and acting in every way contrary to the passion. For instance, when Sir Gareth learned that his brothers had murdered Sir Lamorak (c. 552), he disassociated himself from them by loudly proclaiming his unhappiness and disloyalty to his family. Reducing a passion in this way may be done over the winter, but is the only activity which can be performed, as noted in the Winter Phase rules. Thus the character cannot perform his 1d6 skill training or other options if he reduces his passion. He lowers its value by one point each Winter Phase. Eventually it will be eliminated. The gamemaster may permit more than one point to be eliminated per year at his option, based on roleplaying.

A character will, at some time, receive a failed passion roll in time of a crisis. This means that his feelings failed him at that moment and he may do what he wishes. However, the failure may cause an immediate loss of one point (always ask the gamemaster before you subtract the point. Some circumstances will not warrant the subtraction).

States of Passion

Inspiration

To be Inspired is the object of passion. Inspiration can turn an ordinary character into an extraordinary character. Inspiration is the source for the greatness which the apparently superhuman Round Table knights exhibit.

The result of this inspiration is a vastly increased chance of success in skill use. The selected skill is either doubled (for a critical success passion roll) or +10 (for a normal success). Remember to use the rules for values above 20. Duration of Inspiration is for the length of the task at hand, never more than a day.

Sir Alisander Is Besotted By Love

Sir Alisander has fallen deeply in love with Alis la Beale Pilgrim. Inspired by her, he overcomes all foes, but then falls victim to introspection. He is saved only by the rapid intervention of a young lady who arms and rides out to break his spell.

Then this while came there three knights, that one hight Vains, and the other hight Harvis de les Marches, and the third hight Perin de la Montaine. And with one spear Sir Alisander smote them down all three, and gave them such falls that they had no list to fight upon foot. So he made them to swear to wear none arms in a twelvemonth.

So when they were departed Sir Alisander beheld his lady Alis on horseback as he stood in her pavilion. And then was he so enamoured upon her that he wist [knew] not whether he were on horseback or on foot.

Right so came the false knight Sir Mordred, and saw Sir Alisander was assotted upon his lady; and therewithal he took his horse by the bridle, and led him here and there, and had cast to have led him out of that place to have shamed him.

When the damosel that halp him out of that castle saw how shamefully he was led, anon she let arm her, and set a shield upon her shoulder; and therewith she mounted upon his horse, and gat a naked sword in her hand, and she thrust unto Alisander with all her might, and gave him such a buffet that he thought the fire flew out of his eyen.

And when Alisander felt that stroke he looked about him, and drew his sword. And when she saw that, she fled, and so did Mordred into the forest, and the damosel fled into the pavilion.

—Malory X, 39

This is the only case in all of Malory where a lady dons armor, and it is to help the knight, not to encounter another in battle.

Introspection

Knights and ladies in love periodically fall into a dreamlike daze while contemplating the virtues of their fair amor. They get a distant look in their eyes and totally ignore everything going on around them.

This can happen anytime they are not actively doing something important, typically while riding down the road.

The gamemaster may call for a possible incident of Introspection once per game day. A critical success at the character's Love or Amor passion brings it about. Introspection lasts for 4d6 minutes before the knight regains his senses. No Awareness, Heraldry, Recognize, or other rolls can be attempted.

While lost in introspection, the knights are also Inspired normally (+10 to one skill), but only to defend themselves against anyone who attacks them.

Disheartened

A Disheartened knight suffers a -5 modifier to all rolls during the situation that brought on his state. Subsequently he will be Melancholic.

Melancholy

Melancholy may come about as a result of an unsuccessful passion result. The gamemaster may impose melancholy on characters in other appropriate situations as well.

Melancholy is a mental disease which strikes without apparent cause. When it manifests the victim is overwhelmed by his grief. He falls the ground weeping aloud, lamenting his losses and ill luck, crying out from his deep emotional pain. He may fall into a deep and silent depression.

If a Melancholic character is disturbed he will fall into an absolute rage, hoping to overcome his misery through violence. he always attack the disturbing individual unless it is a female. The only way a man can hope to calm a melancholic individual is by using "reverse psychology." The would-be healer attempts a trait roll, which automatically provokes a roll on the opposite trait. If the melancholic character wins the resolution he attacks, but if he loses he calms down and goes to sleep.

Melancholy usually lasts a day.

Sir Lancelot Goes Mad

Queen Guenever discovers her lover, Sir Lancelot, in bed with another woman, and does not know that he was bewitched to do so. She wakes him:

And then he knew well that he lay not by the queen; and therewith he leapt out of his bed as he had been a wood [mad] man, in his shirt, and the queen met him in the floor; and thus she said:

"False traitor knight that thou art, look thou never abide in my court, and avoid my chamber, and not so hardy, thou false traitor knight that thou art, that ever thou come in my sight!"

"Alas," said Sir Lancelot; and therewith he took such an heartly sorrow at her words that he fell down to the floor in a swoon. And therewithal Queen Guenever departed.

And when Sir Lancelot awoke of his swoon, he leapt out at a bay window into a garden, and there with thorns he was all to-cratched in his visage and his body; and so he ran forth he wist not whither, and was wild wood as ever was man; and so he ran two year, and never might man might have grace to know him.

— Malory XI, 8

Lancelot wanders, mad and wild, leaving the queen to bitterly regret her harsh words.

Shock

Shock occurs when a knight fails to perform a deed which he was Inspired to perform. Normal Shock means that the character gets one roll on the Aging Table. The gamemaster determines whether failure occurred.

Other likely circumstances would be the abandonment by a lord or lover to grave danger or a dire fate. The gamemaster is encouraged to note other appropriate applications of Shock.

Madness

A character may also be driven mad. In such circumstances he must immediately give the character sheet to the gamemaster, who will describe what ensues, based only on what the other player characters know.

Normally, mad characters run away immediately. For the duration of their madness, they will attempt to avoid the scene of their disastrous experience at all cost.

The madman is out of play until the gamemaster wishes to reintroduce him into the campaign, perhaps never. Storytelling considerations should be dominant in determining how long a madman is gone.

If recovered, the madman will have undergone unusual, unknown circumstances which can result in changes to some statistics and/or skills at the gamemaster's option. Players should simply accept these changes, which should not always be negative. The character's player will be unaware of what has been experienced, but may search for knowledge, and may eventually determine what events took place during the period of madness.

Your Home

You are a native of Salisbury, a county in Logres. Logres is the most important kingdom in Britain.

IN THIS CHAPTER we present information about your homeland. Salisbury is the area about which you know the most. We give you all this detail to familiarize players with their homeland. Consider this to be the type of information which you would get just by growing up at the court of Salisbury. Remember that no accurate maps are available — the type of map we are used to is a relatively late invention.

Assume that characters from any region know about this much and this type of information about their own homes. However, remember that your characters will not know this much about other regions, and also remember that if you have a character from another region he won't know this much about Salisbury, either. This ability to separate personal knowledge from character knowledge is one of the marks of good roleplaying.

Salisbury is one of the most interesting and exciting places to live in Arthurian legend. It is one of the most densely populated areas. Many great events occur here: the early Battle of Badon which established Arthur as king of Logres was here, and so will the final Battle of Camlann which concludes the campaign. Many interesting places are here: Stonehenge, most famous of the ancient monuments, and Amesbury Abbey, where Arthur's mother retired and where Queen Guenever will eventually retire. It has many interesting landmarks, especially the dozens of prehistoric mounds, stone circles, and the unusual White Horse. Camelot is also nearby. Salisbury is a good place to be from.

This description, like the rest of this book, is from the era during which Arthur's reign is strongest. During other phases of Arthur's reign things might be very different.

The County of Salisbury

SALISBURY COUNTY CONSISTS of all the holdings of the Earl of Salisbury. This fief consists primarily of a large land area on Salisbury Plain, and secondarily of the lands around Uffington, known as the White Horse Vale, an area to the north which is separated by other fiefs. The fief also includes other forms of income for the duke: fisheries, taxes on merchants, and tolls from the bridges.

Two maps are provided for the County of Salisbury: a large color map showing major features, and a smaller map showing travel times, in terms of one or more days of travel.

The county includes one large city, Sarum, which is described in detail below, three smaller walled cities (Wilton, Warminster, and Tilshead), and dozens of much smaller towns and villages which are not shown on the maps, but are generally clustered in the river valleys around the cities. It has two very strong, modern castles (Salisbury, in Sarum; and Devizes) and three older, motte and bailey castles (du Plain, Ebble, and Vagon).

Note that two significant sections of Salisbury Plain are not part of the county but are held by other landowners. One is the town of Upavon and the surrounding area, held by the Duke of Leicester. The other is Amesbury Abbey, held by the Church. In like manner, the Earl of Salisbury holds a large piece of land outside his own area in the White Horse Vale.

Several towns and cities are cited in this description as "local markets." This means that they are the central collection points for the nearby farmers, who go there to buy most goods and to sell their extra grain. The central market is at Sarum, and is the only place that some types of goods, such as good cloth, clean salt, and anything from outside the county, are available for purchase.

The roads shown on the maps are the best travel routes available. Thus there is no decent road from Tilshead to Warminster, even though they are but ten miles apart. The good roads are more heavily travelled, and the only ones used by travellers passing through the territory. The poor roads are less used, mainly by locals travelling within the region. The Old Tracks have been known since the bronze age, and traverse high ground. Though they are usually dry, they are difficult for horses, which are reduced to travelling a mere 5 miles per day, hence they are used mainly by peasants on foot.

The City of Sarum

Sarum is your home base. Educated, Latin-speaking persons call this city *Sorbiodunum*. The old Cymric name is *Caer Caradduc*. It sits upon a steep, wind-swept mound amidst the rolling Salisbury Plain. A massive ditch and rampart encircles the city of Sarum. This was originally built by your character's ancestors, during the time before iron was used, in the days when people still worshipped the sun at Stonehenge. A series of concentric rings surround the city: a massive ditch on the outside, then a huge rampart, then another large ditch and another rampart. A great curtain wall surmounts the inner ditch. It is 12 feet thick and 40 feet high. Battlements give its top a serrated shape, made by merlons (the upright stone) and crenelations (the indentation between merlons).

Two gates, to the east and west, pierce the walls. They are defended by towered gateworks, each with its huge iron-shod portcullis, murder holes, and drawbridges. As with all cities, these are closed at night and normally admit no one.

Sarum and Salisbury Castle

In the center of the city is a great motte, or artificial mound, upon which sits the magnificent castle of the earl. Four ditch-and-rampart spokes radiate from the castle almost to the outer wall, and divide the city into quarters. The north-western quarter is given over to the magnificent cathedral and church buildings, a part of the fief of the Bishop of Salisbury. It is occupied by churchmen and the bishop's retinue. The cathedral is dedicated to Saint Mary, the Mother of God.

The city occupies the rest, and serves as the outer bailey for the castle. It is large and relatively rich. It serves as the trading center for all of the county and the earl receives rich revenues from its taxes, part of which go to the High King. A royal mint is here which stamps out silver pennies that show King Arthur's image on one side, and the name of the mint and the moneyer on the other. The earl receives no income from this source.

Salisbury Castle

This is one of the finest castles in the realm, incorporating the latest in castle-building features. It sits upon the great motte, or hillock, in the center of the city of Sarum, and is the main seat for your lord, the Earl of Salisbury.

Great curtain walls, 15 feet thick and 40 feet tall, surround the inner bailey, which is roughly circular and about 300 feet in diameter. Within this bailey are domestic buildings, including the bakery by the east gates. The castle well is in the center of this bailey.

Two regular gates and one postern gate pierce the wall. The regular gates have defensive works, including towers and drawbridges which cross the ditch surrounding the motte. The east tower protects the postern gate, which goes through it. The south tower is large and stands attached only to the wall, while the northern tower is attached to the keep.

The keep, or donjon, is the center of domestic and administrative activities. Four rectangular, three-story tall buildings, all surmounted by battlements, surround a central courtyard which is paved with crushed chalk to cast more light within its enclosure.

Like all similar structures, the keep can be entered only over a drawbridge on the second floor. The lowest, ground floor, is used mainly to store food and supplies. The private chambers of the earl, his family, and county officers occupy the eastern and northern buildings. The north tower, situated along the wall, is connected to the keep. The western building holds the great, high-ceilinged hall where the earl meets his petitioners and otherwise holds his court. Here most of the household knights sleep at night. The south contains the kitchen and chapel, and above it more private chambers for county and castle officers, and guests.

The Great Hall

When your knight visits his lord he, like most people, does not have private chambers. Your knight, like most people, sleeps at night in the same place that he works in the daytime. Thus cooks sleep in the kitchen, bakers in the pantry, and grooms in the stable. As a knight, your character sleeps in the Great Hall. This is also the permanent home of the earl's household knights. They each have a big chest to store personal possessions.

By day the great hall is the lord's courtroom. The floor is cleared of furniture except for the lord's high chair, which remains upon the raised dias at the far end of the room. In the evening trestle tables and benches are brought out for the evening meal. At night the tables and benches serve as beds, or people sleep on the floor.

People You Know

These are the most important people in your character's home, the County of Salisbury. Few except Earl Robert are well known outside Salisbury.

Since your character is personally acquainted with these people, their Glory

The Great Hall

numbers and, for the ladies, Appearance statistics and holdings, are given here.

The Knights

Earl Robert

Glory 7,740

Earl of Salisbury, this grizzled old warrior is famed for his prowess, exhibited while fighting under King Arthur during the early wars. He is noted for his deadly feud with the Steward of Levcomagus, and for his burning desire to acquire the rights to the rich lands around Silbury. Another of his habits is to grumble volubly about his wife's extravagant clothing expenses.

The Earl's arms are blue and gold (yellow) horizontal stripes.

Sir Gondrins

Glory 1,375

The only son of the Earl of Salisbury. He is a young man, newly knighted and anxious to prove his prowess in any way. Both valorous and reckless, Gondrins has sworn to kill the Steward of Levcomagus and all his kin some day. He is often away patrolling the borders with a band of knights, including your character on occasion. You know him to be a proud but just knight, and a good leader considering his youth.

Sir Yolains

Glory 3,237

Castellan of Devizes. He has the habit of challenging all new knights to combat "for love" when he encounters them. He often boasts of his part in Arthur's war against the Romans, and jealously guards the trophy legionary shields which decorate his hall.

Sir Jaradan

Glory 5,208

Marshal of Salisbury. He is an old veteran of many wars, including the Battles of Badon, Carlion, and Bedegraine. He has trained most of the knights at court, and loves to tell his war stories to anyone who listens. He is the earl's right-hand man for council.

Sir Briadanz the Hunter

Glory 2,850

A middle-aged man, cheerful and helpful to anyone who expresses interest in the chase. When in his cups he casually mentions the werewolf which he slew years ago on the Yorkshire Moor.

Sir Magloas of Du Plain

Glory 2,768

Castellan of Du Plain Castle, he is hotheaded and pious, claiming to have God's approval for any action he undertakes. He dislikes Sir Briadanz, who he says is a great liar.

The Ladies

Countess Katherine

Glory 2,470

APP 10

Countess of Salisbury and Lady of the White Horse Vale. She is neither greatly beautiful nor intelligent, but is heiress of the White Horse Vale. She loves to gossip about Camelot, and spends extravagant amounts of money (over 40 £. per year!) to employ many skilled seamstresses to keep up with the latest fashions.

Lady Orlande of Devizes

Glory 1,786

APP 26

Holding: Castellancy of Devizes Castle, 3 demesne manors, 7 enfeoffed manors. 96 Glory/year.

A maiden, the only child of Sir Yolains, and the most beautiful woman in the county. She is known to extend the magnificent favor of a kiss to men who gift her with expensive jewelry.

Lady Gaille of Wilton

Glory 5,340

APP 14

Holding: 2 demesne manors, plus 10 £. extra income/year. 22 Glory/year.

Widow's Holdings (Gifts): 3 manors in Salisbury, 2 in Clarence. 30 Glory/year.

A middle-aged woman, the richest heiress of the county, holding rights to the city of Wilton in her own right. She has been widowed four times and is in no hurry to marry again, though she does not discourage any suitors.

Lady Jeanne of Broad Chalke

Glory 856

APP 16

Holding: 2 demesne manors. 12 Glory/year.

She is the chief handmaiden of Countess Katherine, and a devotee of the chaste expression of Amor. She is heiress of two manors up river from Ebble Castle. Her last two suitors disappeared in Camelot Forest while seeking to defend her estate from robber knights.

Lady Anne of Longcot

Glory 258

APP 18

Holding: 3 demesne manors. 18 Glory/year.

She is a beautiful woman who professes to embrace Amor, but whose reputation is for embracing any available man who catches her fancy. She is also owner of her father's magic sword named Bone-Biter (+1 skill) which she is holding for her son to use. (Longcot is a manor in the White Horse Vale.)

Lady Madule of the Raven Hair

Glory 554

APP 13

Holding: 2 demesne manors, 5 enfeoffed manors. 42 Glory/year.

She is the only child of the deceased banneret of West Lavington, and thus the heiress of a rich holding on the Salisbury Plain. She is an unusual young woman, who studied at Amesbury with Morgan le Fay and was expelled from the convent with her for studying sorcery. Everyone believes this, for she has a huge collection of seven books in her manor. She usually lives at her manor house, near Tilshead.

Places

In the following section is the information your character knows about specific locations in his homeland. *CAPITAL LETTERS* indicate places within the fief lands of the County of Salisbury. *Lower Case* letters indicate places outside the fief of Salisbury. Travel times are based upon 15 miles per day, always following the roads.

See the map of the County of Salisbury and the associated Travel Times map, which shows the same area in terms of how many days' ride places are from one another.

AMBROSIUS' DIKE

Aurelius Ambrosius, the first Pendragon, built these massive earthworks as a part of a defense system against the Saxons in the east. Too large to be manned as walls, these were used to observe the moving army, hinder his approach, and to hide am ambushing army. They now mark the northern boundary of the county.

Amesbury Abbey

Aurelius Ambrosius established this monastery, which is still supported by royal funds. It is a double-abbey, having facilities for both men and women. King Arthur's mother, Queen Ygraine, retired here. Although this is within the county, it is actually a fief of the Church and contributes no income to the earl.

AVON RIVER

This river is one of several of the same name in Britain. It is the main drainage of the Salisbury Plain, and continues to flow southward through the Camelot Forest and Dorset to the British Sea. It is navigable by coastal ships which sail all the way up to Wilton.

Badon Hill

This is an ancient hill fort where King Arthur fought his greatest victory against the Saxons. Many people report hearing the angry howling of the Saxon ghosts on the anniversary of their mass deaths.

Bath

The main city of Somerset, it is called in Latin *Aqua Sulis*, or the Baths of Sulis, because of the magical healing properties of its springs. It is three days' ride from Sarum.

BOKERLY DIKE

This is a north-facing bank and ditch built in Roman times to separate tribes which have, since then, become extinct. It now marks the boundary between the counties of Salisbury and Dorset.

BOURNE RIVER

A tributary to the Avon River. Many villages and farms dot the valley.

Calne

This is a fortified city which serves as the local market, and is part of the fief of Somerset. It is about two days' ride from Sarum.

Camelot

Camelot is the city built and ruled by King Arthur after his kingdom was consolidated. It is the preeminent place in Britain and a site of many wonders, especially the Round Table. It is about two days' ride from Sarum.

Camelot is called Winchester by the Saxons. It was briefly the capital city of the Kingdom of Wessex. Before that it was an important Roman city, but deteriorated badly before and during the Saxon occupation.

Camelot Forest

This is a dense forest which forms the southern border of Salisbury County. Though close to the center of civilization it has of late become more inhabited by fabulous beasts, as if they have come to please the High King during his hunts.

Campacorentin Forest

This dense forest lies several days' ride north of Sarum. It stretches for many miles, primarily east and west, and encloses many holdings, some of which are still independent from the High King's rule. Like all forests, it houses many strange creatures, but is especially noted for a pair of huge night-black lions which periodically terrorize nearby peasants. A persistent rumor about the forest tells of a rich princess imprisoned in a tower surrounded by a garden of giant, thorny roses.

Cirencester

This was once an important Roman city, and is now the primary seat of the Duke of Clarence. It is about four days' ride from Sarum.

Clarence

The Duchy of Clarence is ruled by Duke Galegantis, a nephew of King Arthur who delights in tournaments and in skirmishing with the nearby Gloucestermen. He was deprived of his hereditary rights for fighting, with his father, against Arthur, but subsequently received this honor for his loyal service to the High King.

COLINGBOURNE WOOD

This woodland is a favorite hunting place for knights and commoners both. It probably has no exotic animals or faeries.

DEVIZES

This is a fine, modern castle. It includes a shell keep, barbican with drawbridge, and three other towers. It is about 1-2 days' ride from Sarum. It is the fief of Sir Yolains, who holds it of the earl and has an obligation of 5 knights.

DU PLAIN CASTLE

One day's ride from Sarum, this castle marks the eastern boundary of the county. It is small and simple: a motte and bailey, surrounding a single very high stone tower. It was built during Arthur's Saxon wars.

EBBLE CASTLE

This is an old, motte and bailey castle made mostly of wood, but still serviceable in defense. It is the most southern settlement of the county.

EBBLE RIVER

A tributary of the Avon River, this river valley is not densely inhabited. Menaces often come out of the surrounding Camelot Forest. Of late the river has been plagued by a school of repulsive water leapers (see the "Characters and Creatures" chapter) which prey upon small boats.

FIGSBURY

This is one of numerous hill forts on the Salisbury Plain. It has been abandoned since ancient times. Sometimes, on midsummer's day, the sounds of groaning men and clanking chains can be heard coming from underground.

Glastonbury

Glastonbury is one of the most sacred places in Britain, for it was here that the first Christian church was built. Before that it was sacred to Don, the earth mother, and was a magical entrance to the Otherworld. An abbey is there now. It is about four days' ride from Sarum, and is within the County of Somerset.

Gloucester

Gloucester, called *Glevum* in Latin, is the most important seaport of the western coast, located near the mouth of the Severn River. It is ruled by the Duke of Gloucester, a rival of the Duke of Clarence. It is about five days uninterrupted ride from Sarum.

GOFFANON'S SMITHY

Goffanon is the ancient British god of smiths. At this place he forged shoes for the White Horse which is cut into the nearby hills. Any traveller can leave his horse and a silver penny here overnight, and in the morning his horse will be freshly shod. It is an 180-foot long barrow, and anyone who spends the night

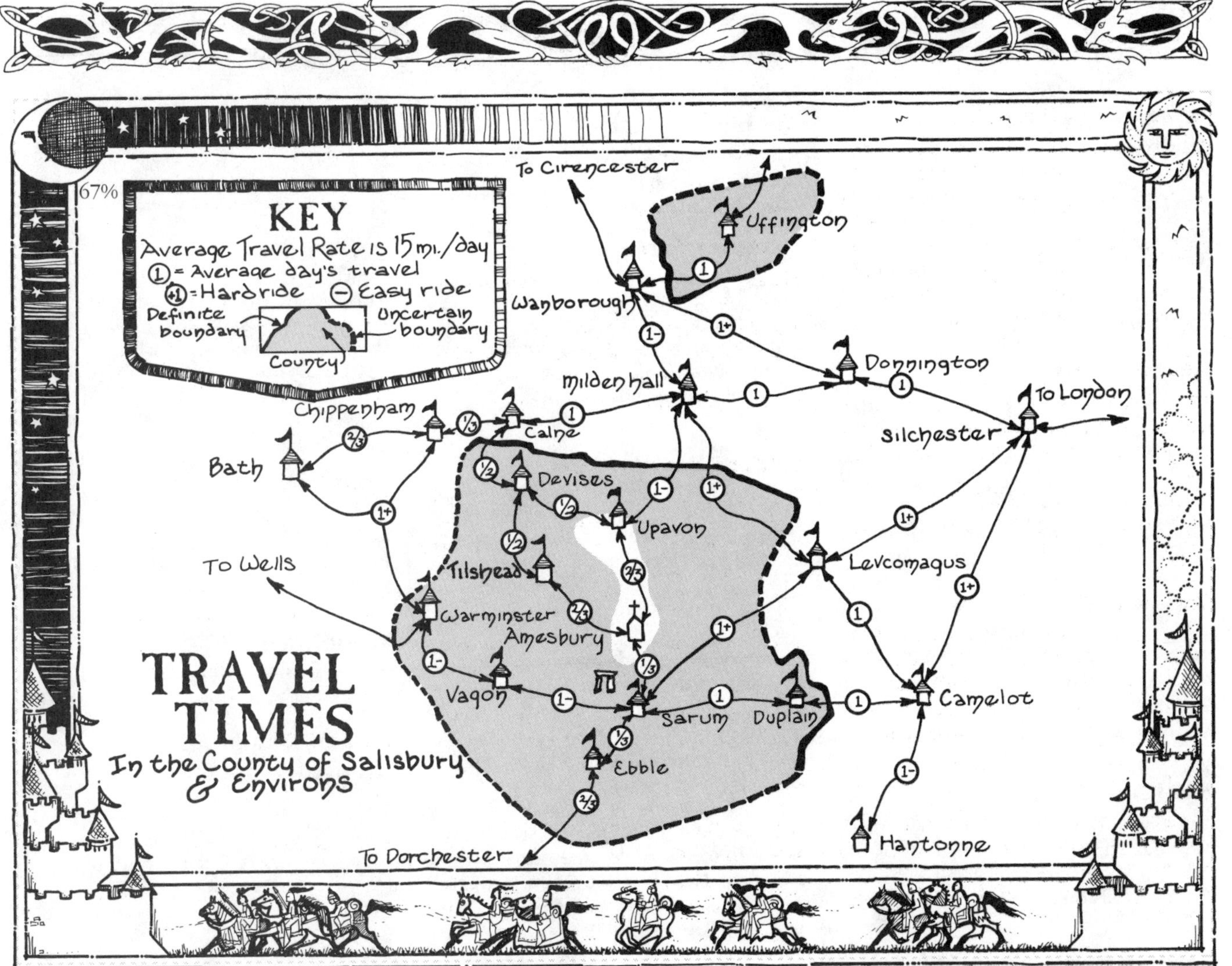

to watch inevitably falls asleep and wakes up robbed of his goods by the faeries.

GROVELY CASTLE

This is an ancient hill fort of great earthworks, now mostly overgrown with thorns and wild flowers.

Hantonne

This is a part of the Kingdom of Wessex, and is the nearest sea port to Sarum. Its inhabitants are surly Saxons. It is two days' ride from Sarum.

Jagent

This city is the center of a county ruled by a militant lord who fiercely defends his ancient rights. He is plagued by the lack of any heir.

Kennet River

A large, eastward flowing river which is a tributary which joins the Thames far to the east.

Levcomagus

This city is part of the fief of the Duke of Silchester. Its steward holds a fierce grudge against all men of Salisbury because the old earl, father of Robert, slew all of the steward's brothers in combat. He keeps many knights guarding the roads to Salisbury to enforce his grudge against Salisbury.

London

London is the largest and most important city in Britain. It has no lord but the High King, and is ruled by a council of its most important merchants. King Arthur first pulled his sword from the stone here. It is about eight days' ride from Sarum.

Marlborough

This is a fine castle. It is built atop a large ancient mound, believed by many to be the burial mound of an ancient wizard. It is held by the Knight of Red and Black, a vassal of the High King. It is about two days' leisurely ride from Sarum.

Mildenhall

This unwalled city is the local market for the farms along the Kennet River, and is held by the castellan from Marlborough. This knight, who wears an unusual suit of red and black armor, refuses passage across his bridge to any knight who will not joust with him.

Morgaine's Forest

This dense forest which lies to the west of the county is named after an ancient goddess of the Britons. It is rumored to be inhabited now by the legions of Morgan le Fay, the wicked sorceress sister of the High King, who has mustered all the

wicked faeries and beasts to her command.

NADDE RIVER

This is a heavily-populated river valley. The river is a tributary of the Avon River.

OCK RIVER

This is the main river which flows through the White Horse Vale. Its farmers visit Uffingham for their local market. It is a tributary of the Thames River.

SALISBURY PLAIN

The Salisbury Plain is a gently undulating plain whose rivers are populated by many villages of farmers. It also has many ancient, bronze- and early iron-age settlements, mostly long abandoned but occasionally resettled, as at Sarum. Only the largest of these are shown on the map, and many are unrecognized as such by the natives.

SARUM

The main county seat, this is a fortified city and castle built within one of the many ancient earthworks of Salisbury Plain. Details on it are given elsewhere.

SAVERNAK FOREST

This border forest is within either or both the lands of the Earl of Salisbury and the Lord of Marlborough, and has been the cause of considerable dispute between the lords. No faeries have been reported here, though the earl's mother once saw a unicorn there.

Silchester City

This is one of the Roman cities of the past, now much diminished in size and importance, but great nonetheless. It is about two days' ride from Sarum. It is part of the holdings of the Duke of Silchester.

Silbury Hill

This in a huge mound, the remnants of some mysterious building program of the ancients. The Earl of Salisbury claims all the land in this valley as his own, but the Banneret of Silbury recently changed his loyalty to the Lord of Calne. He has been constantly thwarted by the Duke of Leicester whose claim is more recent.

Silchester Duchy

Silchester is the dukedom which commands most of the lands east of Salisbury. It is ruled by Duke Ulfius, whose sons are noted for their arrogance.

Somerset

This county includes all the lands to the north west. Formerly the domain of an independent king, it is now part of the realm of King Arthur.

STONEHENGE

This monumental structure was built by giants in ancient times and dedicated to the sun, stars, and ancestors. In consists of five concentric rings and horseshoes of standing stones and a few outlying stones, all surrounded by a mounded ditch.

Two generations ago a great treachery occurred here when Vortigern the Traitor betrayed the nobles of Britain to the Saxons.

One generation ago it was refurbished by Merlin the Enchanter, who reestablished some of the old magic by stealing some great, magical stones from Ireland. Now it is also the burial site for the first two Pendragons: Aurelius Ambrosius and his brother Uther, who was King Arthur's father.

Swindon

A city to the north of Salisbury, held by the Duke of Clarence. It is important because of the quarries which lie nearby. It is about three days' ride from Sarum.

Test River

A river which flows southward to the British Sea, its valley is still largely deserted as a result of the war against the Saxons. Part of it is the boundary between Salisbury and Wessex.

TILSHEAD

A fortified city which serves as the market for the local farmers. It is a one day ride from Sarum.

Uffingham

This is an unwalled city and local market for the numerous farms throughout the White Horse Vale. Although it is separated from the rest of the county and is about four days' ride from Sarum, it is still a part of the fief of the Earl of Salisbury.

UFFINGHAM CASTLE

An ancient hill fort, not used currently. It consists of a ditch and bank. It is about eight acres in area.

Upavon

This is a large, unwalled town which serves as the local market for farmers of the upper Avon river. It is about one day's ride from Sarum. Although located upon the Salisbury Plain, Upavon is actually part of the 10-manor fief of the Duke of Leicester.

VAGON

Vagon Castle sits about one day's ride from Sarum. It is old, being a reinforced motte and bailey.

Wandborough

A city which is held by the Duke of Leicester. It is three days' ride from Sarum.

WARMINSTER

This is a fortified city which serves as the local market for the farms of the upper Wylye River. It is surrounded by the Morgaine Forest, and defends the country from incursions from Somerset. It is two days' ride from Sarum.

Wessex

Previously an independent Saxon kingdom, this is one of the regions conquered by King Arthur during the Saxon wars. Its king, Cerdic, was the son of the traitor Vortigern, the high king who preceded the Pendragons. Cerdic's mother was Rowena, daughter of King Hengest of Kent. Cerdic was thus doubly Arthur's enemy, and was lucky to be exiled after the Saxon wars. His lands are now divided among Arthur's loyal followers.

WHITE HORSE

A large horse was cut from the topsoil here, revealing the chalk beneath. It is shaped like a horse, said to be the steed of Rhiannon, the ancient horse goddess of the Britons, and is older than all memory.

WHITE HORSE VALE

This valley is drained by the Ock River, and is now part of the fief of the Earl of Salisbury. The peasants here persist in pagan practices.

WILTON

This fortified city is the local market for the many farms of the Nadde River and the lower Wylye River.

WYLYE RIVER

This river is a tributary for the Avon River. Its farms are divided between Warminster and Wilton.

YARNBURY

This is one of many ancient earthworks. It encloses almost 30 acres within its bank and ditch. Every Beltaine the local peasants bring all their cattle here and drive them between two big, smokey fires.

The Progress of Salisbury

The Earl of Salisbury spends most of his year at Sarum, the natural collection point for excess goods. His progress can go in any direction or order, and given here is a typical example:

— at Sarum for late autumn, all winter and early spring (16 weeks total).
— to Vagon, stay for 3 weeks
— to Warminster, for 4 weeks
— to various hunting lodges in Morgaine Forest for 2 weeks.
— to Devizes Castle for 3 weeks.

Start of Summer

— to Tilshead for 4 weeks.
— to Amesbury, stay there 2-3 days as guest of the abbott.
— to Sarum for 1 week.
— to Ebble Castle for 2 weeks, hunting and searching for robbers.
— to Sarum for 1 week.
— to du Plain Castle for 2 weeks, lead a raid against Silchester.
— travel along the Bourne River valley and hunting in Collingbourne Woods, 2 weeks total.
— to Mildenhall, 1-2 days as guest.

Start of Autumn

— to Wandborough, 1-2 days as guest.
— to Uffingham, 3 weeks of duty and hunting in the Campacorentin Forest.
— to Wandborough, 1-2 days as guest.
— to Mildenhall, 1-2 days, perhaps including a hunt in Savernake Forest.
— to Upavon, 1 days visit as guest.
— to Devizes Castle again, 1 week.
— Morgaine Forest hunting, 2 weeks.
— Warminster, 2 weeks.
— Vagon, 1 week.
— to Sarum again, preparing for winter.

The Earl's Army

Given here is the usual distribution of the 75 knights and 150 footsoldiers of the earl's personal armed force. Note several interesting features:

- Du Plain and Ebble both have far more men than are minimally necessary, due to trouble or potential trouble from robbers and raiders from the earl's enemy in Levcomagus.
- Vagon is undermanned.
- The earl's entourage always has at least 12 knights, including the earl himself.
- A patrol of knights, usually led by the earl's son, roams from area to area to make random spot checks.
- Uffingham, unwalled, has two knights to oversee affairs there anyway.
- Almost any place will be minimally garrisoned if the resident knights depart, as they would certainly do if real trouble or opportunity occurred in the county.
- Hard-riding knights can reach Sarum from anyplace within the county (Uffingham excepted) within 2 days: 1 day for messengers to go out, and another for the knights to ride in, assuming they are at home. Thus within 2 days most of the county's knights can be mustered at Sarum. This is actually extremely optimistic, but certainly within 4 days from sending out word, almost all the knights can reach Sarum.

The Army

Place	*Min.Garrison**	*Actual*
Devizes	5	5 kts + 5 foot
Du Plain	5	5 kts + 20 foot
Ebble	5	10 kts + 20 foot
Sarum	34	20 kts + 55 foot
Tilshead	14	2 kts + 15 foot
Uffingham	0	2 kts
Vagon	19	5 kts + 10 foot
Warminster	11	2 kts + 15 foot
Wilton	24	2 kts + 25 foot
Entourage	0	12 kts
Patrol	0	10 kts

**Minimum Garrison needed for normal defense.*

The Salisbury Manors

Twenty manors have been selected as the immediately available manors for player knights. They are shown on the nearby "Manors of Salisbury" map. This map reveals a portion of the main Salisbury map in detail (which does not show any population centers of manor size). This one does. It also includes several places which are also mentioned later, in the "Scenarios" chapter.

Your Manor

THE MANOR IS THE BASIS of your character's wealth. A vassal knight holds a manor with 6 £. of income. What is this, really? Given here is a typical knight's holding of a manor, plus the other factors necessary to the holding.

An illustration showing a typical manor is presented nearby.

The Hall

This is a fine house for the knight and his family. Its mark is a great hall. Sometimes, in fact, a manor is called a "hall," naturally implying everything which lies around it as well.

The knight's squire and a couple of the manor's chief servants (a bailiff) probably live in the hall too. Other servants (the pig boy, gardener, stable hand, and so on) live in the buildings they work in: a stable for the horses, a barn for the other livestock, chicken coop, pigsty, and storage sheds. This is, basically, the nicest farm in the area.

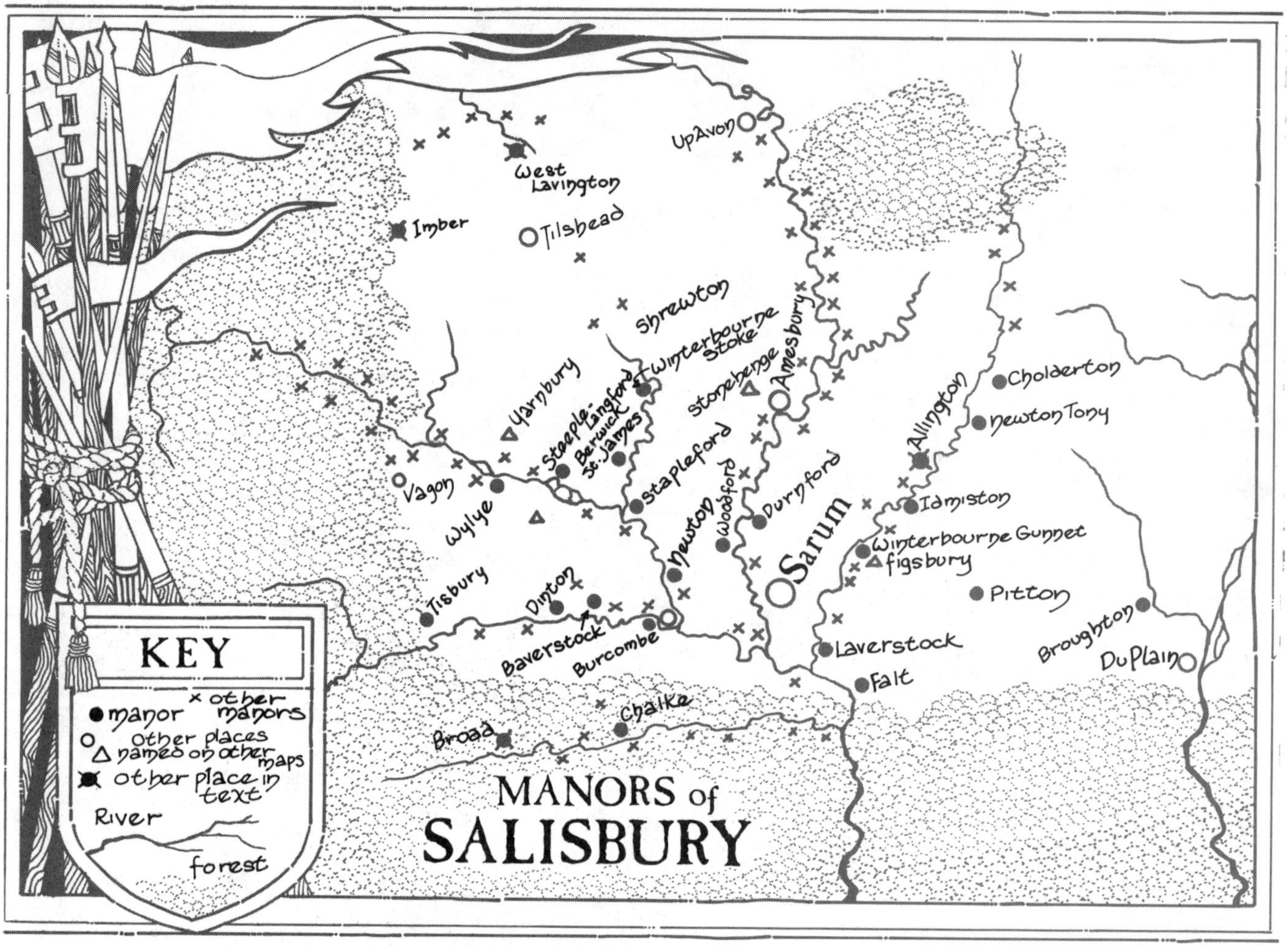

MANORS of SALISBURY

Demesne

These are lands which are owned by the knight. The peasants from the holding send men and plows to work the land. They are planted mostly in wheat for people and oats for horses.

Other Manoral Land

The knight also owns strips of land scattered among the other plow lands. Most landholders have their land in scattered strips this way, which increases community cooperation and cohesion.

The Town

This town is the local market where craftsmen (blacksmith, carpenter, cooper, etc.) can be found, and where itinerant peddlers meet once a week to set up market. A couple of nice houses for the richer farmers are here, but most buildings are peasant shacks and cattle huts. The population is around 120 people, including those of the Hall.

The Church

A small, poor church is at the center of the town. It is the largest building around, and made of stone. The priest, himself nearly as illiterate as the farmers, is in charge of the local congregation. The church is called the *baptistery* because baptisms, marriages, and funerals are performed and recorded there.

Villages

Three villages, each about a mile away, are part of the manor. They each have about 100 residents who are all farmers. They all come to the town for church, festivals, and to work their share for the lord. The village might have a dilapidated church, but most buildings are huts and cattle sheds.

Plow Lands

Plow lands are usually crowded into the quarter-mile around a village or town. Much more distance than that and the work day is too short for the oxen to be herded out daily from the village. Most fields grow barley which makes the bread and ale of daily life. Oats are a secondary crop, while wheat is a luxury crop.

Fallow Lands

Half the fields are plowed each year. The other half are left fallow, and used to graze livestock.

Wasteland

Between the plowed lands of each village lie lands which are not cultivated, but instead supply wood, occasional wild fruit, and as the place where pigs eat. Hunting is not allowed to the peasants, but unless it is a royal forest the knight can hunt on his lands.

Mill

Several mills work to grind the grain for the daily bread of the peasants. The big-

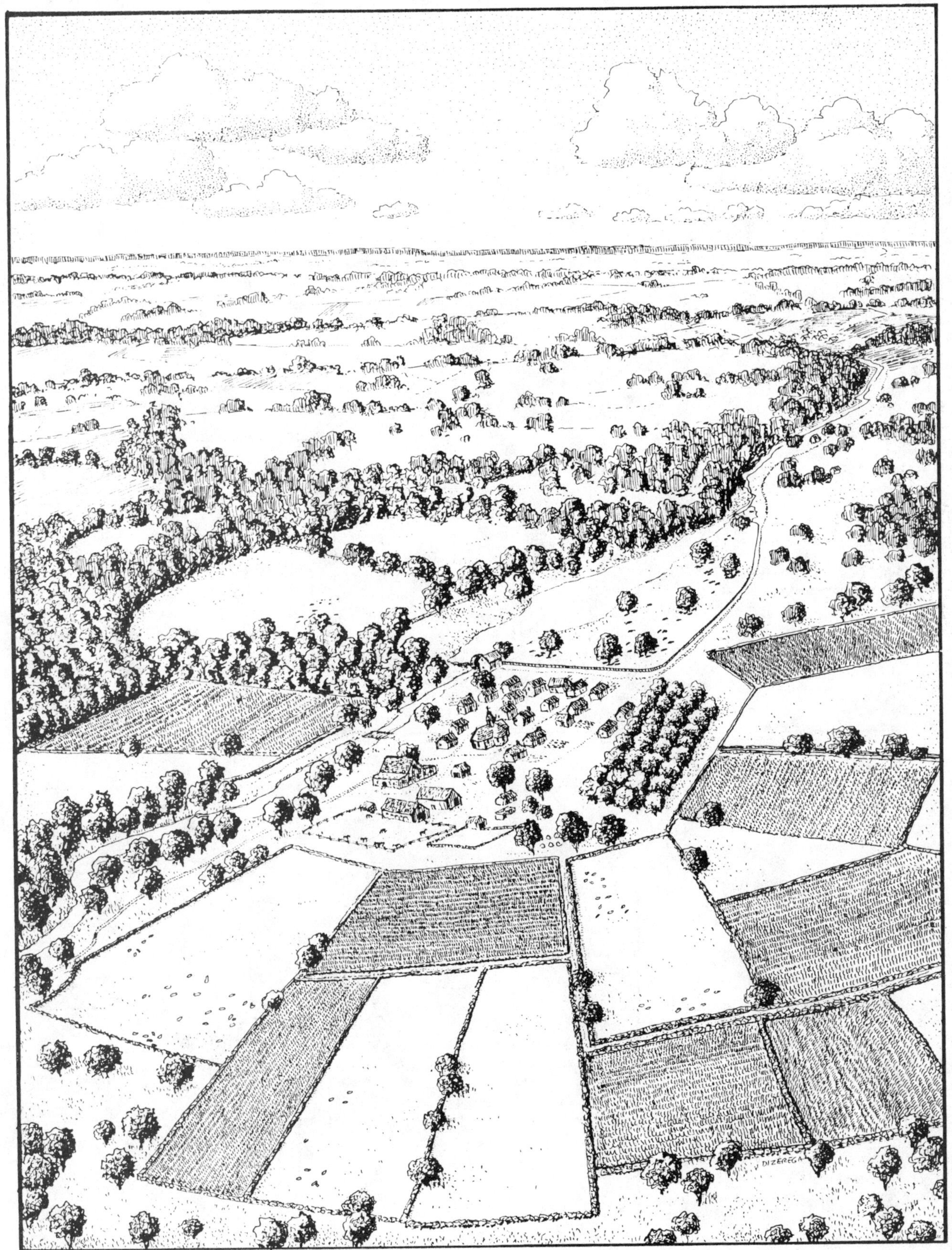

A typical manor

gest one is owned by the manor lord, and all the townsmen must grind their grain there. The lord collects a percentage for this service. He also collects a smaller tax on the other local mills.

Animals

Horses: The knight needs at least five working horses at all times (1 charger, 1 rouncy for himself, and rouncys for his squire, wife, and a servant). Only the first two rouncys normally leave the manor.

Unfortunately, knights do not have the resources to raise chargers and the herd is usually restricted to raising rouncys, sumpters, and cobs, and sometimes a good courser or palfrey (see the "Characters and Creatures" chapter).

The horse herd for the manor has about 10 horses (1 stallion, 4 mares, 2 yearlings, 2 colts, 1 gelding being trained.)

Cattle: Cattle provide meat, leather, and work animals (plow oxen are castrated bulls.) The manor has a herd of around 20 cattle (1 bull, 1 yearling bull, 6 oxen, 5 milk cows, 2 unseasoned oxen, 5 calves).

Sheep: Sheep provide food and wool. A herd of about 20 serves the manor (1 ram, 14 sheep, 6 lambs)

Pigs: Pigs provide the most meat per pound of hoof of any domestic animal. The herd is around 31 animals (1 boar, 6 sows, 24 piglets) and is loosed into the wasteland each year to fatten on wild acorns. They are rounded up in the fall.

Castles

Castles abound in Arthurian legend. Castles are the natural abode of knights. Your character will spend most of his time not adventuring in one castle or another.

Literature occasionally describes the castles, but more often does not. The medieval storytellers simply left out all of the most obvious facts because their listeners or readers would already know about them. Players and gamemasters are not so prepared, so this brief overview is offered.

Castles are the ultimate expression of power in *Pendragon*. They are both homes and tools of war. They offer refuge from danger and serve as a base for cavalry raids and major expeditions. Extraordinarily expensive to build and maintain, castles are essential for controlling areas of the land. They also gain the owner great prestige. Without a castle, your lord would be just another knight.

Pendragon provides four "standard types" of castles as a starting point of knowledge. The illustrations nearby show representative castles for each of the four types. Details like the shape of the walls, the presence of a moat, and the overall position of the castle, as shown in the illustrations, are not the only arrangements possible, but simply examples.

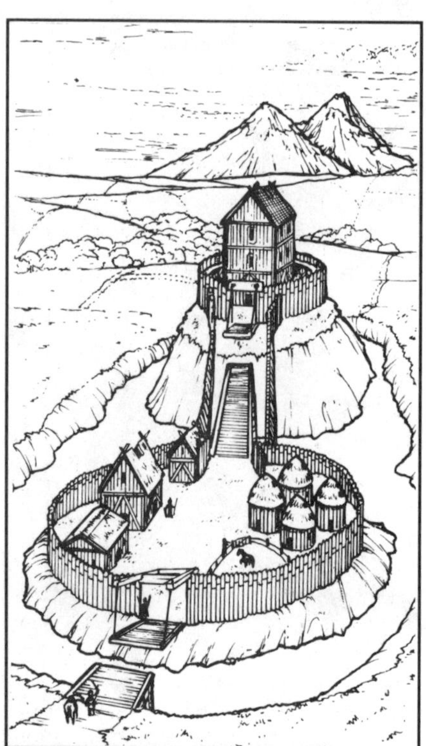

An old-style castle.

A small castle.

A common castle.

A large castle.

Old-Style Castles

The most common castle is a crude wood and earth structure called a "motte and bailey." Such castles are of the old style, known for many decades. Some persons claim that these edifices should be called forts rather than castles.

The motte is the hill, often artificially constructed, atop which sits the lord's stronghold, a great log or (sometimes) stone tower. The bailey is a large courtyard enclosed by log buildings which contain the followers and possessions of the lord: stable, blacksmith, servants' quarters, cattle pens, etc. A log stockade and ditch surrounds the bailey, which can be crossed only by means of a drawbridge.

Small Castles

Since Arthur came to power, castle technology has progressed almost magically. A whole new style of military architecture can be seen nowadays.

Small castles are made of stone. Its heart is a central keep which is the lord's stronghold. It is three floors high, with a basement, and can be entered only through a door on the second story. A courtyard, still called the bailey, surrounds the keep. A tall, thick stone wall surrounds the bailey, and encloses many wooden buildings. The ditch can be crossed only by the drawbridge.

Common Castles

The common castle is like a small castle with towers. At least two square towers stand at the corners of the walls, while a third overlooks the drawbridge, creating a gate tower.

Large Castles

A large castle is like the common castle, but with taller walls, towers at each corner, a large gatehouse, and a larger keep. The inner buildings may be wood, or perhaps even stone.

Fortified Cities

Fortified cities are occasionally seen in Britain. Some have ancient Roman walls, while others are more recent and strengthened by towers.

Travel in Britain

YOUR CHARACTER WILL spend much time travelling. Travel through Arthurian Britain is a risky, time-consuming business. Difficulties of which modern people are unaware create problems for everyone moving from place to place.

Maps

Maps are nearly nonexistent, and those which do exist are nothing similar to the maps of our day. See the color map of Logres for an example. First of all, most people are illiterate and thus unable to read any map. If anything, a map will be a list of stops along the way, probably indicated by a coat of arms of the castle or other stop along the way. Some symbol might indicate whether the stop is a manor, castle, monastery, city, or other landmark.

The usual manner of getting around in strange places is to have a general idea of direction and to ask for more specifics every time someone is met along the way. Since most people met will be locals they will have a pretty good idea of their locality, which in the case of peasants is only the five-mile radius around their homes, or for knights the extent of their native domain. People will have only vague, and often incorrect, information of areas outside their homelands. Directions are not usually given in miles, but rather in vague travel times, like "a long time," or "until noon," or "a little while." Landmarks are better, and may be specific, like "the ford," but can be confusing too: "the big tree," or "where the rocks fall down" or "the ruin." Information about dangerous areas will be particularly sketchy, and will often be plain wrong. Vast areas of forest in Britain are unknown to anyone.

Even moderately settled areas may be lost to the knowledge of nearby folk should a group of enemies cut off the roads and trails to the settlement. A modest quest for a group of young knights might be to travel into an area that has been lost track of, and return with an accurate description of landmarks and so forth.

It is not uncommon to get lost and have to backtrack to the last secure place.

Travel Times

Travelling is not just a matter of going from one unknown place to another. Besides the problems of knowing where to go are the problems of travelling safely and finding accommodations. This increases travel time.

Travel is usually safe within the close demesne of a lord, unless of course the lord lives by robbing travellers weaker than himself, which is regrettably quite common outside Logres. Bands of bandits often hide within forests to waylay the unwary. Thus journeyers must always be on the look out for themselves, perhaps even sending out scouts, slowing them down considerably.

Stopping to eat and rest are common. Persons not used to travel, especially women or children, require more frequent stops.

Turquine

Travel Accommodations

Knights normally stay at any castle, manor, or other settlement along the way. Hospitality is an honored tradition, and standard custom is to help any traveller according to their status. See the chapters entitled "What Your Character Knows" and "Ideals and Passions" for more information on the laws of hospitality.

Most people travel very little, and are likely to be starved for information and gossip about the outside world. Thus strangers who are known not to be enemies are welcome, and if they are entertaining then they are the more welcome. No payment is expected from the visitors.

Of course not everyone is allowed entry. The normal procedure is for a party to ride to the gate and knock, blow a horn, ring a bell, or simply shout until someone comes to listen to them. This person is usually called the *porter,* because his job is to tend the *port,* or door. Being porter is a pretty prestigious job at any location since he determines who enters immediately or later. The porter then asks who is there, and what they want. He may decide to allow entry right away, especially if the visitor is known, but more likely will go to his lord and relay the information before making a decision. The travellers wait patiently outside, perhaps in the rain or the dark.

If it is an enemy who has inadvertently come to the door the porter simply stalls for a while, perhaps exchanging bitter or insulting words with the travellers, while knights and soldiers arm and prepare to rush out and capture the foe.

Once guests enter a castle or manor they are shown to the long hall or bedroom where the lord welcomes them, interviews them, and instructs them to be shown to their accommodations. Occasionally they are shown to a place to wash up before seeing the lord.

Accommodations are normally in the great hall, where the household knights and ladies also sleep, unsegregated. Honored guests may be given a chamber or tower room for themselves, but more likely will share it with the rest of their party. Only a truly great place has enough space to give people separate sleeping accommodations.

A worthy visitor will have pages or women assigned to help him disarm and wash. Washing may be from a public basin or, luxury of luxuries, a hot bath. Women commonly help men bathe, without any sexual implication (but plenty of opportunity).

Monasteries have similar customs. Separate rooms are often available for the different social ranks, thus keeping the nobility away from commoners. High ranking individuals may actually be offered the quarters of the abbott.

Where no noble accommodations exist knights may seek to stay at peasant dwellings. The traveller goes from building to building asking for hospitality until someone tentatively agrees. The commoner complains that he is poor with nothing to spare, and the traveller offers to compensate somehow. They dicker over price until agreement is reached. Nothing is guaranteed except what is agreed upon by both parties. Remember that commoners are usually reluctant to let powerful strangers into their houses, and may recommend someone in town who is less suspicious. Out of these individuals' hospitality grew public inns.

Inns are still a novelty in *Pendragon.* They are frequented mostly by pilgrims and merchants. Cities usually have inns, but they are rare elsewhere. Inns are generally of very poor quality. They are unlikely to have private accommodations, a menu to choose from, or food other than common peasant fare. The building is likely to be a single room with a single fireplace where everyone sleeps.

Finally, if no accommodations can be found, knights do what soldiers do: camp out on the cold, hard ground.

Wealth

Wealth is one of the measures of a knight.

EACH PLAYER MUST choose how much he wants to become involved in economics. It is possible to ignore economics completely. A vassal knight normally receives enough income from his land to easily maintain the standard life style for his station.

Extravagance, however, requires more attention to detail. In this section the basic economic aspects of your character's world are discussed. Part of the enjoyment of *Pendragon* comes from spending money freely and lavishly in the game. Your character starts the game well-off, and may become rich. And there are many things to spend money on in the sumptuous Arthurian world of *Pendragon*.

Understanding Wealth

Coinage and Value

£. = *Librum* (plural, *Libra*). 1 £. = 20s. = 240 d.

s. = shilling (plural, shillings). 1s. = 12 d. = 1/20 £.

d. = *denarius* (plural, *denarii*), also called penny (plural, pence).

Libra, shillings, and pence are the basic units to measure value. Value is important because wealth is measured as standard of living and property, not necessarily cash on hand. Thus household knights do not get money every Christmas. Instead the lord will spend that much to keep him up to standards. Thus the knight gets his clothes patched by the castle ladies for free, gets his food at the common meal, and has his armor repaired by the lord's blacksmith. None of this business is recorded or roleplayed: it is just normal.

Coins in use are the silver penny and the gold Librum. If you wish to get into shillings, sovereigns, crowns, and so on, you certainly may. But for simplicity's sake *Pendragon* values are figured in £. and pence.

Standard of Living

The daily measure of wealth is that which can be seen and partaken of: clothing and daily food. Rich people wear fancier clothes and eat better, more varied foods. Knights, members of the noble class, wear very nice clothing and eat well, whether fed at their lord's board or on their own manor.

A knight's basic standard of living in *Pendragon* is set at 2 £. This means that it takes about 2 £. worth of food and goods to maintain a knight and his squire at ordinary, expected standards. This standard includes meat at every meal, nice clothing worth about 1 £. for the knight, and good ale at every meal.

Horses are the most expensive cost to a knight. To maintain all his horses (at least one healthy charger, oat-fed, and several rouncys and sumpters) costs another 2 £. Replacement of chargers is not included: rouncys and sumpters can be replaced from the herd, but chargers are an extraordinary expense.

A family also needs to be cared for. Family expenses at a knight's level adds another 2 £. This expense covers the costs of housing, clothing, and feeding a wife of good station and children in suitable fashion.

Thus the full annual expense of a vassal knight, maintained at an ordinary level of quality, is 6 £. per year. He receives this amount in income from his manor.

Should a vassal knight have no wife or children the 2 £. are not saved, since the wife's daily work (see the Industry skill listing) and her household management are not available to the knight.

It is useful to compare knights' standards with those of a peasant family of two adults and three children. The common peasant exists in a self-sufficient world where money is unknown, and the family makes, grows, or barters for everything they need. But in money-value, annual expense and income for a peasant family equals 1 £. per year.

The Manor

A vassal knight's manor must generate at least 6 £. to maintain him in his station. A manor is an economic unit and not one of area or population, and so a manor can vary widely from the standards given here. However, the sample manor described in "Your Home" is typical of one found in Salisbury or most other river communities of Logres.

The Market

Every city has a permanent market. This economic nucleus, in fact, defines what a city is: a place where you can buy anything on the *Pendragon* Standard Price List (see below). Towns and manors do not usually have any market beyond a weekly meeting of itinerant peddlers.

Most of the cities in *Pendragon* have about 1,000-2,000 inhabitants. Three are in the 4,000-5,000 range: York, Lincoln, and Norwich.

Two cities are truly large, Camelot and London, and have much larger markets with more exotic items for sale. They are not covered here. On the continent annual fairs temporarily create a market large enough to match the large cities of Britain.

Whatever the size of the city, these rules for buying and selling are always the same.

Buying

Things can be purchased at a market at the Standard Price List costs. A shortage or abundance may reduce values temporarily.

Selling

Knights can sell goods at the market as well. This is done by going to a merchant and negotiating with him for the price.

Selling goods at market nets the buyer half the price shown on the price list. This half-price is a law of marketing,

Sir Galeron Eats a Fine Feast

Sir Galeron of Gallowey has come to court to challenge Sir Gawaine for some lands which were granted to Sir Gawaine, who receives the visitor with great courtesy in an extraordinary pavilion, complete with stove and stable.

Sir Gawaine escorted him out of the hall to a pavilion of linen decorated in purple with tapestries, cushions, and magnificent hangings. Inside was a chapel, a chamber, and a large hall. A charcoal stove had its own chimney to warm the knight. His horse was led to his stall and racks filled to the top with hay.

In the pavilion they set up boards and cloths for dining and ordered the coffers, napkins, and salt-cellars, torches, candlesticks, and standards between. They served the knight, his squire, and lady with the most tasty food in silver services, all carefully prepared. They offered him wines in glasses as well as cups, and meats cooked in a special glaze. In this way Sir Gawaine delighted his guests.

— from *The Adventures at Tarn Wadling*

and one of those damnable things which commoners delight in because it pesters the gentry so much.

Trade

Knights will find it most advantageous to trade goods with their own lord. In such trades the lord usually grants the full price as shown on the Standard Price List. Thus it is always better to try to trade with your lord than to sell treasure at a market.

However, trading armor to lords other than your own is not generally possible. Instead they will send the knight to the blacksmith, who will grant a value in trade of only half the listed value. (These commoners must have a conspiracy or something!)

Equipment

Standard Outfits

These outfits list military equipment, knight's dress clothing, and horses. They are given for two reasons: first, to help gamemasters outfit a non-standard gamemaster or player character when he is generated; second, to help players evaluate relative wealth and poverty. It is assumed that these characters are the sons of a knight, or have been equipped appropriately by their lord.

Squires are not included in these outfits. Poor knights may not have a squire, while Superlative knights may have several very well-equipped squires.

Various essential minor equipment is assumed to be present in this list, but is not stated, including saddles, tack, spurs, weapon belts, and so forth. These items will be of better quality for wealthy knights.

Outfit 1: Poor Knight
Norman (10-point) chainmail armor.
Spear, shield, sword, dagger.
Clothing worth 1/2 £.
2 rouncys.

Outfit 2: Ordinary Knight
Reinforced chainmail (12-point) armor.
2 spears, shield, sword, dagger, 5 jousting lances.
Clothing worth 1 £.
Charger, rouncy, sumpter.

Outfit 3: Rich or Superlative Knight
Partial plate (14-point) armor.
2 spears, shield of peace, shield of war, 2 swords, any one other weapon, dagger, 8 jousting lances.
Clothing worth 2 £.
Destrier, charger, courser, sumpter.

The following outfits have yet to be discovered, but may be found in your campaign soon (remember that the starting year is 531).

Outfit 4: Superlative Knight, during the Period of Apogee (540-555: see the chronology in the chapter entitled "Welcome to Pendragon")

Full plate (16-point) armor

4 spears, shield of peace, shield of war, 2 swords, any other weapon, dagger, 10 jousting lances

Clothing worth 4 £.

Destrier, charger, courser, palfrey, 2 rouncys, 2 sumpters.

Outfit 5: Superlative Knight during the Period of Decline (555 and later)

Gothic plate (18-point) armor.

6 spears, shield of peace, shield of war, sword, two other weapons including a two-handed weapon, dagger, 15 jousting lances.

Clothing worth 6 £.

2 destriers, courser, palfrey, 2 rouncys, 3 sumpters.

Gear

Personal Gear

Everyone has personal gear to start. This includes: under clothes (which double as night clothes), hair brush, towel, blankets, and maybe a razor. It is a small bundle, generally able to be carried on a riding horse.

Travel Gear

Tent, blankets, stakes, cooking and eating utensils, cold weather and rain cloaks, curry brushes, horse blankets, and similar material is a knight's travel gear. It is about a quarter horse-load.

War Gear

Extended military campaigning requires war gear. This includes more warm socks, rope, paint to fix shields, whetstones, spare parts of armor, a mail-polishing keg, spare weapons, a couple bottles of wine, and so on. With the travel gear, it is about a horse-load per knight. Knights must normally have a sumpter to carry this on campaign.

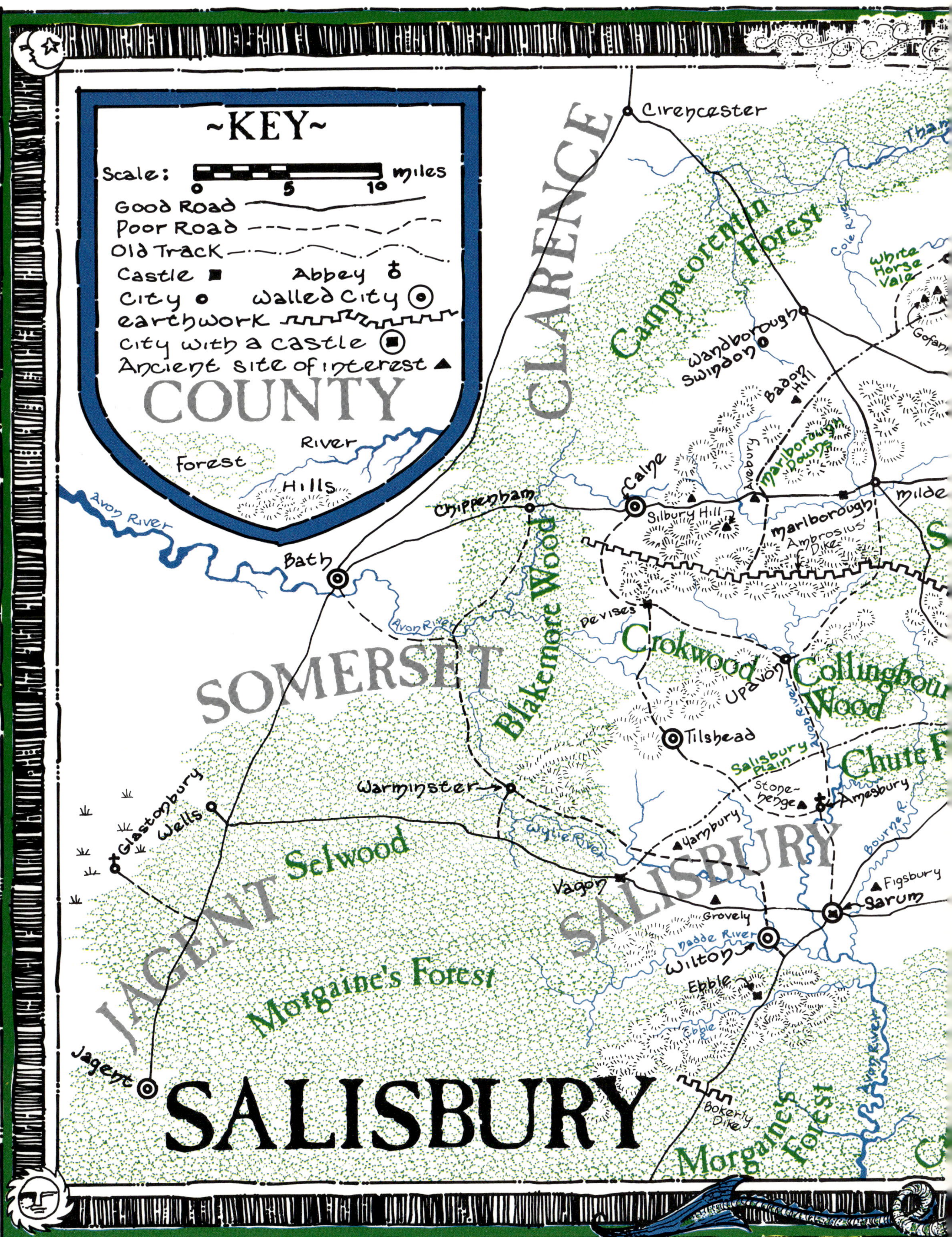
~KEY~
Scale:
0
5
10
miles
Good Road
Poor Road
Old Track
Castle
Abbey
City
Walled City
earthwork
City with a castle
Ancient site of interest
COUNTY
River
Forest
Hills
Cirencester
CLARENCE
Campacorentin Forest
White Horse Vale
Cole River
Wandborough
Swindon
Badon Hill
Marlborough Downs
Avebury
Calne
Chippenham
Avon River
Bath
Silbury Hill
Marlborough
Ambrosius' Dike
Devises
Crokwood
Upavon
Blakemore Wood
SOMERSET
Avon River
Tilshead
Salisbury Plain
Stonehenge
Amesbury
Warminster
Wylie River
Yarnbury
Glastonbury
Wells
Selwood
JAGENT
SALISBURY
Vagon
Grovely
Figsbury
Sarum
Bourne R.
Wilton
Ebble
Morgaine's Forest
Avon River
Bokerly Dike
Jagent
SALISBURY

es River
Ock River
Thames River
Uffington
White Horse
Ridgeway
Uffington Castle
Lambourne Downs
on's Smithy
Lambourne
Ang River
Kennet River
SILCHESTER
Donnington
Kennet R.
nhall
avernake Forest
Enbourne River
To London
Silchester
Levcomagus
ne
orest
Harewood
WESSEX
Camelot
Du Plain
Test River
Itchen R.
Hantonne
nelot Forest
Camelot Forest

Prerogatives of Wealth

The Lord's Progress

Most lords have a main residence, but also travel about their lands in an official "progress." It is usually easier for them to go where the food is rather than move the food. Thus the lord goes from place to place within his own demesne, stopping in to visit vassals, moving with his family and household. This process has the further advantages of checking to see how the site is doing economically and politically, testing the loyalties of the vassals and servants, and conducting whatever business is beyond the capability or responsibility of the resident overseer. If a vassal is reluctant or untrustworthy a lord may choose to stay a long time, eating up the wealth and thus restricting future activity.

Heralds

Announcements are often made at court. While a banneret has his serjeant-at-arms bawl out proclamations, higher-ranking nobles employ heralds for that duty.

Heralds announce visitors by name and distinctive titles. They proclaim cases discussed, the judgments rendered, and also record pertinent facts. Gamemasters should beware of boring the players with too much idle verbiage.

Heralds read proclamations from scrolls. Writing records the attendance of every nobleman and knight at a feast or tournament. Scrolls are made of parchment (scraped lambskin) and, in royal circles, are calligraphed, illuminated, and decorated with gold or silver leaf and pasted-on jewels.

Fanfares blown on long trumpets announce the entrance and exit of important persons. The definition of important is left up to the nobleman. (Here is an opportunity to offend or insult someone, intentionally or not.) Fanfares are also used to announce major decrees and to punctuate ceremonial functions such as sworn homages, naming of officers, champions, and others.

Retinues

The traveling entourage of a fully-accoutered knight is quite something to behold. Every ordinary knight has his warhorse for combat. But no one would ride such a magnificent steed for ordinary travel. The creature would be too tired when the fight comes up.

Due to the complex military saddle born by the warhorse, it is most comfortable to ride a simple riding horse, a rouncy or palfrey. Nor, in most cases, does a knight ride around the countryside all armored, due to the discomfort caused by weight and heat.

A warhorse cannot be used as a packhorse and vice versa: the equipment and saddles are so different that either steed would soon have serious saddle sores if used for the other purpose.

An ordinary knight's full field entourage would, then, normally include a total of 3 people and 6 steeds:

1 knight, 1 squire, 1 page.
2 riding horses, for knight and squire.
1 warhorse.
2 sumpters, one for armor and one for tents and food.
1 pony for the page.

Add the knight's wife and the entourage grows greatly. She has two maidservants and her own page, all of whom would ride. At least another packhorse is needed for their supplies, plus a groom for the horses (the squire performs this duty for the knight). Thus her party would total at least 5 people and 6 horses.

Thus an ordinary knight, traveling with his wife, would have a party of 8 people and 12 horses and ponies.

There may also be sergeants, footsoldiers, messengers, children and their nurse, cooks, heralds, and musicians with assistants of their own.

For further illustration, let us assemble the retinue of a banneret knight who travels to a tournament with his whole entourage:

1 banneret knight, with his 2 squires and 2 pages. 9 steeds required (2 warhorses, 4 riding horses (1 spare), 2 ponies, 1 sumpter).

3 ordinary knights, with 3 squires among them. 12 steeds required (3 chargers, 6 riding horses, 3 sumpters).

4 servants: herald, messenger, cook, assistant cook. 6 steeds required (4 riding horses, 2 packhorses).

1 wife, with 3 maidservants and 4 pages. 9 steeds required (5 palfreys (1 spare), 4 ponies).

4 wife's servants: 2 butlers, 2 grooms. 6 steeds required (4 riding horses, 2 packhorses).

2 children, with 1 nurse. 3 steeds required (1 palfrey, 2 ponies).

Total: 30 people and 45 horses and ponies.

Note that there are 4 knights here, plus 26 more people. Thus the entourages that arrive at a tournament for 100 knights add a total of about 750 people, including the knights themselves, to the local population (if every 4 knights = 30 total people). This might create an encampment equal to the entire population of the sponsoring castle and nearby town. Imagine the multitude at a tournament five times the size!

Spending Money

Prices

All prices given here are the minimum charged. When a statement is "per knight" it also includes his squire.

Some goods, which might be known or rumored, are not available for any price. Especially notable is the absence of destriers and horse barding, which, though attainable as gifts, are not yet for sale to any but the greatest lords and kings.

These are prices to be found in any city in Britain.

Prices are non-negotiable. (It is beneath a knight to bicker with a merchant, anyway.)

Major Investments

Knights may have opportunity to make major investments. Most of the time this isn't necessary – it is sufficient to just say "I'm spending 10£. on my manor," for instance. But sometimes the details are important, so this price list offers prices for some really large items, if desired.

All prices are +/- 25% at any time, according to the gamemaster's whim.

Getting Money

Noblemen are notoriously short of money. being important is expensive! a noblemen's virtue is reflected by his largesse (generosity), and if he wants to be famous within his social circle then he will have to reward favorable behavior with an open hand. King Arthur leads everyone in the largesse which he bestows.

Historically, noblemen had many methods of deriving income from their holdings and vassals. The most important are the agricultural and material goods which a knight or lord regularly collects to maintain himself, his family, and his household. Every feudal lord had other methods as well; most are so unique that we ignore them.

Land

Land is the basis for measuring the economic success of a knight. Land provides the basics of life, the people to provide the basics, and the raw materials which are turned into profit.

The manor is the basic source of economic measure for knights. Other sources may be granted or gifted to individuals at the gamemaster's whim.

The more land a character gains, the stronger will be his economic position.

Ransom

Ransoming captives from battle is the single most lucrative (and dangerous) way to get money. Everyone captured alive in battle is worth money to his captor. Prisoners are, by the rules of war, owned by their captors. By further rules of war, it is gentlemanly to return the captive alive, for a ransom. It is very generous, although foolhardy, to release enemy captives for free.

✳ Standard Price List ✳

THE GAMEMASTER MUST adjust these prices as needed, based on common sense. For example, if a lady wished to buy fur trimmings, but required the fur of a pure white bear, the price might be triple the given amount. Or such a rare fur might simply be unavailable.

Inn Prices

Price includes staying in the common room, with a fire in cold weather, and a meal of common food.

per knight per night .... 1 d.
per horse, hay feed .... 3 d.

Inn Luxuries

private room, with door .... 12 d.
Knight-quality dinner .... 4 d.
Wine, 1 serving, British .... 10 d.
Oats for horse .... 8 d.

The Food Market

Supplies

By the horseload.

Knight's fare, good for 1 week .... 7 d.
Commoner's fare, good for 2 weeks ...... 4 d.
Hard rations, good for 4 weeks .... 2 d.

Food Stalls

One knight's meal .... 1 d.
Four commoners' meals .... 1/2d.
Small bottle of wine .... 3 d.

Ordering a Feast

Includes all edibles and drinkables, delivery, cooking, clean up, and service. Prices are per person.

Ordinary feast .... 1 d.
Quality Feast .... 2 d.
Superb feast .... 4 d.
Grand feast .... 8 d.
Regal feast .... 16 d.
per 4 commoners, common fare .... 1 d.

The Horse Market

All steeds are trained for their station. None are trained to fight. All are various shades of brown.

Charger .... 10 £.
Palfrey .... 5 £.
Courser .... 5 £.
Rouncy .... 1 £.
Sumpter .... 100 d.
Cart horse .... 80 d.
Nag .... 50 d.
Mule .... 100 d.
Donkey .... 60 d.
Special color or appearance
(black, white) .... above prices x2

Tack and Decoration

Basic tack .... 16 d.
Fancy .... 24 d.
Special tack (engraved, etc.) .... 100 d.
Caparison (1 pt. armor) .... 24 d.
Caparison, fancy (1 pt. armor) .... 80 d.
Trapper (5 pts. armor) .... 12 d.

The Stock Yards

Common Beasts

Sheep, goat .... 10 d.
Fat sheep .... 15 d.
Ewe and lamb .... 25 d.
Ram .... 60 d.
Sow .... 60 d.
Yearling ox, cow .... 60 d.
Milk cow .... 120 d.
Ox .... 180 d.

Noble Beasts

Young Hawk .... 15 d.
Trained Hawk .... 80 d.
Common Dog .... 5 d.
Unusual Dog .... 25 d.

The Beer Merchant

Per keg, good for 4 meals.

Ale .... 1 d.
Beer .... 1 d.
Mead .... 4 d.

The Wine Merchants

Per bottle, suitable for two people at a meal.

Good Local Wine .... 1 d.
Better Local Wine .... 2 d.
German Wine .... 25 d.
Occitan Wine .... 25 d.

Musician's Market

Harp .... 1-5 £.
Lute .... 60 d.

Services

Compose a mocking poem .... 60 d.
Compose a love poem .... 40 d.
Compose a heroic lay .... 70 d.
Sing a poem at a specified
time and place .... 5 d.
Entertain for a night .... 20 d.

Wagon Market

Wagon (4-wheel) .... 10 d.
Cart (2-wheel) .... 7 d.

Tent Makers

Camp Tent .... 2 d.

Ransoms may also be gained during tournaments, and from combat in general, if appropriate. The primary restriction is that the combat must be serious, not "for love."

The minimum values of ransoms are established by custom and law and are not usually open to bargaining or debate, except in the case of very important or famous people.

The ransoms given here are based on three years' average income, the minimum acceptable amount. Proud knights will naturally pay more for their release, but modest ones will be satisfied to offer the ransoms below to their captors.

Ransoms

ransom	rank
6 £.	squire
12 £.	knight, bachelor
18 £.	knight, vassal
150£.	knight, banneret
550£.	baron
1100£.	count or praetor
1600£.	duke or pennath
2150£.	king, independent

The ransom value is equal to the blood price. When someone is murdered, his kinsmen pursue the murderer to death, according to all known customs. One acceptable alternative exists, and that is for the murderer to pay to the kinsmen a blood-price (or *weregeld* to Saxons). If this is accepted the feud is over, passions are supposedly ended, and tranquility reigns again.

There is no compunction to accept weregeld if the kin do not wish to. The Orkney clan, for instance, never accepted blood price for the death of King Lot, but hunted down and murdered their enemies instead.

Ransoming Vassals

As explained elsewhere, vassals have the obligation to ransom their lord. But what about knights with no vassals, particu-

Pavilion . . . . .1 £.
Nice Pavilion . . . . 2-3 £.
Fancy Pavilion . . . . 4-6 £.

The Armorer

Note that heavy crossbows, destriers, plate armor, and chainmail barding are not for sale here.

Armor, full suit

Padding (felt or cloth, 2 pts.) . . . . .7 d.
Leather (4 pts.) . . . . .15 d.
Cuirbouilli (6 pts.) . . . . .60 d.
Norman Chain, inc. pot helm (10 pts.) . . . .2 £.
Reinforced Chain, inc. great helm (12 pts.) 6 £.

Weapons

Axe . . . . .25 d.
Dagger . . . . .5 d.
Flail . . . . .50 d.
Great Axe . . . . .50 d.
Great Spear . . . . .2 d.
Great Sword . . . . .100 d.
Javelin . . . . .1 d.
Halberd . . . . .60 d.
Hammer . . . . .30 d.
Lance (jousting) .3 d.
Mace . . . . .30 d.
Morning Star . . . . .75 d.
Spear . . . . .1 d.
Sword . . . . .75 d.
Warflail . . . . .75 d.

Hunting Weapons

Spear, boar . . . . .2 d.
Bow . . . . .10 d.
5 arrows . . . . .1 d.
Crossbow, light . . . . .140 d.
6 light bolts . . . . .1 d.
Crossbow, medium . . . . .200 d.
4 medium bolts . . . . .1 d.

Shields

Common . . . . .3 d.
Knightly (painted) . . . . .5 d.

Horse Barding

Light (8 points) . . . . .2 £.

The Tailors

Clothing

Current fashion, knightly materials . . . . . . .1 £.
Current fashion, noble materials . . . . .4 £.
Old fashion, knightly materials . . . . . . .120 d.
Old fashion, noble materials . . . . .2 £.

The Weavers

Tapestries

Each is about the size to cover the short end of a manoral hall. Six would line a whole hall.

Inexpensive, plain . . . . .120 d.
Nice, sturdy, quality . . . . .1 £.
Simple designs . . . . .2 £.
Excellent quality, beautiful designs . . . . . .4 £.
Embroidered scenes . . . . .6 £.

Clothier

Everything is measured in a bolt large enough to make one knight's or lady's set of clothing.

Knightly materials . . . . .35 d.
Noble quality materials . . . . .80 d.

Trim

Measured in enough for a single set of clothes

Lace . . . . .12 d.
Ribbons . . . . .8 d.
Unusual furs . . . . .18 d.

The Gold and Silver Smiths

Simple seal ring . . . . .60 d.
Silver finger ring . . . . .40 d.
Gold finger ring . . . . .1 £.
Silver brooch . . . . .1 £.
Gold brooch . . . . .5 £.
Common earrings . . . . .10 d.
Silver earrings . . . . .25 d.
Gold earrings . . . . .160 d.
Diamond (needs setting) . . . . .1 £.
Unusual diamond (needs setting) . . . . . . 2-5 £.
Any of above, but
extremely fancy . . . . price x2
Gold dish . . . . .7 £.
Silver dish . . . . .1 £.
Golden goblet . . . . .12 £.

Miscellaneous Mixed Goods

Travel Gear

per knight, ...60 d.

War Gear

Includes Travel Gear.

per knight, ...2 £.

At the Abbey

Read a letter . . . . .1 d.
Write a letter . . . . .3 d.
Copy a book . . . . 5 d./page
Buy a book . . . . impossible
Copy and illuminate a book . . . . . 25 d./page
Have a Mass said .5 d.
Deliver a letter: per day's estimated travel .5 d.

larly poor, errant knights without a lord and household knights?

Poor knights, alas, have no hope. They might be captured while questing, while serving as a mercenary, or perhaps while engaged in a bit of knightly procurement. They can beg for help from their family, but most families of poor knights are too poor to afford ransom. A friend may lend aid, or the poor knight can pledge himself to some task for his captor. But in general his fate is glum.

Household knights can expect to be ransomed by their lord. They are not strangers to their lord but rather his everyday companions. They are the chosen few who reside close to the lord, and who have presumably exhibited valor and loyalty to prove their worth. The feudal bond guarantees that a lord will provide for the safety and well-being of his vassals. A landed vassal has his well-being guaranteed by his property. The household knights get theirs from their lord.

The lord must roll his Loyalty (vassals) passion. Success means that the lord is motivated by his vow and will do everything to try and fulfill it. A failed roll indicates that he will not probably not do so.

Failure to fulfill this basic obligation of ransom means that the lord automatically loses 1 point of Loyalty (vassals) per knight abandoned, plus he loses 1 point of Honor per knight. Furthermore, the captured knight is released from his oath of vassalage (if he survives and returns home).

A nobleman may volunteer to ransom even his landed vassals if he wants. Opportunities to exhibit his largesse are limitless. Such behavior is extraordinary and warrants an experience check for his Generous trait.

Whenever any vassal, landed or not, is ransomed by his lord the knight receives an experience check for Loyalty (lord) to reflect his gratitude.

Four Universal Aids

Four universal customs of European feudalism reward lords with special income. These four taxes give the lord the right to collect income from his holding whether the vassals like it or not. These are called aids.

Each of these four methods may be imposed once by a lord, with exceptions carefully noted below. When imposed, the holding pays an amount equal its average (normal) yearly income.

1. Knighting of the Eldest Son

Creating a new knight is expensive — 8 £. minimum. This money is raised to outfit a man with the equipment listed for an ordinary knight.

The tax may not be enough to outfit the candidate. A father has choices to make here: he can squeeze his people (and incur their hate), he can pay from his own treasury, or he can just outfit his son as a poor knight. If outfitted improperly the young man might not be accepted for the office and not receive the honors of knighthood.

On the other hand the collection may make much more than the 8 £. necessary. The money can be kept, though the father gets a Selfish check for it. Usually it is all squandered in a lavish feast, perhaps even a tournament, to mark the event.

✳ Major Investments List ✳

Public Works & Buildings

commoner's dwelling	3 d.
ox shed	2 d.
barn	12 d.
manor hall	2 £.
small stone tower	10 £.
small chapel	8 £.
fine church	50 £.
stone bridge	5 £.
a village worth 1 £. of income per year	25 £.

Castles

motte and bailey (DV=5/3)	25 £.
reinforced motte and bailey (DV=1/10/5)	65 £.
small (DV=16/10)	82 £.
medium (DV=26/10)	102 £.
large (DV=32/19)	147 £.

Mercenaries

per month

50 footsoldiers	10 £.
10 sergeants	10 £.
10 knights	20 £.
100 laborers	1 £.
engine crew (4 men)	1 £.
Chief Engineer	1 £.

Land

Cost to purchase a fief from a liege.

a manor	50 £.
a village	10 £.

Siege Equipment

"DV" is a term indicating a castle's Defense Value, to be used in future Pendragon supplements. Tortoises, penthouses, cats, rats, and sows all are siege engines. Each 1 £. of siege equipment reduces a castle's DV by one. 1 £. of siege equipment equals the following:

5,000 arrows
250 ladders
100 pavis, mantlets
4 espringle (ballistae)
2 medium mangonel (catapults)
1 large trebuchet
1 siege tower
3 tortoises (penthouse, cat, rat, sow), including the ram, pick, or bore

Water Craft

rowboat, coracle	5 d.
fishing boat	20 d.
small trade ship	5£.
large trade ship	15 £.
war ship	20 £.
pleasure barge	10 £.+
horse transport	15 £.

Manoral Improvements

To the Hall

tile floor	1 £.
fire place and chimney	1 £.
fish pond	120 d.
flower garden	75 d.
small orchard	1 £.
glass windows	80 d. ea.
good tapestries	1 £.
suite of bedroom furniture	1 £.
suite of solar furniture	150 d.
suite of chapel furniture	2 £.

Around the hall and its village

stockade	6 £.
ditch and rampart	1 £.

All Glory gained for the expenditure of money at a knighting goes to the new knight as well as the father. Thus if a nobleman spends more than 8 L. on his son then his son gets a bit of additional Glory.

Sometimes a ranking nobleman will knight many other knights along with his son. This is a rare opportunity for qualified, but impoverished, individuals to become household knights at the nobleman's expense. Each of the extra new knights gets his 1000 Glory, as usual, and all extra Glory for expenses over 8 £. is accrued by both the knights and their new lord, at the usual rate of 1 Librum for 1 point of Glory (for sums under 100 £. total).

2. Wedding of the Eldest Daughter

The family of the bride usually pays for the wedding. A nobleman whose daughter is wed receives Glory for the money spent on the event. To cover the expense the tax is collected. Part of it may be spent on the festivities, and part may be included in the dowry which every wife is expected to provide.

3. To Ransom the Lord

The ransom of the lord is the duty of the vassals. This tax provides the money needed. In all cases the noble vassals will receive at least their usual year's income from the tax, although sometimes they must squeeze their peasants to raise so much. The rest of the necessary sum is collected from the citizens of the towns of the holding, unless the vassals volunteer to pay more, earning Loyalty (lord) and Generous checks if the amount is great.

If a lord is ever captured a second time the vassals are not obliged to pay his ransom again. Taking money from them to pay another ransom is done as an Impost or as Voluntary Tallage (see below).

4. To Support a Crusade

Fighting the infidel in the Holy Land is a venture financed by all the vassals so that they can share in the Glory and expense. Crusading in *Pendragon* will be explored in future supplements.

Fighting a nearby kingdom of infidels does not qualify as a crusade and this tax should not be used in campaigns restricted to the European area.

Tallage

A fifth method of taxation, called *tallage*, is invoked whenever a lord tries to raise extra money. The purpose might be anything: to raise an army to invade an enemy, to defend the realm, to build ships, to finance a tournament, to build a town, or to outfit an expedition. The lord calls together his court (knights and lords who hold land rights) and the leading citizens of his towns (commoners who control the mercantile wealth). Before them, either as one group or separately, the lord pleads his case. The vassals and citizenry discuss the situation, and return their verdicts to the lord.

Results of the request can vary widely. The court might agree to make the payments, and if inspired (perhaps by the threat of an oncoming army) might even volunteer more money or additional labor. They might pay part of the request because they like their lord. They might pay half, but only if the lord makes some sort of concessions in return. They might not pay anything because they don't like him, or because they too are broke, or because they disagree with the intent. Many factors affect their decision.

Impost

An impost is something which is imposed upon the commoners. It can be used to describe a legitimate fine, perhaps imposed for violating the lord's law, or arbitrary, as was all too common historically.

Imposts are simply declared, and then collected from the commoners with whatever force necessary. The payment is usually collected (remember that each peasant family has a yearly income in goods of about 1 £. equivalent), and the only cost is the undying hatred of the people who supply your daily bread.

Other Sources of Wealth

Service at Court

Noblemen holding royal offices get income for holding down an extra job or two. Key offices are lucrative. They include the offices of Seneschal, the person in charge of feeding the court, and Marshal, the commander of field forces, also responsible for the protection of the household. Other minor offices include the tasks of collecting taxes on roads and bridges, collecting import tariffs at borders, keeping forests, etc.

Good Stewardship

Noblemen ought to maintain effective stewards of their properties to encourage efficiency and profit. Wives are traditionally good at this, or the younger brother of someone important may suffice.

The value of good stewardship is illustrated in the amusing tale told of William, Lord of Hemricourt, a knight who loved to tourney but who lost and lost again, almost paupering himself each year with ransoms and remounts. Yet he never went broke. One day while returning from another disaster, Sir William watched his sheep being driven away to pay his ransom. Another flock remained behind in his fields. He asked his friend whose sheep remained grazing on the other side of the hill. "Why, your wife's, Sir," said the friend. Thus William learned that his wife's stewardship had kept him solvent for years. Both chagrined and delighted, the good knight William went happily home to show his appreciation to his wife.

Tournaments

Some *Pendragon* tournaments can be expensive for losers, who forfeit horses, equipment, and perhaps even ransoms. Some noblemen make a profession of arms, conquering many opponents at tournaments just for the money.

War and Raid

War sometimes yields great profit. Successful raiding of lands can net many herds of cattle and sheep for food. Taking cities by storm yields rich plunder, and surrendering towns pay a fee for their liberation. Castles are a lord's treasure house and usually hold many riches. Ransoming his prisoners can make a knight rich.

Conquer and Seize Land

The feudal theory of protection is fine, but sometimes fails. Arthurian stories are full of widows and weaklings beset by an oppressor intent upon enriching himself at their expense. A land which is seized can be kept by the conqueror.

Marry Well

War leaves many widows.

Chivalric Duties

A knight has many duties, and the rewards to be derived are manifold.

THE EVERYDAY ACTIVITIES of knights include visits to court, participation in battle, hunting, tournaments, and more. This chapter, written for both players and gamemaster, tells what your character will expect during these activities.

Although recurrent and routine, these events are not insignificant or dull; on the contrary, they are the primary focus of your character's life. The gamemaster can use these activities as recurrent components of a campaign, or with some additions, as the basis of an adventure

For example, one could begin with a visit to a distant neighbor's court, with everything exactly as described below, except for one thing — the accommodations. Perhaps everyone sleeping in the great hall for the first time would have to follow a strange custom that involves their sleeping under a naked spear suspended from the ceiling by a single thread. A Valorous roll would be needed to obey the custom.

Courtesy

COURTESY IS COURT BUSINESS, and knowledge of what to do at court. Given here are the important things which every knight knows about courtesy. When you make your character's Courtesy roll, you are testing to see if he remembers this material.

Court

"Court" refers to three things: a ceremony, the members of a ruling body, and the location they meet.

Ceremony

Holding court is an activity during which nobles perform their public duties, including legal and property judgments, rulings on criminal charges, public announcements, receiving fealty from vassals, and knightings.

Membership

It is the duty of all vassals to offer advice in their lord's court, so they are often there. They must come whenever summoned, and are welcome to come whenever they want or need to. Appointed household officers are always at court. The important persons of a court are called courtiers.

Location

The location where court is held may be an outside courtyard. Often that is the only place large enough to hold the assembly.

Court may also be held inside the bailey of the castle. Some ancient customs insist that the meeting occur outside on a hill, near an ancient landmark, or by some sacred grove.

In large places the court might be held inside a building, in which case the building is called a courtroom.

In any setting the presiding lord will have a high seat or throne set up from which he listens to petitioners and decrees his judgments.

Court Protocol

One of the most frequently occurring event in *Pendragon* is to visit the court of a lord, either your own or a stranger's. Certain rules are followed in such circumstance. The rules are the same at any court, whether the barbaric halls of the Out Isles or the refined court of a Logres nobleman.

Upon arrival at any court a knight or other nobleman is obliged to go to the lord and present himself. He will then be treated according to his station.

To be at court unannounced (or to depart without permission) are both grave insults to the host lord. When the lord discovers either to be true he will undoubtedly get a Suspicious (person) directed trait (see the "Ideals and Passions" chapter).

In general, a knight visiting a strange court goes to the lord, then expects to:

1. Be interviewed
2. Be feasted
3. Receive appropriate accommodations
4. Depart when finished

The Interview

Visitors should always go before their host and announce themselves, their business and so on to their host. Only in this way will everyone know and recognize the visitor and their correct station at court. Also, the lord determines just what kind of person has come into his home.

The Feast

Everyone eats together at night. The great hall is converted to a great dining room. Noble guests are always invited to stay and are given a place to eat which is appropriate to their station. If they are of great Glory they will sit at the high table, while lowly errant chivalry will be relegated to eat among the other poor knights.

Accommodations

Accommodations are simple. Visiting knights are usually invited to spend the night in the main hall, with the household knights of the lord. They may alternately sleep in the stables, occasionally on the ramparts, or in the outer court. Most of the rest of the castle is, of course, occupied.

Ranking noblemen are given more private accommodations. Groups of knights might be given a tower room.

Departure

Protocol demands that departure be approved by the lord. Under normal conditions this is granted without problems. However it can also be used to political purposes. For instance, in history Duke William the Bastard detained Eorl Harold until the latter swore an oath of homage. To depart without consent was a grave social offense worthy of all defense: King Uther went to war against Duke Gorlois on the excuse that the duke and his wife departed from his court without consent.

Typical Home Court Session

Any court requires the presence of witnesses and advisors for the lord. These are his vassals. The advisors might be knights, probably include the lord's wife, might include other lords, priests or druids, or whatever other advisors the lord finds useful or necessary.

When entering court, noblemen enter in reverse order of precedence, meaning that the least important enter first and the more important later. Visitors, plaintiffs, and others with court duties wait outside at the door until summoned.

Court is opened with a solemn announcement, the lord sits, and everyone else begins business. The lord and advisors are at one end, guards and courtiers along the walls, and others in the rear or outside. The center of the room is open for speakers.

During the session several pages and squires, and occasionally knights, clear a path for entry of their lord. Guards take positions to protect the throne. As a fanfare is blown heralds announce, "All rise for (name and title)," as the lord enters and takes his seat.

Matters of the court are addressed in order of precedence. The matters dealing with the highest ranking petitioner are acted upon first, with the lowly waiting patiently for their turn later.

The lord acknowledges gifts, receives envoys, and greets important visitors. Petitions are presented, boons are sought, feuds are adjusted, and criminal actions are judged.

After business ends the lord rises, fanfare is blown, and the lord departs with his officers and men-at-arms

The Hunt

HUNTING GREAT BEASTS is the sport of nobles. Hunting is done from horseback, with packs of hounds to lead the pursuit and a train of commoners to assist and to pack the meat back. Hunting is not entertainment. The food gathered is necessary for survival. The lions and bears are killed are for the public good as well as for the glory of chivalry.

Commoners are allowed to hunt only from foot, and usually with snares and deadfalls, or with bows, to take squirrel, hare, birds, and such beasts, or those like badgers which are a danger to chicken coops, but not to humans.

Deer are usually reserved for the noblemen to hunt. In some places the king has set aside forests for himself alone, and to take them without permission is an offense of High Treason, punishable by death.

Monsters may be discovered. It is always the duty of knights to destroy monsters.

Hunting is not war. Any kind of finery may be worn. Practical men wear good leather hunting clothes, similar to light (1 point) armor. Boar spears and swords are the main weapons taken. It is not dishonorable for a knight to use a bow when hunting deer.

The process of the hunt begins slowly, and is suitable for ladies. At dawn the hounds and dog boys go out. Knights

Faerie horses

The Boar is Found

They beat the bushes boldly then to start him,
And he in sudden fury seeks escape,
Lunging at the line of men in vain.
The boar whose brunt they bore there was a beauty,
A longer than had long since left the herd,
Grown, aggressive, greatest of all swine,
And when he grunted, grim; and then men groaned,
For three he thrust to earth at his first thrust
But did not further damage as he charged.
The hunters halloo Hi! and cry Hey! Hey!
Clap their horns to their lips to sound recall.
Many are the mouths of hounds and men
That crowd the boar with cry and roar until the copse resounds
He turns and stands at bay,
Savaging the hounds,
And piteously they
Run howling at their wounds.

— Gawaine and the Green Knight

and ladies have a light breakfast, a stirrup cup for luck, and at the sound of the horn set off to pre-selected sites. These are centrally located and, hopefully, suitable for a picnic. From there the knights can hear distant horns and the cries of hounds which signal beasts to pursue. The women can't usually follow the rapid coursing of the chase after this stage and remain behind, ready to succor whatever knight returns.

The hunter follow the cries of hounds until they see the animal, then blast their horns to signal the others that the creature is in sight. Manners insist that the highest-ranking guest be allowed to slay the beast, though he can graciously decline in favor of others if desired. Skinning and cleaning the animal, then cutting it into parts (called "breaking") is a task every knight knows.

It is not unusual to get lost during the chase. Most of the time hunting is done in familiar territory with lots of noise all around. This makes finding the way back relatively simple, probably to join the picnickers at the field until another sighted quarry calls the knight away. The skinned and dressed animals will be collected here, and at the end of the day the party gathers up everything and returns to the castle.

Boar Spears

The distressing habit which many wild animals have of continuing to fight after they are dead led to the invention of the boarspear. This is a long two-handed spear with a cross-bar attached behind the head. When lanced, an animal cannot push its way up the spear to fight that last round after death.

Use a character's great spear skill when armed with a boar spear.

If the boar spear attack roll is the winner, the hunter must still make his own unopposed strength (STR) roll. Success indicates he held the dying animal off. Failure indicates he did not quite do so, and he is knocked down and takes 1d6 damage from the violent fall, though the animal still does not get to attack him. A fumble of the strength roll indicates the hunter did not hold the creature off and it gets its final attack, unopposed.

What to Do

In a hunt most activity is in making successful Horsemanship rolls with various modifiers, plus rolls for your horses' statistics, and for your own Hunting skill. You will fall behind or pull ahead, probably get lost, and perhaps get in on the kill.

Cornered animals may be fought hand-to-tooth, using normal melee rules. Remember that it is courteous to allow the most highly ranked person to attack first, if possible.

Tournament

A TOURNAMENT IS a friendly competition which provides opportunity for knights to exercise their martial skills in a non-lethal situation. It is also a market, a fair, and a general gathering for merry-making. Thus a tournament also provides chances to win Glory, mix with other knights and ladies from around the country, and gain experience in war and courtly skills.

A tournament is a formal affair which, over the years, developed a set of rules and procedures governing the events occurring there. Tournaments have undergone some changes since their introduction several years ago. Now four types are recognized, the older styles being practiced in the lands most distant from trend-setting Camelot. The styles are called: Old, Full, Classic, and Elegant. Most tournaments will be Full Tournaments, which is the standard form described here.

Another factor determines the type of tournament: whether or not dulled weapons are used. Weapons so-dulled are called *rebated*. The rebated sword and lance with coronal are called "arms of courtesy," (*a plaisance*). Regular, sharp, weapons are called the "arms of war" (*a outrance*.)

Tournament Glory

Knights attend tournaments for the primary purpose of gaining Glory. A knight gains Glory points for every fight during the joust, grand melee, or challenge, but equal to the value of 1/10 the normal combat Glory. This is because non-lethal weapons are usually used. He gains this glory no matter what his status is once the tournament is concluded (i.e. whether he won the joust, was eliminated after two rounds, suffered a disabling wound, etc.).

Knights who win the elimination joust receive additional Glory. Furthermore, one knight is chosen as the Tournament Champion and receives glory equal to the number of knights at the tournament (as well as a handsome prize.) Both the tournament champion and the winner of the joust may be the same person, but not necessarily.

Finally, the tournament host receives glory for sponsoring the tournament.

Tournament Sizes

The smallest size of tournament is a Neighborhood Tournament, in which only 100 knights or so participate. 50 Glory is gained by the Melee Champion and Champion of the Joust for this size tournament. The same amount is gained by the sponsor. Typical participants gain ordinary Glory (10 points).

Most tournaments are Local Tournaments, typically sponsored by an earl and pitting his knights against a neighbor's knights. Volunteers are welcomed, and added to the team of their choice. Between 500-1000 knights compete in these tournaments. Participants typically get 10-20 points of glory. Sponsors, Melee and Joust Champions of these tournaments are awarded 100 Glory.

Regional tournaments are more unusual. Sometimes a rich earl gets extravagant and sponsors a regional tournament which draws knights from far and wide. Dukes might sponsor a tournament of this size. On whole, in Logres, they occur once every few years. Two thousand knights typically compete. Sponsors and Champions of the Melee and Joust get 200 Glory points each. Participants typically get 20 Glory.

Regal tournaments have 3,000 or more knights competing. King Arthur's annual Pentecostal Tournament is regal in size and nature. When a new king ascends to his throne he typically sponsors a regal tournament. King Arthur sometimes sponsors them in distant corners of his realm. They are otherwise rare. Sponsors and Champions of the Melee and Joust receive 300 Glory each, and participants typically receive 30 Glory.

What You Do

People of Importance

The patron, or sponsor, is the most important individual at the tournament. He is usually the lord of the estate where the tournament is held. His wife, the lady, bears half the responsibility and glory for the tournament.

Heralds are important. They are official announcers for the events.

The Marshalls of the List are also important. They include two knights and two squires whose duty is to act as judges, arbiters, and overseers of the event.

Knights normally expect to participate in three events at a tournament.

The Joust

First is the Joust, a single-elimination tournament which will result in a single winner. Glory is gained as through normal competitive combat, but at peaceful rates of 1/10 normal. Thus you collect 1/10 the normal glory for each round which your knight succeeds (usually 1-2 points). In addition, the winner gets a bonus amount whose value varies with the size of the tournament.

The Melee

Second is the Grand Melee, a mock battle between the host's team and the visiting team. All combatants fight at once, with one side declared the winner. All participants must join either the host's or visitor's side.

Glory is given to all participants as in a normal battle, but at 1/10 the rate.

Result Modifiers and Victory Modifiers are granted, and the winning team gets a bonus dependant on the size of the tournament.

Finally, judges select the single outstanding fighter, chosen from either side and named Champion of the melee. He is the winner of the tournament, and wins the grand prize.

Dinadan

Challenges

Third are the Challenges, where one contestant can challenge other contestants to various forms of combat for various reasons including: proving skill or strength, resolving stated disputes in a civilized manner, to increase one's standing in the eyes of his peers, or simply for love of the fight.

> **Sir Marhaus Takes the Prize at a Tournament**
>
> *Then Sir Marhaus departed, and within two days his damosel brought him whreas was a great tournament that the Lady de Vawse had cried. And who did that best should have a rich circlet of gold worth a thousand bezants [a type of coin]. And there Sir Marhaus did so nobly that he was renowned, and had sometime down fourty knights, and so the circlet of gold was rewarded him.*
>
> — Malory IV, 25

Other

Interspersed among these battles are lavish feasts, amorous quests, courtly socializing, and other opportunities to engage in *Pendragon* roleplaying.

Before the Tournament

Upon arrival at the tournament site a knight must present himself to the host, as at any time he enters a lord's domain. Then he must present himself to the Marshall of the List, to sign up for the events. There he must decide whether he will join the melee on the host's team, or the visiting team. Once present, he may enter the rest of the social activity.

Before the competition begins the participants are inspected to make sure that they qualify. Other activities are aimed at obtaining a lady's support for the event.

Inspection

The *helm show* is an occasion when all tournament participants show up for inspection without their helmets. This gives the viewers a chance to review them and, if any are found guilty of reproach, name them.

The *making of windows* serves a similar function. Banners of the participants are hung from battlements and windows so that the viewers can check to see who is participating.

Reproaches Which Disqualify Tournament Competitors

These are the reasons for which a knight may be refused entrance into a tournament:

1. violators of churches.
2. hardened excommunicants.
3. slanderers of womankind, or men who have done ladies dishonor.
4. murderers of malice prepense.
5. men false to their oaths or sealed pledges.
6. fugitives guilty of cowardice on the field.
7. men who have been discomfited in the duel on an issue of honor.
8. arsonists.
9. leaders of free companies.
10. pirates of the sea.
11. robber knights.
12. Usurers (moneylenders who charge interest on their loans.)

Historically a participant in a tournament also had to prove his noble blood. Usually he had to prove that his male ancestors were all knights for the last three generations. This rule was often suspended for men who proved themselves to be of natural nobility and thus qualified. Since the average *Pendragon* game will last only three or four generations, and since the first generation (in Uther's time) were the first knights ever made, this rule is a bit silly for the campaign and is ignored.

Ladies' Favors

A favor is a conspicuously-worn token given by a lady to a lover or a knight in a tournament. Knights seek a lady's favor to inspire them and guide them safely through a tournament's perils. The usual favor-token is a scarf or sleeve, though a glove, necklace, or ring are also used.

The favor is often either tied to the knight's arm-armor or tied to the tip of a lance and driven through the enemy's shield.

Tournament Events

The Joust

The Joust event is a chance to show off individual skill and luck. It is the popular knightly sport of knocking each other off horses with sticks. Riding a horse and using their Lance skills, knights battle one another in a single-elimination contest. Each knight who wins continues in the contest and meets another opponent. For each victory he can mark one win in his Joust Score box. If he loses he is eliminated from the contest and must mark one loss in his Joust score box.

Each knight jousts as many rounds as necessary until either he is eliminated or he has eliminated all the other knights. If the latter occurs, he wins the joust.

In the event that one or both jousters break their lances but not eliminate each other, new lances are available. Up to three lances may be used. If all three break, and no one has yet been eliminated, the matter is settled with swords on foot. The winner is the first man to knock the other to the ground.

Jousting is a martial art and although not intended to hurt, damage can occur. It uses the jouster's Lance skill, but with blunted, hollow weapons rather than pointed and barbed spears.

Special rules apply to jousting. See the "Game Mechanics" chapter.

Always remember to mark the jousting wins and losses in the appropriate box on the character sheet. This will allow you to figure your character's average, like keeping hitting averages in base ball.

Fight Challenges

A knight may issue a challenge of whatever sort he wishes.

Some example challenges might be: to anyone, to fight Joust and Sword; to any Saxons, a fight with maces; to anyone, sword fighting on foot; to anyone, a fight to Knockdown with two-handed weapons; to any Somerset knight, a Joust to first blood; to any Round Table knight, a Joust and Sword, both horse and foot.

Any individual may accept these open challenges. Glory is accumulated in the normal way.

A knight may also challenge a single knight, by name, to a combat. This is an individual match, and although Glory will be gained for it there are often other motives in this sort of match. To refuse such a challenge, without some reasonable excuse (such as wounds) will likely bring a Cowardly check, and maybe worse rumors as well.

Fighting challenges will likely net some Glory, but there is a danger of getting too wounded to participate in the big event: the Melee. Sometimes, in fact, challenges are fought after the Melee.

Fight in the Melee

The Grand Melee is the main event. It is a mock battle. All combatants are expected to use blunt weapons or to withhold their blows. Use of either method lessens the killing and maiming power of blows. Their results are identically expressed in the *Pendragon* rules: halve the total damage inflicted when using either blunted weapons or withholding blows.

The rules are exactly those used for Battle.

Combatants remain in the fight until they voluntarily withdraw or are sent out by marshals, who act as judges to eliminate contestants. Simply being unhorsed does not eliminate a knight — sometimes his squire can bring a steed; he can capture one from a mounted foe; or he can receive one from a friend.

Marshals' rulings are final and no one may reenter melee afterwards. Marshals also separate combatants whose passions overcome their chivalry. Such bad behavior, or other bloodshed, usu-

ally results in the elimination of the offender.

Remember that not all action on the tournament field is continuous fighting. Squires ride about with new horses and lances for their knights, to administer first aid, and to lead prisoners off the field. Knots of reserve knights wait patiently for their opportunity, sipping wine and critically observing the fight. Marshals ride about in heraldic garb shouting announcements and judgments. Leaders hold conferences to decide where reserves should be sent. A charge erupts here, a counter charge there. When a valiant fighter is unhorsed a raging melee boils all around him as friends seek to rehorse him before he is discharged by the marshals.

Rules of the Melee

No striking foes from behind.

No striking opponents who are unhelmeted.

No striking horses — injury to a man's steed warrants immediate dismissal from the tourney.

Romance

FINE AMOR, or Courtly Love, is an important activity for many knights and ladies. At the court of Camelot Courtly Love is a popular type of entertainment. In a sense, it says that the duty of women is to flirt with well-spoken guests, and to receive flattery from them and from passing troubadours.

Fine Amor is an invention of ladies and poets to recognize and reward the gentler sex. It is love for love's sake – romantic and passionate love which must be contrasted to the emotionless, political attitude of arranged marriage.

Historically, courtly romance gave social power to women. The experiment was utterly novel at the time, though perhaps a bit trite now. How much of it was just a parlour game, a pretty conceit for the debutantes, a castle-bound girl's dark age soap opera of dreamy emotional outlawry? It is hard for us today to tell these things. Was fine amor was actually practiced? Yes. We have records of some historic knights who did the loony and dangerous things demanded by romance. Although these may have been isolated cases they were admired by many contemporaries for their idealism.

A critical aspect of fine amor is its aspect of being forbidden. Fine amor is directly opposed to the sacrament of matrimony, for True Love is liberating while matrimony is bondage. Thus the most intense of all romances have a married woman cheating on her husband. The purity of their bliss sets both lovers free from the gross material concerns of the world and places them into the rarified realm of emotional commitment. The fact that adultery is forbidden by both Church and State makes its success all the sweeter.

But courtly romance is not just the work of a back-door man: simple lust is a gross reflection of true love. Thus courtly romance is formalized, and required to go through the stages outlined below.

Queen Guenever has recently instituted the Courts of Love, over which she and selected court ladies preside, and with everyone else as audience. Women may come to court to inquire of the rules, to complain of their lover (who nonetheless remain anonymous, of course), and to receive the judgment of the court whether an action ("A theoretical activity, of course...") is romantically correct or not. If the Court of Love condemns an affair, or an activity in the affair, the court may even rule that the love be ended!

Troubadours are an important part of the romantic scene. They write and sing passionate songs which praise the lady's beauty, grace, generosity, and chastity. The poems are often disguised, using the names of ancient lovers so as not to name the lady directly. Thus the poet pretends to be entertaining everyone, but in secret sends his love and messages to someone in the court.

Men must adore women. Adoration, in word, thought, and action is an overwhelming preoccupation. When problems occur, and only failure and frustration ensue, men must be nourished by their agony until love becomes the all-encompassing passion of his life.

Men are subordinate to their lovers. The man takes the role of vassal to the lady's role of lord. This humble and submissive attitude of the manly lover was an idea entirely new to its time, when patriarchy was increasingly dominant in social and clerical circles. The deliberate role reversal was an outright rebellion of emotions against the bondage imposed by prevailing materialistic attitudes. It exalted Love, and transformed it into something new.

The basic procedure for an affair is for the man to court the lady, who marks his success by granting favors. The granting of favors is always up to the lady. The man has no rights other than whatever she deigns to grant him. Usually the woman demands awesome proof from the lover that he is sincere. Knights perform great deeds, compose immortal poetry, and wait patiently in sincere silence for the moment that their lover grants a smile, a glance, or a gentle word. To a true lover frustration only intensifies passion. Troubles are welcome as tests to prove their ardor.

ROMANTIC AFFAIR TABLE

The romantic love affair moves through these stages:

1. Worship through passionate declaration of the love (in private of course).

2. Virtuous rejection by the lady.

3. Renewed wooing, with proofs and oaths of fidelity to the lady.

4. Deeds of valor and heroism to prove courage and strength.

5. Acceptance of the lover by the woman, followed by consummation of their secret affair.

6. Subterfuge and troubles, keeping their affair secret and alive.

7. A tragic ending when the affair is discovered, made more poignant by the depth of the tragedy.

Chastity

Fine amor is often chaste and formalized. Some lovers consider the chaste affair to be the highest form of amor, gaining the

King Mark of Cornwall

benefits without the dangers. Such an affair took place between Sir Galahad, the world's purest knight, and Lady Amide, Percivale's sister. Everyone thought that the courtly romance of Lancelot and Guenever to be the same, and its subsequent exposure brought about the greatest tragedy: the downfall of the Round Table.

Unmarried women must always be chaste. Virginity is the highest virtue for young women. Lack of it brings shame and guilt in abundance, often resulting the woman being forced into a convent as atonement and punishment.

Married women are also expected to be chaste in their exercise of Fine Amor. To maintain their bloodline nobles imprison their wives in marriage, for only then can they be sure that their heir is in fact their son. Laws state that a man may kill his wife and her lover if they are discovered in adultery. Such murder is frowned upon, but is often excused because it is a "crime of passion." Many women work hard to maintain their chastity and use every device to make their lover work for each touch, glance, and kiss. Obstacles are not cause for sorrow, but opportunities for the knight to expresses his devotion and prove that he is made powerful by the love and can overcome anything for it. In this manner a woman may not even be attracted to the man for him to develop a passion and devotion. Sir Palomides, for instance, was never loved by La Beale Isoud, yet he often gained superhuman skills because he knew she was watching him.

So, despite the oppression of society, chastity was often a relative commodity in many affairs. Courtly manners sometimes allow a gentle knight to kiss the hand or cheek of a lady if he has performed some marvelous deed for her. Meetings even between chaste lovers are supposed to be secret, so who can tell what goes on after a discreet public kiss?

Isn't Romance Silly?

Knights in love act like fools. Sir Palomides,one of the finest fighters and most noble knights in the land, spends his spare time weeping, starving to death, and otherwise moping around. Likewise another lover, Sir Alisander le Orphelin, looks at his lover-to-be and is struck so dumb "that he wist not whether he were on horseback or on foot." (Malory, X, 39). They are not sensible or rational. It is hard for most of us to imagine why anyone would even pretend to act that way. What's going on here?

Modern readers should be aware of two facts of medieval emotional life: the expression of all strong emotions by everyone in the stories, and the new idea of love portrayed.

Strong emotions are a mark of the impassioned practices of chivalry. King Arthur weeps when he hears news of tragic deaths, and one time falls onto the floor because he is laughing so heartily. The fury of Guenever's jealous outbursts drives Sir Lancelot mad. The expression of love was as fervent.

The idea of love as portrayed in courtly amor was brand new in the twelfth century when it was written into the Arthurian legends. Love existed before: all the myths of older times had love stories. People are known to have felt the emotion. Previously, however, love was an emotion with extraordinary power, but whose results were as likely to bring about disaster. The story of Helen of Troy is the ultimate love story: great fun for Paris and Helen, but an absolute social disaster since the flower of two great races was exterminated by Aphrodite's passion.

The idea that love was a worthy, redeeming activity was new. In fact, love was noble because it respected women so much. For the first time in Western history women obtained some recognition as individuals worthy of something besides making bread, clothing, and children. Thus was born the "Woman on a Pedestal" attitude – trite and unworkable today, but brand new then.

The people who supported the ideals of romantic love were mostly disgruntled members of the fringes of the ruling noble society: wives oppressed by church, husbands, and daily work; and young unimportant knights who usually owned so little that it was easy for them to swear that their loves were more important than any earthly property. Opposed to them were the nobles and the Church.

Malory prefers romance and its rules to those of society and church. In Malory's works Lancelot is guilty of heinous crimes: disloyalty to his liege, deceitful adultery, insincere oaths, and rebellion. Yet Malory holds him so guiltless that Lancelot catches a glimpse of the immaculate Holy Grail and, much later, even rises immediately to heaven upon his death. To Malory, Lancelot was guiltless to the end, always because he was a staunch upholder of a true and faithful love which sometimes caused him to do rash things. The unswerving loyalty of Lancelot's love, patient and always according to the rules, generated a stability which gave Lancelot his reason to live.

Malory's views on love are stated clearly in an essay where he compares love with a passing year. He was dismayed by the whimsy and vacillations of lovers in his own day.

"Right so fareth love nowadays, soon hot soon cold; this is no stability. But the old love was not so; men and women could love together seven years, and no lecherous lusts were between them, and then was love, truth, and faithfulness: and lo, in likewise was used love in King Arthur's day.

"Wherefore I liken love nowadays unto summer and winter; for like as the one is hot and the other cold, so fareth love nowadays; therefore all ye that be lovers call unto your remembrance the month of May, like as did Queen Guenever, for whom I make here a little mention, that while she lived she was a good lover, and therefore she had a good end." (Malory, XVIII, 25)

Is that silly? Perhaps so to us today. Do not try to run a chivalrous love affair using today's standards. In *Pendragon* chivalrous love is a virtue, a noble passion which inspires and gives meaning to life.

The Queen's Knights

The Queen's Knights are a formal extension of the chaste affair of Fine Amor. These knights are an honor guard noted for their chivalry and for their true love

dedicated to Queen Guenever, the highest, untouchable authority on Love. Knights are chosen for a year at a time at an annual contest, taking winners from various martial and romantic contests. Thus knights may exercise the latest fashion of the court without danger of being killed by jealous husbands, or endangering their immortal souls by going against the beliefs of their Christian religion. Thus many knights harbor genuine affection for the Queen, knowing full well that they will never be fulfilled.

Entertainment

Women characters often entertain strangers and friends through the use of certain skills. These skills are the ones useful to a man who wishes to entertain and impress a woman, and may be used in competitions.

Whenever a woman wishes to learn more about a man she uses these skills: Courtesy, Dance, Flirt, Game, Hawking, Intrigue, Literacy, Orate, Play (Instrument), Sing.

However, simple playing of games is not the entire point, for there are things to be discovered in the banter and talk which passes across the boards between moves. Here behavior comes to the fore, and personality is revealed. A lady may decide to escalate her passion in the affair only after learning the facts about her lover, careful to make sure he is the right kind of man.

In game play the gamemaster may state that the conversation is taking a direction towards a specific personality trait. The participants can then attempt resolution rolls on that trait. If one player wishes to change the subject, while the other wishes to continue on the original, an opposed resolution must be made. In every case the winner of the resolution knows (or thinks) that his virtue is more important to him than the other one is to the loser.

Religion

RELIGION IN THE MIDDLE AGES was very different from religion today. To capture the feelings and attitudes of medieval literature it is important for players to understand the basic, accepted attitudes held about religion by their characters, who are members of the ruling class.

One religion is known: Christianity. All knights from Salisbury are Christian, as are most of the people of the Kingdom of Logres and nearby lands. Other, Pagan faiths, are still held by the barbarians living at the fringes of humanity, but wherever civilization and high culture exists, Christianity reigns. Other religions are possible, and discussed in *Knights Adventurous.*

Christianity is of one type, the Roman Catholic Church. Other types of Christianity are known, but not to beginning player knights from Salisbury, and are covered in *Knights Adventurous.*

The Roman Church is a strict, hierarchal form of Christianity.

The actual influence of the Church on the rest of society in the Middle Ages varied widely during the two eras compressed into *Pendragon.* In the sixth century it was busy solidifying its position as the One Church, and clarifying its beliefs into dogma. In the 13th century the same dogma was strangling the Church and the rest of Europe nearly to death as the Pope tried to rule politics as well as religion.

During the actual Arthurian era, the sixth century, several variations of Christianity were practiced, though the Roman Church was well on its way to claiming to be catholic. Throughout history the Church gradually became stronger, until it became a vast political machine which tried to rule both the temporal an spiritual spheres.

Naturally this growth of temporal power offended many people whose traditions and privileges were being eroded, most notably the noblemen and knights. Conflict, especially as the Church entered the temporal realm, was inevitable. It is appropriate to note here, for instance, that all the saint's Lives in which King Arthur appears portray the king with considerable hostility and unkindness.

Despite this, the religious attitudes in Arthurian literature vary widely, and none of the good knights return this type

Swearing

Knights regularly swear, usually in a subtle way acceptable to the tender ears of their courtly times. The favored way is not, as in our day, to insult some body part or act, but instead to insult something sacred. Since we have more sacred institutions than body parts the knights had many more things to say than we do, and now it is sometimes hard for us unimaginative moderns to tell that the knights were, in fact, cursing.

Cursing itself is forbidden, of course, by the second commandment: *Thou shalt not take the name of thy Lord God in vain.* So instead everyone says things close to Him, but not using His name, thereby satisfying the letter of the law.

Popular oaths of this nature are:

"Gadzooks" which means God's Hooks, referring to the nails which hung Him upon the cross.

"God's Blood," or more popularly, "Bloody" in general, refers to God's Blood, the most precious part of the Body of God, and was coming extremely close to profanity, and so usually discouraged.

"God's Teeth" was the favored oath of King John of England. Other king's oaths recorded to have been in use were: "God's Head," "God's Death," and "by the Holy Face of Lucca."

Swearing by saints was popular among knights, as if invoking the saint's name would keep his attention turned towards the speaker. Some popular saints in King Arthur's time were:

St. Michael, the Archangel of Battle.

St George, the dragonslayer.

St. Theodore, called "the Recruit."

St. Demetrius, "the Proconsul."

St. Procopius, "the Officer."

St. Mercury, a Scythian soldier-martyr.

St. Maurice, head of the Theban Legion which mutinied rather than participate in pagan sacrifices.

of hostility overtly. The least religious knights only ignore their spiritual obligations, although in history many went further and plundered the rich abbeys, especially during foreign wars. Most of the knights in literature attend Mass more or less regularly, but seem to show their spiritual interest the most when they swear either oaths or profanities. The most religious knights are fanatics, though they pursue an officially unacceptable form of Christianity in the Holy Grail.

Rather than judging the past, *Pendragon* presents the two versions of the Church. Gamemasters must choose what mixture of the two will be applied to their campaign.

The Good Church

The Church has done limitless good for humanity.

The Church is the primary organization within which commoners can raise themselves from their humble origins to a position where they can use their talents.

The Church is the only institution which fosters education, both for itself and for others. They have preserved the knowledge of the ancients.

The Church provides protection and peace in a violent, brutal age. Church men continually plead for mercy for their followers against the violence and hostility of the knights and lords.

The Church provides for the poor, sick, and homeless.

The clergy are selfless servants of the Lord, working hard to meet the demands of their faith and provide for the welfare of the people.

Finally, the Church alone can provide true solace for the suffering by offering Salvation for the Eternal Soul.

The Bad Church

The Church has done limitless harm to humanity.

In the name of God it has perpetuated itself to control every aspect of humanity's existence.

It is a materialistic and greedy organization, interested only in enriching itself and its clergy at the expense of all else.

It is foremost among the hypocritical organizations known, selling and buying spirituality like bread.

The clergy are deceitful, grasping men without belief in their own preachings, interested only in enriching themselves and in extending the influence of the Church for their personal benefit. They sell spirituality and pardons rather than following the correct spiritual order.

Morality

Religion is traditionally the guardian of a culture's morality. The exemplary behavior pattern of traits underlined on your character sheet is an interpretation of Christianity's virtues for *Pendragon.* They are the things which the religion has taught to be ideals, for better or worse.

Since magic is also real in the game, and religion is an institutionalization of magic, following certain moral behavior brings about a reward. The reward for being an exemplary Christian is +3 Healing Rate.

Religious Conflict

Religious conflict is always a possible theme in *Pendragon,* but will generally be ignored throughout the game. Religious conflict was not a very important part of most Arthurian literature. The single long story which emphasizes religious conflict (*Perlesvaus*) reflects all of the worst aspects of religious dogma, spiritual bigotry, and the murderous crusader spirit.

My experience in *Pendragon* has revealed that players have a wide variety of attitudes about Christianity, ranging from ignorance and indifference through curiosity and willingness to play, down to fanaticism or overt hostility. The strongest attitudes come from those who have been offended or harmed by one or another of our modern Christian institutions. These people should be urged to play a different type of character which can generate fun and enjoyment as well as hysteria. Constant argument and displayed bigotry in a *Pendragon* game will quickly destroy it. Religious conflict is not a theme in the literature, and I advise you to inflame it only with great care in your campaign.

Religious Attitudes

Attitudes can be summed up within four categories for *Pendragon:*

Fanaticism: Religious attitudes are placed before anything else, including loyalty to one's family, lord, or anything else which interferes with dedication to the religious life (or, in the Bad Church, dedication to the Church.)

Sir Galahad is the best example of this type of knight.

Interest: Most people have been brought up on the ideas and accept them without thinking one way or the other. They regularly attend functions, believe what they are told, and define the core of the mainstream belief. Most practitioners are in this category.

Indifference: Most knights of Arthur's era show monumental indifference towards their religion, just as most people do today and probably always have. They are subject to its invisible, cultural influence, but don't really care. They might attend Mass regularly, or as needed, but think it's probably a waste of time.

Sir Gawaine is regularly accused of being this type of knight.

Hostility: Some knights hate the church and plunder it with glee. Reasons can vary widely, and a few examples of these types appear in literature, and more in history.

Sir Thomas Malory is my favorite example of an Arthurian knight who is of this type.

Changing Religions

The importance of religion to your character is entirely a personal decision. He may be devout, pay only lip service, or ignore it altogether.

Characters are born into a faith, as shown in the Character Generation chapter. However, they need not retain that belief. If devout at all, they will probably choose whatever religion matches their lifestyle and personality.

Changing religions is simple, but cannot be done during character generation. During play, a character may seek out a holy person of the faith he wishes to join. He must speak with the person and seek conversion. He will receive a date (probably a holy day of the faith) and a place for the conversion.

Once formally converted, the knights cultural mores change and he must underline new traits to emulate. The character is eligible to gain the benefits from the traits of that new faith (as detailed below). However, actual personality traits do not change just because of conversion. Thus, a pagan newly converted to Christianity is likely to have problems with chastity.

Adventuring

A spriggan

A PRIMARY ACTIVITY of the famous knights is to adventure. Adventuring, in fact, is the activity which most sets them apart from the ordinary knights who stay at home and acquire Glory passively (out of play).

Adventuring is an activity which is recognized as a legitimate knightly duty by the Arthurian court. Under the reign of King Arthur, knights have a duty to quest which is as important as their duty to stand garrison and serve an active 40 days in the field.

Most knights do not take the job. For them the everyday activities of guard duty, tournaments, and battles, are enough to satisfy their sense of adventure. Other knight, like the player knights, seek more, and undertake to seek adventures.

Most of the lords of Logres are in favor of the new sport of questing, and are happy to oblige their knights who wish to engage in it. The recent lull in peace has left the castles full of boisterous fighters with nothing to fight. Adventures send the knights to work off their energy elsewhere, if not far away from Logres at least far away from home. Perhaps the sponsoring lord also hopes that the questing knights will arouse something from the other, less enthusiastic knights as well.

Adventures abound. Even the normal, stay-at-home knights have ordinary adventures as part of their routine, without having to seek them out. Adventures include going to tournaments, participating in battles, engaging in romance, visiting unusual sights, and encountering unusual beings and other adventuring knights come to plague the home land.

Adventuring is the excuse for player knights to wander the roads and trails of Britain. Adventuring is the activity which sets an Arthurian knight apart from the ordinary knight.

Thus, whereas knighthood is the heart of *Pendragon*, adventuring is its soul.

Quests

Quests are all adventures, but not all adventures are quests. A quest must include several elements to qualify as such: going to an unknown place, encountering something mysterious or unusual, facing strange dangers, and (always) facing death.

Quests must, by definition, occur in unknown territory. In those strange lands waits High Adventure, and opportunity to test the neat ideals of the heartland of civilization.

Thus knights must request a leave from their lord and normal duties to quest and adventure. A knight, even in such lands, represents not only himself, but also his lord, and so the lord will try to send only individuals who he will not have to get out of trouble, or who will not bring shame or dishonor to them.

A time limit is often imposed on absentee time for questing. The proverbial "year and a day" is a good starting time period. At the end of the time the knight must return to court and report the results of his activities. Later on the time limit may be longer, indefinite, or geared to the specific task. Note that this cycle is the same as that which occurs with the Round Table knights at Arthur's court.

The Quest for the Holy Grail is the best-known of the many quests. However, others of impressive story also exist, and can tempt characters who seek success other than the severe tests of the Holy Grail.

Battle

BATTLES ARE A LARGE part of a knight's life. Individual heroism on lonely adventures represents the new type of knighthood. Old knighthood glories in organized mass killing, and reserves for itself the right to regularly use violence. These combats, called battles, occur often.

Your knight's experience in combat with masses of men is contained in his Battle skill. This determines how well he is able to assess and react to situations, to remain within support distance of his group, to recognize good and bad situations, and to be lucky.

Once in a hand-to-hand melee your character's weapon skill(s) determine his relative success each Battle Round. A Battle Round is not a single fight, or an exchange of blows, but is a half hour of riding about exchanging blows with groups of enemies which form and dissolve almost randomly. The die roll does not indicate a single exchange of blows, but many exchanges over the half hour.

The standard battle tactic is for small groups of men to follow the commands of a leader whose banner they follow. This unit is the only step of the army organization which is important for a player knight. In a large battle this leader would be your own earl.

The Feudal Army

The makeup and organization of most medieval battles and armies follows a tra-

ditional and predictable pattern. Army tactics rarely vary. Military sophistication is at a historical low. The feudal lords have enough difficulty just getting the armies to the field without having to *maneuver* them too!

The *Pendragon* battle system assumes that standard battle tactics are always followed. Variations in military strategy may be introduced in later *Pendragon* supplements or by the gamemaster, but they will be applied to this basic system.

When a feudal lord goes to war he summons his vassals. Through feudal obligation, they come fully armed and equipped with provisions for a 40-day period (though service time is of indefinite length if the homeland is being invaded). If he has been invaded the lord probably calls up the local levy, a mob of untrained peasants armed with farming tools. Rich lords might also hire mercenaries, especially specialty troops such as archers, engineers, and spear men; or simply additional soldiers if the campaign is going to last more than 40 days.

Assembled for battle, medieval armies are divided into three sections. Each is given a unique name for the order in which they march on the road, but is called in general a *battaille* or battalion.

The *vanguard* marches first, commanded by the second-highest leader. At the pre-designated battle field the vanguard lines up on the right side of the battle line.

The *main battaille* marches in the center, is led by the highest commander of the army, and assembles for combat in the center of the battle line.

The *rearward battaille* is commanded by the third ranking noble, marches at the end of the line, and assembles on the left side of the field of combat.

Battailles are sub-divided into *units*. A unit is defined as any group of knights following a designated Unit Leader.

Battle, a Poem

Bertrand de Boron was a thirteenth-century nobleman of Aquitaine, and both a friend and enemy to King Richard the Lion-hearted of England. He was a noted warrior, troubadour, and troublemaker. He wrote this piece to describe his pleasure and ecstacy at performing knightly duties. This reveals one of the prevalent attitudes of knights during the era when the King Arthur stories were first written, and reflects the behavior which knights are expected to exhibit.

My heart is filled with gladness when I see
Strong castles besieged, stockades broken and overwhelmed,
Many vassals struck down,
Horses of the dead and wounded roving at random.
And when battle is joined, let all men of good lineage
Think of naught but the breaking of heads and arms,
For it is better to die than be vanquished and live. . .
I tell you I have no such joy as when I hear the shout
"On! On!" from both sides and the neighing of riderless steeds,
And groans of "Help me! Help me!"
And when I see both great and small
Fall in ditches and on the grass
And see the dead transfixed by spear shafts!
Lords, mortgage your domains, castles, cities,
but never give up war!

— Bertrand de Boron, Vicomte de Hauteforte

Types of Troops

Several kinds of troops accompany a lord into battle.

Knights — well-trained and well-outfitted — form a core of the professional, mounted warriors. They are the heart of the army.

Serjeants are professional troops, decently armed and trained, but lacking the skill, confidence, and horses of knights. Poor knights without a liege, unattached squires, and ambitious men-at-arms with good equipment and a horse also count as serjeants. Many mercenary units are composed of serjeants.

Hobilars are mounted but unarmored troops used as scouts and messengers but never mustered for battle as a unit.

Infantry are unmounted troops who are normally used to garrison a castle, to assault walls, and to build camps. Infantry are armed with shield and spear or with great spear, long knives, bows, crossbows, or axes depending on their nationality. They usually wear leather armor, often augmented by miscellaneous parts of real armor plundered from the dead. Only kings regularly outfit their footsoldiers with good armor.

Engineers are men who can build and work the mighty engines used in siege, such as trebuchets, managols, and belfreys. They also oversee making siege works and digging tunnels. Without engineers it is usually hopeless to beseige a city or castle. They are also responsible for building castles able to withstand engines.

Others: many other people also accompany armies, although they are worthless as combat troops. Knights bring girlfriends or wives and servants. Spectators, suppliers, well-wishers, and hangers-on congregate to trade with or cheat the soldiers. These followers are a constant nuisance on the march and are always a great trouble to feed, yet few medieval leaders ever forbade them.

Heralds, because of their special status, play an important part in battle. Heralds are recognized as neutral messengers and may not be attacked by anyone. Prior to a battle they carry messages back and forth between commanders to plan where the armies will meet. Just before the armies engage the heralds

The Army Marches

King Arthur has mustered his army to march to war.

WIth him were nobles and barons and rugged knights, the mightiest ever raised in Britain, warriors fully armored, most skillful with their weapons, and the most resolute in the world. Dukes and worthy lords, strong and beloved, assembled at Arthur's call, all soldiers of great renown, magnificent kings in their golden crowns.

So the king, mighty and rich, with his Round Table moved out in royal array. Never in the world, except in lies and fables, was there a finer gathering of the flower of knighthood in one place, powerful and determined men mounted on their steeds. Many a stern warrior took to the road, banners glittering in the sun, silver and black, others gold and vermillion, still more silver and blue, a brilliant column joyfully riding over the fair meadows and glades.

— from *Golagros and Gawaine*

from both sides withdraw to the same hilltop, steeple, or silo to watch and record events of the fight. They help each other to identify combatants. The victorious side chooses the name of the battle. Afterwards heralds may carry further messages between the combatants, commonly to make a temporary truce for burying the dead.

Definitions

To smoothly and effectively stage a battle, the gamemaster should understand the following terms.

Time Scales

The Battle Round is the basic unit of time.

Battle Round — is about 1/2 hour.

Battle — lasts up to all day; is divided into 2-12 Battle Rounds.

Battlefield Locations

At any point in a battle, the player knights must always know where they are.

Front Of The Battle means that the knight is in the area of fighting.

Back Of The Battle means that the knight is at least 1 Battle Round away from the actual area of fighting. This usually means he is safe to perform actions without being attacked. Knights in the Back of the Battle are Disengaged.

Out Of The Battle means the knight is back at camp, too far to see what is going on and (almost) certainly in an area safe enough not to be attacked. However, he can reach the Back of the Battle in 1 Battle Round. No Glory is awarded for men here.

Commanders

There are three main commanders of importance to the player knights in any battle.

The **Army Commander** is the individual who commands everyone. His Battle roll is important one time, when the battle starts.

The **Battalion Commander** is one of three in the army. His Battle roll is important the first time the battalion enters combat, usually during the First Charge, and is modified by the Army Commander's Battle roll result.

The **Unit Commander** is the person to whom a knight formally reports in battle. The unit commander's standard is where a individual knight rallies to charge or countercharge during melee. In general, even when unable or unwilling to join the commander's standard a knight stays close by, where his companions and friends will be sure to aid him if necessary. They are the men who have agreed to protect him, who know and recognize him, and who are depending on him for aid.

What to Do In a Battle

Make sure you know who your unit commander is. Then just make sure you follow him.

The First Charge

At some point, hopefully the right one, the Army Commander orders the whole or part of his army to charge. The attack is sounded and the entire battle line rushes at the enemy. The opposed commander gives the order to countercharge at (hopefully) the optimal moment for his troops. The placement of troops and the timing of the attack are some of the major details included in the Army Commander's Battle Roll.

Battalion commanders are responsible for the specific details important to the First Charge. Each attempts his Battle Roll, modified by the Army Commander's results, to see how well he placed his troops and is now leading them into battle. This, in turn, provides a modifier to the skill of each individual knight involved in the charge.

Each player must make an opposed Lance roll, with his knight's skill modified by the leadership results of the Battalion Commander. Each knight stands a good chance of being killed in this first charge.

The armies crash together! Immediately men and horses are killed and wounded. After a moment's pause, as the survivors drop shattered lances and draw swords, knots of men fall to fighting in confused masses, called the melee.

The Melee

The melee is the central part of the fight — the armies mingled madly on the field. Units of men work together as best they can, riding back and forth attacking smaller groups to try to raise the odds in their favor. Much of the fighting is indecisive: groups clash and separate. One flees wildly while another dissolves as members go off in different directions. Unit leaders try to rally their men to their standards for another charge to sweep the field free of foes. Comrades charge heroically into larger masses to break them up and prevent a charge. The

✣ THE BATTLE SYSTEM ✣

PLAYERS MUST KEEP TRACK of information which occurs in the battle round: the total number of rounds which you had a critical success, won, lost, and fumbled. This later determines the amount of Glory obtained. Also, you will need to record the losses to your nonplayer Followers.

Squires perform a wide variety of duties in battle, all for the simple trouble of a Squire Roll. They may:

- bring a new horse or weapon.
- escort prisoners away.
- drag a unconscious knight off the field.

Once a squire is used in a battle he is gone for the duration, unless he is sought after and found during a disengaged session. Thus the usefulness of multiple squires is apparent.

Before the Battle

Decide whether everyone is in the same unit, and what battalion the unit is with. Everyone in a battle must be with a unit, which is always assigned to a battalion.

To participate in the First Charge your knight must have a horse, a lance, and be in a unit which is going to charge. The knight lines up at the Front of the Battle. If not in the First Charge the knight begins at the Back of the Battle.

Select Commanders

Each army has an Army Commander. Each battalion has a Battalion Commander. Commanders may be either player-knights or knights determined by the gamemaster and the storyline.

If player-knights, note their battle skills. If randomly determined, the Battle skill of an Army or Battalion Commander equals 15+1d6. Unit commanders, if chosen at random, have a Battle skill of 8+2d6.

Determine Battle Size

Battle Size is determined by the number of total participants on both sides, calculated in *knight-value.* A fully-equipped knight, with the usual armor for the time, riding a charger, and with one squire, is one knight-value. Knight values increase depending upon the individual's relative wealth, expressed as the number of squires. Poor knights, and other inferior troops, are counted at reduced knight-values.

Army Commander Roll

Selection of the battlefield is critical. Some sites offer great advantages to one of the opponents. The results are determined by the Army Commander Battle Roll. Modify the Army Commander Battle Skill by the following appropriate value, roll 1d20, and consult the Commander Battle Roll table.

Outnumber foe at least **2-1**: +5
Outnumber foe at least **5-1**: +10
Outnumbered by foe at least **2-1**: -5
Outnumbered bv foe at least **5-1**: -10

KNIGHT VALUES
Superlative Knight = 3 knight-values.
Rich Knight = 2 knight-values.
Regular Knight = 1 knight-value.
Poor Knight = 1/2 knight-value.
Foot Soldier = 1/5 knight-value.
Rabble = 1/25 knight-value.

BATTLE SIZE
Skirmish = Fewer than 500 knight values.
Small = 500-1000 knight values.
Medium = 1000-2500 knight values.
Large = 2500 to 5000 knight values.
Huge = over 5000 knight values.

wounded are taken to the rear of the battle to receive first aid. Knights have too many targets to remember, and may be fighting several knights at a time each round. Occasionally, the fighting lulls to a stop.

The best tactic in a melee is for a unit to remain disengaged until the right moment, and to avoid being charged until ready. When a suitable target presents itself, the unit strikes at the right time to kill or drive away the foe, or engage it in melee. Optimal conditions are difficult to arrange, and much of a battle consists of bands of men jockying for position, clashing, and separating again.

A typical battle lasts 2-12 Battle Rounds, covering up to a full day of combat. Participants in the melee use the normal combat rules, but instead of man-to-man it represents a larger scale of conflict.

Players must jot down the facts of their fight each battle round on a piece of scrap paper. The normal book keeping for wounds must be followed, plus more. Each round, record whether you made success, a critical success, loss, or fumble. These facts will determine the amount of Glory obtained. Also write down any prisoners captured, horses caught, or other plunder taken.

During each melee round you will be asked whether you are: Leading, Attached, or Alone; and whether you are mounted or on foot. All of your training tells you to remain Attached (except lords, who are usually leaders.) Avoid being Alone — then you are a prime target for groups of enemies.

If you are badly wounded there is no dishonor in withdrawing to the Back of the Battle. Fighting is your trade, not dying. In any battle emergency, call for your squire: attempt a Squire roll. He will come and give you his horse, administer first aid, or try to drag your body out of the battle.

After the Battle

Eventually the battle ends, either because darkness falls and everyone is too tired to continue, because nothing decisive has occurred, because one or both commanders orders a withdrawal, or one of the armies is decisively beaten. Afterwards the wounded are helped, the dead stripped of goods, the enemy camp plundered, and the dead buried.

Knight Status in Battle

In each Battle Round each knight decides on his status. He is either Leading, Attached, or Alone.

Leading — Leading knights have some other knights ready to follow them for at least this round of the fight. Any knight may become a Leader if he successfully Rallies nearby men (see the Disengaged options under Statement Of Intent). Leaders almost always gets a bonus in Melee. There are really no disadvantages to being a Leader.

Attached — Attached knights have committed to following a leader. Each knight looks around and contributes his infor-

The First Charge

In the First Charge the knights are at the mercy of their Battalion commanders' Battle skills. The commanders set things up, then order a charge at the right moment. The participating knights can only follow, and make the best of their Lance skill.

Battalion Commander Roll

Modify the Battalion Commander's Battle skill by the Army Commander's result, if any. Roll 1d20 and check the Commander Battle Roll Table for results. This modifier affects the individual knights' Lance Roll for the First Charge. The Unit Commander has no affect on the First Charge. He, like everyone else, is just an individual following the Battalion Commander's orders.

Commander Battle Roll Table

result	modifier
Critical	+5
Success	0
Failure	-5
Fumble	-10

Determine Enemy Skill

There are two methods which you can use determine the skill of knights opposing the players:

Story Method: your story may have determined what foes you face. Simply quantify them according to their knight-value on the table below.

Random Method: Roll 1d20 on the Battle Enemy Table to determine how good the foes are for this attack. This table is used in the First Charge, and for each round of Melee.

Random Battle Enemy Table

d20	Kt.-val.	Skill	Damage	Group
01	Pretender	05	3d6	1d6-2
02	Poor	10	3d6	1d6
03	Regular	10	3d6	1d6
04	Rich	10	3d6	2d6
05	Poor	12	3d6	2d6
06	Rich	12	4d6	2d6
07	Superlative	13	4d6	3d6
08	Regular	13	4d6	1d6
09	Poor	14	4d6	2d6
10	Rich	14	5d6	2d6
11	Regular	15	4d6	1d6
12	Superlative	15	4d6	3d6
13	Poor	16	5d6	1d6
14	Rich	16	5d6	2d6
15	Regular	17	5d6	1d6
16	Superlative	17	5d6	3d6
17	Rich	18	6d6	2d6
18	Regular	19	6d6	2d6
19	Superlative	19	5d6	3d6
20	Superlative	20	6d6	3d6
21	Superlative	25	6d6	3d6

**This shows the range of possible followers. Roll the dice shown, then roll the usual d6 to find possible modifiers to their skills for melee.*

Fight

The First Charge is determined by using the usual *Pendragon* Lance combat rules, although the gamemaster may use either the Simple or Longer Methods to determine results.

Statement Of Intent: players state whether they are Alone, Leading, or Attached.

Simple Method: the gamemaster throws a single d20 which is used as the enemy's response against all participants. Everyone else rolls their Lance skill opposed to the result.

Longer Method: the gamemaster rolls separately opposed to each player knight. The results are the same, above.

Follower Results

Each Leader should roll Battle again to determine the fate of his followers. Check the results against the Followers Fate Table. On the First Charge, always ignore results of capturing prisoners.

Follower's Fate Table

Critical Success = no damage, and they captured a prisoner.*

Success = 10% losses (2% killed, 8% wounded)

Failure = 50% losses (10% killed, 15% captured, 25% wounded)

Fumble = 75% losses (50% killed, 25% captured)

**prisoners are not captured on the First Charge*

Melee

Preparation

Start each Melee Round by checking your status. You will need to know if:

you are alone, leading, or attached,
you are mounted or afoot,
you have a prisoner or not,

Roll on Unit Events Table

Roll 3d6 and check this table. The modifier is applied to your character's subsequent Battle, Melee, and Followers Fate rolls.

Unit Events Table

3d6	Modifier	Event
03	-15	Your Battalion Routs
04	-10	Your Unit Retreats
05	-10	Surge of Enemy Knights
06	-5	You are Outnumbered
07	-5	More Enemies than Friends
08	-5	Enemy Pushes Forward
09-12	0	Could Go Either Way
13	+5	Enemy is Confused
14	+5	More Friends than Enemies
15	+5	They Pull Away
16	+10	A Surge of Victory
17	+10	Enemy Unit Retreats
18+	+15	Enemy Battalion Routs

Battle Roll

Knights who are Alone, and Leaders, make Battle rolls. Followers do not make this Battle roll. Knights who are Alone get a -10 (!) modifier to their Battle skill.

If You Are Mounted:

- Critical Success, = you can engage, or remain disengaged. If you have a Lance, you can get a Charge bonus.
- Success = you can engage, or remain disengaged
- Failure = you are engaged
- Fumble = you are engaged to your disadvantage, -5 on weapon roll

If You Are Afoot:

- Critical = you can start the round engaged or disengaged
- Success = you are engaged, or can become disengaged IF the next Unit Events Table results is 09 or more
- Failure = you are engaged
- Fumble = you are attacked from the rear, additional -5 on your next melee Weapon roll

Statement of Intent

Leaders and Alone knights must make a statement of intent for the round, based upon what they know now. Engaged knights may choose to fight or flee. Disengaged knights have many choices, listed below.

Disengaged Knights Disengaged knights have can either remain disengaged (with a variety of possible actions open to them); or re-enter combat.

Remain Disengaged: While disengaged many possible actions can be attempted. They include:

- get and/or give several treatments of First Aid
- check someone for life, give First Aid, get them on a horse, and ride them to the Back of the Battle
- look for your squire (attempt Squire roll: success=he shows up. Failure=he doesn't.)

- look for your group (attempt Awareness roll: success= you see them and can travel there next Battle Round)
- take off a set of armor (you are unarmored for the duration)
- put on a set of armor (you are unarmored for the duration)
- pillage a corpse or living person of his goods and armor
- ride away to the Back of the Battle
- run away to the back of the battle
- Look for, find, and attempt to catch a riderless horse (roll Riding minus 2d6 modifier: success=you got it, roll 1d6: 1-4=Charger, 5=palfrey, 6=cob).
- Rally a group (roll your Battle, modified by plus (your Glory/1000) minus (2d6); success=you are a Leader and 1d6 knights are ready to follow you next Segment. Failure=you are still alone.)

Re-enter Combat: A disengaged Leader or Alone knight may either: go to where friends are in combat, usually to rescue unit members who were unhorsed; or attempt an Awareness roll to look for a target.

Help Friends: Knights are often dismounted in a fight. A Leader or Alone knight can choose to return to melee and help these individuals. If so chosen, reentry to combat is allowed.

Roll 1d20 on the Melee Target Table:

Melee Target Table

d20	*result*
01-05	Advantageous attack, +3 to weapon roll
06-10	normal targets
11-15	Disadvantageous targets, -3 to weapon roll
16-18	Enemy Hero
19	Enemy Standard
20	Enemy Battalion Commander

Decide To Attack Or Not

The Leader or Alone knight may choose to ignore the target and, instead, remain disengaged despite his Statement of Intent. However, if this is done then *no other actions can be undertaken that round.*

Combat

Engaged and mounted nights have two choices: fight or flight. Knights engaged on foot can not attempt to escape.

Fight

Find the Enemy Skill: Use the Random Battle Enemy Table to find the foe this round. The foe will change every round.

If attacking a group with the Hero, add the appropriate modifier to the Random Battle Enemy Table results.

Find Group Bonus: Find your group bonus, if any, and apply it.

Attack: Fight the melee, using normal combat rules. As with the First Charge, the gamemaster may choose to use the Simple or the Long method.

Flight from Combat

While Engaged, knights may choose to flee rather than fight against bad odds.

To flee knights must attempt their Ride skill opposed to the enemy's Weapon skill.

Battle Flight Table

Critical = You escaped, get double shield protection if necessary

Success = you escaped undamaged

Partial Success = you escaped, but they struck you

Failure = you did not escape, and took damage

Fumble = you did not escape, and took damage, and dropped or broke your weapon

Surrender

Knights may surrender if in danger of being slain. It is customary for knights to accept surrender from other knights, and ransom them afterwards.

If Unhorsed This Round: If you were unhorsed this melee round you will begin next round Alone and On Foot.

Effects on Followers

Roll on the Followers Results Table each round to see what has happened to your followers. This affects your possible modifier if you lead only a small number of troops.

Retreat, Rout, and Pursuit

Some results of the Melee Unit Events Table have special results, as detailed here. They include Retreat, Rout, and Pursuit.

Retreat

Retreat indicates an orderly withdrawal of forces from the battle field. The armies will fight as they withdraw if necessary, usually with a designated rear guard unit sacrificing itself if necessary for the escape of the rest.

Battalions can be forced to retreat only on a roll of triple 5's or triple 2's.

Retreats are treated as part of normal battle. Units in retreat are likely to rally again and re-enter the battle.

Rout (by your battalion)

Rout indicates a panic withdrawal from the field. Soldiers, even knights and nobles, abandon the field and camp in absolute haste, often throwing away their equipment.

Rout can occur only on a roll of 3 or 18. Entire battalions rout at a time.

Knights whose battalions Rout have a choice of action depending on whether they are Engaged or Disengaged.

Disengaged knights may Escape, Run Away, or Stand.

Engaged knights may Run Away or Stand.

Escape — To Escape, attempt a Flight from Combat *without modifier.* This indicates that your knight saw what was going on, and got out before things got too difficult.

Run Away — Your knight is one of the majority who are running from the field. Attempt Flight from Combat, with the appropriate -15 modifier.

Stand — You are determined to stand and rally your unit, or die in the attempt. Fight a Melee round, as per usual Battle methods, with this special result:
Critical Success = your heroic stand stymies the enemy! The Battalion rallies! Get 100 Glory, and the attention of your leaders.

Pursuit

A statement of intent of Pursuit means that the enemy has routed, and that your knight is among those who have broken ranks to run them down.

Only knights who are mounted may pursue a mounted foe. Mounted knights pursuing dismounted foes get +5 to their roll. Men on foot may pursue dismounted foes.

First Pursuit Round: the first round of pursuit is like a battle. To pursue, a knight must:

- Make a Statement of Intent to Pursue.
- Roll his Weapon skill, as usual, modified.

This simulates chasing the enemy off the battlefield.

Subsequent Pursuit Rounds: Once the foe has fled, pursuit may continue. Now,

however, instead of melee it is like a hunt, and a Hunting roll is used instead of Melee weapons. No battle modifiers apply to the Hunting Roll.

Subsequent pursuit results are:

Pursuit Results Table
Critical Success = You found their camp. Add 2d6+2 £. booty. Add two more rounds of Pursuit Glory.
Success = You killed 1d6 more of them, and captured 1 more man. Add one round of Pursuit Glory.
Fail = You killed 1d6 more of them, add one round of Pursuit Glory. But you were also variously hurt, so take 1d6 damage without armor.
Fumble = you were ambushed! Take 6d6 damage from the surprise lance strike. Get no Pursuit Glory round.

After the Battle

Determine the Victor

Determine whether the battle was a clear victory, indecisive, or a loss for your side.

If the story has not determined the results, find modifiers, then roll on this table for the results.

Modifiers:

- A battalion on your side routed = +10
- Enemy battalion was routed = -10

Battle Results Table	
01-02 or less	Decisive Victory
03-18	Indecisive
19-20or more	Decisive Defeat

Count and Bury the dead

Burial of the dead is a major task after the battle. The losing side usually asks for a truce to bury their dead, and it is usually granted.

Tend the Wounded

Wounded who are too hurt to travel must be tended nearby. Others are taken by cart and wagon to cities and monasteries to be healed.

Many characters, including player knights, may need extensive time to recover. The army may march on to campaign, leaving them behind.

Determine Plunder

After a Decisive Victory the winners in the army collect Plunder. The amount of plunder for the winning side is:

Battle Plunder Table

size	*plunder*
small	1 palfrey, 1 cob, 1-2 £. in goods
medium	1 charger, 1-2 palfreys, 2-6 £. in goods
large	1-2 chargers, 2-4 palfreys, 5-10 £. in goods

Collect or Pay Ransoms

Negotiation for ransoms is carried on through the Heralds. Prisoners are listed with them, and the lists then taken to each side for confirmation. Alternatively, knights may be released on their own recognizance if they swear by their knighthood and honor to pay the ransom.

Payment usually comes several months after the prisoner's release. After all, he must return to his estates and raise the value, then convert it to cash and treasure to transfer.

Prisoners may be traded as well as ransomed. Thus if one of your band was captured, but you captured an enemy, you can normally trade one man for the other, neither collecting nor paying anything.

Calculate Glory

Glory for battles is determined by its size, and the number of rounds which the knight fought, and how well he did in the fight.

The procedure is to find the Basic Battle Glory, then multiply it by the other factors to find your total Battle Glory.

Size Of Battle

Glory shown is the amount of Glory per successful combat round. The First Charge is one Combat Round, and each Melee Round is one.

- Small = 15 Glory per round
- Medium = 30 Glory per round
- Large = 45 Glory per round

Results Multipliers

- Critical Success = x2
- Success = x1
- Failure, Fumble = x0.5
- Disengaged = x0.1

Victory Modifiers

- Your side won clearly = x2
- Indecisive = x1
- Your side lost clearly = x0.5

Other Modifiers

- You were outnumbered more than 2:1 = x1.5
- You were outnumber at 5:1 or more = x2

mation, but are with the group for better or worse. If the player has stated their character is attached, then the knight must *always* stay with the leader and do what the group does. To do otherwise is an act of desertion. The advantage is that attached knights usually get the leader/follower bonus to their skills, because they are in a group. Disadvantages are that individual knights do not get their own Battle roll during melee, nor do they have an opportunity to choose a target, or to leave the group to help friends.

Alone — Alone knights are still within their unit, but taking responsibility for their own actions. The advantage to being alone is that the knight controls his own fate and gets his own Battle roll results. The disadvantage is that the single knight must often fight multiple foes, perhaps without getting any help from other knights that round. This is reflected by a large negative modifier to the knight's Battle skill that round.

Engaged, Disengaged

In each Battle Round a knight is either Engaged (in close hand-to-hand combat) or Disengaged.

The Leader/Follower Bonus

Both leaders and followers in a battle may get an advantage for remaining close together. This applies to melee, but not to the First Charge.

The leader rolls 1d6, and he and his followers all get a bonus equal to the die roll if the number rolled is equal to or less than the number of followers. The bonus is added to their melee weapon roll. This indicates the number of riders who have stuck close together.

More than 6 followers gives a bonus to the d6 roll. Each follower more than 6 adds one to the die roll. Thus a leader with 9 followers gets a d6+3 modifier. A leader with 11 or more followers has a +6 while leading.

The maximum bonus attainable through Leader/Followers is +6.

Scenarios

Game play occurs when your characters interact with their environment, a situation, and each other.

SCENARIOS PROVIDE the elements of a story for your characters. A scenario includes the setting, gamemaster characters, and a potential plot to challenge or beguile the knights. Scenarios supply the interface between your imagination, your character, the setting, and the game.

The word "scenario" is the general word used for any kind of game event that can be experienced by players. This section introduces the basic concepts, types, and terms used in the creation of *Pendragon* scenarios. A complete Introductory Scenario is provided. Examples are also given for several sub-types of scenario: Solos, Adventures, and Stories.

You will need to refer to the "Chivalric Duties" chapter while using this chapter. The "Duties" chapter presents the recurring components of *Pendragon* scenarios: crucial but routine events such as visits to court or battles that the characters will experience many times. These events should occur often during the campaign, but not as the high point of a scenario.

The Introductory Scenario is a series of simple training sequences designed to help new gamemasters learn the game and teach new players at the same time.

Solos are designed for a single person, a player with no gamemaster. Several examples are given: Home Service, At the Crossroads, and Lost In the Woods.

Adventures are stories in which the player knights are the main participants. About half of the game play in a *Pendragon* campaign is spent on adventures, with the other half spent in courtly, romantic, family, and other interpersonal activity.

The Adventure of the White Horse is the sample given here.

The *Short Adventures* section provides the kernel of information for many more adventures. Material not provided must be filled in by the gamemaster, but these short adventures always include rather common activities, and although you will enjoy playing the activities out, there is no point in printing material here.

Stories are parts of the campaign which are taken directly from the on-going chronology of the Arthurian legend. They can be a basic source for *Pendragon* scenarios. Stories are individual events, but over time the individual scenes, adventures, encounters, and gossip about a single famous character create a longer tale. The gamemaster can use events in a story to create a scenario. Thus the players will witness, and perhaps participate in, some of the major events in the lives of other well-known Arthurian characters.

Given here are three stories, all occurring on the first year of play, 531: "Keeping Up with Sir Lancelot", "Meeting Sir Mordred", and "The Irish Tournament".

Introductory Scenario

PENDRAGON CONTAINS MANY innovative and unusual concepts. The game takes on its greatest depth of meaning and enjoyment when all of the rules are used. The game may seem intimidating and imposing; beginning gamemasters, especially, face a challenging task in mustering the courage to run a game. Even gamemasters with experience in other game systems may find aspects of *Pendragon* intimidating.

Here we present a suggested way to start your *Pendragon* campaign. It contains suggestions on running your campaign, additional background information, and an introductory adventure to get your *Pendragon* campaign started with the right spirit. The adventure acquaints players with the game and characters with their homeland.

It is important to time events so that they will be knighted at the end of the play session. Keep an eye on the clock and cut events short, if necessary, to perform this act.

Suggested Campaign Objectives

To start things off, be thinking of the following while you run this first scenario.

- teach dark age morals, illustrate the primary passions.
- introduce gamemaster characters.
- introduce Logres, the setting.
- witness some of the marvels of Britain.
- prepare to meet King Arthur.
- establish the player knights' initial power base.
- establish families.

Prepare Beforehand

Material components which gamemasters will need: this book, copies of the blank character sheet, copies of the four default knights, copies of the "Character Generation" chapter, copies of the Winter Phase section of the "Game Mechanics" chapter, copies of the Price List (see the "Wealth" chapter), pencils, d20's, d6's.

Immaterial components which gamemasters will need: energy and enthusiasm, a generous and helpful nature, a sense of fairness, a kind disposition, a modest and cooperative sense of ego, and courage to start.

Your First Players

Unless you come from an established gaming community getting game players may be difficult. Even in places dense with gaming enthusiasts, like colleges, a gaming group is often made up of strangers who may meet for no reason other than to game. The initial difficulty lies in getting everyone together for the first time.

The first place to find new gamers is among your friends. Presumably you have some common interests, and if someone shares your interest in literature and medieval panorama they may share your interest in participation through roleplaying games.

Brush up on what you will say to explain what the game is like. I suggest that you explain the game like this:

"*Pendragon* is a game where you make up imaginary characters who run around and do medieval things in King Arthur's realm. It is mostly talking back and forth. You tell me what you want your knight to do, then either I tell you what happens as a result, or you roll dice to see if it works. It is like playing Cops 'n' Robbers, but instead of saying "I got you" and "No you didn't" you roll dice. It is sort of like I am the producer of the movie and you are the actors, but you have the power to determine the script."

If they are willing to go along, you will have to get into some of the details of the game system and overall plan. Cover the broadest aspects: the Arthurian panorama and background, Glory, jousts, battles, chivalry, families, heraldry, and so on.

Do not expect them to read the rules before the first game. Encourage them to if they wish, but many players will be too intimated by the book to even attempt to play. Many of my best players have not read the rules of a game, and they therefore play their characters from the roles they take on, and trust the gamemaster and other players to interpret the game rules in precise situations where measurements are needed. Other players are what we call "rules lawyers" and insist upon scrutinizing every die roll for accuracy and sometimes delight in arguing over rule judgments. Your job as gamemaster is to balance both types of players, and everyone else in the game.

Prepare yourself by reviewing exactly what you will have to do. This is a training session for you as well as the players, but you must be at least one lesson ahead of them.

The adventures suggested below may be compressed or expanded according to your needs and those of your players. You might rush through several in one evening's session, then take several more to work out a single adventure. Play it by ear and time it so that the game moves from action to contemplation and back again.

Your First Talk

Explain you are new at this, that you have a fair grasp of what to do, and that you hope everyone can work together. Read the chapter entitled "What Your Character Knows" and explain the basics of the game setting, particularly these important areas:

- Knighthood
- The Feudal World
- The Universal Laws of Society
- The Christian Church
- Magic

You will have to keep talking to explain various things. Players will not wait for your instructions and will barrage you with many questions. Don't worry about this; have fun!

First Characters

This entire book is set up for new players. Be sure to go through the Character Generation system and be familiar with it yourself. You must answer questions which will come up during the process, even though it is recommended that your first shot at creating characters be to simply use the default knights provided, instead of using the designed method.

Give everyone a copy of the character sheet (see the back of the book for blank character sheets). Pass around copies of the default characters, and simply have the players copy their favorite characters' values onto the blank character sheets, without trying to actually generate characters completely.

As players create their characters, the gamemaster should be ready to lead them through confusion, and to talk, filling in details as necessary and starting to provide descriptive background of the people, places, and things used by characters. Start by talking about names: read the list of names out several times, and explain why frivolous names will spoil the game experience.

Urge everyone to think on how their character looks, and on what motivates their character. It is likely that someone will choose a bad knight. Let him, but warn him how his contemporaries feel about this, and that he may be killed for anti-social behavior.

Talk about the County of Salisbury (see the chapter entitled "Your Home." Remind everyone that the characters have known each other, more or less, during most of their lives. Help everyone work something out about their character which is interesting. Learning more about characters is an on-going process, especially through the first sessions.

Encourage the players to discuss their characters' previous history.

At the end of character generation everyone will have a character who has completed his training with excellent results, and at age 21, is a respected and experienced squire, fully anticipating being knighted soon.

Have everyone introduce their characters. To show them how to do it, introduce Sir Jaradan first, as follows.

A Day of Training

State that the squires are at Salisbury Castle. Show where it is on the map. Show the picture of the castle, and the Great Hall. Introduce the first gamemaster character of the game now. He is Sir Jaradan, the castellan of Vagon Castle and marshal to the Earl of Salisbury. He is in charge of training the best of the squires to be knights and directing their activities.

Sir Jaradan and the player characters go outside to the training grounds of the castle. It is springtime and the sun is shining already, though it is only early morning. The usual day's activity is martial practice and training, and today is no exception.

In this short sequence you will teach the resolution system and get the player started on the idea of roleplaying.

First Game System Explanation

Tell them they are going to practice their Lance skill, first using a simple wooden target and then against a quintain.

The target is a small wooden plate attached to a post. Success at this attack is by a simple unopposed d20 roll versus the character's Lance skill. Make sure everyone knows how to read the d20: equal or under = success.

Next they use the quintain. This is a vertical post with a rotating horizontal arm, one end of which has a shield and the other a rope and stone. Lance practice consists of charging against the quintain, striking the shield, and ducking the swinging rock as it comes around from the force of the blow.

Success at this is by using Lance, again unopposed and unmodified. Failure means they are thwacked, harmlessly, by the rock.

First Roleplaying

Be sure to ask everyone two things throughout play. First, *what they intend doing* when something occurs. Second, how their characters *feel* about their own and others' success or failure. For example, are they embarrassed if hit by the rock? Make sure they refer to their traits before they decide. Cruel characters might tease others, while modest characters might not mind. If anyone wants to roll a trait to see what they do, great. But no rolls are mandatory here.

A Horse Race

Next is a horse race. Characters will have many opportunities in the future to try to outrace each other, and this is the procedure which will be used.

Explain that they will use opposed Horsemanship rolls. Tell everyone to get their best (fastest) horse. It is probably their charger. It is possible that someone will choose a rouncy for personal reasons. Note the relative speeds of each horse.

Draw ten lines on a piece of paper. These are the steps which will measure relative distance travelled in the race. Basically, every successful Horsemanship roll will allow the riders to move ahead one space. A critical success will allow a movement of two spaces. Failure means that the rider falls back a space (remember, the ten lines are relative distance, not absolute). A fumble means the rider falls off and takes 1d6 damage (no armor), and falls two spaces behind.

If a horse is faster than the others, it will move one additional space ahead as well, no matter what the Horsemanship die roll result is. If there are three different horse speeds, then the faster will get this bonus to move ahead, and slowest will get a negative bonus and move backward.

The winner is the one who passes the goal first. A tie is possible.

Once the race is concluded, everyone can rest. It's noontime now. Encourage the players to voice how their characters feel. Speaking in character as Sir Jaradan, compliment those who did well, and gently tease or rebuke those who did poorly.

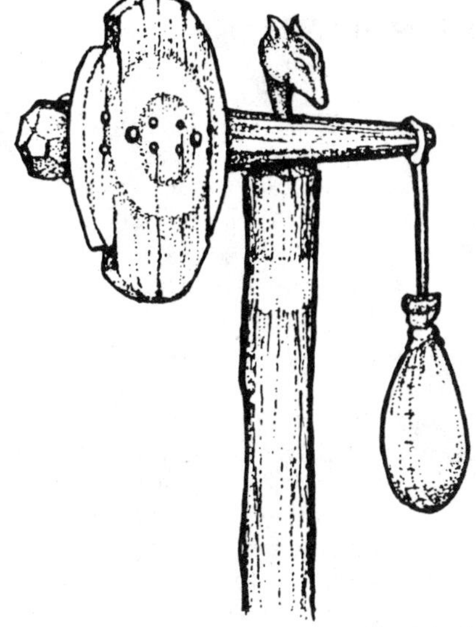

The quintain

Your First Adventure: A Hunt

Since Sir Jaradan is growing infirm he does not usually ride on ordinary missions: thus he will choose a leader from among the player characters after discussing the task at hand. Speak in character: begin your comments with "He says..."

Sir Jaradan says, "Men, we have need for your talents. Will you take on a small task for the good of the county?" Encourage the players to speak their answer aloud. If they are shy, tell them that Sir Jaradan smiles and says "Speak up, lad — don't be afraid to speak your mind!"

Let the players ask questions too. They may be from the players, directed to the gamemaster, or they may be from the characters, but these are usually directed at the gamemaster too. If it is something which the characters are likely to know then feel free to answer it. If it is not, then point the fact out and ask the player who the character is asking. If the character asks something which no one knows, then you need not answer.

By the same token, if the players do not know something which their characters know, it is the gamemaster's duty to inform them of it.

Sir Jaradan speaks. "The peasants have reported a man-eating bear in the west acres. I never heard of such a thing. It's probably a rabid dog. Even if it is a chipmunk but you must go and take care of it because they claim it is too dangerous for them to come and work the lord's fields." (He shakes his head ruefully).

A Joust

"Before you leave, I want everyone to joust until only one person is left. That person will act as leader for this hunt."

Explain that a joust is a non-lethal sport which uses blunt, breakable lances. Opponents use their Lance skills in opposed resolution: the higher success wins. The two first players, designated at random, joust. Do it slowly, leave the dice on the table after they have been rolled, and make sure everyone understand who won and why. By the time a leader is determined everyone ought to understand the mechanics.

The marshal congratulates the leader. "Go to Imber and ask for Old Garr, the priest. Any questions? Anyone?" Remind the players that their characters will not have time to ask anything later, except of local personnel.

The marshal asks, "Do you want to leave this afternoon or tomorrow morning? It is a half-day ride to Imber." Start them thinking in character.

Half of the job is for the gamemaster to propose questions to the players which they answer for their characters. The other half is talk and discussion, much of which may not be game-related. Just let them do as they wish, describe the passive events as well as you can, and keep asking questions when something exciting is happening.

A Short Journey

The gamemaster should open the book to the map of Salisbury and trace the route of travel from Sarum to Imber. Indicate the points of interest as they go. Be sure to note Amesbury, Stonehenge, and anyone's manor which they pass along the way.

The Village of Imber

Imber is a village at the boom of a valley of the down. Ask the players for Stewardship rolls. Success allows them to judge the quality of the village: large but poor. The fields around it are small, and judging by the hides stretched to dry much of the income of the village is from hunting. Rather than a stream, it has a spring pond. The mill is ox-driven.

Once they reach the town use Old Garr as your mouthpiece. He is the only priest for the couple hundred residents of Imber. Like many of this type, he is almost illiterate, having memorized several of the Latin verses he needs to know. He is the younger son of an obscure knight, living sinfully off the money he gets for his job as priest. He loves hunting, and will go along as guide, if the players supply a horse. Alas, they have no spare here at the village. Old Garr has a Hunting skill of 7, but is too old to fight.

Before the hunt begins, remind the players that their characters must remove their armor and wear appropriate hunting clothing (1 point of armor).

The Hunt

This hunt is a modified form of a longer format which will be given in the next *Pendragon* book, *Knights Adventurous*. It is cut down to include only the relevant material for this scenario. It teaches the primary game rules for the hunt. Use these rules for the Hunt Solo Scenario, as listed below, and for any hunts depicted without the use of *Knights Adventurous*.

Step 1. Preparation

A hunt is normally divided into segments of about an hour in length. A single day allows up to 6 segments in winter, 8 in spring and autumn, and 10 in summer. The gamemaster must decide on how long the player squires will have for this hunt (8 are suggested, since it is spring). Once the segments have elapsed, the hunt is over for the day.

During each hunting segment the hunters engage in many activities: mostly searching for tracks, finding the best way to ride through the brush, listening for sounds of the chase, and so on. Tracks and trails are fairly easily found, and pursued with the help of dogs and peasants.

Leaders and Followers: Some characters may not have much faith in their Hunting ability. They can choose to just follow someone else with a better Hunting value. The followers will not get to make a Hunt roll, but then they will not mislead the others, either, and will probably arrive on site for the kill.

Gamemaster Preparation: Draw about six parallel lines on a piece of paper. Put a marker for each participating character on the center line. This marks the spot where they begin. Each time someone fails a Hunting or other roll to overcome an obstacle, they fall one line behind. This way you can keep track of when the laggards catch up with the quarry. Note that this is quite similar to the method use in the Race, done earlier.

Step 2. Search

Finding game is not difficult in these wild forests – it is a matter of finding the right prey. Each character should make a Hunting roll to see if the dogs can find a trail. Old Garr, who knows the marks of the bear well, is able to point out a good spoor to start the trail, so there is a +5 modifier to the squires' Hunting skills for this initial roll. Success or critical indicates a trail was found by the character and any followers. Failure or fumble indicates that the character's marker is moved back one line. Try again next segment.

Old Garr will follow the character selected as leader during the joust. He is cautious, and makes no rolls himself.

Step 3. Chase!

For those characters and any followers who successfully hunted, the track of the bear is found and the horses spurred onward to thunder through the woods in pursuit. Each hunter must rely upon his own Hunting skill to keep on the track to the end, unless he is a follower. The bear will attempt to escape the hunters.

3A. Find Modifiers: This table gives a modifier for terrain which is subtracted from each character's Hunting skill value during the chase.

Hunting Terrain Modifiers

modifier	*terrain*
+5	Your home county
+4	Clear Ground, wastes
0	Forest
-3	Hilly

3B. Track: The bear hears the dogs and attempts to escape. He is a cunning beast with stealth above the ordinary.

Each player makes an opposed Hunting Roll, modified as above (+5 for your home county, 0 for forest), versus the bear's Avoidance value of 10 (rolled by the gamemaster).

Hunt Versus Avoidance Results Table

Winner, success or critical = You found the prey at the end of this segment. Move marker to last line and go to Step 5.

Loser, partial success = You are still on-trail. Move character up one line, cross off a segment. Try this step again next segment if the last line was not crossed. If so, go to Step 5.

Loser, failure = Move the character's marker back one line, cross off a segment. Obstacles block your way, go to Step 4.

Loser, fumble = You lost the trail. Move marker back two lines. Go back to Step 2.

Step 4. Overcome the Obstacles

Hunters who failed their Hunting roll were delayed by an obstacle. Roll on the following table.

Obstacles Table

d20	*obstacle*
01-02	Oops! You rousted the wrong animal! Roll on the standard Prey Table (below), ignoring results of 1, and deal with the creature you and your followers have encountered.
03-04	Jump a fallen tree: Horsemanship roll.
05-06	Jump a stream: Horsemanship roll.
07-10	Birds flushed underfoot: Horsemanship roll.
11-12	Thick brush: Horse's DEX roll.
13-14	Men shouting somewhere: Awareness.
15-16	Hidden ditch: Awareness.
17-18	An animal growls. Awareness roll.
19-20	A horn blasts somewhere: Awareness roll.

If the hunter can succeed with the required roll he overcomes this obstacle and is still on the trail. Go back to Step 3. If not, he is out of the hunt.

Normal Prey Table

d20	creature (Avoidance Roll)
01	Bear (7)
02-04	Boar (10)
05	Bull (5)
06-10	Red Deer (15)
11-17	Fallow Deer (18)
18-19	Wolf (10)
20	Special. Roll again on Special Creature Table below.

Special Creature Table

d20	creature
01-02	Giant (5)
03	Griffin (30*)
04	Hippogriff (30*)
05-07	Lion (10)
08	Manticore (10)
09-11	Panther (15)
12	Lesser Unicorn (25)
13-14	Greater Unicorn (15)
15	Wyrm (7)
16	Wyvern (30*)
17-20	Yale (10)

*flying creatures are extremely difficult to track.

5. The Kill

Once found, use the statistics for the Bear from the "Characters and Creatures" chapter. As noted before, this bear is more cunning than normal, and has an Avoidance value of 10, not 7.

5A. First Attack: The first character to arrive gets one free attack. You have drawn close enough to use the weapon of your choice against an unprepared beast, unopposed. Determine damage normally, remembering that the bear has hide and fat worth 6 points of armor.

If more than one squire arrives on the same segment, the character with the highest Movement Rate (or DEX) gets the first attack.

5B. Second Attack: If the bear lives, as many as three of the hunters may attempt a second attack while it tries to escape. This is an opposed roll, pitting your weapon skill roll versus its Avoidance roll. If several squires attack, it must divide 10 among the three, or ignore one or more.

Weapon Versus Avoidance Results Table

Winner, critical success = double damage, it will turn angrily and begin fighting next round if still conscious.

Winner, success = normal damage, it begins fighting next round unless hurt badly, in which case it will Avoid again.

Loser, partial success = it escapes. Go back to Step 3, with a +5 modifier.

Loser, failure = it escapes. Go back to Step 3.

Loser, fumble = it escapes. Go back to Step 3.

5C. Continue Melee: If the beast does not escape, it continues to fight or attempt Avoidance. Subsequent attacks are done as in a normal melee. A bear has little actual chance against several armed and mounted men, but might wreak great havoc among reckless beginning players. Remember that the characters have only 1 point of armor, not their usual 12.

If the bear escapes, a segment passes, and the characters must go back to Step 3.

Unless the bear escapes, the other squires will not arrive in time to see the kill. Glory gained for killing the bear is 10 for the creature, plus another 10 Glory for completing a ordinary but significant task. Divide 20 among the characters who killed the bear.

Back to Imber

A brief celebration occurs in the village when the characters return with their trophies. The bear is dead! Once the festivities are concluded, the characters rearm for the ride home.

Again, as always, ask the players how they feel about the events.

Another Encounter

On the way home the young squires encounter a band of bandits, caught red-handed beating up a farmer and stealing his cows. The farmer is known to the player squires and reminds them of it ("You have seen me at our lord's court many times! Help me!"). Ask the players if they know what their character's duty is, then state it if the players do not. Their duty is to aid their lord's peasant.

This is their first test of man-to-man combat, and a fairly sure win, since the characters are mounted and armored, and the bandits are on foot..

Use one bandit per squire. See the Bandit statistics in the "Characters and Creatures" chapter. They will stand and fight as long as half of them are still fighting. Then they will turn and run.

Be slow and patient with everyone to make sure they understand how the combat works. You, the gamemaster must train the players now, the way the marshal is trying to train the characters. When they have a chance to kill a helpless foe, ask them to determine their Merciful and Cruel traits, and go through the traits procedure. Cruel checks are gained by those who kill helpless or surrendered bandits. Tell them that their characters know that taking these types of outlaws as prisoners is usual. But they don't have to spare them.

After the fight the squires should return to court. Allow everyone to present their own tale to Sir Jaradan, who is pleased. Assign Glory as relevant. Each bandit killed or captured is equal to 10 points, and everyone gets another 10 points just for being along on this fight.

A Visit to Court

The squires, with a bear skin and possibly several bandits as prisoners, have ridden back to Sarum. If any bandits escaped, Sir Jaradan announces that the squires ought to report these bandits to their earl. If any bandit prisoners are present they will be brought along, too. This is a courtly, non-combat, part of the scenario, and the squires have a chance to mingle in High Society for a while. Use this opportunity to show what a higher standard of living is like.

Upon entering the bailey of the castle a squire and stable boys rush forward to take the horses. The player squires know to take their personal goods with them to the Great Hall, where Marshal Jaradan immediately leads them.

Your First Court Scene

Gamemasters should be familiar with the rituals of court activities. An essay in "Chivalric Duties" describes the process. First, the gamemaster should state the general setting, show the picture of the Great Hall from the chapter entitled

"Your Home," and describe what is different now: the court is in session, and in the illustration, it is not. During this period the gamemaster should stress courtly etiquette and fashion. Courtesy rolls may be appropriate.

Note that the porter, the man in charge of letting people through the door (the *port*) recognizes Jaradan immediately and treats him with great deference. After all, the Marshal is a very important man in this castle. Nonetheless, the Marshal and squires wait quietly in the back of the hall.

After only a short wait the herald calls forth Sir Jaradan. The marshal indicates the squires to come forward with him, and then explains recent events. If some bandits are alive they are dragged forth and turned over to the earl. He is pleased, and thanks the player characters for the service. The earl addresses the squires directly, asking how many bandits were killed, and being pleased with that result too. The earl then dismisses the squires, asks Sir Jaradan to remain with him, and goes on to the next matter of business. The squires are left to their own devices at court.

The squires can go about and mingle. The gamemaster should bring forth the important people of the county who will be active in the future (see "Your Home").

Let the characters meet people who are full of news, gossip, rumor, scandal, and tidbits of background information for upcoming adventures.

The squires will spend a lot of time in this castle and city. Urge them to wander around a little bit. Some of the possible pursuits include:

- Visit the City. Get to know the slick city ways of the merchants. See big buildings, the biggest of which is the cathedral. Visit the market – the gamemaster should hand out photocopies of the price lists from the "Wealth" chapter.
- Visit the Castle. This is a first-class, very modern example of the castle-builder's art. Take the time to educate players and characters on the details to show reasons why castles are so invincible.
- Heiresses. An important sideshow at the castle is the opportunity to view, from a suitable distance, the heiresses whose husbands are to be chosen by the earl. Crudely said, they are the prizes for whoever pleases the earl the most. Until then, the earl collects the revenues from their lands. Other available women, the younger daughters of knights, serve as ladies in waiting to the Countess and other noble ladies. They are the social equivalent of the player characters at this point. The five most eligible heiresses are listed in the chapter about your home.

In the evening the squires join in the meal in the hall. They sit at the far end, away from the earl's table, of course. They receive good fare, but not as good as the knights who sit closer to the earl.

Earl Robert creates a new knight

Knighthood

That night, after dinner, Earl Robert announces that he has decided to grant knighthood to those deserving it, so that they can serve him. He asks the men of his court who are the available candidates, and one of those asked is the marshal, who sits at the high table near the earl. Of course, the player characters are put forward.

The earl agrees, and calls the characters forward to ask them if they feel they are ready to become knights. They should agree. If not, they can continue play as squires later. The earl announces that next day the ceremonies will begin.

The Knighting Ceremony

For most knights, the ceremony of knighthood is the most important event of their career. Extraordinary Glory will be gained, and a solemn oath spoken.

Refer to the nearby boxed article on "The Knighting Ceremony". Explain the basic form of the ceremony. Explain that the characters, as vassal knights, will simultaneously be invested with the rights to their inheritance.

✣ The Knighting Ceremony ✣

INITIATION INTO knighthood is a solemn occasion which will occur only once for each knight. Your gamemaster will probably conduct a game session when new characters are knighted so that you can speak their oath aloud during play.

Several men are often knighted at the same time. In that case, the order in which they are called forth depends upon the importance of their fathers. The gamemaster determines precedence.

The ceremony is always done with full panoply. This means the lord sits upon his high seat or throne, banners are displayed, courtiers are present in their best clothes, and heralds make announcements.

Herald: "[Name of candidate], come forth and kneel before the throne." Sword, armor, shield, and spurs are placed nearby.

Herald [reads]: "Be it known to all men that I, [name of noble] am minded to raise [name of candidate] by virtue of his honor, loyalty, valor, and skill at arms, to the high rank of knighthood."

Herald [to candidate]: "[Name], do you swear and acknowledge [noble] to be your true and lawful liege?"

Candidate: answer affirmatively.

Herald: "Do you swear fealty to [king of land], to defend and obey him until he depart the throne, or death shall take you?"

Candidate: answer affirmatively.

[Noble rises, goes to candidate.]

Noble: "Let this be the last blow you receive without just recourse." [The Noble delivers the coulee and strikes the knight across the face or on the shoulder, sometimes hard enough to knock the man down. The candidate then kneels before his liege with hands palm-to-palm and raised. The Noble places his hands over the knight's.]

Herald [to candidate]: "Repeat after me, 'I, [name], do solemnly swear and pledge my sword to [noble], my liege, to defend and obey him until he depart the throne or death shall take me, and to uphold the honor of knighthood.'"

Candidate: repeats, using his own name.

Noble: "And I, for my part, do swear to defend and honor [candidate] as befits a true knight." [The noble then receives the sword and taps the candidate lightly on both shoulders with the sword.] "I dub thee Sir [name]. Receive now your spurs [receives spurs], your right to suitable arms [receives shield], and take this, my sword [girds on sword], to your side to serve and defend me well.
"Arise, Sir Knight."

Ceremonial Flourishes

In addition to the standard knighthood ceremony, there are sometimes additional ceremonies which may be added by regional custom or by the desires of the lord.

Additional Christian Ritual

Religious lords may use a more elaborate ceremony. Typically, the knight spends the night preceding his ceremony in a vigil of prayer and contemplation. The sword, armor, coat of arms, and spurs which he will wear as a knight are placed upon the altar to receive a blessing from God or the knight's favorite saint. Blessings are bestowed by a priest or bishop, and the knight makes further oaths to support the church.

In this ritual the candidate may be dressed in special clothing which symbolized his future as a knight. In such cases his white overtunic symbolizes purity; his black tunic, hose, and shoes denote death; a red cloak indicates blood (both that which may be shed and that which runs in a nobleman's veins); and the white belt denotes the chastity of a good Christian man.

The Leap

Many lands follow an informal ritual held immediately after the knighting ceremony is concluded. The new knight, armed and armored, dashes outside and leaps into the saddle. If he makes it into the saddle, the knight is praised and honored, but if he misses, then everyone laughs. No other meaning is attached to the rite.

In *Pendragon* some lords follow this custom. To see if your character is successful, roll d20. If the number rolled is equal to or less than your character's DEX, he is successful and earns an additional 10 points of Glory.

Short Ceremony

Knighting may also occur without all the pomp and ceremony. This ceremony, for instance, might be used on a battlefield to instantly promote someone.

Lord: "Kneel before me, [name of candidate]." [Candidate kneels.] "Do you acknowledge me as your true and rightful liege?"

Candidate: answer affirmatively.

Lord: "Do you pledge fealty to me, and swear your sword to me, to be forever at my service?"

Candidate: answer affirmatively.

Lord: [Takes sword from candidate] "Then I dub thee Sir [name], and return this, my sword, to you to be wielded in my name. Arise, Sir Knight."

The court of Salisbury is Christian, so start with the vigil (see "Additional Christian Ritual" in the nearby box). Ask the players whether their characters are really trying to pray, or if they are just going through the motions. Ask for Religion (Christian) and Piety rolls. Energetic rolls are useful as the night passes to see whether the candidates stay awake.

During the ceremony, insist that the players speak the oath of knighthood for their characters, and describe what is happening to them in some detail. Many knightings will be performed later, but this first one is always important. Try to do as well as possible by reading the script, spoken here by an anonymous herald, and by Earl Robert, the lord.

Be sure to use the Leap option. It is good for a little bit of Glory, and a few laughs.

For the moment, the characters are the center of attention, radiant in the splendor of their new knighthood. Men will offer respect, women perhaps more. Allow everyone to make the best of it, with opportunity for behavior checks in almost whatever trait they wish.

A New Year

If there is time, continue the session by starting a new year. Otherwise, begin the next game session with the Winter Phase. Hand out copies of the Winter Phase section of the book and read through it word by word, if necessary, to help everyone see how to do it.

The characters have gained at least 1000 points of Glory over the previous year, and will now receive a bonus point. Explain that gaining a bonus point is a very rare and important occurrence, seldom repeated: ordinary knights who simply perform routine duties may never gain another bonus point during their whole careers. Suggest that they use the bonus point on something that cannot be increased easily (like SIZ, or a skill above 15, or a trait or passion).

Explain that the process just completed denotes the passage of a game year and the beginning of a new one. Remind them that many game years will pass during their characters' careers.

Further Adventures

Continue the new year with the characters travelling around their county, and also exploring the nearby lands. The exploration of Logres is a regular theme of this phase of the campaign. Let characters get to know the noblemen who are important, and meet other gamemaster characters of interest.

Insert the various Short Adventures below where appropriate in your campaign, interspersed between skirmishes, visits to court, weddings, and so forth. They are typical of the types of smaller adventures which characters will meet throughout their lives. The short adventure especially suited to beginning players is "The Skirmish at Allington" below.

Your campaign has begun. Congratulations!

Adventure of the Skirmish of Allington: Sir Gondrins, Lord of Uffington and only son of the earl, regularly rides patrol around the lands of Salisbury. The player characters must accompany him on patrol. This familiarizes the players with the setting, and gives a practical idea of the scale of the county.

When the patrol rides in the east, travel along the Bourne valley and point out the manors every mile or so along it. Note that these do not show up on the main maps, but such settlements are common along most of the rivers of Logres. Note which, if any, of the characters' manors are along the Bourne.

While on patrol along the Bourne valley a young man mounted on a pony comes galloping to the young lord and delivers his message breathlessly. Knights are raiding nearby! Without hearing more Sir Gondrins orders his men to prepare for battle.

This will introduce the players to knight versus knight combat. This is a much more dangerous prospect than fighting bears or poorly armed bandits. Combat is an important facet of play so teach it carefully. Play it slowly, make sure people understand what is going on, and keep events simple the first time.

At the end of the battle the knights know that a neighboring lord, the steward of Levcomagus, led this raid. He is an enemy of the earl's family, and perhaps of the player characters now as well.

Solos

Solo scenarios have several uses:

Additional Experience. These provide relatively painless ways to try to get experience checks for some of the traits or skills.

Previous Experience. These scenarios can supplement the Previous Experience section of character generation, with gamemaster approval. You might want a character to be older than 21 years, and a solo scenario adds more interest and history to a new character than the standard character generation system can offer.

Compensatory Play. Maybe your character missed a couple of games and you want to learn what he did while gone. Alternatively, your character might have chosen not to participate in an event or adventure, and is "Out of the Story". These scenarios offer something for the player and character to do while the rest of the game continues.

Private Business. Some things are done primarily in private – specifically the practice of Romance.

Several types of common solo experiences are given here:

Your Own Land. This tells what you do when you are spending your time taking care of your manor and other property.

Vassal Service. Knights spend a fair amount of their time doing work for their lord, and this solo tells you what you did on that service.

At the Crossroads. Knights in the stories spend a surprising amount of time idling away the weeks by waiting at a crossroad, a bridge, or ford and jousting "for love" with every knight who comes along. This solo allows that activity.

Lost In the Woods. This is the most-often invoked activity when someone is "Out of the Story." Gamemasters should request that players use this solo whenever they refuse to have their characters participate. Such players can go through the Lost In the Woods solo, rather than sitting with nothing to do while the other players continue on.

Romance. Pursuit of love is a private business, and this solo tells what to do and how to do it.

Your Own Land

Knights who own their own land also spend time on it, doing all of the things which land lords and farmers must do.

Short Form: For spending all his time on his lands a vassal knight gets experience checks to Intrigue, Stewardship, Folk Lore, and Just or Arbitrary at player option. The long form follows:

A. Income

Determine annual modifiers:

Annual Income Modifier Table

d6	*type of year*
01	Terrible.* Blight, drought, etc.
02	Bad*
03-04	Normal
05	Good
06	Excellent

* indicates that the result has an effect on your knight: see B3, below.

B. Usual Events

B1. Lord Visits: Get Roll in Intrigue.

B2. Review the estate: Get a Roll in Folk Lore.

*B3. In Poor Years (only for * above):* Roll Stewardship. If successful, enough money and grain was conserved to maintain health and status. If failed, the knight is Poor, unless he comes up with some other way to pay his maintenance costs.

B4. Sit in Judgement: Roll 2d6 twice to find contestants in the argument. The first is the *plaintiff* who makes the complaint, the second is the *defendant*, who must defend himself against the claim.

Common Court Participants Table

2d6	result
01	a rich farmer, who offers you 2£. to settle for him
02	the priest
03	a rich farmer, who offers you 1£. to settle for him
04	a poor old widow
05	a peddlar
06-08	a farmer
09	a tradesman (blacksmith, cooper, carpenter, miller, tanner)
10	a poor farmer
11	an attractive and flirtatious widow
12	a childhood friend, who offers you 1£. "to help you think."

Next, find out what they are arguing about: roll 1d20 to find dispute.

Dispute Table

d20	dispute
01	ownership of a cow
02	ownership of a pig
03	ownership of an ox
04	time to use the plow
05	unpaid debt
06-08	exchange of verbal insults
09-12	a brawl
13	a knifing
14-15	theft of petty property
16	theft of real property
17	something about a wife...
18-19	something about a daughter...
20	a killing

You can either:
Choose a party and decide in their favor, and collect the promised reward, getting an Arbitrary check;
or
Attempt a Just/Arbitrary roll.

Glory: Ordinary activities get no Glory, although the mere act of holding land always get 1 point of Glory per £. of income. Thus a vassal knight's manor gets 6£. per year.

Vassal Service

Vassal service includes all the things vassals must do for their lord: standing guard at castles or manors, riding the borders, participating in hunts, giving advice, and otherwise performing the knight's business.

1. Events

Find out which event, among all the things done, was of significant interest this year. Make one roll. Checks received for traits are at player choice.

Knight Home Service Table

d20	service performed
01-10	garrison
11-14	border patrol
15-16	escort someone to nearby place
17	escort someone far away
18	participate in a local tournament
19	battle
20	siege

Garrison: Check to Awareness, Intrigue.

Border patrol: Check Horsemanship, Awareness, Merciful/Cruel, Prudent/Reckless, Trusting/Suspicious.

Escort someone to nearby place: Check Horsemanship, Courtesy, Intrigue, Temperate/Indulgent.

Escort someone far away: Checks to Courtesy, Intrigue, Awareness, Horsemanship, Temperate/Indulgent, Trusting/Suspicious.

Participate in a tournament: Checks to Lance, Sword, (or other best weapon), Awareness, Horsemanship, Forgiving/Vengeful, Merciful/Cruel, Modest/Proud, Prudent/Reckless, Temperate/Indulgent.

Battle: Raiders attacked the fief, and your character engaged in a small battle or siege as a leader. Go to 2.

2. Battle

2A. Discover Battle Results: Roll on the Random Battle Results Table to find result and modifier.

Random Battle Results Table

This table determines the result of all the possible modifiers to the battle. Apply the result as a modifier to the knight's Battle skill value.

d20	results
01	Brilliant leadership and prowess, a great victory! +10. (Siege = +5)
02-03	Overwhelming victory! +7 (Siege = +2)
04-05	Victory! +5 (Siege = 0)
06-08	Contested victory. +3 (Siege = -5)
09-12	Draw. +/-0 (Siege = -10)
13-15	Contested defeat. -3 (Siege = -15)
16-17	Routed! -10 (Siege = -20)
18-19	Major disaster! -15 (Siege = -20)
20	Utter disaster. -20. (Siege = -20)

2B. Individual Fate: Bypass the First Charge, and fight a round of Melee, as per normal Battle rules. Your character is a leader. Ignore all other options and consider it a 1:1 fight.

If your character is killed, ignore the result and presume instead that he received a Major Wound, but survived. *Pendragon* does not believe in killing player knights out-of-game.

3. Glory

Normal Glory is gained for participating in a local tournament, a round of a small battle, and so on. See the "Glory and Ambitions" chapter. Any other activity gets 15 points.

A Hunt

1. Preparation

Refer to the Introductory Scenario for the basic pattern of a hunt, and the relevant tables needed below. You have 6 hunting segments to find prey.

2. Search for Prey

You have found a trail or spoor. Roll on Normal Prey Table. Determine Avoidance skill value. See the "Characters and Creatures" chapter for attributes.

3. Chase!

3A. Find Modifiers: You are in your home county. Roll 1d6, where any result but 1 indicates forest, and a 1 indicates open terrain.

3B. Attempt Hunting Roll, modified, versus prey's Avoidance Roll. Check the Hunting vs. Avoidance Results Table.

4. Overcome the Obstacles.

Roll on Obstacle Table. Success = continue Chase. Go back to 3. Failure = lost trail. Go back to 2.

5. The Kill

5A. Get 1 free attack.

5B. Attempt second attack versus its Avoidance roll. If your attack wins, it will turn and fight. If not, it escapes into the woods. Cross off a segment, go back to 2.

The Lover's Solo

Fine Amor is a long process for a knight, but one surely worthy of his efforts to improve the world. Success is evasive, and usually takes years to accomplish, if ever. However, perseverance through suffering is one of the virtues of this kind of love, and the Glory gained grows with time.

This side plot is designed so that it can be done solo, over the winter, in secret from the other players. It is used to determine success in a progressive *fine amor* carried on with a nonplayed character. This does not mean the events should be kept secret from the gamemaster, for the results should always be reported in case he can use it as part of his campaign. But some players can be allowed to perform this on their own without his supervision.

The same process can be used to court a woman to become a wife.

STEP 1: Passionate declaration of love

The player must tell the gamemaster, perhaps by secret note, that his character wishes to declare love, in private, to a lady. Determine the strength of the passion for both characters, as detailed earlier and repeated here:

Starting Amor (Individual) passion = 3d6

Possible Modifiers (Maximum =+10):

- She (or he) Flirted successfully = +1d3
- She is an Heiress = +1 per 1£. annual income
- She (or he) is Famous = +1 per 1000 Glory
- Stunning Beauty = +1 per point over 20
- She brought him back from the brink of death = +6
- He saved her from a dire fate = +6
- She/he is an enemy = –1 per Hate

Because one important factor in the love game is secrecy, it may suffice to just write in Amor (Individual) for a while. Thus other knights will know he is courting someone on the sly, but not exactly who.

If the knight has one particular lady in mind, the player ought to write her name down someplace on his character sheet. She might be a well-known gamemaster character, perhaps an heiress or maybe even a Queen.

Step 2: Virtuous rejection by the lady

The Amor is always reluctant. Figure her Reluctance Factor, which is the length of time which she is willing to resist, even if she has been favorably impressed.

Starting Reluctance = 20 minus her Amor (Individual) for him, if any.

Possible Modifiers: If her Chastity is greater than 15 = +5. From this point on it is a matter of chipping away at her reluctance through flattery, gifts, and performance of deeds.

Step 3: Wooing, by proof of deeds

Each winter, when the knight and his lover are together (or if they spent considerable time, perhaps non-played time, together during the year) the wooing may proceed.

3A. Gift, and Approach: Each Winter the knight must give the lady a gift worth at least 1£., and make a successful Amor (Lady) to get her attention. Failure at the roll here ends the attempt and no further action on this Amor may be attempted this year. No Glory is gained.

If successful, she pays attention and then imposes a task. (Go to 3B.)

3B. A Task Imposed: She imposes a task. During this stage relatively simple tasks are requested. Roll 1d6+6 to get the difficulty of the task imposed. Some samples of the types of difficulties for different levels are given in the Task Table below.

3C. Attempt the Task: The knight then attempts to perform the task. This is done by refering to the Lover's Task Table below. This gives a deed to be done, and an appropriate skill to use.

To succeed, subtract the difficulty of the task from the knight's appropriate skill or Trait value, and attempt a d20 roll.

Success indicates that he satisfied her. Each successful attempt gets:

- Increased Friendliness. Her Reluctance Factor is reduced by 1 point. With a Critical Success roll here, Reluctance Factor is reduced by 3.
- Increased Glory. Each successful attempt gets increasing amounts of Glory equal to a multiple of 50. The first success gains 50 Glory, and each subsequent success gets an additional 50 points. Thus the third success gets 150, the sixth 300, and the tenth gets 500 by which time, incidentally, a total of 3,200 Glory has been earned.

Increased Familiarity. At successive stages of success the lady allows her lover more liberties: to address her affectionately, to kiss the hem of her dress, her hand, her arm, receive a hug, to receive a little kiss on his forehead, rest his head on her lap, and so on. When the last point of resistance is overcome at this stage she may allow her lover a soulful, lip-to-lip kiss.

3D. Continue the Process: This same process is followed each winter phase. When only 3 Reluctance points remain, go to the next step.

Lover's Task Table

This table gives an idea of the type of deeds performed to reach the Difficulty Factor shown. (In parentheses are the rolls whose success indicates that the task was overcome.)

Difficulty 1: sit around, sighing and looking moonstruck (roll Amor, again)

Difficulty 2: make her smile (roll Flirting).

Difficulty 3: get some fresh flowers from far away (Roll both Energetic, Horsemanship)

Difficulty 4-5: sing a pleasant song, which surprises her in the garden (roll Singing)

Difficulty 6-7: recite a traditional love poem at court (Roll Orate)

Difficulty 8-9: create an original love poem at court (Roll Compose)

Difficulty 10-11: be seen pacing the ramparts late at night (Roll Energetic, Amor)

Difficulty 12-13: carry her favor at a tournament and win prize of Champion (go to "Tournament" scenario)

Difficulty 14-15: recite a personal love poem at court (roll successful Compose, Orate)

Difficulty 16-17: recite a love poem addressed to the lover, but disguised (roll successful Compose, Deceitful)

Difficulty 18: joust with all strangers for a day (go to "At the Crossroads" solo)

Difficulty 19: fight a boar, without armor (play out combat)

Difficulty 20+: enter a tournament, and fight in every event (roll successful Tourney, Lance, and best weapon)

The gamemaster is encouraged to add other tasks to this list.

3D. More difficult deeds:
This second stage of deeds begins when the lady's Reluctance is equal to 3, and continues to her submission.

3E. Gift, and Approach: As above.

3F. A Task Imposed: The lady now selects a more difficult task to be performed. This is equal to 2d6+6.

3G. Attempt the Task: As above.

3H. Collect Rewards: Successes at this stage lead towards more liberties. During this stage the lady will allow her lover to lick her lips, to whisper softly into her ear, to touch her ears with his lips, to feel her breasts, to place his tongue into her mouth, to lick her neck, to fondle her naked breasts, and kiss them.

When all the Reluctance has been erased, go to Step 4.

Step 4: Consummation

If this has been a wooing, the lady admits her deep and abiding love, then agrees to marry her suitor.

If this has been Amor, the lady sees the light. Ah, sweet success, bliss and pleasure. The love is joined on all planes. The passion changes from Amor (individual) to Love (amor). It is still secret. See the "Ideals and Passions" chapter for more information. Stop and look back and compute the Glory acquired in this quest. Was it not worth it?

(Go to step 5.)

Step 5: Subterfuge and troubles

Now that the lovers are in accord, they must keep their burning desire a secret. This is not easy since their natural desire is to be together, and she is usually married.

5A. Determine Discovery Factor

Starting Discovery Factor = 1d6 + husband's Suspicious Trait.

Modifiers to Discovery Factor:
+1 per year's duration of the successful affair.

Sample Discovery Factors

This table gives some idea of the seriousness of the efforts towards discovery by the husband, and the kind of outside influence that can occur. Increased factors indicate more severe exposure.

factor	*possible events*
4-5	husband discovers gifts from someone else.
6-7	husband has seen longing glances too many times.
8-11	someone is following you!
12-13	overeager lovers slip up in public.
14-15	meddlesome busybody interference.
16	consistent malicious gossip.
17	spiteful maids expose their knowledge.
18	a deliberate trap is set to catch lovers.

5B. Attempt Consummation: Roll Love (Amor) minus Discovery Factor. Success, go to 5C. Failure, go to Step 6.

5C. Collect Rewards: Besides the normal pleasures of love, for each year of a successful, undiscovered affair, the lovers each get 50 Glory.

Step 6: Exposure, shame

Her husband? Oh, him! The lovers have been discovered, exposed, or otherwise caught.

Exposure Results Table

Roll 1d20 to find his reaction:

01	wants to fight to the death.
02	will try to strip the knight of his rank.
03-05	will publicly shame knight, exile denounced wife.
06-10	will seek to exile knight without punishment, beat wife.
11-18	will privately threaten knight, and forgive wife.
19	will privately threaten knight, denounce and exile wife.
20	nothing. He doesn't like women anyway.

Step 7: Pregnancy? and other complications

Be sure to check whether the lady becomes pregnant or not over each winter, especially after consummation (see the "Winter Phase" section). Her resultant child may be her lover's or her husband's. Could she have more than one lover? Oh, what tangled webs love and genetics weaves...

Where all of this leads is up to the players, gamemaster, and flavor of the campaign. It is quite possible that the lover, his beloved, and her husband all neatly forget it now that it is over. Perhaps he harbors a secret grudge. Maybe she doesn't really want to end it. There is no end to the intrigue...

At the Crossroads

Arthurian stories are full of encounters with knights who are waiting at a road crossing, ford, or bridge to joust with any and all comers. This duty is often self-imposed to gain the knight some Glory. Sometimes it is imposed by a lady.

This set of tables is designed to make such duty easy for the players to perform. Such activities might be done completely solo by a player during a year in which the character did not actively participate in the active campaign. Alter-

nately, a gamemaster can use these to determine which knights might be at a crossroads encountered during play.

Various sections of the *Pendragon* game are necessary to use this system.

Step 1: Type of Road

The types of road will determine the amount of traffic, and hence the number of opponents. If one (or both) of the roads is a Royal or Trade Road, then use the Trade Road Encounter column. If both are paths, use the Path column. All others use the Road Encounter Column.

Step 2: Encounters

Determine the number of encounters. Roll 1d20 each month to see how many opponents pass by.

Crossroads Encounter Table (number of opponents)

d20	*Trade Road*	*Road*	*Path*
1	3	2	1
2	4	2	1
3	5	3	1
4	5	4	1
5	8	4	2
6	10	4	2
7	10	5	2
8	10	5	2
9	10	5	3
10	12	6	3
11	12	6	3
12	14	6	4
13	14	7	4
14	15	7	4
15	15	7	5
16	16	8	5
17	17	8	5
18	18	9	6
19	19	10	6
20	20	10	7

Step 3: Opponent Quality

Determine quality of opponent knights. For each opponent, roll 1d6 on this table, and refer to the "Characters and Creatures" chapter.

Quality of Knight Table

d6	*result*
1	Young
2-3	Ordinary
4	Notable
5	Famous
6	Special, roll again on Special Opponent Table

Special Opponent Table

d6	*result*
1	Enemy Knight, roll again for quality
2-3	Bandits (1d6+1)
4	Saxon war party (1d6+1)
5	Pict War party (1D6+2)
6	Extraordinary Knight, roll again on table below.

Extraordinary Knight Table

d6	*result*
1	Lancelot
2	Lamorak
3	Gawaine
4	Ywaine
5	Bors de Ganis*
6	Kay the Seneschal*

* Use standard Extraordinary Knight attributes as listed in the "Characters and Creatures" chapter.

Bandits: Bandits will attack to capture the knight for ransom. If captured, they can be sold into serfdom (1 £ each).

Saxon Raiders: These foes will try to kill the knight. If captured, they can be sold into serfdom (1 £ each).

Pict War Party: These foes will try to kill the knight. If captured, they can be sold into serfdom (1 £ each).

Enemy Knight: This knight is, or will become, a personal foe of the jouster. He fights to capture for ransom. If you player character has no permanent foes then make up a name, or ask the gamemaster for one.

Step 4: Fight

The solitaire player must make the Lance rolls for both his character and the opponent. Remember to keep track of wins and losses, damage, and of Glory gained each time.

Each opponent is fought separately and successively. If the player character is wounded, captured, or loses all his horses then the rest of the month will be affected.

When healing, each week subtracts 5 from the number of knights not yet encountered. For instance, a character on a trade road rolls a 12, thus expecting to fight 14 enemies that month. But if the first one wounds him badly enough to require 2 weeks healing, the player must subtract 10 from 13. After recovery he would then encounter only 3 more opponents; remember that he already fought one.

Victorious jousters who release their opponents only for ransom will collect the money in 2d6 months. See the "Wealth" chapter. Characters may keep their defeated opponents' warhorse, armor, and weapons if they wish, without incurring a Selfish check. However, returning the equipment at least half the time will get a Generous Check.

Lost in the Woods

Most of Britain is wooded. This table can be used as a guide to wandering in unknown forests. It can also be used as a compensatory solitaire. Characters will often find themselves departing the company of the other characters and going off on their own, out of the game. This little chart can be used as a solo in such cases.

Step 1. Each day, roll on the Woodland Encounter Table until a 20 is rolled, whereupon the character can find his way home again. If modifiers are applied, any number less than 1 equals one, and any number greater than 20 equals 20.

Step 2. Each roll is one day of wandering. Keep track of the number of rolls.

We assume that the knight has some food, and is able to feed himself with hunting and gathering as he goes. He also stops to feed his horse, perhaps to pray, and so on.

Lost In The Woods Encounter Table

d20	result
01-05	Irrevocably lost, wandering hopelessly without encounter.
06	Find a shrine. Attempt Piety, success gets a +2 modifier for next roll.
07-08	Bandits. See Bandits, below.
09-10	Wild animal encountered. See Wild Animal Table.
11-13	Unfriendly Village. Subtract 5 from your next roll.
14-16	Friendly village. +5 to your next roll.
17	Hermit found. +5 to next roll.
18-19	Manor Found. See Manor Encounter Table.
20	You have reached a familiar area, and can find you way home now without further difficulty.

Bandits: Fight against 1d6 bandits. They are desperate and foolish and attack with intent to kill or capture. The knight must fight them.

The bandits will fight until half of them have been killed or made unconscious. This constitutes a successful encounter against them. If successful, the knight gets 1d20 pence.

If unsuccessful the knight will be killed or captured. If captured, he can be ransomed. He will be stripped of all equipment and held prisoner until winter, when his ransom will have been paid by the liege lord. After collecting ransom the bandits will take him to the nearest road and let him go.

Wild Animal Table: These are all hostile beasts which will attack the knight. Players must fight it out, acting both the part of the knight and of the animal.

Wild Animal Encounter Table

d6	hostile animal
1	bear
2	boar
3	lion
4-5	bull
6	small giant

Manor Encounters: These are generic encounters. In a solo game you may wish to elaborate upon these individuals, making friends or enemies for the future. In a normal, fill-in type of adventure they are of less consequence and should not be elaborated upon.

Manor Encounter Table

d6	result
1-2	Friendly manor; Add 10 to next d20 roll
3-4	Jousting knight; Knight must joust, then treat as Friendly Manor.
5-6	Hostile knight; Fight to the death! Success means the knight gets no modifier to the next d20 roll.

ADVENTURES

Adventures are challenges or tests that follow a standard format. Here I offer two versions of a sample adventure, the Adventure of the White Horse, with varying amounts of detail. The format for each version is the same. The short, outline version is given here first, followed by a longer version that shows beginning gamemasters the type of work needed to expand an outline into a complete adventure.

The remaining adventures in the book are all in the short, outline form. Gamemasters should create an outline like the ones here for any adventures they prepare.

Note that the short form of the White Horse is slightly different in plot from the longer form, which contains more possibilities and dialogue.

The standard adventure format I recommend is as follows:

Title: This is always preceded by the words "The Adventure of" and gives a convenient title of the event to add to the character history (on the character sheet back).

Time: Some adventures cannot begin before a certain date or event, in which case this entry gives relevant facts. Most scenarios can occur any time, and thus have no "Time" entry.

Setting: Sometimes this is very specific, sometimes dependent on variables, and sometimes irrelevant.

Problem: A synopsis of the problem or challenge to be overcome is given.

Characters: Gamemaster characters who are important or likely to be used are given here, either in a verbal synopsis or with attributes, as is necessary.

Secrets: Things are not always what they seem, or sometimes critical information is not publicly known. The gamemaster must figure out how to divulge this information, according to the capacities of his players.

Solutions: Possible solutions are given here. Often players will discover or create their own solutions.

Glory: Glory awards are listed here.

Afterwards: Further events may ensue, or a legacy be left.

The Adventure of THE WHITE HORSE *(Short Form)*

Problem: The players have an opportunity to view or participate in an unusual, magical event: a Horse Blessing. However, they have been misled about the location, and must race to the right place. At least one Horsemanship roll out of three tries is needed for success, and the horses will become exhausted by the end. Once there, they are tested by a priestess to see if they are worthy of the blessing.

Several events occur to slow the knights on their race. These include: temptations from pagan celebrants (roll Temperate and Chaste to pass by); a chance to pursue an exotic creature, the Red Stag (move to a separate adventure); and a challenge from a jousting knight (Notable) that tires the knights, forcing a challenge to the character's willpower (roll Energetic to avoid sleep and missing the adventure).

Settings: The White Horse Vale; Salisbury Plain; Westbury Vale; the magical Plain of Emerald and Epona's Hill.

Characters: The Knight of the Old Way, Father Peter, the jousting knights, Dame Paulette. The Knight of the Old Way knows all the secrets and helps the characters along. Father Peter, a monk, reveals the existence of the second horse. Dame Paulette, a beautiful young woman, administers the test and the blessing.

Secrets: Besides the well-known chalk horse in Salisbury, another White Horse exists in Westbury Vale, generally unknown even to neighboring peoples. Also, the horse blessing depends upon how the horses are treated. Characters are asked by Dame Paulette whether they will choose to continue to the reward, or pass up the chance in order to let their tired steed rest. Those who choose to let their steed rest gain the blessing anyway, which is to ride across the magical plain of Emerald to Epona's hill. Those who are greedy gain nothing but a dead horse.

Solutions: Race across Salisbury Plain to the other location, making at least one successful Horsemanship roll. Choose rest for your steed when asked if you will give up the reward by Dame Paulette.

Glory: 10 for each trait test success. 100 for passing Paulette's test and gaining the magical hill.

Afterwards: Characters gain +1 to STR and CON for making it to Epona's Hill, while horses gain +3 to CON. They may also gain Paulette's respect or interest, with luck and gamemaster approval.

The Adventure of THE WHITE HORSE (Long Form)

Introduction

The player knights must learn of this event. They might learn it from anyone. I have chosen to use a gamemaster character from my campaign called The Knight of the Old Way. This adventure is best performed with at least four player characters. All must own chargers.

Character: The Knight of the Old Way

He is a mediocre warrior, but a famous horseman, and an expert on folklore, superstition, and the Old Way. He is present primarily to give useful information to the characters.

Attributes: Use Ordinary Knight attributes; plus, Awareness, Horsemanship, Faerie Lore, Chaste, and Temperate all at 20. His riding horse is a superb beast (a courser) with a CON of 16. The most unusual thing about him is his religion. When queried, he responds:

"I just want to live at peace with all the spirits, and so I did what the priests said their heroes did, and went wandering without food in the wilderness and did nothing but ask Christ to help me get through. Later I did what the old witch lady did and went wandering in the rich forests for as long, asking only that the Lady and her servants help me. I was not normally a pious person, but those things can change a man. Well, I got the same answers from both about Love and Life and The Knight's Duty. So now, naturally, I am a Grail Christian by practice. It lets me get everywhere: Beltaine feasts, Christmas at Court, Midsummer, wherever is convenient. But in truth, I do not think the Holy Grail is real, except as some sort of symbol to inspire idealism in young knights."

The Story

This is a special year, a centennial anniversary of the foaling of Epona, the horse goddess. The Knight of the Old Way has heard that anyone who is present at the Great White Horse during the next full moon will have an opportunity to receive a great gift. It is something good for horses, but he knows nothing else about it.

Characters must plan to be at the Great White Horse of Uffington. Arrangements must be made to stay nearby, and to get to the White Horse shortly before nightfall/moonrise. The Knight of the Old Way will be going along, of course.

Characters must take their rouncy, charger, and squire, and should bring weapons and wear leather armor (4 points), since they know that the night is a time both mysterious and dangerous, especially on an evening of magical significance.

The White Horse

The White Horse Hill gets its name from the huge shape which is cut from the turf on the side of the hill. The earth beneath the layer of topsoil is chalk, so that the outline of the horse is white, shining from the green grass. The shape is quite abstract, and although many people doubt that it is a horse, it has had that name for centuries. It is 374 feet long.

At the Hill

When the knights arrive at the site they find only a young Christian monk at the site, already lost in prayer. He is wearing a monk's robe, has a funny haircut, and so on. Stuck into the ground before him is a white-headed hobby horse. As the sun sets the full moon simultaneously rises, gigantic on the horizon. When it rises viewers can actually see it rise for the few minutes it takes to pass the line of the horizon.

The moon rises. After an hour of fooling around the priest starts to pray more loudly, and says a prayer to God in Latin. Characters may roll their Religion (Christian). Success = the character recognizes the words. It is an invocation.

The priest ends by standing, shouting aloud in plain talk (Cymric), asking God to send a miracle and convert these heathens. He raises his hands to heaven, holding the hobby horse aloft, arms spread. For as long as everyone waits, nothing happens. The player knights must make the first move, but if they wait for an hour and nothing happens then the young man finally shrugs and, shoulders drooping, avoiding looking at the knights, the priest begins walking home, away from the knights.

If no one else pursues him to ask what is going on then the Knight of the Old Way will.

At first there is confusion: he is Father Peter, a monk from an abbey near Wanborough, who came to convert the heathen by proving that their magic came from God, not some petty demon masquerading as a goddess. He is surprised to see the knights, because he thought that the Lady Paulette, a pagan sorceress, and her followers, would attend. Although he verbalizes disappointment, Peter is also obviously relieved not to be confronting her. He complains aloud that she must be "at the other horse."

"What 'other horse?'" asks someone.

"Why, the Westbury one, of course," he says. "Surely you know about. Everyone knows about it."

Knight of the Old Way: "I have heard of Westbury, a pleasant vale in the Campacorentin Forest, but I never heard of a White Horse there."

"Well, there is, and if your lordships are finished I would like to go home." All Father Peter's subsequent action is geared towards leaving. He will not, in any way, accompany the party, save for being threatened with death not to. But he is a terrible rider and will inevitably fall off and either delay the party intolerably or be left behind (as he wishes).

Knights should discuss their options. Most knights will be from Salisbury and therefore familiar with the terrain. The Knight of the Old Way can provide a map if necessary. Note, however, that it is not the best map because he is not a native of this area. Let the player knights discuss the best route. The distance is about 35 miles, as the crow flies, and longer to follow the best paths. The time left until moonset is about 5 hours. The conclusion: "We can make it to Westbury before the moon sets if we ride as hard as we can." Knights who do not ride at the breakneck pace will miss the ceremony.

The Knight of the Old Way points out that "Wearing armor beyond leather will slow the horses down, and rouncys are not fast enough to make the trip in time, so our chargers will have to be ridden. Also, the squires are not skilled enough to keep up with us. So this will be a risky adventure. Who knows what the darkness holds tonight?"

Challenge 1: the Race to Westbury

The knights can attempt a hard-riding race across Salisbury on their chargers. Two factors are significant to the ride: Horsemanship and horse's CON rolls. Interspersed between the three Horsemanship and CON rolls are several other challenges. Three Horsemanship rolls are required, one after every challenge given below.

When a knight fails, he falls behind the riders who do not fail by 1 hour per roll missed. Thus knights may outdistance each other as some are successful and others are not. The knights arrive at their goal in order of their skill at Horsemanship. Whoever misses none of the three rolls is first, whoever misses one is next, and those who miss two are last. Fumbles cost the usual 1d6 damage for the fall, but do not delay characters worse than normal failure. Anyone who fails all three rolls is too slow and misses the entire ritual, arriving at the site after the sun has risen.

Each successful Horsemanship roll also requires a subsequent horse's CON roll to see how tired the horse has become. Success = no effect; failure or fumble = no immediate effect, but note the number of failures. Thus the steed continues to the goal even if it misses its CON roll.

Challenge 2: The Moonlit Celebration

A couple of hours after the knights have been riding hard they might hear sounds of a celebration [Awareness roll.] Even if they do not they will ride up to the frolic, which is some sort of peasant moonlight celebration, complete with lavish food and drink which, though of peasant fare, is plentiful and fresh.

The peasants offer refreshments to the thirsty knights, who may be tempted by the delicious smell of the food and drink. This is a test of the Temperate trait: a successful roll is needed to pass by.

They also see that, a little distance away, the peasants are dancing in increasingly sparse clothing. Several very lovely girls can be seen dancing in the soft moonlight, wearing nothing but their long, unbound hair. A Folk Lore roll reveals that this must be one of those pagan fertility festivals. This is a test of the Chaste trait: roll to avoid.

Anyone who succumbs to one or more of their desires [Indulgent or Lustful] dismounts and is welcomed heartily to the festivities. The knight receives a check in the appropriate trait, and is pleasantly occupied for the rest of the night. All who fail the challenge are out of the adventure.

Those knights who avoided temptation should now make the first set of Horsemanship and horse CON rolls. See below for Glory.

The Knight of the Old Way naturally makes his trait and skill rolls successfully. However, roll for his horse's CON, which may result in failure or fumble, and record the result as for the player knights.

If *none* of the player knights succeed in passing this challenge, the Knight of the Old Way will go back and help them, permitting another attempt at the roll(s) missed, this time with a +5 modifier due to his expertise or strong virtue.

Challenge 3: The Red Stag

After a couple of more hours the knights may attempt another [Awareness] roll. If successful, they see a great red stag, larger than any natural stag ever seen in Britain, sedately watching them dash past from a hillside. It shakes its head once, and the sound of silver bells is clearly audible across the still night. Success at [Faerie Lore] tells the knight that whoever pursues this magical animal, and corners it but does not kill it, will be guaranteed a fine healthy son. The Glory for catching it would be great, as well. The Knight of the Old Way makes his rolls and pulls up his horse. If no one else noticed, he calls to the player knights and tells them of the creature. "This is indeed a magical evening, gentlemen." he says. However, he wants to push on to the White Horse, and avoid the chase.

Pursuit is possible. See the Creatures chapter under "Red Deer" for the stag's attributes. Give the Red Stag an Avoidance value of 20, and see the hunt in the Introductory Scenario. But if the stag is pursued, the pursuing knights are out of the story. The gamemaster should ensure that the reward of a fine son come true if someone fulfills the ritual of the stag correctly. See Glory section below for Glory from the quest.

Those knights who choose to ride on should now make the second set of Horsemanship and horse CON rolls now. Again, roll for the Knight of the Old Way's horse.

Challenge 4: A Midnight Joust

At the edge of Campacorentin Forest, where the trail enters the forest to Westbury Vale, several knights wait to joust any passersby. They block the only way through.

They are gentlemen about it, but insist on a joust "for love." They are from Somerset, and were told to wait here all night by a mysterious woman they call the "Adventurous Maiden." They actually know little about her except that her requests are followed by all chivalrous knights. Use the Notable Knight attributes. Every rider must joust once, with the normal Glory for victory. They can borrow armor from one of the jousters.

After jousting, the leader of the Somerset knights notice how tired the men and horses are, and they invite the knights to stay and eat with them. This is a test of the Energetic trait: even though the ride to the White Horse is important, jousting on top of many hours of riding is

The White Horse

very fatiguing. Failure or fumble indicates that the knight falls asleep after the meal, exhausted. No check to Lazy is necessary, nor would such a check be appropriate. See below for Glory.

Those knights who ride on should now make the third and last set of Horsemanship and horse CON rolls now. This time, CON rolls have a -10 modifier, due to fatigue. Fumbled CON rolls will still permit the knights to continue, but note the fact for reference later.

Again, roll for the Knight of the Old Way's horse. Also, if no one has made all three Horsemanship rolls except the Knight of the Old Way, he will stick with the character who is first in the race, instead of outdistancing all the characters ("There may be danger ahead, and we should stay together if possible." he says).

Conclusion

As the knights straggle through the woods to the hidden vale each individual or group is treated the same by Dame Paulette, the young woman described below. Therefore the gamemaster should settle results of the race first, then move on to this scene. Because it happens the same to everyone he can save having to describe things more than once this way.

The knights who make it (succeed in at least one Horsemanship roll) reach the vale as the moon is sinking into the west. The first group (no missed rolls) sees the moon high in the west; the second group (one roll missed) sees it low towards the horizon; the last group (two rolls missed) sees it looming on the skyline, moving down out of sight.

A band of commoners, led by a tall young woman in country dress, are performing some sort of dance. A large group of ponies waits quietly at the bot-

tom of the vale. As the characters ride up, the peasants turn to greet them. [Roll Awareness. Success = you see some who are not commoners; and you see some people wearing horse costumes.]

As the knights approach the scene, on the hillside beneath the horse's feet, every horse which failed or fumbled one or more CON rolls collapses. The woman comes forward quickly, glances in concern at their exhausted chargers, and speaks.

"Your steeds are sorely wearied, gentlemen. You have a choice," she says, "Will you ride onward tonight when the time comes, or let your horse rest?" Each knight must answer, and arguments or questions are ignored. She accepts either answer without comment. All players must note whether they choose Ride or Rest. Players who cannot make up their characters' minds must make a Merciful/Cruel roll.

Once every knight has given his answer, the woman touches each charger in turn, whispering quietly when touching one whose knight has chosen Ride rather than Rest. Then the dance resumes, and continues until the moon is touching the skyline. During the dance, inquiries are met with smiles but no answers. Every character who did not fail all three rolls has arrived by this point.

The dance is concluded, and the crowd goes to their ponies. The young woman sweeps her hand across all the steeds before her, and any exhausted animals stop panting and wheezing, and briskly rise to their feet. The horses neigh with excitement. The lady cries out, "Mount up, friends, and ride on the wind into the arms of the moon!" Those horses which were exhausted no longer are. The commoners leap atop their ponies and dash away. Some folks in costume join the stampede.

Knights' choice: join in the wild ride, or not. If not, they remain on the hilltop and see the others ride into invisibility. If they chose "Rest" when questioned, and hesitate to ride now, the young woman turns back and waves to them, saying "Your horses are rested enough: join me, and catch me if you can!"

Knights who join the chase ride up the hillside, over the white horse figure cut into the sod, catching the ponies at the top of the hill, then outdistancing them on the hilltop. Without trouble they charge onto a great open plain which was not there before. As the moon sets and the sun rises, the grass of the plain is revealed to be of an extraordinary emerald green.

The ride is too wild to let anyone see images in the flashing emerald landscape until, far ahead, shines a golden hill. Without warning, some people are thrown from their horses. This includes: 1. All knights who exhausted their steeds, but did not choose to Rest them; 2. All knights who made a Cruel roll rather than a Merciful roll; 3. sufficient gamemaster characters to impress the players. These riders land back on the hillside, beside their dead horses or ponies, near the white horse. They are out of the story. It is daylight. The priestess and other people are all gone.

The other knights, those who chose Rest, or any who managed to get lucky with their horse's CON rolls, continue on to the small hillock that rises from the bright green plain. As the horses dash up the hill the knights see it is covered with yellow flowers. At the top the horses stop, and circle a large wooden tub full of sparkling, silvery water. The horses all drink eagerly. Nearby is a stout oak chest, the only other thing on the hilltop. Its lid is thrown open, and it is filled to the brim with silver coins with the image of Epona on them.

Knights can drink from the tub when the horses are finished, and/or take the silver from the chest, or do nothing. The young woman, the peasants, and the others who made it this far do both.

If characters drink, but take no silver, they add 1 point to their CON and STR. If they drink, and take silver, they add 1 to their CON, and get 1d6 £. worth of silver coins. If they only take coins they get 3d6 £. of silver. All horses get +3 to their CON.

After a time a mist surrounds the knights. They may choose to ride or to stay. Either way the mist clears with the characters having arrived near to wherever the gamemaster wishes them to be.

Glory: 10 Glory for anyone who began the ride; 10 points for each successful trait test (Temperate, Chaste, and Energetic); 10 points for successfully defeating a Notable knight in the joust; and 100 for reaching Epona's Blessed Hill and partaking in the magic.

Anyone who succeeded at all three Horsemanship rolls gains 10 Glory for his impressive display of expertise.

The Glory for succeeding on the quest of the Red Stag is heroic, 100 points.

Afterward: The young woman introduces herself to any characters who made it to the hill. "I am Paulette, a follower of the old ways," she says. She might tell those characters a few minor secrets of Epona if they impress her (up to the gamemaster to determine).

Short Adventures

SHORT ADVENTURES ARE IMPORTANT components of a *Pendragon* campaign. They add color and excitement, and serve as a break between the day-to-day concerns of court and castle.

Short adventures can be used alone, each requiring about a single session to resolve. Alternately, these are simple building blocks used to make more complex scenarios. The gamemaster should mix and match the parts according to his whim or other plot development. By weaving them together using the methods described here the story is enriched, and character knights are integrated into the legends of King Arthur.

The Short Adventures are listed in alphabetical order.

Make a Longer Plot

Typical Arthurian narratives often begin with a simple event which leads to a second, a third, and perhaps many more until the final event is resolved.

The Adventure of the Basilisk, for instance, cannot be solved by knights. But perhaps the witch queen found in that adventure will catch the magical weasel if the knights will do a favor for her: a powerful knight is blocking the road to her castle. Will the knights help her? If so, this leads to the Adventure of The Knight Of The Moon. The Knight of the Moon

agrees to let the knights go ahead of his army and fight his foe, who is described in the Adventure of the Headless Dead. The characters win. This finishes the tasks initiated by the witch queen and, conveniently, kills the sorcerer who has created the basilisk.

Make the Characters Important

Most of the Short Adventures use characters designated by title rather than a specific name. Gamemasters are urged to develop the characters as they are needed. They might be great knights. The Knight of the Moon might be Sir Agravain in disguise, or the Damsel of Sun Flowers be Lady Nimue testing the knights, or the Castle of the Beard may be Sir Brus Sans Pitie's own castle.

The characters might be closely related to the player knights. For instance, the Lady of the Bridge may turn out to be a player knight's long-lost mother, or lover, or a potential love.

Reuse Gamemaster Characters

Weave them through the tale: a nameless gamemaster character in one adventure can reappear later and become more significant. Each successive reappearance will help you to build the character by revealing facts slowly.

Warn the Characters!

Always warn characters of the potential dangers in these adventures. Some of them are just plain hard, while others are destined *never* to be solved until the appearance of Lancelot or Galahad, though gamemasters may wish to alter that version of the tale to give these feats to player characters. But part of the long-term campaign concept is to have some adventures which are not immediately solved, and which can be revisited years later, either by player knights or gamemaster characters.

Remind the players that the modifiers to Valorous rolls, which are required upon sighting some monsters, indicate the likelihood of fatality in combat. Running from a creature with a -10 or more modifier gets the knight a Cowardly check, but no loss to Honor. And he will be alive. See the "Characters and Creatures" chapter for more on Valor modifiers.

Adventure of THE ADVENTUROUS SHIELD

Setting: An abbey of the White Monks. It is very isolated, in a forest in Logres.

Problem: An ancient shield hangs on a pole behind the alter. It is white, except for a blood-red cross across its face. If anyone attempts to take it the monks warn them away saying, "Sirs, this shield ought not to be hanged about no knight's neck but he be the worthiest knight of the world, and therefore I counsel you knights to be well advised."

If questioned why not, they will say, "No man may bear this shield about his neck but he be mischieved or dead within three days, or maimed forever."

Anyone who takes it away meets a knight dressed all in white within three days. He is a terrific fighter, and always kills or wounds the adventurer and then returns the shield. No one has ever succeeded in carrying the shield away.

Characters: The monks. No attributes are needed.
The White Knight. His armor is almost blinding. The knight is an angel in disguise, has the attributes of a faerie knight plus 100 more hit points and a Valorous trait of 30, and always makes a critical hit against his opponent. If one hit is not enough to make the knight helpless, the angel will attack until it can remove the shield and bear it back to the abbey. The angel behaves with strict chivalry, and will not kill a disarmed, unconscious, or surrendered foe.

Secrets: The shield is from Joseph of Arimathea, who brought the Holy Grail to Britain. It is destined to be used by Sir Galahad.

Solutions: No one can take it away, for it is fated to be used by Sir Galahad on the Quest for the Holy Grail.

Glory: 25 for attempting to take it away, plus up to 100 more if the unsuccessful fight against the angel is performed in a heroic manner.

Adventure of THE AVANC

Setting: on the waters of Llyn Barfog (in Gwynned). The name means "The Bearded Lake." Alternatively, on any large lake or river.

Problem: A monster, the avanc, is terrorizing the neighborhood.

Characters: The Avanc. The avanc is a carnivorous whirlpool spirit which looks like a huge black beaver. It is malevolent and capable of creating whirlpools which can spin and capsize boats, draw down swimmers, or clutch at the ankles of horses or men walking a ford. It roars like a waterfall, and splashes whenever it walks on dry land, leaving a wet trail behind it.

Avanc

SIZ 20	Move 5	Armor 5
DEX 10	Damage 6d6	Unconscious 13
STR 40	Heal Rate 7	
CON 32	Hit Points 52	

Modifier to Valor: -5, +5 to Prudent

Glory to Kill: 200

Attacks: 2 claws @15, against 1 or 2 targets; plus Dodge (DEX roll) against a single foe. (Monsters do not subtract natural armor modifiers from DEX rolls).

Special Whirlpool Attack: In the water, the avanc is extremely dangerous. Each melee round the strength of the avanc's whirlpool increases by 5 points, starting from 0. The number is received as a modifier to attributes. When crossing a ford, the victim must receive a successful modified STR roll to overcome the whirlpool. Success indicates he stands where he is and may move next round, advisedly to flee to dry land. When swimming, a modified Swimming roll against the whirlpool must be made. Men in boats suffer the modifier to Boating when in the whirlpool. Once a victim fails an attribute roll, he is sucked into the whirlpool, helpless. When in the water the avanc cannot be struck by weapons, but cannot strike with its claws either. However, it will probably be drowning its foes or drawing them into an underwater lair for dismemberment.

Secrets: The avanc is less formidable when out of the water, but it is impossible to get it out except by subterfuge. The knowledge to draw him out is known only to witches or to characters who are successful recipients of a Faerie Lore roll.

Solutions: Avancs are attracted by the charm of virgin women, and so the virgin ploy can be used. The avanc will sleep with his head in the girl's lap. Handling a sleeping avanc presents a major problem. The poor girl cannot sit forever. The avanc of legend was held with heavy chains attached to a team of hauling oxen. Several strong knights with armor and weapons might be able to do the job as well. Keep the avanc's STR a secret, or roll it randomly on 10d6 if everyone has a copy of this book.

Glory: 300 to kill.

Adventure of THE BASILISK

Setting: Anyplace.

Problem: A Basilisk, the King of Serpents, has moved into the area and is devastating it.

Characters: a Basilisk. The basilisk is an unnatural creature hatched from a cock's egg by a sitting toad. It has powers from the devil himself. Everyone knows that a basilisk can kill as easily as looking at you. This monster must be avoided, and a knight loses no Honor for running from its deadly glance. It looks like a huge snake with a feathered cowl, wearing a crown, and its body is decorated with six white lengthwise stripes.

The basilisk is composed of living poison. This poison is so potent that nothing can touch the beast and survive. If it is speared, the poison eats away the weapon and creeps up to attack the wielder. Its venom can be spat as well, doing terrible damage to anything touched. The basilisk is so accurate that it can lie down on its back and spit into the air at birds which, when slain, fall right into the beast's mouth.

Basilisk

SIZ 5	Move 5	Major Wound 50
DEX 25	Damage special	Unconscious 13
STR 10	Heal Rate 3	Knockdown 5
CON 50	Hit Points 55	Armor 20

Modifier to Valor: -15, +15 to Prudent

Attacks: spit venom @21 with a range of up to 25 yards. The venom does 10 points of damage once in contact with a victim, with the damage received every melee round until the gamemaster rolls a 1 on 1d6, indicating that its potency is exhausted. Armor does not protect after the first round (except for the Armor of Honor). Several doses of venom may hit the same victim, for a severe cumulative total.

Basilisks dodge one attack with DEX and may spit once per round as well.

Solutions: Drive it away using missile weapons, or weapons used to strike it once and be discarded.

Secrets: The only thing dangerous to a basilisk is a certain type of weasel. A weasel is a petty thing for a knight to hunt, and he will have to get someone else to do it for him. For instance, a witch or priestess may offer to catch it in return for some other favor, as mentioned in the introduction to this chapter.

Glory: 100 to drive it from a territory, 500 to kill it.

Adventure of THE DAMSEL OF THE SUN FLOWERS

Setting: the only nice campsite, at the end of the day. A nice pavilion, with the banner of a sunflower hanging before it, stands beside a small clear pool.

Problem: an ugly dwarf tells the player knights they cannot stay here unless they joust with his master, Sir Arfonen, who is here because of an evil custom. The knight is already prepared, ready to joust. Suspicious rolls are in order.

Characters: Sir Arfonen of Lincoln, a Notable knight; Lady of the Sun Flowers.

The Avanc

Solutions: Joust with Sir Arfonen.

Secrets: The Lady of the Sun Flowers, a very ambitious young sorceress, has set the rules here. Every knight who wins the joust must remain with her until he is defeated by another. If the knight is defeated, he may go on. If the knight wins, but refuses to stay until he loses, then his land is struck by a blight which makes the knight Poor or even Impoverished. Household knights suffer illness to themselves or their family which have the same effect. Only two things can change this effect: 1. Going back to keep the custom; or 2. Death of the knight.

Glory: Only the normal for jousting. Thus it is 10 for defeating Sir Arfonen of Lincoln.

Afterwards: Use the "At the Crossroads" solo to see what jousting your character does for the interim of his stay with the damsel.

Adventure of THE DOLOROUS GARDE

Setting: in Garloth. This castle is the haunted lair of an evil, dead enchanter. In English its name means Sorrowful Castle. Now inhabited by monsters and ghosts, it is also believed to be the site of great hidden treasure.

Problem: Many knights have entered it and never returned. A huge rock, prophesied to be picked up by the fated lord of this castle, lies unmoved in the courtyard (-25 to STR to lift).

Characters: About 30 guardians, active at various times during the day and night.

Lions: see "Characters and Creatures" chapter.

Celtic Ghost Knights: These corpses in rusting armor moan as they attack. Use Ordinary Knight attributes, or headless dead from the adventure of the same name. (Reduce knight armor by 5 points). 50 Glory to defeat.

Copper Giants: These huge warriors have metallic skin made of ringing copper, and huge swords and round shields also of that metal.

Copper Giant

SIZ: 30	Move 5
DEX: 10	Damage 9d6
STR: 25	Hit Points 38
CON: 8	Armor 25 + 10-pt. shield
APP: 10	

Attacks: Sword @18
Modifier to Valorous: -5
Significant Traits: Cruel 16
Significant Passions: none
Significant Skills: Awareness 5
Glory to defeat: 200

Secrets: Sir Lancelot achieved this quest and changed the name to *Joyous Garde* (Joyous Castle). Although supposedly fated for him, player knights can try to contribute to his pre-success, try to beat him to it, or just accumulate Glory here. In my house campaign consistent (and unexpected) successes against the guardians by player knights were resolved by one of them finally finding his own name upon the rock.

Glory: 100 to claim it, plus whatever monsters may be defeated.

Adventure of THE HALF-A-GIANT

Setting: A very useful shortcut through the woods is not used because of a giant which lives there. It can be heard roaring at various times. A huge bare footprint, with six clawed toes, is visible in the rocks nearby. It is as long as a horse.

Problem: To clear the trail.

Characters: A giant, whose head and one arm only are visible. The rest of him is buried in the ground.

Use normal Giant attributes.

Solutions: The great roaring comes through the dense brush of the woods. Horses cannot enter and investigation must be on foot. Everyone must make a Valorous -5 roll, or else hesitate when entering the dense brush and thereby fall behind at the rate of 1 melee round per Valorous attempt.

Investigation reveals a giant head and arm above the ground. The rest is buried. His big leather hat is crushed, like he'd been hit on the head. The neck and arm are rather bony and thin (for a giant).

Some knights might immediately charge, in which case combat ensues. Give the other players time to watch the fight and to discuss what they can and should do. Ask for an Awareness Roll, where success indicates that the knights hear the giant say, in big and slow and deep giant-speech, "Spare me!" Point out that the giant is clearly helpless, and ask for a Merciful Roll. Success indicates that the character is moved by the giant's helplessness. Ask if the player wishes to act on that feeling, and if they will then the character gets the Merciful check and makes some sort of statement to spare the creature.

If (on player decision) the knights try to forcibly resist any efforts to kill the giant (probably by fighting on the giant's behalf) they also get a Justice check.

If, after the player knights have made their statements to earn Merciful checks, any of the knights not yet in combat enter into the fray then they automatically receive Cruel checks.

If spared the giant will be friendly. He is mostly hungry and, if fed, will volunteer information about himself. After eating he laughs out of pleasure and happiness. It is a fearsome sound, ironically similar to his previous roars.

He has been here for centuries since an enemy, a much *bigger* giant, pounded him into the ground. But he considers himself lucky because his companion was thrown up into the sky by the big fellow, and hasn't landed yet — he's probably starved to death by now!

If asked, he thinks that the footprint in the rock is probably his enemy's. Who is his enemy? Llew of the Long Hand, who used to be king of this whole land before the humans came.

Gamemasters should decide how much they wish to use this character. The giant might know nothing useful, having been isolated since plunked down here. Even if he is stupid he might be a useful source of information about fairy lore, pre-human history, or dragons. On the other hand he might be suave and funny, the witness to many travellers along this secret path, and source of much information. He cannot be released.

Adventure of THE KNIGHT OF THE MOON

Setting: Along the road someplace.

Problem: The Knight of the Moon, called because of the arms he bears, refuses to let anyone pass without a joust. His terms are unusual: the loser pays six-month's knight-service or the equal scutage, starting next Pentecost at a castle to be named. The Knight of the Moon states beforehand that if he loses he will pay the scutage, which is 1 £., to the winner.

A famous bard, whose skill is readily apparent, is nearby, ready to make up songs about whatever occurs, especially to satirize cowards who refuse to joust.

Characters: The Knight of the Moon. Use Famous Knight attributes.

Secrets: The knight is gathering an army to attack Castle Spidora, where an enemy has imprisoned his lady-love. Thus he needs good men to take into his force.

Solutions: Joust with him. If you win, accept the money and go away. If you lose, either join his army, pay, or renege and lose a point of Honor.

Glory: Normal for the joust: 25 if you beat him.

Afterwards: The gamemaster must choose a battle to run afterwards.

Adventure of THE KNIGHT OF THE WOLF

Setting: On the road someplace. A squire, half terrified to death, is stumbling slowly down the road. He is too exhausted to be panicked. If helped along with some water and kind words he explains his problem.

Problem: His lord has been attacked and killed by the Knight of the Wolf, so-called because of the huge shaggy beast which accompanies him everyplace. Archers hidden in the woods cut down the squire's good lord. And his daughter has been seized.

Characters: The Knight of the Wolf, always accompanied by a dozen evil archers and an scurvy-looking Irish Wolfhound. Use Famous knight attributes for the Knight of the Wolf.

Secrets: The Knight of the Wolf, though ruthless, is avenging his own father, who was killed by the ambushed lord using hidden crossbowmen. From the point of chivalry, the knight's attack was dishonorable, but from the point of view of Love (family), he is justified in carrying out a blood feud with such viciousness.

He has not mistreated the dead either, and will show a small plot in the church yard where the dead lord and retainers are buried to any who challenge his respect for the deceased.

Solutions: Visiting the Knight of the Wolf immediately reveals his secret. Furthermore, although the lovely daughter is refusing to eat and generally being difficult, she is not being harmed.

The Knight of the Wolf agrees to release the daughter to the care of the player knights if they will perform a deed for him.

The knight wants the player to regain a family heirloom which was taken from him many years ago by the dead lord, and then lost. A knight known as the Lord of the Ivy Tower has it, but will give it up only if he is defeated in mortal combat. The Knight of the Wolf would go himself, but he took an oath swearing never to again to seek it when he was defeated by the Lord of the Ivy Tower many years ago.

Glory: None for getting this far. To continue, fight the Knight of the Wolf, or go to the Adventure of the Lord of the Ivy Tower. If that one can be solved, then the artifact is regained, and if returned to the

Knight of the Wolf, then an additional 50 points are distributed among the party, for performing a significant task.

Adventure of THE LADY IN PINK

Setting: along a trail someplace.

Problem: A mournful squire, alone beside the path, entreats the character knights to stop and help him. If they do, he explains that his lady has been kidnapped by a villainous knight, who is holding her in a tower a few miles away. He begs the knights to help him and her.

The squire says he cannot give her name, but she is a noblewoman whose father will reward whoever delivers the lady home.

If the knights agree they must travel to the tower, which is the stronghold of an old motte-and-bailey castle. The lady, obvious by her pink clothing, is hanging out a window and waves a scarf at the knights. She is too far away for voices to be heard.

While viewing the castle, the drawbridge lowers and the lord and ten knights ride out.

The lord knight is a chivalrous knight, who has taken the lady only in sport and has not harmed her. He will surrender her to anyone who beats him and all his men at jousting. Any losses result in her continued imprisonment for that day. Anyone may joust once per day against him and his men. Resting and First Aid are permitted.

The lord knight is chivalrous and very courteous, welcoming all challengers to his hall. The Lady in Pink is there as well, apparently a party to this scheme.

Characters: The Squire. Attributes are not necessary.

Lady in Pink. Use Lady attributes.

Lord Knight. Use Famous Knight attributes.

10 Knights. Use 5 Notable Knights, and 5 Ordinary Knights.

Secrets: none.

Solutions: Win the 11 jousts.

Glory: 25, in addition to Glory gained in jousting

Afterwards: The Lady in Pink can fulfill any of the female roles in your campaign.

Adventure of THE LADY OF THE BRIDGE

Setting: At a bridge.

Problem: A young girl stands at the end of a bridge and asks passing knights to help her. She has been taken prisoner by a wicked knight, who waits yonder.

Characters: The Lady of the Bridge. Use Damosel attributes. The knight. Use Notable Knight attributes.

Secrets: The knight is a man of good character, though sometimes of questionable methods. He is off on a money-making spree and has taken this woman to be his bait. He has not harmed her, nor intends to. He offers to free her if the challenger offers his own armor, horse, and weapons as his wager, against the woman.

Solutions: The knight offers to fight for love, "for there is no reason for either of us to die over the trivial event of this lady's abduction."

Glory: 10 for defeating the knight in the joust, plus 10 if the rather ordinary task of rescuing the Lady is achieved.

Adventure of the LADY OF VALAINE

Setting: On a road. A knight rides towards and then past the player knights. The rider ignores the player knights, proudly disdaining any speech. A squire follows, leading a heavily loaded pair of pack horses. A second squire leads a mule upon which sits a sad lady. [Awareness] The lady appears to have been crying. She looks at each knight, gestures, and says out loud, "Oh Sir Knights, I am a captured lady taken by this knight from the home of my father. I beseech you to help me, as is the task of all good knights."

Problem: She is the only child of the banneret of Valaine, a nearby holding. The knight has killed her father and intends to forcibly marry her so that he can hold the land.

Characters: The woman. Use Damosel attributes.

The knight. Use Notable Knight attributes.

Solutions: Challenge the knight. His terms are not unusual, though harsh: fight to the death for her.

Glory: 50 to rescue her, plus 100 Glory to whoever conquers the knight.

Afterwards: Her identity could be expanded into being a heiress, an enchantress, a saint, or a lover; or she might just say "Thank you" and be dropped off at home, out of the game.

Adventure of THE LORD OF THE IVY TOWER

Setting: an old country castle in a poor district.

Problem: Every May 1st a bad thing happens on this property, and no one knows what it is. Something enchants everyone to sleep. The next day one half of all the calves are gone, and one half of the stored grain too. The Lord of Ivy Tower knows it is something from Faerie, and is unable to confront it. But he has made a very generous reward offer of "anything which will not stain his honor or his family" to whoever can drive off the curse.

Characters: The Lord of Ivy Tower; a faerie creature.

Solutions: Stay awake through the night. The only way to do this is to make three successive Energetic rolls, the first one unmodified, the second one at -10, and the third at -15. Once done the knight will remain awake to see what it is that comes.

Secrets: It is, of course, something magical which does this. The precise cause is left to the gamemaster. Some possibilities are:

1. A witch, with a band of hungry dwarfs. Kill or capture the dwarves to end the curse.

2. A malicious faerie, shaking a sleeping wand. Trick him in a duel of wits and riddles.

3. A very hungry goblin. Fight or capture.

4. A lonely magical cow which collects the calves to raise as her children, and the grain to feed them. Buy her own herd.

5. A noble elf knight, collecting tribute which he has collected since time immemorial. Fight or attempt to appeal to his Mercy.

6. A lovely elf maiden with a sleeping flute, and a horde of hungry white mice. Praise her beauty and her mice and she might move to your lands instead.

The Questing Beast

Glory: 50 points for overcoming this challenging task, plus whatever is gained by overcoming the foe.

Adventure of THE PERILOUS CEMETERY

Setting: An abandoned cemetery. A small chapel, in the center of the graves, offers the only shelter around. It is untended, with tall weeds between the graves, and a broken-down fence surrounding it. In the chapel is a shattered altar, over which is hung a rusted spear with the remains of a great war banner hanging from its tip.

Problem: Appearing to be just an abandoned cemetery by day, this place is haunted by hostile, tormented ghosts by night. Being nearby invites attack, and staying here guarantees attack by supernatural agents.

As the sun sets the stars and moon do not appear to rise. A chill sharp wind keens around the graves. After a time of indeterminate darkness and silence, spectral figures can be seen mustering at the edge of the cemetery. Another army, moaning, rises from the graves. The outsiders rush forward. The forces clash. Howls and screams shred hearing and sanity as dead and immortals clash. A Valorous roll is called for, with a fumble indicating flight.

Sometimes figures detach themselves from the battle and attack the knights hiding in the chapel. Thus anyone in the chapel will be fighting all night long.

Knights nearby will be attacked if they are within sight of the fighting, but may be able to run away if they are not killed by the ghosts.

Characters: The Ghost Knights. Use a mixture of knights. This should be a challenging task to defeat, so use attributes appropriate to party strength.

Solutions: Fight to survive. Appropriate Piety and Love (deity) rolls may be relevant for inspiration, at gamemaster option. Then gain the altarcloth and put the tormented ghosts to rest.

Secrets: If the party survives, towards morning they will notice that the altar is glowing slightly. A white altarcloth has magically appeared, draped over the altar. However, if anyone tries to touch it, it suddenly flies up into the air. Only if someone makes a critical success at Pious, Merciful, or Honest can it be held, and then only long enough to cut or tear a piece off the corner.

The cloth can be used to heal. When applied to a wound like a bandage it automatically gives 10 points of magical healing. But it can be used on only one wound. Afterwards it can be washed in holy water and used again.

If the cloth is touched to a Ghost Knight of the cemetery, he disappears. If all the cemetery army is put to rest, the opposing army fades away as well.

Glory: 100 for surviving the night, 50 per Ghost Knight killed (regardless of quality), plus 100 for a piece of the cloth, and another 100 if the curse is ended.

Adventure of THE PROUD KNIGHT OF LANDOINE

Setting: along a road someplace:

Problem: a wounded knight, carried about in a wagon, cannot have his poisoned wounds healed until his attacker is slain. His attacker is the Proud Knight of Landoine, which is in eastern Logres.

The suffering of the knight is pitiful. Anyone who volunteers to help him without making any die rolls gets a Just check. Anyone who makes a Merciful roll would like to help, and if they volunteer they get a check.

Characters: The Proud Knight of Landoine; the other knights of Landoine. The Proud Knight should be of similar Glory and strength to the player characters.

Secrets: The Proud Knight of Landoine has a magical sword which is made of poisoned steel. Any time it makes a major wound, then that wound can never be healed while the wound-maker lives. The Proud Knight is a very skilled fighter, and notorious for invoking his Passion of Hate (chivalrous knights).

Solutions: Fight and kill him, and all who carry the poisoned wounds are healed.

Glory: Usual for combat, plus 150 for achieving this challenging and significant task.

Afterwards: The sword is a good prize, but costs the bearer a check to Cruelty each time he uses it.

Adventure of THE QUESTING BEAST

Setting: Anyplace away from civilization where a source of water exists.

Problem: The knights hear something strange and spooky in the distance. [Awareness = the sound of supernatural hounds, like the Wild Hunter.] It draws closer rapidly, but though the noise grows nothing comes into sight. [Valor, where failure or fumble = the knight hesitates to investigate, or rides in the opposite direction, and misses the rest.]

Abruptly the noise stops, and next to the nearby stream or pool of water a fabulous creature appears and slinks down to drink. As it drinks the howling and barking stops. At this time the knights can get a good look at the creature. [Faerie Lore = they recognize it as the Questing Beast.]

After a short time, [Awareness = something else is approaching, which sounds like a mounted, armored man crashing through the brush.] The perceptions are correct, and a mounted knight gallops towards the pool as the beast turns and slips into the brush, once again accompanied by the sound of a pack of pursuing hounds.

The knight is either King Pellinore (early in Arthur's reign) or Sir Palomides the Saracen (now or later.) Subsequent actions depend upon the needs of the gamemaster: perhaps the knight bounds away, perhaps he arrogantly demands a steed from the knights, or he may be challenged to joust by one of the player knights.

Characters: Questing Beast; Extraordinary Knight (Pellinore or Palomides).

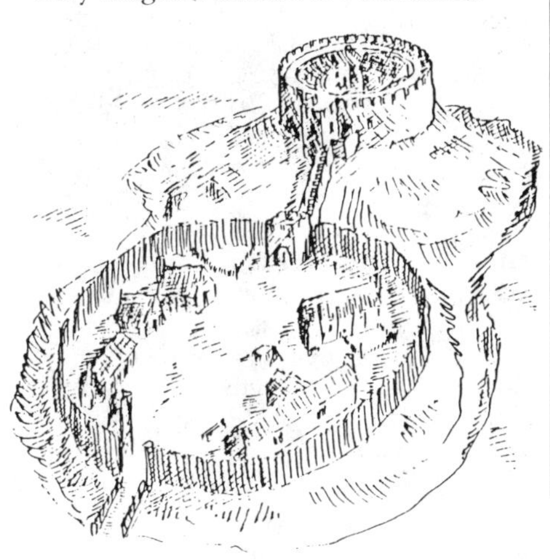

The Questing Beast

Named Glatisant, or the "Barking Beast," this miraculous beast was pursued first by King Pellinore and later by Sir Palomides. It was never reported caught, and was never fought when pursued.

SIZ 65	Move 15	Major Wound30
DEX 45	Damage none	Unconscious 24
STR 25	Heal Rate 6	Knockdown 65
CON 30	Hit Points 95	Armor 10

Modifier to Valor: none.

Attacks: none discovered. Instead, it uses its Avoidance skill of 35, opposing any Hunting, Awareness, or even weapon skills used against it. See the Hunting rules.

Secrets: The sound of the hounds comes from inside the belly of the Questing Beast.

Solutions: Glatisant lives to be hunted, but not to be caught. Though adept at fleeing and hiding, the noise always betrays its hiding place eventually.

Glory: 15 to see it, 100 to get close enough to strike it. 250 to kill it, and 500 to capture it alive.

Adventure of THE RAVEN TOWER

Setting: Near Gloucester. The Tower of Ravens is an ancient structure, built by giants before the Romans came. It has no doors to enter at ground level — only by flying can you enter. It is the home of a coven of Raven Witches, powerful sorceresses, who are jealous of their privacy. The peasants thereabouts are silent, surly, and hostile. A band of fierce warriors works for the witches, living within the stockade which surrounds the tower. They protect the approaches to the tower, and are periodically carried up into the tower for a pleasant while as payment for services.

Problem: A powerful lord wants information about a nearby holding. They always refuse to pay homage to any lord, and sometimes raid their neighbors, usually rob travellers, and generally ignore all social niceties altogether.

Characters: The Raven Witches. These are a special coven of pagan witches who can transform themselves into wicked ravens to help their friends and harm their foes. They appear as sorceresses and warrior women in the story "Peredur" and as fighting birds loyal to Owein in the story "The Dream of Rhonabwy," both from *The Mabinogion*. Six to twelve individuals appear at a time, and they also masquerade as armed human women with pagan magic powers. Use Ordinary Knight attributes for the warrior women.

Raven Witch, in Raven Form

SIZ 10	Move 10(fly)	Major Wound 20
DEX 25	Damage 3d6	Unconscious 8
STR 15	Heal Rate 4	Knockdown 10
CON 20	Hit Points 30	Armor 4
APP 18		

Modifier to Valor: -5

Glory to Kill: 100

Attacks: 1 dodge (use DEX) *and* 1 peck done while flying @18; or a lift, wherein multiple birds grapple a foe and lift him into the air, where they then peck him with unopposed rolls, and the lifted foe can only strike at one of the ravens at a time at half his ability with Dagger or Grapple. To lift, the gamemaster must roll the ravens' combined STR in opposed resolution against the STR of the foe, rolled by the player.

The Warriors. Use a mixture of Bandits, Saxon Warriors, and foot soldiers, all led by officers of Sergeant quality on good chargers. For their chief, use a Notable Knight who has the traits of a bandit.

Secrets: everything stated about them is true.

Solutions: Get the help of Sir Peredur, who is seeking help to wipe out these family enemies of his (see the literature related to Peredur).

Glory: 100 per witch killed, 200 to drive them out of the tower for good, plus whatever is gained in combat with the defenders.

Adventure of THE REDCAP

Setting: A ruined tower.

Problem: A man with a red hat has lived here for centuries, killing anyone who approaches, and sometimes ranging afield from his lair.

Characters: The man is a redcap, a murderous man-eating monster who only appears to be human. There is only one approach to get close to the entry of his tower, and a good supply of rocks to drop on the heads of invaders. He cannot be surprised.

This evil faerie lives in a ruined place where wicked deeds were done by men. He is tall and broad-shouldered, but cadaverously gaunt, with gleaming red eyes, fangs, talons on his fingers, and a red cap which he soaks in the blood of his victims.

The best-known redcap of legend could not be beaten in combat. When he was finally defeated through exorcism, the only remaining part of the redcap

was one of his long teeth. The individual detailed below, perhaps somewhat weaker, is still monstrously formidable.

Redcap

SIZ 12	Move 6	Major Wound 40
DEX 12	Damage 8d6	Unconscious 13
STR 35	Heal Rate 8	Knockdown 12
CON 40	Hit Points 52	Armor 20
APP 14		

Modifier to Valor: -15

Attacks: barbed Greatspear @28; if disarmed he uses 2 claws @20 each, normal damage.

Secrets: Some people claim that they can be weakened by prayer or by magic.

Solutions: If the secrets are not true, then only a fierce combat can solve this problem.

Glory: Glory to kill: 300

The Adventure of THE TOMB OF LIONS

Setting: A forest — the exact location is left to the gamemaster. A beautiful and elaborate marble tomb stands alone in the woods. From a distance, a successful Awareness roll reveals that the walls inside the tomb are coated with fresh, running blood. A critical success reveals a lion hiding in the shadows.

Very close by, a pool of water boils furiously, so hot that anyone touching it receives 2d6+2 damage per round in contact with it. A successful Awareness roll allows the knight to see the helmeted head of a knight within the water, apparently quite unaffected by the boiling. The head cannot be plucked out in any way except by Sir Lancelot or another of his family.

Close up, the knight can see an inscription in Latin which explains that the knight was murdered feloniously, and that this mystery will not be solved except by one of this king's lineage.

Problem: The dripping blood has miraculous healing properties: one touch of it heals all wounds. However, the place is hard to find and the blood is hard to gather, due to the pair of lions guarding it.

The lions prevent anyone from entering the tomb by blocking the single entryway. One lion fights at a time, and a maximum of two knights can reach him to fight. When one lion is wounded he leaps back into the tomb and the other leaps out to fight. Inside, the lion licks a wall and, after one round, is fully healed and able to fight again!

Characters: The pair of lions.

Secrets: The body was King Lanceor, the grandfather of Sir Lancelot.

The dead king is Sir Lancelot's grandfather. After that knight visits the site and plucks the head from the well, the water will stop boiling.

Solutions: the lions may be fought and killed, and some of the blood taken. No matter how much blood is taken, only one dose of healing per knight is allowed. After the knights depart, two more lions take up residence.

Glory: 25 per knight for attempting the adventure, 250 for slaying a lion, 100 more per lion if they have access to the healing blood, and 100 more for slaying them both and taking some blood.

Adventure of THE TOWER OF THE HEADLESS DEAD

Setting: A tower in an area known as the Forest of Skulls. The many skulls amidst the forest are the heads of the victims of others who tried to go to the tower. One can still speak, and will try to warn the knights not to go.

Problem: A sorcerer has been doing something bad. The gamemaster must determine the specific act, which is sufficient to motivate the player knights to try to stop him. This is only the most recent of his evil deeds, which have become legend in these parts. Two challenges must be met to enter the tower.

Characters: A panther; the Sorcerer; the Headless Dead.

Headless Dead: Animated by magic, these warriors have remarkable skill for beings without heads. Some of the dead are recent, but others wear decayed ancient armor: Romans (from 8-12 points), Greek (6-14), Phoenician (2-8), perhaps even — gasp — Atlantean (8-20)!?

Normal Headless Dead

SIZ: 10	Move 1
DEX: 5	Damage 3d6
STR: 10	Hit Points 18
CON: 8	Armor varies

Attacks: Mace @10, Spear @10

Big Headless Dead

SIZ: 20	Move 2
DEX: 8	Damage 6d6
STR: 18	Hit Points 32
CON: 12	Armor varies

Attacks: Mace @10, Spear @10

These creatures cannot be knocked unconscious and must be reduced to zero hit points to be stopped. To break a leg so the creature cannot move properly, do a Major Wound.

The Sorcerer: The sorcerer is a necromancer of moderate skill at making the dead walk, but the wracking work of his profession has ravaged his body, as has age.

The Sorcerer

SIZ: 5	Move 1
DEX: 7	Damage 2d6+1d6*
STR: 8	Hit Points 15
CON: 10	Armor 2 (clothes)
APP: 5	

Attacks: Great Sword @22* (tell the players that he always attempts a beheading stroke)

*damage for Great weapon.

Significant Traits: Cowardly 16

Significant Passions: Hate (knights) 18

Significant Skills: Alchemy 27

Secrets: Killing the sorcerer will slay all the undead. If the knights can get past the undead and into the tower, they can more easily stop the menace.

Solutions: Challenge 1: The Panther's Way. The woods are vast and enchanted, and move around when no one is looking. To find the way through to the tower, knights must make two successive Hunting rolls, each with a -10 modifier. Each day of travel requires two rolls. Each night a panther frantically attacks the horses, ignoring all attacks upon it, intent only upon destroying horses.

Challenge 2: The Headless Undead. A large number of walking headless corpses, still wearing their armor, will fight the knights outside the tower. They may not be decoyed from their appointed area, but might be distracted or caged. Once defeated or bypassed, the knights may enter and kill the sorcerer, who is too cowardly to leave the safety of his home.

Glory: 5 points for each of the two successful Hunting rolls, and 75 for killing each Panther. 35 points for each undead. 25 for the sorcerer. 150 for completing the task of ending the curse.

Afterwards: The knights may be granted the tower as their own holding.

Stories

THE *PENDRAGON* CHRONOLOGY lists three major events of interest for the year 531. Given here are three scenario outlines for that year.

A gamemaster has many ways to use these. He might offer three distinct choices for the players to make. Alternately, he may choose to save a couple, and have them occur in upcoming years, out of the suggested chronology.

However they are used, they are given here with suggestions on integrating them into the campaign.

The Adventure of KEEPING UP WITH SIR LANCELOT

At an obscure manor, an insignificant stopping point on the way to adventure, a young knight stops in and asks if he can join your party. Player knights make Heraldry rolls or, if they have been to Camelot, Recognize rolls. They get a huge positive modifier and cannot fail, for this is Sir Lancelot himself. See the "Characters and Creatures" chapter for Sir Lancelot's Glory and attributes.

Challenges: Keeping up with Sir Lancelot is challenge enough for most characters, even though he is still young, and has not yet reached his full degree of prowess by the year 531.

Run one of the Short Adventures, and let the player knights observe the ways of the greatest of knights. Lancelot is generous and is willing to let the other knights attempt any challenges before he does.

Secrets: Before this adventure, the player knights should have had some chance to test other, more specific challenges appropriate to Lancelot's history. If they had visited Dolorous Garde, for instance, they might tell Sir Lancelot about it. They could then help him out, and perhaps witness Lancelot's discovery that his name lies under the slab of stone. Similarly, if the players have wisely withdrawn from combat with a Huge Giant, they will have an interesting dilemma when Lancelot charges right in against the monster, as he does in the story.

Remember, too, that Sir Lancelot might appear out of nowhere and rescue the players knights from a disaster.

Whatever the case, meeting with major characters like this is great fun for players. Don't be afraid to use such events.

The Adventure of MEETING SIR MORDRED

A handsome young knight asks to join the player knights. Success at [Heraldry] rolls shows that he is of the famous and powerful Orkney clan, kin to Sir Gawaine himself. He is Sir Mordred, the youngest of the clan, just come to court. He desires to prove himself for a while before visiting his uncle, the High King.

Challenges: This is a chance for player knights to meet and interact with important characters in a natural, innocent manner without bending any rules or social norms. Because first impressions are lasting impressions, the way this is played is very important.

Some sources portray Mordred as a good guy at first, not having any of his evil recognized by anyone. If this is the gamemaster's choice then player knights are likely to befriend Mordred just to know such an important person. Later this friendship will cause conflict for the player knights when their former experiences are shattered by Mordred's subsequent actions.

Other sources show him as being unctuous and dishonest from the start. If players choose this sort of friendship, perhaps they deserve the consequences.

The Adventure of the IRISH TOURNAMENT

Setting: Castle Anguish, in Ireland

Event: The King of Ireland has proclaimed a tournament to promote good will between his people and the knights of Britain. Heralds and messengers are traveling far and wide, and everyone agrees it will be a great event.

Characters: King Anguish, the sponsor.

Princess Isoud, daughter of the King.

Sir Gawaine, leading the contingent of Round Table knights.

Sir Palomides, a foreigner from Africa.

Sir Tramtrist, an unknown knight who has been staying at the Irish court.

Challenges: To participate in the tournament. It is a Regal tournament, and offers Glory for everyone.

Secrets: Sir Tramtrist will carry the day in this tournament, despite heroic efforts by Gawaine, Palomides, and the player knights. He is actually young Sir Tristram in disguise (use Sir Lamorak's attributes, as given in the "Characters and Creatures" chapter, plus Inspiration). Gamemasters should read of this event in Malory VIII, 9-10.

Event: The wife of King Anguish discovers that Sir Tramtrist is the killer of her brother and threatens to kill her guest. King Anguish upholds the laws of Hospitality and offers to let Tristram depart in peace. Tristram challenges the nobles of the court to fight him "man to man and body to body, here and now" if they think he did wrong. No one accepts, Tristram gets a Justice check, and departs.

This event is very illustrative of many important social customs, especially hospitality and challenge by combat.

Glory: As for Regal Tournament.

Afterwards: In later years, as gossip grows, recall to players that they witnessed the start of the love between Tristram and Isoud.

Characters and Creatures

Unique individuals and standardized people and creatures are detailed here.

Ordinary Characters

STANDARDIZED ATTRIBUTES FOR categories of people who are commonly met during play are given here. Actual individuals may vary from these, according to gamemaster desire and need.

These lists of attributes are given to fulfill the needs for combat. Any of these can be used as the base to establish a real individual with his own personality.

Traits, passions, and skills are noted if important or unusual (Honor for the Picts, for instance.) Unlisted skill values are around the minimum listed on the character sheet. Unlisted traits are 11, with 13s in the character's religious virtues. Unlisted passions have a value of 11, or are not held.

Note that Movement Rates for both characters and creatures not bearing heavy loads are increased as per the Movement rules in the "Game Mechanics" chapter.

Knights

Standard Knights

The first four knights can be taken as statistically standard knights. These are the nameless and faceless knights who are in the background of every story, but (for whatever reason) never distinguish themselves. The final knights listed are also nameless, but are distinguished. The Extraordinary knight can be used for most of the great knights like Sir Sagramore who are not described specifically in this chapter (but fine-tuning by the gamemaster is a good idea).

Young Knight

Current Glory 1200

SIZ: 14 Move 2

DEX: 11 Damage 4d6

STR: 11 Hit Points 28

CON: 14 Armor 10 + shield

APP: 11

Attacks: Sword 15, Lance 13, Spear 6, Dagger 5; Battle 10, Horsemanship 10

Significant Traits: Valorous 15

Significant Passions: Loyalty (lord) 15

Significant Skills: Awareness 10, Courtesy 5, First Aid 10, Heraldry 5, Hunting 5, Tourney 10

Horse: Charger (6d6)

Other Equipment: .5 £. clothing

Ordinary Knight (Middle-aged Knight)

Current Glory 1800

SIZ: 14 Move 3

DEX: 11 Damage 5d6

STR: 14 Hit Points 28

CON: 14 Armor 12 + shield

APP: 11

Attacks: Sword 20, Lance 15, Spear 10, Dagger 10; Battle 15, Horsemanship 15

Significant Traits: Valorous 15

Significant Passions: Loyalty (lord) 15

Significant Skills: Awareness 10, Courtesy 10, First Aid 10, Heraldry 10, Hunting 10, Tourney 10

Horse: Charger (6d6)

Other Equipment: 1 £. clothing

Old Knight

Current Glory 2500

SIZ: 11 Move 2

DEX: 8 Damage 4d6

STR: 11 Hit Points 22

CON: 11 Armor 12 + shield

APP: 8

Attacks: Sword 21, Lance 18, Spear 10, Dagger 10; Battle 18, Horsemanship 18

Significant Traits: Valorous 1d6+12

Significant Passions: Loyalty (lord) 15

Significant Skills: Awareness 15, Courtesy 15, First Aid 15, Heraldry 15, Hunting 15, Tourney 15

Horse: Charger (6d6)

Other Equipment: 2 £. clothing

Notable Knight

Current Glory 3000

SIZ: 15 Move 3

DEX: 11 Damage 5d6

STR: 14 Hit Points 30

CON: 15 Armor 12 + shield

APP: 11

Attacks: Sword 21, Lance 16, Spear 10, Dagger 10; Battle 16, Horsemanship 16

Significant Traits: Valorous 15

Significant Passions: one or more at 16

Significant Skills: Awareness 12, Courtesy 10, First Aid 10, Heraldry 10, Hunting 10, Tourney 10

Other Equipment: 2 £. clothing

Famous Knight

Current Glory 6000

SIZ: 16 Move 3

DEX: 13 Damage 5d6

STR: 14 Hit Points 31

CON: 15 Armor 12 + shield

APP: 13

Attacks: Sword 22, Lance 18, Axe 15 (+1d6 vs. opponents bearing shields), Spear 10, Dagger 10; Battle 18, Horsemanship 18

Significant Traits: Valorous 16

Significant Passions: one or more at 16

Significant Skills: Awareness 13, Courtesy 13, First Aid 13, Heraldry 13, Hunting 13, Tourney 13

Horse: Charger (6d6)

Other Equipment: 4 £. clothing

Extraordinary Knight

Current Glory 9000

SIZ: 17 Move 3

DEX: 16 Damage 6d6
STR: 16 Hit Points 33
CON: 16 Armor 14 + shield
APP: 16

Attacks: Sword 23, Lance 21, Spear 18, Axe 18 (+1d6 vs. opponents bearing shields), Mace 18 (+1d6 vs. opponents in chainmail), Dagger 10; Battle 18, Horsemanship 20

Significant Traits: Valorous 18, Prudent 16

Significant Passions: one or more at 16

Significant Skills: Awareness 16, Courtesy 16, First Aid 16, Heraldry 16, Hunting 16, Tourney 16, others at 5 or more

Horse: destrier (8d6)

Other Equipment: 8 £. clothing

Adjustments

Economics

Poor: downgrade steed, clothing worth only 1/2 £.

Rich or Superlative: upgrade the steed, add 1 £. clothing. Also see the "Wealth" chapter.

Chivalrous

Significant Traits: All chivalrous traits will total 80. Chivalrous knights get the Armor of Honor, 3 points of magical protection.

Religious

Significant Traits: Religious knights have all virtues at 16. Religious knights gain a bonus for virtue: see page 122.

Lovers

Significant Passion: Love or Amor for someone at value 16+. The main significance of this is that knights who are lovers can be temporarily Inspired, and get a bonus thereby.

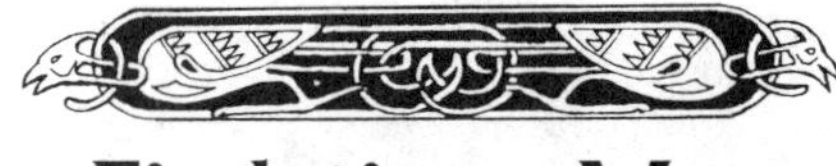

Fighting Men

Bandit

SIZ: 12 Move 2 (+1)
DEX: 10 Damage 4d6
STR: 12 Hit Points 24
CON: 12 Armor 4 + shield
APP: 8

Attacks: Great Spear 8, Light Crossbow 8 (1d6+10), Dagger 8

Significant Traits: Cruel 13, Valorous 8, Suspicious 16

Significant Passions: Hate (knights) 12

Significant Skills: Awareness 18, Hunting 16

Footsoldier

SIZ: 10 Move 2 (+1)
DEX: 10 Damage 3d6
STR: 10 Hit Points 23
CON: 13 Armor 4 + shield
APP: 10

Attacks: Spear 10, Sword 10, Dagger 6

Significant Traits: Valorous 12

Significant Passions: none

Significant Skills: Awareness 10

Archer

SIZ: 9 Move 2 (+1)
DEX: 10 Damage 3D6
STR: 10 Hit Points 24
CON: 15 Armor 4
APP: 10

Attacks: Bow 18 (3d6), Sword 8

Significant Traits: Valorous 10

Significant Passions: none

Significant Skills: Awareness 12, Hunting 8

Royal Guardsman

SIZ: 13 Move 3
DEX: 13 Damage 4d6 +1d6*
STR: 13 Hit Points 28
CON: 15 Armor 10
APP: 10

Attacks: Halberd* 17 (negates reflexive modifier for height), Great Sword* 13, Medium Crossbow 15 (1d6+13), Dagger 8

*damage bonus for using Great weapons

Significant Traits: Valorous 15

Significant Passions: Loyalty (Lord) 16

Significant Skills: Awareness 15

Sergeant or Mercenary Knight

SIZ: 13 Move 2
DEX: 10 Damage 4D6
STR: 13 Hit Points 28
CON: 15 Armor 10 + shield
APP: 10

Attacks: Lance 13, Sword 13

Note: rides on a poor charger, 5d6 damage

Significant Traits: Selfish 15, Valorous 13

Significant Passions: none

Significant Skills: Awareness 10

Experienced Sergeant or Mercenary Knight

SIZ: 13 Move 2
DEX: 10 Damage 4D6
STR: 13 Hit Points 28
CON: 15 Armor 12 + shield
APP: 10

Attacks: Lance 19, Sword 20

Note: rides on a charger, 6d6 damage

Significant Traits: Selfish 18, Arbitrary 17, Valorous 16

Significant Passions: none

Significant Skills: Awareness 15

Saxon Warrior

SIZ: 16 Move 2
DEX: 8 Damage 5d6
STR: 14 Hit Points 30
CON: 14 Armor 6 + shield
APP: 12

Attacks: Spear 13, Axe 14, Javelin 13

Significant Traits: Valorous 12

Significant Passions: Honor 10

Significant Skills: Awareness 15, Boating 12, Swimming 10

Saxon Chieftain

SIZ: 17 Move 2
DEX: 10 Damage 5d6+1d6*
STR: 13 Hit Points 30
CON: 13 Armor 12 + shield
APP: 12

Attacks: Spear 20, Axe 21, Javelin 17; Battle 15

*Bonus from following Wotanic religious virtues

Significant Traits: Valorous 17, all Wotanic virtues at 16

Significant Passions: Honor 15

Significant Skills: Awareness 15, Boating 18, Swimming 12

Saxon Berserk

SIZ: 17 Move 3
DEX: 13 Damage 6d6+2d6*
STR: 17 Hit Points 35
CON: 18 Armor 10
APP: 6

Attacks: Javelin 20, Great Axe 19*

*Damage bonus from Wotanic Religious Bonus, and for using Great weapons. Also regularly uses Berserker combat option.

Significant Traits: Valorous 22, all Wotanic virtues at 16

Significant Passions: Love (Wotan) 16; Honor 6

Significant Skills: Awareness 5, Boating 3, Swimming 4

Wild Pict Warrior

SIZ: 8 Move 3 (+2)
DEX: 14 Damage 3d6 +1d6*

Secondary Famous Knights List

1. Kalahard. Sable, 3 concentric orles or.
2. Sibilias. Or a fire gules.
3. Arphazat. Sable a saltire argent.
4. Agricol. Ermine.
5. Gallindes. Argent a martlet sable.
6. Dalides. Argent 2 dolphins hauriant addorsed sable, a circle around the eye gules.
7. Haran. Vert 3 pine cones or.
8. Malequin. Purpure, a bend argent charged with 3 lions gules.
9. Argahast. Or a bull passant gules, unguled armed and langued azure.
10. Ferrandon. Or 3 bars gemmel vert.
11. Radouyn. Sable a chaple artent opened sable.
12. Armon. Or a griffin vert, armed and beaked argent.
13. Lupin. Azure semey of crescents or.
14. Abilen. Sabe an escarbuncle or.
15. Felix. Vert a winged stag trippant or, unguled sable.
16. Fryadus. Party per chevron or and gules.
17. Rostelm. Or a wild man facing the dexter sable, holding upright in his dexter hand extended a club gules.
18. Sadach. Undy azure and argent.
19. Lambourc. Purpure a lion guardant argent armed and langed azure.
20. Ferrant. Gules a bear stantant or.

STR: 11 Hit Points 19
CON: 11 Armor 3 (magic)**
APP: 7

Attacks: Great Spear 14, Great Axe 15*, Javelin 18

*Damage bonus for Great Axe.

Picts also use the Double Feint Combat Tactic.

**Picts usually have magical armor tattooed on their bodies.

Significant Traits: Valorous 16

Significant Passions: Honor 12, Love (Goddess) 12

Significant Skills: Awareness 18, First Aid 15, Hunting 18, Faerie Lore 15

Ordinary Folk

Good Monk

SIZ: 10 Move 2 (+2)
DEX: 10 Damage 3d6
STR: 10 Hit Points 23+6*
CON: 13 Armor 1 (clothes)
APP: 10

Attacks: none

Significant Traits: Chaste 16, Forgiving 16, Merciful 15, Modest 17, Pious 16, Temperate 17, Valorous 5.

*He gets the Christian Religious Bonus.

Significant Passions: Love (God) 17

Significant Skills: First Aid 18, Chirurgery 18, Stewardship 12, Read (Latin) 6, Religion (Christian) 18

Possessions: bible, simple silver crucifix, bandages, simple travel gear

Bad Monk

SIZ: 10 Move 2 (+2)
DEX: 10 Damage 3d6
STR: 10 Hit Points 23
CON: 13 Armor 1 (clothes)
APP: 10

Attacks: Cudgel 14

Significant Traits: Chaste 4, Forgiving 10, Merciful 8, Modest 10, Temperate 4, Valorous 4

Significant Passions: Love (God) 3

Significant Skills: First Aid 4, Chirurgery 2, Stewardship 4, Religion (Christian) 4

Possessions: a cudgel, two bags of 2d20+6 pennies each, small silver crucifix, four fake relics

Common Farmer

SIZ: 8 Move 2 (+2)
DEX: 9 Damage 3d6
STR: 12 Hit Points 18
CON: 10 Armor 1 (clothes)
APP: 8

Attacks: hoe* 8

*treat as axe at gamemaster option

Significant Traits: Valorous 5

Significant Passions: none

Significant Skills: First Aid 10, Faerie Lore 5, Folk Lore 12, Hunting 2, Industry (Farming) 10, Stewardship 8

Rich Farmer, Merchant

SIZ: 14 Move 2 (+2)
DEX: 10 Damage 4d6
STR: 10 Hit Points 28
CON: 14 Armor 2 (heavy clothing)
APP: 8

Attacks: Sword 8

Significant Traits: Valorous 6

Significant Passions: none

Significant Skills: Awareness 15, First Aid 10, Folk Lore 16, Hunting 2, Orate 12, Stewardship 8

Possessions: 3d20 pennies, a fine sword, 2 £. clothing

Village Blacksmith

SIZ: 10 Move 3 (+2)
DEX: 13 Damage 5d6+1d6*
STR: 20 Hit Points 24
CON: 14 Armor 1 (apron)
APP: 7

Attacks: Great Hammer* 16 (*add damage for Great weapon)

Significant Traits: Valorous 12

Significant Passions: none

Significant Skills: Awareness 8, First Aid 10, Faerie Lore 8, Folk Lore 12, Industry (Smithing) 15

Women

Women characters given here are not primarily for combat, and require attention to personality rather than hit points and attack skills. These are provided as standards, from which interesting characters can be developed.

Typical Serving Girl

SIZ: 10 Move 2 (+2)
DEX: 13 Damage 3d6*
STR: 9 Hit Points 23
CON: 13 Armor 1 (clothes)
APP: 14

Attacks: Dagger 6 (*subtract one die for dagger)

Significant Traits: Chaste 10, Valorous 3

Significant Passions: none

Significant Skills: Awareness 10, Courtesy 3, First Aid 10, Folk Lore 13, Chirurgery 10, Industry 10

Maid-in-waiting

SIZ: 11 Move 2 (+2)
DEX: 14 Damage 3d6*
STR: 8 Hit Points 24
CON: 13 Armor 1 (clothes)
APP: 14

Attacks: Dagger 10 (*subtract one die for dagger)

Significant Traits: Chaste 13, Valorous 4

Significant Passions: none

Significant Skills: Awareness 8, Courtesy 8, First Aid 12, Chirurgery 9, Industry 13, Stewardship 7, Battle 3

Lady

Current Glory 250

SIZ: 10 Move 2 (+2)

DEX: 13 Damage 3d6*

STR: 10 Hit Points 25

CON: 15 Armor 2 (heavy robes)

APP: 15

Attacks: Dagger 10 (*subtract one die for dagger)

Significant Traits: Chaste 15, Valorous 5

Significant Passions: Hospitality 17

Significant Skills: Courtesy 14, Dance 12, First Aid 16, Chirurgery 17, Industry 15, Stewardship 12, Battle 10

Holding: 1 manor

Damosel

Current Glory 850

SIZ: 10 Move 2 (+2)

DEX: 11 Damage 3d6*

STR: 9 Hit Points 24

CON: 14 Armor 1 (clothes)

APP: 15

Attacks: Dagger 10 (*subtract one die for dagger)

Significant Traits: Chaste 17, Valorous 8

Significant Passions: Hospitality 16, Honor 17

Significant Skills: First Aid 16, Chirurgery 10, Industry 10, Stewardship 10, Battle 10

Holding: 9 manors

Famous People

GIVEN HERE ARE statistics for important gamemaster characters. Given first is a short description with notes on personality, to tell how he or she should be played. Significant Traits, Passions, Statistics, and/or Skills list notable attributes, and finally I provide notes for unique features of the character.

Most of these characters have gotten ahead in life through some unusual means: Lancelot was raised by the Lady of the Lake; Turquine had a sorcerous giantess for a mother; Guenever is the most beautiful woman in Britain; and so on. Of them all, Sir Ywaine is the closest to normal, and is at the height of Glory to which most character knights can hope to attain. Compare Sir Lancelot and the

King Arthur

King Arthur is the epitome of royalty, embodying all which is good in a king. Arthur is an accomplished warrior, despite the demands of his role as king which keep him at home. Much is said about him elsewhere.

Glory: King Arthur is "off the charts" for most *Pendragon* Glory measurements. The number of 100,000 is given as the ultimate number comprehensible.

Traits: Arthur is chivalrous, of course. His Justice and largesse (Generosity) are the highest in Britain.

Passions: Loyalty (Vassals) is renowned.

Stats: Although extremely stable physically, Arthur does not rely on his physical stats to impress people.

Skills: Arthur is expert at all courtly practices.

Combat Skills: Arthur is not a chessboard king. He is a great general, and excellent warrior as well.

Equipment: In court, Arthur's clothes cause everyone to attempt a Greedy and Worldly roll when they see them. Excalibur [Magic sword] — +10 to Sword Skill; Scabbard [Magical, now lost] — allows a maximum of 6 points of damage in one wound; Rhongomiant [Magic spear] — +5 Spear skill, +1d6damage, never breaks; Wynebgwrthucher [Magic shield] — The image of the Virgin Mary is like a portable Passion, in which a successful Piety roll while using the shield gives the benefits of being Inspired.

Special Notes: The High King is surrounded by pomp and almost unapproachable. If met personally he is disarmingly human, warm and friendly unless aroused to wrath; conciliatory until aroused to conquer.

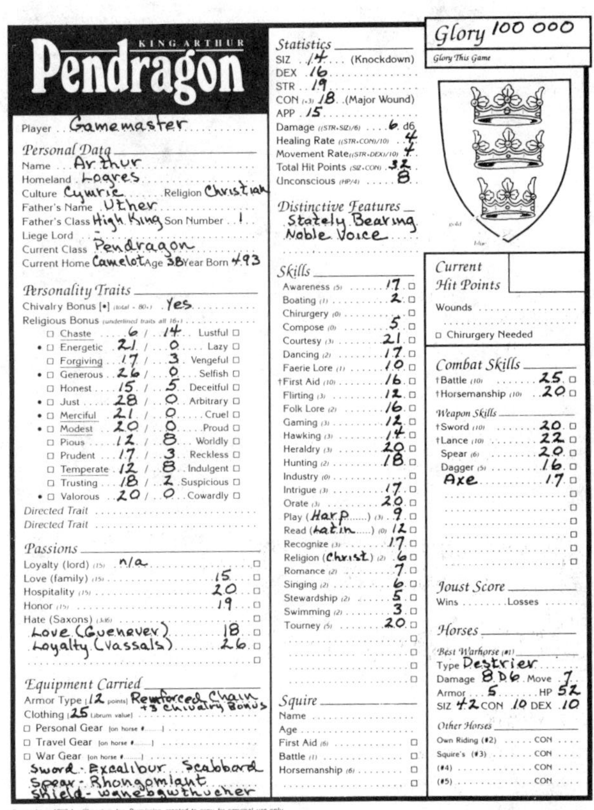

KING ARTHUR
Pendragon

Player: Gamemaster

Personal Data
Name: Arthur
Homeland: Logres
Culture: Cymric — Religion: Christian
Father's Name: Uther
Father's Class: High King — Son Number: 1
Liege Lord: -
Current Class: Pendragon
Current Home: Camelot — Age: 38 — Year Born: 493

Personality Traits
Chivalry Bonus [•] (total = 80+): Yes
Religious Bonus (underlined traits all 16+)

	Trait	Value	Value	Trait
	Chaste	6	14	Lustful
•	Energetic	21	0	Lazy
	Forgiving	17	3	Vengeful
•	Generous	26	0	Selfish
	Honest	15	5	Deceitful
•	Just	28	0	Arbitrary
•	Merciful	21	0	Cruel
•	Modest	20	0	Proud
	Pious	12	8	Worldly
	Prudent	17	3	Reckless
	Temperate	12	8	Indulgent
	Trusting	18	2	Suspicious
•	Valorous	20	0	Cowardly

Directed Trait
Directed Trait

Passions
Loyalty (lord) (15): n/a
Love (family) (15): 15
Hospitality (15): 20
Honor (15): 19
Hate (Saxons) (3d6)
Love (Guenever): 18
Loyalty (Vassals): 26

Equipment Carried
Armor Type [12 points]: Reinforced Chain +3 Chivalry Bonus
Clothing [25 Librum value]
Personal Gear [on horse #]
Travel Gear [on horse #]
War Gear [on horse #]
Sword - Excalibur, Scabbard
Spear - Rhongomiant
Shield - Wynebgwthucher

Statistics
SIZ: 14 (Knockdown)
DEX: 16
STR: 19
CON (+3): 18 (Major Wound)
APP: 15
Damage ((STR+SIZ)/6): 6 d6
Healing Rate ((STR+CON)/10): 4
Movement Rate ((STR+DEX)/10): 4
Total Hit Points (SIZ+CON): 32
Unconscious (HP/4): 8

Distinctive Features
Stately Bearing
Noble Voice

Skills

Awareness (5)	17
Boating (1)	2
Chirurgery (0)	
Compose (0)	5
Courtesy (3)	21
Dancing (2)	17
Faerie Lore (1)	10
†First Aid (10)	16
Flirting (3)	12
Folk Lore (2)	16
Gaming (3)	12
Hawking (3)	14
Heraldry (3)	20
Hunting (2)	18
Industry (0)	
Intrigue (3)	17
Orate (3)	20
Play (Harp) (3)	9
Read (Latin) (0)	12
Recognize (3)	17
Religion (Christ) (2)	6
Romance (2)	7
Singing (2)	6
Stewardship (2)	5
Swimming (2)	3
Tourney (5)	20

Squire
Name
Age
First Aid (6)
Battle (1)
Horsemanship (6)

Glory 100 000
Glory This Game

gold
blue

Current Hit Points
Wounds
Chirurgery Needed

Combat Skills
†Battle (10): 25
†Horsemanship (10): 20

Weapon Skills
†Sword (10): 20
†Lance (10): 22
Spear (6): 20
Dagger (5): 16
Axe: 17

Joust Score
Wins — Losses

Horses
Best Warhorse (#1)
Type: Destrier
Damage: 8D6 — Move: 7
Armor: 5 — HP: 52
SIZ: 42 — CON: 10 — DEX: 10

Other Horses
Own Riding (#2) — CON
Squire's (#3) — CON
(#4) — CON
(#5) — CON

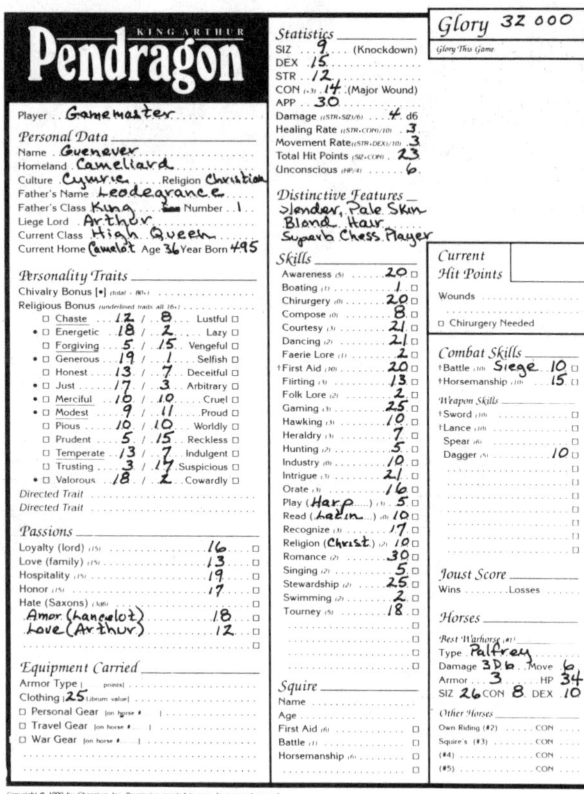

KING ARTHUR Pendragon

Player: Gamemaster

Personal Data
Name: Guenever
Homeland: Cameliard
Culture: Cymric — Religion: Christian
Father's Name: Leodegrance
Father's Class: King — Number: 1
Liege Lord: Arthur
Current Class: High Queen
Current Home: Camelot — Age: 36 — Year Born: 495

Personality Traits
Chivalry Bonus [•] (total = 80+)
Religious Bonus (underlined traits all 16+)

	Trait	Value	/	Value	Trait
	Chaste	12	/	8	Lustful
•	Energetic	18	/	2	Lazy
	Forgiving	5	/	15	Vengeful
•	Generous	19	/	1	Selfish
	Honest	13	/	7	Deceitful
•	Just	17	/	3	Arbitrary
•	Merciful	10	/	10	Cruel
•	Modest	9	/	11	Proud
	Pious	10	/	10	Worldly
	Prudent	5	/	15	Reckless
	Temperate	13	/	7	Indulgent
	Trusting	3	/	17	Suspicious
•	Valorous	18	/	2	Cowardly

Directed Trait
Directed Trait

Passions
Loyalty (lord) (15) 16
Love (family) (15) 13
Hospitality (15) 19
Honor (15) 17
Hate (Saxons) (3d6)
Amor (Lancelot) 18
Love (Arthur) 12

Equipment Carried
Armor Type (points)
Clothing (25 Librum value)
Personal Gear (on horse #)
Travel Gear (on horse #)
War Gear (on horse #)

Statistics
SIZ 9 (Knockdown)
DEX 15
STR 12
CON (+3) 14 (Major Wound)
APP 30
Damage ((STR+SIZ)/6) 4 d6
Healing Rate ((STR+CON)/10) 3
Movement Rate ((STR+DEX)/10) 3
Total Hit Points (SIZ+CON) 23
Unconscious (HP/4) 6

Distinctive Features
Slender, Pale Skin
Blond Hair
Superb Chess Player

Skills
Awareness (5) 20
Boating (1) 1
Chirurgery (0) 20
Compose (0) 8
Courtesy (3) 21
Dancing (2) 21
Faerie Lore (1) 2
†First Aid (10) 20
Flirting (3) 13
Folk Lore (2) 2
Gaming (3) 25
Hawking (3) 10
Heraldry (3) 7
Hunting (2) 5
Industry (0) 10
Intrigue (3) 21
Orate (3) 16
Play (Harp) (3) 5
Read (Latin) (0) 10
Recognize (3) 17
Religion (Christ) (2) 10
Romance (2) 30
Singing (2) 5
Stewardship (2) 25
Swimming (2) 2
Tourney (5) 18

Squire
Name
Age
First Aid (6)
Battle (1)
Horsemanship (6)

Glory 32 000
Glory This Game

Current Hit Points
Wounds
Chirurgery Needed

Combat Skills
†Battle (10) Siege 10
†Horsemanship (10) 15

Weapon Skills
†Sword (10)
†Lance (10)
Spear (6)
Dagger (5) 10

Joust Score
Wins — Losses

Horses
Best Warhorse (#1)
Type: Palfrey
Damage 3D6 — Move 6
Armor 3 — HP 34
SIZ 26 — CON 8 — DEX 10

Other Horses
Own Riding (#2) CON
Squire's (#3) CON
(#4) CON
(#5) CON

Queen Guenever

Guenever rules by personality. She is an expert at discerning men's motivations and using them to do her bidding. Fortunately for Britain, her bidding is always for the good of the kingdom, and she feels no need to exercise her power for her personal needs.

Guenever has not yet succumbed to her desire for Lancelot, though he Passions indicate a certain potential beyond the chaste Amor which now exists.

Glory: Guenever is heiress in her own right of a kingdom.

Traits: Arthur finds her Courage and Recklessness exciting.

Passions: Her Hospitality and Generosity are famous, but not fanatical. Note that her Amor (Lancelot) is more than both her Love and Loyalty (Arthur).

Stats: Guenever's APP is the highest in Britain.

Skills: Guenever has all the skills needed to run a diplomatic court, whether openly (with Courtesy, for instance) or in secret (Intrigue). She is also the Mistress of Romance.

Combat Skills: Guenever's Battle skill is restricted to withstanding a siege.

Equipment: The clothing of the High Queen is so rich that knights must attempt a Selfish and Worldly roll, where success gets a check and indicates a desire for the goods.

Special Notes: Guenever is a regal, aloof personage when appearing in state, every bit the High Queen. In person she is keen and intelligent, politely formal to everyone but her closest household, but surprisingly adept at learning the hearts of men and women.

KING ARTHUR Pendragon

Player: Gamemaster

Personal Data
Name: Ywaine
Homeland: Gorre
Culture: Cymric — Religion: Pagan
Father's Name: Uriens
Father's Class: King — Son Number: 1
Liege Lord: Arthur
Current Class: Round Table
Current Home: Camelot — Age: 31 — Year Born: 500

Personality Traits
Chivalry Bonus [•] (total = 80+) Yes
Religious Bonus (underlined traits all 16+) Yes

	Trait	Value	/	Value	Trait
	Chaste	4	/	16	Lustful
•	Energetic	18	/	2	Lazy
	Forgiving	10	/	10	Vengeful
•	Generous	18	/	2	Selfish
	Honest	17	/	3	Deceitful
•	Just	16	/	4	Arbitrary
•	Merciful	16	/	4	Cruel
•	Modest	4	/	16	Proud
	Pious	10	/	10	Worldly
	Prudent	13	/	7	Reckless
	Temperate	10	/	10	Indulgent
	Trusting	7	/	13*	Suspicious
•	Valorous	18	/	2	Cowardly

Directed Trait: * of mother +5
Directed Trait

Passions
Loyalty (lord) (15) Arthur 15
Love (family) (15) 16
Hospitality (15) 17
Honor (15) 17
Hate (Saxons) (3d6)
Love wife 20

Equipment Carried
Armor Type (14 points) Partial Plate +3 Chiv
Clothing (18 Librum value) Red & Gold Silk Jupon
Personal Gear (on horse #)
Travel Gear (on horse #)
War Gear (on horse #)

Statistics
SIZ 13 (Knockdown)
DEX 21
STR 17
CON (+3) 17 (Major Wound)
APP 16
Damage ((STR+SIZ)/6) 5 d6
Healing Rate ((STR+CON)/10) 3+2
Movement Rate ((STR+DEX)/10) 4
Total Hit Points (SIZ+CON) 30
Unconscious (HP/4) 8

Distinctive Features
Raven Black Eyes
Black Hair
High Cheek Bones

Skills
Awareness (5) 19
Boating (1) 3
Chirurgery (0)
Compose (0) 10
Courtesy (3) 16
Dancing (2) 5
Faerie Lore (1) 21
†First Aid (10) 17
Flirting (3) 12
Folk Lore (2) 15
Gaming (3) 5
Hawking (3) 15
Heraldry (3) 11
Hunting (2) 19
Industry (0)
Intrigue (3) 3
Orate (3) 7
Play (Harp) (3) 11
Read (....) (0)
Recognize (3) 16
Religion (Pagan) (2) 5
Romance (2) 12
Singing (2) 3
Stewardship (2) 3
Swimming (2) 5
Tourney (5) 16

Squire
Name
Age
First Aid (6)
Battle (1)
Horsemanship (6)

Glory 9000
Glory This Game

silver
blue

Current Hit Points
Wounds
Chirurgery Needed

Combat Skills
†Battle (10) 17
†Horsemanship (10) 21

Weapon Skills
†Sword (10) 20
†Lance (10) 20
Spear (6) 17
Dagger (5)
Great Sword 24

Joust Score
Wins — Losses

Horses
Best Warhorse (#1)
Type: Arab Charger
Damage 5D6 — Move 10
Armor 3 — HP 40
SIZ 30 — CON 10 — DEX 21

Other Horses
Own Riding (#2) CON
Squire's (#3) CON
(#4) CON
(#5) CON

Ywaine

Sir Ywaine is a nephew of King Arthur and the son of Morgan le Fay, the infamous Pagan priestess. Ywaine is the epitome of the Pagan knight, holding fast to the Old Ways of his northern ancestors.

Glory: Ywaine's Glory is typical of successful Round Table knights.

Traits: Ywaine is chivalrous, of course. He is the paragon of Pagan virtues (Lustful, Energetic, Generous, Honest, Proud) and gets the Pagan Religious bonus of +2 Healing Rate. He has learned to distrust his mother, Morgan le Fay.

Passions: Ywaine is unusual in having a hard-earned Love (Wife) passion which often inspires him in desperate moments.

Stats: Ywaine's DEX is his highest, and he sometimes applies his Inspiration to it for using the Double Feint attack.

Skills: Ywaine is competent in knightly skills, and is an expert at Faerie Lore.

Combat Skills: Ywaine is an excellent warrior, and uses the Double Feint attack when possible.

Equipment: Ywaine has a richly decorated suit of the latest partial plate armor. His horse, an Arab Charger, is the only one of its kind in Britain, and is one of the fastest horses known.

Special Notes: In the wilds Ywaine is often accompanied by a great lion which he befriended on an adventure.

Lamorak de Gales

Sir Lamorak is the current knight errant *par excellence*. He travels without cease, seeking danger and its subsequent glory. Lamorak is a tragic figure. The feud between his family and Sir Gawaine's is incessant, and interferes with Lamorak's time at court.

Lamorak is friendly and courteous, but overly proud of his rights and obligations as a knight.

Glory: 18,000 is the most Glory which a knight has gotten through war, adventuring, and hard work.

Traits: Lamorak is Chivalrous, of course. His Valor is among the highest known.

Passions: His Loyalty (Arthur) and Honor, though sometimes slipping during these years of ill-luck, are notable.

Stats: Lamorak is called "the fastest knight in Britain," thanks to his high DEX. He is a master of the Double Feint tactic.

Skills: Lamorak is a great hunter, like his father was, thanks to the years of adventure spent traveling through the forests.

Combat Skills: Lamorak is a great warrior in his own right. He also uses the Double Feint when he can.

Equipment: Though a wanderer, Lamorak (like most Round Table knights) has gotten the latest in armor: partial plate. He also has an exceptional horse: a Spanish horse trained both as a courser and as a charger!

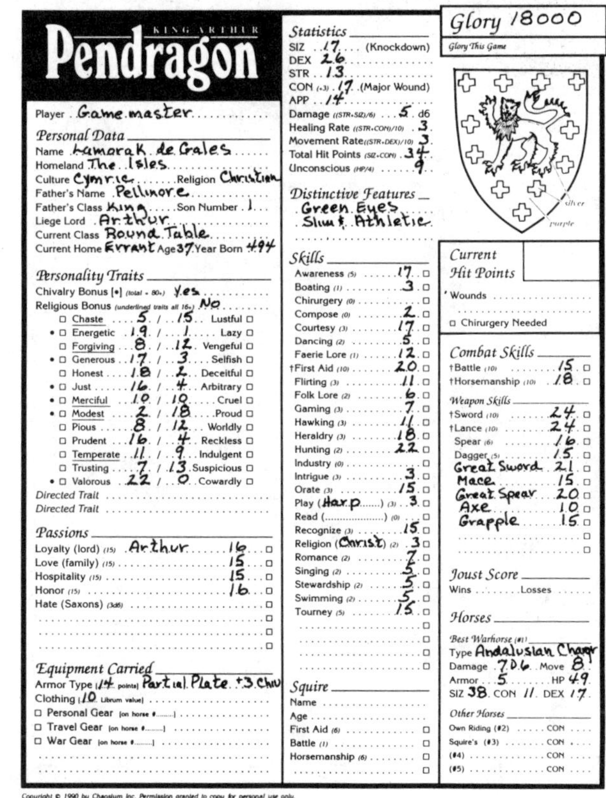

King Arthur Pendragon

Player: Game master

Personal Data
Name: Lamorak de Gales
Homeland: The Isles
Culture: Cymric — Religion: Christian
Father's Name: Pellinore
Father's Class: King — Son Number: 1
Liege Lord: Arthur
Current Class: Round Table
Current Home: Errant — Age 37 — Year Born 494

Personality Traits
Chivalry Bonus [•] (total - 80+): yes
Religious Bonus (underlined traits all 16+): No

	Trait	Value	/	Value	Trait
	Chaste	5	/	15	Lustful
•	Energetic	19	/	1	Lazy
	Forgiving	8	/	12	Vengeful
•	Generous	17	/	3	Selfish
	Honest	18	/	2	Deceitful
•	Just	16	/	4	Arbitrary
•	Merciful	10	/	10	Cruel
•	Modest	2	/	18	Proud
	Pious	8	/	12	Worldly
	Prudent	16	/	4	Reckless
	Temperate	11	/	9	Indulgent
	Trusting	7	/	13	Suspicious
•	Valorous	22	/	0	Cowardly

Directed Trait
Directed Trait

Passions
Loyalty (lord) (15) Arthur: 16
Love (family) (15): 15
Hospitality (15): 15
Honor (15): 16
Hate (Saxons) (3d6)

Equipment Carried
Armor Type (14 points): Partial Plate +3 Chiv
Clothing (10 Librum value)
Personal Gear (on horse #)
Travel Gear (on horse #)
War Gear (on horse #)

Statistics
SIZ 17 (Knockdown)
DEX 26
STR 13
CON (+3) 17 (Major Wound)
APP 14
Damage ((STR+SIZ)/6): 5 d6
Healing Rate ((STR+CON)/10): 3
Movement Rate ((STR+DEX)/10): 3
Total Hit Points (SIZ+CON): 34
Unconscious (HP/4): 9

Distinctive Features
Green Eyes
Slim & Athletic

Skills
Awareness (5): 17
Boating (1): 3
Chirurgery (0)
Compose (0): 2
Courtesy (3): 17
Dancing (2): 5
Faerie Lore (1): 12
†First Aid (10): 20
Flirting (3): 11
Folk Lore (2): 6
Gaming (3): 7
Hawking (3): 11
Heraldry (3): 18
Hunting (2): 22
Industry (0)
Intrigue (3): 3
Orate (3): 15
Play (Harp) (3): 3
Read (........) (0)
Recognize (3): 15
Religion (Christ) (2): 3
Romance (2): 7
Singing (2): 5
Stewardship (2): 5
Swimming (2): 5
Tourney (5): 15

Squire
Name
Age
First Aid (6)
Battle (1)
Horsemanship (6)

Glory 18000
Glory This Game

silver
purple

Current Hit Points
Wounds
Chirurgery Needed

Combat Skills
†Battle (10): 15
†Horsemanship (10): 18

Weapon Skills
†Sword (10): 24
†Lance (10): 24
Spear (6): 16
Dagger (5): 15
Great Sword: 21
Mace: 15
Great Spear: 20
Axe: 10
Grapple: 15

Joust Score
Wins ... Losses

Horses
Best Warhorse (#1)
Type: Andalusian Chargr
Damage 7D6 — Move 8
Armor 5 — HP 49
SIZ 38 — CON 11 — DEX 17

Other Horses
Own Riding (#2) ... CON
Squire's (#3) ... CON
(#4) ... CON
(#5) ... CON

Lancelot du Lac

Lancelot is a relative newcomer to court. He was raised in a magical place, under the tutelage of the Lady of the Lake who so strongly instilled in him all the virtues of chivalry that he is a fanatic for the cause.

Note that Lancelot has already begun to conceal his feelings about Guenever. At this stage in the campaign it is still Amor, not carnal Love.

Glory: Lancelot's astonishing Glory is from several sources: his ancestry, his connections with Faerie, the treasures he brought to court, his actions in the Roman and Irish wars, his fanatical devotion to chivalry and romantic knighthood, and his non-stop adventuring to prove himself to be the best of all Arthur's knights.

Traits: Lancelot is a fanatical devotee of Chivalry, and an accidental paragon of Christian virtue as well. Thus he gets the +3 Armor of Honor, and the +6 Hit Points for the Christian Religious Bonus. However, the flaw of his feelings for Guenever has begun to show in his self-deceit about her.

Passions: Lancelot has a perfect Loyalty (Arthur), balanced with a perfect Amor (Guenever).

Stats: In addition to great statistics, Lancelot has a magical shield (below) which can double his strength. Lancelot is endowed with supernatural statistics, thanks to his childhood spent in the faery realm under an enchanted lake, from whence he gains his name "du Lac."

Skills: Lancelot is good at everything that knights do. He is exceptional in Awareness, Romance, and Tourney.

Combat Skills: Lancelot is good at every weapon, and exceptional at Horsemanship and Sword. Best of all, he always gets a critical success at Lance.

Equipment: Lancelot has magical silver armor from the Lady of the Lake. His shield, which bears his coat of arms, also has the power to double his STR during combat. Lancelot's horse is a one-of-a-kind destrier, complete with the first set of barding seen in Britain, which is also trained as a courser.

Special Notes: Lancelot has a devoted old man as his personal, lifetime squire.

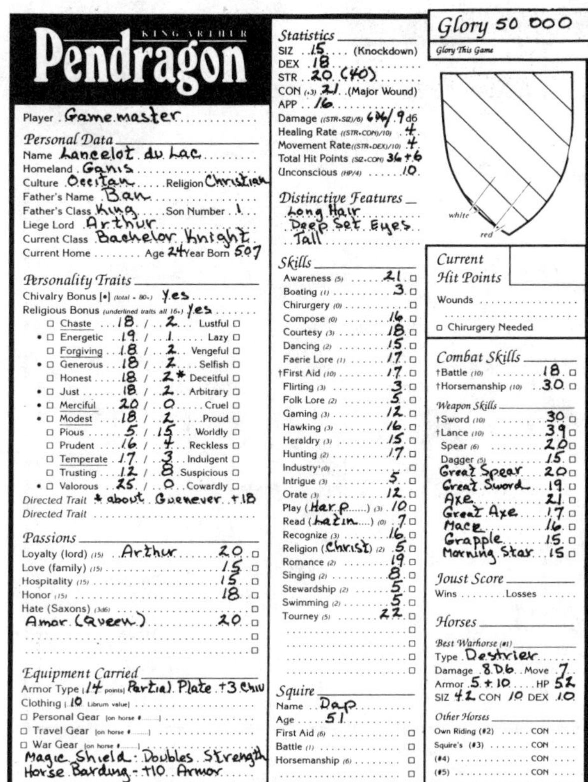

King Arthur Pendragon

Player: Game master

Personal Data
Name: Lancelot du Lac
Homeland: Ganis
Culture: Occitan — Religion: Christian
Father's Name: Ban
Father's Class: King — Son Number: 1
Liege Lord: Arthur
Current Class: Bachelor Knight
Current Home — Age 24 — Year Born 507

Personality Traits
Chivalry Bonus [•] (total - 80+): yes
Religious Bonus (underlined traits all 16+): yes

	Trait	Value	/	Value	Trait
	Chaste	18	/	2	Lustful
•	Energetic	19	/	1	Lazy
	Forgiving	18	/	2	Vengeful
•	Generous	18	/	2	Selfish
	Honest	18	/	2*	Deceitful
•	Just	18	/	2	Arbitrary
•	Merciful	20	/	0	Cruel
•	Modest	18	/	2	Proud
	Pious	5	/	15	Worldly
	Prudent	16	/	4	Reckless
	Temperate	17	/	3	Indulgent
	Trusting	12	/	8	Suspicious
•	Valorous	25	/	0	Cowardly

Directed Trait: * about Guenever +18
Directed Trait

Passions
Loyalty (lord) (15) Arthur: 20
Love (family) (15): 15
Hospitality (15): 15
Honor (15): 18
Hate (Saxons) (3d6)
Amor (Queen): 20

Equipment Carried
Armor Type (14 points): Partial Plate +3 Chiv
Clothing (10 Librum value)
Personal Gear (on horse #)
Travel Gear (on horse #)
War Gear (on horse #)
Magic Shield: Doubles Strength
Horse Barding - +10 Armor

Statistics
SIZ 15 (Knockdown)
DEX 18
STR 20 (40)
CON (+3) 21 (Major Wound)
APP 16
Damage ((STR+SIZ)/6): 6 / 9 d6
Healing Rate ((STR+CON)/10): 4
Movement Rate ((STR+DEX)/10): 4
Total Hit Points (SIZ+CON): 36 +6
Unconscious (HP/4): 10

Distinctive Features
Long Hair
Deep Set Eyes
Tall

Skills
Awareness (5): 21
Boating (1): 3
Chirurgery (0)
Compose (0): 16
Courtesy (3): 18
Dancing (2): 15
Faerie Lore (1): 17
†First Aid (10): 17
Flirting (3): 3
Folk Lore (2): 5
Gaming (3): 12
Hawking (3): 16
Heraldry (3): 15
Hunting (2): 17
Industry (0)
Intrigue (3): 5
Orate (3): 12
Play (Harp) (3): 10
Read (Latin) (0): 7
Recognize (3): 16
Religion (Christ) (2): 5
Romance (2): 19
Singing (2): 8
Stewardship (2): 5
Swimming (2): 5
Tourney (5): 22

Squire
Name: Dap
Age: 51
First Aid (6)
Battle (1)
Horsemanship (6)

Glory 50 000
Glory This Game

white
red

Current Hit Points
Wounds
Chirurgery Needed

Combat Skills
†Battle (10): 18
†Horsemanship (10): 30

Weapon Skills
†Sword (10): 30
†Lance (10): 39
Spear (6): 20
Dagger (5): 15
Great Spear: 20
Great Sword: 19
Axe: 21
Great Axe: 17
Mace: 16
Grapple: 15
Morning Star: 15

Joust Score
Wins ... Losses

Horses
Best Warhorse (#1)
Type: Destrier
Damage 8D6 — Move 7
Armor 5 + 10 — HP 52
SIZ 42 — CON 10 — DEX 10

Other Horses
Own Riding (#2) ... CON
Squire's (#3) ... CON
(#4) ... CON
(#5) ... CON

KING ARTHUR **Pendragon**

Player: Gamemaster

Personal Data
Name: Gawaine de Orkney
Homeland: Lothian
Culture: Cymric — Religion: Christian
Father's Name: Lot
Father's Class: King — Son Number: 1
Liege Lord: Arthur
Current Class: Round Table
Current Home: Camelot — Age: 36 — Year Born: 495

Personality Traits
Chivalry Bonus [•] (total = 80+): yes
Religious Bonus (underlined traits all 16+)

Trait	Value		Value	Trait
Chaste	3	/	17*	Lustful
• Energetic	18	/	2	Lazy
Forgiving	2	/	18	Vengeful
• Generous	16	/	4	Selfish
Honest	16	/	4	Deceitful
• Just	13	/	7	Arbitrary
• Merciful	16	/	4	Cruel
• Modest	4	/	16	Proud
Pious	6	/	14	Worldly
Prudent	6	/	14	Reckless
Temperate	10	/	10	Indulgent
Trusting	10	/	10	Suspicious
• Valorous	18	/	2	Cowardly

Directed Trait: * -15 for married women
Directed Trait:

Passions
Loyalty (lord) (15): Arthur 23
Love (family) (15): 22
Hospitality (15): 15
Honor (15): 18
Hate (Saxons) (3d6):
Hate (de Gales Clan): 20

Equipment Carried
Armor Type (14 points): Partial Plate +3 Cha[in]
Clothing (20 Librum value)
Personal Gear (on horse #)
Travel Gear (on horse #)
War Gear (on horse #)

Statistics
SIZ: 17 (Knockdown)
DEX: 15
STR: 18
CON (+3): 19 (Major Wound)
APP: 17
Damage ((STR+SIZ)/6): Special d6
Healing Rate ((STR+CON)/10): 4
Movement Rate ((STR+DEX)/10): 3
Total Hit Points (SIZ+CON): 36
Unconscious (HP/4): 9

Distinctive Features
Red Hair
Charming Smile
Robust Voice

Skills
Awareness (5): 16
Boating (1): 5
Chirurgery (0):
Compose (0): 7
Courtesy (3): 25
Dancing (2): 20
Faerie Lore (1): 12
†First Aid (10): 17
Flirting (3): 27
Folk Lore (2): 2
Gaming (3): 12
Hawking (3): 17
Heraldry (3): 17
Hunting (2): 17
Industry (0):
Intrigue (3): 6
Orate (3): 12
Play (Harp) (3): 10
Read (Ogham) (0): 2
Recognize (3): 10
Religion (Christ) (2): 2
Romance (2): 23
Singing (2): 12
Stewardship (2): 10
Swimming (2): 6
Tourney (5): 22

Squire
Name
Age
First Aid (6)
Battle (1)
Horsemanship (6)

Glory 32 000
Glory This Game

gold
purple

Current Hit Points
Wounds
Chirurgery Needed

Combat Skills
†Battle (10): 18
†Horsemanship (10): 23

Weapon Skills
†Sword (10): 26
†Lance (10): 27
Spear (6): 20
Dagger (5):
Mace: 10
Hammer: 17
Great Sword: 15
Grapple: 15

Joust Score
Wins — Losses

Horses
Best Warhorse (#1)
Type: Faerie
Damage: 6D6 — Move: 10
Armor: 5 — HP: 35
SIZ: 30 — CON: 14 — DEX: 10

Other Horses
Own Riding (#2) — CON
Squire's (#3) — CON
(#4) — CON
(#5) — CON

KING ARTHUR **Pendragon**

Player: Gamemaster

Personal Data
Name: Brus sans Pitie
Homeland: Kent
Culture: Cymric — Religion: Christian
Father's Name
Father's Class — Son Number
Liege Lord: None
Current Class: Outlaw
Current Home — Age — Year Born

Personality Traits
Chivalry Bonus [•] (total = 80+)
Religious Bonus (underlined traits all 16+)

Trait	Value		Value	Trait
Chaste	20*	/	0	Lustful
• Energetic	18	/	2	Lazy
Forgiving	4	/	16	Vengeful
• Generous	5	/	15	Selfish
Honest	2	/	18	Deceitful
• Just	1	/	19	Arbitrary
• Merciful	0	/	20	Cruel
• Modest	5	/	15	Proud
Pious	5	/	15	Worldly
Prudent	17	/	3	Reckless
Temperate	17	/	3	Indulgent
Trusting	3	/	17	Suspicious
• Valorous	2	/	18	Cowardly

Directed Trait: * +8 with noblewomen
Directed Trait:

Passions
Loyalty (lord) (15): None 2
Love (family) (15): 10
Hospitality (15): 3
Honor (15): 4
Hate (Saxons) (3d6):
Hate (Arthur): 21

Equipment Carried
Armor Type (12 points): Reinforced Chain
Clothing (10 Librum value): Black with Sapphires
Personal Gear (on horse #)
Travel Gear (on horse #)
War Gear (on horse #)

Statistics
SIZ: 17 (Knockdown)
DEX: 23
STR: 21
CON (+3): 17 (Major Wound)
APP: 8
Damage ((STR+SIZ)/6): 6 d6
Healing Rate ((STR+CON)/10): 4
Movement Rate ((STR+DEX)/10): 4
Total Hit Points (SIZ+CON): 34
Unconscious (HP/4): 8

Distinctive Features
Close Set Eyes
Snarl

Skills
Awareness (5): 18
Boating (1): 5
Chirurgery (0): 7
Compose (0):
Courtesy (3): 20
Dancing (2): 20
Faerie Lore (1): 7
†First Aid (10): 17
Flirting (3): 3
Folk Lore (2): 2
Gaming (3): 3
Hawking (3): 3
Heraldry (3): 7
Hunting (2): 15
Industry (0):
Intrigue (3): 19
Orate (3): 3
Play (Drum) (3): 3
Read (..........) (0):
Recognize (3): 7
Religion (Christ) (2): 2
Romance (2): 2
Singing (2): 2
Stewardship (2): 2
Swimming (2): 10
Tourney (5): 5
Disguise: 17

Squire
Name
Age
First Aid (6)
Battle (1)
Horsemanship (6)

Glory 13 000
Glory This Game

white
black

Current Hit Points
Wounds
Chirurgery Needed

Combat Skills
†Battle (10): 10
†Horsemanship (10): 20

Weapon Skills
†Sword (10): 20
†Lance (10): 25
Spear (6): 20
Dagger (5):
Great Sword: 20
Axe: 20

Joust Score
Wins — Losses

Horses
Best Warhorse (#1)
Type: Faerie
Damage: 6D6 — Move: 12
Armor: 5 — HP: 35
SIZ: 30 — CON: 14 — DEX: 10

Other Horses
Own Riding (#2) — CON
Squire's (#3) — CON
(#4) — CON
(#5) — CON

Gawaine

Gawaine is the leading knight at King Arthur's court, and works hard to epitomize the chivalrous ideal. He is gracious, generous, and strives to make newcomers to court feel welcome. He is the master of courtliness. He does, however, have a weakness for women, and a relentless streak of vengeance where his family is concerned. This latter is especially apparent in his hatred against the de Gales family.

Glory: Until Lancelot came, Gawaine had the highest Glory of all the Knights of the Round Table.

Significant Traits: Gawaine is Chivalrous, of course. He is also Lustful, except with married women. Though Christian, his pattern of Traits is functionally Pagan.

Significant Passions: Gawaine works to make his Loyalty (Arthur) the highest known. His Love (Family) is fanatical to the point of weakness. His Hate (de Gales Clan) is total.

Significant Stats: Gawaine's STR is magically enhanced; see Special Notes (below).

Significant Skills: Courtesy, Flirting, Romance, Tourney

Combat Skills: All weapons are known. A cautious fighter, Gawaine sometimes uses the Defense tactic to wear down his enemies. Also see below under special notes.

Equipment: Gawaine's clothing is second only to the High King's. His armor, the most up-to-date, is also jeweled and etched and worth twice as much as normal armor. Gawaine has a magical Faerie horse which he earned in an adventure, which is the only way to get them.

Special Notes: Sir Gawaine has a secret magical power, unique to him, and unknown outside his immediate family. Gawaine's strength increases in accord with the position of the sun. It increases every day from dawn until noon, then decreases. Thus, although he is normally no stronger than most player knights in the evening and morning and at night, he is twice that at noon. Estimate the time of day, and use this schedule for his Damage value: Before 7AM = 5d6; 7AM-9AM = 6d6; 9AM-11AM = 7d6; 11AM-1PM = 8d6; 1PM-3PM = 7d6; 3PM-5PM = 6d6; After 5PM = 5d6. Gawaine, great gentleman that he is, usually withholds his full strength during any combat for love, and may even take rebated (blunted) weapons into a fight to ensure the safety of other fighters.

Brus sans Pitie

Sir Brus without Pity is a dastardly knight without virtue or honor. He kills women and children without remorse, and has survived through lies, deceit, and cowardly flight from his betters.

Brus is often inspired by his Hate (Arthur) passion.

Significant Traits: Energetic, Vengeful, Deceitful, Arbitrary, Cruel, Prudent, Temperate, Suspicious, Cowardly

Significant Passions: Honor, Hate (Arthur)

Significant Stats: DEX, STR

Significant Skills: Lance, Other Weapons

Special Notes: Brus owns a faerie horse which has saved his life many times.

Turquine

Sir Turquine is a notorious Saxon outlaw knight. From his hidden castle, the Dolorous Tower, someplace in Essex, he leads bands of Saxon outlaws to raid and plunder surrounding lands. However, he is a warrior *par excellence* and admires others of like ability. Thus he does not kill anyone who puts up a good fight, but imprisons them in his castle.

Glory: Turquine is immensely successful in his rebellion against King Arthur and his British ways. He is the most Glorious of all the knights who are not kings.

Traits: Turquine qualifies for the Wotanic religious bonus (Generous, Proud, Worldly, Reckless, Indulgent) of +1d6 damage.

Passions: Turquine's basically excellent character is ruined by his driving hatreds. However, these hates serve him well for Inspiration in a fight.

Stats: The stats, especially SIZ, are the result of having a giantess for a mother.

Skills: Turquine's skills reflect his ability to survive, and express no refinement.

Combat Skills: Turquine is an expert fighter at almost anything. As a last resort in a stalemated fight he will Grapple. He enjoys the Berserker tactic on occasion.

Equipment: Turquine's horse is the best he has been able to get by conquering knights, but is not the latest type (destrier). His armor is likewise good, but not up to latest Round Table standards.

Special Notes: Turquine's sorcerous mother has enchanted his skin.

KING ARTHUR **Pendragon**

Player: Gamemaster

Personal Data
Name: Turquine
Homeland: Essex
Culture: Saxon — Religion: Wotanic
Father's Name: ?
Father's Class: Noble — Son Number: 2
Liege Lord: None
Current Class: Knight
Current Home: Dolorus Tower — Age: ? — Year Born: ?

Personality Traits
Chivalry Bonus [•] (total = 80+): NO
Religious Bonus (underlined traits all 16+): +1D6 Damage

	Chaste	10	10	Lustful
•	Energetic	16	4	Lazy
	Forgiving	2	18	Vengeful
•	Generous	17	3	Selfish
	Honest	10	10	Deceitful
•	Just	10	10	Arbitrary
•	Merciful	10	10	Cruel
•	Modest	0	21	Proud
	Pious	4	16	Worldly
	Prudent	3	17	Reckless
	Temperate	4	16	Indulgent
	Trusting	10	10*	Suspicious
•	Valorous	17	3	Cowardly

Directed Trait: * Non-Saxons +10
Directed Trait:

Passions

Passion	Value
Loyalty (lord) (15)	
Love (family) (15)	19
Hospitality (15)	17
Honor (15)	16
Hate (Saxons) (3d6)	
Hate (Cymri)	19
Hate (Lancelot)	21

Equipment Carried
Armor Type (12 points): Reinforced Chain*
Clothing (8 Librum value)
Personal Gear (on horse #)
Travel Gear (on horse #)
War Gear (on horse #)
* Enchanted skin +6 armor

Statistics
SIZ 25 (Knockdown)
DEX 18
STR 19
CON (+3) 19 (Major Wound)
APP 15
Damage ((STR+SIZ)/6): 8 d6
Healing Rate ((STR+CON)/10): 4
Movement Rate ((STR+DEX)/10): 4
Total Hit Points (SIZ+CON): 44
Unconscious (HP/4): 11

Distinctive Features
Yellow Hair
Horny Skin*

Skills

Awareness (5)	18
Boating (1)	12
Chirurgery (0)	
Compose (0)	2
Courtesy (3)	6
Dancing (2)	5
Faerie Lore (1)	7
†First Aid (10)	18
Flirting (3)	5
Folk Lore (2)	12
Gaming (3)	15
Hawking (3)	3
Heraldry (3)	7
Hunting (2)	21
Industry (0)	
Intrigue (3)	5
Orate (3)	18
Play (Horn) (3)	5
Read (Runes) (0)	7
Recognize (3)	5
Religion (Wotan) (2)	10
Romance (2)	2
Singing (2)	5
Stewardship (2)	6
Swimming (2)	17
Tourney (5)	8

Squire
Name
Age
First Aid (6)
Battle (1)
Horsemanship (6)

Glory 16 000
Glory This Game

Black
white

Current Hit Points
Wounds
Chirurgery Needed

Combat Skills

†Battle (10)	20
†Horsemanship (10)	20

Weapon Skills

†Sword (10)	20
†Lance (10)	23
Spear (6)	20
Dagger (5)	18
Great Axe (+1D6)	24
Axe	20
Crossbow	18
Great Spear	18
Grapple	15

Joust Score
Wins — Losses

Horses
Best Warhorse (#1)
Type: Andalusian Chargr
Damage: 7D6 — Move: 8
Armor: 5 — HP: 49
SIZ 38 — CON 11 — DEX 17

Other Horses
Own Riding (#2) — CON
Squire's (#3) — CON
(#4) — CON
(#5) — CON

other famous people to the Standard Knights to appreciate how far above the ordinary these heroic characters are.

These characters show many minor traits not explained in this book. See the horses, for instance. These are explained further in *Knights Adventurous*.

Alternative Round Table Knights

Most of the famous knights of the Round Table have complex stories attached to them which significantly affect their behavior towards each other. Your campaign may not want to bother with those old tales, but still have the weight of authenticity to give flavor. Thus the nearby Secondary Famous Knights list gives 20 knights cited as Round Table knights, but about whom we know almost nothing except their name and coat of arms. We are supposed to presume that each had as complex a tale as (say) La Cote Mal Taile, but we do not have it recorded in literature, so the tale of each knight may be created by the gamemaster.

The arms are listed according to standard heraldic nomenclature. We regret that we were unable to supply illustrations.

The Stable

Types of Steeds

The training which a horse receives is more important than its breed or type. A large pony can be trained for combat, for instance, although most of them are too small to be of significant value in combat. Custom determines what a horse is trained for, as well as knowledge of equestrian husbandry. This section assumes that ordinary custom has been followed.

carthorse: small, inexpensive horse used by peasants to pull carts

charger: a war-trained horse; the standard knight's horse; most chargers are crossbreeds of native ponies with the Great Horse or larger foreign breeds.

courser: a large, fast light horse used as a knight's riding animal. Coursers may be trained for battle, and are the steeds especially trained for the hunt.

destrier: a large, war-trained horse. In this case the term also indicates a breed, for only the Great Horse is big enough to be a destrier.

nag: a broken or old horse of any type, capable of carrying goods but nothing else.

palfrey: an excellent riding horse. Some are noted for gentleness and easy handling, making it favored for women. These gentle beasts are sometimes classified as amblers, trotters, or pacers.

rouncy: a standard riding horse, slow and small, but comfortable and hardy.

sumpter: a pack horse or pony.

Combat Training

Horses can be trained for combat, and must be if the rider is to concentrate fully on his task. All horses labelled Charger, Courser, Rouncy, and Destrier are assumed to have been battle trained, as reflected in their price and usage. Because they have this training no extra rolls must be made in a fight, as with riding horses.

At this time in *Pendragon* no horses which fight are known. The gamemaster is warned against introducing rules for attack-trained horses. See *Knights Adventurous* for information on fighting horses.

Horses which are not combat trained are difficult to handle during the press and panic of a bloody fight. In combat riders on non-combat trained horses must attempt a Horsemanship roll on the Normal Horses in Combat Table before any other actions every combat round. Combat-trained horses do not require this roll.

Normal Horses in Combat Table

Critical success = the horse does not need another Horsemanship roll for the rest of this fight.

Success = the character may fight, as normal.

Failure = the character cannot fight, but can try to evade attacks with another Horsemanship roll.

Fumble = no fall is suffered, but the horse broke control and bolted out of battle. It will run until another Horsemanship roll is made.

Hunting Horses

Some horses, especially coursers, are trained for the hunt. When required to make a Horsemanship roll while hunting, or otherwise chasing through the woods, add +5 to your skill as a modifier while riding a trained hunting courser.

Magical Horses

Magical horses are extraordinary, but well-known. They may only be gained from adventures, never purchased. They usually have magical armor or movement rates, but other game effects are possible.

To win a magical horse requires a heroic effort or deed, as determined by the gamemaster. Possibly the trust of the steed must be established, if it is to accept its position in your stable. Or mastery must be gained, through a grueling series of Horsemanship rolls or other efforts.

Ruining Horses

Horses are sturdy, but breakable. Horses can be permanently ruined for combat work and hard labor if they are broken. A horse is broken if:

- It takes a major wound; or
- It fumbles a CON roll during a Forced March or other extended exertion.

Steeds

Destrier

SIZ 42	Move 7	Major Wound 10
DEX 10	Damage 8d6	Unconscious 13
STR 38	Heal Rate 5	Knockdown 42
CON 10	Hit Points 52	Armor 5

Destriers are combat-trained.

Charger

SIZ 34	Move 8	Major Wound 12
DEX 17	Damage 6d6	Unconscious 12
STR 30	Heal Rate 4	Knockdown 34
CON 12	Hit Points 46	Armor 5

Chargers are combat-trained.

Courser

SIZ 30	Move 9	Major Wound 15
DEX 25	Damage 5d6	Unconscious 11
STR 24	Heal Rate 4	Knockdown 30
CON 15	Hit Points 45	Armor 5

Coursers are hunt-trained, and combat-trained.

Rouncy

SIZ 26	Move 6	Major Wound 14
DEX 10	Damage 4d6	Unconscious 10
STR 18	Heal Rate 3	Knockdown 26
CON 14	Hit Points 40	Armor 4

Rouncys are combat-trained.

Palfrey

SIZ 26	Move 6	Major Wound 8
DEX 10	Damage 3d6	Unconscious 9
STR 16	Heal Rate 2	Knockdown 26
CON 8	Hit Points 34	Armor 3

Sumpter

SIZ 22	Move 5	Major Wound 16
DEX 12	Damage 3d6	Unconscious 10
STR 15	Heal Rate 3	Knockdown 22
CON 16	Hit Points 38	Armor 3

A squire tends several horses. From the left, we see a courser, a destrier (in the back), and a rouncy.

Carthorse

SIZ 15	Move 4	Major Wound 10
DEX 10	Damage 2d6	Unconscious 6
STR 15	Heal Rate 3	Knockdown 15
CON 10	Hit Points 25	Armor 3

Nag

Any of the above which have been broken are classified as nags. Thus their attributes can range widely, but all are unspirited, slow, and uninspired.

Donkey

SIZ 15	Move 5	Major Wound 15
DEX 15	Damage 4d6	Unconscious 8
STR 20	Heal Rate 4	Knockdown 15
CON 15	Hit Points 30	Armor 3

Mule

SIZ 25	Move 6	Major Wound 18
DEX 8	Damage 6d6	Unconscious 11
STR 25	Heal Rate 4	Knockdown 25
CON 18	Hit Points 43	Armor 4

The Kennel and Mews

Dogs are almost as valued as horses. Dogs are important for a successful hunt, and a -5 or greater modifier should be given to the Hunting skill if prey is being followed without dogs.

Dog breeds are unusual, and almost all of them are either brachets or gaze hounds. The first hunts by scent, the second by sight. A pack of hounds usually includes some of each.

The Mews are a special bird house where the falcons and hawks are kept.

Dog

All kinds of dogs are included in these statistics. Every household has some type of mutt which barks at strangers and feeds on scraps. Very rare or valuable dogs would have better attributes than this; an example is given, the Irish Wolfhound.

SIZ 4	Move 8	Major Wound 12
DEX 25	Damage 2d6	Unconscious 4
STR 12	Heal Rate 2	Knockdown 4
CON 12	Hit Points 16	Armor 1
Bite 8		

Irish Wolfhound

This unusual animal is a rare, very valuable domestic dog. It is more common in Ireland, and sometimes is given as a prize in Britain.

SIZ 12	Move 7	Major Wound 12
DEX 20	Damage 3d6	Unconscious 6
STR 13	Heal Rate 3	Knockdown 12
CON 12	Hit Points 24	Armor 2
Bite 10		

Hawk

All hawks are classified under these statistics.

SIZ 1	Move 20	Major Wound 5	STR 5	Heal Rate 2	Knockdown 1
DEX 20	Damage 1d6	Unconscious 2	CON 5	Hit Points 6	Armor 0

Hunted Beasts

CHARACTERS OFTEN HAVE occasion to meet these creatures on the hunt, and so their precise attributes are given.

Note the new attributes given here for some creatures. If an animal does not have these attributes, values for both are zero.

Avoidance: how well the animal is at hiding in the woods. It will pits its Avoidance against your Hunt skill. If it wins, it escapes.

Modifier to Valorous: Any creature with a negative value here cannot be attacked without a character first making a successful Valorous roll. The modified roll is made upon sighting the creature. Only one roll is needed to initiate the attack. Failure indicates reluctance to close with the beast that round (another roll may be made next round) while a fumble indicates that the character flees in terror. Remember that modifiers for the situation should also be applied; for example, if a helpless character is in danger a positive modifier to Valorous would be appropriate.

Glory to Kill: Average amount of Glory gained by slaying the creature with its attributes as given.

Bear

The brown bear is the only bruin native to Britain. It tries to avoid humans, but if trapped can be deadly. A popular entertainment is to pit a bull versus a bear in a pit or arena.

SIZ 25	Move 8	Major Wound 18
DEX 10	Damage special	Unconscious 11
STR 25	Heal Rate 4	Knockdown 25
CON 18	Hit Points 43	Armor 6

Avoidance: 7

Modifier to Valorous: 0

Glory to Kill: 10

Attacks: 2 paw swipes @13. Bears may attack only one target per melee round. If the bear wins the round with an attack roll, it makes two 3d6 damage rolls instead of the usual single attack. This simulates the bear's mauling and slapping attacks. When combating a mounted foe, a bear usually attacks the rider first.

A bear always completes one more attack after his hit points reach 0, he becomes unconscious, or receives a Major Wound. Thus a bear fights one round after he is dead.

Boar

The wild boar is a cunning and savage creature, deadly when cornered. As a species they are quite pugnacious, and the old solitary boars are very dangerous.

SIZ 20	Move 8	Major Wound 25
DEX 15	Damage 6d6	Unconscious 11
STR 30	Heal Rate 6	Knockdown 20
CON 25	Hit Points 45	Armor 5

Avoidance: 10

Modifier to Valorous: 0

Glory to Kill: 15

Attacks: tusk slash @18, trample @18 against prone foe.

When combating a mounted foe a boar always attacks the horse first since he cannot reach higher. Boars try to charge their foes and make a tusk slash as they pass.

Boars fight for a round after death, unconsciousness, or a major wound.

Bull

The male domestic cattle can be fierce in combat when defending the herd or provoked to fight in an arena.

SIZ 30	Move 8	Major Wound 20
DEX 10	Damage 6d6	Unconscious 13
STR 30	Heal Rate 5	Knockdown 30
CON 20	Hit Points 50	Armor 6

Avoidance: 5

Modifier to Valorous: +2

Glory to Kill: 10

Attacks: charge @15, +2d6 damage; horn gore @10, trample @18, at normal damage

Bulls try to charge and impact their foes, then trample them. If cornered or otherwise unable to charge, a bull fights with its horns to knock down a foe.

Red Deer (elk)

The red deer is a large woodland deer similar to the American Elk.

SIZ 20	Move 9	Major Wound 20
DEX 25	Damage 5d6	Unconscious 10
STR 25	Heal Rate 5	Knockdown 20
CON 20	Hit Points 40	Armor 4

Avoidance: 15

Modifier to Valorous: +10

Glory to Kill: 5

Attacks: charge @18, +2d6 damage for success; antlers @15, hooves @15, normal damage.

Stags normally try to elude their foes, but when cornered or exhausted they fight to the death. Each round the stag either charges and impacts a foe or fights with both antlers and hooves.

Fallow Deer

The fallow deer is large, with a reddish coat that is covered with white spots. Its large antlers are similar to those of an American moose.

SIZ 17	Move 9	Major Wound 15
DEX 20	Damage 3d6	Unconscious 8
STR 15	Heal Rate 3	Knockdown 17
CON 15	Hit Points 32	Armor 3

Avoidance: 18

Modifier to Valorous: +10

Glory to Kill: 1

Attacks: Charge @14, +1d6 damage for success; antlers @10, hooves @10.

Stags normally try to elude their foes, but when cornered or exhausted they fight to the death. Each round the stag either charges and impacts a foe or fights with both antlers and hooves.

Roe Deer

This is a tiny deer, unworthy of being hunted by a knight. It is included because the roe buck is important in several myths and fairytales, and may appear in an adventure as well. It is so small that we give no statistics.

Wolf

Wolves generally travel in packs. They rarely attack humans under normal circumstances, but are a menace to livestock.

SIZ 4	Move 8	Major Wound 12
DEX 22	Damage 2d6	Unconscious 4
STR 12	Heal Rate 2	Knockdown 4
CON 12	Hit Points 16	Armor 2

Avoidance: 10

Modifier to Valorous: 0

Glory to Kill: 5

Attacks: bite @20

Monsters

CREATURES DANGEROUS TO a knight are rare, and fortunately so. As a group they are referred to as monsters, although several are more than that.

Many of these creatures have special attributes, such as unusual or extra attacks, which must be considered during combat.

Monsters are truly fearsome entities. A Valorous roll is required to initiate combat with one. Some monsters also have modifiers to the Valorous roll. This modifier is a survival factor for player knights: creatures too large to kill should be abandoned. Thus a Prudent modifier is also given where appropriate. However, groups of knights confronting a single monster have a better chance, and so the modifier should be *divided* among them. Glory is, likewise, divided among them.

Monsters often flee or surrender. The duty of a knight is generally to rid the world of such creatures, so killing is usually needed for Glory to be gained. However, at gamemaster option, a tenth of normal Glory can be gained for such a partial victory over a monster.

Faerie Knight

This is a powerful faerie knight. Others might exist with greater or lesser attributes.

SIZ: 20	Move 4
DEX: 20	Damage 7d6
STR: 20	Hit Points 40
CON: 20	Armor 18 + shield
APP: 20	

Attacks: Sword 23, Lance 21, Great Spear 21, Dagger 10; Battle 15, Horsemanship 21

Modifier to Valorous: -5

Significant Traits: Valorous 16

Significant Passions: gamemaster choice

Significant Skills: Awareness 15, Courtesy 15, First Aid 15, Heraldry 8, Hunting 15

Other Equipment: Faerie charger, 7d6 damage, Move 10, other eerie magical items

Glory to Kill: 200

THE RACE OF GIANTS

This race long-ago ruled the world before the good gods drove them into waste places. They are bigger than men, but slow of wit and body. Their foul habits are more like those of bears than men, and they delight to eat the flesh of humans. They wear crude hides, make nothing with crafted skill, and use only natural weapons. Their skins are stony and hard, like armor. Their unnatural lusts extend to human women, most unchivalrously.

Small Giant

This guy is not much bigger than a huge Saxon can be, but is big nonetheless.

SIZ 25	Move 4	Major Wound 25
DEX 8	Damage 8d6	Unconscious 13
STR 20	Heal Rate 5	Knock Down 25
CON 25	Hit Points 50	Armor 15
APP 5		

Modifier to Valorous: 0

Glory to Kill: 100

Attacks: club @13. Grapple @15 does 3d6 damage.

Giant

An immense monster of gargantuan proportions, the giant is almost invunerable.

SIZ 40	Move 7	Major Wound 30
DEX 5	Damage 14d6	Unconscious 18
STR 50	Heal Rate 8	Knock Down 40
CON 30	Hit Points 70	Armor 25
APP 3		

Modifier to Valorous: -5, to Prudent: +5

Glory to Kill: 250

Attacks: Club @15, or two Stomps @10 each.

Huge Giant

A monster of fairytale proportions, this monster of a being is to be avoided by all right-thinking knights. Fortunately, it is very slow, and easily avoided by riders.

SIZ 85	Move 5	Major Wound 35
DEX 1	Damage 22d6	Unconscious 24
STR 65	Heal Rate 10	Knock Down 85
CON 35	Hit Points 120	Armor 40
APP 3		

Modifier to Valorous: -15, to Prudent: +15

Glory to Kill: 500

Attacks: club @7, or two Stomps @4 each.

Griffin

This monster has the rear body of a lion and the wings, head, and foreparts of an eagle. It is huge, has a special taste for horse meat, and also hates humans. It comes from the land of Hyperborea, and chooses bleak mountain chains for its habitat.

SIZ 40	Move 14(fly)	Major Wound 25
DEX 20	Damage 8d6	Unconscious 16
STR 40	Heal Rate 7	Knockdown 40
CON 25	Hit Points 65	Armor 10

Avoidance: 30

Modifier to Valorous: -5

Glory to Kill: 250

Attacks: 2 clawed paws @17 each against one or two targets; or 1 grapple @10, whereupon it flies upward and drops the hapless foe. Both forms of attack are done while swooping from the air.

Hippogriff

This creature, perhaps born of heraldic quartering, is part lion, part eagle, and part horse. It has one attack per round.

SIZ 30	Move 16(fly)	Major Wound 10
DEX 25	Damage 5d6	Unconscious 10
STR 15	Heal Rate 3	Knockdown 30
CON 10	Hit Points 40	Armor 10

Avoidance: 30

Modifier to Valorous: 0

Glory to Kill: 200

Attacks: hooves @12, striking while swooping upon the foe.

Lion

The legendary lion is found throughout Malory. Sir Ywaine has one for a friend, Sir Percivale aids one on the Grail Quest, two of them live in the Tomb of Lions in Ganis, four of them escort the magical white stag through the forest.

SIZ 40	Move 8	Major Wound 20
DEX 20	Damage 7d6	Unconscious 15
STR 30	Heal Rate 5	Knockdown 40
CON 20	Hit Points 60	Armor 10

Avoidance: 10

Modifier to Valorous: -5

Glory to Kill: 250

Attacks: 2 paws @21 each, separate attacks against one or two targets. Alternately, one bite against a prone foe @20, +2d6 damage (remember to add the reflexive modifier).

Manticore

This man-eating beast has three rows of wicked teeth and the stinging tail of a scorpion. Its red eyes glow at night and its voice resembles the sibilant notes of a flute. Although it originates in far-away India, an individual or two have been seen in the rugged mountains of Britain, coming out only to feed upon humans. It is so powerful a leaper that no walls can hold it. Contrary to some legends it does not have wings.

SIZ 45	Move 11	Major Wound 25
DEX 20	Damage 9d6	Unconscious 18
STR 45	Heal Rate 7	Knockdown 45
CON 25	Hit Points 70	Armor 10

Avoidance: 15

Modifier to Valorous: -10, +10 to Prudent

Glory to Kill: 300

Attacks: 1 bite @10 at full damage rate, and 1 tail sting @20 for 6d6 damage.

Panther

The panther is a legendary cat which inhabits Britain. It is smaller than a lion, and prefers to lie in ambush to attack solitary foes in the deep woods. When surprised, perhaps on a hunt, it is considered wonderful sport. According to White's Bestiary the panther was considered to be of "truly variegated color, and it is most beautiful and excessively kind." Also, the panther was a sworn foe of dragons, and had an incredible belch which was proof against the great monsters.

SIZ 15	Move 9	Major Wound 15
DEX 25	Damage 4d6	Unconscious 8
STR 25	Heal Rate 4	Knockdown 15
CON 15	Hit Points 30	Armor 5

Avoidance: 15

Modifier to Valorous: 0

Glory to Kill: 75

Attacks: bite @15, with +1d6 damage; or 2 claws @10 each against 1 or two targets, normal damage.

Unicorn

Several types of unicorn exist in legend. Two are given here. When presenting information of an unicorn sighting, the gamemaster need never differentiate between types. Most people in the world of Pendragon know of only one type or another, not both.

Greater Unicorn

This creature is normally shy and retiring, and can easily Hide from most hunters, using Glamour to hide its tracks and disguise itself from dogs. However, it can be attracted using the virgin ploy, and is sought since its parts are valuable to magicians, their steaks a rare delicacy to most palates, and their heads priceless trophies to noble hunters. Though they can be killed, they cannot be captured alive.

SIZ 25	Move 12	Major Wound 25
DEX 40	Damage 5d6	Unconscious 12
STR 25	Heal-special	Knock Down 25
CON 25	Hit Points 50	Armor 5

Avoidance: 15

Modifier to Valorous: 0

Glory to Kill: 100

Attacks: horn @16. Also has Awareness @18. Knows simple Glamour magic (gamemaster option for effects).

Special Healing: this kind of unicorn can heal all wounds with a touch of its horn, if it so desires. It cannot heal during a fight, but in quiet moments can even heal itself.

Lesser Unicorn

This diminutive animal would never harm any innocent creature. Nonetheless, its horn has miraculous properties, and it is still attracted to virgin women.

SIZ 15	Move 10	Major Wound 15
DEX 45	Damage 3d6	Unconscious 8
STR 15	Heal-special	Knock Down 15
CON 15	Hit Points 30	Armor 3

Avoidance: 25

Modifier to Valorous: +5

Glory to Kill: 25

Attacks: horn @10. Hide @18. Knows simple Glamour magic.

Special Healing: this kind of unicorn can heal all wounds with a touch of its horn, if it desires. It cannot heal during a fight, but in quiet moments can even heal itself.

Water Leaper

Shaped like a legless frog with fin wings, this terrifying monster leaps from the water and glides along its surface to snatch boaters from their craft and drag them underwater to drown. It is almost helpless if beached or trapped on deck, although its frantic thrashing is dangerous to anyone struck. A Water Leaper has no redeeming virtues.

SIZ 10	Move 5(fly)	Major Wound 15
DEX 20	Damage 3d6	Unconscious 6
STR 15	Heal Rate 5	Knockdown 10
CON 15	Hit Points 25	Armor 5

Avoidance: n/a

Modifier to Valorous: +0

Glory to Kill: 100

Attacks: Bite while in flight @15, holds on with a winning STR vs. STR roll and drags victim into the water; or thrashing about @10, doing 4d6 damage.

Wyrm

These giant serpents are undoubtedly of demonic origin, for they exude an essence discernible to all good knights. They can breathe fire and have very tough hides. Also, they have the ability to rejoin their severed parts and regenerate damage.

SIZ 35	Move 10	Major Wound 25
DEX 30	Damage 7d6	Unconscious 15
STR 35	Heal Rate special*	Knockdown 35
CON 25	Hit Points 60	Armor 15

Avoidance: 7

Modifier to Valorous: -10, +10 to Prudent

Glory to Kill: 400

*Regenerates at rapid rate, receiving 1d6 points per melee round.

Attacks: bite @15; breath @10, tail lash @10. May only be used against two different foes. Fire breath does normal fire damage, at a rate of 1d6 damage, ignoring all armor, except for the first time hit, unless the wyrm changes targets.

Wyvern

This dragon-like creature is two-legged and winged. It is smaller than most of its draconic kin, but usually lives in family groups of 2-6 individuals.

SIZ 20	Move l3(fly)	Major Wound 20
DEX 60	Damage 5d6	Unconscious 10
STR 25	Heal Rate 5	Knockdown 20
CON 20	Hit Points 40	Armor 8

Avoidance: 30

Modifier to Valorous: 0

Glory to Kill: 100

Attacks: bite @12; or (while flying only) two claws @15, 3d6 damage each.

Yale

This hoofed animal is rare, but can be hunted in the deep woods. It is amazing in that its two horns are jointed and can be moved independently of each other. Thus this fabulous creature can fight two foes in one round.

SIZ 30	Move 8	Major Wound 15
DEX 10	Damage 5d6	Unconscious 12
STR 15	Heal Rate 3	Knock Down 30
CON 15	Hit Points 45	Armor 8

Avoidance: 12

Modifier to Valorous: 0

Glory to Kill: 50

Attacks: 2 horns, against 1 or 2 targets, @12 each.

Allegorical Medieval Beasts

Some creatures, by their very nature, provoke an emotional response. Some perform unusual or allegorical roles and require the viewer to recognize what is occurring to achieve the experience. Such events may occur often or rarely, depending upon your own sense of humor and manner of portrayal of these medieval truths.

Meeting these animals offers a chance to receive personality trait or passion checks. No statistics are given for these mythic creatures because such numbers would be meaningless.

These examples are taken from T. H. White's *Bestiary,* which every gamemaster should read for further examples.

Beaver

This creature is hunted for its testicles, which make a very powerful medicine. When hunters close in upon it, the beaver castrates itself and flings the organs to the hunter, thereby escaping with its life. Observers of this fact may receive a Chaste check.

Coot

This bird is often found in company of eagles, with nests lower down the cliff. Coots adopt any orphan or rejected eagle which is cast down from its home nest. The coots raise the eagle like their own to healthy adulthood.

Observing this fact yields a Generous check.

Eagle

These imperial mothers of the sky test their offspring by holding the nestlings to stare at the sun. If they flinch, the young are rejected as unworthy and ejected from the nest.

The parent does this out of a sense of unyielding justice, and observers gain a Just check.

Hawk

These sleek raptors withhold food from their fledglings, and are quick to kick them out of the nest to fend for themselves. They do it because it will make the young birds tough.

Anyone who sees this receives a Cruelty check.

Lynx

The lynx is a type of spotted wolf whose urine hardens in seven days into a precious stone called a carbuncle. Lynxes know this, and so bury their urine as deeply as possible to prevent humans from finding and using the stones as ornaments.

Observers of this act receive a Selfish check.

Pelican

These water birds annually slay their young through righteous anger, then three days later pierce their own breasts until blood pours out over the chicks, which return to life.

If the players characters see this, they receive a Piety check.

Stork

Storks are family-oriented birds. They are monogamous and always return to the same nests. The parents incubate the nest so intently that they lose their feathers, and afterwards are cared for by their young for an equal length of time.

Continued observations, perhaps constantly over a year, or intermittently over many years, can allow players a Love (Family) check.

More Monsters

Some unique creatures, found rarely or only in specific locations, can be found in the Short Adventures section of the "Scenarios" chapter.

The Redcap

Appendix

Designer's Notes

First edition *Pendragon* was released in 1985 and met with rave reviews, rapid sales, and immediately upon its heels, financial and personal crises which kept it out of print until this revised release.

During that period I took time to touch the game up a bit. I wanted to address the primary complaint about the first edition: many would-be gamemasters lacked the background to confidently run a believable game. So I reorganized it, collecting parts from the other books of the first *Pendragon* series and adding a lot of new background material.

It was very hard to decide on what to keep and what to save for later. Some sort of rational parameters had to be imposed on its size, simply to keep it within a size which was affordable, and even to be finished at all!

I decided that the center would be a hard and strict version based on the Romantic Arthur, despite the fact that it omitted some of the players' favorite parts of my own campaign: the previous history, ladies and Pagans. But I did omit these, just to provide a social standard which was understandable by most players who cared enough to read the book. Finally, Romantic Arthur is definable: everyone who is informed on the subject agrees on what constitutes the genera. Its core is a story-telling style which was popular when the first stories about King Arthur and his cohorts were written down. The Romantic Arthurian literature is also the trunk from which most modern story versions of the Pendragon and the Round Table are drawn.

Any or all of the other options disrupts the Romantic structure mildly or greatly, and so are covered in book two. They are not the kind of thing which everyone expects to find at the center of Logres. They are, however, the most interesting and fun types of knights encountered when they are found (Sagramore le Desirious, Dinadan, Palomides, and others).

Since the purpose of *Pendragon* is to allow every player to create a character who is individual, I decided that it is most critical to understand what the norm is. Hence the structure and content of this 3rd edition *Pendragon* determines the core of the Arthurian legend. The first supplement, *Knights Adventurous,* expands the options beyond even the wildest extant literature. It is what "everyone thinks." It is all of the things that "they say." It is the ancestor of our culture, and of its myths.

Joseph Campbell has urged everyone to create our own mythology. Imagination is the first key to such a thing, and the Arthurian realm holds fascination for many of us. It provides a setting for our imagination. I hope that *Knights Adventurous* can provide a vehicle for anyone's imagination in the world of our cultural ancestors.

Pendragon has lots of rules. Both *Knight Adventurous* and *The Boy King* have far fewer. But they include more text and explanation than hard rules. They don't provide for much outside the actual Arthurian (i.e. European feudal) realm, but should have everything inside of that.

More *Pendragon*

Arthurian roleplaying does not end with this book! *Pendragon* restricts itself to the single realm of Romance literature. But King Arthur was bigger than that, and so is the game.

Supplements will demonstrate this: *Knight Adventurous* expands player options in the Arthurian world. It is ours to explore outside of the conventions of established literature and legend. Thus where the basic *Pendragon* book provides a base from which to operate, the second book provides a wide range of variant knight roles.

The Boy King steps backward in *Pendragon* time to put player characters at the start of Arthurian history. Background and character attributes are provided to begin play before Arthur was king and experience life during his early reign. In effect, the players roleplay the grandfather of a character generated here in basic *Pendragon.* Perhaps he can witness the drawing of the sword from the stone, participate in the great battles of Arthur's early reign, and work his way to Arthur's inner circle of friends. Its emphasis is on adventuring as part of history.

Prince Valiant is a different game, with rules radically simplified from these in *Pendragon.* In fact, they take only one page! Based on the world-famous comic strip by Hal Foster, this setting is very similar to that of *Pendragon.* If you don't want to bother with rules or history or literature, *Prince Valiant* is for you.

Want to Write *Pendragon* Adventures?

Chaosium Inc. is interested in receiving your submitted manuscript for consideration of publication. Write to us, at the address in the front of the book, and ask for Submission Guidelines. Send a self-addressed, stamped envelope and ask for the Pendragon Prospectus.

Bibliography

The following books are recommended for players and gamemasters wishing to obtain familiarity with the legend of King Arthur and with the history that surrounds it.

Barber, Richard. *The Knight and Chivalry.* Harper & Row, 1970.

A historical reference which traces the development of knighthood from its obscure beginnings to its decadent end. This book gives an excellent synopsis of the historical background and development of knighthood, and is highly recommended to gamemasters wishing to maintain historicity.

Bloch, Marc. *Feudal Society.* University of Chicago Press, 1964.

Although over 50 years old, this text provides the definitive scholarly history of the development of the aspects of society which are critical to the *Pendragon* game. Concise, but not for the casual reader.

Gies, Francis. *The Knight in History.* Robert Hale, 1984.

Several life histories of famous knights from different periods of history illustrate the historical trends in chivalry which are detailed in this book.

Hall, Louis B. *The Knightly Tales of Sir Gawain.* Nelson-Hall, 1976.

Several lesser-known, but excellent, tales of Sir Gawaine are here, taken from the Old English. It is the source of some of the quotes in this book, including "Golagros and Gawain."

Karr, Phyllis Ann. *The King Arthur Companion.* Chaosium Inc., 1983.

This definitive, and highly readable, catalog lists hundreds of character, places, and things from Malory and the Vulgate. It delightfully reconstructs the lives of many lesser characters, turning them into complete personalities.

Keen, Maurice. *Chivalry.* Yale University Press, 1984.

Knighthood as an aspect of nobility is the main theme of this excellent book, which traces the development of this class through its history.

Malory, Sir Thomas. *Le Morte D'Arthur.* edited by Janet Cowen, Penguin Books, 1969 (two volumes).

Sir Thomas Malory was a fifteenth-century knight who compiled the most important version of the legend in the English language, published by Caxton, the first modern printer in Britain. Malory's book is the basic text for the *Pendragon* campaign.

Many editions of this work are available, but this one is my favorite. It has just the right mix of modernization and archaic vocabulary. Entries given in the text are in the format of (X, Y) where X is the book, and Y is the chapter number of Caxton's edition (this is the format for the quotations in this book as well).

Silverstein, Theodore (trans.) *Sir Gawain and the Green Knight*. University of Chicago Press, 1974.

This is an excellent rendition of the most famous Arthurian poem in Old English, and an excellent example of the chivalrous ideals.

Steinbeck, John. *The Acts of King Arthur and his Noble Knights*. Ballantine Books, 1977.

A great American novelist pours forth his love for this subject, bringing the characters alive for the modern reader. It is not perfect, having too much psychoanalysis for my taste; and is not finished, excluding the Grail Quest and final phases. This book provides my favorite portrayal of Sir Lancelot.

White, T.H. *The Once and Future King*. G.P.Putnam's Sons, 1939

This modern rendition of Malory's works is a great source for detailed information about the Middle Ages, as well as being perhaps the most readable modern version of the legend. If you read only one book, this is the one I recommend. It combines medieval lore with the story in a delicious mix of literature. It has my favorite versions of King Arthur and Mordred (a real rotter.)

Measurements

Distances are measured in inches, feet, and miles. Metric conversion are given here:

- 1 inch = 2.5 cm
- 1 foot = 12 inches = 30 cm
- 1 hand = 4 inches = 10 cm
- 1 rod = 16.5 feet = 5 meters
- 1 mile = 0.66 km
- 1 league = 3 miles = 5 km

Weights:

- 1 ounce = 30 gm
- 1 pound = 16 oz. = 0.48 kg
- 1 stone = 14 pounds = 6.5 kg
- 1 ton = 2000 pounds = 0.9 metric tons

Watch your C's and K's

The C-sound used in foreign words in this game in almost every instance is pronounced as a hard C, a K-sound. This is especially important for these words:

Celtic is pronounced Keltic

Cymric is pronounced Kymric. Remember, the Celtics (seltiks) are a basketball team, a selt is a stone knife without a handle, and Celts (kelts) are an ancient culture.

Glossary and Abbreviations

Many words used in this game are, inevitably, medieval and no longer in current usage. Others are in use, but have been transformed over time to have a new meaning. Effort has been made to use these terms consistently as given here.

APP. Appearance. One of the Statistics.

AREA. How much ground a city or town takes up. This is important primarily for battles and economics. 1 Area is about 1 acre. Not used in this book.

Attribute. The various areas in which a character is rated: traits, passions, statistics, skills, and combat skills. All attributes have numerical values for use with a d20 roll.

Character. An individual person or being encountered during the game. Player characters have their actions determined by players, while gamemaster characters are controlled by the gamemaster.

Combat Skill. A skill used in war or tournament.

CON. Constitution. One of the Statistics.

d6, d20. Dice used in the game, six and twenty-sided.

d. Denarius (plural denarii). The Roman equivalent of a pence, or penny. 240 d. = 1 £.

Dame: Title for a woman which is equivalent to "lord," used when the woman is the head of her own household.

DEX. Dexterity. One of the Statistics.

DV. Defense Value. Factor used to determine the relative value of a castle, city walls, or other defensive fortification.

Glory: A measure of a character's success, notoriety, and power. Does not measure reputation directly. Value is measured in Glory points, which are received for most significant events or actions during play.

Knight: A warrior who has undergone the ceremony of knighthood, and sworn allegiance to a lord. A nobleman.

Lady: The wife of a nobleman of any rank.

£. Librum (plural Libra): A Roman monetary unit, also commonly called a Pound, equal to 240 denarii. or 20 s.

Liege Lord: The lord to whom a knight owes primary loyalty. Through marriage and inheritance a knight may have many lords, but he must choose one to be pre-eminent, who is called the liege lord.

Lord: A knight, and a nobleman, holding other knights as vassals. A banneret knight is the lowest lord. The High King is the highest lord.

Manor: A land holding which is capable of providing enough income to support a knight.

Noble: A person of the highest social class, including all lords and knights, and some squires.

Passion: An attribute. A powerful specific emotion that can inspire or prematurely age a knight. Also measures reputation.

Penny: See Denarius.

POP. Population. A measure of the monetary value of a population. About 120 people. Not used in this book.

Roll: A random roll of a die to determine events during the game impartially.

s. Shilling. A monetary unit equal to 12 d, or 1/20 £.

SIZ. Size. One of the Statistics.

Skill: An attribute. A measure of ability and knowledge in a specific ordinary activity such as singing or swimming. Combat skills are more important than ordinary skills and are placed together in a separate section.

Squire: The servant of a knight. Squires may be nobles if they are the sons of nobles, or commoners if they are the sons of commoners or of squires.

Statistic: An attribute, measures innate aptitude or physical ability. Does not include mental factors.

STR. Strength. One of the Statistics.

Trait: An attribute. A psychological factor indicating preferences for certain actions over others, such as courage rather than cowardice. Also measures reputation in conjunction with passions.

Value: The numerical value of an attribute.

Weapon Skill: A subset of Combat skills, involving weapons.

Index

ff = more follows
t = table
b = boxed item

Actions, melee 85
Adventures 179ff
  see also Scenarios
Adventuring 28, 159
Aging 110, 129
Aggravation of damage 107
Ambitions 64
Amor, see Romance
APP 39
Armor, primary rules 82
Armor, human 82
  horse 87
Avoidance, used by animals 170, 171
Badges 27
Balance 80
Banishment 29
Banneret 67
Berserker Attack 89
Bastardry, see Illegitimacy
Battle 159ff
  System 163b
  skill 98
Brawling 80, 97
Britain 16ff
  map 21
Brittany 20
Cambria 19
Camelot 22ff
Castle 131, 140
Character 4, 32 ff
Character Generation 32ff
  of a son 54
Character Sheet 35, 36
  Sheets for major characters (Arthur, Lancelot, etc.) 195
Childbirth 112t
Chirurgery 92, 108
Chivalry 27, 68
  duties of 150ff
Christian Knight 69
Christianity 30, 96, 157
Chronology 9
Church, Christian 29, 158
  See also Clergy, Christianity
Classes, social 13ff, 64b
Clerical Class 13, 14
Climb 80
Coat of Arms 27, 42
Coinage 143
Combat System 81ff
  for Conquest 28
  for Love 28
  Glory 59, 97
  Tactics 80, 89
  Options 87ff
Commoner Class 13, 16
Companions of Arthur 69
CON 39
Cornwall 20
Court 150
Courtesy 92, 150ff
Critical Success 72
Cumbria 19
Damage 39, 82, 108
Death 7, 50
Defense 89
Degradation 29
Deterioration of health 106
DEX 39
DEX rolls 79ff
Dice 71
Directed Traits 122
Disheartened 129
Dishonor 123t
Distinctive Features 40
Divorce 22, 25
Dodge 80
Double Feint 80, 89
Economics , see also Quality of Knights, Wealth, Price Lists
  annual circumstances 110
Enchantment of Britain 31
Encumbrance 77
Escape Melee 89
Europe 20
Evasion, in combat 77, 80
Experience 76ff
  previous 41
  annual 109
  for traits 121
Faerie 4, 93
Family 9, 18, 22ff, 46, 48ff
  creation 51
  annual events 111
Fealty 12
Feudalism 11
Fief 12
First Aid 93, 103
Fumble 72, 117b
Gamemaster 6
Gentry 14
Gift 11
Glory, general 9, 56ff
  Basic Awards 58t
  Beginning 42
  Bonus Points 62, 113
  Range of Awards 57, 58t
  Ranking Table 57t
  Sample Awards 60t
  from Skills 91
  from Combat 97
Grant 11
Healing Rate 39
Health 102ff
Heraldry 42ff, 94
  see also Coat of Arms, Shield
Hit Points 39, 102
History, family 48
Holy Days 31
Homage 12
Honor 20, 91, 123
Horsemanship 99
Horses 45
  in combat 86
  survival Table 111t
  prices 146
  attributes 200ff
Hospitality 17
Hunt 151, 170ff
  Hunt segment 170
  Hunt solo 175
Ideals 7, 68ff, 115ff
Illegitimacy 24ff
Income, knightly 65
Inheritance 22, 25
  underage 53
Initiative 77
Inspiration 128
Ireland 20
Jousting 153
Jousting Lances 88
Joust Score 42
Jumping 81
Justice 27
Kin 18
  see also Family
Knight Bachelor 26
Knight Lord 26, 67
Knight Mercenary 26
Knight Vassal 26, 66
Knighthood 6, 25ff, 42
  Ambitions 64ffCustoms 27
  Grades or Ranks 26, 66ff
  Ideals 68
  Qualities (economic) 65
  Qualifications 42, 90
Knockdown 39, 82
Lance in combat 86
Laws, Universal 17
Laws, Justice 27
Leap, the 42
Librum, Libra 143
Logres 17ff
Lords 14
Loyalty 19
Luck Benefits 45t
Madness 129
Magic 10, 30, 31
Manor 137, 143, 146
Marriage 22ff
Mechanics (game) 71ff
Melancholy 129
Melee Round 76, 82ff
Modifiers, 73ff
  to beginning skills 63
  to DEX roll 79
  to combat
Monsters, attributes 203
Motivations 7
Movement System 77ff
Movement Rate 39
Noble Class 13, 14
  See also Lords, Knighthood
Oaths 28
Outfits 144
Outlawry 29
Page 25
Passions 8, 34, 115ff, 122ff
Personal Gear 45, 144
Pictland 19
Price Lists 146ff
Progress 137, 145
Punishments of knights 29
Qualities (economic) 65
Questing 29, 159
Ranks, knightly 66
Ransom 147, 149, 166b
Recovery from Damage 102, 106
Religion, see Christianity, Church
Resolution System 72
Restrictions, on statistics 39
Retinue 145
Roads 18
Roll (die) 71
Romance 96, 125, 128b, 155ff
  Lover's Solo 176,177
Romantic Knight 68
Round Table Knight 69
Rounding Off 71
Salisbury 130ff
Sacraments 31
Scenarios 167ff
  Introductory Scenario 167ff
  see also Adventures
Shield, also see coat of arms
  in combat 88
  of Peace 27
Shock 129
SIZ 39
Skills System 90ff
  in character generation 41
  Optional 90
  Non-knightly 90
Skirmish 98
Sneaking 81
Squire 25, 45
Statistics 34
  restrictions on allocation 39
  Yearly Increases 39
STR 39
Swearing 157b
Throwing Objects 81
Time 8, 74ff
  Calendar 75
  Chronology 9, 49ff
  Current 14b
Tournament 152ff
Traits 34, 116ff
Traits, directed 34, 122
Travel 78, 80b, 141
Travel Gear 45, 144
Unconsciousness 39
Vassal 11, 47
Virtue 121
War Gear 45, 144
Wealth 143ff
Weapon Skills 100
Winter Phase System 109
Wounds 104